The Kremlin Device

The Watchman

Chris Ryan

arrow books

Arrow Books Limited
The Random House Group Limited
20 Vauxhall Bridge Road, London, SW1V 2SA

Random House Australia (Pty) Limited
20 Alfred Street, Milsons Point, Sydney,
New South Wales 2061, Australia

Random House New Zealand Limited
18 Poland Road, Glenfield
Auckland 10, New Zealand

Random House (Pty) Limited
Endulini, 5a Jubilee Road, Parktown 2193, South Africa

The Random House Group Limited Reg. No. 954009

www.randomhouse.co.uk

A CIP catalogue record for this book
is available from the British Library

Papers used by Random House are natural, recyclable products made
from wood grown in sustainable forests. The manufacturing processes
conform to the environmental regulations of the country of origin

ISBN 0 09 191105 2

Printed and bound in Great Britain by
Bookmarque Ltd, Croydon, Surrey

THE KREMLIN DEVICE

'For what is a man profited,
if he shall gain the whole
World, and lose his own
Soul?'

For Janet and Sarah

ACKNOWLEDGEMENTS

I wish to give special thanks to someone who shall remain anonymous but without whose editorial help I would never have finished this. To all my family and friends for all their patience and understanding. Also to Mark Booth, Liz Rowlinson, Katie White and Rachael Healey at Century.

GLOSSARY

ATO	Ammunition technical officer
Bergen	Rucksack
BG	Bodyguard (noun or verb)
Blue-on-blue	Accidental strike on own forces
Casevac	Casualty evacuation
CND	Compact nuclear device
COBR	Cabinet Office Briefing Room
Comms	Communications
CQB	Close-quarter battle
CTR	Close target reconnaissance
DF	Direction finding
Dicker	Lookout
Director	Officer commanding special forces, generally a brigadier
DOP	Drop-off point
DPMs	Disruptive pattern material, camouflage garments
DZ	Drop zone
EMOE	Explosive method of entry
ERV	Emergency rendezvous
Exfil	Exfiltrate
FMB	Forward mounting base
FOB	Forward operating base
FSB	Federal Security Bureau, part of former KGB

GPS	Global positioning system, navigation aid
HALO	High altitude, low opening
Head-shed	Headquarters
Incoming	Incoming fire
Int	Intelligence
IO	Intelligence officer
Kremlin, The	SAS headquarters
LO	Liaison officer
LUP	Lying-up point
LZ	Landing zone
MAC	Military Air Command
Magellan	Brand-name of GPS
Omon	Special forces, Russian Ministry of the Interior
OP	Observation point
PJI	Parachute jump instructor
PNGs	Passive night goggles
PUP	Pick-up point
QRF	Quick-reaction force
Rat	Radio alarm trigger
RTU	Return to unit
Rupert	Officer
SAM	Surface-to-air-missile
Satcom	Satellite telephone system
SAW	Subversive Action Wing
Scalie	Signaller
SCR	Satellite Communications Responder
SEAL	Sea, Air and Land American special forces unit
SOCO	Scene-of-crimes officer
SP	Special projects
Spetznaz	Russian special forces
SSM	Squadron sergeant major
US	Unserviceable
VCP	Vehicle control point

RUSSIAN EXPRESSIONS

Babushka	Granny, little old woman
Chush!	Rubbish!
Chyort!	Damn! (literally 'devil')
Davai	Carry on
Dosvidanya	Goodbye
Huinja!	Bollocks!
Idyom	Let's go
Isvinite	Sorry, excuse me
Kak dela?	How goes it?
Kakovo khuya sidite?	Why the fucking hell don't you shift your arse?
Khorosho	Good
Khuyevo dyelo!	Shit!
Konechno	Of course
Kontraktnik	Professional soldier
Mne zhalko	I'm sorry
Nichevo	Not to worry
Orushiye k boyu	Stand by
Otlichno!	Great!
Pojaluista	Please
Polkovnik	Colonel
Poshli!	Go!
Poyekhali	Bottoms up
Prinyato	Roger, got it
Spasibo	Thank you

Starik	Old man, veteran
Starshina	Warrant officer
Tochno	Precisely
Uchodite	Get lost
Valite otsyuda	Piss off
Vas ponyal	Roger, understood
Vot beda	Pity
Vpered!	Go!
Vstali i poshli!	Shift your ass!
Vzdrognem	Cheers
Ya ne znayu	I don't know
Yefreitor	Corporal
Yestj	OK
Zdorovo	Brilliant
Zdravstvuite	Hello

ONE

With the tailgate open, the cabin depressurised and five minutes to run, we'd all gone on to individual oxygen. That knackered voice communication: for one thing, we had masks over our mouths, and for another the Herc's four turbo-props were deafening. We were wearing covert radios, with throat mikes on our necks and earpieces under our helmets, but we couldn't use them until we were in the final stages of our descent, because of the risk that they'd foul up the pilots' comms.

Our PJI – the Parachute Jump Instructor from Hereford – stepped along the line of bulky figures, giving our kit final checks. The hold was so dark he was doing most of the work with his hands, following lines and straps with his fingers, pulling on rings and clips. Then the red jump-warning lights came on, like half ping-pong balls one either side of the tailgate. Two minutes to go.

Our kit made us cumbersome: GQ-360 chutes on our backs, oxygen tanks on stomachs, 120lb bergens clipped upside-down on the backs of our legs and tucked high under our chutes, so that they rested against the backs of our thighs from knee to arse. Our weapons,

1

203s or Minimis, were tied with para-cord to our left legs. With that lot on I had a job to waddle to the rear of the plane.

As leader of the team, I'd be the first to jump.

Stars wheeled across the big, square opening as the pilot put in his final turn. I glanced to my left at Harry Price, known to all as Pavarotti, the hefty Welshman famous for singing in the showers and for the eyes tattooed on the cheeks of his arse. He'd had them done one night when he got pissed in Cardiff, by a Chinese bloke for a fiver a side, and the eyes were a bit slitty.

Now, under his helmet, goggles and oxygen mask, not much of his face was showing, but I could see the muscles in his jaw working as he swallowed. He was thinking the same as I was: for fuck's sake, let's get out of this damned aircraft and on our way.

Anyone who says he's not nervous when about to free-fall at night wearing full equipment is bullshitting. All eight of us were crapping bricks. A night-time HALO – a high-altitude, low-opening drop – is no picnic, however many times you've done it before. After two seconds you're heading for the ground at 125 miles per hour. You roar through the first thousand feet of air in ten seconds, the next in five, and so you keep going.

A clean free-fall is one thing; a drop with full kit something else, because of the risk that your load may move and render you unstable. Tonight we were jumping at 22,000 feet and dropping to 4,000 before we popped our chutes: a free-fall of ninety-five seconds.

This way, on this moonless night, we'd come out of the blue – or rather, out of the black – as far as anyone on the ground was concerned: until our chutes deployed nobody would see a thing.

Our target was a clearing among the chestnut forests of the Cevennes where, according to the exercise scenario, partisan forces would be waiting to guide us in, meet us and take us to safe houses.

The captain of the aircraft had given the wind as eight knots on 260 degrees – just south of west. We were going to jump four ks west of our target and fly ourselves in towards it. The sky was clear but the air was full of turbulence, and the Herc kept juddering and twitching so that the guys were being jostled against each other as we huddled on the ramp.

Somebody gripped my right arm. I twisted and saw it was the head loadie, asking with thumb up if I was all set. I nodded and gave him a thumb in return. He raised a single finger. One minute to go. Cushy bastard: we were going out into the black night while he was safely tethered to his aircraft by a harness and long webbing strop. By the time we hit the deck he'd be well on his way back to Lyneham and a warm night tucked up in bed . . . I caught myself up. Geordie, I told myself, stop pissing around. You're in the SAS, and this is what it's all about. If you did the crew's job you'd be bored out of your mind.

I passed the signal to Pavarotti and glanced down at my altimeters, one strapped on either forearm: both dials were registering 22,000. I felt the angle of the floor change slightly as the pilot throttled back, dropping speed for his final run-in towards the DZ. Screwing my head round, I got a glimpse of Whinger Watson, my second-in-command. All I could see was the red light glinting off his goggles, but I could imagine the oath he was muttering to himself: 'Firekin ell,' again and again. He and I were the old men of the party: at thirty-six and thirty-seven, we could almost have been some of the guys' fathers.

Time for last-minute checks: harness straight, bollocks clear of crutch straps, bergen in position, weapon secure, mask tight, gloves on. I reached round and bent the Cyalume light velcroed on to my bergen, cracking the glass phial in the middle and setting the chemical reaction going so that everyone would have a marker to steer towards when they followed me out of the plane.

Thirty seconds to go. Into my mind came a sudden vision of Moscow. For a moment I imagined we were doing a night drop into the heart of the city, heading down towards all those red-brick towers and golden onion domes. I knew that the dark land below us was France, not Russia, and that we were only on a preliminary exercise; but Moscow was our ultimate destination, and for the past few days we'd heard so much about Spetznaz, Omon, Alfa Force, the Mafia and the break-up of the KGB that I'd started seeing red in my sleep.

Then I felt the head loadie grip my arm again. I tensed myself and hunched forward.

4

The two little jump-warning lights were still on. Still on . . . Still on . . . Then the bottom half of each ping-pong ball sprang to life. *Green on!*

GO!

All I had to do was tumble forward, head-first into the black space outside. Lean forward – gone.

As I cleared the belly of the aircraft upside-down, the slipstream hit my front with a huge thud. Head up, chest out . . . An instant later I was horizontal and falling in a good position – face down, arms and legs spread, chest thrust out, steering with my hands turned up and out. The engine scream had been replaced by the roar of air blasting past my helmet.

So far, so good. Now I needed to get eyes on the other guys, make sure everybody was OK. Pavarotti had jumped a couple of seconds behind me, the others after him. I wanted to slow my descent so they could catch up. Bending in the middle, I de-arched myself – that is, curled my body into a banana shape to increase resistance to the air.

Staring down, I saw long streaks of haze between ourselves and the ground: a thin layer of cloud. As I hit it, drops of water stung my cheeks and forehead like fire. A second later I was through, and aware of someone coming down on my right, a black shape slanting in at an angle, monochrome, but more solid than the surrounding darkness. Another appeared, then another. There was no way of telling who was who, but I was glad they were keeping a safe distance from me, facing inwards in a wide ring.

I stuck out my chest again and straightened out to pick up speed and keep pace with them.

Below us the wooded hills were crow black, not a light in sight. Then, at three o'clock to me, I saw a brilliant spark flare up: a Firefly, our reception committee. Now I could count six other guys around me, all more or less level. Good work. But where was the seventh? Maybe behind me, out of my vision.

For a few moments I positively enjoyed myself. Hurtling through the night, keeping control, gave a feeling of terrific exhilaration. I was free as a bird, flying; everything seemed easy. Inside the thin gloves my fingers were freezing, but what the hell!

Again I thought irrationally, Moscow, here we come!

Against the illuminated faces of my altimeters the hands were unwinding fast. My mind was making continual checks: I'm fine. Eighteen thousand. My position's stable. Sixteen. Keep that posture. Left hand down a bit. Now you're OK. It's fourteen. You're good. It's twelve.

Then *wham!* Some heavy object flew down from the side and slammed into the back of my right leg with a terrific blow. Jesus, I thought, a meteorite. No – a falling human body. The impact knocked me out of the posture I'd been working to hold. Worse, it knocked my bergen from its central position behind my knees and pushed it over to the outside of my left leg. In an instant I was destabilised, still face-down, but spinning.

I knew I was in the shit. A spin is the worst thing that can happen to a free-faller, the fate everybody dreads. If one starts on its own it may wind up slowly, and you stand some chance of correcting it. But after an impact of that kind, you're away. The combination of momentum and air pressure is so ferocious that you're rotating like a propellor, and that's you gone.

I struggled with hands, arms and legs to adjust my posture, to regain control. But whatever I did, I just spun faster. For the first few seconds my mind stayed clear. Maybe one of the lads will see what's happening, I thought. Maybe someone will steer in to give me a hand. Then I realised, No, they can't. This is too violent. If anyone tried to make contact I'd smash them, or they'd smash me. We'd break limbs, knock each other out. If they've got any sense, they've pulled off to a safe distance. I'm on my own.

All this went through my mind in a flash. Then I thought, I'm going to have to cut my bergen away. Pull the cord to dump it. Lose all my kit. But by the time I'd taken that decision it had become physically impossible. The centrifugal force of the spin was so great I couldn't get my hands anywhere near my body. No way could I reach my knife, still in its sheath on my right leg. My arms were locked straight out, hands and fingers throbbing with the pressure of blood forced into them. They felt as if the skin was going to burst. My head seemed to be swelling, too, the skin round my eyes bulging, vision deteriorating. Geordie Sharp, I told myself, this is it. During your career in special forces you've got out of plenty of tight corners, but this time, finally, you're fucked.

I wasn't exactly frightened; everything had happened so fast there was no time to worry. I just seemed to accept that fate had got me by the short-and-curlies, and I was going in at 125mph. Obliteration, I thought. Fair enough.

In fact I must have been losing consciousness. Then an almighty jolt brought me back to my senses. It was as if a huge hand had arrested me in mid air. The thump knocked the breath out of my lungs, and I was still spinning, but much more slowly. It took me a few seconds to realise that the auto-release had fired my main chute, and that I was descending more slowly, in a sitting position.

Instinctively I reached up and pulled on the webbing strops to test the reaction. Something wrong: a rough, grating feeling, too much resistance. Glancing up, I saw from the outline of the chute against the stars that the canopy was lopsided. Instead of being rectangular, it was all sharp angles. The rigging lines had tangled round each other in the spin. Instead of working down to a position just above my head, the spreader bar had become jammed in the twisted ropes.

Because it wasn't properly deployed, the chute started spinning as well, winding me around like a fairground ride. But by then, thank God, my mind was back to normal. I saw my options clearly. I was descending much too fast. If I couldn't free the main chute in the next few seconds I'd have to cut it away and deploy my reserve. Also I'd have to ditch my bergen, because its weight was too great for the reserve

8

chute to support.

I held the strops and started giving violent twists, turning my body hard to the left. The third jolt did the trick. Above me there was a hefty *smack* as the chute deployed fully, then a twitch came down the lines. When I next looked up, the spreader bar had slid down to its proper place and everything was back to normal. I took a few deep breaths, thanked my lucky stars and turned my attention to the ground.

As far as I could tell, I was little the worse. My eyes felt funny and my face was glowing red hot, but nothing was broken. My breathing was OK, vision fair. There was the Firefly, away to my left. Because of the spin I'd drifted several hundred metres off my heading.

I'd just started steering back towards the DZ when I became aware of someone else flying in dangerously close to me. What the hell was he doing?

'Piss off, you stupid git!' I shouted. Still he came at me, slanting in.

Belatedly I realised that, now that we were under canopy, the others should already be on comms. I switched on my set and immediately heard guys coming up to check in: 'Seven, roger . . . Eight, roger.' Then Whinger was saying, 'Come in, One. One, are you OK?'

With a jab on my pressel switch I said sharply, 'One, roger. I'm all right. And I'd be even better if some cunt hadn't flown into me. Now get off the air.'

After that close call, the rest of the exercise seemed

pretty tame. Our reception committee met us in the forest clearing. They'd seen nothing wrong, and didn't realise we'd almost had a fatality; when they heard, there were a good few *mon Dieu*s flying about, but I'd recovered my composure, and we let down the tension by having a laugh. We quickly established that it was Pavarotti who'd nearly written me off. I couldn't hold it against him, because it turned out that he himself had gone unstable when clearing the aircraft, and he'd had a load of trouble of his own. The result was that he'd got separated from the rest of the group. He'd been flying back in to re-establish contact when the collision occurred, and he'd never seen me until the impact.

'Christ, Pav,' said Whinger. 'With eyes in your arse like you've got, you ought to be able to see in every fucking direction at once.'

As we gathered up our chutes, Pav and I felt our legs stiffening from the bruises we'd sustained, and knew we were going to be pretty sore in the morning. But our French colleagues spirited us past the opposing forces and put us in position to take out the power station that was doing duty as the enemy's comms centre.

No snags there – and after a wash-up next morning, we moved into the civilian phase of our exercise, which required us to make our way back into England under assumed identities. Use of the tunnel was banned, so we had to travel by sea, using either Dover or Folkestone. The rules laid down that we had to land between midday and midnight – and we knew that the immigration authorities had been briefed by the Int

Corps guys from Hereford. In other words, the bastards were poised to intercept us.

We travelled up to the Channel individually, and by the time I reached Calais at about 6.30, after two nights with no proper sleep, I was knackered.

One of the first people I saw on board the ferry was Whinger, easing his nerves with a quick pint of lager in one of the bars. It wasn't beyond the bounds of possibility that someone had put dickers on the ship, trying to eyeball us before we'd even landed; so I went past without giving any sign of recognition. With his Mexican moustache, Whinger looked every inch a veteran SAS operator, and I had myself a private bet that the watchers would pick him up. His face was deeply lined, with telltale furrows up his cheeks and across his forehead, giving it that strained, prematurely aged appearance brought on by years of pushing yourself to the limit.

If I was being honest, I'd have to say I looked much the same, with the odd grey hair appearing. Worse, my eyes were so bloodshot from the centrifugal force of the spin that I looked like Count Dracula after a satisfactory attachment to some young lady's jugular.

One thing I knew for sure was **that I did** *not* **want to get caught in the net and have to submit to** prolonged interrogation. I'd been through all **that six** years earlier, during my first tour with the Subversive Action Wing, the most secret unit within the SAS. That first time I'd been pulled in and put through the mill. Now, as then, everyone assigned to the SAW had to be able to maintain a cover identity for up to thirty-six hours: it was an essential part of our training, especially when a delicate task like our trip to Moscow was in prospect. It wasn't that, as commander of the team, I felt I should be exempt from such indignities: just that I was tired, and the thought of answering endless questions gave me a pain in the arse.

I'd toyed with the idea of wearing shades when I came to Immigration, but I dropped it, because all they do is attract attention. Instead, I'd gone for a white baseball cap with a long peak, green on the underside, that came well forward over my face. What with that, a blue T-shirt, jeans and trainers, and a scruffy little civilian haversack on my back, I hoped I could pass for the self-employed carpenter I was claiming to be. I'd also taken the precaution of loading up with booze, like all the genuine tourists and day-trippers around me.

I found myself a seat in the forward upper lounge and settled down. All round me people were laughing and chatting, kids screaming; but I pulled the peak of my cap down and closed my eyes, which were itching and aching, and the next thing I knew a voice on the tannoy was blaring out that we would dock in five minutes' time. I'd managed to sleep the two-hour trip away.

I had time for a wash and the hundredth run-through of my own cover identity, just in case I was pulled. According to my passport I was Malcolm Barrow, aged thirty-six, from Alnwick in Northumberland. I'd been to France to visit friends who'd bought an old pub in Normandy and wanted some restoration done. I had the name of the place in my head – L'Auberge au Vieux Puits – but, conveniently for me, it was very primitive and had no telephone, so no quick checks could be made.

Our cover stories had been created by the Firm – our name for MI6 – and were adapted from our own real backgrounds. Because I'm obviously a Geordie, by my accent, my phoney address was in the correct part of the country: Castle Row, Alnwick. The first names of my parents were Derek and Mabel. The telephone number I'd use – a real one – was that of my brother, who'd been primed to tell anyone calling that Malcolm was on a job in France. Often the lads got muddled when they gave the names of imaginary parents, and, under cross-questioning, confused them with the real ones. But for me it's easier: being an orphan brought up by my Uncle Phil, I never knew any real parents, and so had no trouble remembering Derek and Mabel.

We were off the ship in short order. Normally these days there's practically no passport control at the Channel ports; but that evening immigration staff manned all the desks, probably for their own training, and certainly as part of our exercise. But as the crowd was lining up to go past the desks I got a lucky break. Immediately ahead of me was a stunning black girl in a lime-green top and skin-tight, lemon-yellow satin pants, lugging two bags of bottles in one hand and dragging a small, coffee-coloured kid along with the other. I didn't deliberately position myself behind her, you understand: she just happened to be there. The point about her was that one of her carrier bags was splitting.

'Eh,' I went, 'watch yourself. You're about to lose a few bottles.'

I bent down, picked up the child and held it on my hip – a boy, by the look of him.

'What's the matter?' she said sharply. 'I'm OK.'

Probably she thought I was trying to pick her up. Maybe she didn't fancy my fiery eyeballs.

'No, really,' I said, 'it's no bother.'

A second later we were side-by-side in the immigration queue, looking like any other couple coming back from a holiday. She smelt of lemon, too: lemon pants, lemon scent. Nice.

She was glaring at me and I saw that she was really *very* pretty, with a wide mouth and big hazel eyes. She looked so suspicious that I couldn't help smiling.

'I've got a kid of my own,' I said. 'Older than him, but much the same. It's quite a way to carry him. Maybe you can take my passport and hand it over. How's that?'

'It's a deal.' She relented and gave a dazzlingly white smile: 'What's your name?'

'Malcolm. Mal.'

'OK. I'm Jane.'

We closed on the cubicle as a pair, and the short, sandy-haired guy in occupation was so riveted by her cleavage that he scarely got his eyes on our documents or on me. In a couple of seconds we were through and waltzing through the Customs hall. Glancing back, I saw Whinger in another of the queues, still on the wrong side of the barrier.

As soon as we were clear, I said, 'Thanks. Where would you like him taken?'

'We're on the train.'

'OK. This way.'

When I sneaked another glance behind me I saw that Whinger had been rumbled: the man on the desk had stopped him, poor bugger, and called in a superior.

We started walking again and I said, 'Where are you going?'

'London. Don't tell me – you're coming as well?'

'Wish I was. No – I'm driving. But I'm not in any hurry. I'll see you on board.'

In the terminal a train was already standing at the platform, so I did as I'd promised and sat the child down and waved goodbye, not without a touch of regret. Lemon Jane could have been a lot of fun.

Then, as I stepped back on to the platform, I was jerked out of my reverie by the sight of a stocky, fair-haired young guy walking past. There was something familiar about his shape and gait – a bit of a roll in his walk – but at first I didn't recognise him. Then suddenly I saw that it was Rick Ellis, one of our team, wearing a blond wig. I almost called out to him but stopped myself just in time: it was still conceivable that someone was tailing him, and I didn't want either of us compromised.

Crafty sod! His disguise had carried him clean past Immigration, and it looked like he was away.

I knew that anyone captured would be taken to the Intelligence Corps headquarters at Ashford, which was running the exercise, so I dug my mobile phone out of my pack and called the Ops Room. After being passed around for a bit I heard a familiar Scottish voice – Jock Morrison, the Assistant Int Officer from Hereford, who was monitoring the interrogations.

'How are we doing?' I asked.

'They've got two of your guys here already, and they reckon they've just picked up a third at Folkestone.'

Whinger, I thought. But all I said was, 'OK – I'm through, and I'm coming in.'

I knew the lads would have been taken across in blacked-out vans so that they wouldn't know where they were, and although they wouldn't get physically knocked about, they would have a hard time of it all the same, being deprived of food and sleep, and repeatedly brought back for re-interrogation throughout the night.

Having hired a Golf from the Avis desk in the terminal, I shot up the M20 and reached Ashford in under half a hour.

'How did *you* get through?' Jock demanded when he saw me.

'Walked,' I told him. 'What's the crack?'

'They're questioning two of the lads now.'

The Central Control Room had a bank of TV monitors ranged high along the front wall, each connected to one of the interrogation rooms. A couple of guys in shirtsleeves were watching them and making notes, exchanging the odd remark.

On one screen was Johnny Pearce, one of our weapons specialists, twenty-eight years old, black-haired and high-complexioned, looking even darker than usual under a couple of days' stubble. His long eyelashes gave him a deceptively gentle appearance, though in fact he was as hard as they come, and an ace at martial arts. A Scouser, he'd practised kick-boxing ever since he was a kid. He always said he'd needed it to survive in school, fights taking place every day in front of appreciative audiences, and every boy having to look after himself.

Johnny was wearing an open-necked, short-sleeved blue shirt and sitting on an upright wooden chair in the middle of the cell-like room. Facing him across a bare wooden desk sat a detective in a pale grey suit. The camera was looking straight at Johnny from somewhere behind the interrogating officer, whose head and shoulders were visible at the bottom of the screen. Johnny looked tired but calm, and whenever one of the controllers turned up the sound on his channel, his answers sounded perfectly composed.

'You said you went to school in Worcester?'

'That's right.'

'How come you have a Liverpool accent, then?'

'Born there. Never lost it.

'All right. What was the name of the school again?'

'Hadlow Comprehensive.'

'Address?'

'It's on Kidderminster Road.'

'Does it have its own sports fields?'

'Yes.'

'Where are they?'

17

'Right behind it.'

'Swimming pool?'

'I dunno about now, but it didn't then.'

'What dates did you say you were there?'

'Let's see.' Johnny paused. 'I must have gone there in eighty-three, left in ninety-one.'

'That's funny.' The detective's voice remained level and polite. 'We've checked the records, and they don't mention anyone called Martin Turner attending between those dates.'

'Really?' Johnny raised his eyebrows and looked coolly at the man opposite. 'You know they had a big fire the year after I left, in the spring? I think a lot of records got burnt.'

'Well, we'd better check again . . .'

Good on yer, Johnny, I was thinking. Great stuff! I knew his cover story nearly as well as he did, and I could see that he was sticking to it. The home team was probably bluffing: Johnny certainly was, and he seemed sure they were. Since this was Saturday, and in the school holidays, how could they have checked the school records?

'Good!' said one of the supervisors in the control room. 'He's doing well. I like that.'

Next door, things weren't going so well. Pete Pascoe, a Cornishman, was letting his temper get the better of him. His reddish hair and moustache hinted at his Celtic origins: he could be a fiery devil and needed to watch himself.

His interrogator seemed to have realised this. 'Your

18

family,' he said. 'Your brother's how old?'

'Twenty-four.'

'And he's a mechanic?'

'That's right.'

'What's his address?'

'Twenty-eight . . . twenty-eight Northcourt Avenue, Reading.'

'That's where you said your *sister* lives.'

'It is. She does. Simon lodges with her.'

'He's not married, then?'

'No.'

'But she is?'

'Of course. I told you.'

'And her married name?'

'Jenkins.' Suddenly Pete's patience ran out. 'For Christ's sake!' he snapped. 'We've been through all this before. Have you got nothing better to ask?'

'Just checking,' said the detective smoothly. On the monitor I could see Pete's nostrils working in and out – a sure sign that he was getting steamed up. Beside me, one of the supervisors made a grimace and wrote something on his notepad.

I watched for a while longer, but then I thought, To hell with this. It was amusing to see the guys getting grilled, but I decided the time could be better spent: we still had a long way to go in preparing for our Russian trip, and not many days in which to get everything done.

I looked at my watch: 9.35. The exercise had gone on long enough. That sort of thing's OK if there's no big deal in prospect, but we had a hell of a team job to tackle. What we should all have been doing was learning Russian, not pissing about with cover stories in pissy Ashford. It was time we went back to Hereford and got stuck into our final training.

A guy from Spetznaz, the Russian special forces unit, was due in on Monday, coming to have a look at our set-up and give us advice on kit. On Thursday our advance party would fly to Balashika, the base outside Moscow, to suss out the accommodation and facilities, with the main party following within two weeks.

I slipped out of the control room and found Jock Morrison. 'Listen,' I said, 'do we have to go through with this?'

'What's the matter?'

'I want to stop it. For one thing, they've only caught three of our guys. I'm through, and I know Rick Ellis is too – I saw him boarding a train. I bet the other three are clear as well. And anyway, we've got more important things to do than sit around here playing games.'

'Well . . .' Jock looked doubtful. 'It's not my decision.'

'I know. It's down to me. Tell you what – we'll give it another hour and see how things are going then. I'm going to call the Feathers and find out who's made it.'

The Feathers Hotel, on the old London road, was the RV for anyone who'd passed through the screen. We'd got rooms booked, but it was a sure bet that the lads would be in the bar, so I had my call put through there.

'Have you got a Mr Terry Johnson there?' I asked, using Rick's cover name.

'One minute,' the guy replied. There was a pause, during which I could hear the buzz of conversation, then Rick came on the line.

'Mr Johnson?' I said in a phoney, genteel voice. 'I saw you, you poncified twit.'

'Who's that, for fuck's sake?'

'Geordie. I was behind you at the station.'

'Never saw you.'

'No, but I saw you. Who else is there?'

'Dusty, Mal and Pavarotti.'

'Four of you! That's everyone accounted for, then.'

'Where are you, Geordie?'

'In the torture chamber. They've got Whinger, Pete and Johnny. But listen – I'm going to call it off in a minute. Are they still doing food over there?'

'Just about.'

'Ask them to keep four dinners, then. We'll be across in an hour.'

Back in the control room, Pete Pascoe was still on the second screen, but one glance told me he'd got hold of himself and settled down: he was now looking quite comfortable. As for the first screen – there was Whinger, claiming to be an undertaker called Solomon Grice, and bombarding his detective with outrageous remarks. He'd always been a bit of an actor, had Whinger, and in situations like this he could crack an extra edge on to his native Cockney accent, making himself sound almost like a caricature of what he is

21

anyway – a true East Ender. Throw in the horrible rhyming slang, and no interviewer has a chance.

When a second interrogator took over and asked him to confirm his name, he instantly said, 'Hell of a price.' Only after a few seconds of blank silence did he come up with the second half: 'Solomon Grice.' In the next minute he said, 'Give 'em a chance' for 'South of France', then, when asked where his father lived, he replied, 'Ask some boffin.' Again he waited before completing the equation: 'In his coffin.'

'You mean he's dead?'

'Course he's fucking dead. Been dead for twenty years, ennie?'

I looked at the nearest controller, who was trying to suppress a laugh, and said, 'You'll not get anywhere with him. Not a chance. He's done this too often.'

'You could be right.'

'Let's pack it in, then. The guys are all doing OK. The rest are at the RV. We might as well join them there.'

So it was that we piled into the Feathers for big plates of lasagne and a few pints of Shepherd Neame's Spitfire ale, while we shot the shit about how we'd reached the Channel.

TWO

The moment we'd got wind of a team job in Moscow, word had spread through SAW like a charge of electricity. Russia! The very notion had put the wing on an immediate high. The Regiment had never worked there before. In the Communist era, of course, the idea would have been unthinkable. For as long as anyone could remember, Russia had been the arch-enemy, the big, ugly bear on the eastern horizon, threatening the rest of the world with nuclear destruction.

My only personal involvement in the Cold War had been during the early eighties, on stay-behind exercises in which members of the Regiment had literally gone to ground on the West German border, opposite the Soviet and East German troops on the other side of the line. We'd dug ourselves in, camouflaged the shelters, and spent three weeks at a stretch underground. Buried on top of each other, breathing the foul air, shitting into plastic bags . . . It had been a filthy experience which had almost driven several of the lads round the bend. The plan was that, if the Russians launched World War Three, their front units would roll over us, and we could come up behind them, to report troop movements, direct Western air strikes and suchlike. Everyone had known that, if it happened for real, we'd be on a one-way ticket. So, what with that and the discomfort, the whole experience hadn't been very cheerful.

Now things were entirely different. As part of the programme of co-operation between our Prime Minister and their President, the Subversive Action Wing had been tasked to go out and train Tiger Force, a special unit newly formed to fight the ever-increasing menace of the Russian Mafia. With the rupert who normally commanded the SAW away in the Far East on another assignment, it had fallen to me to lead the training team and take it out.

I'd never say it to any of them, but the seven guys under my command were a first-class lot – seasoned all-rounders who'd each done at least five or six years with the Regiment.

The oldest and best known to me was Whinger Watson, whose laid-back attitude concealed his high abilities. We'd worked together in Ulster, Colombia and other hairy places, and understood each other perfectly. His nickname was slightly misleading, in that it referred to his habit of making deliberately stupid remarks, rather than complaining about things. That was one of his best features, in fact: he never complained, but always got on with the job in hand.

The others were all in their late twenties, although Rick Ellis, our best linguist, looked younger, being fresh faced, with curly light-brown hair already receding from his forehead. He had a very good brain, and had worked closely with the Det – the intelligence-gathering unit – in Northern Ireland. Maybe it was his appearance that caused him so much trouble with women. The thing about Rick was that he could never burn his bridges: as each affair petered out, rather than simply saying goodbye he'd keep phoning the woman or sending flowers, in case he became desperate for a shag at any time in the future.

Pavarotti Price's speciality, apart from singing in the bath, was explosives. He took great delight in dropping anything, from a bridge to an obsolete cooling tower – the bigger the better. A hulking six-footer, he came from a mining family in the Rhondda valley, and was probably the strongest man in the party. Sometimes, after a few pints, he could be persuaded to perform his party trick of bending six-inch nails with his bare hands. Yet he had one failing which he tried to keep under wraps: a fear of confined spaces, which seemed to stem from his background. For generations his ancestors had worked in the mines, but his elder brother had been killed in an old shaft; they'd been playing with some other boys when part of the roof had collapsed. Pav had escaped unhurt, but the disaster had left him with a horror of mine-workings and tunnels in general.

Another big fellow was Mal Garrard, a dark and rather quiet man who had originally came to the UK on a two-year secondment from the New Zealand SAS, then did Selection at Hereford, passed, and served for six years as a fully fledged member of the Regiment. For a few weeks after his arrival people had given him stick about his accent, pretending they couldn't understand what he was saying; but he'd taken it in good part, and had made himself well liked, not least because he was brilliant on computers.

The team medic was Dusty Miller, son of a Yorkshire blacksmith, much addicted to horses, racing and betting particularly: a compact, dark-haired fellow with a very powerful upper body, heavily into weight-lifting. You could see him coming a mile away, because he had a peculiar walk: he moved with his toes turned out, and rose on to the balls of his feet like a duck. Doctoring was only one of his skills; apart from anything else, he was a hell of a pistol shot, and often went out on unofficial rabbit-shoots around one of the training areas, blowing the heads off his quarry with some grossly over-powered weapon like a Colt .45.

Johnny Pearce, as I said, was as tough as they come: a fearsome kick-boxer and an ace mountaineer. No doubt his physical nature, and the many hours he spent in the open air, contributed to his ruddy complexion.

Last, but of equal calibre, was Pete Pascoe, the carrot-headed Cornishman, whose special skill was signalling. He, too, was an excellent all-rounder, his one defect being his volatile temper. In his first years with the Regiment this had been a real handicap, and he'd almost been RTU'd after he rammed a civilian car in the outskirts of Hereford. He claimed his brakes had locked and he'd skidded on a wet surface, but he only just escaped prosecution. Afterwards he had admitted that the fellow he bumped had been knocking off his girlfriend while he was away on a Squadron trip. Now though, at the ripe old age of twenty-seven, he was calming down a bit and had become more reliable.

Our first action, when we heard about the Russian job, had been to put the team on an intensive language course, so that by the time we went across we'd at least be able to exchange courtesies with our opposite numbers and read Cyrillic script. Personally I found the language a pain, because so many of the characters were similar, which made words hard to read, let alone understand. But the lessons were enlivened by our Russian teacher, Valentina, a big, dark woman in her fifties, with steel-rimmed spectacles, a lot of teeth, and hair pulled back into a short pony-tail. Three times a week she swept in from London, gave us hell laced with smutty jokes, and swept out again, a whirlwind of energy. The only person who didn't like her was Pete: she teased him once too often when he forgot something basic, and although he didn't actually flare up at the time, for ever after he referred to her as BOB: the Bloody Old Bitch.

Lectures from a member of the Firm introduced us to the Russian Mafia. The main point seemed to be that it wasn't a single organisation like its namesake in Sicily, under the control of one godfather, but comprised a whole lot of criminal gangs battling each other for supremacy. Since Russia had converted to a free-market system, our informant told us, every kind of racketeering had broken out: by sheer power of money the Mafia had risen above the law and made themselves impervious to normal justice. The police couldn't control them, and corruption was spreading through every kind of business. 'Once the disease had taken a hold,' the guy from the Firm had told us, 'there was no stopping it. Now it's even eaten its way into government. Leading politicians are being bribed and pressured and threatened. If they don't play ball, they're eliminated. There's a real fear in Western capitals that the whole of Russia is soon going to be ungovernable.'

Within a week of the request for a training team, we'd set a timetable. A recce party – consisting of myself, Whinger and Rick – would fly to Moscow on 15 September and spend a day checking the facilities of the camp and training area. We'd return on the seventeenth and have three weeks in which to make final preparations. The whole team, with all our kit, would go out early in October.

Before any of that, though, the Russian course leader, Major Ivanov, was due to spend a couple of days seeing how we did things in Hereford – and as his opposite number I went to meet him off the plane at Heathrow.

I cut it a bit fine. By the time I'd put my car in the stack and walked over the bridge into the Terminal Two arrival area, Aeroflot's flight SU247 from Moscow had already landed and passengers with hand luggage only were coming through the Customs screen. By arrangement, I was carrying a white square of cardboard bearing the word ACTIVE in big black capitals, and I stood by the barrier holding it in front of my stomach.

In the end it wasn't needed, because I spotted my guest before he saw me: a big fellow, a good six feet, and broad with it, walking very upright. He had a wide forehead with mid-brown hair swept across it, a rather flat face, and a quick, alert look as his gaze swept back and forth across the waiting crowd. I also noticed a fuzzy vertical scar on his left temple. As he came towards me I had time to think that in the old days you would have expected a Russian officer to carry duelling scars, but this one was clearly the result of a burn.

The guy was wearing jeans and a black leather jacket that looked rather expensive, and was carrying a hold-all slung over one shoulder. As he drew level with me I raised my right hand to attract his attention, and said, 'Major Ivanov? *Zdravstvuite.*'

He stopped, focused on me and said, 'Sergeant Major? *Zdravstvuite.*' His face broke into a smile, revealing that his two front teeth were made of metal, and he said, '*Vui gavarete pa Russki?*'

The words slipped out so fast that I took a second to recognise them. Then I managed, '*Nemnogo.*'

'*Khorosho!*' He looked delighted. We shook hands over the barrier and I motioned him towards the exit. As he came through, he fired off something else in Russian, and my bluff was called.

'Sorry,' I went. 'When I said *nemnogo*, I meant it. Only a very little.'

He smiled again and said, 'Doesn't matter. I speak English OK.'

I tried to take his hold-all off him but he wouldn't let me, and we set off for the car. He walked fast, with a springy gait, and I could see straight away that he was fit.

'Good flight?'

He shrugged. 'The pilot – he landed it like a ton of shit.'

'But you survived.'

He smiled. 'It remind me of when I get these teeth. Hard landing in Siberia. Into seat before.'

He was all eyes as we walked out on to the third floor of the stack, past ranks of shiny new vehicles.

'Cars!' he exclaimed. 'Such types of cars!'

'This is ours.' I unlocked the Passat, opened the boot and put his bag inside. Automatically he made for the right-hand front door.

'This side.' I pointed.

'Excuse me!'

'Rassat,' he said as he ran a finger over the car's logo.

'It's a P,' I said. 'Passat.'

'Of course! He is English?'

'German.'

Soon I realised that, although he spoke English with fair fluency, he had trouble recognising letters, as if he'd picked up the language by ear, rather than by reading. I could see him mouthing words to himself as we passed the hoardings. I had to stop myself smiling at his accent, which was tremendously Russian. His Hs were very hot: he pronounced Os like As, and jacked Y sounds on to the front of Es – *prafyessional*. He also made 'kill' into

30

keell. His L's were beautifully liquid, as if he were rolling a mouthful of vodka round the back of his tongue.

In a few minutes we were heading west on the M4.

'Your first time in the West?'

'*Da.*'

'How come you speak English so well?'

'I learn in school. Also from American attached to our unit.'

'I see. Can I call you Alexander?'

'Sasha, please. Sasha is small name of Alexander. The diminution. Your name is George?'

'Geordie. That's a kind of diminutive, as well.'

'*Khorosho!* And second name?'

'Sharp.'

'That is family name. I mean patronymic.'

'What's that?'

'Your father name. My father is Vassily. So I am Aleksandr Vassilyevitch Ivanov. Your father is . . . ?'

'Was. Michael, I think.'

'You think? You don't know?'

'I never knew him.'

'I am sorry. Well – anyway, you are Geordie Mikhailovitch.'

His accent made him pronounce my name 'Zheordie', but who was I to complain? His English might be fractured, but at least he could get along in it – whereas my Russian was limited to about twenty words.

Already I liked his enthusiasm, the keen interest he took in everything he saw – for instance, the surface of the motorway. 'This street!' he said. 'He is vairy good. Our streets are full of holes. Cars soon break. The suspenders – always breaking.'

Another thing that fascinated him was the smallness of the suburban houses, and their gardens.

'How many families live in such a house?' he asked, pointing at a row.

'Those are what we call semis – semi-detached, two joined together. Two front doors, you see. Probably one family in each side.'

'In Russia we have all big house. Not like this.' He saw me glance across and said, 'Apartment blocks. Fifteen, twenty pieces high. These are like *izbas*.'

'What's that?'

'*Izba* is old house in the country. Peasant house.'

'A cottage?'

'Yes, but very old. And such a house . . .' He gestured at a thirties villa standing in a large garden. 'This belongs to government?'

'No, no. I'm sure it's private. A private individual. I think I read somewhere that you can buy houses in Russia now.'

'Yes – it is just starting.'

'And land? Could you buy a farm, for instance?'

'By no means. No land can be sold, except for gardens.'

The afternoon traffic was light and the fast lane was often clear, but I kept my speed down to eighty and let the BMWs whip past. I explained the system of number-plates: how S indicated the current year, just started in August, that next autumn there'd be a scramble for Ts, and that freaks paid huge sums for special numbers. Just at the right moment to illustrate my point, we were overtaken by a hell-driven Peugeot 205 with the number P1NTA.

We started to compare British and Russian special forces, and I asked about the base at Balashika.

'It is home of our famous Dzerzhinsky division. That belongs to Ministry of Interior. They have many facilities at Balashika. Beeg *strelbilshze*.'

'Barracks?'

'*Nyet*. Barracks is *kazarma*. *Strelbilshze* is ranges. Beeg ranges, beeg training area. Between town and forest. Town this side, forest this side. Only thirty kilometres from Moscow, to the east. All behind concrete fences.'

'Fences?'

'Walls. Concrete walls, two metres tall. From outside you see nothing.'

When I brought up the subject of the Mafia, he instantly became indignant and twisted round in his seat to look at me. 'They keell everybody! Half the population has become what we call *vor v zakone*. That means "thief in the law". In other words, creeminals.

'They keell businessmen, bank managers, property men – anyone. Last year they even kill Larisa Nechayeva!'

'Who?'

'Nechayeva? Boss of Spartak football club. They shoot her in her *dacha*, her country house. Another woman with her. And why? Because she refused to pay

33

them money. Also they kill Valentin Sych, ice hockey president.'

'What's the motive?' I said. 'Why kill all these different kinds of people?'

'Marney!' Sasha held up his right hand, rubbing thumb and forefinger together. 'Marney, marney, marney! Everyone wants more. Always US dollars. Russian money no good. You know how we call it? *Deregannye dengi* or *deregannye rubli*. That means wooden money, wooden roubles. Throw it in the stove!'

'But you've just had a revaluation. Didn't they divide by a thousand?'

'*Konechno*. Of course. Before, it was seven thousand roubles to one dollar. Now it is seven. But what is the difference? Prices are still crazy. No change.'

'These murders – who's carrying them out?'

'Contract killers. Almost all. With one bullet, a man can earn half million dollars.' He looked at me and went on in a soft, menacing, ingratiating voice: 'Eemagine. You are manager of bank, big boss, yes? Somebody telephones. "Look, Meester Sharp, you should pay us some marney." You tell them, "Get to hell."

'Another call. "You know, Mr Sharp, you are in danger. You need pratyection. We do not like you to be hurt. We can pratyect you. We can look after your family. But it will cost you: two per cent. Two per cent of bank takings – a lot of money."

'Again you say, "Get lost."'

He paused, and when he went on, his voice was even more reasonable, more wheedling, more sinister.

34

'A week passes. Another call. "Now look, Meester Sharp. Are you not concerned for your safety, for your little children, for their lives?"

' "No," you say.

' "All right, then. Wait. Wait. Just wait."

'You think you are safe. Why? Because you have closed-circuit TV on your block. You have modern security system. You have former KGB on duty outside. But you are under terrible pressure – from your bosses to resist the threat, from the criminals to pay.

'Then one morning you go out to your car. Sunny day. Very nice. Guards are sitting there. Only twenty-five metres to walk, but that is enough. *BASH! Bang!* The contract killer fires one shot from his car – finish.'

'Nasty,' I said.

'Is very bad, and always getting worse. Now all politicians are in danger, even the President and the Prime Minister.'

'That's why we're coming over, I guess.'

'*Konechno.*'

He gave me such a long run-down on Mafia activities that we reached camp almost without noticing it. 'Here we are,' I said as we turned in towards the gate. 'Welcome to Stirling Lines.'

The police on security duty had been briefed to expect him, and I checked him through without difficulty. Then we headed for the officers' mess, where a room was booked. At that time of the afternoon the place was deserted except for Larry, the steward, who was busy cleaning the regimental silver, so I took Sasha through to show him his room, which was small but cheerful, with a shower and lavatory cubicle attached.

'Even own bathroom!' Sasha grinned. Then, pointing at the washbasin, he recited a little poem: '*Tolko pokoynik, Ne ssit v rukomoynik.*'

'What's that?'

'It is joke about Russian hotels. Usually bathroom is a kilometre away along passage. It means, "Only a dead man does not piss in the basin."'

He was delighted with the accommodation; but when we got back into the anteroom, with its sofas and armchairs and little tables, and scenes from regimental history on the walls, he became nervous.

'Zheordie,' he said. 'I am shamed.'

'What's the matter?'

'This place . . .' He gestured round the room. 'My clothes . . .' He looked down at himself, pointing to his black jacket, his faded jeans, his ancient trainers. 'Not smart.'

'Don't worry. Everyone's very relaxed round here. No formality.'

'Perhaps . . .'

Still he looked anxious, so I said, 'Tell you what. I'll run you into town and we can buy you some new stuff at Marks and Sparks.' I saw him hesitate, and explained, 'That's a chain store. Good cheap clothes. Have you got money?'

He produced his wallet, opened it and fished out some notes. 'This is enough?'

He had two fivers and two ten-dollar notes.

'Is that all you've got?'

He nodded.

Jesus! I thought.

'Zheordie, you must understand. In the army, now, we do not get paid. Five months, no marney.'

I stared at him. 'In that case, *we'll* get you something.'

'No, please. You should not pay.'

'Not me – the system. There's a fund for this sort of thing. I can square it away.'

I dived into my room in the sergeants' mess to pick up a chequebook. Thus equipped, we drove into town and got Sasha kitted out with a lightweight, dark-blue blazer, grey slacks, a pair of black moccasins, a couple of shirts and a tie. The bill came to nearly £200, but I knew I could recover the money from Bill Tadd, the quartermaster.

By 5.30 we were back in camp, and I realised that to Sasha it was already 8.30 – so I suggested that he had a shower and got his head down for an hour before I came back and collected him for supper.

The meal went fine. There were one or two young ruperts about, but we two sat in a corner of the dining-room and no one bothered us. Sasha's new gear did him proud. He couldn't help preening himself a bit, shooting the cuffs of his pale-blue shirt and brushing invisible bits of fluff off the sleeves of his blazer.

As we chatted it became apparent that he'd had quite a lot of fighting experience – more than I had. One of the pictures on the wall was of the Jebel Akhdar in

Oman, where the Regiment had won a famous victory in the fifties, and it set him reminiscing about Afghanistan, where he'd been posted for a year in hellish conditions. The mountains, he said, looked very similar – but in contrast with the heat of the Gulf, the winter cold in Afghanistan had been horrendous.

Towards the end of the meal, though, our conversation became rather stilted. Several times Sasha didn't understand something I'd said, and he seemed to be preoccupied with his behaviour, eating his cheese carefully and often glancing round. So I proposed we go out for a couple of beers and his mood lightened again.

The main thing was to steer clear of other guys from the Regiment and of the local slappers, whose intelligence network is shit hot. Bush telegraph keeps all the Hereford talent fully informed about who's who and who's where – who's on the standby squadron, who's on the SP team and so on. The last thing I wanted was for those women to see a Russian walking around with me in the evening – so we drove off to The Lamb, a pub in one of the outlying villages, and Sasha put down his first pint of Theakston's Old Peculier like he hadn't had a drink in months.

With the beer came relaxation.

'Cheers!' He raised his glass for the third or fourth time. 'Tell me your family. You are married?'

'No. I was. How about you?'

'The same.'

'What happened?'

'My wife – she was killed.'

'I'm sorry. How?'

'She was shot. It was street battle. Some Mafia persons were shooting a bank manager from their car. They keelled him, but also three persons on the pavement. Olga was one.'

'An accident, then?'

'By no means!' He turned on me indignantly. 'On purpose. The Mafia keell all witnesses.'

He paused before adding, 'Olga came from Alma Ata, in Uzbekistan. That was her home.'

'You didn't have children?'

'She was pregnant. Six months. I think it was a boy. My son.'

'When was this?'

'Ninety-three . . . ninety-four. Four years ago.'

'Well – that makes two of us.'

'Excuse me?'

'My story's much the same.'

Keeping it short, I told him about my marriage to Kath, a Northern Irish girl, and how she'd been killed by the premature explosion of an IRA bomb outside a supermarket in Belfast. 'Our son Tim was only three then, so he went to live with Kath's parents in Belfast,' I explained – and that led on to an account of my feud with the man I held responsible for her death, the leading IRA player Declan Farrell.

Sasha listened sympathetically, then said, 'It is your own Mafia, I think, the IRA.' He pronounced the name 'Ee-ra'.

'Not really. The IRA's driven by politics and

religion. Political and religious hatred, more than money. Anyway, because we couldn't get this guy on legitimate operations, I was stupid enough to go after him on my own.'

In a few minutes my reminiscences led me to describe the kidnap of Tracy and Tim.

'Tracy?' Sasha interrupted. 'She is who?'

'A girlfriend . . . Jesus!' I hadn't meant to get into all this. I pushed back my stool, looked at my companion and said, 'We need another drink.' When I stood up and went to the bar to fetch two fresh pints, Sasha came with me, pulling out his wallet.

'Put it away,' I told him. 'In England, you're our guest.'

He gave a little nod by way of saying thank you.

'Yes,' I resumed as we sat down again. 'Tracy. A great girl. At least, she *was*. A redhead. Taller than you. Good fun to be with. She worked as a receptionist at the med centre, in camp. There'd been nothing between us before, but after Kath was killed we gradually got together, and a few months later she moved in with me. It was fantastic the way she took over Tim as if she were his mother . . .

'That was great – until the IRA grabbed her and Tim.'

I described the desperate struggle we'd had to recover her. 'It took us two months – more – to get her back. And when we did, I found she'd flipped.'

'Flipped? What is this?'

'She'd gone out of her mind. The stress had made her

ill. She was a different person. We tried everything: rest, a holiday in the sun, a shrink – a psychiatrist – but nothing worked. She recovered physically, but not emotionally. She blamed me for the whole episode. If I hadn't been in the SAS, it never would have happened – all that crap. As a couple we couldn't get back to where we'd been before.'

'And?'

I sat back and took a deep breath. 'She went away to her family, somewhere in the north. It's more than a year since I last heard from her.'

'And the boy?'

'He's seven now, doing well. He's living with Kath's parents in Belfast. He's growing up a little Ulsterman.'

'You see him?'

'Oh yes, from time to time. We're good buddies.'

Sasha's mind was evidently dwelling on the IRA. 'Why be so soft with such terrorists?' he asked. 'Why not eliminate all? In Chechnya we shoot many rebels, no problem.'

'Yes – but down there a lot of innocent people got killed as well.'

'Chechens vairy primitive people,' Sasha said scornfully. 'If they come to Moscow they go beggars. They make things worse.'

'And in any case,' I persisted, 'you didn't win the war.'

'And why? Because our army has such bad equipment. Many, many shortages. No guns. No ammunition. No food. But Zheordie – I tell you something . . .'

'What's that?'

'The Chechen Mafia – vairy clever at stealing gold. They have more gold than all the other Mafias collected together. Chechens are gold specialists. Drugs also. They bring drugs from Central Asia and send to Europe.'

'What about the army?' I asked. 'How's morale?'

'The army? The Russian army?' He looked round wildly. 'Zheordie – if I am to speak of army, I need vodka.'

'Is it that bad?'

He nodded.

'Vodka, then. Anything with it?'

'No thank you. Just vodka.'

When I handed him a double, neat, he raised the glass in my direction, smiled, called out, '*Vzdrognem!*' and tipped it straight down. I'd got myself the same amount of water in another glass, and tipped that down with an answering 'Cheers!'

'Good vodka,' he said. 'No *samogon*.'

'What's that?'

'Vodka made at home, from potatoes, wood even. What the soldiers get. It is very dangerous.'

'Don't they drink beer?'

'Beer too expensive. And anyway, drinking in barracks is strictly forbidden. So the soldiers go out at night and buy secretly from *babushkas*, old women. Then one junior soldier stands in the passage – guarding, you say? – while the others drink themselves crazy.'

'But morale – you say it's bad?'

'Zheordie, you must understand. There are too many armies. For example, Ministry of Interior has own army, one and half million men – Kulikov's men, we say, from General Kulikov, Interior Minister. That is more than the regular army. Then Ministry of Defence has own army. Special forces for this, special forces for that. You know, there is even special force for underground?'

'You're joking.'

'*Konechno nyet!* It is called GRU. Special troops trained to live in tunnels and work in missile silos. Altogether too many armies, no money. Food is very bad. Soldiers eat shit – on starvation rations all the time.'

'Like what?'

'According to the law, it is such kind of menu. For the morning, it is tea, two pieces bread – one white, one black. Fifty grams butter, but only once a day. Butter only once. And *kasha*, of course. Porridge. Always porridge.

'For dinner, they could get meat in their soup, but very small pieces. Usually young soldiers, for their first half-year, get no meat, because the *cherpaks*, the second-years, grab it. In the evening dishes, every day it is potatoes purée, with piece of so-called fish, bread black and white, tea, and three pieces of sugar.

'For celebration – on important days, state holidays – they have special menu. What does it mean? It means, two biscuits per man, and *makaroni po flotski* – macaroni naval style, with very small meats, like the ship's rat chopped up. Maybe piece of water melon, and one grape per man.

43

'That's what soldiers eat. That's why they are ready to rob, do anything.'

As I fetched another round of vodkas from the bar – with a double for myself this time – I wondered what the hell we'd do about our own food once we got over there. None of our cooks had high enough security clearance to come on an operation as sensitive as this one, so we'd either have to eat with our hosts or fend for ourselves.

Again Sasha knocked his spirit straight down, with another cry of '*Vzdrognem!*'

'Also,' he went on, 'there is much torture of recruits.'

'Bullying, you mean.'

'Torture also. Many beatings. If sergeant does not like junior soldier, he drags him out of bed and makes him stand on one leg half the night. You have heard of *velociped*, the bicycle? No? It is what they do to young recruit. They come to him while he is sleeping, lift up bottom of bed, and put between the fingers on the feet—'

'His toes?'

'Yes – between his toes they put paper or cotton wool, then set it on fire. When flames reach him, he does the bicycle.'

Sasha whirled his hands round in imitation, and I couldn't help but laugh.

'No laughing!' he said indignantly. 'It is very bad. Officers terrorise soldiers – beat them, shoot them—'

'Not really shoot them?'

'Certainly! Many men are shot dead by own officers.

Absolutely incredible.'

'Do people get fined?' I asked.

'Fined?' Sasha seemed astonished. 'How *can* they be fined? They have no so big money. And in any case, it would be very dangerous for commander to punish *kontraktnik*, a prafyessional soldier, in this way. Such persons do not like to pay. Easier just to kill officer with shooting.'

'What about special forces? They must be better.'

'Many, many special forces. Every ministry has special force. Ministry of Defence, Ministry of Interior, Ministry of Federal Security . . .'

'So who's taking on the Mafia?'

'Good question. Under whose jurisdiction is situation going? These too many bodies – in the past they have no joint policy. But now we have new initiative – result of your Prime Minister's visit to President Yeltsin last year. From this has come new agreement. Yeltsin has persuaded Ministry of Defence and Ministry of Interior to create Tiger Force, specially to combat Mafia operations.'

'So who are the guys we'll be training?'

'All *kontraktniks*. That means prafyessional soldiers with contracts – not conscripts. At least two years in the army. All officers, from junior lieutenant to captain. Good types, I hope.'

'Where do they come from?'

'From all different special forces. From Spetznaz, from Omon, from Alpha, from Vympel . . .'

I saw him stifle a yawn.

'Come on,' I told him. 'Time you got your head down. Tomorrow's a full training day. You can meet the guys and tell us what to do.'

'*Khorosho!* Zheordie – let me say thank you for very kind reception. Also for clothings.'

'It's a pleasure.'

One amusing twist that I didn't yet explain to Sasha was that our own headquarters were known in the Regiment as the Kremlin. Valentina had impressed on us that the word simply means 'citadel', but we were chuffed to think that, for the first time in history, our own little Kremlin was about to join forces with its Big Brother in Moscow.

THREE

For the next few days my most important task was to keep up the momentum of our countdown to departure; but at the same time I had to show Sasha round the base and give him an idea of how we did things. Certain areas of camp were out of bounds to him, notably the SAW and the ops room, but there was plenty else for him to see, not least the Killing House, where the CT team laid on a demonstration of hostage-lifting. At first he was cautious about expressing opinions, but the more time I spent with him the more he became prepared to criticise or compare our methods with his.

For us, Killing House demos were routine, but for Sasha they were an eye-opener. The guys put him and me into the left-hand corner of a special room, corralled with two other visitors behind white tape. As usual, the live hostage-figure was sitting on a chair in the middle of the room, with his two guards, in the form of figure-targets, on either side of him. Behind the hostage stood the sergeant in charge, commentating on events.

Just as he seemed to be in the middle of his spiel, giving the principles of close-quarter battle: 'Speed, aggression, surpr—' *BANG!* Loud explosion. Door blown off. Two assaulters running in. *Ba-ba-bom! Ba-ba-bom!* Short bursts from MP5s. Targets riddled, hostage lifted and gone before anyone else could react. Nothing left but smoke and dust.

As our ears recovered, Sasha turned to me, beaming, and said, 'Vairy good! Vairy prafyessional!'

Before we went out he took a close look at the construction of the building, pulling back the metre-wide sheets of thick red rubber, which overlapped each other by nearly half their width, so that he could inspect the steel-plated wall some three inches behind them. Seeing all the crumpled bullets lying on the floor, he understood at once how the rubber caught anything which flew back off the wall, killing its energy.

'This we would like,' he said wistfully, looking round.

'You don't have it?'

He shook his head. 'Only rubber wheels.'

'Tyre houses?'

He nodded.

I knew what he meant, because I'd seen them in the States: skeleton buildings with walls made of piled-up motor-tyres filled with concrete, which, in a crude way, performed the same function as the rubber sheets.

In another room a young assaulter dressed in full black kit had his equipment spread out on two tables for Sasha to look at. The Russian carefully inspected the guy's primary weapon – an MP5 with laser marker and torch attached – and some of his EMOE devices. His close interest offered an unwelcome opening to the range warden, a retired RSM who'd been given a kind of grace-and-favour job keeping the place tidy and sweeping up empty cartridge cases. The old guy could be a pain in the arse, as he always tried to latch on to our guests, and now I had to prise Sasha away from him before we got any awkward questions about where he came from.

From Sasha I gained a more precise idea of our task. He had already explained that the personnel of the new Tiger Force were being drawn from various sources. Most were from Spetznaz, the elite military special force, controlled by the Ministry of Defence, or from Omon, the civilian militia, which came under the jurisdiction of the Ministry of the Interior. Normally, Sasha told me, Omon dealt with problems inside Russia while Spetznaz worked in foreign countries; but the point of Tiger Force was that it should be a highly trained and highly mobile unit, ready to tackle emergencies either at home or abroad. When I remarked that this made it rather like the SAS, Sasha seemed surprised: he had always supposed that we only operated overseas.

He told me that Tiger Force would be directed by the Federal Security Bureau, the FSB, the largest remaining constituent of the old KGB, which had now been broken up into several parts; the bureau was in charge of security and counter-intelligence. The person in charge of our tour, our liaison officer and interpreter, would be an FSB officer.

'And who will that be?' I asked.

49

He spread his hands. 'So far, no information. I find out when I am back in Moscow.'

As I guided Sasha round camp, his meetings with the CO, the ops officer and the rest of the team all went fine; but where he came into his own was in polishing up the diagrams we were preparing for the course. Technically he was way behind because we were working on computers, aiming to project three-dimensional diagrams from our laptops, whereas the Russians apparently were still using blackboards and overhead projectors – but he was very quick on the uptake.

Among the diagrams Sasha had brought with him were two of the weapons that Tiger Force personnel would be using: the Stechkin Mark 5 9mm automatic pistol, and the latest creation of the Rex Firearm Company in St Petersburg, the 9mm Gepard, a modular weapon which can be instantly adapted for use as rifle, sub-machine gun or pistol. I thanked Sasha as gently as possible for bringing them, then let him know that, as well as better diagrams, we had an actual example of the Gepard which we'd acquired via another channel. In fact I'd arranged that Johnny would give the rest of the team a lesson on stripping down and reassembling the weapon, with Sasha present.

This demo proved a big success. For one thing it gave Sasha a chance to start getting to know our guys, and for another, he hit top form during the talk, acting up and joining in Johnny's commentary.

'*Gepard* is Russian for cheetah,' he told the team. 'Very fast, very light.' He made springing, bounding movements with his hands. 'It was developed from the Ryss, which is lynx. Lynx is OK, but cheetah is faster and lighter.'

'That's right.' Johnny took him up, holding the weapon across his knees as he sat at the front of the classroom. 'It's a beaut. It's got everything bar the spots.' He hefted it in one hand. '*Extremely* light. Under four and a half pounds without a mag. As you see, there's a strong resemblance to a sawn-off Kalashnikov AK74U: more than half the parts are interchangeable. But it's a hell of a lot more versatile. From what we've seen on the range so far, it's accurate and nicely balanced. Handles exceptionally well. Looks like it could be a winner in CQB and law enforcement.'

He demonstrated how the tubular steel butt-stock could be flipped out to turn the weapon into a rifle, or downwards to form a grip for sub-machine-gun mode. Then he rapidly stripped it, removing the bolt and bolt-carrier, the return spring, the upper hand-guard and gas chamber. As he brought each component away, Sasha gave us the Russian names.

'Two models of magazine,' Johnny went on, having reassembled the pieces. 'This one holds twenty-two rounds, this one forty. The selector switch here has three positions. On safe, the bolt is locked half-way back so you can just see down into the magazine. Second position, O, as you know, stands for *odin* – one. *Odinochniy* is single fire. Is that right, Sasha?'

'*Konechno.*' The Russian grinned. 'And next position, AV, is for *avtomaticheskiy* – automatic.'

So they went on, back and forth. The Gepard's greatest novelty lay in the fact that it could fire several different types of 9mm round without having to change the barrel. Sasha reeled off eight possibilities, ending with the 9 × 30 hard-alloy-core bullet called the Grom. 'You know what *grom* means?' he asked jokily. 'It means thunder! Very big impact and penetration. Will pierce body armour at three hundred metres.'

Sasha also sat in on a couple of language classes. When he and Valentina found they came from the same city – the place the Communists had called Gorki, now back to its original name of Nizhni Novgorod – they really hit it off. There was one hilarious session when somebody asked Val for a few swear-words, just to put us in the swim, and she pretended to be greatly shocked.

'Swear-words?' she said. 'In Russia, there are no such things. The Communist system was so pure that after seventy-five years of it, all obscenities were eliminated.'

Her teasing kept everyone in good spirits. Of course there was no question of her joining the team in the field, but as we broke up from one lesson, to butter her up, I said, 'Val, I wish to hell you were coming with us.'

'Get me a visa and give me a Gepard,' she quipped back, 'and I'll be there.'

One little task I set the lads was the creation of lapel badges bearing their names in English and Russian. Obviously we didn't want anything that would flap about, so I told everyone to make up a cream-coloured linen patch, with black writing on it, that could be stitched on the tunic of the Russian DPMs we would be wearing. My own name came out as ZHORDI, Mal was exactly the same – MAL – and Rick was RIK, pronounced as if he stank. Johnny became ZHONNI, Dusty DOSTI, and Pete PYOTR. Even Pavarotti could be easily transliterated. But the one name that knackered everybody was Whinger. His real name was Billy, but he'd been known as Whinger for so long that none of his mates could call him anything else. The trouble was, the Russian alphabet has no W, and the nearest we could get to it was VUINZHA.

Among the lads there was a good deal of talk about money, because this looked like being a lucrative trip. What with allowances for food, accommodation, laundry, arduous conditions and so on, our pay was going to build up to two or three times its normal level. The expenses for the whole trip had been reckoned at £6,000 per head, and four grand of this had been paid up front. Anyone prudent put most of the cash into his bank account, but Pavarotti went straight into Monmouth and put down a deposit on a thirty-five-year-old scarlet XJ120 Jag which he'd been fancying for months. I put three grand into my building society account and changed the rest of the money into dollars, insisting that the paymaster got me new notes from the bank, with no year earlier than 1997 on them and in low denominations, because I'd heard that fifties and older notes wouldn't be accepted in Russia.

When we asked Sasha about the black market for money, he said that it had collapsed. He explained that

Moscow, like all Russian cities, had become so flooded with US dollars that anyone could get them, and the rate of exchange was the same everywhere – about seven roubles to the dollar, ten or eleven to a British pound. In the previous year, he told us, following rampant inflation, the rate had swollen to outrageous proportions: 7,000 roubles to the dollar, 10,000 to the pound. But then on 1 January the Russian government had divided the currency rate by a thousand in an attempt to simplify things and calm the economy down.

More briefings about the Russian Mafia came from another visiting professional from the Firm, this one a smooth, silver-haired fellow called Edgar (his surname). Again, Sasha was able to supplement his information, which had been collected from intelligence reports, with first-hand knowledge. The briefings confirmed what Sasha had already told us – that the main Mafia activity was extortion, and the worst threat was against people with big money: leading businessmen, heads of companies, bankers. We learnt that over the past few years various branches of the Mafia had risen to prominence and then faded away. The first to show had been the Solntsevo gang, named after the scruffy suburb on the south-western fringes of Moscow where its members lived. Lately, however, that lot had apparently yielded supremacy to the Ismailovskaya Mafia, also based in Moscow and led by a notorious crook called Sergei Askyonov. This group, with its strong military connections, claimed to have a private army of more than a thousand men.

Edgar, an intelligent guy, quickly appreciated Sasha's worth, and started asking for comments about what he himself was saying. 'One reason for so much crime,' he told us, 'is that there's a fantastic amount of paper money actually in circulation. One the one hand, people don't trust the banks. On the other, inflation's moving so fast that they reckon they get a better return by having dollar bills in their possession. So there's cash everywhere, and a big incentive for robbery. Is that right, Major?'

'Certainly!' Sasha gave a vigorous nod. 'More dollars in Russia now than in rest of world.'

'Outside the States,' Edgar corrected.

'Of course. But that is very much money.'

The lectures helped us all to refine the aims of our course. With kidnappings so common, hostage rescue was obviously of prime importance, and we decided to concentrate on that. EMOE – explosive method of entry, or blowing in doors and windows – was clearly going to be another key area. A third vital subject was ambush drills, and a fourth, the bodyguarding of VIPs. Strictly speaking, BG work fell outside the remit of the Subversive Action Wing, but as all the members of our team had been on specialist close-protection courses it seemed natural to include the subject in our syllabus.

Sasha's tales of the Mafia were so lurid that they acted on the team like shots of adrenalin. All right, we were going in on a training task, but soon every one of the lads was dreaming that we would somehow become directly involved in a Tiger Force hit and get some action ourselves. And it was obvious from the relish with which he described anti-Mafia operations that Sacha was a born killer.

'In Gorki, my home town, is this godfather figure,' he told us one evening. 'Real name Borzov. But he calls himself *Nepobedinyi* – Unvincible.'

'Invincible,' I suggested.

'Yes – Invincible. He thinks nobody can keell him. He is former criminal, many years in gaol. Like I told you, he is true *vor v zakone*, a criminal in the law. Now his chauffeur drives him in bullet-proof Mercedes. Always four bodyguards with him when he moves around. He lives in a palace – like the Winter Palace in St Petersburg, almost. At night, in the yard round his house, a Siberian tiger is wandering. Like a guard dog. A guard cat, you say?'

'Some cat,' said Pavarotti.

'Two hundred kilos,' Sasha said, not joking. 'We heard he feeds this cat on human flesh, his enemies. This Invincible wears a Patek gold watch. His body is covered in pictures . . . tattoos. Small Mafia are not allowed such pictures. If some man gets one without authority, he can be keelled. But Invincible has on his chest a portrait of Lenin. And why? Because no one would dare to shoot at our great Communist leader. On his knees, he has pictures of stars. And why? That means he never kneels for anyone.'

Sasha broke off and gave a quick, rather nasty laugh. 'But one day soon, I think we make him kneel.'

When Sasha flew back to Moscow we missed his cheerful company, and I looked forward to seeing him again when he met our recce party at Sheremetyevo Airport.

'What's the weather going to be like?' I asked him before he went.

'In Russia, autumn is one month ahead. Days warm, nights cool. Typical September.'

His final instruction as I saw him off was, 'Breeng plugs.'

'Plugs?'

'For bath and basin. In Russian hotels, such things do not exist.'

FOUR

We had the weekend clear for our own preparation, then on Monday morning we set off for Heathrow – myself, Whinger and Rick. Obviously the commander and second in command had to go, and we selected Rick as a third partly because he was one of our signallers – he and Pete Pascoe were level when it came to radio work – but mainly because he was our best linguist. He had an incredible knack of picking up languages informally, learning wherever he went: already he spoke French and German, and Russian seemed to be giving him no problems.

In the event, our flight was delayed for nearly three hours by technical problems – one aircraft went tits-up on the runway, and another had to be brought into service – with the result that the whole day seemed to disappear, and dusk was already settling on the land by the time British Airways' flight 262 began its descent into Sheremetyevo.

In the distance and far below us on the starboard side of the plane, I saw lights glowing in the dark, and as we came closer I realised I could see the whole of Moscow enclosed within a single ring of illumination. 'Look at that,' I said to Whinger. 'Ten million people inside that circle. Can you imagine it?'

'Yeah, and a couple of well-placed nukes would finish most of the bastards.'

'Come on,' I laughed. 'They're our friends now.'

But there wasn't much sign of that when we landed. We were travelling on civilian passports made out in our own names, and so had to go through Immigration along with everyone else. The hall was hot and dimly lit. Everything looked dirty and dilapidated – walls, doors, lights, the local staff. Worst of all was the ceiling, close over our heads, which looked as if someone had nailed ten thousand copper saucepans to it, rims downward.

'Jesus!' I said quietly. 'This is worse than Africa.'

For forty minutes we sweated shoulder-to-shoulder with passengers from other flights, shuffling forward like snails in queues that stretched towards the booths manned by the immigration officials. As we inched closer, I saw that the lady we were heading for could have walked straight off the set of a James Bond movie: grey uniform with lieutenant's bars on the shoulders, a mane of long, straight streaky blonde hair and half-inch false eyelashes.

Finally reaching her booth, I summoned up my best Russian and said, '*Dobriye vecher.*'

She glared at me, glared at my passport, glared at her video monitor and punched my details into her computer terminal, then shoved my documents back across the shelf without a word. It was definitely the wrong time of the month for her.

'Friendly lot,' Whinger observed as he came through behind me. 'Roll on the fucking Customs!'

To our surprise, they gave us no trouble. We took the green channel and nobody even looked in our direction. On the far side of the screen a swarm of taxi-drivers engulfed us, all shouting and trying to snatch our luggage; but through the middle of them came Sasha, dressed in civvies and smiling as he shouldered the mob aside. I recognised his shirt as one of the pair we'd bought in Hereford.

He greeted us warmly and led us out to a battered grey saloon which he'd parked on the pavement. We put our hold-alls into the boot and climbed aboard, myself in the front, the other guys in the back. Because the hinges had worked loose, it took three slams to make my door shut securely.

'I am sorry,' Sasha said as he drove off. 'You are in Intourist Hotel.'

'What's wrong with that?'

He let go of the wheel to spread his hands. 'Not nice. We wanted the Moskva, but no rooms.'

'Oh, well. It's only two nights.' To change the subject I asked, 'What sort of a car is this?'

'It is Volga. Old, old. I would like to buy new one, something good. But that would be too dangerous. And why? Because the Mafia would take it. One day, in a traffic jam, my mother is driving it, she sees two gun-machines in her ears, this side and that side. "Give me the keys." Finish.'

'Can't the police do anything?'

'Police!' He shot me a hopeless look. 'They are worst. They are cowards. And anyway, half of them are paid by Mafia.'

The highway into town was wide but rough: four lanes in each direction, treacherously pitted with dips and potholes. I realised that when Sasha had described the Russian roads as diabolical he hadn't been exaggerating. We were really getting thrown around – and this on one of the main thoroughfares. We were also being overtaken on both sides simultaneously: anybody with a reasonably fast foreign car was weaving in and out of the traffic like a lunatic.

Set back on either side of the road were terrible, drab tower-blocks of flats, nine or ten storeys tall. Closer to the road, old-fashioned hoardings carried advertisements, many for Western products. When I spotted some familiar red and yellow colours and slowly picked out the Cyrillic letters for McDonald's I couldn't help grinning at my own linguistic prowess.

It took us fifty minutes to reach the city centre, the traffic thickening all the time. I noticed several good-looking older buildings, mostly pale yellow with green copper roofs, but the general run of architecture was abysmal. Then, as we were crawling downhill along another broad street, Sasha pointed ahead and announced, 'There is Kremlin.'

I peered out through the relatively clean area of the windscreen and saw in the distance a red star glowing on top of a steeply pointed tower. Only that one corner of the citadel was in sight, but even so my neck prickled. Here was the centre of Russian power, the focal point of a vast country, the power-base that had dominated world politics for all our lifetimes. If ever there was to be a breakdown of relations between Russia and the West, this was where it would start.

A moment later Sasha pulled the car over in front of a tall, faceless, modern high-rise building on the right-hand side of the road, and parked end-on to the kerb.

'Hotel Intourist,' he announced. 'I help you check in.'

Outside the entrance a few rough-looking young men were standing around, all smoking; they were hard to see clearly, but whenever the glow of a cigarette lit up a face, I didn't like the look of it. They could have been taxi-drivers, yet their presence seemed vaguely threatening.

The little glass-walled lobby was full of security men – half a dozen overweight, slovenly guys with pistols in holsters. The women staffing the reception desk were wearing bright red tunics pin-striped with white – a cheerful touch which wasn't matched by any warmth of greeting. One of them gave us forms to complete and moved off towards her office without a word, carrying our passports.

'When do we get them back?' I asked.

'Tomorrow.'

Her lack of common civility pissed me off. I can't believe *all* the women in Moscow are having their periods right now, I thought. Then I heard Sasha saying, 'Programme for tomorrow: eight-thirty, I collect you and drive to Balashika for inspection of camp. OK?'

I nodded.

'Four o'clock, visit to British Embassy. Meeting with Chargé d'Affaires. Also meet your interpreter and liaison officer. At Embassy, same time.'

'Fine.'

I thanked him for collecting us, and he was gone.

Our rooms were on the fifteenth floor – 1512, 1513 and 1514. We went up in the lift, sharing it with a couple of overweight Yanks, a man and a woman, obviously on vacation.

'Been to the Kremlin yet?' the man asked in a southern accent.

I shook my head. 'Only just arrived.'

'One helluva monument, that place. Sure is. How long are you guys here for?'

'Couple of days.'

A quick inspection revealed that all our rooms were the same: small, hot and stuffy, without air-conditioning, and with only the small upper section of the windows openable. In the tiny bathrooms the tiles were cracked and yellowing, the grout between them black with grime. As Sasha had warned us, there were no plugs in the baths or basins . . . and suddenly – fuck it – I realised I'd left mine behind. I took a quick look round the bedroom for signs of hidden microphones, and although I couldn't see anything I felt sure they were there. We'd already agreed that there'd be no shop talk in the hotel.

'Grotsville,' exclaimed Rick as he emerged into the passage.

'You said it. Have you got your money on you? Don't leave it in there, whatever you do.'

'Got it.' He slapped his bum-bag which he had pulled round to the front, over his stomach.

'You look like that fat git we came up with.'

'*Spasibo*, mate.'

'Let's stretch our legs,' Whinger suggested. 'Eyeball the Kremlin.'

That seemed like a good plan. It was already 9.45 local time, but only 6.45 by our biological clocks, and since we'd eaten on the plane we didn't feel any need for food. Besides, I knew that the British Embassy was somewhere close by, just across the Moscow River from the Kremlin, and I reckoned we might as well suss it out, as I was going to have to report there regularly during our operation.

On our way down in the lift Rick suddenly started shitting himself with laughter.

'What's so bloody amusing?' Whinger said irritably.

'Some cunt left a menu from one of the restaurants in my room. The stuff on offer is incredible.'

'Like what?'

'"Needles in meat sauce", for one. Then there was "frog's paws in paste".'

'That's frog's legs in batter,' Whinger told him.

'I know – but think of it . . .'

It was a fine evening for a stroll: the sky was clear and the air cool. Out on the pavement, we elbowed through the scrum of taxi drivers and walked down the slope towards Red Square. The street was so wide and the traffic was moving so fast that the subway seemed the best way to cross. We went down some steps into a concrete tunnel, past young people busking and old women begging, and up the other side. A minute later we were walking uphill on another short, broad thoroughfare and emerging on to the huge open expanse of Red Square.

'Never realised it was cobbled,' said Whinger.

'Nor that it was so big.'

It gave me a strange feeling to be looking at buildings I'd seen a thousand times in pictures. As a young soldier, during my early years in the army, I'd spent hours in classrooms doing recognition training, staring at black-and-white slides of Soviet tanks and missiles until we could pick out T54s, T64s and T72s in our sleep and name all the main types of ICBM. The place all these weapons were photographed most often was Red Square, during big parades on the anniversary of the 1917 revolution and suchlike – so now the buildings in the background were like echoes from the past.

Rick's mind was moving on the same lines. 'Think of all the military hardware that's rolled along here,' he said.

On our right the low, squat hulk of Lenin's mausoleum sat hunched against the wall of the Kremlin. Wherever a light was shining on the wall, we could see it was made of dark red brick.

'Funny there aren't any guards on the mausoleum,'

said Whinger. 'You'd expect there to be some official presence. Isn't it a national shrine?'

'Not any more,' Rick told him. 'I read on the Internet that they're arguing about what to do with the old bugger. The die-hards are all for keeping him, but a lot of people want him out.'

'Burning'd be too good for that bastard,' said Whinger bitterly, surprising me with the anger in his voice. 'If anyone sent the Russian government a bill demanding compensation for all the misery he and his bloody ideas have caused, this country'd be bankrupt for the next thousand years.'

'That's why they're not paying the Regiment anything for our job here,' I said. 'All the funds are coming from the States or the UK.'

Ahead of us in the distance rose the multi-coloured onion domes of St Basil's Cathedral, some striped horizontally, some vertically, some segmented like the skins of pineapples. Even I, ignorant as I am about church architecture, sensed that there was something wild and barbaric in those amazing shapes and colours.

'What about that German kid who landed a light plane here?' said Whinger. 'Some feat, that. I bet it made them cut about a bit. The Russkies must have been fairly shitting themselves when they found out how easily he'd got through their defences without the aircraft even being called.'

'Rust, his name was,' I said. 'Mathias Rust. He landed up the slope.' I pointed ahead. 'That means he must have come in from that direction, towards us.

Didn't the cheeky bugger get a job at some travel agency in Moscow, once he'd come out of gaol? I think so. It just shows how times change.'

Soon we were walking down the gentle hill past St Basil's. At the bottom we found a bridge over the river, and decided to cross to the other side, so we'd be able to look back across the water and get a view of the Kremlin. We cleared the steps on the far bank, and had just started walking, the river on our right, when Rick said quietly, 'We've got a tail.'

'Sure?' I asked.

'Pretty much. He's been with us at least since the bottom of the square.'

'Keep walking, then. When we get to that bench, we'll sit down and see what he does.'

On the embankment a hundred yards in front, a metal bench faced out over the water. When we reached it, I sat on one end, took off a shoe and proceeded to shake out imaginary bits of grit.

Up on Red Square there had been plenty of people wandering about. Down here by the river the wide road was deserted, and our follower stood out like a spare prick.

'He's stopped,' Rick announced. 'He's leaning over the wall.'

'Let's tip the bastard in,' said Whinger.

'It could be someone Sasha's laid on to keep an eye on us,' Rick suggested.

'Hardly,' I said. 'I don't think he'd do that. More likely a common-or-garden mugger. He could have mates waiting up ahead, though. He may be trying to push us towards them. We'd better sort him.'

Whinger agreed – so we strolled forward, slower than before, then suddenly turned and began walking fast towards our pursuer. He'd started after us again, and it seemed to take him a moment to realise what was happening. Then he also turned round and began to scuttle off. By now we were running, and we were on to him in a flash.

Whinger and I each went for an arm and grabbed him, bringing him to a rapid halt. We couldn't see him too clearly in the lamplight, but he looked a swarthy lad of twenty-odd, with a bit of a ragged beard, wearing a check shirt and a thin jacket of some dark material. He was angry, but also scared.

'What the hell d'you think you're doing?' I snapped.

He let fly a stream of Russian, of which I understood not a word. Rick said something in Russian, and he spat out an answer. Then he started to struggle, and for a moment I was afraid he was going to scream to attract attention. I got my handkerchief scrumpled in a ball, to stuff in his mouth if he opened it any wider, but already Rick was frisking him, and in seconds came up with a nasty, slim-bladed knife which he held in front of the guy's face.

That made his eyeballs rotate and quietened him nicely.

'Into the river,' I said, and Rick flipped the weapon over the wall. We heard the splash as it hit the water.

'No mobile phone or radio?'

Rick shook his head. 'No wallet or money either.'

'In that case he's probably after ours.'

Suddenly I remembered one of the unofficial phrases Valentina had taught us. '*Valite otsyuda!*' I told him, and indicated the direction he could go – back the way we'd come.

He got the message, no problem. As we released him, he shook himself like a dog and set off without a word. I saw that he had a bit of a limp, dipping slightly on his right leg. We watched until he had disappeared up the steps by the bridge, then we carried on along the river.

'What did he say, Rick?'

'Just that he was out for a walk.'

'Like hell he was.'

Rick was the most observant member of our party. He had a terrific knack of noticing any small object or incident that was out of line, and his memory for faces was phenomenal: even a year or more after an event he'd remember a person's appearance. Sometimes it took him a minute or two to place them, but then the setting and date would come back. I'm sure his skill derived partly from all the surveillance work he'd done in Northern Ireland, and often it stood us in good stead.

'Where did he pick us up?' I asked. 'Was he outside the hotel?'

Rick shook his head. 'I don't think so. He must have been hanging around on Red Square.'

Away to our right, across the river, the floodlit Kremlin was a magnificent sight, but we were feeling too unsettled by the incident to appreciate it fully.

'I can see three possible explanations,' I said. 'One, he was after our money. Two, Sasha detailed him to check where we went. Three, he was a Mafia dicker. I don't like any of them. If he *was* just a mugger, it goes to show how dodgy this place is. If Sasha sent him, it means we're not trusted. If he's Mafia, it means we may have been rumbled already.'

I was getting jumpy. I remembered how the Colombians had had dickers posted at all the airports, photographing people as they arrived off the planes. Someone had told me that the secret police got hold of the flight manifests, and that by using computers they were able to match up passengers with pictures, so they could keep tabs on every single visitor to the country.

We walked on, until we became aware of a handsome, old-style building set back from the road behind a courtyard on our left, and flanked by two matching outliers, evidently part of the complex. Beside the gate, in a grey pillbox, were two Russian guards in uniform, chatting, smoking, looking bored and not paying attention. Behind them, further in, was a stone gatehouse containing a guy in a red jumper who sat at a desk behind a glass screen.

'Bet that's a Brit,' I said. 'He's a bit more alert. He'll be controlling the electronic gates and the phones.'

'Look on the roof,' said Rick, 'left-hand corner. There's an infra-red light. They must have good security systems.'

We crossed the street towards the gates, where a brass

plaque announced that the building was the British Embassy. The discovery made me feel a little better: at least we'd carried out one small but useful research task.

We recrossed the river by the next bridge, watching our rear all the way, and returned to base along the north side of the Kremlin, past the Tomb of the Unknown Soldier, where a perpetual gas flame burned out of a horizontal slab, and a cloak made of bronze lay folded over a plinth. We paid our respects and walked on.

Then, only a minute or two away from the hotel, we were nearly caught up in a violent incident. Fifty yards ahead, facing us, a single car was parked against the kerb. Suddenly a grey van hurtled past us from behind. Tyres screeched as it scorched to a halt inches in front of the car, blocking any take-off. From the van burst four figures in uniform – militiamen, by the look of them. They ran at the car, ripped the doors open and dragged out the driver and passengers.

In seconds the three guys from the car were spread-eagled over their own vehicle, taking heavy punishment from batons. Then one of the uniformed men stood back in the road and fired a couple of short bursts from his sub-machine gun, aiming into the air over the river. His purpose seemed to be to scare the shit out of the targets – and I wondered where the bullets were landing in this huge city. As if to emphasise what he thought of his victims, another militiaman ran in and swung his boot, delivering a fierce kick to one of the huddled bodies, catching the man in the small of the back, whereupon he sank to the ground with a groan.

My instinct was to back off as fast as possible. Whinger evidently felt the same, and hissed in my ear, 'Keep walking!' This was nothing to do with us, and we definitely didn't want to get involved. So we crossed to the far pavement and kept going. The last we saw, one of the three had been dragged into the van and driven off, leaving the others slumped in the gutter by their vehicle.

'What the fuck was that all about?' Whinger muttered. 'Were they the cops, or hooligans pretending to be cops?'

'I bet those were some of the guys we're going to have to train,' said Rick cheerfully.

The brawl had made me yet more edgy, and for the last few hundred yards to the hotel, we speeded up. The approach was thronged by hangers-around, but as far as we could see the crowd didn't include our friend who'd lost his knife. Still, I was relieved when we'd pushed through and were back inside.

By now it was nearly 11.00 p.m., and Whinger spoke for all of us when he said, 'Let's get a pint, for Christ's sake.'

We'd already spotted a bar on the third floor, so we took the lift up. Whinger stepped out first on to the landing, and he was hardly through the door before I heard him go, '*Phworrhh!* Firekin ell!'

'What is it?' I rushed out – and instantly saw: leaning against the wall was the most blatant hooker I'd ever set eyes on – fishnet stockings, black leather skirt nine inches long, white blouse open to the navel, blazing scarlet lipstick, hair a dark, coppery colour she was never born with. As we passed within a couple of feet of her she let out a long jet of cigarette smoke through pursed lips and gave us a cool, arrogant stare of appraisal.

'Jesus!' Whinger muttered as we turned along a corridor. 'How was that for an old slag? She could be quite a looker if she wasn't so plastered in make-up.'

'Rather you than me, mate,' I said. 'Wait a minute, though. You're not exactly strapped for choice.'

The entrance to the bar was ahead of us, at the end of the landing; in front of the doorway lurked three more women, all peroxide blondes, all smoking. We pushed past them into a dark cavern thudding with a disco beat and headed for the bar on our right.

'*Pivo, pozhaluista,*' I said, trying out two of my best words. '*Tri.*'

'Three beers?' said the barman in good-sounding English.

I nodded, and he pulled three tall glasses of Heineken, the only brand on offer. The beer was OK, but it cost the equivalent of £3 apiece.

As our eyes became accustomed to the dim light, we realised that the whole room was heaving with hookers, all dressed in minimalist kit. Two were dancing with each other under strobe lights on a small circular floor in the centre; the rest were sitting at tables or standing against the walls, gyrating in time with the beat. A quick head-count put the total at sixteen. The three other men present were paying them no attention whatsoever.

Soon it was clear that Rick had spotted someone he fancied. I saw him getting eye contact, and his gaze kept wandering off across the room.

'Bloody hell!' he muttered. 'There's going to be some crack when the rest of the lads get here.' Then he said, 'Look at that, too.'

Above my head and behind me, on a high shelf in the corner, sat a television set. I turned to look at it, and saw a guy, with his bare arse to the camera, humping a woman, going at her hammer and tongs.

When I turned back, the two girls had left the dance floor and their place had been taken by a single, pasty-faced man. The guy, who looked to be in his twenties, was pissed out of his mind. He could still just about stand upright, but he staggered whenever he tried to walk. Lurching, faltering, tripping over his own feet, he seemed oblivious to his surroundings, but at the same time hell-bent on staging a grotesque solo dance.

Only when he started a strip-tease did he become too much for the management. Two security heavies hustled in and took him away.

We had another round of beers, watched the hookers vainly circulating, and then decided to get our heads down. At least, Whinger and I did. Rick said he was staying on for one more round.

'Watch yourself,' Whinger told him. 'This place is hopping with Aids.'

'How d'you know?'

'I can smell it.'

Out in the corridor we were accosted by yet another

pair of tarts, one dark, one fair. The blonde came straight for me, stopped a foot away and said, 'We go to the bedroom.'

It was a statement, not a question. I twisted a smile into position and said, 'No thanks. I'm happy.'

'I make you more happy.' She moved even closer and ran her fingers down my chest.

'It's OK.' I gestured towards Whinger. 'I'm with a friend.'

'All four go to the bedroom.' She pointed at her companion.

The blonde was slim and quite pretty, with a good set of tits on her, but the dark girl was a nightmare, flat chested, and with a complexion like the surface of the moon. I shook my head, pushed past them and made it to the lift.

Safe inside my room – so I thought – I had a shower and stretched out on the bed to watch CNN news.

The next thing I knew, the phone was ringing. The light and the TV were still on. I looked at my watch: 1.30.

I picked up the receiver.

'Meester Sharp?' It was a woman's voice. 'I think you are lonely.'

'Am I hell!' I spluttered. 'Get lost. *Valite otsuda!*'

I slammed the phone down, switched everything off and lay down again.

Fifteen storeys below, traffic was still surging along Tverskaya. Opposite my window, huge, bright neon advertisements for Panasonic and Technics blazed on the top of another high-rise building. What a place, I thought. What a shit-heap: overrun by commercialism, yet scruffy as hell. Nowhere else in the world had I ever known such unpleasant vibrations: nowhere had I sensed so clearly that if I got into trouble, nobody would help or protect me. When the rest of the team came out, we were going to have to take care.

Back in Hereford Valentina had told us all about *babushkas* – literally grannies – the old ladies who do menial jobs like sweeping the streets, shovelling snow and sitting at desks on the landings of big hotels. Sasha had mentioned how they also run little kiosk shops and sell illicit vodka to soldiers.

Whinger and I clocked our first specimen when we went down for breakfast: eighteen stone if she was a pound, with eyes set too close together in a huge pudding of a face, and a stack of violet-tinted grey hair piled six or eight inches above her head. On the wall behind her was a notice half in English, half Russian: CONTINENTAL ZAVTRAK: 50 ROUBLES, and the *babushka*'s function was to intercept people on their way to the dining room and take the number of their room, so that she could make sure no one sneaked in twice or let somebody else in on their ticket.

Breakfast was self-service: rolls, bread, butter, jam, cheese and so on. There were sachets of instant coffee, tea-bags and a big samovar of boiling water with a tap that spat on your fingers when you turned it. We helped ourselves and went to sit at a table in the outer room. The little packets of butter were Finnish, the redcurrant jam German; the local bread was dry and papery, and the cheese, presumably home-made too, tasted of nothing. But I wasn't in critical mood. I'd slept pretty well, it was a fine morning, and I was looking forward to seeing the camp. Whinger was also in good nick. He too had had a midnight call, but he'd sensibly seen it off.

Then in came Rick, face pale, T-shirt on back-to-front.

'Rough night? What time did you hit the pit?'

'Dunno,' he mumbled. 'Had a couple more drinks.'

'Don't try bullshitting us,' I warned. 'I know what you were hanging around for.'

He leered.

'Don't tell me you . . . Bloody hell! Which one was it?'

'That little blonde in the corner.' He blushed scarlet, then said, 'Wait a minute.'

He put two sachets of sugar into his black tea and got a couple of mouthfuls down him. Then he said, 'Natasha, she's called.'

Whinger went, 'You bastard! How much did she take you for?'

'Nothing.'

'*What?* Come on.'

'Honest. She wants help.'

'I should think she bloody well does after you've been through her a few times.'

'It's not that. It's her sister.'

77

Whinger and I looked at each other. Then Rick began to explain.

Natasha's home was in Rostov-on-Don, a thousand miles south of Moscow, he said. She was eighteen, a student, and supposed to be starting her autumn term at university. But like hundreds of other provincial girls she'd done a runner and come to the capital to earn some money and make a better life for herself. And along with all the rest, she'd fallen into the clutches of the Mafia.

'The point is, she's shit-scared,' Rick went on. 'They all are. They have to hand over half their earnings. If they don't pay, they're liable to have their faces carved up.'

'Is that what's happened to the sister?'

'Not yet. But she's deep in it. Irina, she's called. She went to New York on the job, with a friend, but both of them got caught up in a money-laundering racket run by the Mafia. Apparently it's got a hold on the States like a tick in a dog's arse.'

'So what was this slag doing?' Whinger asked.

'Something in a restaurant. There's drug money pouring through: she has to bank it and make out phoney bills for meals that nobody's eaten. Last week the friend got murdered, and now Irina thinks she's for it too.'

'And what is the great, all-shagging, all-conquering hero supposed to do about it?' Whinger shot a steely look across the table.

Rick scrubbed his eyes. 'Natasha wants me to rescue her sister.'

'Fucking roll on!' Whinger cried in alarm, so loud that a Japanese couple at the next table jumped in their seats. 'Who does she think you are?'

'Part of a film company. Don't worry – I stuck to the cover. It's just that, because I'm a Brit and have dollars, she thinks I can whip across to America, sort the Mafia and bring her little sister safely home.'

'What did you tell her?' I pushed back my chair. 'How did you get rid of her?'

'I haven't yet. She's still there.'

'Where?'

'In the bed.'

'Bloody hell! For Christ's sake, Rick – she's nothing but a whore. Otherwise she wouldn't be in a dump like this.'

'No, no,' he protested. 'She's a really nice kid.'

'What did she *do* to you?' Whinger asked sarcastically. 'She emptied your head as well as your balls.'

Sasha was in the foyer at 8.30, still in civilian clothes, evidently not wanting to show any military presence in the hotel. Leaving the others, I got up, greeted him and walked him over into the area near the ground-floor bar, where a few tables and chairs were so widely scattered round the large atrium that I felt sure they couldn't be covered by microphones.

'These girls,' I began. 'The ones that hang around the hotel. What basis are they on?'

'I'm sorry?'

'I mean, are they employed by the hotel, or what?'

'No, no – Mafia. All Mafia. You have a problem?'

'Just that Rick laid one of them last night.'

'Does he not pay her? She is angry?'

'No – she's OK.'

'And he doesn't tell her who he is?'

'No, no.'

'In such case, not to worry.'

'All right, then. One other thing . . .' I described the incidents on the embankment – first our own little set-to, then the heavy hit.

Immediately Sasha was apologetic. 'This man – nothing to do with me,' he insisted. 'Nothing.' From the way he reacted, I knew he was telling the truth.

'No sweat,' I said. 'We didn't lose anything. As long as the wrong people don't know we're here.'

He shook his head. 'It was only small thief. Teepical Moscow. Zheordie, I am sorry.'

'In that case, forget it. But what about the bust?'

'Probably this was Omon. They get information of criminals in the car. Maybe they hear them on their radio.'

'Their methods aren't exactly subtle.'

He shrugged. 'Moscow is very violent place.'

'Well, we're all in one piece so far. *Idyom!*'

He smiled, like he always did when I hit a Russian word accurately, and said, 'Let's go.'

I piled into the front passenger seat of his car, the other two got in the back. As Sasha pulled into the traffic, he announced, 'One more dead.'

'Who? Where?'

'On radio news this morning. The boss of Russavto, big car import, shot dead in his Mercedes. Or maybe roasted. They found the car burning on Komsomol-skaya Square.'

'Mafia?' I asked.

'Of course.'

'What did he do to annoy them?'

'Refuse to pay money – just how I told you.'

'The women in the hotel,' I said. 'How do they get in there? I mean, is the hotel supporting them?'

'I tell you, all Mafia-controlled.'

'Yes – but d'you mean the hotel or the girls?'

'Both.'

I looked round at Rick and said, 'You'd better watch yourself, mate. You don't want to fuck this whole job just because of one hooker. You could end up floating down the Moscow River.'

We were heading out of town towards the east. The traffic going our way wasn't too bad, but the incoming stream was diabolical: crossing after crossing gridlocked, drivers hooting. When I remarked on it, Sasha said, 'Moscow traffic goes to collapse. It is impossible.'

After I'd asked about the make of a car in front of us, he was quick to point out others. 'That is big-engine Volga. This is tenth-model Lada. This is Zhigudi.' Then he added contemptuously, 'Nobody want Russian cars.' What he coveted, I could see, was a BMW or a Mercedes, a few of which nosed through the rush-hour crawl, sleek and well-polished.

As we drew away from a set of lights, he said, 'Now

we are on Shosse Entusiastov.' He turned to me with a grin. 'All revolutionaries who must go to prison use this street!' He saw me looking puzzled and went on, 'Why? Because in Communist era all people sentenced to gaol passed along this highway to the gulags. They never return! Nobody return! The street goes to Siberia.'

Our journey took less than an hour, and as we drove the morning began to brighten: the air was quite warm, and as the cloud thinned we started getting glimpses of blue sky. After a scatter of new high-rise blocks on the outskirts of the city, we passed under the ring-road whose lights we'd seen from the air, and suddenly Moscow was at an end. The land here was dead flat; enormous fields stretched away on either side, apparently uncultivated, covered in rough grass, punctuated with tussocks a couple of feet high. Then, on our right, we started passing a forest which exactly matched my expectations of Russia: tall, slender silver birches with bark mottled white and grey rising among dark green pines, giving a pleasantly open texture to the wood.

I was admiring the trees when I realised that a uniformed man had walked out into the road ahead and was flagging us down with a black-and-white baton.

'What's the matter?' I asked quickly.

'It is nothing.' Sasha sounded unmoved. 'Only GAI, the traffic police, making checks.'

He pulled in to the verge, and the cop came to the window. He wore a grey uniform with a thin red stripe down the seam of the trousers. Sasha wound down his window and started to give the policeman a bollocking. Even I could understand what he was saying: that he was an army officer on an important mission and had no time to piss about. But the cop gave him as good as he got, and after a minute Sasha gave a sigh.

'*Isvinite*. He demands my documents. One minute, please.'

Muttering under his breath, Sasha leant across me to extract an envelope from the dashboard pocket, got out of the car and followed the man into the flat-topped concrete hut at the side of the highway. Waiting, we had time to take in the decrepit surroundings: the road's edge churned up, rutted mud beyond the tarmac, heaps of rusting metal lying about, broken drainpipes dumped in a heap.

'What it is,' said Whinger thoughtfully, 'is the size of this godforsaken country. At home everything's neat and tidy because we have so little space. Here there's millions and millions of fucking acres, and it doesn't matter if you scatter rubbish about.'

Five minutes later Sasha returned, sliding papers back into his folder. 'Forged documents,' he said as he started up. 'Always they are looking for forged licences. People sell them for fifty dollars.'

'Are these the regular police, then?'

'No – GAI only traffic.'

We drove on. Soon I saw a large sign which I could read easily: BALASHIKA. Behind it, set back from the road and running parallel with it, was a wall of concrete sections topped by coils of barbed wire. The solid part of the barrier was about two metres tall, so that it effectively blocked the view of everything beyond.

'Here is the camp,' Sasha announced. 'Very big.'

Certainly the wall ran for miles. On and on it went, broken at one point by a single-track railway line, but even there baffles of concrete slabs set at angles made it impossible to see inside. At last Sasha slowed and we drew up at what was obviously the main entrance: a double gateway with sliding barriers of heavy metal bars forged in squares, and flat-roofed guardrooms on either side. The roadway was pitted, the buildings badly finished, the wall cracked where it was propped by pillars. Twisting round in my seat, I glanced at Whinger and saw that his reaction was the same as mine: the place had an instantly depressing atmosphere.

When I look back on that day, I realise that from the start I had a feeling of foreboding about our whole operation. There was no friction of any kind – indeed, our hosts were friendly and welcoming – but the squalor of the barrack blocks and the primitive nature of the training facilities made me dread spending two months in such surroundings. Get a grip, Geordie, I kept telling myself. What matters is the training. You can put up with anything for eight or nine weeks.

As soon as we were inside the camp, Sasha disappeared briefly and came back dressed in DPM fatigues, without badges of rank, but with the emblem of a tiger's head on his left lapel. On duty, we soon saw, his manner changed: he became sharper, more efficient

– and that gave me confidence. He introduced us to a couple of fellow officers – who seemed good enough guys, with a positive, open approach – but they spoke hardly any English, and at this first meeting their names didn't stick.

It was Sasha who showed us round and explained the facilities. I said nothing as we toured the camp, because in the Regiment you work with whatever assets you've got, and don't start criticising others when they are doing their best. But I couldn't help noticing that most of what we saw was way out of date: again and again I was reminded of conditions when I'd joined the army nearly twenty years before.

The camp had its good points, one of which was space. Beyond the drill squares, the barrack blocks and other buildings, the land ran straight out into ranges and training areas. Several thousand acres were taken in by the surrounding wall, which struck away through the forest at the back and disappeared out of sight. You could drive or even walk to the various ranges without leaving the base's perimeter.

At the Killing House, our hosts put on a demonstration of hostage rescue – no doubt in return for the one we'd given Sasha at home.

As Sasha warned me, their building was nothing but a hollow square formed out of old lorry tyres filled with sand and cement and stacked on each other to make walls about eight feet high. Because the room had no roof and was open to the elements, we had a good view down into it from our vantage point on the observation tower. As at Hereford, the guards either side of the prisoner were represented by figure targets, much the same as our own, but the hostage between them, far from being a live human being, was only a dummy.

When the assault went down, the explosive charge failed to blow the barricaded door first time, and when the assaulters opened up with their sub-machine guns, instead of firing a couple of short bursts, they sprayed the inside of the house with dozens of rounds. The entire exercise was marked by a lack of precision. There was also a worrying lack of emphasis on safety. The assaulters had no flame-proof clothing like our black gear, only standard DPMs – and as the day warmed up I saw several guys remove the heavy Kevlar plates from the fronts and backs of their flak-jackets. Without the plates the jackets would stop secondary impacts like ricochets, but not live rounds. And whereas at home we always have a fully equipped ambulance standing by, manned by two paramedics, the Russians had nothing but an ancient meat-wagon, with jack-shit kit on board and only two squaddies in control.

Sasha seemed amazed when I told him that the SAS had only ever lost one man in the Killing House. Plenty of guys had broken arms and legs when they fell off buildings while abseiling, but in the Killing House itself only one man had died; he'd been shot in the femoral artery and had bled to death in seconds.

'Reelly!' Sasha seemed impressed. 'We lose one or two men a year.'

I almost said, 'I'm not surprised,' but bit it back and

made a mental note that safety instruction was going to be at the top of our agenda when the team came out.

Another fundamental decision was about food. For lunch, we were taken to a canteen and ate with the rank and file. The menu was exactly as Sasha had described it in the pub in England: *shchi*, cabbage soup with lumps of gristle floating in it, black and white bread. The soup was OK if you avoided the gristle, but I could see Whinger's eyeballs rotating.

As soon as we were on our own outside, I said, 'We're going to get fucking hungry here.'

My spirits sank even lower when we saw what we were being offered for accommodation: the ground floor of a three-storey block which was standing empty and looked as if it hadn't been used in years. There was no shortage of space – a dozen rooms of reasonable size led off either side of a central corridor – but the building itself was in a disgusting state, with plaster coming away from the concrete-block walls, dirty cream paint flaking off, and yellowing newspapers strewn about the bare cement floors. The security was shite, as well: no locks on the doors, and several window panes broken.

Sasha saw the way my mind was working and said, 'We get it cleaned up. No bother.'

'Yes, please – and some means of securing the doors. We're going to want beds, too.'

'How many?'

'Eight – no, better make it ten.' I adjusted my estimate as I counted in the scalies.

As we left to return to the city, we took a short drive

round the town of Balashika – and that depressed us even more. The road verges were sheets of dried mud, flanked by blocks of flats made from hideous yellow brick, with badly fitting windows and cracks gaping in the walls. We looked in vain for shops – and as for a pub, the idea that one might exist in such a place seemed like a bad joke.

We were driving against the tide of traffic once more, and in less than an hour we were alongside the river, passing the spot where the knife had gone over the wall and pulling up outside the gates of the British Embassy.

Sasha, who had changed back into his civvies, glanced at his watch and announced with satisfaction, 'Three hours fifty-eight.'

The security guards had been briefed to expect us. The first two – Russians – checked our documents. The inner post was manned by a Brit, as I'd predicted. He spoke a few words into his radio, then directed Sasha to drive on across the courtyard and round the left-hand side of the main building. Behind the inner post was another open space with an attractive garden, a hard tennis court and, across the back, a low two-storey building which had obviously once been the stable block belonging to the main house. A forest-green Range Rover was parked in one corner with a small, shiny blue Fiat beside it.

By the time we arrived at the front door a man was already standing outside – a tall guy, probably in his early forties, with a shock of thick, grey hair springing forward over his forehead and a bushy moustache to match. He was wearing a white shirt and a navy tie with diagonal stripes that no doubt indicated some fancy school or regiment.

'Sergeant Major Sharp?' He came over and shook hands with a firm grip. 'Pleased to meet you. I'm David Allway, Chargé d'Affaires.'

'Hello,' I said. 'This is Major Ivanov – Sasha – who's looking after us.'

Sasha shook hands and gave a deferential nod in place of a salute. Then I introduced Whinger and Rick.

Allway swept a hand at his forelock, which instantly flopped back into its former position, smiled at everyone and said, 'Your liaison officer's here already.'

'Great,' I said. 'What's his name?'

'*Her* name . . .' he paused, smiling again, 'is Colonel Gerasimova. She's waiting in the office. Let's go in.'

'Just a second,' I said. 'A colonel . . . Is she army?'

'No – she's from the FSB, a section of the former KGB. On formal occasions they still like to use KGB ranks.'

Ah, Jesus, I thought. This is all we need.

If I don't remember much about Allway's office, it's because I was so startled by the appearance and manner of our interpreter. She was dark, with short, straight hair, and very slim – 'lithe' would be a better word, because her movements were quick and elegant. She was wearing a smart suit of cornflower-blue linen with a cream-coloured shirt underneath. After so much squalor outside, she was like a vision. When we entered the room she was sitting down, talking to a red-headed secretary, but when she stood up to greet us, I saw she was nearly as tall as me. Her face caught everyone's eyes as we came in: it was a bit too long and narrow to be classically beautiful, but there was something striking about it, especially her big, dark eyes.

'Sergeant Major Sharp? I'm Anna Nikolayevna. Welcome to Moscow!'

'Thanks.' I took her hand gently. Her English pronunciation was perfect – no trace of an accent – and it was refreshing to hear her sound British, rather than American, as most Russians do when speaking English. She smelled pretty good, too: I was getting traces of some scent that I knew but couldn't quite place.

In a few moments we were all sitting at a rectangular table and the secretary was getting a brew on. Allway sat at one end, on my left, Anna opposite me. She sat back in her chair with her arms folded, very composed, very still, as she listened.

Allway was courteous, brisk and efficient: without any faffing about, he went straight into confirming the details of our schedule.

'You arrive all together next Saturday . . . the eighth,' he said, checking a sheet of notes.

'That's right.'

'Transport is by RAF C-130, which will fly direct into the strip at Balashika. Arrival at 0030 local time.'

'Correct.'

'The aircraft will depart as soon as unloading's finished.'

'Correct. It's going to refuel in Berlin on the way here, so that it can turn straight round and be gone in the dark.'

'Good. Now – your personnel.'

He began to run through the list of names – he had them all correct – and at the end I said, 'I take it you have secure satellite comms with the UK?'

'Of course. I'll give you a list of numbers in a minute. You can call me direct from Hereford – and from Balashika, when you get there.'

I looked across the table. 'Colonel?'

'Please call me Anna.'

'Anna, then. Can you explain what our official status is going to be? I mean, what basis will we be here on?'

Her face, which had been set rather hard, softened into a smile. 'Don't worry. It's all above board. You'll be here as guests of the Ministry of Defence and the Ministry of the Interior, jointly.'

'Does anyone outside the armed forces know we're coming?'

'No. There has been no official announcement. Our aim is to protect you from possible interference by criminal elements.'

'You mean the Mafia?'

She nodded. 'They would hardly welcome the idea of foreign experts coming to train the new unit.'

'So it's important that we don't get seen or recognised coming and going, or outside the camp?'

'Precisely.'

'In that case, what about transport? One or two of us

are going to have to liaise with the Embassy. I imagine we'll be coming in and out.'

'That's no problem. We'll make a couple of civilian cars available. The only thing is, you'll need driving licences. If you give me your names and details, I'll arrange that.'

'Thanks. What if we get stopped by the traffic police?'

'The GAI? There will be no difficulty, provided your documents are in order. We'll fix you up with whatever you need for each vehicle – licence, insurance and so on. And I shall give you a number to ring in case any problem arises.'

'What about your own involvement? Will you be available in the camp?'

'Of course!' She gave another brief smile. 'At your service.'

'Will you sit in on training sessions?'

'I don't know about *sitting*. I'm planning to take part pretty actively.'

'Great. We're going to need you.'

The meeting went so smoothly that it lasted only half an hour. Soon after 4.30, Allway was ushering us out into the courtyard, where a gardener was sweeping up leaves.

'Your English is fantastic,' I told Anna as she was departing. 'Where did you learn it so well?'

'I give you three guesses.'

'University?'

'Well – partly. But really in London. I worked for

two years at the Intourist main office in Piccadilly.'

'Ah! When were you there?'

'Early eighties. Eighty-two to -three.'

A sudden thought came to me. 'No chance of your having supper with us tonight?'

'I'm sorry.' She gave a little shake of her head. 'I have a date already.'

'Oh well – I just thought you could fill us in on background.'

'When you're over again, maybe.'

'Definitely. I'll look forward to that.'

She made for the Fiat, shoe-horned herself neatly into the driving seat and set off.

'Well,' said Allway. 'So far, so good.'

'Yes – thanks.'

I'd been looking at the old stables at the back of the yard, and they'd given me an idea. 'There's one other thing . . .'

'Yes?'

'The security on our accommodation block is . . .' I was on the point of saying it was shite, but ended up saying, 'dodgy. What I mean is, I wonder – is there a secure room here in the Embassy that we could use for storage? A garage or something?'

Allway looked up and said, 'What would you want to store?'

'Maybe some of our comms equipment. On these team tasks we generally have some fairly sensitive kit with us.'

'Well – as it happens, we've just cleared out part of

the cellar, over there.' He pointed into one corner. 'It's a bit rough – really just a garage.'

'As long as it can be locked up . . .'

'Oh yes – it's got a steel door. I'll get the key and show you.'

He disappeared into the office, came out again, and took us across to a steep ramp leading down to an up-and-over door.

'Ideal,' I said after a quick look. The cellar had no windows or other exit and, considering that it was below ground level, it felt remarkably dry. 'This'll be perfect.'

'OK then.' Allway grinned. 'I'll do my best to keep it empty for you. People and things around here have a habit of expanding to fill any space that becomes available.'

We thanked him again and set off to tab back over the bridge to the hotel.

'I give you lift,' said Sasha, pointing to his car.

'Thanks,' I told him, 'but I'd rather walk.'

'Then I say goodbye.'

'We'll see you on Sunday morning. And thanks for all you've done for us.'

'It is nothing.'

With smiles all round, he got into his car and drove off.

As soon as we were clear of the Embassy gates I said to Whinger, 'Anna. Former KGB, for sure. She must have been spying in London. Most of the Russians in England were on the KGB payroll. Certainly most of the diplomats were spies.'

Whinger didn't argue. 'Nice try, Geordie,' he said.

'What d'you mean?'

'Your eyes were all over her like a rash.'

'Piss off, mate,' I told him. But secretly I was annoyed with myself for having let my interest show.

Having scored a point, Whinger was relentless. 'On yer bike,' he said with a sneer.

'Come again?'

'She's a dyke.'

'Could be,' I agreed. 'But I don't care *what* she is. I'm keeping this on a professional basis.'

FIVE

Two days later we were on the training range at LATA, the Langwern Army Training Area just inside Wales, when my bleeper went off.

Beep, beep, beep. I immediately recognised the number that came up in the little window. It was Bill, the adjutant.

Mal might as well carry on,' I told Whinger. 'I'll be back in a minute.'

As I walked away to the range hut, short bursts rattled out behind me, so I closed the door and dialled camp.

'Hi, Geordie,' Bill said. 'Where are you at?'

'Down at LATA.'

'OK. The boss wants an immediate meeting. How soon can you be back up here?'

'Half an hour. Just me, is it?'

'No – the whole team.'

'Bill – is something wrong?'

'No, no,' he went. 'Everything's fine.'

'Has the job been pulled?'

'Not at all. It's definitely on. We'll talk when you get here.'

'Where's the meeting, then?'

'In your briefing room.'

'OK. I'll see you in half an hour.'

The lads grumbled a bit at being dragged off the range, especially Pete Pascoe, whose feelings were always near the surface. I kept thinking there was something strange about the way Bill had said, 'It's definitely on.' I got the impression that the job *was* on, but that it had changed.

Ever since our recce party landed back from Moscow, it had been all singing and dancing. I'd put in a positive report, saying that everybody in Moscow was on net, and that, although conditions in the camp at Balashika were primitive, we'd been given a really good hand by the Russians and by the Embassy. Since then we'd faxed across the names and details of the team, for driving licences and other documentation. We'd also lined up a load of extra stores, and everything seemed to be under control. Thanks to Whinger, Rick's reputation as an instant Russian legover specialist had gone all round the team: he'd had a lot of stick, but he'd taken it well.

Now what?

When I saw the line-up in the wing, I knew for certain that it was something heavy. The Regiment was represented not only by the CO and the ops officer, but also by the Director – a brigadier – who must have made a special trip down from London, leaving at dawn. From the Firm came Edgar, but with him was an older and evidently senior man who was introduced as Mr Laidlaw.

The CO – a small, spare man with a bony face and receding hair – spoke first, and I could tell from the pitch of his voice that he was tensed up. Normally he talked at a deliberate pace, but now he had gone up a gear.

He began with the usual spiel about the secrecy of our operation. 'Until now, as you know, it's been classified Top Secret,' he said. 'That classification was imposed primarily for the safety of the team going into Russia. I need hardly remind you, it's essential that Mafia elements don't get wind of your presence.'

He paused and looked down at his notes. Then he said, 'The name of the operation has been changed. It is now Operation Nimrod. Further, it has become a black operation. I don't need to tell you what *that* means, but I will. It means that absolutely no further mention of it is to be made to anyone except members of the team. The reason will become obvious in a moment. Is that clearly understood?'

We were sitting facing the brass on two rows of chairs, three and five. When I glanced round, I saw everyone nod quickly. The CO's tension had communicated itself to the team.

'Right, then.' The CO cleared his throat. 'Another element has been added to the operation. The training of Tiger Force will go down as planned, but as from today that will serve as cover for a new main task. The first priority of Operation Nimrod is now to plant two compact nuclear devices in strategic positions, where they can be detonated by satellite signal if or when such action is deemed necessary.'

Silence. For several seconds nobody moved. I felt as if I'd been skewered to my seat. When the CO continued, I seemed to be hearing him from a distance.

'We realise, of course, that this action is not in line with overt Western policy. The initiative has come from the United States Defense Department. For some time they've been looking at the concept of infiltrating nuclear devices into the former Soviet Union. Now Operation Nimrod is about to provide an opportunity. Any questions so far?'

'You mean you're expecting *us* to plant nuclear devices?' I went.

'Just that,' the CO replied.

'What – under the bloody Kremlin, I suppose?'

'Exactly. One of them, anyway.'

'Boss – you can't be serious.'

'I am, Geordie. It sounds outrageous, I know. But I am. Totally serious.'

I felt myself growing angry. 'I thought we were supposed to be helping the poor bastards.'

'We are. In the short term, we're on their side. We'll go through with the training programme as planned, and I hope we'll do them a service. The new phase of the operation is a long-term measure designed to keep the lid on things in the event of a take-over by criminal elements.'

'That's one way of putting it,' I said. 'You keep the lid on things by blowing the whole fucking place sky high.'

'Geordie!' The CO's voice sharpened. 'Get hold of yourself. The Regiment has received this request from the Pentagon, via the British Government. We've agreed to carry it out.'

Already I regarded Sasha as a friend, a comrade in arms, who needed all the help I could give him. Now I was going to have to double-cross him in everything I said or did. All my friendly actions were going to be undermined by treachery. Then there was Anna. Even though we'd only met once, I sensed that I could work with her. From day one I'd be deceiving her too.

I heard myself asking, 'Does our embassy in Moscow know about this?'

'No.' The Boss shook his head emphatically. 'Not a thing. They'll never hear of it.'

Immediately I thought, *More* people to deceive: the Chargé d'Affaires, for a start. 'Christ!' I glanced at Whinger and saw he was looking pretty sick. I looked on along the line of faces – Rick, Mal, Pavarotti, Dusty – hoping for back-up, but they all wore blank, puzzled expressions.

'These devices,' I said. 'Are you talking about suitcase bombs – the sort of things that were developed for taking out bridges or dams?'

'A modern version,' the CO conceded. 'Slightly bigger, and very much more powerful.'

'How are we supposed to handle them? I mean, are they portable, or what?'

'More or less.' The CO gestured to his left. 'Mr Laidlaw is going to give you an initial briefing.'

Laidlaw stood up to expound. Plump and rubicund, with dark hair slicked back and a big gut bulging against his double-breasted, navy pin-stripe suit, he looked a bit of a character, a man who enjoyed a glass or two. Yet his manner was anything but frivolous: 'Gentlemen,' he said in a thick, fruity Scottish accent, 'for simplicity's sake I shall refer to the devices by initials. In the trade they're known as CNDs, compact nuclear devices. Ironic that the same initials stood for the Campaign for Nuclear Disarmament, which some of you may remember. Nevertheless, those are the initials that we tend to use.

'The two CNDs you will be placing in position weigh approximately a hundred and fifty kilograms apiece. However, each one comes in two parts the size and shape of large suitcases. One component weighs eighty kilos, the other seventy. Thus each component can be carried without much difficulty by two men. Easier with four. The device is primed by fitting the two halves together. It is then connected to a smaller unit, a radio receiver. The whole is detonated by signal from a satellite in synchronous orbit.'

He stopped, scanning our faces. 'Gentlemen, I can see you looking worried. May I emphasise that the chances of any CND ever being detonated in anger are extremely remote. The devices are being planted purely as a deterrent, which the West will use as a form of control, should the situation in Russia deteriorate to a level which threatens the international community. Think of them as an insurance policy, not as weapons of aggression.'

Seeing Johnny shift on his chair, he prompted, 'Yes?'

'These bombs. How do they get to Moscow?'

'You'll take them with you when you fly in.'

'Where are they now?'

Laidlaw looked at his watch. 'They're due into Lakenheath any time now. They should reach Hereford this evening.'

I was finding it hard to believe that this whole spiel wasn't some crazy test, sprung on us to gauge our reactions.

'How do we know where to site them, once we get there?' I asked.

'Our friends in the Pentagon have got everything worked out for you. I'll give you a quick idea from these maps. Of course, you'll have detailed diagrams which you can memorise, but these will show you the general idea.'

He bent over an open laptop which stood on the table and punched a couple of keys. The big VDU beside him flickered into life – and even before he began to explain the coloured diagram that came up on the screen I knew where we were: on the bank of the Moscow River, opposite the Kremlin wall, practically at the spot where we'd had the showdown with the mugger.

'For security reasons,' Laidlaw was saying, 'as from now, the devices will be referred to only by code names. CND 1 is Apple, CND 2 Orange. All right? Now – this diagram shows the site for Apple. We're right in the centre of Moscow. Here you have the

Moscow River, marked blue, flowing west to east. The river at this point is a hundred and five metres wide. This, here, is the south wall of the Kremlin, running parallel with the river. The interior of the Kremlin lies to the north. Alongside the north bank of the river is a road, then there's a strip of grass. The distance from the water to the Kremlin wall is seventy-seven metres.

'Fortunately for your purpose, the ground beneath the city is honeycombed by tunnels. Not sewage tunnels like in London, because Moscow works on a system of relatively small-bore pipes, which are cleared by high-pressure water jets. Of course, there's the Metro – the underground – with tunnels on many different levels, as in London.' He stopped to clear his throat, and continued in a strange, slightly theatrical voice. 'But there are also various other tunnels, less well known. For instance, there is one major and totally secret system which was built during the seventies, in the depths of the Cold War, to give party leaders an escape route from the Kremlin in the event of invasion or nuclear attack. It's very deep, and one of them's big enough to take lorries.

'At the inner end, access is by lifts from a secret terminal under the Presidium. The tunnel runs roughly here' – he drew an imaginary line with his pointer – 'southwards under the river, and all the way out to a site near Vnukovo Airport, twenty kilometres to the south-west. There, a complete underground city still awaits its first refugees. The place has its own supplies of food, power, water, air and so on.'

He paused for effect, and saw he had us well hooked. 'More recently, in the attempted coup of ninety-three, the rebels were cornered in the White House, the parliament building. You'll all have seen TV pictures of tanks firing on it. Well, when the defenders decided to run for it, they went down tunnels – that was how they got away. The KGB were supposed to be guarding all the tunnel systems, but they just didn't have the manpower.

'Our tunnel, *your* tunnel, is much more modest, but ideal for your purpose: only six feet in diameter, but adequate for pedestrians. Again, it was built as an escape route, but during the twenties, on the orders of Lenin. This is it – the dotted line – running from beneath the Great Kremlin Palace, under the river and away towards the south. Fortunately we have been able to acquire KGB records, which show that during the Khruschev era – some time in the fifties – it was declared obsolete and the section under the Kremlin was filled in with a plug of concrete. But the next section has remained open, and appears to have been forgotten, or at any rate abandoned, by latter-day authorities.'

Once again I couldn't help making a sarcastic remark. 'I suppose it passes right beneath the British Embassy. All we have to do is open a trap-door in the floor of the ballroom and drop into it. Brilliant.'

The CO frowned at me, but Laidlaw wasn't fazed. 'You're not far wrong. In fact it passes about five hundred yards to the east of the Embassy. Here's the Embassy complex, on Sophieskaya Quay, and here's the line of the tunnel.' He drew another invisible line downwards, passing to the right of the Embassy and on towards the south-east.

'How do we get into it, then?'

'Access is via a shaft in a courtyard behind a church. I'll show you a detailed diagram in due course.'

'I know,' said Rick suddenly. 'It's that pink-and-white structure, a bit like a wedding cake. Three arches and a tall tower.'

I stared at him, amazed that he'd noticed and remembered such detail.

'Yeah,' he went on. 'We walked right past it after we'd sorted that interloper. You can look through the gateway and see a little church in the yard at the back. There was a big, wrought-iron gate at the entrance, but it looked as though it hadn't moved in years.'

'Pink and white,' Laidlaw echoed him, clearly impressed.

Laidlaw went back to his laptop and wiped the picture. 'Let me show you something else.'

Up came a close-in photo of two heavy padlocks, their hasps passing through a pair of thick metal rings.

'These,' he said, 'are the locks on the plate sealing the access shaft.'

Pavarotti, who was good on his lock-picking, gave a low whistle. 'Fuck me!' he muttered under his breath, as though immediately sensing a challenge, then louder: 'I could go through those bastards in under a minute.'

'I didn't think they'd trouble you much,' Laidlaw said with a smile.

'So that,' he continued, 'for the moment, is Apple. Now for Orange. Some of you have already been to Balashika, I believe.'

I nodded.

'The second site is less precisely specified.'

His next coloured diagram showed mainly open country, with a few buildings and fence-lines running across it.

'This is the southern boundary of the space control complex at Shchiolkovo, next door to the training area at Balashika. It will be for you to choose the exact location, but the objective is to place Orange within a hundred metres of the perimeter, so that its blast effects will cover the entire space complex. As some of you have seen, the training area in which you'll be operating abuts the complex. It should be relatively simple to bury the device at a suitable depth.'

'Which is . . . ?'

'A minimum of six feet, a maximum of twenty.'

The guy seemed to know all the answers. Yet still I could not quite believe that what we were hearing could be for real.

'These CNDs,' I said. 'How powerful are they? What damage will they cause if they go off?'

'Apple would destroy much of the centre of Moscow, and remove the Russian high command at one stroke. Orange would take out the space complex, removing Russia's ability to launch ICBMs with any precision. In both cases, blast damage would be limited to some extent by the fact that the devices would go off underground – but it would still be extremely severe.

'In the city, the Kremlin would disappear. Every tunnel under Moscow would collapse. The entire Metro system would be destroyed. Escape tunnels and nuclear shelters the same. The city would come to a standstill. Within a two-kilometre radius, I would not expect anyone to survive.'

I took a deep breath. 'Between them, then, the devices would kill a few hundred thousand people. Possibly a million.'

Laidlaw said nothing, so I went on, 'This is all well and good, but we aren't trained to handle weapons of this kind. We won't have a clue about them, and unless we postpone the whole training programme there isn't time to learn.'

'No bother,' said Laidlaw. 'I gather one of your colleagues has been on a course in the United States.'

'That's right,' the boss broke in. 'In fact he's escorting the devices over. He's coming in with them this evening.'

'Who are we talking about?' Whinger asked sharply.

'Steve Lime.'

Steve Lime! The guy whose initial and surname spelt 'Slime'. Whose nickname was Toad. Jesus! This really freaked me. I glanced at Whinger. He hated the bastard as much as I did. Toad! The colleague from hell.

I heard the CO saying, 'He'll be going with you, of course. You'll need him to look after the devices, and prime them when the time for insertion comes.'

Toad had always been a pain to the lads on the

squadron, but over the past few weeks, since he'd been posted to the States for a course in nuclear technology, he'd faded into the distance, as it were, and people had stopped beefing about him. It wasn't his fault that he was ugly, with oily skin and protuberant eyes; what bugged us was that he seemed to have no personality, and never got on with any of the guys. He'd go about with a smarmy smile on his face, but there was no warmth in it, and after a while you came to realise that he was wrapped up in his own affairs. At the same time, he was a real crawler, who'd lick up to anyone if he thought he could gain something from doing so.

How he had ever made it into the Regiment I could never understand. He had come from an unusual source – the Royal Engineers – where he'd worked in bomb-disposal; he was fascinated by explosives – obsessed, almost – and he spent hours tinkering with time-fuses and remote-firing gadgets.

He'd never tell you what he was doing, or have any real crack with the lads. He'd associate with the cooks and drivers rather than with the rest of us. It was no accident that he'd ended up as an instructor on the lock-picking wing, in a dim little world of his own. I know that all SAS guys, myself included, are loners to some extent; but at the same time everyone has to muck in, and Toad never did.

The idea of having to live at close quarters with him in the camp at Balashika was a fucking wind-up. In fact I found the whole scenario a nightmare.

I'd always hated the idea of nuclear weapons because

they're bound to kill thousands of innocent civilians, including any number of children – people who have no idea of what's going on. My career in the SAS has always emphasised the need for precision: what you might call 'economy of violence'. People imagine that guys in the Regiment have a cold-blooded, murderous outlook, and regard anybody as a potential target. It isn't like that. All our training is directed to making surgically accurate strikes on targets that have been properly identified.

For the moment, all I could do was grasp at straws. 'This tunnel under the river,' I said. 'How do we know it's still open?'

Laidlaw checked his notes, gave a half-smile, and replied, 'It was open on the fourth of April this year, and we have no reason to believe the situation's changed.'

'That means someone's been down it. If access is that easy, how do we know that the KGB or some other security organisation isn't sitting in there, waiting for us to arrive?'

'The suggestion is that, once you've got Apple in position, you should block the tunnel on the river side of it by dropping the roof, as if there had been a natural fall.'

'Not that easy if it's concrete.'

'I didn't say it was concrete.' A hint of irritation edged into the Scot voice. 'The tunnel is lined with brick, and it's not in the best of condition.'

I nodded in token conciliation.

'Even if you do drop the roof, it is recommended

that you brick the device into the tunnel wall.'

'Hard to camouflage new mortar.'

'That'll be up to you. I imagine there may be dust or mud that you can smear around.'

Next Whinger came up with, 'How do we get the devices on site?'

The CO looked at Laidlaw, as if asking permission to intervene, and said, 'They'll travel out with you on the Herc, sealed in Lacon boxes. They can be marked the same as ammunition. The weight will be about right. At the other end it'll be up to you to devise ways of moving them to their final positions.'

'What if the Herc goes down with the devices on board?' asked Pavarotti. 'What's the chance of a premature detonation?'

'None,' said Laidlaw. 'Even when the two halves of each device are united, nothing can happen until the control box has been interrogated and primed by satellite signal. You need have no worries on that score.'

Thanks, I thought, feeling crushed with a sudden terrific weight of responsibility. The boss was going on again about the paramount need for security; but although I could hear what he was saying I was wondering how the hell I could carry out the training mission with this knowledge in my mind. Every day we'd be dealing man-to-man with our students, instructing and encouraging them, and at the same time, behind their backs, we'd be plotting to annihilate them.

As the main briefing was coming to an end, the CO drew me aside and said, 'One thing to remember,

** TELEBANCO 4B **

REF.   0049.5884.00

DATE	HOUR	OPERATION	DEPO/AUT
13/12/2006	17:28	39	080039

VISA   **** **** **** 3123   08/08

AID:A0000000031010
VISA DEBIT

AMOUNT
WITHDRAWN ******140,00 EUR

THANK YOU FOR YOUR VISIT

Geordie: whatever happens, don't let yourselves get involved in any live operation, like you did in Colombia.'

'That was different, Boss,' I protested. 'When Peter lifted, we had to do something about it.'

'I know. But what I'm saying is that we don't want any repetition. Even if the Russians beg you to take on a job for them, refuse.'

'Will do.'

From the briefing we went into a close-up study of the two sites. Laidlaw produced large-scale drawings with much detail on them.

'All this information is on compact discs, which you can obviously take with you,' he said. 'The discs are programmed so that if anyone tries to get into one without using the correct password, the contents are automatically destroyed. Nevertheless, you obviously want to handle the discs with the greatest care.'

As soon as the brass had dispersed, I called the team together for a Chinese parliament. We got a brew on, and sat round discussing this amazing turn of events.

Rick remembered that, a few months ago, there'd been reports of the Russians losing a whole load of such devices. 'There was something on the Internet that I downloaded on to our Russian file,' he said. 'Wait one, and I'll pull off a copy.'

While he went to make a search, Whinger and I filled in the other guys on the layout of the Kremlin and the British Embassy, which had suddenly become of critical importance. I felt instinctively that because the Orange site was out in open country, we'd be able to hack it without too much trouble: it was Apple, right under the walls of the Kremlin, that made my neck crawl.

In a few minutes Rick returned with a couple of pages printed off his lap-top. 'Listen to this,' he began, reading out his transcript. ' "A respected Russian scientist and former adviser to President Yeltsin said on Thursday that during the 1970s, under orders from the KGB, Moscow had secretly developed suitcase nuclear bombs. The devices had an explosive capacity of one kiloton – the equivalent of 1,000 tons of TNT. They could be activated by one person, and could kill 100,000 people. The bombs were designed for terrorist purposes. Since the break-up of the Soviet Union in 1991, at least 100 such devices have remained un-accounted for." '

Rick broke off, looked up and said, 'Guess what this respected Russian scientist is called.' When nobody answered, he said, 'Yablokov. We all know what that means.'

Somebody gave a groan. *Yabloko* was one of the first words we'd learnt on our Russian course. It means 'apple'.

'Either it's a fluke,' I said, 'or someone's having a laugh.'

'Maybe someone nicked a couple of suitcases from the KGB, and we're just taking them back,' Pavarotti suggested.

'There's a worse possibility than that,' said Pete. 'If we're doing this to the Russkies, who's to say they haven't done it to us already? What if there's a CND nicely placed in the wall of the Thames, under the House of Commons terrace?'

'Yeah,' Whinger agreed, 'and another under the guardroom, right here in camp.'

'It's no bloody joke,' I told him. 'Don't you remember that time in the seventies when the Finns stopped an articulated truck and found it contained the roof for a Mexi stay-behind shelter, destined for England? If the bastards were getting dug in in the UK then, why should they have stopped now?'

'Here's something else off the Net,' Rick went on, scanning his second sheet. Again he read: ' "Russia is regarded as an increasingly unreliable partner on international issues, because of the power of corrupt officials, crooked businessmen and organised crime, a US public policy research group declared on Monday. A panel of the Center for Strategic and International Studies said that the criminalisation of Russia's economy, if left unchecked, would make normal state-to-state relations with the country unviable. It will become impossible for the United States to have traditional, satisfactory dealings with an emergent Russian criminal state." '

He lowered the paper and said, 'What about that?'

'That's it, exactly,' I said. 'The stupid bastards in the Pentagon have got the wind up. They're bobbing like the shit-house fly, and want us to do their dirty work for them.'

Once in Russia, we were going to need several days for

site recces. Obviously we'd have to get the training course up and running; so no matter how fast we moved there was no way we could install Apple and Orange immediately. That in turn meant that the devices would have to be stored somewhere secure for the time being.

The idea of having them with us in that decrepit barrack block at Balashika seemed impossible, and I rapidly came to the conclusion that we must get them into the cellar at the British Embassy at the first possible moment. There, apart from other considerations, Apple would be practically on-site anyway, only a few hundred yards from its ultimate destination. The trouble was, the devices would travel into Russia with us on the Herc and be off-loaded on the strip at Balashika. How could we account for the fact that we needed to transport heavy boxes into the centre of Moscow?

'Tell the Russians we've shipped in some new comms equipment, at the Embassy's request,' Whinger suggested.

'OK,' I agreed, 'but what do we say to the *Embassy*?'

'That it's some of our own stuff. The security in the Russian barracks is shite, and the equipment's so sensitive that we don't want to leave it lying around while we're out working all day. You pretty well told the Chargé that already.'

'All right,' I persisted. 'Let's think about transport, then. That's going to be a bugger. It looks to me as though we're going to have to whip in to the Embassy pretty often. We don't want to draw attention to ourselves by using a military truck or a Brit car. I hope Anna turns up trumps with those Russian vehicles she promised.'

After a delay to the MAC flight from Nevada, Toad didn't reach Hereford until late that evening. I was having supper when I got a message to say that he was in the SAW. As soon as I'd finished I went over to the wing's special armoury – and there he stood, dry-washing his hands. After a couple of months in the desert sun, anyone else would have had a really expensive tan, but all he'd managed was to turn a sickly yellow.

'Hi, Toad,' I went. 'You made it. Where are your packages?'

'Right there.' He half-turned to his right, pointing behind him, and there, sitting on a wheeled pallet by the wall, were four black steel trunks, each maybe two feet by four feet, and only a foot deep, with a couple of smaller boxes on top of them. The only markings, stencilled in white paint, said 'A-1, A-2, A-R' and 'O-1, O-2, O-R'.

'Jesus!' I said. 'So they come in kit form and have to be fitted together.'

'Oh yes. Early portable devices were in two parts. Then, as technology improved, they started making one-piece models – real suitcase bombs. Those are still around, but when something more powerful's wanted they've gone back to this modular design.'

I was horribly fascinated by the thought of what the

black cases contained and what they could do. But at the same time I couldn't help being irritated by Toad's proprietorial air. There was something in his gestures, in his attitude, which said, These are mine, and you can keep your distance.

'Everything all right?' I asked.

'Sure.' He rubbed his hands some more.

'Good course?'

He nodded.

'Have you been briefed about the operation?'

'Not yet.'

'Well, we're leaving for Moscow the day after tomorrow, so there isn't much time. Better come on up, and I'll give you the bones of it now. Then maybe you can brief me and Whinger on the devices in the morning.'

We went up to the main briefing room, and I un-locked the safe in which I'd stored the site plans and the CDs. Toad hardly spoke as I went through them, but I knew that his quick mind was soaking in every detail.

'The Orange site is out in open country,' I told him. 'Part scrub-land, part forest. As far as I can see, it's just going to be a hole in the ground: either one we find and adapt or one we dig ourselves. So I don't see much of a problem there. The tricky one's going to be Apple. This access shaft, in the courtyard, is at least twenty feet deep.'

'Pulleys,' said Toad.

'Spot on. I've thought of that. Those small titanium pulleys the Mountain Troop use for hoisting heavy machine guns and mortars up steep hillsides. The thing is, how robust are the devices? Can they stand knocks, or have they got to be feather-bedded?'

'Oh no, they're pretty robust. You could probably drop one down the shaft and it wouldn't come to any harm.' Toad frowned and then added, 'Cancel that. Better not drop it.'

'But it couldn't go off, even if we did?'

'Not a chance. Until the two components are united they're inert. We'll have to take them in separately and couple them at the last minute.'

He studied the plan for a minute, then asked, 'What depth is the tunnel running at as it comes to the Kremlin wall?'

'We don't know. But it's a hell of a wall. Must be thirty or forty feet high, so the foundations have to go down some way.'

'We'll need to get the SCR within ten feet of the surface.'

'The SCR?'

'The Satellite Communications Responder. That's the unit which the satellite sends messages to and interrogates.'

'How big is it?'

'Oh – those small black boxes downstairs. Didn't you see them? Like this.' He held up his hands a foot apart.

'Can they be some way away from the device?'

'Sure. The connecting co-ax cables can be any length.'

'Maybe there'll be an old ventilation shaft. Or maybe

we'll have to bore into the tunnel roof.'

'An auger, then.'

'Good thinking. What else?'

Slimy though he was, Toad had his head screwed on, and in the morning he gave the whole team a good briefing. This time he started with the SCR, and described how it needed to be positioned with its antenna coming up to within three or preferably two feet of the surface. The controlling satellite, he told us, would send it signals to check that the system was working. There was no chance of an accidental explosion, because detonation could only be achieved by a complex sequence of questions and answers, and confirmed by coded messages from the Pentagon.

'The SCR contains its own nuclear power source, which gives it an indefinite life,' Toad said. 'One snag is that the generator contains radioactive fuel and could become a health hazard if it gets crushed or broken. That's why it's so heavy: it's encased in a lead jacket.'

'What happens if the Russian security forces do an electronic sweep along the front of the Kremlin, up above?' asked Rick. 'Won't they detect it?'

'Almost impossible,' Toad replied smoothly. 'For ninety-nine per cent of the time the SCR's passive. It's just listening. Its response periods will be pre-set to times like three in the morning, when people are least likely to be about.'

Seeing Rick frown, he added in a patronising voice, 'I wouldn't worry about it. You can take it from me

118

that it'll be OK. I could go into a more technical explanation, but I don't think you'd understand. The bottom line is that the satellite sends signals down, and the SCR only answers for a split-second every twenty-four hours.'

He looked round the row of faces, clearly enjoying his role of teacher. 'For security when the devices are being moved around,' he went on, 'there's this very useful piece of equipment.'

He crossed to the end of the small case marked A–R and applied his thumb to a shallow depression near one corner. The sprung lid of a small compartment flew open, and from it he took out an object the size of a compact mobile phone. 'This is the radio alarm trigger, generally known as the Rat. Whenever this is switched on it has to remain within thirty metres of the device. If it goes farther away than that it automatically triggers a radio alarm in the device itself. The signal can be picked up by satellite. So if you have to move the device in enemy territory, I suggest that the guy in charge keeps the Rat on his belt – like this.'

He clipped the thing on to his own belt, then returned it to its lair.

'What about having a shufti inside one of the components?' I suggested.

'Not a chance.' Toad started dry-washing his hands again. 'They're all sealed down, and I don't want to break them out until they're about to be put in position. There are quite a few checks I'll make then.'

We couldn't argue with him and he knew it. He

wouldn't even come clean about the damage each bomb was likely to do. He pretended the information was classified and kept it to himself. We had to be content with staring at diagrams of bewildering complexity which he brought up on a lap-top from his own CD. We all knew, though, that the destructive capacity packed into the black boxes in front of us was something awesome.

'What would happen if we got the devices in position but didn't prime them properly?' I asked. 'What if you deliberately connected them up wrong?'

'The satellite would detect the fault. That's the beauty of the system. The Pentagon would know there was something wrong. They'd probably send us back to put it right.'

'Well,' said Pavarotti, as if to sum up. 'I'm not going down any fucking tunnel. That's for certain.'

'I wouldn't be so sure,' I told him.

Our 'last-minute' checks seemed endless. We were taking our own main weapons and ammunition – MP5s and G3s – so that we could give demonstrations without having to worry about handling unfamiliar kit. Stun grenades for CQB work; plastic explosive, detonators and det cord for EMOE. Also, I'd cleared it with Sasha that we could take pistols, to carry covertly when we were outside the camp. With crime running at the level it was, he'd agreed that it would be only sensible to have some means of self-defence.

Covert comms equipment was another basic item

we'd need for demonstrations. Also, I foresaw that it would be indispensable when it came to recceing sites for Apple and Orange and then inserting the devices. Plenty of batteries were required, therefore, and recharging kit. For work in the tunnel we needed good head-torches, short-handled picks and jemmies, plus a wire climbing ladder for going down the access shaft, and lightweight pulleys and nets for lowering the component parts of Apple. Also sandbags for removing spoil from the insertion-point, lock-picking kit for the padlocks, shovels for possible digging on the Orange site . . . All this on top of our normal equipment and personal kit.

At one point the CO called me in for a private chat.

'Sit down, Geordie,' he began. 'I can see you're not happy. You've just got to make the best of it.'

I nodded. 'This mass-destruction – it's not like the Regiment.'

'I know. But what you've got to believe is that the devices will probably never be used.'

'Easy enough to say that. One thing I'd like to be bloody sure of is that they're not going to get used while the team's still over there.'

'Don't be stupid. There's no chance of that.'

'How do we know? What if the Resident gets assassinated and there's some kind of Mafia takeover? What if Clinton decides that Russia's going down the tubes and criminals are about to take over? The international situation might go to ratshit in a few hours.'

I stared at the boss, and he said nothing.

'What I'd like to know is, whose finger's going to be on the button? Who's really in charge? If it's the Yanks, I'm not at *all* happy. They're just as volatile as anyone else. Worse, probably.'

The boss gave a non-committal grunt, and I went on, 'It's bloody two-faced of our own government, anyway. All these overtures to the Kremlin about giving them help – and now this.'

'That's politics for you.'

There was no good counter to that, and I came away feeling pretty pissed off. Thinking ahead, I put in a call over the secure satellite link to the Chargé d'Affaires in Moscow. He sounded friendly enough, to the point of asking if there was anything he could do to help.

'Well, thanks,' I said. 'We're coming in tomorrow night, as planned, but we don't start the course till Monday – so I wondered if we could bring some kit to store in the cellar on Sunday evening?'

'Ah.' He sounded a bit taken aback. 'I shan't be here. But I tell you what. I'll leave the keys with the duty officer. That's going to be . . . wait a minute . . . Richard Henshaw. I'll tell him to expect you. What time will you get here?'

I had to think fast. 'I'm not certain we'll have transport by then. But let's assume we will have. We should be there between six and seven in the evening. If there's anything different, I'll call to say so.'

'Right-oh. I'll leave a message at the gate.'

So far, so good. Then, to take my mind off immediate problems, I called Tony Lopez, late of the

US SEAL special forces, but by now working in CIA headquarters at Langley, Virginia. I had come to know Tony after he'd rescued me when I got hurt in Iraq during the Gulf War and we'd been interned together for a month. Then, a couple of years later, he had come over for a tour with the Regiment, and had done brilliantly until he'd had his left arm smashed.

His wound was serious enough to finish his career in the armed forces, and when he'd recovered, he joined the CIA. He'd been too discreet to tell me exactly what areas he was working in, but it didn't take a genius to guess that he would have reponsibility for special forces projects.

Now, when I got through, he sounded his usual lively self.

'Hi, Tony,' I went. 'How are you doing?'

'Good! Good! How about you?'

'Fine. How's the arm?'

'Still improving. About seventy per cent now.'

'Great. Listen, Tony – d'you know people in the Drug Enforcement Agency?'

'Sure do. Why?'

I told him about Rick's friend Natasha, and her sister Irina who'd got sucked into the Russian Mafia operations in New York. I also gave him the name of the brasserie in Brooklyn where the girl was supposed to be working, and asked if he could do anything to help.

He said he'd put in a call to a friend in the DEA, but then in a different voice he added, 'So it's you who's been in Moscow. I might have guessed.'

'What's that supposed to mean?'

'Nothing. But this assignment could be a hot number. When you go back there, Geordie, take it easy. OK?'

'OK.' I wasn't going to ask him anything else. Clearly Tony knew about Operation Nimrod: he knew we'd been over, he knew we were going back . . . and there were obviously things about the task that he didn't like.

SIX

The runway at Balashika was pretty short, and the captain of the aircraft warned us in advance that he'd have to do a tactical landing. In practice that meant that he banged the Herc down so hard on the first impact that it bounced and flew on a bit before coming to earth a second time. Down in the back we all had a good grip of the cargo nets, and although we went weightless for a second or two, with legs and bodies flying up in the air, we were none the worse.

When the tailgate opened the night air struck surprisingly cool. Sasha was there to greet us, and as we shook hands I remarked on how cold it was.

'I told you,' he said. 'Summer is feenished.'

But the temperature was good for unloading and, in spite of numerous well-meaning offers of help from waiting Russians, we insisted on humping all our own kit ourselves.

'It's kind of you to have kept them up,' I told Sasha, 'but we can handle this. Let them go to bed.'

We had everything out on the apron within forty minutes, and as the Herc took off for home I watched its navigation lights disappearing into the sky with the

125

same feeling I'd had when I'd looked at the head loadie before we went out on the HALO jump over France: Lucky bastards, I thought. They're off home. A nice, comfortable stop-over in Berlin, and tomorrow they'll be back. We, meanwhile, were left two thousand miles from base with fearful problems to solve.

As soon as I saw we had everything up together, I insisted that Sasha fall out. I knew he had a room in the officers' mess on the camp, but he'd told me that at weekends he went home to live with his mother in her flat in Ostankino, a northern suburb of Moscow. At that time of night, he said, it was only fifteen minutes by car – so off he went, with promises to be back first thing in the morning.

The important stuff was locked inside green Lacon boxes, stencilled with white numbers – 1 to 27. We never let any of these boxes out of our sight. We lifted them on to hand-trolleys, wheeled them across to our designated block, and carried them up the steps ourselves. I was glad to find that Sasha had got strong hasps and padlocks organised on most of the doors, and I designated two rooms at the end of the corridor as stores, next to the kitchen on one side and the signal office on the other.

By 2.00 a.m. local time we had everything squared away. The cooking equipment was in the kitchen and the edible stores in the room alongside. We designated the best-protected room the armoury, putting the weapons, ammunition and CND components in there. The room next to that had the only telephone, so we made that our office and comms centre, housing (among other things) the lockable filing cabinets we'd brought to contain the classified CDs. I created an instant rule that all lap-tops were to remain in the office, unless being used for giving lessons, and that no Russian was allowed in there on any pretext.

As for sleeping, we billeted ourselves in twos. Whinger and I shared, with the rest of the team similarly paired off. Coarse sheets and blankets had been dumped on the beds, and the water in the showers was hot. A smell of fresh emulsion paint, not unpleasant, made it clear that some hasty sprucing-up had taken place. Mal nearly went ballistic when he saw a rat disappear down a hole in the corner of the corridor, but I told him to push a Lacon box over the place and we'd deal with it in the morning.

The odd man out was Toad, whom I'd detailed to sleep with his devices in the armoury. In fact I'd told him that as long as the CNDs remained in camp, he was to stay with them day and night, except when relieved by somebody approved by me. I also told him he'd got to screw the nut and knock his running on the head for the time being, even if it meant him going short of exercise. In sum, he was to guard his charges with his life, until such time as we could transfer them to the safety of the Embassy cellar.

For our nefarious purposes, the block was brilliantly placed. It backed directly on to the edge of the training area, with no other buildings behind it, and nobody overlooking its rear entrance. Our people would be able to slip out that way, straight down a track and into the scrubby forest. Also behind the block was parking space for several cars, so we'd have little bother loading the CND components into vehicles for transport to the Embassy.

When I realised how well sited we were, I almost changed my mind about the need to move the devices: in such favourable circumstances I thought hard about keeping Orange with us. Then I reckoned, No: I don't fancy being out of the building all day, running the course, with those things sitting here – even if Toad *is* in charge. Better get both of them into the Embassy until we're set up to deploy them. Thus I decided that we wouldn't wait, but would follow my original plan and move them on Sunday evening. For one thing, they'd be gone before Anna came on the scene, at 8.30 on Monday morning; and for another, I already knew from our first visit that the Moscow traffic was far lighter during the weekend than on working days.

It wasn't long before I felt sure I'd made the right decision.

With the course not due to start until Monday morning, we had all Sunday to sort ourselves out; but we'd hardly got a scratch breakfast down our necks when Steve, one of the scalies, came up to me with a face of doom and asked if he could have a word. When I asked what the problem was he jerked his head up and back, meaning, Let's go outside. So we walked out the back, into the edge of the forest, and he said, 'Geordie, they've put bugs in the power points.'

'Where?'

'In the signals room, and in the kitchen.'

'Ah, shite! Are you sure?'

'Hundred per cent. I was making a routine sweep, and they came up loud and clear. Have a listen for yourself.'

Back inside, I borrowed Steve's detector kit and ran the sensor pad along the wall in the signals room. As it passed the dual power-point, a loud *brrraannggg* sounded in the headphones, then died away as I moved the pad on. I said nothing, but shook my head, went through to the next room, and got the same thing.

What should I do? Report the bugs to Anna in the morning? Have a quiet word with Sasha? Say nothing?

In the open again, walking up and down, I asked Steve if he could disable the microphones without his interference being apparent.

'I suppose if I knocked one out, they might think it had just broken down. But if I did both they'd be bound to realise.'

'OK, then. Knacker the one in the signals office. Break one of the connections or whatever you have to do, but leave the other. Have you swept the signals room thoroughly?'

He nodded. 'There's only the one in there.'

'Better do all the rooms the same.'

Now I realised why our hosts had done so much re-decorating: they'd painted over any bits of replastering that had been needed.

The discovery unsettled me. 'I'm really disappointed,' I told Whinger. 'I hoped all that was a thing of the past.'

'Who are we to talk?' he said.

The truth of his remark kept me in a state of permanent unease. I confirmed to Whinger that I didn't intend to mention the bugs: we'd wait to see what happened if Steve took one out.

The day being Sunday, there were few people about on the camp, and we were left to sort ourselves out – which suited us fine. There was more than enough admin and physical work to keep us busy. Sasha was in and out, making sure we had all we wanted.

It was clear that all our lads were going to have to take turns at cooking, and in mid-morning Sasha took Dusty – our master chef – and Mal off on a conducted tour of Balashika's shops, from which they returned effing and blinding. The so-called Supermagazin was a disaster, and the only place they found any half-decent vegetables was in an open-air market, where locals were selling produce brought in from the country. In the Supermagazin they'd bought scabby oranges, and at the other place they had got eggs, onions, carrots, cabbages and potatoes; but still it looked as though we were going to be relying heavily on tins, packets and boil-in-the-bag meals designed for use in the field.

After lunch, under Sasha's supervision, drivers delivered two battered-looking Volgas, one mid-grey, one black, with worn tyres and rust showing through the paint where the mudguards joined the body. He explained that they were a slightly later model than his own, but similar. The grey one had 88,000 ks on the clock, the black 13,000 – which obviously meant that it had been round the dial once at least

When I asked if it was OK to drive around the dirt roads inside the training area, to familiarise ourselves with the vehicles, Sasha exclaimed, 'Why not?'

'How about going into town?'

'Whatever you like. You've got your licences OK. But inside camp, no red-and-white bars, please.'

He meant that we weren't to go through any of the safety barriers that blocked off the danger areas; but there was plenty of other space, and four of us set out for a spin. Before we left, I got Steve to run his bug-hunter over both vehicles just in case, but the result was negative, and that reassured me a little. Nevertheless, we didn't propose to run unnecessary risks, so we took covert radios and kept the Volgas a few hundred metres apart, chatting to make sure we weren't being followed.

The cars were sluggish and noisy, with heavy steering; but even though driving them was a pain, at least we had wheels of our own. I hadn't expected such freedom: I'd imagined we would be more closely supervised. The entire training area was ringed by the concrete wall, so we were in fact enclosed. We soon found that a perimeter track skirted the inside of the wall, heading out north-eastwards in the direction of the space complex; and after a couple of ks we began to see, beyond the wall, amazingly large, white dish-aerials pointing skywards in serried ranks. Although I said nothing, I could immediately imagine why the Pentagon fancied taking that lot out.

The land was almost dead flat, with only a gentle rise and fall to relieve the monotony. Patches of pine and birch forest alternated with wide-open scrub and grass, criss-crossed by dirt tracks, reminding me of the training areas at Pirbright. Here and there a primitive wooden observation tower stuck up above the trees. Clearly the training area was well used, but two things about it made me feel reasonably secure. One was the sheer size of the landscape. In terrain as open as this it would be very difficult for anyone to watch us without our being aware of the surveillance. The other factor in our favour was the decrepit nature of the fixtures and fittings. On several of the wooden watch-towers the ladders had rungs missing, and the red-and-white barriers which Sasha had mentioned were bent and rusting. All this, we felt certain, reflected the cut-down in the Russian forces: clearly, they had nobody to do the maintenance and were generally short-staffed.

Three ks from base, as we were cruising gently, Rick suddenly pointed to his left. There, at the end of a glade with a shallow ditch running out along its base, was a derelict air-raid shelter or bunker – a dome of concrete protruding from a bank of higher ground, with a small rectangular opening in the side that faced us.

I felt my heartbeat speed up. At first glance this looked an incredibly promising candidate for the burial of Orange. The perimeter wall of the training area was only a few yards behind it, the nearest dish aerials a short distance farther off. We'd never get closer than this. I could scarcely believe we'd found one site already.

'Black to Grey,' I called over the radio. 'Stopping to have a pee. Hang off and watch my back.'

'Grey. Roger,' came Whinger's voice.

In the warm afternoon sun Rick and I strolled towards the bunker while Mal stayed at the wheel. Small birds were singing and the place had a peaceful atmosphere. All the same, I was nagged by a feeling that somebody was watching us.

'We won't go any closer,' I said quietly to Rick. 'Turn back.'

From fifty yards short of the structure, I could see planks and spars of wood piled up inside the opening. The shelter, whatever it was, appeared to be full of rubbish. All the better for us.

We slowly wheeled round and walked towards the car again. Facing that way, I realised that there was one watch tower in sight, but it was a long way off, and, as far as we could tell, unmanned. To complete the casual picture, I went over and had a piss against a gorse bush, after which we got back into the car.

'Mobile again,' I told Whinger. 'Nothing moving your way?'

'All clear.'

We returned to base without incident. Had I imagined the unseen eyes? Rick said he had felt nothing – and he normally picked up danger signals before anyone else. Once again I started wavering. My first reaction, as we drove away from the shelter, had been.

133

Right, let's go for it. Let's get the damned CND straight in there and not bugger about taking it into the city centre. Then the feeling of unease returned, making me realise how hasty I was being. Obviously we needed to recce the site properly before we went crashing into it. Even though the building looked as though it had been abandoned for years, it could still be the scene of some training activity. Better keep calm, take time to settle in and get the feel of things.

'Carry on as planned,' I told Whinger. 'We'll aim to roll into town after dark.'

We had a meal – Dusty produced a great corned-beef hash with plenty of onions and fried eggs on top – and waited till it was fully dark. Then we backed both Volgas as close as we could to our block's rear entrance. I could tell that everyone was on edge, from the way they were talking in short bursts. We put dickers out to watch either end of the building, and when they confirmed that the coast was clear, we began carrying the kit out.

From measurements taken earlier, we knew that one Lacon box would effectively fill the boot of each car, and that the rear doors were too narrow to take one at all. We'd therefore opened the boxes up and brought out the CNDs in their original packing. The main components, in their black steel cases, were forty inches by thirty by twelve, and the SCR, an incredibly heavy lump, was a twenty-inch cube. The cases had built-in handles at the corners for a four-man carry.

Before we left the building, Toad opened up the

small compartment in the base of each SCR and brought out its Rat. I hooked one into my belt and gave the other to Pavarotti. Now those two had to stay within a hundred feet of their devices, otherwise the pagers would go off automatically and start transmitting their alarm signal.

I was shitting bricks as we came down the steps with the first of them. Having a thing like that in your hands is no joke. No matter how often Toad had assured us that an accidental impact couldn't set the bomb off, I kept wondering what would happen if one of us lost his footing.

Gingerly we lowered the first case into one boot. That just left room for the SCR box alongside. The second big case had to go on the back seat, and the combined weight put the Volga down on its springs. With two guys up front, the rear mudguards were almost on the tyres.

Sasha had told the guardroom we'd be going out, so we had no problem there. We flashed some big smiles along with our passes, and the sentry raised the barrier, waving us through. Then, on the main road, it was just a question of turning left and heading down the big highway into town.

The traffic was incredibly light. I thought of Sunday night on the M4, with a million cars all trying to pour back into London at the same time. Here, I realised, most of the poor bastards who lived in the city centre had nowhere to go at weekends.

Whinger drove the lead car, the black one, with me

beside him, map in hand. Rick kept the grey Volga four or five hundred yards behind, so that the two vehicles didn't seem to be associated. With him was Pavarotti, and, squeezed into the back seat beside half of Orange, Toad. There was really no need for him to come with us, but at the back of my mind lurked the worry that while we were moving the devices around, something might happen to them. I could hardly imagine what the problem might be, but if one of them started ticking or heating up we might suddenly need Toad to deal with it.

The two cars were in radio contact, in case anyone saw trouble looming. The plan was for Rick to close up in the final stages of the trip, so that he could follow us and not have to worry about navigation. We also had pistols in underarm holsters, concealed beneath our jackets.

When we joined the thin stream of traffic, I realised what good cars the Volgas were to have. Never mind that they had zero acceleration and roared and wallowed like ten-ton trucks: they were anonymous, and scruffy enough not to arouse anyone's interest. As we kept to the right-hand lane at about sixty ks, any number of identical vehicles surged past on the outside.

That first run-in could hardly have been easier. The only threat was from the potholes which, with the huge load we had on board, could have done serious damage. Whinger often had to swerve to avoid a chasm ahead.

To help with the map-reading in the city centre, I'd made a list of the streets we needed to take. In fact, for most of the way all we had to do was follow the same highway right through, almost until we reached the Moscow River.

Once over the river it was plain sailing along the south bank. Ahead of us and to the right, the red stars on the towers of the Kremlin glowed in the sky – familiar landmarks already, giving me the comfortable feeling that I was back on ground I knew. In a few seconds we passed under the bridge we'd walked across that first night. Having glanced in the mirror to make sure there was only one car behind, I called Rick to say, 'Slowing now,' and Whinger dropped our speed to twenty ks so that we could get a look at the pink-and-white gateway and the churchyard.

The drive-past didn't yield much. As Rick had predicted, the tall, elaborate wrought-iron gates were open, and through them we caught a glimpse of a small, low church, set back maybe seventy metres from the road. The light inside the courtyard was exceedingly dim, and we couldn't see details, but I got an impression of ramshackle buildings round the sides, and even some bushes.

'Nice and dark,' commented Whinger.

'Not too tidy, either. Look out, though. Here we are.'

The security guards on the Embassy gate had been briefed to expect us, and let us through without bother. There was a short delay while the Brit guy phoned the duty officer to say we'd arrived: then a message came for us to drive round into the compound. There, an outside light had been switched on, and under it was standing a young-looking fellow with fair hair.

As I jumped out, he came forward. 'Sergeant Major Sharp? Richard Henshaw.'

We shook hands. I introduced Whinger properly, and the others more sketchily.

'Got some stuff for us, have you?' asked Henshaw.

'Well, it's for ourselves really. I'd just like to be sure it's in safe hands.'

'Of course. Well, here are your keys. You know where to go. There are two locks on the cellar door. This key's for the central lock, this one for a padlock that goes through a hasp at the bottom corner. But in any case, the compound's fully secure, so I imagine your equipment will be all right. D'you need any help to unload?'

'No, no. We'll be fine, thanks. Is this the only set of keys you have?'

'No, there's a duplicate set as well.'

'Do you mind if I have them too? I'd rather we didn't have anyone else poking around in there.'

'Oh – all right.' He looked a bit sniffy, but disappeared briefly inside and came back with another set.

'There you are. I'll leave you to it. As it happens, I'm quite busy.'

'Thanks again, then.'

As soon as he was indoors we opened the up-and-over steel door of the cellar and backed the black Volga to the head of the ramp. There was no point in taking the car down the slope, because the approach, between concrete walls, was too narrow for the rear doors to open more than a few inches and we wouldn't have got the boxes out of the back seat. That meant a short carry, and before we began it I scanned round to make certain we weren't being overlooked. No problems on that score: the high wall of the compound blanked off the view from outside. Reassured, I said, 'OK, lads. Here we go,' and we set about dumping our lethal load.

When all six cases were stacked, Toad brought out the two Rats, switched them off and slipped them back into their compartments in the SCRs. To put the final touch on our security, we replaced the padlock on the foot of the door with one of our own.

Toad was obviously impressed by the size of the Embassy buildings, and from the way he started dry-washing his hands I knew he was coming up with some new idea. 'Now we've got the devices here,' he said, 'hadn't I better stay with them? There must be a spare room I could live in.'

'Not a chance,' I told him. 'The kit'll be fine here. Nobody can touch it. You're coming back with us.'

The relief of getting the devices off my hands – even for the time being – made me feel reckless, and I almost went straight into a recce of the churchyard. 'After all,' I said before we re-boarded the cars in the embassy compound, 'we're on the spot. Why not have a look round?'

It was the ever-observant Rick who stopped me. 'When we drove in, there was a guy hanging around out there on the embankment,' he warned.

'Where?'

'About a hundred metres beyond the entrance. He looked everything like a dicker, from the FSB or somewhere.'

'In that case we'll not piss about in the area,' I agreed. 'Especially if he's still there when we pull out.'

He was – a figure in dark clothes, wearing a cap, leaning out over the river wall as if watching boats go by. 'He's moved this way a bit,' said Rick over the radio. 'But it's the same guy.'

'Right then,' I replied. 'That's it. Next stop Balashit-heap.'

I found it a pleasure to start the course the next morning. Our team had all slept well, and the weather was still fine. Whinger and I had gone for a four-mile run at first light, and after a shower and breakfast I felt in good shape. But above all I was chuffed to get back to our proper role of soldiering, and passing some of our skills on to others.

The sight of Anna in her DPMs was enough to put a smile even on Toad's face. I'd arranged with Sasha that all our guys would get an issue of Russian combat kit, so that we blended into the local scenery. Naturally, the garments didn't fit too well; we could disguise short or long sleeves by rolling them up, but the blouses hung away from our waists and the trousers tended to be bulky. Anna's kit, in contrast, was immaculately cut to flatter her slender figure, and looked as though it had been styled by some Western couturier. She wore elegant black boots, a black leather belt that emphasised her narrow waist, and a jaunty peaked cap. Even though she wore no insignia you felt instinctively that she was the senior officer present.

'You got your cars all right?' she asked.

'Yes, thanks. They'll do well.'

'Nothing special, I'm afraid. Not like a couple of BMWs.'

'Oh well – they're fine for getting in and out of town.'

I wasn't sure if she knew that we'd already been in to the Embassy, but I wasn't going to bring the matter up unless she did, so I said nothing on that score and switched to matters about the course.

To open proceedings we got the twenty-four students into the main lecture room and sat them down, while our team lined up across the stage, Sasha hovering at one side. Anna introduced herself to the course, and to the Brits who hadn't met her, with a brief explanation that she came from the FSB and that she had been appointed our liaison officer. I then introduced our lads one by one, using the names they'd chosen to sport on their chest badges. I felt a right prick saying, '*Vot Rik, vot Dosti* . . . This is Rick, this is Dusty,' followed by a couple of words about what each man would be teaching – weapons, unarmed combat, explosive entry, house assaults, vehicle drills and so on. When I came to Whinger – last, because he was last in the line – I asked Anna to explain that Vuinzha was not his proper name but the best approximation we could make of his nickname.

'And what's that?' she asked. When I told her, she immediately came up with, 'Well, we've got one of them too.' She looked around the benches and pointed to a tall, saturnine fellow with sticking-out ears. 'He's called Zanuda,' she said, 'and that means exactly the same thing. He's always moaning and groaning.'

Like us, the Russians were wearing name badges, but I got them to call out their first names all the same. This revealed that we had three men called Nikolai and three called Sergei, as well as two Semyons and two Igors.

'Right,' I said, moving along the ranks, 'I know that really we should call you by your patronymics, but it'll be easier for us if we give you numbers. You're Nikolai *Odin*, you're Nikolai *Dva*, you're Nikolai *Tri*.'

I did the same with the Sergeis and the two doubles. All that, coupled with the discovery of the twin Whingers, caused a good few laughs and broke the ice.

Finding that several of the students were from Spetznaz and some from Omon, I deliberately split the two groups, pairing off each man with one from the other organisation, so that they'd all have to mix and communicate. 'It's important you all know each other really well,' I told them. 'Your lives may depend on knowing how your partner's going to react in a particular situation. Learn everything you can about each other. Our team have been working together for years, and we're still finding out.'

Altogether the Russians looked a lively bunch, and fit: by the glow on them, I guessed they'd all been running that morning. They were all aged between twenty-five and thirty-five, but they were noticeably bigger than us – taller on average, and well built. There were a lot of broad, wide-cheekboned Slavic faces, and a couple of broken noses. When I asked how many had fought in Chechnya, nine hands went up, and a similar question about Afghanistan produced four.

'*Khorosho!*' I said warmly. 'Plenty of combat experience.'

When Anna translated, the remark brought out self-congratulatory smiles all round, and I could see we were going to get on.

The only two I didn't much care for were a pair who, I knew, had come from SOBR, the organisation that had once guarded the prisons and gulags. Sasha told me that, when the camps had broken up in 1992, a lot of these guys were thrown on to the market – and some bunch they were, too. They had the reputation of being the nastiest of all Russian special forces, with their own line in brutality and torture. Certainly the two we'd got, Oleg and Misha, looked pretty low-brow and unco-operative.

As I handed round the course programme, written in both languages, I said, 'OK, we'll be starting right away, with basic CQB. But first we want to take you on the ranges and make sure we're all together on our commands. We want to watch you firing, and see how you do things. This is as much for our benefit as for yours: we need to get to know your methods.'

So we began, with magazine changes, stoppage drills and zeroing. Their weapon-handling proved to be good, although, as I'd suspected, some of the safety aspects wanted watching. We delivered a few bollockings on this score, especially after Sergei Two let off an AK47 round vertically into the air after he was supposed to have cleared his rifle.

Over the next few days, with basic range-work satisfactory, we began teaching the theory of house assaults, starting small, with two-man teams, making the students work in their pairs, showing them how to go through a room and clear it. We then moved on to four-man teams, through an assault on a single room to one on a house with four rooms and a corridor, still using one team. Then we progressed to having several teams operating together: eight or a dozen men entering different rooms at the same instant. Next came multi-floor tactics, with guys bursting in through doors, windows and skylights, all their movements precisely co-ordinated by radio.

At first we worked in classrooms, using magnetic boards and coloured counters to demonstrate formations, but soon we started moving men through actual rooms, and finally took them out for live firing practice in their primitive Killing House. The Russians were full of energy and enthusiasm, and they fairly threw themselves into the work. But what they lacked was precision: several times, when left to themselves to make a plan, they managed to have one assault team come face to face with another in the stair well, and we had to drum into them the vital importance of logical thought in command and control.

All this was interesting and good fun – a challenge for both sides, and one that we all enjoyed. But the trouble was that, for me, the days began to slip away at an alarming speed. In no time at all it was Wednesday, then Thursday, then Friday. Our first week had almost gone, and we'd had no chance to recce either of our prospective nuclear sites.

The other aggravation was that on only the third night Rick did a runner. After supper he simply disappeared, and there were a few moments' panic before Mal, who was sharing a room with him, suddenly said, 'I bet I know where he's at. He's gone to screw that woman he met on the recce. I heard him on the phone to her this morning.'

'Not Natasha!' I said. Bloody hell! I knew he'd taken her address but I didn't realise he'd made contact again.

'Yeah – laid himself on a taxi, too.'

I wasn't going to sit up half the night waiting for the randy bastard to come back, and I never did hear what time he rolled in. But after breakfast I lit into him for taking off without letting me know what he was doing.

'Can't you see?' I told him. 'It's plain bloody stupid. If anything had happened to you we wouldn't have had a clue where you were. If you got picked up by the Mafia, for instance, the whole team would be in the shit.'

He saw the point of that, and apologised, but I still warned him that if he couldn't control himself, I'd have to send him home.

Friendships quickly formed between the two sides, boosted on one occasion when Pete Pascoe, a great hunter-gatherer, returned from a run with a handful of brown mushrooms he'd collected in the forest. The sight of them brought vigorous protests from our own guys. 'For fuck's sake!' cried Whinger. 'Throw 'em out. Don't cook them, Mal, or you'll poison the lot of us.' But when the students saw them they went ballistic. '*Beliye griby!*' they shouted. 'Boletus mushrooms!' and rushed out to the spot where Pete had found them in search of more.

These were the best, most sought-after kind of fungus. Pete became a hero, and Anna confirmed that Russians are crazy about mushrooms. 'Weekends, at this time of year, thousands of Muscovites go hunting for them in the woods. They come out by train, car, everything. They're like locusts, and sweep the place clean. But the training areas are out of bounds to the public, so we're lucky.'

The week also saw an amazingly rapid proliferation of swear words far worse than any Valentina had taught us. The strangest thing was the way each nationality began to curse in the other's language: very soon the Brits had adopted *yob tvoio mat* (fuck your mother) as their basic expression of disgust, and several of the Russians were giving brilliant imitations of Whinger's 'firekin ell'. They'd started calling Dusty 'Dostoievsky', and Johnny, with his high complexion, had immediately become 'Svyokla' – Beetroot.

After supper on Friday evening, before the weekend

break, the students invited us round to their block for a drink. It was a strictly private affair, as drinking in barracks was totally forbidden even to officers. But somebody had slipped out for a few bottles of vodka and some cans of beer, and camaraderie flowered in an impromptu sing-song.

'I hope to Christ this isn't home-brewed,' I said to Whinger as I downed a slug of vodka. 'Otherwise we may wake up blind.'

I turned to Sergei Dva, holding up my glass, and said, 'Not *samogon*?'

He looked outraged. '*Samogon?*' he roared. '*Nyet! Almas!* It is Diamond' – and he grabbed a bottle to show me that it had a big white diamond, flashing reflected light, on its blue label.

Somebody produced an accordion, and it turned out that a man called Yuri had a phenomenal bass voice. To look at him you'd never have suspected it, because he was slim and wiry: the voice sounded altogether too big for such a spare frame, and seemed to come right from his boots. After a few pints of Baltika No. 6 – a powerful, dark brew – he launched into the 'Volga Boatmen's Song', and his mates joined in the choruses with terrific growls of '*Ayee och-nyem, ayee och-nyem*'. When Pavarotti hit back for the visitors with an impassioned rendering of 'Drink to me Only', he won loud cheers.

As merry shouts shook the windows, I sat there sunk in the blackest thoughts. With a couple of exceptions, these Tiger Force guys were ordinary, lively fellows like ourselves. Too many people in Britain still had a Cold War image of the Russians, and thought of them as sinister, alien beings. Now, after a week in the country at grass-roots level, I saw that normal people, like us, had remained human in spite of all the horrors heaped on them. They had their strengths and weaknesses, their good and bad points, the same as us. And an attack on Britain was the last idea that any of them would have entertained.

Nevertheless, the job had to be done – and even as Sergei Three handed me another slug of Diamond I was saying to myself, 'Right: the city centre recce's going down tomorrow night . . .'

SEVEN

When we next went to the Embassy, we left camp at the same time as on our first run, but this time we took just the black Volga. I hadn't told the Chargé we were coming into town: officially, we were going out for a couple of drinks and a bit of a bar-crawl.

Whinger drove, I read the map, and in the back sat Pavarotti, alongside Toad, with his lock-picking kit and two spare padlocks for the cover of the shaft. I'd deliberately nominated Pav as my No. 2 in the tunnel: I'd told him I might well need his height and strength, and that he'd just have to overcome his phobia. We were all wearing civvies, but Pav and I carried thin, dark overalls to wear on top of our other clothes while we were underground.

The weather had turned wet, and rain glistened on the tarmac. We soon realised to our cost that the car's wiper blades were knackered, and created more smears than they removed; but once again the traffic was light and we made rapid progress. On the long, straight run in we turned off the highway a couple of times, waited in a side-road, then came back out, to make certain we didn't have a tail.

No threat presented itself, and this time my navigation was spot-on: we reached the embankment without a false turn. There was a chance that the dicker we'd seen before, or some replacement, might still be on station, so we put in one drive-past, cruising westwards along the gentle, left-hand curve of Sophieskaya Quay, past the pink-and-white gateway, then past the Embassy, both on our left. To our right, across the river, the great buildings of the Kremlin were splendidly floodlit, and faint reflections gleamed in the wet tarmac of the embankment. A couple of cars came from the opposite direction, and a man and a woman were walking away from us, but there was nobody loitering.

At the end, before the bridge approach, Whinger pulled into the kerb and stopped in a dark area between street lamps.

'Right, lads,' I said. 'Just to confirm. The time now is 2105. Drop-off will be in five minutes, at 2110, near enough. A couple of minutes to reach the stable. We'll assume Toad can manage the locks in five minutes. If he has any trouble, Pav, you have a try. That means we should be in the tunnel by 2120 at the latest. Half an hour to suss it out. Back at the ladder by 2150. Pick-up at 2155 from this street, south side, east of the gateway. OK?'

Everyone nodded.

'I don't think the radios will work underground,' I added, 'but everyone stay on listening watch. Pav and I are One, Whinger Two, Toad Three. Our ERV is over there, under the bridge. Right, then – let's go.'

150

Whinger swung round and drove back at a moderate pace. Now the gateway was on our side of the road. One car overtook at speed, and we watched its tail-lights draw rapidly away into the distance.

Whinger was slowing.

'Nothing behind,' I said. 'Now!'

In seconds the three of us were out and under the gateway. I heard, rather than saw Whinger pull away behind us.

I led us forward into the dark courtyard, keeping to the right-hand wall. Above our heads, lights were showing in a couple of windows; straight ahead the little church sat hunched in shadows, jutting from the left wall of the yard, and the inner road swung past its entrance at the right-hand end into a second yard at the back.

From an intensive study of the plans I had every inch of the layout in my head. Five metres past the door of the church we'd come to the end of the building on our right. Beyond it, set back farther to our right, was a run of smaller structures – old stables. The second little building from our end would be open-fronted, or at least without a door. The head of the shaft was in the back of that shed, behind a wooden partition.

Moving quickly, we came level with the door of the church, which stood slightly open with slivers of light shining through top and bottom. Women were talking inside, their voices rising and falling. We reached the corner of the tall building. There, just visible in the gloom, stood the low range, a few metres farther on. A dozen quick steps brought us to an open doorway.

The wooden lintel was sagging, and I ducked to go under it. Inside, the darkness was so intense that I had to use my pencil torch. The beam picked out an old wooden partition of horizontal planks, extending halfway out across the stable. Beyond it the earth floor was covered with rough, half-rotten hay. Raking some aside with my fingers, I felt iron: the shaft cover. Quickly I cleared debris away from two padlocks – the two we'd been shown in the photo, which were not rusty but coated in dust. Clearly it was some time since they'd been touched.

'Stay in the doorway,' I breathed at Pavarotti, and he faced outwards, on guard, as Toad went to work, opening the barrels of the locks with his levers. I held my torch-beam steady on his hands, wincing at every little click and scrape.

The first lock gave itself up easily after no more than a couple of minutes, but the second was more stubborn. As Toad fiddled and shook, Pav let out a sudden hiss over his shoulder. Instantly I doused my torch. Peering past our sentry, through the doorway, I saw two women come out of the church and walk towards the big building.

We let them get clear, then started again. At last there was a louder click, and the hasp of the second lock fell back. As I carefully lifted the cover its two hinges groaned. My torch, pointing straight down, lit up a square shaft with brick walls, and I could see at a glance that it was big enough to take the component parts of

Apple. To make certain, I'd brought with me a piece of string thirty inches long – the maximum dimension we needed – and when I stretched it out from one edge it ended nearly a foot short of the other. That was one problem solved.

The disappointment was the ladder – or rather the lack of one. Instead of a succession of built-in steel rungs there were only two, a foot apart, close to the top of the shaft. From the holes and pits in the brickwork lower down, it looked as though the rest had been ripped out.

'We need the ladder,' I whispered.

I unrolled the springy bundle from my bergen and made one end fast round both hinges. Then I pulled on my overalls, and I heard Pavarotti rustling as he too kitted up.

'All set?' I asked.

'Fine.'

'Right, then, Toad. We'll see you in half an hour.'

I lowered my legs into the shaft and eased my weight down the wire rungs, feeling for them with one foot after the other. Fourteen changes of grip, and my feet touched bottom. As soon as I stepped off the ladder it went slack. I knew they'd feel the change up top, and that Pav would start down.

I heard him scraping on the brickwork as he descended, then felt him touch down beside me. The moment he let go of the ladder, the end went snaking up as Toad reeled it in. His brief was to seal us down with two spare locks he'd been carrying, then to hide up somewhere close by until the time came to release us. That way, if by any thousand-to-one chance somebody did come along to check the padlocks, he'd see nothing amiss. Toad would be in radio contact with Whinger throughout, and could call him in to lay on a diversion if anything started to go wrong.

When I heard the cover come down with a faint thud, I felt a shudder of claustrophobia run through me. If anything serious befell Toad and Whinger, we'd be sealed down here for the duration. Pav was obviously having the same panic, or worse: I could hear him breathing deeply and effing and blinding under his breath.

The air was rowsty and moist, full of a smell of damp decay. Our head-torches revealed a tunnel with a horse-shoe section, lined with bricks. The roof was just high enough for me to stand upright, but Pav, who was a couple of inches taller, had to crouch slightly to keep his head clear.

Somehow – perhaps because of the colour of the Kremlin walls – I'd expected the bricks to be red. In fact they were dirty cream, or had been: much of the surface was black with fungus or slime, and when I touched the wall beside my shoulder my fingertips slid along the wet surface leaving pale streaks. In many places individual bricks had crumbled or fallen out, so that there were frequent piles of rubble on the floor. That gave me encouragement; if the tunnel had been in immaculate condition, any tampering we did would have been that much more obvious.

I bent down and examined the floor. It was evenly

covered with damp dust – paste, almost – the same dull
colour as the walls. There was no sign of any disturbance – not even any traces of rats, which I'd expected
to find. I saw that we wouldn't be able to help leaving
footprints.

We'd measured the distances, and I had them in my
head: 160 metres to the river bank, 110 metres across
the river, seventy-five to the Kremlin wall: 345 metres
in all to our preferred site. When I went forward I was
going to count.

'Ready?' I whispered.

Pav didn't answer.

'Eh!' I went. 'Let's go.'

'*You* go!' he gasped in a peculiar voice. 'I'm staying
here.'

I could tell he was having problems just from the way
he sounded. When I put out a hand and touched his
arm, I felt him shaking violently. I turned the beam of
my head-torch on his face and saw beads of sweat
trickling down his cheeks.

'Get hold of yourself!' I snapped. 'We haven't got
time to piss about.' In my mind I added, A great big
feller like you, too! But I knew his hang-up was getting
to him.

A few seconds later he said unsteadily, 'I'm all right
now.'

'Come on, then.'

I moved forward, counting. For 102 paces the floor
of the tunnel remained level. Then it began to descend.

'Going down under the river,' I said.

'Aye,' Pavarotti agreed. 'I reckon.'

At the start of the slope was a big heap of debris. Such a chunk had fallen out of the upper right-hand wall and roof that the pile of bricks stretched across the tunnel floor to the base of the opposite wall, and we had to scramble over the lowest part of it. When I directed my head-lamp at the raw wall where the bricks had been, I saw that it consisted of moist grey clay.

'At least we can dig into that,' I muttered.

'Pity we can't put the bloody thing in right here. Save messing about.'

'It's too far from the proper site.'

We were still talking in whispers, partly out of habit, partly because we reckoned any sudden noise in a place that had been silent for generations might precipitate a further collapse of roof or wall.

We crept on again, but after a few more steps I stopped. My torch was picking out some difference in the texture of the floor ahead. Instead of light grey, it looked black. I stared for a minute, then said, 'Shit! It's water. The fucker's flooded.'

'Never,' said Pavarotti. 'If part of the tunnel was flooded, the whole thing would be full of water.'

I saw the logic of what he said – but he was wrong. At the point where the water started the floor was still dropping away, so that as we continued forward the flood gradually deepened. The water was cold and black and stank of decay, and we had no option but to wade into it until we were knee, then thigh, then bollock deep. Only when the surface was above our waists could we see that, a few more yards ahead, it came right to the roof.

'Jesus Christ!' said Pavarotti. 'We're knackered. We can't get through this lot.'

We pulled back and started wringing the filthy, black water out of our trousers.

'Pretty obvious, isn't it?' said Pav. 'Of course it's going to be flooded, under the bloody river.'

For a minute I sat on the deck, holding my head in my hands, trying to think constructively.

'There's no way we're going to get closer to the Kremlin anywhere else.'

'Why not forget this bastard?' Pav suggested. 'Get the other one in first and then see?'

'No, no,' I told him. 'This is the one they want. I'm sure of that. We've got to crack it. What we need to get through this lot is breathing gear and dry-suits.'

'Yeah. But how do we know what happens the other side of the water? If there *is* another side. If the rest of the tunnel's flooded we're buggered. Jesus, I hate this!'

'It must be quite a small leak,' I said. 'Otherwise, like you said, the whole tunnel would be full. Maybe the pressure's equalised itself somehow – or mud's filtered into the fissure.'

'Let's get the hell out, anyway.'

I'd been planning to sweep away our footprints behind us, but I realised now that, even if we went to that trouble, we'd still leave fresh marks and it would be obvious that somebody had been down here. In any case, the chances of anyone else coming down in the next few days seemed infinitesimal.

We were back under the access shaft just twelve minutes after leaving it. Eighteen minutes to wait. I tried the radio again but got no response. I wasn't going to shout, just in case some Russian was passing the old stable up top. I imagined Toad, on the lurk up there, and Whinger, on standby in the Volga somewhere along the embankment. Maybe they were chatting to each other on the radio.

'Have to wait,' I whispered. 'Let's take a stroll in the other direction.'

That didn't get us far. This time I wasn't counting the steps, but about a hundred metres to the south the tunnel was blocked by a major fall. The damage to the roof and walls was so extensive that I felt sure they'd been bulldozed in or deliberately dropped by hand. Bricks, rubble and clay were tumbled in an impenetrable mass.

Back under the shaft, we waited. We peeled off our sodden overalls, but still we were soaked to the waist and higher. Soon we were pretty cold. I went over the various levels of our fall-back plan in my mind. The first was that if Toad got accosted in the yard, he'd pretend he was drunk and had staggered in there to sleep it off. The next level was that if we three didn't reappear, Whinger would park the car out of the way and come looking for us. The final stage laid down that if all four of us weren't back in camp by 6.00 a.m., the rest of the team would come out to search. I knew that in an emergency we could seek sanctuary in the grounds of the Embassy, but that could only be a last resort because it would blow the whole Apple programme.

Spot on 2150 we heard faint metallic noises above our head – a clinking and scraping. Then came a slight change of pressure as Toad lifted the cover. A few seconds later the ladder-end flicked down beside us. I sent Pav up first, and heard him grunting with effort as he climbed. When the ladder twitched twice, I started up myself.

In the blackness of the shed I whispered, 'OK?' and Toad said, 'Fine' as he undid the ladder, closed the hatch and slipped the original padlocks back through the securing rings.

We pulled some of the rotten hay back over the cover and stood listening in the doorway.

'There's still something on in the church,' said Toad quietly. 'People keep coming back and forth. They're crossing to that doorway with the light showing.'

We were so wet and filthy we looked like a couple of drunks who'd fallen in the river, so even if we did meet someone there was a chance they'd pay no attention.

'Let's go,' I said.

We hustled along the edge of the yard, past the church door, back to the entrance gate. We'd hardly crossed the road on to the pavement beside the river when we saw a car coming in our direction.

In my earpiece Whinger's voice went, 'I have you visual,' and I knew it was him. Ten seconds later he pulled up beside us, and we were safely on board.

'All quiet up top?' I asked.

'Beautiful. But, Christ, what have you been doing?' He turned and glared at me.

'Eating caviar and drinking vodka,' I told him. 'What's the matter?'

'You stink like the arsehole of the universe.'

'Thanks, mate. That's what it's like down there. Stinking. The bastard tunnel's lined with shit and what's more, it's full of water.'

'Could you get through it?'

'Not this time. We waded as far as we could, but we need breathing kit and dry-suits. Head for base, Whinge. We're soaked to the bloody skin.'

Back at Balashika I called straight through to the duty officer in Hereford on the secure Satcom link. We'd set up our equipment in the office-cum-ops room, with the dish aerial on the roof of the building. Daily sweeps for bugs showed that the microphone in the kitchen was still live, so nobody talked any kind of shop in there; but there'd been no reaction to Steve's disabling of the bug in the office, and we reckoned that room was secure.

We were back at 10.40 Moscow time; England was three hours behind, and I knew the duty officer would be around in the ops room in Stirling Lines. Technically, the connection was perfect; if it hadn't been for the half-second lag in transmission as the message went up to the satellite and down again, I might have been in the next room rather than 2,000 miles away.

I recognised the voice at the other end as that of Bill Bravington: I'd spoken to him a couple of times already since our deployment, and had no need to fill him in on background.

'Bill,' I said, 'we've hit a problem. The Apple site. The approach is blocked by water.'

'Wait one.'

I imagined him reaching for a notepad.

'All right,' he went. 'Carry on.'

'We can't tell if the site itself is flooded. If it is, we'll need an alternative. But even to recce it we need breathing kits, dry-suits and half-hour tanks. Plus some of those Boat Troop rubber bags for the components. And two big underwater torches. Can you organise all that soonest?'

'No problem. How many suits?'

'Two. Correction: three suits and three tanks. Plus rubber bags.'

'Number?'

'For three pieces. You know – two big, one small. But we'd better have spare small bags as well. Say half a dozen small.'

'Got it. Fins?'

'Sorry?'

'Will you want fins?'

'No, thanks. The distance isn't great enough.'

'OK.'

'And Bill – listen. We need this stuff right away.'

'We'll get it all to London tonight, for the next Diplomatic Bag.'

People must have pulled their fingers out all along the line, because the kit reached the Embassy on Monday afternoon, less than forty-eight hours after we'd found the water. On Tuesday night Pavarotti and I were back in the tunnel, with the same back-up team on watch above. On a weekday evening there was more traffic along the quay and more pedestrians about, but we made it into the stable undetected, and down below everything was precisely as we'd left it: the marks I'd scraped in the dirt on the floor were still fresh, the surface of the water still one inch below a horizontal line I'd scratched in the slime on the wall.

The discovery of water and the sight of the various falls had led me to change our plan. I reckoned that if we managed to reach our destination on this second recce, we might as well start opening up the site for the CND. My reasons were: first, that the chances of any inspection team coming through the water within the next few days were zero, and second, that even if somebody did come snooping, a hole in the wall wouldn't in itself excite suspicion as there were plenty of other natural cavities already.

So it was that this time we had jemmies and small picks in a bergen. Having zipped each other into dry-suits over our clothes, we fitted our tanks and breathing kits and waded into the inky water. On our outward trip the water was fairly clear, and our torch beams reached a few feet ahead – enough for us to spot two submerged heaps of rubble before we blundered into them.

We'd been through all the measurements again, and I'd calculated that the fully flooded section of the tunnel couldn't be more than fifty or sixty metres long. So I wasn't surprised when, after two minutes half-walking, half-swimming, my head broke the surface again. As we continued to advance, an upward slope lifted us steadily clear of the water. Soon we were back on dry land.

The orginal distances given us by the Firm turned out to be spot-on. A total of 340 metres from the old stable, we came to a circular hole in the roof – the ventilation shaft. When I stood upright with my head in the bottom of it, my helmet lamp revealed that it did not rise vertically, but turned at an angle to my right. I could feel cool air flowing down, so I knew it was open at the top.

'Shit hot,' I told Pav. I brought out my tape and held it across. 'Twenty-eight inches. That's easily big enough to accept the SCR – and anyone making visual checks down the manhole won't be able to see round this corner. Made to measure.'

Five metres beyond it, the tunnel had been sealed with a wall of concrete blocks. Yet providentially, just on our side of the barrier was another big fall.

'Look at that,' I said to Pav. 'Made to measure again.'

'Yeah – and we won't even need to move any spoil. We can just add whatever we bring out to the heap that's here already.'

We'd prearranged with Toad that we would stay down for ninety minutes. That gave us an hour of work-time, so we stripped off our dry-suits and took turns to put in concentrated attacks on the clay subsoil. Soon we were both in a muck sweat and having problems with our breathing, perhaps because the air was so damp. None the less, before our hour ran out we had enlarged the cavity to about half the size we needed. We kept the overhanging roof and edges rough, and left a pile of rubble on the base of the hole so that, when we returned to install Apple, all we'd have to do would be to enlarge the hole, clear the bed and lift the components about two feet from the floor before pushing them sideways into their final resting place.

Our return to the surface posed no problems, and once again the pick-up went without a hitch.

'So it's a foot on the brake, is it?' Whinger asked as we drew away.

'What's that?'

'Piece of cake.'

'I wouldn't call it that. But it's possible – wouldn't you say, Pav?'

'Oh, yeah,' he agreed. 'It's definitely on.'

So we drove back, feeling quite chuffed.

But as we arrived in camp, the shit hit the fan. We hadn't even drawn up at the back of the accommodation block when Mal came running down the steps to meet us.

'Geordie,' he said, 'I need to have a word.'

'Walk this way, then.'

We went a few yards down the track into the woods, and as soon as we were out of earshot Mal said, 'Somebody's been tampering with number two laptop.'

'How d'you know?'

'They've killed the disk with the plans on it.'

'Killed it?'

'The contents have been wiped. Somebody must have tried to get into it without using the password.'

I stopped walking and turned to stare at Mal, who was barely visible in the dark. 'Is it possible the person could have read the contents and then deliberately destroyed them?'

'Not a chance.' He sounded fairly confident. 'They tried a wrong password, and that did it.'

Jesus, I was thinking. Are we compromised, or what?

'If they'd got into the disk they wouldn't have wiped it,' Mal added. 'They'd have left it intact to cover their traces.'

'True. But who the hell was messing about in the office?'

My first instinct was to blame Toad, whose duty it was to maintain security. But of course he'd been with us in the city. In his absence, the two scalies, Steve and Terry, should have been in occupation.

'When did this happen?'

'It must have been some time this evening, while everyone was out working.'

'So who was in the block?'

'Only the scalies.'

'What do they say about it?'

'I haven't asked them yet. I only just discovered it. I tried to boot up the laptop and found the floppy was still in the slot.'

165

'Grip them, then.'

I was enraged. Trust those arseholes of signallers to foul up our entire enterprise.

I rushed into the building and dragged Terry off his pit. 'Dozy wanker!' I yelled. 'Get into the ops room, NOW!'

No. 2 laptop, a Toshiba, stood open on the ops room table with its screen raised and the floppy disk still in the port on the right-hand side.

'There's been a major breach of security,' I started. 'Who used that computer last?'

I glared round, but one by one the lads shook their heads. None of them had been on the laptop that day, they declared. They'd been out of doors, on the ranges, then on a night-movement exercise.

'Well then, how the fuck did that programme disk come to be in the port? It should be locked inside the filing cabinet. Everyone here knows that.'

Still there was silence.

Suddenly Rick said, 'Wait a minute. There was the Colonel.'

'The Colonel?'

'Anna!'

'Jesus!' I said. 'You mean she came in *here*? What did she want?'

'She said something about her phone having gone down. She asked if she could use ours.'

'And you let her in here?'

'Well, yeah – she being a colonel and everything. I didn't think I could tell her to fuck off.'

'So what happened?'

'She dialled a number and started talking in Russian.'

'What was she saying?'

'I couldn't understand a lot of it. Something about transport – cars.'

'And you stayed in the room with her?'

Rick shook his head. 'No – I let her carry on. I was working in the kitchen and I went back in there.'

'Ah, Jesus! How long for?'

'Five minutes?'

'Cunt!' I was almost on the point of whacking him, so angry did I feel.

Obviously he realised it, because he blurted out, 'I mean, with her being our OC, more or less, I thought everything was above board.'

'Rick,' I said, 'that's the second time you've dropped a bollock. And this one's serious. This is your last chance. Any more cock-ups and you're going home.'

I took a deep breath. It was too late. The damage had been done. But how the hell had Anna got her hands on the disk so fast? She must have had a duplicate set of keys for the filing cabinet. But how far had she managed to get? Had she been dictating stuff straight off the computer screen to some FSB colleague? Or was the conversation Rick had heard just cover for her attempt to get into the program?

'What happened at the end, when she left?' I demanded.

'I came back in here. I was going to offer her a cup of tea.'

'Bloody hell! What was she doing?'

'She was sat there at the table.'

'With the lap-top in front of her?'

Rick frowned. 'I never noticed. She was still talking on the phone.'

'And then?'

'She rang off, put the phone back on the hook. Then she said thanks and went out.'

Now what? It was the same dilemma as when we'd found the bug. Should we reveal our suspicions, or should we keep quiet? Even if I didn't accuse Anna of trying to break into our computer programs, should I drop some casual remark about her having used our phone, just to show that her visit hadn't gone unreported? Should I confide in Sasha and see what he thought?

'Wait,' was Whinger's advice. 'Let it develop. Say nothing. See what happens. If she has managed to bust into the program, the next thing we can expect is a massive search. If they suspect we've got a couple of suitcase bombs about the place, they're going to go mad trying to find them. On some pretext or other, they'll turn everything upside-down tomorrow.'

'What about Hereford?' asked Pavarotti. 'Are we going to report this to base?'

'Wait out on that one too,' I said. 'They'd shit themselves if they heard about it, and they've no means of assessing the position from that end. No point in stirring things up unnecessarily.'

Mal – our best computer buff but always a worrier –

said, 'Yeah, and I for one wouldn't blame them.'

'Who?'

'The Russkies. If they made a search. It pisses me off that we're doing what we are, anyway.'

'Me too,' I agreed.

Most of the guys, Mal in particular, were confident that it was technically impossible for Anna to have accessed the program. They reckoned that her visit was nothing more sinister than a repercussion from her past – a return to her old KGB habits of snooping – and that she couldn't have discovered anything damaging. So, after a bit of a Chinese parliament, we decided to keep quiet.

Until that moment I'd had no cause to suspect the woman of duplicity. Quite the opposite: she'd seemed fully on side, and had been a terrific asset. She'd thrown herself into the training with real zip, and had never shown the slightest irritation when people kept calling on her for translations. Her physical presence had been enough to give everyone a lift: she was very fit and energetic, and went up ropes or over the assault course as fast as any man, often joining in for the fun of it when there was no real need. And the students liked her as much as we did. They were slightly in awe of her, and referred to her as *Polkovnik* – the Colonel – in a way that was partly sarcastic but had an edge of respect as well. Several times she'd reinforced my impression that she was right behind us visitors by telling indiscreet stories about her days in the old-style KGB. She'd joke about how clumsy and stupid and suspicious all her

Communist comrades had been — with the implication that nowadays everything was sweetness and light.

Her private life, though, had remained mysterious. Like Sasha, she had a room in the officers' mess at the other side of the camp, and she'd dropped hints about a flat somewhere in town. Beyond that I knew nothing about her. On a personal level I was still fancying her in a cool sort of way, and I was planning to ask her out to dinner one evening when the time seemed ripe, suggest a meal at a place of her choice and see what developed. So far, though, I'd been so busy and had so much on my mind that I hadn't got round to issuing an invitation.

For a long time that night I couldn't go to sleep. My mind kept returning to the tunnel, to the hollow we'd made in the brickwork, right under the wall of the Kremlin, and to the chaos that would follow if we'd been rumbled. Arrest? Gaol? Deportation? International incident? Should the whole team do a runner while the going was good?

No matter which way my thoughts turned, they were anything but soothing.

EIGHT

Through my sleep I heard a hammering on our door, and in burst Johnny, shouting, 'Geordie, get up! There's a panic on.'

For a moment I thought, Christ, the search has started already. They're turning us out of bed. But at least they can't search the Embassy – so sod them.

Across the room Whinger protested from under his pillow, and I groaned, 'For fuck's sake – what time is it?'

'Six-fifteen,' said Johnny. 'It's Sasha. He's desperate to see you.'

'Where is he?'

'Here. In the passage.'

'Bring him in. Sasha!' I shouted, rolling out of bed. 'What the hell are you doing?'

Sasha appeared in his DPMs, writhing with embarrassment at having crashed into our preserve and finding me naked.

'Zheordie, I am sorry . . .'

'Forget it. What's the problem?'

'We need your help.'

'Now?'

'Immediately.'

'Tell me, then.'

I began pulling on clothes as Sasha spilled his story: how a 'beeg Mafia feesh', self-styled Keet, the Killer Whale, who normally ruled the roost in Chechnya, had been sighted in Moscow. He and his two brothers, known as Akula (Shark) and Barrakuda, were the godfathers of the Chechen Mafia. Now Keet had been traced to an apartment which belonged to another known criminal in a new, sixteen-storey block in the suburb of Lianozovo, on the northern fringes of the city. His presence in the capital, reported by a tout, offered the authorities a rare chance of getting at him on their own ground.

Senior officers in Omon were anxious to take him out, but they were nervous of the firepower he commanded. Not only did he have a team of four bodyguards armed with sub-machine guns for close-protection; the apartment block in which he'd holed up was equipped with the latest security systems, including closed-circuit television, remote-controlled locks and so on. The whole block was under Mafia control, from the team running the security on the ground floor to the janitors who passed out information about people's comings and goings. In other words, any attempt to storm the building would inevitably end in a major gun battle, probably with a load of casualties, and certainly with more publicity than anyone wanted.

All this Sasha poured out in a rush.

'So I come here,' he ended. 'And why? Because Omon ask, can the British experts of the SAS help?'

'Help? How?'

'Make the plan of attack. Give advice.'

'Well . . . it's not what we're here for.'

'Zheordie, I know. But this is special problem.'

Poor Sasha looked so anxious that I almost laughed. I turned to look at Whinger, who had come round far enough to prop himself on one elbow.

'Hear that, Whinge? They're needing assistance. What d'you reckon?'

'We could look at it. No harm taking a shufti.'

Pavarotti, who was hanging into the room round the door, raised his eyebrows. 'For fuck's sake don't get involved,' he said. 'Christ knows what it could lead to.'

'What about the course?' I said. 'It's an EMOE day, isn't it? You can sort them on that, Pav. Wait a minute, though. Sasha – are you planning to use some of the students on this?'

'*Konechno*. You have teached them well.'

'They're only half-trained at the minute . . .'

'All the same, it is best. We want to make attack quickly.'

At the back of my mind I heard the voice of the CO in Hereford, warning me that on no account should we get involved with any live operation. And I heard myself solemnly promising that we'd steer well clear. Then I thought, Ah, bollocks! Easy to say that from a distance. Still, I'd told the boss we'd keep our hands clean . . .

But I heard myself saying, 'OK, we'll come.'

With a big smile Sasha went, '*Zdorovo!* Breelliant!'

'How many guys d'you need?'

'You say.'

'Two teams of four? That means Whinger, myself and six more. You choose them.'

'I do that now. You and Vuinzha, please prepare immediately. It is important you start planning.'

'What about Anna? Does she know about this?'

'She's in control room already.'

The time was 6.40 a.m.

Pavarotti had gone off to the washroom in disgust, and was shaving when I poked my head round the door. 'Sorry, mate,' I told him, 'we're going to have a crack at it. You'll have to take charge of the course today.'

'You're nuts, Geordie.'

'I dunno. All good for international relations.'

In the kitchen the lads already had a brew on, so Whinger and I got some tea and a piece of bread down us, picked up our personal weapons and a few bits and pieces, and were ready for the off.

Sasha had come in some different car, newer and more powerful than either of ours, with a driver in DPMs. We piled in and set off at speed through the dawn, first towards the city centre, then right-handed into the northern suburbs, crossing one main thoroughfare after another. In less than quarter of an hour we were pulling up at the gate of another barracks, where the sentry took one look at Sasha's card and whipped up the barrier pole. Next stop was a briefing room full of men in black Omon uniform, grouped round a large-scale plan spread out on a table.

At first I thought the guys from the course must have moved like shit off a shovel, because they were there ahead of us. Then I realised that Sasha had probably detailed them already, before speaking to us. I recognised Sergei Tri, Volodya, and one other. As we entered there was a bit of muttering in Russian, and a few smiles were beamed in our direction.

Introductions to the top brass were perfunctory, but I cottoned on to the fact that the guy in charge, a major, was called Ivan – a heavily built, swarthy fellow of about my age, with dense black hair cut short into a kind of point, like a little roof over his head, and mean, yellow eyes that put me in mind of a bear. He spoke some English, but didn't understand much of what I said.

Anna glided in, her normal, suave self, quite at home in a room full of men. Staring at her, I kept asking silently, What the hell were you doing with our computer, woman? But when she caught me looking at her she gave a terrific smile, and entered into the business of the day with infectious enthusiasm.

It seemed that Keet, the target, had been reported arriving at the block in the early hours of the morning, and had gone up in the lift to apartment number 128 on the twelfth floor. Omon's information was that a meeting between him and other godfathers was due to take place in the flat at nine that evening. It seemed there'd been an argument over whether the security forces should go straight in, to make sure of arresting one man, or wait and hope to catch several.

To Whinger and myself, the plan for seizing Keet

seemed amateurish in the extreme. The proposal was for an assault group to drive up to the ground floor, shoot their way in through the main entrance, secure the lifts and staircases, and then blast their way into the flat.

'It's a fucking shambles,' I muttered to Whinger. 'The guards on the door downstairs will raise the alarm with mobile phones or bleepers, and the villains will disappear from the flat like rats down holes before anyone gets near them. The assaulters'll end up killing half the people in the block; there'll be civilian casualties too, and a tidal wave of bad publicity.'

When Ivan the Bear asked my opinion of the plan, I said tactfully, 'I'm sure your basic idea's right, but maybe we can refine it a bit. Let's think this thing through.'

Ivan told us that his men had the block under surveillance, and that armed guys were posted in cars along the boulevard leading to it. If Keet did try to make a getaway they could always have a go at gunning him down. But his bullet-proof Mercedes might save him, and they didn't want to run any risk of losing him.

'Even so, you surely want to wait for tonight's meeting,' I suggested. 'Even if he goes out somewhere during the day, he'll come back. To catch four or five of them together would be fantastic.'

He agreed, and asked, 'So – what do you suggest?'

'Surprise is what you need,' I told him. 'The element of surprise. It would be much better to come down on the apartment from above.'

'From the roof?'

'Yes.'

He nodded and said something in Russian, which Sasha translated as, 'We land from helicopter.'

'Too noisy.' I shook my head. 'Too obvious. Everyone in the building would hear us coming. Immediately Keet and his party would know something was happening. They might go and hole up in other flats. You'd lose the advantage of surprise.'

At Ivan's shoulder was a tall, cadaverous fellow with a thin, long, rather grey face, a big mouth and unusually red lips. If Ivan was a bear, this guy was a wolf. I wasn't sure of his status, but he seemed to be the second-in-command. Although I couldn't understand many of his words I got the gist of them clearly enough: 'For Christ's sake let's go in and shoot the bastards,' he was saying. 'Let's not ponce about with these pissy British ideas . . .'

Ivan, however, ignored him and asked me to carry on. When we looked at a large-scale plan of the site we saw that it comprised not a single tower block, but two structures set at right-angles to each other in the shape of an L, only a few feet apart at the inner corner. I'd noticed several pairs of buildings with this plan as we had driven around town on other days.

Now Whinger and I had the same idea at the same moment.

'Cross from the other roof,' he said.

'Exactly.' I knew that in Hong Kong he'd practised this very technique with the fire brigade, laddering across from one high-rise block to another and coming down on the target from above. Here, with the flat on the twelfth floor, five down from the roof, it would be child's play to abseil and come in through the windows, while another party stormed the door from the internal corridor.

I looked at Ivan and asked, 'This other building. Is that Mafia as well, or is it clean?'

'No Mafia,' Sasha answered. 'No guards on door.'

I pointed at the plan. 'How wide is this gap between the buildings?'

Ivan gave an off-hand shrug and said, 'I don't know.'

'It's important.'

'Maybe ten metres.'

'No more?'

'*Nyet.*'

'That's OK, isn't it?' I asked Whinger. 'Forty feet?'

'Piece of cake.'

I felt my adrenalin levels rising rapidly, and, almost before I knew what I was doing, I was outlining a complete new action plan.

'Call them Block A and Block B,' I began. 'Block A to the west, B just east of it. Keet's on the twelfth floor of Block A, facing west, right? We maintain surveillance on that block, as you're doing already, but to avoid arousing suspicion we keep well away from the entrance. Instead of a direct approach, two assault teams go up to the roof of Block B and ladder across to the roof of Block A. There we split. One party makes its way down the emergency stairs and comes out on the twelfth-floor corridor. The other abseils down the outside of the building. When both parties are in position, we blow the internal door and the windows simultaneously, come in from both sides with stun grenades, and overpower everybody inside.'

As Anna translated, I saw Ivan following my scenario with ever-growing incredulity.

'All this is possible?' he asked.

'Of course,' I replied confidently – but even as I did so I suddenly realised what I'd done. Carried away by my own excitement I'd been saying 'we' when I should have been saying 'you'.

Ivan was under fire from Wolf-face, but he shut him up again with an irritated wave, and showed that he hadn't missed the implication of my words with his next question: 'So, you will lead the assault?'

'No, no. We can't. We're not authorised for anything like that. We're here purely on a training mission.'

Ivan's dismay was painful to witness. '*Starshina*,' he pleaded, 'Sergeant Major – we very much need your help. We do not have your experience in assaults of this kind.'

I looked at Whinger and saw that he was thinking the same as I was. If we did our hosts a good turn, it would ease our consciences. Besides, it would be a great gas to take part in an anti-Mafia hit. The idea was outrageous, of course – the Regiment would never sanction it. But would the Regiment ever *know* about it? Not until afterwards, if at all – provided we didn't say anything.

I looked at Whinger and said quietly, 'What d'you reckon?'

'All right by me.'

I turned back to Ivan and said, '*Yestj*. We'll help as much as we can. At least we can show you what to do.'

This led to knuckle-crunching handshakes and big grins all round.

But my decision shifted the initiative to myself and Whinger – and thereafter we had to make the running.

I'm bound to say that the Omon leaders pulled their fingers out: whatever we asked for they got, and fast.

The first things we needed were architectural plans of both apartment blocks. It looked as though the pair would be essentially the same, but we wanted to be sure. In particular, we needed to know the internal layout of the flat we were going to hit – the disposition of its rooms, and details like which way the doors opened. As the buildings were only three years old it should have been easy to find drawings, but when somebody phoned the construction firm who'd put the flats up the people there began making difficulties, claiming that their computers were down, and that without them they couldn't produce plans. I heard a good bollocking go down the line, and that seemed to produce results. 'Half an hour,' was the eventual answer.

'In that case,' I said, 'let's do a drive-past. We need to get a look at the blocks. Somebody bring a video camera.'

'Better not go dressed like this.' Whinger pointed at his DPMs.

'Good point, Whinge.'

A quartermaster figure produced sets of thin grey overalls which smelt of mothballs, and soon we were rolling northwards in two cars: myself, Ivan (who had a camera), Anna and the driver in one, Whinger, Sasha and the Wolf-man in the second.

'Tell him we don't want to get too close,' I warned Anna.

'What d'you call too close?'

'Nothing under a couple of hundred metres, anyway.'

By now it was fully light, and rush-hour traffic was pouring down the main arteries into the city centre. Heading outwards, we could move freely, and it was only five minutes or so before Ivan said something, pointing ahead and to the right.

'Those are the buildings,' Anna translated. 'The target's in the left-hand one, as we're looking.'

Two slender blocks rose out of a wasteland. They were made of pale-grey concrete, relieved by small square panels of sky blue ranged along the balcony-fronts on each of the sixteen floors. At ground level the entrances were imposing: on the end of each building was a grandiose porch with square pillars, under which cars could drive, and marble facings round the doors. Either side of the doorway into what we'd named Block A stood a guard in grey fatigues armed with a sub-machine gun.

Round the base of the buildings some attempt had been made to establish a garden or park: there were patches of grass and a few saplings had been planted, but further out much of the area was still bare earth, no doubt awaiting development. On the approach road leading to Block A numerous cars were parked end-on at forty-five degrees to the kerb, including a high proportion of Mercedes, BMWs and Audis.

The road to Block B came in from the far side and had far less transport sitting on it.

I glanced at Ivan and saw that he was already filming.

'Ask him to get close-up footage of the roof-line,' I said – and in response to Anna's request he tilted the camera upwards.

'Just to confirm,' I said. 'The target's in this near block.'

'Correct.'

'And the apartment's facing this way?'

'Correct again.'

'In fact we can see the windows now.'

'Yes. The fifth floor down from the top.'

I was looking for sniper vantage points, and immediately saw one: a third high-rise block of the same model, but with green panels rather than blue, maybe 200 metres away on our left.

'Can we drive back down the far side of Block B – over there, behind it?'

'Not very well.' Anna pointed. 'You see that long wall? Behind that's a railway line and marshalling yards. There's no road in that area.'

'What about those roofs just over the wall?'

'Those are railway offices.'

'OK.'

A kilometre or so beyond the site we made a U-turn and came back for a second pass. Again I concentrated, fixing details in my mind. The run confirmed my earlier impression that a direct daylight approach from ground level would have been disastrous: there was no cover close to Block A's entrance, and a gun-battle would have led to many casualties.

Back in the Omon briefing room we found architectural drawings of Blocks A and B awaiting us. As Whinger and I went into a huddle over them, mugs of sweet black tea beside us, we had no difficulty coming up with a plan.

When we were ready, I signalled to Ivan, and we began an informal presentation.

'I don't know if they want to make notes,' I said to Anna, 'but maybe you'd suggest it.'

Wolf-face let fly a few more disparaging remarks, but the others ignored him, and Ivan produced a notebook and pencil.

'Right,' I said. 'First thing, the assault should go down at night, after last light. If the Mafia meeting's due to start at 2100, I suggest 2130.'

I had to take it slowly, phrase by phrase, letting Anna translate in between. For a few exchanges the delays irritated me: then I realised that they were useful, as they gave everyone time to take in what I was saying.

'Next, there will be three assault parties, designated Red, Blue and Black. Red and Blue will enter Block B and cross on to the roof of Block A by ladder, as outlined. Red will deploy on the roof of Block A and prepare to abseil down the outside of the building. Blue will enter the building via the fire exit on the roof – here – then descend the fire stairs and position themselves to assault the apartment from the corridor.

'Black will deploy on the ground by vehicle. Their job will be to drive up to the front of Block A and secure the building by capturing or shooting the two guards we saw. Timing will be critical. They'll need to reach the door at the moment the assaults on the flat go in – not before.

'If possible, we'll position sniper/commentators in Block C – the green block. From there they'll be able to observe the windows of the target flat and report movements. When everyone's deployed, we'll use EMOE to blow the door and at least one window from both sides of the flat and simultaneously. The actions and timings of all three teams will be co-ordinated by radio.

'I'll be the leader of Red team. Whinger here will lead Blue team. Red and Blue will each consist of the leader and three men. Black team will be commanded by an officer nominated by Ivan. For comms purposes, the snipers will be designated Green.'

Ivan asked Anna a couple of questions in Russian, and she gave him answers herself. Then she said, 'He is afraid control will be difficult because of the language.'

'I've thought of that. If we can have you at the command centre, there'll be no problem. You'll be able to translate and pass things on. The only English commands your colleagues need to understand will be the two I'll use at the end: "Stand by, stand by" and "Go! Go! Go!"'

Anna immediately translated these. ' "Stand by" is *Orushiye k boyu*,' she said. 'That means literally "weapons ready". Go is *poshli*. Easy!'

Ivan smiled briefly as he nodded his agreement.

I went on to emphasise that Whinger and I were not in the business of killing Russian citizens, whether Mafiosi or otherwise. All we would do was get the assault teams into position and blow the door and windows: it would be up to the Russians to clear the flat. Again, there was a murmur of agreement. I could see that Wolf-face was still ticking with irritation.

'Ask Ivan, please: what are his intentions? Is he aiming to capture Keet or kill him?'

As Anna translated, a faint smile spread over Ivan's face – but it did not extend to his eyes. The only answer he gave was, 'It depends.'

'In any case,' I went on, 'what we need immediately is a forward mounting base. Those railway sheds behind the wall – any chance of your taking one over?'

Ivan sent a colleague to make a telephone call. I began going into the nitty-gritty: ladders, ropes, explosive charges, weapons, comms. I said that Whinger and I would carry pistols only, for self-defence in an extremity, but added that the Russian members of Red and Blue teams should take Gepards with short magazines as well as their pistols. The guys in the Black team should have silenced weapons, to whack the ground-floor guards with minimum disturbance.

Within a couple of minutes an answering call came back: inside the railway complex, it said, were the offices of a company operating steam trips in a joint venture with a Swiss tourist firm. The place had modern communications, and also a large, empty engine shed in which we could assemble our kit and lay on some quick training.

Once Ivan had nominated the men for each of the teams, we had only a few hours in which to sort them out. My three – Nikolai Two, Igor and Misha – were all built like brick shithouses, and well versed in abseiling.

The railway office and shed turned out a big bonus. By midday Ivan had sent the normal staff home, taken the place over and set up a command post and control centre in the main office, with a dish aerial on the roof. The engine shed was high enough for us to put in some abseil practice: with ropes anchored to the steel girders under the roof, we had about fifteen feet clear below us. Ivan's video showed quite a few possible anchor-points on the roof of Block B – the tops of lift-shafts, ventilation pipes and so on – and I foresaw no trouble there.

From our study of the architects' plans we knew that the flat had two bedrooms and a living room ranged along the southern balcony face, down which we'd be coming. On the other side, along the internal corridor, were the kitchen, hallway, separate lavatory, a bathroom and a big storage cupboard. To us on the outside

– and to the snipers positioned in Block C – the apartment's windows were the first four from the right-hand end on the twelfth floor. I named them *Okno Odin, Okno Dva* (Window One, Window Two) and so on, numbering from the right. One was the first bedroom, two the second, three was the top half of a door which opened inwards from the balcony into the sitting room, and four another window in the same room.

Ivan agreed that we should time the hit for 2130, in the hope of catching the big players in the sitting room. Therefore we decided to blow the window-door and go in that way.

Whinger, meanwhile, was sorting a route for his team to enter via the fire-escape door on the roof, and come down the emergency stairs to position themselves outside the flat entrance.

I tried to impress on Ivan how easy it would be to create a blue-on-blue – to have the Red and Blue teams firing at each other. But in fact the layout of the flat gave us two natural territories in which to operate. For Red, the balcony team, the obvious field of fire was the sitting room; for Blue, entering from the corridor, the hallway would be the main theatre. We made it a fundamental rule that Red team members would only engage targets remaining in the sitting room and not fire at anyone running through into the hall. Blue would be free to fire into the hall or either of the bedrooms.

Of the three guys allotted to me, I was happy enough with Nikolai and Igor. The one who worried me was Misha, one of the relics of SOBR. Sasha had put him in my team because he'd done abseiling, but our experience so far suggested that he had a low IQ, and wasn't all that co-operative either.

No good worrying about that now.

I took the team through our sequence of actions again and again. We'd abseil down to the balcony, aiming to establish ourselves on it thirty seconds before the raid was due to go in. We'd need to be extremely careful in our movements: not to clank our weapons against the metalwork of the balustrade, not to let a boot or elbow bump on a window. For the last few seconds we'd crouch against the wall of the flat, under the windows. As soon as I confirmed by radio that Whinger's team was in position, I'd call, 'Stand by, stand by . . . Go!', then crack off the door charge and follow it instantly with a stun grenade.

Seeing the blank looks on their faces, I started to flap a bit. I knew what standard they'd reached, and it wasn't as high as we needed. A fully fledged SAS assaulter is so highly trained that his reactions are instantaneous. These guys were nowhere near that level. Nevertheless, since Igor was the sharpest of our team, I detailed him to be first into the room. 'The second the grenade blows, you're through.' I told him via Anna. 'When you go in, stay on your feet and move to the left. None of this rolling-around we've been practising.

'You other two, give him covering fire through the blown-out window. Aim outwards into the corners of the room. Don't fire straight at the door into the hall, otherwise rounds may go through and hit your own guys coming from the other side.'

When Igor protested about being first in, I told him he didn't need to worry. The godfathers inside would be deafened and blinded by the stun-grenade.

Suitable ladders took a bit of finding. There were some in the Omon stores but they were too short and heavy for our purpose. It was Sasha who had the idea of borrowing better kit off the nearest branch of the fire service. They came up with an extending set of four three-metre sections, made from aluminium, well machined and snugly fitting. The overall length was eleven metres, and since the gap between the corners of the buildings showed on the architects' plans as nine metres, we would have a one-metre overlap at either end.

Once we'd held several practices at assembling the ladders and crossing gaps on them, we bound the ends with foam and masking tape to reduce the risk of making a noise, and handed them over to another team. These two guys, who appeared to be television technicians, drove to Block B and took the ladders up the fire stairs on to the roof, under the pretence of realigning the aerials.

By 4.00 everything was in hand. Omon had discovered an empty apartment on the thirteenth floor of Block C and installed a pair of snipers, armed with Dragunov 7.62mm rifles fitted with telescopic sights. Their brief was to watch for movements in the target flat with binoculars and report any change to the control room. When the assault went down, they were to engage anyone who tried to make a getaway by coming out of a window and escaping along a balcony.

At 4.30 Whinger and I got Sasha to drive us back to Balashika. Rather than handle Russian detonators and det cord of uncertain vintage, I wanted to pick up some of our own. At the base we found everything in order: the lads back from a good day in the open, and no further scares. We had time for a quick meal and a cup of tea.

As I sat down to eat I said to Whinger, 'I don't think very many Mafiosi are going to come out of this alive.'

By 5.15 we were back at the railway command centre for a final run-through of the plan. I made up my explosive charge for blowing the window – a ring of det cord taped on to a sheet of expanded polystyrene about fifteen inches square, to which I'd fitted a short broom-handle – and explained to my three how, once we reached the balcony, I'd apply the polystyrene gently – and silently – to the glass of the door, holding it out with the end of the handle, before I cracked off the charge.

I emphasised that, once we had launched the hit, we must go quickly through with it. If anyone saw us crossing between the buildings, for instance, it was possible that the alarm could be raised. Once we were established on the roof of Block B, we couldn't afford to hang about.

My big worry was the weather. All afternoon the wind had been getting up, and by 8.00 a gale was blowing and driving blasts of rain before it. In a way it was good, as the roar of the storm would cover any small noises we might make; but I also reckoned there'd be hellish turbulence around the edges of those tall buildings.

Everyone was nervous – myself and Whinger no less than the students. As before all operations, our watches seemed to stop or at least slow down to a ridiclous crawl, the hands hardly moving. The snipers came on the air with the occasional bit of news – 'Green One. Curtains being drawn in Window One . . . Light switched on in Window Two' – and by 8.05 all four windows had been curtained off. That suited us fine.

As we rehearsed the action sequences again and again, the only person who seemed unmoved was Anna.

It felt very strange to be dressing in Russian kit. Their flak-jackets were heavier and stiffer than ours, and made us pretty clumsy. My helmet fitted my head inside but still felt very big. Realising that it would be difficult to control my explosive charge on its panel while I was crossing on the ladder, I had Nikolai lash it flat to the small of my back, with the handle pointing up behind my head like a short antenna.

When I glanced across at Whinger I was amazed: he looked every inch a member of Omon, with his features hidden under a black rapist's mask, and only his eyes and mouth showing.

For the tenth time, it seemed, I checked all weapons and magazines.

At last it was time for the off. We went out on foot into the cold, swirling wind through a gate in the railway compound wall, over the wasteland. The odd street lamp was burning in the distance, but the area we crossed was good and dark. With us we had one guy in civilian clothes, to range ahead as a scout and radio back a warning if he met anyone on the stairs. The covert comms system was working well: in my earpiece I could hear the Black team lining itself up in the van they'd arranged for transport, and the occasional remark from a sniper. With the finger and thumb of my right hand I settled the throat mike more comfortably in position.

In the underground car-park of Block B we waited while our scout started climbing. 'Red and Blue at foot of stairs,' I reported, and immediately Anna's voice answered, '*Vas ponyal. Khorosho.*'

A few moments later the scout called to tell us that all was clear as far as floor five, so both teams went scuttling up. After another pause there, we took the next eleven flights straight, and arrived at the top panting.

Out in the open, the wind was formidable. There was no point in telling people to watch themselves. They wouldn't have heard me, anyway, and anybody with the slightest sense of self-preservation wasn't going to start pissing about in a place like that.

All Moscow, it seemed, was spread out at our feet. Immediately below us the patches of wasteland were dark, but to the south blazed an immense galaxy of lights, and the main thoroughfares were like brilliantly illuminated rivers down which flowed endless streams of headlamps.

The ladders were lying where the pseudo-TV crew had left them, and we had no trouble locking the sections together. But when we tried to raise the whole length upright, the force of the gale nearly lifted two of us off our feet. Quickly I got a second rope round the top of the ladder and secured our ends to vertical stand-pipes. That way, we could exert enough friction to lower the whole bridge gently into position. Once it was down, we lashed the near end to a rail, in case it got blown overboard after we were across; even though the ladder was lightweight, it wouldn't have improved the health or temper of anyone it landed on after dropping sixteen storeys.

By now I was shitting bricks. 'Wish to fuck I'd never volunteered to lead,' I said in Whinger's ear.

'I'll go if you like,' he said – good old bugger that he is.

'No, no. I'm fine really.'

I was, too – once I'd started. '*Khuyevo dyelo!*' I said to myself. 'Shit, shit, shit!' – and then I was on my way.

With a safety rope round my waist and belayed on to the guy next in line, I crawled forward, each knee on one sharp-edged rung at a time, hands clutching the side-rails with a grip like a Scotsman's on a five-pound note. The ladder swayed horribly as gusts of wind hit me. I tried not to look down, but far below and away to my left I couldn't help catching glimpses of cars that looked like toys. Half-way across I decided it was better to keep my eyes shut.

Even without seeing I could tell how far I'd got from the bend in the ladder. It flexed most when I was in the middle. Russian ladder, I kept thinking. Russian aluminium. I hope to hell it doesn't break.

At last it began to stiffen again as I drew near to the far side. I opened my eyes and saw that I had only feet to go. A few more seconds and I was safe on the roof of Block B. As I scrambled on to the rough asphalt I was appalled to find that the ladder's overlap was more like a foot than a metre. The blocks were obviously slightly farther apart than the architects had prescribed. I watched, fascinated, as I saw the end of the ladder creeping in and out, and realised that the high buildings were swaying in the wind.

Igor came across next, and made it with no fuss. So did Nikolai, who hadn't even bothered with a safety rope. It was Misha who got into trouble. Exactly what happened, I'll never know. All the rest of us saw, as we crouched shoulder-to-shoulder in the gale, was that he stopped half-way across the bridge. Whinger came up in my earpiece saying, 'Blue – got a hold-up. Oh, for fuck's sake . . .' and then, 'Get on, yer twit.'

Obviously Whinger didn't shout. Even if he could have been heard it would probably have been counter-productive, because in that situation, if someone loses his nerve, yelling only intensifies the fright. But seconds were ticking away. From exchanges on the radio I knew that Black team were starting their final approach to the front of the building. We couldn't afford to lose time.

Another dark figure started crawling out on to the ladder. With a double weight on it, the aluminium sagged horribly. The second man reached the feet of the stationary Misha, who was frozen in a face-down attitude. The back-up guy began talking, first in a low voice, then louder. When bollockings had no effect, the newcomer turned physical. From the blurred movements it looked as though he had started thumping Misha with his fist on the backs of his knees.

Still there was no reaction.

The wind and rain were hitting our faces so hard that, even from close range, it was impossible to tell exactly what happened next. It looked to me as though the second guy had tried to crawl over Misha's prostrate body. He was right on top of him when there came a sudden eruption of movement. I saw a flurry of limbs, much faster than men crawling, as if the two were wrestling.

An instant later one of them was falling. Without a sound he dropped away into the dark.

Jesus! I thought. Too low for his chute. But of course he had no chute.

He went straight down, 150 feet on to concrete.

I grabbed the pressel of my radio and hissed, 'Red leader. We have a casualty. One guy's fallen.'

'Roger,' came Anna's unemotional voice. She said something else in Russian. Then, 'Can you recover him?'

'Not a chance. He's gone right to the ground.'

'Proceed, then.'

'Roger.'

The guy who'd survived the mid-ladder encounter reached us. Not Misha. It was Volodya from the Blue team. Misha was written off. Peering over the edge of the roof, I could just make out a little dark heap splatted on the deck. At least the controllers knew what had happened. It was up to them whether or not they made any move to help him. I was pretty certain there'd be no point. No way could he have survived that impact, especially with the weight of the weapon on his back, the ammunition in his pouches and all his other gear. All I could think, selfishly, was, I hope to hell nobody saw him go past their window.

The rest of Blue team quickly came across, Whinger last. He gave me a strained look, but never said a word about the setback – just a quick '*Idyom!*' to his guys, and they were gone, round the end of the lift-housing to the point where the emergency stairs reached the roof.

I led the two surviving members of Red team along the roof to the far end and round the corner, until we were positioned above the target windows. There we quickly laid out our ropes. We found ideal anchor-points in the form of a strong metal rail that skirted the raised top of the lift shaft, and in a couple of minutes we were ready to descend.

'Red leader,' I called. 'Can I have a sniper report on the windows? Are all curtains drawn?'

Anna instantly passed the request. I heard Green come in: '*Da, da. Vsyo,*' and in a second I got, 'Yes, all curtains closed.'

My watch said 9.24. 'Red leader,' I reported.

196

'Starting descent now.'

Abseiling down a building in the dark is never a picnic. Still less is it easy in a high wind. The longer your rope, the more you swing about, and the greater the danger of accidentally bumping against a window. But it was no good pissing about. I stuck my arse into space, walked backwards over the edge of the roof, and started down.

Luckily the shape of the building was kind to us. All the doors and windows were set back about a metre inside the balconies, so that as we came past each floor there was very little chance of any accidental contact with the inner wall of the building.

Inches at a time I tip-toed down the wall and dangled in space above the top half of the first balcony. On down past the metal rails. Sixteen done. Fifteen the same. Slowly on past fourteen. My two guys were doing OK, to the right and left of me. Between fourteen and thirteen a terrific gust of wind swung us so violently that all three of us bumped against each other. Luckily the windows were closed and curtains drawn all the way down, courtesy of the wild night.

My boots touched the top rail of the twelfth-floor balcony. I eased myself down gently until my backside was on the rail, then got my feet on the floor of the balcony itself. I'd landed in front of Window Two. The greenish curtains were drawn tight, but light was shining out round the edges.

The second I was out of my ropes I turned to guide Igor in.

By 9.28 all three of us were in our prearranged positions: myself crouching beside the door, Nikolai on my right, Igor on my left. Even in the relative shelter of the balcony the wind was blustering loudly, and there was no need to keep my voice down when I reported in. 'Red leader, on target. Blue, report your state.'

'Blue, preparing charge,' came Whinger's voice. 'Wait out.'

'Red, roger.' My heart was going like a hammer. I imagined Whinger deftly taping a length of det cord down the centre of the door. I glanced either way at the dark, helmeted faces beside me and gave a reassuring twitch of my head. The lads had heard Whinger in their earpieces, but naturally hadn't understood what he said, so I made taping motions round our own doorway. Both got it, grinned back and nodded.

But I was wrong. Suddenly I heard Whinger say, 'Blue. We have a problem. I can see through a glass panel in the fire-escape door. There are two guards sitting outside the apartment, in the corridor. Wait one.'

I made an instant decision. 'Red. You'll have to drop them. I'll use your shots as the signal to go.'

'OK,' said Whinger softly. 'Ready when you are.'

'Red. Roger. Control – is Black on schedule?'

'*Da, da. Chyornii gotovi*,' came Anna's voice. I could tell that the excitement was getting to her as well because for a moment she forgot to translate. Then she said, 'Yes. Black ready.'

'Red. Starting countdown now. Sixty, fifty, forty . . .'

I imagined the Black team wagon speeding towards the Mafia entrance, silenced weapons at the ready. The gale was certainly going to help mask any noise they made.

'Twenty . . . ten . . .'

Jesus, I was thinking, I hope this goes our way, because we shouldn't be anywhere near here.

'Ten, nine, eight, seven, six, five . . . Stand by, stand by . . . GO!'

The hammer of rounds going down in the corridor came clearly through to us. With my charge held flat to the glassed upper half of the door, I knelt with my head tucked down, away from the blast, and squeezed my clacker.

BOOM! The blast made the inner wall shudder. I raised my head. The entire glass panel had vanished. Through the hole I lobbed a stun grenade and ducked again, eyes averted.

BANG! A sharper, louder explosion. I came upright again. Pieces of glass were tinkling down. The lights in the room had gone out.

'*Poshli!*' I shouted at Igor. 'Go!'

In he went with a wild yell, head-first through the gap. I heard a thud as he hit the floor and scrabbling noises as he scuttled sideways. Then Nikolai was at the opening, hammering long bursts into the room with his Gepard. He was screaming obscenities too.

Hardly had he opened up when there came a second explosion as Whinger blew the door from the corridor. More rounds started going down inside the flat – bursts of seven or eight. Too long to be properly selective.

Empty cases cascaded on to the floor of the balcony beside me. Nikolai threw down an empty magazine, smacked home a full one and continued to fire. For a moment I felt a bit of a prick, lying there against the safety of the wall while guys were risking their lives inside.

Then the bursts of fire died away. Single shots cracked out – one, two, three, four. I knew what they meant: the assaulters were using their pistols to pop rounds into the heads of their victims, making certain they were dead.

One more single shot, then silence – except for the wind.

'Boris!' I shouted. '*Yestj?*'

'*Da, da.*'

'*Khorosho!*'

I held in my pressel and called, 'Red to Blue – all secure at your end?'

'Blue,' came Whinger's voice. 'Affirmative. All inner rooms secure.'

'Red. Roger. This side secure also. You can come on through.'

Standing up, I walked in through the shattered window-door. The air in the living room was hot as hell and thick with cigarette smoke, shot through with the sharp reek of cordite. Something had caught fire, ignited by the stun grenade. The blaze wasn't serious – just enough to give flickering illumination and light up the gory scene. The lights had gone down and for the time being I let it burn.

The Mafiosi must have been in conference round a rectangular table. Now, overturned chairs and five bodies lay all round it. Igor, crouched in the left-hand outer corner of the room, was still covering Nikolai as he scurried round checking each one. The door into the hallway was closed, so I went straight over and called through it, 'Whinge?'

'Yeah, yeah. We're here.'

'OK. I'm opening up.' I turned the handle and pulled, to find the door was locked. Peering down, I saw the key was in the lock, spun it and pulled the door towards me. The two teams were safely reunited.

'Red leader to Control,' I called. 'Target secure.'

'*Vas ponyal*,' went Anna. 'Roger.'

'Piece of cake!' said Whinger. 'What's the Russian for that?'

'I don't know. How many have your guys taken out?'

'Four. The bodyguards. Two in the passage, two more watching TV in the end bedroom. We got them as they came out the door.' He flashed his torch into the bedroom doorway, and I saw two bodies lying across each other on the floor.

'No casualties on your team?'

Whinger shook his head. 'The stupid bastards never got a round off. The two outside were asleep on their chairs, and the others had left their main weapons in the hallway. There.' He shone the beam on a little stack of sub-machine guns in a corner. 'Didn't even have time to draw their pistols.'

201

I found myself shaking with reaction. 'Jesus!' I said. 'What happens now?'

After a hit of that kind in the UK, the assault teams would be instantly spirited away from the scene in a hostage reception van, and any prisoners would travel with them, to get the whole lot clear before any journalists or TV crew turned up. Then a quick-reaction force would move in and take over. The most important guy in the aftermath would be the SOCO, the scene-of-crimes officer, from the police. Until he arrived, the key rule was that nothing must be touched or moved.

Not so in Moscow. Satisfied that all the villains were dead, Igor got up, walked over and kicked one of the bodies contemptuously, rolling it over.

'Stop!' I called, waving my hands about to tell him to lay off. But that was the limit of my Russian, and he probably thought I was crazy.

Somebody found the electricity control panel. A trip switch had been thrown by the blasts, and once it was flipped back up enough of the lights went on for us to survey the wreckage.

It looked as though four of the sitting-room victims had been gunned down where they sat at the table. They were all flabby-looking, middle-aged men with bellies bulging out into their shirts and their sleeves rolled up. Their faces had probably never been pretty, and they certainly weren't now, because Nikolai had gone round and popped each one with a bullet through the head. One had an eye out on a stalk; another had

202

spewed out half his teeth. Pools of blood were spreading over the pale carpet. Their jackets, still hanging over the backs of their chairs, had been riddled by bullets. The fifth guy, a younger man in a dark-blue polo shirt, had got half-way to the door before being dropped. On the right-hand wall, looking from the windows, water was dripping from the shattered remains of a glass fish-tank, and the wretched occupant was flapping its last in a puddle at the bottom. Another victim was an old tabby cat, which lay in a corner without a mark on it and seemed to have died of fright.

The table was covered with papers, evidently the subject of the meeting, and expensive-looking brief-cases sat on the floor beside the chairs. The fire had started in a waste bin containing more paper, and I had no problem stamping it out. But I'd hardly finished when there was a commotion outside the door and in strode Ivan the Bear, with Sasha at his heels.

Ivan advanced towards me, grinning, and said something which Sasha translated as, 'Breelliant! He congratulates you very much.'

'Your guys did it.' I gestured round. 'They were first class. *Ochen khorosho.*'

Ivan accepted the praise with a nod and turned his attention to the bodies. Almost at once he gave an exclamation and began to talk at speed into a mobile phone.

'It is Keet – the Whale,' Sasha translated, pointing at the corpse of a huge man with close-cropped grey hair that lay on its back almost under the table. As he was speaking, Ivan bent down and unceremoniously ripped open the perforated, blood-stained shirt to reveal a foot-long tattoo of a whale's head and open jaws, tilted upwards towards the man's left shoulder. From the half-open mouth the feet of a human being were protruding. By a horrible fluke one round had gone in almost exactly through the whale's eye, leaving a bloody hole.

With a jerk on one arm Ivan rolled the body over and kicked the shirt up round its head. There, between the shoulder blades, was a tattooed portrait of Stalin.

'Old Uncle Joe didn't save that bugger, did he?' Whinger was staring at the effigy, fascinated. Then, as he surveyed the scene, he added, 'I like the delicate way they handle things round here, I must say.'

Ivan brought out a pocket knife, slipped the blade inside one leg of Whale's trousers, at the ankle, and slit the grey material open to half-way up the thigh. Then he pointed contemptuously and gave a short laugh.

'He has stars on the knees,' Sasha translated. 'Like I told you. The sign he would never kneel.'

It seemed that all the villains bar one were known to Ivan. By any standards it was a terrific coup for the security forces: five godfathers at one hit, plus four bodyguards and a haul of incriminating papers. Nor was that all. The two most fancy briefcases – crocodile leather by Gucci, no less – were closed with gold combination locks. Ivan picked one up, laid it on the table and started trying to open it. Frustrated, he called to Igor, who produced a small jemmy.

'Hey, wait!' I said, thinking of Toad and Pavarotti.

'That thing's worth a few grand. One of our guys will open it without wrecking it.'

But Ivan wasn't in a mood to wait, and in a few seconds he'd burst both locks. When he lifted the lid, everybody who could see gave a gasp, because the case was packed solid with fifty-dollar bills done up in little paper sleeves holding bunches of twenty notes: a thousand bucks a throw.

When you see cash in that kind of quantity, you realise how little space it takes up: I could have put ten grand in my hip pocket, no bother.

As if reading my thoughts Ivan plunged a hand into the case and brought out a fistful of bundles, holding them in my direction.

'Take,' said Sasha. 'He wants you to have it.'

'No, no.' I waved it away.

'Yes, please. He inseest. He thinks like Russian soldiers you not being paid well. You need more.'

Looking round under the table, Ivan spotted a far cheaper briefcase made of imitation black leather, with a flap closure and no locks. Having tipped the papers it contained on to the table, he proceeded to stuff it with handfuls of fifty-dollar bills and thrust it at me.

From this point things became more and more surreal. Somebody discovered bottles of special, high-octane vodka in the freezer compartment of the fridge, brought them out and began pouring slugs into short, squat glasses. Whinger and I declined, but as the icy spirit went down other people's throats in repeated doses, the volume of voices rose. While a minion collected up the papers from the table and stowed them away, Ivan himself carefully removed gold watches from three dead wrists and a couple of crocodile wallets from the jackets still on the chairs.

'Present to English friends!' he beamed, holding a watch out in my direction.

'No, for fuck's sake!' I exclaimed. '*Spasibo* – but keep them.'

Then some of his guys arrived with body bags, and at last bundled the corpses out of sight.

Outside, in the corridor, there was a great commotion as other inhabitants of the block argued with the guards on the door, trying to get in and find out what had happened.

'Let's get the hell out of here,' Whinger muttered. 'There's going to be a monster piss-up.'

'We'd better sign off with Ivan.'

'He's busy. Another day.'

'OK.'

I looked round for Sasha and beckoned him over. 'We need to get back to Balashika,' I told him. 'Can someone give us a lift?'

'*Konechno*. I drive you.'

'How many vodkas have you had?'

'Vodka? Nothing! Two only.'

So it was that we pushed our way past the new guards on the door, through the crowd outside and into the lift. Downstairs there was a heavy military presence on the entrance to the block, but Sasha spirited us through it, found the car he'd been driving, and set off.

I felt plagued by guilt – first by the thought that we should all have been in a formal debriefing session, recalling and recording every move of the raid; second by the knowledge that we had lost a man; and third by the fact that I was carrying a small fortune of ill-gotten gains in a Mafia briefcase.

'Misha,' I said. 'He was dead?'

Sasha nodded. 'Absolutely. We found his body. How did he fall?'

'Just lost his nerve.'

'It is a pity. But – *nichevo*!' He smiled broadly. 'We have beeg victory. Like in football – Arsenal nine, Tottenham Hotspot one!' He gave a merry laugh and drummed his hands on the steering wheel. Then he added, 'Only one problem.'

'What's that?'

'Mafia bosses will be angry. For sure, they make counter-attack.'

'On Omon?'

'No, on government. The President, the Vice-President, the Minister of the Interior. Perhaps one of them will be their next target.'

NINE

I thought I was going to have nightmares, but in fact I slept like the dead, and woke up unable to remember where I was. Until I heard Whinger snoring, that is: then everything flooded back.

'All in a day's work,' I'd said cheerily to Rick when we came in the night before – and a hell of a day we'd had. But it had been exhilarating too, and a sharpening change from the routine of training.

Naturally we'd had a wash-up with our own lads as soon as we had come in: they'd got a brew on, and we'd sat up till after midnight analysing the hit. We had also had a discussion – not quite an argument – about what had come to be known as the 'diplomatic bag'. A count had shown it to contain 110,000 dollars.

When the lads saw that amount of money tipped out on the kitchen table they uttered, 'Firekin ell!' in a kind of chorus.

If there's one thing that makes SAS lads take leave of their senses it's money. Normally they're pretty straight-up, but somehow the sight of cash sends them bananas.

'There's my Jag!' Pavarotti cried with his eyes glazing over.

'Bugger the Jag!' Pete told him. 'What about my kitchen extension?'

'Bet it's all forged,' said Dusty, ever the cynic.

'Never,' Mal told him. 'Big Mafia players wouldn't be carting fake stuff around. Whose is it, anyway? Geordie's and Whinger's, I suppose.'

'No, no,' I said. 'If it belongs to anyone, it belongs to the team.'

'Buy a team Merc,' said Pavarotti. 'Get a five-hundred or something. Smoked-glass windows. Then we can take on the hoods at their own game. *How* much did you say they had?'

'Meellions,' I said, imitating Sasha. 'Christ knows. It was a big briefcase and it was jam-packed. This lot was only a fraction of what we saw. There could have been stuff we didn't see as well. We never looked in the other croc briefcase or in drawers or cupboards. The flat could have been full of money. Drugs too, I daresay. God knows what they were at: it looked as though they were carving up their empire.'

It was Rick who produced the idea of sending the cash back to the UK. 'Put it in the Diplomatic Bag,' he suggested. 'Then at least it'll be safe, and a nice little bonus for when we get home.'

'Bollocks to that,' said Pav. 'Split it up now. Then we can go out and start spending.'

'What on?' demanded Dusty derisively. 'Rotten onions? Crappy cabbage? You'll get fuck-all else in Balashika.'

'Funny,' said Mal. 'At Sandhurst it's the other way

round. It's the students who have the money. Arabs slip their instructors gold watches to get an early look at exam papers. Here, the students are penniless and the instructors are loaded.'

Whinger, who'd been keeping quiet, butted up and said, 'They offered Geordie a gold Rolex as well.'

'You bastard!' roared Pav. 'Where is it?'

'I told him to keep it.'

'Bloody idiot,' Pav cried. 'I'd have taken it.'

'I know you would,' I told him. 'But the person who needs money is Sasha. I bet that mean bugger Ivan didn't give *him* anything. The poor sod hasn't been paid in months.'

I brought up the saga of my having to buy clothes for him in Hereford, which the lads hadn't heard, and finished with, 'I vote we slip him a couple of grand, anyway.'

Our Chinese parliament passed the suggestion unanimously – with the exception of Toad, who, as usual, was lurking at one side of the room, outside the main circle, listening, watching. He said nothing – just gave us a sly look – so I considered him over-ruled and said, 'Right then – here's a couple for Sasha,' and separated out two of the little bundles.

'What about the rest?'

In the end it was agreed that we keep it all together for the time being, and send it back to UK as Rick had suggested.

'All right, then,' I said. 'It's going in a Lacon box for

now, and the next time we go in to the Embassy, it heads for home.'

Next morning Sasha was on top of the world, beaming at everyone, bringing thanks and congratulations from Omon's highest brass. He also brought a personal invitation.

'My mother,' he began, as we stood in the sunshine outside the back of our building. 'She would like so much to meet you. She asks, please come to supper one evening.'

'Sasha! You haven't told her about yesterday?'

'*Konechno nyet!* She knows nothing about yesterday. She knows nothing about my work. This invitation is from many days old.'

'Well – thanks. I'd like to meet her.'

'Good! Good!'

'When would it be?'

'She suggest Friday. And please, bring one friend.'

'Thank you. That's really nice. Now look – I've got something for you. Hang on there a minute.'

I nipped inside to fetch his dollars. It wasn't the ideal moment, because it looked slightly as if I was trying to pay in advance for a couple of dinners, but I thought it best to get the presentation over with.

'Listen,' I said. 'We want to give you this.'

When he saw the money he blushed bright red and tried to push it away. 'No, Zheordie. No, please . . .'

'Take it.' I caught his right hand with my left and pushed the notes into it. 'You know where it came from. We got more than we need. We want you to have a share. And change it quickly, before somebody decides it's fake.'

For a second or two I thought the silly bugger was going to cry, as he blinked and looked down at the notes. But he soon got hold of himself and said, 'Too much. Too much.'

'Put it in your pocket and shut up!' I grinned and gave him a clip on the shoulder. 'It's time we got the lads down to the range.'

The students were in fine form, and gave an ironic cheer when we appeared. Apparently there'd been a clip about the raid on the morning's TV news, and bush telegraph had whizzed a full account of it round more efficiently than the Internet. Nobody seemed in the least put out by the loss of Misha, least of all his former colleague in SOBR, who appeared to regard him as entirely dispensable.

I'd been intending to play the whole thing down, and I asked Anna to explain that, for political reasons, it was essential that Brit involvement in the bust remained under wraps. But the Russians were so enthusiastic about the hit that I decided to make a virtue of it and called a special seminar at which we took everyone – the students who hadn't been there, and our own guys – through all the stages of the raid: planning, equipment, preparations, execution.

It proved an inspired idea: everybody was gripped by the analysis and discussion, and learned useful lessons. Of course I said nothing about the handout of dollars, but I did deplore the lack of a formal debriefing session. 'I'm not criticising anyone,' I said. 'That isn't my business. But at home we'd have done it a different way – and in fact it's what we're doing now. It's always important to talk through what's happened. That's the way you avoid mistakes in future.'

'Misha,' somebody started. 'Why did he fall? Why no safety rope?'

'He was supposed to have one. I told everyone to rope up, but it seems he hadn't bothered. Your special forces people are like us: you don't take kindly to orders.'

I saw two of the Russians exchange glances, and added, 'That's not criticism. It's a statement of fact.' Finally I said, 'I must emphasise that our participation in the raid was completely unofficial, so we can't have any mention of it leaking to the media. Otherwise we'll be in the shit with our own people. Understood?'

All through that day I felt I was blundering deeper and deeper into a moral maze.

Almost making matters worse was the fact that the course was going really well. Our relationship with the students had never been better. Maybe it was the success of the hit that fired them up; whatever, a lot of jokes were flying about and morale was great. Sasha was all over the place in his desire to be helpful.

At lunchtime Anna and I went for a walk. I'd already had some food when she appeared at the back of the building, yet I offered her lunch – God knows what we would have given her if she'd accepted. But she said she'd had an apple, and otherwise didn't intend to eat until the evening.

So it was that we strolled off down one of the tracks into the training area.

I think her intention was just to be friendly, and to thank us again for leading the raid; but gradually her talk turned to the present good relations between East and West, and the contrast with the bad old days of the Cold War, when the KGB was crazily suspicious and went to fantastic lengths to penetrate foreign embassies in Moscow.

'You know what happened in the Japanese Embassy?' she asked.

I shook my head.

'It was an old merchant's house, like your British Embassy. It still had fireplaces and chimneys. So the KGB decided that the way to penetrate it was by sending a man down a chimney to plant microphones. They found a very thin man, trained him to climb, and sent him off.'

She stopped, looking at me.

'And what happened?'

'Nothing! The man was never seen again. That was the end of him. Did he get stuck? Is he still there, perhaps? Did the Japanese catch him and feed him to their tame fish? Nobody knows. Of course the KGB couldn't ask, so they never found out.'

I laughed and said, 'When you worked in London, I suppose you were spying too?'

'Naturally! All Russians abroad were spies then. We were running the Intourist office, of course, but every day we were sending in reports to the KGB.'

'What about?'

'Oh, prominent people who booked air tickets or tours, foreign visitors to London, economic activity in general . . . I'm sure most of the information was useless, but we thought we were tremendously important.'

'But how did you get into spying in the first place?'

'To see the world. Isn't that what you say about your navy? "Join the navy and see the world"? That was it with the KGB, exactly. In those days, the only chance you had of getting out of the Soviet Union was by joining the Ministry of Foreign Affairs or the KGB. Those were the two best careers on offer.'

Several times during our chat I almost challenged her about the business of our lap-top. But I decided on balance that it was better not to stir things up.

So, on the surface, everything was brilliant; and yet, undermining the cheerful atmosphere, was the presence of Apple and Orange, sitting there in the Embassy lock-up.

The CNDs were a lead weight on my mind, and Sasha's invitation to supper made everything worse. How could I chat up his old mother with this in the back of my brain?

All afternoon my mind kept wandering as I tried to think up ways of wriggling out of our commitment. What if we dropped both devices, unprimed, off one of the bridges into the Moscow River, and told Hereford there'd been an unfortunate accident – a crash which had flung the cases out of the back of the van and over the parapet? Even if they believed it they'd probably react by simply getting two more CNDs sent post-haste from America, and we'd be back in the shit, neck deep, with even less time to extricate ourselves.

What if we dumped the cases in the river but reported that we'd installed them correctly at the two sites? Obviously the satellite wouldn't pick up the right signals – but maybe we could attribute this to faults in the systems. I needed to consult Toad on that one.

What if I posted Anna an anonymous typewritten note about the contents of the Embassy lock-up? A quick raid by Omon, an almighty diplomatic row, Embassy staff expelled, SAS sent packing, international stand-off, countdown to World War Three . . .

When I confided my anxiety to Whinger that evening, his reaction was typical. 'For fuck's sake, Geordie,' he went. 'You're getting old. The only thing to do's to get the bastards in place and forget about them. It's a thousand to one they'll never get used. So let's bury them, have done with it – and don't get caught, 'cause life's too short.'

I stared at the deep lines in his face and the curls of grey in the light-brown fuzz of his hair. 'You always were a mean bastard,' I told him, 'but I reckon you're right. We'll go for it.'

Our next decision was to shift our early-morning run in the direction of the potential Orange site, to clear that one down. During the past few days we'd made a couple more passes along the track that went by the old air-raid shelter, but we'd still not looked inside, and now we needed to suss it out properly.

The nights were growing steadily longer, so the next morning we set off in the dark, and we'd covered the three kilometres to the site before the light was at all strong. This meant we had to hang around a while before we could see, but at least we felt confident that no one else was about.

The shelter proved to be not much more than a tunnel driven horizontally into a piece of sloping ground – a primitive structure with an arched roof of corrugated iron which was about ten feet high in the middle and dropped down to ground level on either side. From the front we could see that the tin was only the inner lining: on top of it was a layer of concrete maybe a foot thick, and then earth. In the front wall, made of concrete blocks, was a small opening at shoulder height, designed to let in light and air, and the entrance was to one side. Since the only illumination came through those two apertures, the inside was dark as a cave and we had to feel our way past the edge of the heap of old planks dumped in there.

'Should have brought a torch,' Whinger muttered.

'Yeah – but we can hack it enough for now.'

The shelter ran about thirty feet into the side of the hill and was all one space – no divisions. When our eyes had adjusted to the gloom we could see that the wall at the back was like the one at the front – concrete blocks

– but in less good nick: damp had worked its way through, cracking the mortar and producing dark stains. Pressure from the earth behind had pushed two or three of the blocks forward so that they stood proud of their neighbours. When I ran my fingers down the wall they came away wet and smelling faintly of iron.

'What we should do is get behind the blocks and dig out a hollow,' said Whinger. 'Then put the wall back up. With the blocks loose like that, it's a piece of cake.'

'It would be if we didn't have to dispose of the spoil.' I bent down and scuffed my hand over the floor. 'Feels like bare earth. But the stuff coming out of the bank's bound to be a different colour.'

'Yeah – but who's coming in here to see it?'

'A hundred to one, nobody. But if somebody did we'd be buggered. Better to get rid of it. Let's recce a dump site outside.'

Back in the open, we found an ideal place within thirty metres of the entrance: pushing through scrub, well away from the track, we nearly fell into a deep pit with gorse bushes growing over it. Sand or earth dumped through the branches would vanish into the hole, which would have taken tons and was far bigger than we needed.

'That's it, then,' I said. 'When we come, it's going to be all hands to the pumps. We've got to do the whole job in one night: drop the wall, dig the recess, place the device, rebuild the wall, skim it with mud to mask the new joints, and away.'

The simplicity of the task seemed to steel my resolve.

As we trotted back towards the camp I realised that for the past few days I'd been postponing the insertion of Apple on the grounds that there was no hurry. Now I'd swung round to Whinger's point of view: the sooner we got both devices squared away, the better.

'You're right,' I panted. 'There's no reason to hang about. We'll go for the Kremlin tomorrow night.'

TEN

We planned everything in as much detail as we could, but the timings inevitably remained untidy. I arranged with the Chargé d'Affaires that we'd remove some of our stuff from the lock-up during the evening. We'd be bound to arouse suspicion if we swept into the compound at midnight; equally, it was quite possible that watchers in the Kremlin had the Embassy's entrance under continuous video surveillance from across the river – if anyone saw a car emerge from the gates and vanish straight into the churchyard down the road, the forces of law and order would be on the scene within minutes. The same would apply if we attempted to move the Apple components on foot. We couldn't trudge out of the Embassy gates lugging heavy containers and struggle with them along to the churchyard: video cameras or not, somebody would be bound to notice. The only safe way of shifting the device to the old stable was to load it up, drive off, disappear for a while and then return from the opposite direction, cruising in through the gateway arch and straight past the church door.

Our earlier visits had shown that there were people

about until quite late in the evening, and we reckoned that 10.00 p.m. would be a safer time to kick off than 9.00. That meant we'd have nearly an hour to kill.

For the tunnel team I'd nominated Toad, Pavarotti and myself. Rick would man the head of the shaft: with his reasonable Russian, he might be able to bluff his way through if anyone accosted him while we were down. During our recce Whinger had stood off in the car, and this time I wanted him in command on the surface once again; but we were going to need two vehicles, because we would never fit five guys and the Apple components into one of the Volgas. That meant I had to detail Mal as our second driver, leaving only Dusty, Johnny and Pete in barracks.

I was worried by the knowledge that the guys back on the base had no vehicle in which they could come out and recover us if anything went wrong. In fact I was worried by a hell of a lot of niggling possibilities – which all seemed to become probabilities as the day ground on. We'd get a puncture driving out of the Embassy gates, with Apple on board (we'd had three punctures already). We'd meet hostile natives in the churchyard. We'd drop one of the heavy components down the access shaft and wreck it. We'd crack the casing of the SCR and absorb fatal doses of radiation. We'd find the tunnel booby-trapped. We'd find the tunnel flooded along its whole length. We'd run out of oxygen while making final excavations at the site. We wouldn't be able to lift the device into its resting place. It would turn out that the two components were incompatible. The satellite wouldn't pick up signals from the SCR . . .

Before we left I put through a call to Hereford and confirmed that we were under starter's orders. Until then I'd been economical with information about our progress. I'd reported our successful recce of the Apple site but I hadn't told anyone what we'd done with the devices. Now I simply said that it should be possible for Washington to make contact with Apple from 0200 next morning.

At last 8.00 came, and it was too late to agonise any more. I rode passenger in the black wagon, with Mal driving and Toad in the back. Whinger drove the grey car, with Rick and Pavarotti as passengers.

Unfortunately it was a still evening. The noisy gale that had blown up during the Mafia hit would have suited us fine, but tonight we had to make do without.

As we headed into town we passed one GAI team who'd set up a temporary check-point on the other side of the road: they'd got three of their little blue-and-white Gaz jeeps set out to form a funnel, and were pulling in about one driver in three. Sasha had told us that by the end of each month these traffic police were frantic for money, and imposed instant fines for any offence they could dream up – as he put it: '*for* documents, *for* speed, *for* lights, *for* breaking rules, *for* not having seat-belts done up.'

We had our documents, we had roubles, we had dollars . . . but luckily tonight there was no purge on vehicles going in our direction.

The route was familiar by now. Over the bridge, swing down on to the embankment, head west. We made one precautionary drive-past in the black car while the grey one stood off out of sight; then we came back round the block, joined forces, and both turned into the Embassy compound at 8.55.

So far, so good. But from that moment things persistently went a little bit wrong. The first shock came when, as we pulled up in the Embassy's rear yard, the Chargé himself came out to greet us. I'd assumed he'd be off duty by now.

In fact Allway was harmless enough – he'd obviously had a couple of drinks, and was braying in a loud, hearty voice that he'd only emerged to wish us well. But his mere presence outside the lock-up was a pain.

'How are you doing?' he boomed. 'All tickety-boo?'

'Yes, thanks.'

'Getting enough to eat out there? Hope they're not starving you.'

'No, no. We're fine. Just come in to pick up a couple of items of kit.'

'Ah! Some of those ammunition boxes, what?'

'Those are the ones.'

'Want a hand?'

'No thanks. We'll manage fine.'

'Well – any problems, just let me know.'

'Thanks.'

I thought the bastard was going back indoors, but he turned and said, 'Oh, by the way, the security forces had a big success against the Mafia the other day.'

'Is that right?'

'Caught several of the godfathers in a flat, right here in the middle of town. Killed four or five of them. It was on the news next day. Surprised you haven't heard about it.'

'No . . .' I shook my head. 'We've been pretty busy – don't have much time for watching TV.'

'Maybe the Russians are getting better at Mafia-hunting, what? Maybe they don't need you fellows so much after all. Or maybe you've taught them something already? Well – ta ta!'

I took several deep breaths, forcing myself not to utter a sound until the door had closed behind him. Then I just whispered, 'Jeeesus Christ! Let's get moving.'

Unless you were colour-blind there was no way of muddling the components, because Apple's three pieces were all marked with a light green circle, Orange's with orange. We backed the black Volga as close as we could to the cellar door and carried the three green-marked cases out, four men on each of the heavy ones. Once again they pushed the car right down on its springs. Toad removed the Rat from its lair and clipped it on his belt.

As soon as we'd secured the up-and-over door of the cellar, we drove off. I'd felt as if my exchanges with the Chargé lasted for ever, but still we had fifty minutes to kill; so, rather than hang about in the area, we followed our plan and drove up to the terrace in front of the univerity, on the edge of the Sparrow Hills. Sasha had taken us there during our first visit, and I remembered it as a favourite view-point, popular with tourists and sightseers, where strangers hanging around wouldn't attract attention.

If you ever want to get your adrenalin going, try driving through Moscow at night with a nuclear bomb in the boot of a rickety, underpowered car. Every traffic light spelt possible disaster, every vehicle that overtook seemed certain to be full of Mafia gunmen bent on a hijack.

'What we do *not* want,' I said grimly, 'is to be stopped by the fucking GAI with this lot on board.'

'Nah,' said Pavarotti. 'They don't seem to operate much in the centre – more out on the highways.'

Luck favoured us. With me map-reading we managed to avoid the cops and find the way, and soon came out on to the huge, level esplanade, where one can park and walk forward to look out over the city. Whinger, following at a distance, pulled up some fifty yards to our right, and a couple got out of each car to take in the sights.

The prospect was spectacular, I had to admit. Behind us, the monstrous skyscraper of the main university building towered into the sky, topped by a slender spire that gleamed golden in its spotlights. On either side of it the lower towers sprouted pinnacles, and hundreds of lighted windows made the campus look like a city on its own.

In front of us, immediately over the wall was a steep

drop, with a couple of rickety-looking ski-jumps – not yet in use – poised over it. Below them, the centre of Moscow was laid out in a million more lights. It reminded me of the view from the top of Block B – except that here the illumination was far more varied and concentrated. Close in the foreground was a large stadium; farther out, the floodlit buildings of the Kremlin glowed magnificently. We could also see the White House. I remembered Sasha telling us of how it had been rebuilt after the coup: apparently the workers had stayed in the nearby Kiev Hotel, and their demand for whores was so phenomenal that busloads of extra women had had to be imported from out of town.

I glanced around. There were a few other people up here, but nobody close to us. Away to our right I could see Whinger and Rick, also looking over the wall, but correctly keeping their distance.

'I feel that hepped up, I reckon if I jumped off here I'd fly,' I told Pavarotti quietly.

'Don't try it, mate. You might just keep going, never come down.'

We admired the view for a few more minutes, then returned to the car and hung around some more. As usual at such moments, our watches seemed to have gone on strike.

But at last it was 9.45, time to head down.

'Moving off now,' I told Whinger over the radio.

'Roger. I'll let you get clear.'

Mal turned the car and started to back-track our route – but we were hardly under way before Whinger came through again with, 'Watch yourselves. I think you've got a tail.'

Mal said, 'Shit,' studied his mirror and said, 'Is it that buff Lada?'

'Roger. It pulled out when you did.'

'I'll watch it for a minute.'

'Roger.'

Turning in the passenger seat to face Mal, I saw the car they were talking about. Now what? Our options were severely limited by our lack of speed and the great weight we were carrying. Shooting red lights was no good: hundreds of drivers did that anyway; the Lada would simply follow us through any crossing. And in any case we didn't want to risk a brush with the GAI. We certainly couldn't outrun a pursuer. Nor could we afford to tangle with one. We all had Sigsauer 9mm pistols, and if things turned nasty we could use them – but only as a very last resort. A collision might shunt the nuclear components clean out of the car, taking the boot lid or rear door with them, and damage the devices beyond repair . . .

'How many on board?' I asked.

'Three,' came Whinger's voice.

Mal said, 'I'm going to head away from our target area.'

'Roger.'

Before we started down through the bends of the hillside, he took a left, heading south. Then another left. The Lada followed. When a light turned red way ahead, he changed down to decelerate without using the brakes. The Lada slowed as well, keeping its distance.

'Definite tail,' I told Whinger. 'Can you sort them for us?'

'I'll try.'

'Do they realise we're a pair?'

'Don't think so. I'm driving on sidelights and keeping well back.'

Whinger was – and is – a hell of a guy behind the wheel. He'd done a stint as instructor in special driving techniques at Llangwern, the training area in Wales, and what he didn't know about J-turns, ramming and breaking up illegal VCPs wasn't worth knowing. The trouble was that in England or Northern Ireland he'd probably have been driving one of the Regiment's souped-up intercept cars, which have extra power, armour, strengthened suspension and belly plates, and can whack anything else off the road with one flick of the rear end. Whereas here he had a lumbering, light-weight Volga with little power and no protection. I knew what he was thinking: that although it would be no trouble to knock our tail into the gutter, the last thing he wanted was to end up immobilising his own vehicle.

Somehow we'd got on to a big boulevard which my wrist-compass told me was heading south-west, out of town. At a crossroads I got a glimpse of a sign and deciphered it as Leninskii Prospekt.

The Lada was still behind us.

Shit! I was thinking. We should never have come up into this area. I've dropped a bollock here. We should just have made a loop and risked going into the church-yard early.

Then I remembered a friend of mine – Andy, a Tornado pilot – saying that a key element in training to fly fast jets was that pilots must have the ability to dump bad decisions behind them. In the air, especially at low level, events happen so fast that the pilot has to take dozens of decisions every minute, and the essential skill is to dump whatever's just happened, so that your mind's free to look ahead.

OK, I told myself. Forget that one. Now what?

'Take that right,' I told Mal suddenly.

He hauled the wheel round. Our tyres squealed under the load. Sixty yards behind us the Lada copied our every move, turning through the crossing just as the lights changed.

'Whinger's got through as well,' Mal said tersely. 'Must have shot the red.'

'I've a mind to stop suddenly and sort the bastards ourselves,' I said, reaching down to draw my Sig. At the back of my mind I knew that the very idea of opening up on unidentified strangers in the middle of the city was outrageous. In London I'd never have dreamt of it. But here in Moscow the level of lawlessness was so high that any form of self-defence seemed in order.

We appeared to be driving in orbit round the univer-sity; the colossal tower was still quite close on our right. If we stayed near it, at least we'd know where we were.

'Right again,' I said.

Now we were on another wide boulevard, heading

back towards the esplanade. The big road stretched ahead, empty of traffic. Suddenly I heard Whinger say, 'Slow down, Mal. Come down to fifty ks.'

'Roger,' went Mal, and eased off the accelerator. He'd been doing about sixty-five, and let the needle fall back. With one eye on the mirror he said, 'Stand by. The Lada's closing. No – cancel that. They've eased off again.'

The next thing we heard was Whinger calling, 'Stand by for contact. I'm going in.'

I knew what he'd done: on the long straight he'd built up speed and was coming in at the opposition on one fast run. I twisted round in my seat just in time to see a wild flare of headlights sweeping sideways, then the black silhouette of a vehicle momentarily on end, standing on its nose for an instant before hurtling off the near side of the road. Seconds later there was a brilliant flash, and flames leapt from the wreck.

I braked and pulled in to the kerb.

'Nice one, Whinge,' I called. 'You OK?'

'More or less.' He sounded well hyped up. 'Sustained a bit of damage, but we're still mobile. *Davai, davai!*'

We carried on for a couple of blocks. Then Mal said, 'No – he's dropping back.'

'Whinge,' I called. 'You got a problem?'

'Yeah – front tyre's going down.'

'Next right, then. Get off this fucking great road.'

We turned into a tree-lined side-street and came to a halt a hundred yards from the junction. Behind us the grey Volga crawled round the corner and crept under a tree.

'Turn and park on the other side,' I told Mal. 'Face this way, so you can cover us.'

I jumped out and ran across to Whinger's car. The air was full of the stink of burning rubber. Smoke was rising from the off-side front wheel. Rick and Pavarotti were already grappling with spare and jack, with Whinger standing back on the alert against the trunk of a tree.

'Tyre's knackered,' said Rick. 'The bumper got pushed into it by the impact. The bastard's almost on fire. It's worn right through.'

'Steering OK?'

'Should be when we get this wheel on.'

I went over to Whinger. 'What was all that about?'

'Ask me another. There were three young guys in it. At least one of them had a pistol, too.'

'You up-ended them, anyway.'

'Yeah. I got up to eighty ks and came at them without lights. Took their back end away.'

'*Zdorovo!* That party won't be doing any more driving tonight.'

We could have done without that little episode. It broke our concentration and meant that, as we finally approached the churchyard, we had to go through our mental preparation all over again.

This time Whinger made the drive-past, dropping Rick and Pav off on the embankment to walk in and recce the stable on foot. Only when they reported all clear did we prepare to move in.

Never in my life had I felt more nervous. I kept thinking, Once we get underground I'll be OK. What I do *not* want is any confrontation with all this hardware on our hands. We had no plausible explanation to offer if we were caught. We were prepared to shoot our way out of trouble if we had to, above or below ground, and we hoped that if the police found bodies, they would chalk them up as victims of some Mafia feud. But as for being grabbed in possession of the bomb – to that we had no answer. If we were forced to run for it, we might not even get back to the barracks at Balashika. I had visions of a gigantic escape and evasion scenario.

Mal remained perfectly cool, and that helped steady me. He hadn't seen the yard before but I'd briefed him on the layout, and now I talked him in, yard by yard. 'Here's the gateway, coming up. There's the church ahead. Keep round to the right. Stop opposite the doorway. Here we are – GO!'

Rick materialised from the stable, opened the rear door of the Volga and dragged section one of Apple half-way out. 'Pav's done the locks,' he whispered.

'Great.'

Mal remained in the driving seat with his engine ticking over in case he needed to take off suddenly. Toad grabbed the handles on the other end of section one. Together with Rick he carried it into the stable. I seized the SCR canister from the boot and staggered in with that. A moment later Toad and Rick brought in section two. Last out of the car was my bergen, containing lightweight hoist, ladder, nets, rubber bags, dry-suits, digging tools, head-torches, spare batteries, overalls and other essential paraphernalia. The pack alone was one hell of a weight.

'That's it,' I hissed at Mal through his open window. 'See you later.'

He eased the Volga gently forward, through the bend into the rear yard, swung round and came back past us. We saw his brake lights glow for an instant before he nosed out on to the main road. Then he was gone.

In the ink-black stable we stood and listened. I found I was hyperventilating, but I knew that now the most immediate danger – of having the hardware discovered in the car – was over. Now, in an emergency, we could do a runner or shoot our way out, leaving the stuff behind, and, if challenged, deny all knowledge of it.

The yard was very still, the church dark. We waited a couple of minutes. Nobody moved or spoke. Then I whispered, 'OK.'

Our individual tasks were carefully pre-planned. Toad kept watch on the doorway. Pav, the tallest, slung a loop over the main roof beam to take the top hook of the hoist. I broke out the nets, which were made of thick green nylon with a three-inch mesh, and manoeuvred the steel cases into them.

We'd just got the first one trussed when Toad let out a hiss. Torches snapped off. Everyone kept still. But it was only the usual problem – women crossing the yard from the church – and in a moment we moved again.

With all three cases netted, I pulled on my dry-suit,

got Rick to zip up the back, and took over from Toad at the door while he got his suit on.

Pavarotti had the hoist well secured, the pulleys running smoothly. 'Looks good,' I whispered, running my torch beam over his ropes. 'Rick?'

'Hello.'

'I'm going down. We'll aim to be back at the base of the shaft at midnight. Lift the lid and have a listen then, anyway. If we're not back, try again every half-hour.'

'Roger. Happy landings.'

Feet into the top of the shaft. Ease down the ladder. Once my feet touched, I took a careful look round the floor in my immediate area. No signs of disturbance other than our own. The same damp, muddy smell of decay.

I switched off my head-torch to save the battery, jerked the ladder and felt it rise past me as somebody lifted it clear. Then I heard scuffling noises as the first of the loaded nets – the SCR – started down. I was tempted to peer up the shaft and watch it coming, but didn't fancy being under it if a rope should break or anything went wrong with the hoist; so I stood to one side and waited until the heavy bundle sank gently to the floor, then released the shackle.

Before the second net came down there was quite a pause. I imagined the guys struggling to manoeuvre the heavy case into position, on end above the mouth of the shaft, without letting it bump or scrape. Then more scuffling, scratching noises started, and I switched my torch on again in time to see the bulging net appear.

Once more I released the shackle and twitched the rope, then walked the case out of the way on its corners and laid it gently on its back. Its weight was formidable, and I knew that the third component, section two, was ten kilos heavier still.

The pause was longer this time. The guys were obviously having more problems. Then came a thump, and some strangled curses. At last the scraping noise began again, and I stood clear in anticipation.

Suddenly a loud, sharp *crack* ripped down the shaft. A patter of particles landed by my feet, as if there'd been rapid movement above. Jesus, I thought. Somebody's fired a shot.

I stood frozen. All movement in the shaft had ceased. Some bastard's stumbled on them, I thought. They've dropped him. But they can't close the cover with the pulley ropes in the way. Why the hell don't they get on and lower away? Maybe there are more guys in the yard.

In the silence of the tunnel I could hear my heart beating. Not a sound came from above. Irrationally, I felt that if I moved or spoke I might precipitate disaster. All I could do was keep still.

For many long seconds I waited motionless in the dark. My heartbeat seemed to grow louder and louder. Then at last I heard more noises above. They sounded different from the earlier scrapings, but at least something was happening. More bumps and thuds. I shone my torch quickly up the shaft and saw that the whole of its section was filled by the third and last net. Yet, in spite of the noises, the thing wasn't moving. Had it jammed?

I tried my radio and got no response. My instinct was to yell up the shaft and find out what in hell was going on. But I realised that they couldn't shout back for fear of being heard, so I steeled myself to wait.

In the end movement resumed and the big case came on down, Toad and Pav close behind it.

'What the fuck were you doing?'

'Didn't you hear that?' Pav asked.

'I sure did. Did somebody fire a shot?'

'No, no. That was the main beam in the stable going.'

'Jesus!'

'Yeah. The whole roof dropped several inches. Shit rained down all round. We thought the place was falling in on us.'

'Nobody else heard it?'

'Don't think so.'

'What did you do?'

'Found an old timber lying at the back and managed to get it under as a prop so the beam couldn't drop any lower. Then we carried on.'

We'd lost quite a bit of time already, so we made haste to catch up. First we had the laborious task of getting the cases out of the nets, loading them into the rubber bags, then bundling them into the nets again. Experiments with nets full of sandbags, filled to the equivalent weight, had shown us that the best way of shifting our loads in the confined space of the tunnel would be by fitting slings of wide webbing to the nets, fore and aft, and advancing as a pair in line-ahead, one leaning forward and the other back, to levitate the burden between us. It wasn't easy or comfortable – because the laden net tended to crash into the heels of the person leading and drag the back marker off his feet – but it was better than hauling a huge weight along the floor.

It was obvious that three journeys would be needed, so we set out on the first with me leading, Pavarotti behind, Apple's section one between us, and Toad carrying his own bergen full of tricks. My plan was that, once we reached the site, we'd leave him there with the first half of the device so that he could start preparing it while we went back for the second.

All went well until we were on the downward slope, leading to the river. Then, as the beam of light from my head-torch danced around in front of me, I sensed that something had changed.

'Stopping,' I said.

I slackened off my end of the net and stood still.

'The water,' said Pav. 'It's gone.'

'Exactly. I'm sure my marker was just here somewhere. Look – there it is.' I pointed to the horizontal scratch-mark on the wall.

'Some bastard's been in here draining it,' said Pav incredulously.

'Can't have been.'

'Where's it gone, then?'

'You tell me.'

In fact only some of the water had gone. A lot remained. Soon after we'd moved forward again we saw its surface lying still and black ahead of us. As we advanced to the edge of it I realised that even at its deepest point it no longer reached the roof: there was a gap of about a foot under the arched yellow bricks, and I could see right through to the other side.

'Well, damn!' Pavarotti sounded very Welsh in his indignation. 'The tide's gone out.'

'Tide be buggered!' I snapped. 'We're a thousand bloody miles from the sea.'

'Only joking. We don't need our masks now, that's for sure. Hardly need the suits, even. We can walk straight through with our heads above water.'

'All the better,' I told him. 'But . . . hey, what's this?'

On the right-hand wall ahead of us, just above the water line, the top of an arched recess was showing – clearly the opening to a side-tunnel. It was bricked in, but some of the cement had washed out and I could see water welling in and out through the gaps.

'That's where it's gone,' I said. 'Or where it came in from. Part of the system.'

'So what?'

'So nothing. We carry on.'

And through the flood we went, moving slowly to create as little disturbance as possible. Once in the water the steel case, with air trapped round it inside the rubber bag, was almost floating, and towed along easily.

Very soon we were out of the water and at the site itself. We laid the case down a few feet short of the end of the tunnel, to make sure no debris fell on it when we started digging.

'There you are,' I told Toad. 'It's going in that recess. And there's the shaft for the SCR. You get cracking, and we'll be back.'

One of Toad's unnerving features was his silence, the fact that he spoke so little. You felt that his brain was turning over smoothly like a well-oiled mechanism, but you hadn't a clue what he was thinking. Now, as we left him, he stood there dry-washing his hands without a word.

'I wouldn't mind sealing the bugger down here,' I said as we started out with our second load. 'That'd stop him annoying me.'

By the time we returned, Toad had the lid off the case, and for the first time we got a glimpse of its contents: a terrifying maze of bright blue and white wires snaking round compartments of different shapes. He was wearing latex gloves and a pair of headphones, listening carefully as he touched a probe on one point after another. He had small socket spanners, Allen keys and battery-driven screwdrivers laid out on a mat beside him, occasionally picking one up to tighten or loosen a connection. But as soon as we delivered the SCR, he turned his attention to that, because he was anxious to have it up and working first.

Rather him than me, I thought as Pavarotti and I peeled off our dry-suits and got stuck into the digging. Secretly, though, I felt a bit like a navvy labouring in the presence of a technician who understood things that would always be beyond me.

We were already sweating when we started to dig, and soon we were positively pouring. The ground was neither clay nor rock but something in between – a hard, shaly, grey-brown compound that sometimes broke away in lumps and sometimes split up into flakes with sharp edges. To save batteries we worked with minimum light, using only one torch at a time, whacking our short-handled picks into the face, levering out whatever the blades had got hold of, and shovelling loose spoil away with our hands. From past experience I already knew that Pav stank like a badger when he got hot – Pavagrotti, he was sometimes called – and now, at close quarters and in the confines of the tunnel, he was overpowering. But I realised I was smelling probably as bad to him, and said nothing.

Toad, as always, worked in silence, but after twenty minutes or so he stood up and said, 'This one's ready.'

Out of its cover, the SCR reminded me of the head of a robot, with twin aluminium antennae, linked by a cross bar near the base and rigged on the top like a pair of miniature rugby goal posts. I knew that Toad wanted it installed as high up the ventilation shaft as we could get it, and we'd worked out a means of fixing it in position. From behind our block at Balashika we'd scavenged three pieces of angle-iron and had cut them into twenty-four-inch lengths so that they'd jam across the shaft at an angle beneath it, and lock in position when its weight came down on them.

Standing with my head up the duct, I chopped at the

brickwork above me with hammer and chisel to make three notches that would take the lower ends of the struts. Chips of brick kept flying into my eyes, but the grooves didn't need to be very deep, and after one trial with a length of angle-iron, to make sure it would seat itself properly, we were ready to lift the SCR into place.

As a temporary support, we'd brought an aluminium pole made of short sections that slotted into one another. It was part of another satellite aerial system, and we'd worked out that we could stand it upright, with a circular pad on top, to take the receiver's weight between lifts.

When Pavarotti and I raised the box to waist height, Toad slipped the first section of pole in vertically beneath it.

'OK,' he said, 'rest there.'

Another lift, to chest height, and he got another section in.

The pole, longer now, started to wobble and flex as it took the weight. 'Keep it steady,' said Toad.

A third section propped the receiver at head height. The final hoist, into the shaft, could only be done by one person, pushing up with both arms above his head. I delegated the job to Pavarotti, as he's taller and stronger than me.

'I'll give you what lift I can on the pole,' I told him, gripping it with both hands. 'Ready?'

'Right.'

'Three, two, one – *lift!*'

Up went the black box, scraping against the sides of

the shaft. Toad snapped one more length on to the bottom of the stalk and said, 'OK – steady again.' While I held the pole in the middle, Pav bent his knees, lowering the box on to the pad.

'Angle-irons next,' I said – but when I went to slot them into position, I found we still hadn't got the box high enough. We needed another three or four inches to give us the necessary clearance. While Pav and I both grabbed the pole and lifted, Toad slipped his steel tool-box under the bottom and wedged it there. That gave us the space we needed; I got the struts into position, arranged some bubble-wrap padding on top of them, and called to the others to lower gently.

All that had taken a lot of effort and concentration. When I checked my watch I was amazed at how much time had gone by. Our torch batteries were faltering and needed changing.

'Got to keep moving,' I said as we took a quick break for a drink of water. Our next task was to chip out a gully for the co-ax cables that would connect the SCR to the device – another aggravating job at which only one person could work. Again we took it in turns, going all out for a few minutes, then resting. As soon as we had a channel clear Toad moved in to connect the cables, and we went back to our main excavation.

I'd realised that our best plan was to form the spoil from our cavity into a ramp, so that we'd be able to slide the Apple components up it and into position. The trouble with this was, the ramp itself began to get in our way. Digging became progressively more awkward as we had to lean over our own heap to reach the back of the recess. By the time we had a hole of the right dimensions, we were both knackered.

All this time, when he wasn't tinkering with the cables, Toad remained bent over his charges, tightening, adjusting, listening through his headphones. Then, as we paused, I noticed he was into his hand-washing routine again, a curious look on his face.

'What's the matter?'

'Just trying to imagine it all white in here.'

'White?'

'When the device is detonated, everything in here will be vaporised in blinding white light.'

'Charming. I hope we're not here to see it.'

'You wouldn't see anything,' he said. 'You wouldn't *feel* anything. You'd be obliterated, just like that.' He snapped his fingers – and suddenly, as if he'd conjured up a genie, we became aware of a noise.

'What the . . . ?' Pav was crouching beside me on our ramp of spoil. He raised a hand. 'Listen!'

At first we could feel it rather than hear it: a deep vibration more than a sound, a shudder so low that it seemed to come through our boots. But in seconds it built into an audible flutter, then into a rumble, then into a roar which filled the tunnel and made it shake. The water behind us had long since settled back into stillness after our passage through it. Now I saw a ripple on the black surface, and I was convinced that the roof was about to cave in.

I looked round at the concrete blocks behind us. We

were trapped between the wall and the water in a section of tunnel about fifteen yards long.

The pulsating roar built up still louder until it seemed to come from right over our heads. Particles of brick dust started to fall from the roof. I looked up at the brickwork right above us, fearful that I'd see water break through the joins, expecting to be swamped any minute. I made a grab for my mask and breathing kit.

Into the din Pav yelled, 'Fucking Metro!'

'Bollocks!' I shouted. 'No Metro line anywhere near. I checked it on the street plan.'

'Gotta be a boat, then.'

'A boat?'

'On the river.'

'Some boat.'

We were bellowing at the tops of our voices. Toad stood there looking vacant, but I think he was just as scared as we were. Then I realised that the racket was diminishing, and I felt sure Pav was right: a boat had gone up or down the river, close over our heads.

After that scare, it took Toad only a few more minutes to complete his preparations.

'OK,' he announced, 'we're ready to go.'

Anywhere else, the idea of taking orders from Toad would have made me see red, but here we were entirely in his hands and it didn't bug me at all to follow his instructions. With him directing and helping, we raised the base section of Apple – the heavier of the two – and eased it sideways on to the rough shelf we'd created. That was relatively simple. The harder part was to lift the top section, turn it over in mid-air, then manoeuvre it into position above its mate without letting the two touch or knock together until they were perfectly aligned. The second part weighed just on 150lbs, and even for two fit guys, holding that amount out at arm's length was no picnic.

Toad had had the simple but brilliant notion of bringing three slender spars of wood, an inch thick, to act as temporary buffers, and he laid these across the top of the base unit so that we could lower the top on to them without letting it touch the metal beneath until we were ready. Then, while Pavarotti and I held up one end of the top component, he withdrew the bars one at a time and we lowered away the last inch. As we stood back, he quickly went to work inserting six stainless-steel bolts – one at each corner, one half-way up each long side – and carefully screwed them down with a ratchet-handled socket spanner. Then he plugged one of the two black co-ax cables into the lower half of the package and locked it in position, using an Allen key to turn the sunken nut.

As he took hold of the second wire, I said, 'Listen, Toad. Are you quite certain this fucking thing isn't going to go?'

'Don't worry,' he replied, not even looking up. 'My instinct for self-preservation's as good as yours.'

In went the end of the wire. Again he tightened a nut down.

'OK to cover up?' I asked.

'Hold on. I need to check.'

Once more he put on his headphones, lifted a small flap at the bottom corner of the device and plugged in the lead from a control box slung across his stomach. For a minute or two Pav and I waited, running with sweat, itching with the grit that had worked its way down the necks of our shirts. My anxiety about possible premature detonation wouldn't die down. I could only hope to hell Toad knew what he was doing. Glancing sideways at Pavarotti, I could see him thinking the same.

At last that sly, secret smile stole back on to Toad's face.

'What's happening?'

'I can hear it.'

'What?'

'It's talking to us.'

'What is, for fuck's sake?'

'The satellite.'

'Jesus! What's it saying?'

'I don't know. I just recognise the signal they gave me. Listen.'

He pulled off the headphones and handed them to me. All I got was a distant chirruping and beeping that rose and fell.

'How far up is the satellite?'

'Twenty-two thousand five hundred miles.'

I handed the set back and said, 'OK to cover up, then?'

Toad nodded and began to pack up his tools.

I'd decided in advance that we weren't going to

ponce about mortaring over cracks in the brickwork. The chances of somebody else reaching the site were remote – and anyway, new mortar wouldn't pass a close inspection. Now that Apple was live, I wanted to get the hell out of the tunnel as soon as possible. So we simply covered the casing with a loose mound of bricks and spoil, as though the heap had fallen from the roof, and pushed some lumps into the conduit that we'd cut for the connection, to hold the cables in the duct. Then we collected up our kit and prepared to withdraw.

'Toad,' I said, 'what happens if the water level comes right up and the thing gets flooded?'

'It shouldn't make any difference. Now the units are sealed together they're waterproof. There'd be problems if the level got as high as the SCR, but I don't reckon that's possible.'

There was one last precaution I'd decided was worthwhile. Back at the edge of the water, we used one of the empty rubber bags as a water carrier, filled it, and dragged it to the base of the blocking wall. There we tipped the lot out at once, retreating backwards before a little tide that pursued us down the tunnel. By doing that four times, we washed away every sign of disturbance and left the silt on the floor in a smooth, unbroken carpet.

Then we waded away through the flood.

We were back under the shaft by 0020. We'd missed the midnight rendezvous, but in only ten minutes Rick was due to make his next inspection. Our last batteries were all but spent. As we waited in pitch blackness, my mind wouldn't leave the twinned cases, buried under the mound across the river. I thought of the device as a time-bomb, ticking away towards detonation. I knew that wasn't how it worked, but the idea wouldn't fade. How could we be sure that some idiot in the Pentagon wouldn't set it off by mistake? We had only Toad's word to give us hope that accidents were impossible.

We waited, sweat congealing, grit itching inside our shirts. I found myself thinking of the occasion, years before, when we'd buried an old aunt in the churchyard of my village, in the north of England, how the clods of earth had rained down on her coffin as the gravediggers started to fill the hole above her. There was something uncomfortably similar about the way we'd heaped the spoil back on top of Apple's black and green casing.

On the dot of 0030 we heard a creak of hinges above us, and a beam of light flickered down the shaft.

'Anyone for the up?' Rick called softly.

'Three,' I told him. 'Can't wait to get out. Everything OK on top?'

'Fine.'

'Let's have a rope for the bergens, then the ladder.'

So we came back to ground level. The moment we were clear of the shaft and the cover was closed, Rick slipped the original padlocks into place and scattered hay over the top.

'Where's our transport?' I whispered.

'Dunno exactly. Somewhere close. We've been talking to them. Give 'em a call.'

I switched on my radio and said, 'Green One to Black, do you read me? Over.'

'Black,' came Whinger's voice immediately. 'Standing by for pick-up.'

'Roger,' I went. 'We'll come out two and two, as planned. First pair one minute from now. Second thirty seconds later.'

By then all the nuns – or whoever they were – seemed to have gone to bed. Only a single light was burning at the back of the inner yard; everything else was dark. All the same, we stuck to our plan of coming out in separate pairs.

'Away you go,' I said, and Rick and Toad vanished towards the gate. I counted thirty, then set off with Pavarotti.

Through the gate we turned right and started walking along the pavement. The asphalt gleamed wet after recent rain, and across the river the Kremlin buildings were still floodlit. There was nobody walking on the embankment. The first pair had disappeared – picked up already.

About a hundred yards ahead of us I saw some object lying half on the pavement, half in the road. As we approached, I saw it was a man, or maybe a body, legs out in the carriageway, head in the gutter. From the horrible angle of his feet I could tell that his legs had been run over, maybe several times. One hand was clutching the neck and shattered remains of a bottle, and round it a dark puddle had spread, more like blood than vodka.

'The poor bastard's snuffed it,' said Pavarotti as we passed. But no: at that moment the figure let out a gurgling groan and shifted slightly. On any other night, anywhere else in the world, I'd have pulled him to safety on the pavement. But here, so close to the scene of our infiltration, I didn't want to know.

The contrast between the splendid buildings opposite and the sordid brutality of life in the gutter said everything about the way in which seventy-five years of Communism had brought a vast country to its knees.

We walked on. A second later we heard an engine and saw lights coming up behind us. I tightened my right hand on the butt of my Sig, just in case; but then the lights flicked up and down in recognition. Whinger called, 'I have you visual,' the vehicle slowed, and a second later we were safe on board his Volga.

'Good on yer, Whinge,' I said as we pulled away. 'No problems?'

'The whole place is lifting with drunks – but apart from them, nothing. How about you?'

'We managed it, just about. The bastard's in place. Toad said he could hear the satellite talking to it, so we presume it's all set up. But I tell you – even if it isn't, I'm not going back down that fucking tunnel in a million years.'

'You couldn't smell any worse if you did,' Whinger observed.

'Thanks. And by the way – what made that fearsome racket?'

'When?'

'About an hour ago. It sounded as though an aircraft carrier went up the river.'

'Oh, that. It was just a barge with a load of sand on board.'

'Christ – it scared the shit out of us. We thought the tunnel was coming in.'

'Oh, well.' Whinger sounded unimpressed. 'It didn't. So that's it for tonight, is it? One down and one to go.'

ELEVEN

In the morning we felt, and looked, pretty shattered. When our students noticed some pale faces and started asking questions, we pretended we'd once again been on the piss. In fact we were rapidly gaining a reputation – quite unjustified – as leading piss-artists, and we claimed to have been so smashed that we couldn't remember the names of any of the bars we'd allegedly visited.

In fact we'd got back to barracks by 1.30 a.m., and I'd sent Hereford a coded message through the patrol radio to report the insertion of Apple. Late as it was, the lads were far too hyped up by the success of the operation to feel sleepy. As we had sat round the kitchen table with a brew, Pavarotti had croaked, 'What the fuck have we done?' perhaps partly in amazement because we'd managed it, partly in alarm at the possible consequences. 'That's put the frighteners on the bastards, anyway.'

'Not yet it hasn't,' I'd corrected. 'It may do at some time in the future, but they don't know about it yet.'

'If that thing went off now,' Johnny had said, 'what

effect would it have on us here?'

'Ask Toad.'

Toad, as usual, was hovering at a distance from the rest of us.

'Eh, Toad!' Pav had shouted. 'Would Apple do for us here, now, if it went off?'

'Not immediately,' he'd replied. 'We'd hear it, of course. We'd feel the shockwave. But the big danger would be the radiation.'

'How long would that take to get here?'

'Depends on the wind. An hour?'

'Would we feel anything from it?'

'Not until it was too late.'

'Firekin ell!' went Whinger.

'Duty, old boy. Must do your duty.' Rick could take off the CO to perfection.

We'd gone on shooting the shit till nearly 3.00, so it wasn't surprising that morning found us a bit jaded.

What brought me to my senses was an encrypted message that came in while we were having breakfast. Decoded, it read simply: WEST END CONFIRMS APPLE PIE ORDER. West End was Washington, and the rest was obvious. The Pentagon must have put out a test transmission and made contact with the SCR.

'Can you believe it?' I said to Rick. 'They're talking to the fucking thing, as if we'd buried a person there.'

'I hope they're being polite to it,' he said.

The fact that Apple was up and running gave me a jolt. I suppose I'd been subconsciously hoping that somewhere along the line the system would fail, and that, through no fault of our own, the satellite would be unable to make contact with the bomb. In that happy event we'd be absolved from responsibility.

Speculation was cut off when Anna appeared at our back door proffering a small package.

'I brought you a present,' she began.

'Great! Come in. Have a cup of coffee. We've got a few minutes.'

Perching neatly on a chair in our mess-room, she said, 'This is by way of saying thank you for your help the other day.'

'Oh, come on. We got a big thank you anyway.'

'I know. But this is more important. Your security people in London may like to have it. MI5? Yes – MI5.'

'What is it, then?'

'Only a computer disk. But it contains full details of the Mafia organisation in London.'

'In *London*?'

'Yes. They've made rapid progress there lately. Drugs, banking, prostitution – all the usual things. The London network is spreading fast: links into Paris, Brussels, Amsterdam, Rome and other cities. This is a copy of a disk we picked up in the apartment after the raid. It's in Chechen, I'm afraid, but I'm sure your specialists will manage to translate it.'

'Is Chechen different from Russian, then?'

'Absolutely.' She saw me looking blank, and added, 'All educated Chechens speak Russian, of course. But the languages are entirely different.'

As she talked, my mind was moving at speed.

Another computer disk. Had this presentation got something to do with our own disk that had been destroyed? Was this supposed to be an apology for that accident?

'Well,' I said. 'As you know, that kind of crime isn't really our field. But I'm sure the guys in London will be grateful. Thank you.'

'You're welcome. Please send it with the compliments of the FSB.'

'Sure. I'll get it off today. The guys can take it when they go into town on the post run.'

A couple of the other lads were present at this informal meeting, but as Anna and I walked out and down the steps of the building she and I were alone for a few moments. Suddenly she said, 'I'd like to offer you a more personal thank you as well.' She gave me a sideways, come-on look. 'Will you come and have supper?'

The invitation took me by surprise. Until now she'd been so formal and so correct – so impersonal, although always friendly – that the idea of trying to take her out had almost faded from my mind. Still less had I imagined that she'd ever invite me. Apart from that brief walk we'd taken one lunchtime we'd never been alone. Now, for a moment, I was stuck for an answer.

'You don't *have* to come. That wasn't an order!' She gave me that sidelong glance again and burst out laughing. She also started to raise her right hand, and I thought she was going to take me by the arm; but luckily at that moment Mal came running round the corner with a cry of, 'Forgot my flaming notes.'

Once he'd passed, I looked back at her and said, 'Terrific. I'd like that. When were you thinking of?'

'One day next week, maybe? Friday?'

'Fine.'

'I'll come and pick you up at seven-thirty. I suggest that to avoid gossip, we say we've been summoned to see the Minister.'

In the mean time I was glad to keep our rendezvous with Sasha and his mother. Since he'd asked two of us, Whinger was my obvious choice as No. 2 – but that afternoon he had developed a filthy sore throat, and by the evening he was more or less speechless. So in his place I nominated Rick, first because of his Russian, second because, if he was with us, I'd know for sure that he wasn't shagging Mafia women.

Sasha came and collected us at 7.00, and for this excursion no subterfuge was necessary, so we went off openly, casually dressed in jeans and sweaters.

At first, Sasha was on a high. He had more information about the victims of the raid on the apartment, and it had emerged that one of the five at the table had been Ruslan Beno, another big player in the Chechen mafia.

'You don't mean Keet?' I asked.

'By no means,' Sasha replied quickly. 'This Whale, Keet – I showed you, he was one. His name was Gaidar, one of three brothers, very notoriotous. Beno is also from Grozny, but younger man.'

'I know which he was,' I said. 'That dark young

fellow who got dropped half-way to the door of the living room.'

'Yes. That man.' Sasha turned to me with a big grin. 'Fantastic creeminals, Chechens. They make fabulous amounts of money. For example the Lazanskaya gang, based on Lazania restaurant, here in Moscow – they got enormous riches from stolen cars. They operate very much in Brussels, stealing big cars from diplomats. Then, you know *avizo* system?'

I shook my head.

'A*vizo* is promise note. A bank signs it, to say they will pay so much money. The criminal makes forged promise note in one city, gets it signed, takes it to another city and cashes it. Simple! By such means Chechen *avizovshchiki* made meellions. No – not meellions. Beellions! In early nineties, such kind of Chechen gang got sixty billion roubles.'

The idea of Mafiosi making fortunes obviously excited Sasha as much as did the idea of knocking off big-time players, and he talked enthusiastically for most of our short journey. But then, as we drew near his flat, he fell silent. After a couple of minutes he said, 'Zheordie – you must know. My mother – she is very simple woman. Not very educated. Peasant woman.'

'That's OK,' I said. 'I expect mine was too.'

'You don't remember her?'

'I thought I told you. I never knew my parents. I was brought up by my uncle and aunt.'

That seemed to ease his mind, and his cheerfulness returned.

257

'Here is my house,' he announced as he pulled up outside a tower block. 'Please, this way.'

We walked down an asphalt path between patches of grass, with a few young trees scattered about. Other tall blocks rose all round, at a reasonable distance. In the dark, with only a few lamps glowing here and there, it was difficult to judge the state of the area, but it looked run-down, with litter blown up against the walls of the buildings.

We entered a cavernous lobby with bare concrete walls, and took the lift to the eighth floor. As we went up slowly, juddering and jerking, I sent Rick a glance that said, 'Might try the stairs on the way down.'

Sasha stepped out first, sifting through a bunch of keys, and ushered us towards a door – one of four on a small, dingy landing. Turning the lock, he led us in. 'Please,' he said, 'welcome to my house.'

His apartment was very small. That was my first impression as we stepped straight into the living room, which was cluttered with furniture and lined with shelves. Some held books and magazines, some vinyl albums. In one area Sasha's hi-fi equipment was stacked – Teac amplifier and turntable, dating (by the look of them) from the seventies. At the right-hand end of the room a table was laid for supper: blue-and-white check tablecloth, glasses, knives and forks, but only three place-settings. Beyond it a doorway gave on to a tiny cubicle of a kitchen, and in the opening stood a little old woman, rather bent, with her silver hair swept back into a bun, and wearing a shapeless dress of dark-blue covered in white polka-dots.

'Here is my mother,' said Sasha, following up with a few words of Russian.

Rick, in the lead, did brilliantly, cracking off a '*Dobriye vecher*' (Good evening) and a couple more Russian phrases.

The broad old face – startlingly like Sasha's – creased into a smile, and the woman gave a little bob, inclining towards us. As we shook hands, I asked Sasha her name and he said, 'She is Lyudmila.'

The first few minutes were pretty difficult. Sasha insisted that we sat down, so I perched in an armchair and Rick on a sofa.

Because the flat was extremely warm, I asked what powered the heating. The answer was that all apartment blocks in Moscow are centrally heated – that is, not from boiler rooms in individual buildings, but directly from power stations via underground pipes. Sasha said there was always plenty of heat in winter, even when the outside temperature was twenty below zero, but I noticed that there were no controls or thermostats on the old-fashioned radiators.

'How many rooms d'you have?' Rick asked.

'Living room, here. My mother's bedroom. Bathroom. Kitchen. And balcony.'

'Where d'you sleep, then?'

'There – where you are!' Sasha laughed and pointed at the sofa Rick was occupying. 'I make bed.' He obviously sensed that we found the place rather small, because he added, 'For Moscow, this is *good* apartment.

Besides, I am not very much here: always I have been away in army — in Africa, in Afghanistan, in Chechnya. Not much time in Moscow.'

In spite of his protestations, I felt a pang of guilt at having accepted hospitality in surroundings as humble as these. The idea of living in such cramped quarters eight floors up also brought on a surge of claustrophobia.

Looking round, I realised that there was a huge ginger cat asleep on a shelf above a radiator — a welcome diversion.

'What's he called?' I asked.

Back came the answer, 'Tigr.'

Tiger the cat, Tiger Force. Of course. What other name could he have?

'Isn't it awkward for a cat; living high up like this? I mean — how does he go about his business?'

'No problem,' Sasha answered airily. 'He has box on balcony. But two times every day, my mother takes him down in the lift for walk in the park. Also, he is very good hunter.'

'What — mice?'

'Birds. Here on the balcony. He can go for three flats along. He is very quick' — a swiping motion with one hand — 'he catch many birds.'

I had a fleeting, uncomfortable vision of Tigr missing his grip and toppling eight floors to the ground — only half the distance that wretched Igor had fallen. Even a cat with nine lives would hardly survive such a drop.

When I turned my head to look farther round, I

realised that one wall was dominated by a large sepia portrait photograph, framed in a border of carved wood. I was startled, because the subject looked so familiar.

'Surely that's our old king, George V?' I asked.

'Not English king. Russian king! It is Tsar Nicholas.'

'But it looks exactly like George.'

'*Konechno*. These men were cousins. My mother, she is beeg fan of royal family.'

'But the Russian royal family's long gone—'

'English royals she likes. Prince Charles she likes very much. When Princess Diana was killed she felt *vairy* sad.'

During our conversation Lyudmila had been bringing dishes of food out of the kitchen and setting them on the table. Now she murmured something to Sasha, who jumped up announcing, 'Please! Dinner is ready.'

He went to the head of the table, and indicated that we should sit either side of him. But his mother continued to hover in the doorway, and it soon became clear that she didn't intend to join us.

'Isn't your mother going to eat?' I asked

'Later. She prefers to serve us. Now, please, we have teepical Russian meal. First, *zakuski*.' He gestured lavishly over the spread of dishes. 'Such kinds of smoked fish, fish eggs, smoked meats, cheeses, cucumbers – help yourselves.'

I would have felt bad had I not known about the Mafia dollars which had obviously financed this banquet. As it was, I started eating fast, to provide some bedding for the vodka which Sasha kept pouring freely from a litre bottle. The food was delicious, and the vodka made a perfect foil for the sharp, salty, smoky tastes, especially of red fish roe. Whenever one of us paused for breath Sasha exclaimed, 'Please, eat! Dreenk!' and waved us on.

'Take it easy,' I muttered to Rick. 'I'm sure this is only the start.'

Sure enough, the next course was *bortsch* – thick soup, not full of beetroot as it usually is in England, but more subtle, with a meaty stock for background, small slices of various vegetables floating in it, and a good, peppery overall taste. Next came *bitochki* – meat balls in a rich tomato sauce, with mashed potatoes – and after that a special cake full of nuts, made by our hostess, with which Sasha served sweet Georgian champagne.

Throughout the feast his mother waited on us with embarrassing anxiety to please, bringing new dishes, removing empty ones, watching us, fussing around, gently urging us: '*Yest! Yest!* Eat! Eat!' Sasha, though clearly devoted to her, did nothing to help, but ate and drank to keep up with Rick and me.

By the later stages of the meal, the vodka had got to all three of us. Sasha was gabbling away about how his brother, a taxi driver, had made millions of roubles from illegal sales of booze in the period when Gorbachev tried to bring alcoholism under control. 'It was a kind of *prahibeetion*,' he kept saying. 'Everyone was crazy for vodka.'

'You mean booze was banned altogether?' said Rick

incredulously.

'Not absolutely. But rationed. One half-litre of vodka a week – that was all.'

'Why, though?'

'Russian people were drinking all day, all night. They were falling down in street, running over by cars. They couldn't work. Very many died. Alcohol was our national disease.'

'And did the prohibition have any effect?'

'*Konechno nyet!* Black market was immense.'

Rick began to converse freely with Lyudmila in Russian. I sat listening, smiling genially at everyone, but my spirits were sinking. Once again guilt was clawing at me.

After many entreaties, we finally persuaded Lyudmila to join us for tea, and she sat at the other end of the table, obviously pleased that we had enjoyed ourselves, but still watching anxiously for any possible deficiency in her arrangements.

Suddenly Sasha raised his glass and shouted, 'Your Queen!'

'The Queen!' we echoed, slurping champagne.

'My mother, she say your Queen is beautiful woman.'

'Thank you!'

'My mother is big monarchic.'

'Monarchist.'

'Yes – big *monarknik*. She make beautiful book of royal peoples.' He switched into Russian, asking Lyudmila to fetch her prize tome. With a show of simulated reluctance she got up, opened a drawer and produced a large, cheap scrapbook carefully jacketed in tissue paper, which she laid on the table for our inspection. The pages contained dozens of photographs cut from newspapers and magazines, almost all to do with England, but including a few of Tsar Nicholas II and his family, taken in the last few months of their lives before they were executed by the Bolsheviks in 1918. Towards the end, the cuttings went fast-forwards, and pride of place inevitably was accorded to Diana, Princess of Wales.

'Such kind of tragedy,' Sasha kept saying, repeatedly translating a remark of his mother's.

'I know,' I said. 'But she'd become a bit of a loose cannon.'

'Excuse me?'

I explained that the phrase was used about people whose actions tended to be unpredictable.

'Yes, yes,' said Sasha impatiently. 'But British people loved her. When she died, they came in millions.'

Lyudmila had gone off on another tack. 'Something about the Second World War,' Rick said. 'Can't quite get it.'

'Heetler!' cried Sasha. 'My mother would like to say thank you to British and American soldiers for help in beating Nazis. She thanks you and your fathers. Her father was killed at Stalingrad, famous battle. She does not like Germans. British and American armies very brave.'

'I'm glad to hear that,' I told them. 'I've read in

Communist history books that it was the heroic Soviet army who defeated Fascism single-handed.'

'*Kommunizm!*' shouted Sasha derisively. '*Kommunizm* is shit. My mother does not say that, of course, but it is what she believes. *Kommunizm* all lies and rubbish.' He turned and in Russian loudly sought confirmation from Lyudmila, who nodded and went, '*Da, da.*'

The next thing we knew, Sasha had brought out a bottle of Georgian brandy and was pouring huge slugs. His mother did not touch the spirit.

The conversation became ever wilder, with stories of army brutality.

'You know how they treat prisoners in Russian army? This soldier in Murmansk . . .'

'Murmansk?' yelled Rick. 'Where the f—' He stopped himself just in time and and finished up, 'Where's that?'

'In Russian Arctic. Far north from Moscow. Terrible place. This man is soldier in garrison. Very poor, like I told you – no money. But he is also musician, used to moonlight. He played accordion in restaurant in the evenings to earn roubles. He went *maskarad* - in disguise – with glasses and some beard. But an officer went to the restaurant and recognised him.

'So, to punish him, they put him in a cell, with acid on the floor, deeper every day. No shoes. They wanted to leave him for a week, but after three days his hair had gone grey, so they took him out. Such tortures they make in army.'

It was midnight before we reeled out. We tried to say

we'd walk or get a taxi, but Sasha wouldn't hear of it and insisted on driving us back. When we went down in the lift, Lyudmila came with us to give Tigr an extra run, and as we said goodbye she kissed our hands, holding the cat against her. Rick did his best to thank her gracefully, but I felt too choked to say anything except '*Spasibo! Bolshoi spasibo!*'

Morning brought shock after shock to exacerbate our hangovers. The first came on the news, when somebody heard that the Russian Foreign Minister, had been assassinated. There'd been a shoot-out on Leningradski Prospekt, the main thoroughfare running out towards the north-west. The Minister had been on his way to Sheremetyevo airport, en route for Washington, when a car had come up alongside his Zyl limo – in spite of the police escort – and gunmen had riddled it with bullets. The Zyl had run off the road at speed and crashed head-on into a concrete wall, and the bulletin didn't make clear whether he'd been killed by gunshots or by the impact. In any event, he was dead. So were the driver, two of the bodyguards and one policeman. The gunmen had got clean away, but blame had immediately been placed on 'criminal elements' – in other words, the Mafia.

'Chechens, for sure,' said Sasha, the moment he arrived in camp. 'And why? They make retaliation for losing their Beno. I told you.'

'It's a war, going on in the middle of Moscow,' I said.

'Zheordie, this war will last fifty years.'

Like us, Sasha was feeling rough, and we gave him a cup of strong black coffee before starting for the ranges.

Then Toad appeared, washing his hands like crazy.

'Heard the news?' he went.

'The hit on the Foreign Minister?'

'Yeah – but the stand-off it's creating.'

'What are you on about?'

'It's just been on the BBC World Service. The American Ambassador was in that same car.'

'Jesus!' I sat up. 'Did they kill him as well?'

'Not quite. He's in intensive care. But the United States is threatening to break off relations with Russia. Clinton's been on the hotline to the President, giving him a bollocking. He reckons the whole country's going to ratshit.'

'He's not far wrong,' I said. I felt my gut contracting. Now we're really in it, I thought – and as if to confirm my misgivings, in came another unexpected punch from a different direction.

We were on the point of leaving the building when in burst Rick, looking chuffed to bollocks. 'You'll never believe it!' he yelled. 'Irina's back!'

'Take it easy,' I told him. 'Who's Irina?'

'Natasha's sister. The one who went to the States.'

'What about her?'

'They've got her back!'

'Who have? For Christ's sake, explain.'

'The FBI turned up at her apartment in the Bronx. They grabbed her and a few of her friends and deported them – put them on a plane for Moscow.'

'Ah,' I said. 'This is starting to make sense. You've Tony Lopez to thank for that. He must have got his finger out.'

Then suddenly I thought, Wait a minute. How does Rick know about this? He must have been talking to Natasha. Hadn't I told the prick to lay off?

I felt my face colour up and I said quietly to Sasha, 'If you don't mind, we'll meet you in a couple of minutes outside the armoury.'

He got the message and took himself off. The moment he'd gone, I turned on Rick.

'You stupid bastard! You realise what you've done?'

'No. What's the matter?'

'There's a very good chance you've compromised the entire operation. Listen. How did that woman get hold of you?'

'She phoned.'

'Exactly. And how did she know your number?'

'I'd given it to her.'

'Exactly. Jesus Christ! Are you out of your mind? Who d'you think she's busy giving your number to now?'

'What do you mean?'

'THINK, cunt! Her sister's been in the grip of the Mafia in New York. The FBI have kicked her out, along with a bunch of other slags. They snatched the whole lot and sent them home. But now she's in Mafia territory again, worse than New York. The wide boys here have access to the airlines' passenger lists. They know she's come back to Moscow. They've got her address from before. She's probably got a Russian pimp here anyway.

'In other words, they know precisely where she is. And now, because you can't stop following your prick around, they know precisely where *you* are. The next thing'll be a group of four charming young men with Gepards up their jumpers coming to the gate to ask for a fucking interview!'

I wasn't exactly shouting, but I was talking a lot faster and louder than usual. From the stricken look on Rick's face, I might as well have been hitting him.

'They don't know what I'm doing here,' he said defensively. 'All I told Natasha was that we were making a film.'

'To hell with that. Listen, Rick. You know the score. We're on a military telephone exchange, for fuck's sake. One look at the number must have told them where we are.'

To ease my feelings I started walking up and down. 'Things aren't looking good for you,' I said. 'This is the third time you've screwed up. I told you before – and that was a last warning. I've got a feeling you're on your way home. And if this doesn't end in your getting RTU'd I'll be bloody amazed.'

He started to say something, but I cut him short. 'Don't bloody well argue! There'll be time for that back in the UK. Get down to the armoury and tell Sasha I'm not coming out with the team this morning. I'm going to have to stay here and sort this mess out. In fact, you can ask Sasha to put an hour's delay on the start today.

If any of our lads are down there already, bring them back. Tell them I'm holding a meeting immediately.'

He'd hardly disappeared before I made up my mind. Yes – he'd have to go. He'd already done serious damage, and was too great a liability.

I called the Embassy, asked for the Chargé, and got put through to Kate, the red-headed secretary.

'Is David there?' I asked.

'Not yet. He had to pick something up on his way in.'

'Could you do us a favour, then?'

'I can try.'

'Thanks. It's just that we need to get someone back to UK soonest. I want him on a plane today. Could you be an angel and book a ticket?'

'Return?'

'No – one way.'

'What's the passenger's name?'

'Ellis. Richard Ellis.'

'What flight shall I go for?'

'Any flight – the earliest he can catch. He'll have to get from here to the airport, that's all.'

'All right, then. I'll call you back.'

I urgently needed to speak to the CO in Hereford, but the time there was still only 6.30 a.m., so I decided to wait until he came into his office.

When Kate rang back, she gave me another jolt. 'I'm sorry,' she said, 'I can't get through to any of the airlines. The reservation lines are all jammed.'

'Is that normal?'

'Certainly not. I phoned a friend in the Lufthansa cargo department, and she says there's some sort of a panic on. People are trying to get out of Moscow in a hurry. There are no seats available before next Thursday.'

'Jesus! It must be this thing about the American Ambassador.'

'That's right. There's a lot of really nervous talk coming out of the FCO.'

'Like what?'

'The international situation deteriorating, that sort of thing.'

'Well, listen. I really need this guy on a plane as soon as possible. Can you keep trying?'

'Of course.'

Ten minutes later she rang again and said, 'I got through in the end, but no luck. I tried BA, Aeroflot and Lufthansa, and they're all fully booked. There are no seats available before next week. The only chance is to send him first class. Lufthansa may have a seat at 1520 this afternoon, but it's via Berlin, I'm afraid.'

'That'll do,' I said. 'Take it.' Privately I was thinking, I don't care if he goes via Timbucfuckingtoo, as long as I get him off my hands. The idea of Rick sipping champagne in a first-class seat gave me a royal pain in the arse. But then I consoled myself by thinking, If he's getting binned, back to the Green Army, it's the last time he'll be travelling like *that* for a while.

'I'll charge it to the Embassy for now,' Kate was saying. 'Then we'll send the bill to Hereford. He'll have to collect the ticket from the Lufthansa desk at the airport. He needs to be there by 1400 at the latest.'

'No bother. I'm very grateful to you. Has David appeared yet?'

'Just this moment. D'you want a word?'

'Yes please.'

I hung on, then heard Allway say, 'Good morning.'

'Good morning,' I went. 'Can you fill me in on what's happening?'

'The situation's pretty confused at the moment.'

'What's causing the panic?'

'Clinton said something about Russia being on the point of becoming ungovernable.'

'Don't you feel that's exaggerated?'

'Personally, yes.'

'So what line's London taking?'

'No special line yet. But Washington is advising Americans to leave unless they have urgent business here. Are you people all right out at Balashika?'

'For the time being. Everything's been going fine. I don't know how this will affect things, though.'

'No,' Allway said cryptically. 'I get the impression that your team may be off home fairly soon.'

'Oh, really?' I went. 'We'll have to wait and see.'

I rang off, and called Hereford on the secure satellite link. By good luck the CO was already at his desk, and sounding cheerful.

'Hi, Geordie,' he went. 'How are things?'

'Rough. You've heard the news?'

'Yes. It sounds a bit dicey. How does it feel at that end?'

'Can't tell yet. But listen, Boss. That's not what I'm calling about. It's Rick Ellis. I'm sending him home.'

'Oh God!' he said. 'What's happened?'

I told him in short, sharp sentences. He didn't query my decision, and I was glad of that. He saw my point. I summed up by saying, 'He's dropped us right in it. At the very least, the Mafia know there's a Brit presence in the barracks here. That means there's a threat to our lads, quite apart from the potential disruption of Operation Nimrod.'

'Are you going to need a replacement?'

'Not worth it. We can manage as we are.'

'OK, then. I'll see Rick as soon as he gets back.'

'Do you need a report immediately?'

'It can wait. I'm sure you've got plenty on your hands. You can give me a full statement when you get back.'

'Will do.'

'What's the state of play with the operation?'

'Apple's in place, as you know. We've got a site for Orange, and we're just waiting for a chance to do the insertion.'

'Sooner the better,' said the CO sharply. 'If the situation gets much worse we may have to pull you out.'

'Roger. But – Boss?'

'Yes?'

'There's no chance the Yanks are going to start playing funny buggers and press the button on Apple?'

'Don't be silly, Geordie. Things aren't *that* bad.'

273

Then suddenly he switched mode and made what seemed to me a lousy joke. 'But if they were, you'd be the last people to know anything about it.'

'Ha ha,' I said.

'Sorry, Geordie.' He realised he'd pissed me off. 'Seriously, things look OK from this end.'

'They don't from here, I can tell you. People are pouring out of Moscow like fucking lemmings.'

'Is that right?'

I told him about the airlines, then said, 'What I'm saying is this. Isn't that exactly what these bloody devices are for – to use as blackmail if things get tense, to bring the buggers to their senses in an emergency?'

'Precisely. But we're nowhere near the stage of using them yet.'

'I hope to hell you're right. Once Orange is underground we're going to be in the killing zone ourselves, never mind any radiation that might drift this way from Apple.'

'Take it easy, Geordie. Your imagination's running away with you.'

'I hope you're bloody well right.'

The lads reassembled, looking rather surprised. Having sent Rick away to his own room, I got everyone sat down and went straight into it.

'I'm sorry to say that there's a high probability Operation Nimrod's been compromised.'

Everyone sat very still. Several seconds passed before Whinger said, 'For Christ's sake, what's happened?

Have they found the bomb?'

'I hope not. But next worst: Rick's sent the Mafia a message saying the SAS is in town.'

'Don't be stupid!' went Whinger.

'I'm not,' I told him. 'I exaggerated slightly, but only a little.'

I explained what had happened. Mal – careful, steady Mal – surprised me by starting to stand up for Rick. 'If he stuck to the cover story about the film, we don't need to worry.'

'We bloody do! That woman's obviously in the hands of some pimp or other. It'll take the guy about ten seconds to recognise the number Rick gave her. I bet you the Mafia have got us pinpointed already.'

'Eh!' said Johnny. 'Let's fuck off out of here while the going's good.'

'That's what Rick's going to do,' I said. 'I'm sending him home right away. The lucky bastard's flying first class because there are no other seats. And Toad – I want you to take him to the airport. OK?'

Nobody put up any good reason for keeping Rick on the team. Mal saw the point of what I was saying and finally agreed that Rick should go. The only argument was about his share of the Mafia dollars – and in the end we voted that he should still get it, provided he kept his mouth shut about the whole episode when he reached home.

So the day's training got under way an hour late. I stayed in barracks, fighting to catch up with paperwork – mainly the course reports on the students, which we were supposed to be continuously updating.

All morning I kept remembering how, at the climax of the siege of the Libyan Embassy in London, the police negotiators had kept the terrorists in play by telling them direct lies: that the Libyan Ambassador was on his way, that a coach was coming to take them to Heathrow, and so on. Even Trevor Lock, the policeman trapped inside the building, couldn't get any straight answers from the police. Several times he asked for an assurance that the building wasn't going to be assaulted – and at the very moment when the SAS men were laying out their abseil ropes on the roof, the cops promised him blind that all they were trying to arrange was the villains' getaway.

Now we seemed to be in an unpleasantly similar situation. The boss would go on saying, 'No, no, Geordie, everything's fine,' until the very moment when Clinton or some other jerk in Washington pressed the button. The CO was bound to toe the line. But for us poor sods at the sharp end it was different. Maybe we'd see a brilliant white flash. Maybe we wouldn't.

At midday I called the Chargé again and heard that the American Ambassador had died from his wounds. All US flights into Moscow had been suspended, and American citizens advised not to travel to Russia by any means. More and more I was needled by apprehension that this whole train of events had been set off by us – by our participation in the hit on the apartment. Then I told myself that if we hadn't gone along with it the result of the shoot-out might have been much the same, with a few more casualties to the forces of law and order – but still the feelings of guilt were building up.

Before Toad left I took him aside and asked, 'Is there any way you can disable Apple?'

'Not unless we go back down the tunnel,' he replied. 'Now it's live, it's live.'

TWELVE

We seemed to have two options. One was to call in an RAF aircraft and lift the whole team out, taking Orange with us, on the grounds that the situation was too dangerous to stay. That definitely went against the grain: it would be unprofessional and would smell of panic. If we quit, we'd have failed in one of our main objectives.

The second option was to carry out our task and get Orange into place as soon as possible – after which we could assess the position again, and decide whether to carry on with the training course or leave immediately.

To reach a decision we held a Chinese parliament out in the open, in the middle of the assault course, well away from any bugs. Toad, as usual, remained silent, but the rest of the lads were emphatically for Option Two. The only disagreement was about what we should do once we'd buried Orange in the old air-raid shelter.

Whinger, croaking through his laryngitis, was all for playing it straight. 'We might as well see the course through. Nobody's going to push any button. They wouldn't fucking well dare.'

Johnny and Pavarotti agreed with him. But Mal, who'd done a two-year tour attached to the US Marines, had a low opinion of American decision-taking in general, and reckoned somebody in a key position in Washington might easily lose his cool under pressure. Dusty and Pete tended to go along with that, and so did I. That meant that three of us were for remaining on the team task, and four for opting out: the narrowest possible majority. In the end we agreed to debate the matter again once Orange had gone down.

Our plan for the second device was perfectly simple. Whinger and I had already decided we couldn't start digging on the site before we were ready to insert: otherwise somebody might see the spoil. Therefore, we'd fetch the components from the Embassy that evening, bring them to the camp, stash them temporarily, and take them out to the shelter the next night, starting and finishing the insertion in one shift.

Or so we thought.

For this next run we adopted the same tactics as before: using both cars and keeping well apart, in radio contact. We left Balashika at 8.00 p.m., and reached the Embassy at 8.55. Taking our normal precautions, Whinger put in a drive-past with the grey Volga; he had Johnny riding passenger with him, and when they reported all clear, Pavarotti, Toad and I went in with the black vehicle to load the components. We'd done what we could to make the Volgas more roadworthy, getting them both a service and replacing three of the worst tyres.

As we drove along the embankment and over the line of the tunnel, I got a peculiar fizzing sensation in my stomach.

I'd already sent word to the Chargé that we were coming in. My spiel had been that, because of the international tension, we wanted to recover the last of our bits and pieces so that we'd have everything in one place if the Regiment decided on a quick evacuation. Allway had said that was OK by him: there'd be no one to meet us, but he'd leave word with security, and we could hand them the keys of the garage on our way out.

That suited us fine. We loaded up at leisure, locked the door and handed in the keys. In the car, before I drove off, I got Toad to hand me Orange's Rat, and clipped the device to my belt.

We were rolling again less than ten minutes after we'd arrived. Pav was beside me in front, Toad in the back.

'Clearing now,' I called to Whinger.

'Roger,' he answered. 'I'll fall in behind.'

On our way out through the city centre I couldn't distinguish his lights from all the others behind us; but I knew he was there, because we kept exchanging messages. The traffic began to thin out, and on the highway the vehicles were well spaced. Fine rain had set in, reducing visibility. The black Volga wallowed on the wet road like a boat under its heavy load, and I kept our speed down to sixty-five ks to give myself time to avoid potholes. That meant we were one of the slowest cars on the road, and we kept getting overtaken, but I felt in no particular hurry.

So we cruised on until we were within about five ks of base. Out in the country the rain was heavier, the air murkier. We'd just gone under the outer ring-road when everything went ballistic.

'Look out,' said Pav. 'There's a flashing blue light up ahead.'

At the same moment Whinger came on the radio with, 'I think we've got a tail.'

I glanced in my mirror and exclaimed, 'Jesus! I think we have one too. There's a police block up ahead as well. Listen, Whinge. We're being pulled in by the GAI. Get off the road and wait out.'

In the road ahead, beside the vehicle with the flashing blue lamp, a man was waving us down with one of those white-ended batons. As I braked, I saw in the mirror that the car behind us had swung in close on our tail.

'Shit, Pav,' I said. 'Looks like the GAI are having a purge. What do we do?'

'Bluff our way. Stop – if he tells us to – for Christ's sake. Don't piss him off – otherwise we'll be in the nick for resisting arrest.'

A man in grey GAI uniform, with the red stripe down the side of his pants, was guiding us in towards the verge. As I pulled up, another man appeared beside the window and said, '*Dokumenti.*'

I reached down under my seat for the package Anna

had made up for each car and handed it to him. He took it, but motioned for me to go with him to a hut at the edge of the highway. Then he started saying, '*Klioucha, klioucha,*' and making twisting movements with his hand.

'Keys,' said Toad. 'He's after the keys.'

'Suspicious bastard,' I said. 'He thinks we're going to try and drive off.'

'Ah, fuck it!' exclaimed Pavarotti. 'Shall I deal with him?'

'It's all right,' I said. 'I'll go. You two sit tight.'

I took out the ignition key and handed it through the window. I was on the point of getting out when I remembered the Rat. Better leave it in the car, I thought. Then, measuring the distance to the hut by eye, I thought, No – that isn't a hundred feet. It'll be OK.

As I stepped out of the car I glanced into the back, and was reassured to see that the component beside Toad was covered by an old blanket.

I started to follow the GAI officer. He pointed towards the hut, gesturing to me to carry on. Then he turned back to the Volga.

The hut was set just off the tarmac, down a bit of a bank and on the edge of the wood. At first my main concern was that I wouldn't understand what the cops were asking, and I wished to hell my Russian was better. Then, second by second, step by step, I began to get the feeling that something was wrong. The hut didn't look like one of the regular GAI stations, which were lit up like little guardrooms. This thing was only a roadsmen's cabin, and dark. Besides, the other cars parked by it weren't GAI vehicles, but ordinary saloons. Worst of all, there were at least five men standing in the shadows, not in GAI uniform, but wearing leather jackets that gleamed when the headlights of a vehicle went by on the road. There was something odd about their body language; their postures unnaturally rigid and alert.

At that instant I suddenly heard, through my earpiece, Pavarotti call, 'CONTACT!' Before I could react, the guys in front of me started to move in my direction. I glanced over my shoulder at the Volga and saw two men with sub-machine guns closing in from either side.

I jabbed my pressel switch and said sharply, 'Contact! Contact! Whinger, in here! Get in! Get in!'

'Negative,' came his answer. 'We can't. We're in a contact too.'

Over the radio I heard a rattle of shots. An instant later the shots came live, through the air.

The five men on the edge of the forest were in a ragged group only ten feet from me. They started moving towards me. Instinctively I pulled out my pistol and dropped the nearest one with a single shot to the forehead, which jerked his head violently backwards.

I looked back at the Volga. Rounds cracked past my head. As I went down on one knee. I could see that the pseudo-policeman was at the driver's door. A second guy was trying to force his way into the back seat.

Another burst ripped past me. I felt a sharp tug and a stab of pain in my left shoulder. The impact spun me round, only to find one of the others almost on top of me. Automatically I fired a double tap into his chest, and he went down, but he was so close that his impetus carried him past me, and he narrowly missed me as he fell. I then emptied my magazine into the area where his three remaining mates had suddenly taken cover, and sprinted the last few yards for the safety of the woods.

The trees were pines, fairly well spaced. By luck I went between the first few, then ran smack into spiky dead branches, ripping my face. I backed off, skirted left and kept going.

Behind me, pandemonium erupted. Men began yelling like lunatics. Engines started up and revved furiously. Tyres scrabbled and squealed as cars pulled away. Somebody cracked off a few more bursts from a sub-machine gun, and rounds came snapping through the trees, but by then I was a hundred metres into the woods, and relatively safe.

For a few seconds I lay prone, head-on to the road in line with a thick trunk, gasping for breath, more from shock than from exertion. 'Jesus!' I went. 'What the fuck happened?'

Out on the highway everything had gone quiet. I jabbed the pressel of my radio and called, 'Black to Grey. Can you hear me?'

'Grey,' went Whinger. 'We've broken the contact. We're mobile.'

'Where are you?' I gasped.

'Heading on in your direction. Where are *you*?'

'In the forest behind the hut. Give me one minute. I'll come back to the roadside a hundred metres past the hut.'

'Roger.'

I tore through the trees, parallel with the road, with my left arm raised in front of my face to ward off branches. I had a stinging sensation on the outside of my left shoulder, and I could feel blood running down my side. But the arm was working, and the wound didn't feel bad. Already my night-vision was establishing itself, and I could see enough to make rapid progress.

I counted a hundred and fifty steps, then turned left, running back towards the road. I burst out of the trees and looked back, to the left. I was about the right distance from the hut. Through the rain I saw one car coming fast towards me. In my earpiece Whinger said, 'OK, we have eyes on you.' I stepped farther out into the road, and the car swung in towards me. As it pulled up, I saw that windscreen and rear window had been shot out.

'Get in! Get in!' shouted Whinger. 'Where's the other Volga?'

'They've got it.'

'Jesus! The bastards went that way. Back into town.'

'After them!'

I dived into the back and slammed the door.

'Watch your hands on the glass,' yelled Johnny. 'It's all over.'

With a howl of tyres Whinger spun the car and

screamed up to high revs in each gear. Wind came whistling through the cabin, fore to aft.

Johnny was trying to tell me something, but with the internal slipstream roaring it was hard to hear. Also, after the gunshots, I was slightly deaf.

In a few seconds we passed a car burning on the other side of the road.

'Who's that?' I shouted.

'That was the lot that came for us,' went Whinger. 'What happened to *you*?'

'Ran straight into an illegal VCP. They had a man out in GAI uniform, waving us down. He demanded documents and keys. Made me go with him towards the hut. Then I saw all these other guys on the lurk. That was the moment you called "Contact". What about you?'

'This car came up behind. Somebody put a burst through the rear window. The rounds must have gone right between me and Johnny, on out the front . . .'

'Slow down!' I shouted.

We'd come round a bend. Through the murky dark we could see nearly half a mile up a long straight ahead. There wasn't a car in sight.

'Either they've got right away or they've pulled off into the forest. Look for side-roads. There! Just ahead. Stop!'

Whinger slid to a halt across the mouth of a dirt track that ran into the trees at a right angle to the highway. Johnny and I leapt out, flashing torches over the surface in search of fresh tyre marks.

'Nothing doing,' I called.

We jumped back in and set off again.

'OH this fucking car!' Whinger groaned, exasperated by the lack of acceleration.

'Keep talking,' I told them.

'The car that was harassing us,' went Johnny. 'I dropped the driver with my Sig. That fucked them. They were struggling to get him out of the driving seat, so I cracked a couple more rounds off into the front of the car. Bit of luck – the thing blew up. Bullet must have severed a fuel pipe. The whole thing went *woof*—'

'THERE!' I yelled.

Another small road had loomed up. Whinger hauled on the wheel and we squealed round. This track was surfaced and quite smooth – no point in looking for tyre marks. We followed it for a minute, scanning frantically for any spur or layby among the trees where the villains could have pulled in. Then I shouted, 'This is fucking useless. We've lost them. You're sure they turned back?'

'Yeah, yeah!' Whinger was emphatic. 'Just after you'd called for the pick-up, a whole shower of cars went flying back towards Moscow. A dozen at least, going like the clappers.'

'Was the Volga in among them?'

'Couldn't tell. There was a Merc at the front. The rest were in a bunch. Really motoring.'

My mind was churning. Blood had reached my waist and was sogging round my belt.

'Back to base?' Even Whinger sounded temporarily defeated.

'I guess so.'

'What happened to Pav and Toad?'

'I couldn't tell. The last I saw of them they were both still in the vehicle, with an armed guy on either side of them. I tried to get back to them but I was taking fire from the car behind ours. I got a nick in the shoulder, as it was.'

'Not serious?'

'I don't think so. More of a burn, really. It's bleeding, though.'

As we drove the short distance back to camp, the scene ran through my mind again and again like a closed loop of film. Already I was blaming myself for making mistakes. Maybe I should never have got out of the car. Maybe I should have just driven off. But then, if I had, our lumbering vehicle would certainly have been cut out by one or more of the faster cars I'd seen lined up. But again, once I *had* got out – once I realised things weren't right – maybe I should have made a greater effort to get back to the Volga. But if I'd done that, I'd almost certainly have ended up getting shot dead. The guy in the back-up car couldn't have gone on missing for ever.

'Where's the Rat?' Whinger asked suddenly.

'Christ!' I felt for it, on my belt. 'I've still got it. It must have activated the bomb's alarm signal. The thing will be transmitting by now. I hope to hell the Yanks can track it.'

Before the lift my moral confusion had been bad enough: now it was acute. What the hell was I to tell Anna and Sasha? Obviously we couldn't conceal the fact that we'd lost two guys, or that they were probably in Mafia hands. Apart from anything else, we needed the Russians to launch a search.

The lads we'd left in camp were appalled by the news. As we compiled a coded message for Hereford, they got a brew on and we brought them up to speed on what had happened.

My shoulder wound turned out to be little more than a groove cut through the skin. Dusty got out his medical pack, swabbed it thoroughly, bombed it with disinfectant and smacked a wound-dressing over the top.

'You'll live,' he pronounced. 'But you were lucky. A couple of inches lower and your shoulder would have been a mess.'

'If it *was* Rick's whoring about that put them on to us,' I said, 'he wants to be well away from Hereford before we get back. If I see him I'll bloody murder him.'

'Maybe the Mafia have been doing better surveillance than we thought,' Mal suggested. 'Maybe they'd got us marked down anyway. D'you think somebody slipped a hundred dollars to one of the guys on the gate, to shop us?'

'It was that fucking hit on the flat that did it,' said Whinger savagely. 'Somehow the bastards got wind of the fact that we were involved.'

'What if we got followed to the church?' said Dusty. 'Maybe there was a dicker out, somebody who saw us going in and out of the Embassy.'

'Possible,' I agreed. 'Jesus – now I suppose we'd better get our arses back there and check the padlocks on the shaft.'

I thought for a moment and changed my mind. 'Cancel that,' I said. 'There's no way the Mafia could have known about Apple or Orange. Our security on that front's been one hundred per cent. Even if they got eyes on the cars going to and from the Embassy they couldn't have known what we were doing.'

'Extortion,' said Pete. 'That's what we were up against. They're after money. They've scented a chance of making a quick fortune. And now, in handing them Orange, we've given them the biggest fucking lever in the world. God alone knows what ransom demand they'll make: ten million? A hundred million?'

I said, 'The question is, will they go public, or will they do it under cover?'

'If they go public we're buggered,' said Dusty. 'If they start honking about how they're holding two SAS guys, the whole operation's blown.'

'Will they realise what the components are?' asked Mal. 'After all, they're not nuclear specialists.'

'No,' said Dusty, 'but I bet they'll have access to someone who is. It won't be long before they find out. And anyway, they've got Pav and Toad to tell them.'

There was a moment's silence. Although nobody spoke, I know we were all thinking the same thing: that our guys were going to get badly knocked about. They were in for a hard time, whatever happened. And if they refused to talk, there was a high risk they'd be topped. We needed to find them fast.

We had local maps out on the table, but they were precious little use.

'Let's think where they're likely to put the thing,' said Johnny.

'Lock-up garage, probably,' Whinger suggested. 'Leave it in the car, drive in. Easy.'

'What about its alarm signal?' Mal asked. 'Will that still reach the satellite if the device is inside a building?'

'I don't know. Toad could tell us. Listen, I'm going to call Anna. She can get a search going.'

'What are we going to tell her?' Mal, ever careful, had been making notes with pencil and pad.

'That two guys have been lifted.'

'What about the bomb?'

'Not a whisper.'

I had to use the local line, which I knew was insecure. But that now seemed the least of our worries. I tried the emergency number she'd given us, and got some Russian-speaking female.

'Anna,' I said several times. 'Anna Gerasimova.'

A torrent of Russian came back.

'Y*a Anglichani*,' I went. '*Ni ponemayo*.'

Another incomprehensible rush of words. For a moment I half-wished Rick was with us. At last the woman stopped and said, '*Moment*.' A second later a man came on, speaking slow, heavily accented English.

'Anna no here.'

'Can you give her a message, please?'

'A message? Yes. It is what?'

'Telephone Zheordie immediately.'

'Zheordie?'

It was beyond me to spell the name in Russian letters, so I repeated it several times, gave the number slowly, and rang off.

'Jesus!' I gasped. In the state I was, any small delay seemed a massive aggravation.

'What about Sasha?' asked Pete.

'Good idea.'

As the number rang, I thought of old Lyudmila and her bloody great cat, tucked up there on the eighth floor.

'*Da?*'

'Sasha, it's Geordie. Sorry to bother you, but we're in big trouble.'

I told him what had happened. As soon as he got the gist of it, he said, 'No, it is impossible. Not real.'

'It's real enough,' I told him. 'They've gone.'

'I come in.'

'Well, if you can.'

'No problem. Twenty minutes.'

'Thanks.' I rang off and said to the lads, 'Sasha's on his way. Watch yourselves when you're speaking to him. This is where we need to start juggling the story.'

'The Embassy,' said Whinger. 'What about them?'

'Christ, yes. Better inform them.'

'What about the bomb?' Mal asked in his voice of doom.

'Same thing. Not a whisper.'

'They know you went in to collect kit,' Mal persisted.

'OK, we collected it.'

'So where is it now?'

'It was in the car that got through.'

Even as I dialled the Embassy number on the secure link, I felt amazed at how easy it seemed to be to invent plausible falsehoods. They were fairly whipping off my tongue. At the same time, I was aware of how easy it would be to make one fatal mistake and bring the whole edifice of lies crashing down.

'British Embassy,' said an unfamiliar voice.

'Geordie Sharp,' I said. 'I need to speak to the Chargé.'

'I'm sorry. He's not here. It's the duty officer speaking. Can I help you?'

'I need to talk to him urgently.'

'I'm afraid he's not available on this system.'

'Can you ask him to come in, then?'

'Is it that urgent? Can't it wait till the morning?'

'No.'

There was a pause. Then the guy said, 'All right. In that case, I'll pass the message. Has he got your number?'

'He'll have it there in the office, yes.'

I rang off, thinking of Hereford. Where the hell was the boss? He was taking his time to come through. Maybe he was out at a party. By now it was midnight – 9.00 p.m. in the UK. Not late.

Mal looked up from his notes and asked, 'Who's controlling the tracker satellite?'

'The Americans,' I told him. But his question prompted a sudden idea.

'Jesus!' I exclaimed. 'That's a thought, Mal. I'm going to call Tony Lopez right away.'

'Who's he?'

'American, ex-SEAL. He was seconded to the Regiment before you joined. Now he's working for the CIA. It was him who put the ferrets in after Rick's girlfriend's sister. But he's a hundred per cent on side. He'll help. What time is it in Washington?'

'Five o'clock,' somebody said. 'Correction. Four.'

'He'll still be in the office.'

I jumped up, dug out his number and punched it in. Two rings, and an American voice answered.

'Tony!'

'I'm sorry, sir. Major Lopez is in a meeting.'

'Break in on him, please. This is an emergency.'

'May I ask who's calling?'

'Just say Geordie.'

'One moment, sir.' The guy had that ultra-polite, deferential American manner that gives me a pain in the arse.

I put my hand over the mouthpiece and said, 'He's coming.'

A second later Tony was on the line – but he didn't sound himself. His voice was quick and sharp.

'Tony,' I began, 'we're in the shit.'

'OK, I know what it is.'

'You *know*?'

'Sure. Hereford have been in touch. That's what we're discussing right now. The satellite tracker system's up and running.'

'Thank God. Can you let us know if you get a line on where they've taken the thing?'

'Sure can.'

'OK. I'll speak to you later.'

As I replaced the receiver, the phone rang.

'Geordie?' It was the night comms clerk in Hereford. 'I've got the CO for you.'

'Put him on.'

The first thing the boss wanted to know was which two guys we'd lost.

'Pavarotti and Toad,' I told him.

'Toad!' he said. 'Jesus!'

'Exactly. The next thing's going to be a ransom demand. We've got to recover Orange, and fast.'

'The Americans are tracking it already.'

'I know. I just spoke to Tony Lopez in Washington. He seems to be on the tracking team. Boss – what do you advise?'

'Very difficult. You'd better stand by to come out. The political situation's extremely volatile. The Director's coming here for eight tomorrow morning. We're going to take a decision then on whether or not we pull you.'

'We can't come out with two guys missing.'

'I don't know. We might take the view that it's better to lose two rather than risk losing nine. The shit's hit the fan in London as well.'

'Why's that?'

'The computer disk you got. The information on it has sent the police ballistic, in London and New York. They've made fifteen arrests in London alone.'

'Russian Mafia?'

'Leading players.'

I took a deep breath. Then I said, 'How does that affect us?'

'Too early to say. Your kidnap could be a reprisal for the arrests in Europe. But losing Orange complicates the issue still more. We've got a QRF on standby. We may establish an FMB in Berlin in any case. That would put them within three hours of you.'

I told him I'd be through again if there was any news, and hung up. Seconds later Sasha appeared, and we started going through everything again. He was upset about the disappearance of our guys, and kept apologising.

'Come on, Sasha,' I said, forcing myself to smile. 'They're not dead yet. We'll get them back.'

Before he could answer, the satellite phone beeped again. It was Tony.

'We got it!' he announced triumphantly. 'Your hardware's still with you.'

'Wait one.' I looked up and saw Sasha watching me eagerly.

'Sasha,' I said. 'It's our base in Hereford. This may take a few minutes. Could you get on the local line and set up a police search?'

'*Konechno!* Immediately!' He sprang to his feet and

headed for the other phone. I felt a turd, lying to his face – but what else could I do?

'Tony,' I said. 'Carry on. Where is it?'

'In the south-western sector of the city. We can give you the location within a couple of hundred metres.'

'Fantastic! Can you give me the co-ordinates?'

'Sure. Ready?'

'Fire away.'

He read out a series of figures, which I took down and checked back. 'Brilliant,' I said. 'Let me know if it moves.'

'Roger – and good luck.'

'Miracles of modern science,' I told the lads. 'Correlate these on to a street plan and we can go right in and get them.'

'Wait a minute,' said Mal. 'How do we know this? I mean, what are you going to tell Sasha?'

Once again a plausible lie rose effortlessly to the surface of my mind. 'Pav has a tracking device fitted into his jacket,' I said. 'Some of our guys always do, in case this very thing happens.'

'Yeah, but if we organise a hit, with the Russians, they're going to find Orange at the end of it.'

'We'll play that one when we get to it . . .' I broke off because Sasha reappeared.

'General police alert,' he announced. 'All Moscow forces to search. I give car number. And Zheordie, I make suggestion.'

'What's that?'

'We can stop training course, freeze everything.

297

Instead of lessons, we make students rescue your hostages.'

'Great idea!' I went. Privately I thought, Christ!

Luckily I was distracted by yet another beep from the secure phone.

This time it was the Chargé. Hell, I thought when I heard his voice. I can't send Sasha out again. Then suddenly I realised I didn't need to: the Embassy knew nothing about Orange.

I started into the whole spiel again. I said that Sasha had got a search under way, that I'd been through to Hereford, and that we were expecting a decision about a possible pull-out in the morning.

'Yes,' said Allway. 'Your people were talking to us earlier in the day.'

He nattered on for a minute about the general situation, which he described as 'jittery'. As he spoke, I was thinking, Do I tell him we've traced the signal? No, I decided. If we get our guys back, yes, of course, we tell him, but there's nothing definite enough yet.

It was just as well I didn't bother, because within five minutes of that call Tony had come through again to say, 'It's moving.'

'Ah Jesus!'

'Yep. I've got it on a computerised map screen. Heading south-west. It's already five miles out from the location I gave you. You want to stay on the air till we see what's happening?'

'Sure. I've got the map in front of me.'

'OK. It's coming up to a place called Vnukovo. Hey

298

– wait a minute. That's marked as an airfield.'

'Vnukovo,' I said to Sasha. 'What is it?'

'Main airport for southern departures.'

'Tony,' I said. 'It's Moscow's airport for the south.'

'Then I guess they're putting it on a plane. Target now stationary. Can you organise an intercept?'

'What – in the air?'

'No, on the ground.'

'I'll ask.'

I put the question to Sasha. He frowned at the size of the problem, but headed back to the local phone.

'How far are you from that field?' Tony was asking.

'At least an hour. Our Russian contact's phoning the police down there.'

'Target still stationary. If it is Mafia, they'll have a big armed escort round it.'

'Precisely.'

'There's a major highway heading out of the city due south–west. Which side of that is the airfield?'

'Immediately to the north.'

'That's it, then. They're on the field.'

He went quiet for a few moments, then added sharply, 'Signal lost. Wait a minute . . . no. Confirm signal lost.'

'What does that mean?'

'Most likely they've loaded Orange into a plane. That would mask the transmission. Yep. It's gone dead. I'll come back if we get it again.'

'Thanks, Tony.'

I found Sasha glued to the other phone, talking hard,

as if he was having to galvanise the police into action against their inclination. I left him at it, returned to the mess room and called Hereford again.

'Boss,' I said. 'It looks like they're being taken south.'

He already knew that the moving signal had given out at Vnukovo, and had come to the same conclusion.

'What destinations does that place serve?'

'Rostov-on-Don, Sochi, other Black Sea resorts.' I reeled off names that Sasha had told me, and added, 'Word here is that the villains could be Chechens.'

'Who says that?'

'I don't know . . .' I hesitated, suddenly aware that I was on the point of dropping myself in the shit by revealing our participation in the bust on the flat. 'The idea came from Sasha, our main contact here.'

'Chechnya!' went the CO. 'Bloody hell. If that's where they're heading, we'd better scrub Berlin and start looking for jumping-off points further south.'

Sasha reappeared, scratching his head.

'Private jet has just made take-off from Vnukovo,' he said. 'Unofficial departure. No clearance from tower – no lights, nothing. This can only be Mafia.'

'Can the air force track it?'

He raised both hands in a gesture of helplessness. 'I have passed message. But you know, little co-operation between police and armed forces . . .'

'These criminals,' I said. 'D'you think they're Chechens? Is this a reprisal for our raid on the apartment?'

He nodded vigorously. 'I think so. Yes. These

Chechens will demand big money for ransom.'

'When would you expect them to start?'

'Tomorrow morning.' He looked at his watch. '*This* morning – later.'

'Sasha,' I said. 'I'm afraid a couple of guys got killed in the contact on the highway.'

'Only Mafia!' he said, as if they'd been rabbits. 'No problem.'

I saw him yawn and said, 'Listen – you've been great. Thanks for coming in.'

'It is nothing. Zheordie, I am sorry.'

'Don't start all that again. It's not your fault. Off you go now.'

I ushered him out in a friendly way, and said to the lads, 'Better get your heads down. There's nothing to be done for the time being.'

'You too, Geordie,' said Whinger. 'You look knackered.'

'I feel it. What I'm going to do is bring a bed in here, in case Tony comes back on the blower.'

Two of us dragged my bed into the room. I took off my boots, but stretched out otherwise fully dressed. Gradually the place quietened down, but I couldn't sleep. Would the kidnappers try to use the bomb themselves? Would they have the technical capability to detonate it?

But my worst worries now were about our two missing men. I shrank from thinking what they might be going through. Much as I disliked Toad, I didn't want him hurt. I had to admit that on this task, so far, he'd pulled his weight and caused no trouble. As for Pav – still less did I want him to get beaten up. I clung to one small straw of hope. Neither of them had been involved in the bust on the apartment, so they could deny all knowledge of that.

But what were they to say about the bomb?

So far as we'd worked it out, our cover story – in the event of getting bumped – was that the device belonged to the Russians, and that we'd been moving it on their behalf. Toad had repeatedly assured me that every part of the device was anonymous and deniable: nowhere on the casing or any of the contents was there a single letter of Western writing. If he and Pav claimed to be ordinary squaddies, and professed complete ignorance about how the thing functioned, they might get away with it for a few hours. As always when someone is captured, their policy would be one of controlled release – letting out as little information as possible, as slowly as possible. The best I could hope was that they'd be able to hold out until we discovered their destination and got after them.

THIRTEEN

It was the telephone that roused me.

Tony's voice sounded incredibly close. Half asleep, I thought he'd flown into Moscow. Then I came round fully and realised he was calling again from New York.

'I think I woke you,' he said. 'Sorry.'

'No sweat. What time is it?'

'Here, we've got a quarter of nine. I don't know about you.'

'Still dark. Wait a minute. Quarter to five. What's happening?'

'We've found your missing Orange.'

'Fantastic. Where is it?'

'A nice quiet place called Grozny.'

'Ah, Jesus! Chechnya. Just what we thought.'

'That's where it is. It came back on the air ten minutes ago, and it's now proceeding westwards into the mountains.'

'OK. Can you continue monitoring it?'

'Sure. How about we update you every quarter-hour?'

'That'd be brilliant. I'm going to get right on to Hereford, ask them to establish a forward mounting base.'

'Eastern Turkey's where you want to be looking. Kars – somewhere like that.'

'I bet they're on to that already.'

They were. It was just before 2.00 a.m. GMT when I got through to the ops room, but the place was up and running. The ops officer and the CO were both there, planning to launch the QRF.

'Orange has turned up in Grozny,' the boss told me. 'We'd been talking to the Firm, and we were expecting it. We've also been in touch with the Turks about using an airforce base in the east of the country.'

'Kars?'

'Probably. That looks like being our FMB. We should have that confirmed by eleven ths morning.'

'When are you launching?'

'If all goes well, later tonight. The stand-by squadron's squaring everything away right now.'

At the risk of stating the obvious, I said, 'We're not certain where the target's going to end up. The last I heard, Orange was still moving.'

'Yes. But we can only assume it's the Chechens who lifted our guys, and that the hostages are with the device. There's no point in hanging about. We're going to stage through Cyprus, so we'll get the squadron on its way. If the Turks play ball about Kars, the Herc can change crews at Akrotiri, refuel and fly straight on.'

From that moment the Satcom phone was in continual use. At 5.30 Tony came back on to say that Orange had stopped at a point just north of a village called Samashki, fifty kilometres west of Grozny.

'There's a river running east and west,' he said. 'The terrain is hilly – looks like the foothills of the main Caucasus range. The site's one kilometre north of the river.'

'Samashki,' I said. Somewhere, sometime, I'd seen that name before. 'Thanks, Tony. Tell me if the target moves again.'

An idea had developed rapidly in my mind. The site was going to need recceing. The Russians were stipulating that Sasha should co-ordinate the hostage recovery. He'd told me earlier in the night that they didn't want foreigners crashing around unsupervised in their territory, and I reckoned the same would apply, although more so, in Chechnya. What better plan than that I and he should drop in together? A HALO descent.

He was a trained parachutist, but had never done free-falling. Therefore we'd have to go in tandem, strapped together under one canopy. As it happened, at that time I was one of only three tandem masters in the Regiment. Where the other two were, I didn't know, but I decided to try it on the head-shed, anyway.

They remembered Samashki in Hereford, all right. 'Jesus!' said Dick Trafford, the ops officer. 'That's where the Russian army murdered more than a hundred people. Burnt the houses. It was tactically pointless – just a show of strength. It became one of the most notorious incidents in the war.'

'Listen,' I said. 'I've had an idea about the recce . . .' I explained what I'd been thinking, and added, 'I want to volunteer for the job. We can get down to it much quicker from here than you can from there. Why don't we do it?'

'OK,' said Dick cautiously, 'but who's Sasha?'

'Major Ivanov, commander of Tiger Force, big operational experience in this region.'

'It's possible,' Dick agreed. 'I'll check it out and let you know.' Then he added, 'We've made one bit of progress. The Turks have cleared us to use Kars as our FMB.'

'Brilliant.'

I went into the kitchen and put the kettle on, then went back on the Satcom to Hereford. This time I got the CO, and outlined my scheme. 'The recce party needs to include a Russian,' I emphasised. 'If we bump into anyone on the ground and can't communicate, we're buggered. The ideal guy's Sasha Ivanov, our contact here. He's a hundred per cent on side, and I've got to know him pretty well.'

The CO must have already been discussing my idea with Dick, because he agreed at once. 'Don't get carried away, though,' he warned.

'Has the squadron left yet?'

'No – they're going in about an hour. You'd better have a word with Pat Newman. He's right here.'

Pat Newman, leader of the HALO team, was an old mate. 'Hi, Geordie!' he said. 'Stirring it up again, I hear.'

'Just a bit. Great to hear you, Pat. Listen. I've been looking at the map. The best way to hack this is for me and my Russian colleague Sasha to meet you at Kars.

I'm going to need a full patrol kit and a tandem rig. Can you make sure it's all brought out?'

'Don't worry,' he said. 'I know the score. I've been fully briefed. Your kit'll be on board. Just tell the SQMS what you want.'

'OK, then. Put me over, please.'

The squadron quartermaster sergeant was Larry Tompkins, another good friend. 'Listen, Larry,' I said, 'can you get your finger out?'

'Might be able to. Why?'

I ran through a list of what we needed: tandem rig chute, two free-fall suits, two oxygen sets working off one cylinder, harness and clips for attaching Sasha to me, GPS, Satcom phone, camcorder and lap-top computer for videoing the site, kite-sight, binos . . . 'And Larry,' I ended, 'those suits. Medium will do for me, but the guy I'm taking in's a big lad. Six one at least, and broad with it. We need a large for him.'

'Got it,' said Larry. 'We're pulling the stuff out already.'

'Thanks.'

I went back to Pat and asked, 'How about timings?'

'Depart Lyneham 0530 . . .' I could tell he was doing calculations on a sheet of paper – a habit of his. 'Six hours thirty to Cyprus. Akrotiri at 1200 – that's 1500 local. Ninety minutes to change crews and refuel. Take off for Kars 1630 local. Two hours twenty, approx. Into Kars by 1900 local.'

'So if Sasha can get me and him to Kars by then, the recce can go down tonight?'

'Yes – it'll have to.'

'And the squadron assault the night after.'

'Exactly.'

Back in the kitchen, I found the kettle had boiled dry and heated up to a fearsome degree over the gas burner. When I wrapped a cloth round the handle it gave off a smell of singeing, and the first gush of fresh water exploded into steam when it hit the base.

One or two of the other lads were starting to come round. Whinger blundered into the kitchen, scrubbing at his eyes and muttering, 'Fucking phone – it's never stopped all night.'

As if to back up his complaint the local line rang. It was Anna, spitting with rage. She'd only just got the message I'd left the night before. Her people were useless, she said, idle and stupid. Now – how could she help me?

The older you get, the more cynical you become. I couldn't help wondering if she was really that furious – or was she acting up a bit? Had she got my message hours earlier and deliberately done nothing about it?

Whatever the truth, she caught up fast. I'd barely finished outlining events when she said, 'If it's Samashki, it's certainly one of the Gaidar brothers you're dealing with. You know the big man who was shot in the apartment?'

'Of course.'

'That was Aslan, so-called Keet, the Whale. His second brother, Usman, calls himself Akula, the Shark. He's been building a big house for himself down there near Grozny, a kind of fortified palace, in the mountains. That's the Gaidars' home territory. The three of them *are* the Chechen Mafia.'

'Who's the third?'

'The young one, Supyan, calls himself Barrakuda. That hardly needs translating.'

'Are there pictures of this place at Samashki? Any air shots?'

'The FSB have some, but they're poor quality. The Chechens tend to shoot at any aircraft that comes over. And anyway, the pictures are out of date.'

'You mean the house is still being built?'

'The house is complete, but there's still work in progress on the perimeter fences and some of the outbuildings.'

'Listen,' I said. 'We're going to hit that place – provided we can confirm the hostages have been taken there. Can you bring over any information you've got about it – the pictures, exact location?'

'With pleasure. But I can tell you the location anyway. It's one kilometre north of the River Sunzha, half-way between Samashki and the next village, Sernovodsk.'

'Say those names again.'

As she spelled them out, I scribbled them down in the notebook tied to the phone for message-taking.

'Thanks, Anna. How soon can you get here?'

'In an hour?'

'Terrific. Do you have any photos of this fellow Shark?'

'Certainly. There were some on the disk I gave you. But I can bring you prints as well.'

Already the Satcom was ringing again.

'Geordie,' went Tony. 'It's still there. Hasn't moved.'

'Can you give me the co-ordinates?'

'Sure. Coming up.'

I took down his figures.

'I know where that is,' I said. Parroting Anna I added, 'One kilometre north of the River Sunzha, half-way between Samashki and Sernovodsk.'

'I'll be damned!' Tony exclaimed. 'How in hell did you know that?'

'A little bird called Anna told me. Seriously, any chance of satellite imagery on the site?'

'I knew you'd want that. I started to check out orbits. It's looking good. We'll have a satellite in the right place two hours from now. Also I got a met report for the Caucasus area, and the weather's fine: frost in the night, clear sky, no wind – gonna be a beautiful day. We should get some great pictures for you. I'll fax them just as soon as I can.'

The last person I had to convince was Sasha. 'Very big search, just for two persons,' he said doubtfully when he came into camp.

'Typical of the Regiment,' I told him. 'They don't like losing people. They'll go to any lengths to get them back.'

As to my suggestion of his own involvement in the recce, he didn't hesitate: as soon as he knew I was going with him, he was delighted to come.

'The point is,' I said, 'can you get us down there for insertion tonight? What I want to do is join up with the squadron at Kars – here.' I put my finger on the map.

'Hars!' he exclaimed, aspirating the initial letter. 'But that is in Turoktsiya.'

'Turkey.'

'Yes, Turkey.'

'We need to be there by five tonight. Earlier if we can.'

'Timing no problem,' Sasha said confidently. 'It is three-hour flight, not more. Plane also no problem. We get small military jet. The difficulty is diplomats. Do they give permission to enter Turkish airspace?' He spread his hands and stuck out his lower lip.

'Maybe Anna can help on that.'

'No!' He bridled. 'I arrange it through my own bosses.'

'Think you can manage it?'

'Zheordie – for you I arrange *anything*: even to become beautiful!'

When Anna swept in at 7.30 she brought good mug-shots of Usman Gaidar, aka Akula, the Shark – a mean-looking fellow, in his forties, with short, dark hair, heavy eyebrows, lean, hollow cheeks and a prominent jaw. In the photos his teeth and gums seemed to protrude, pushing his lips out – hence his name, maybe? Anna said the man was obsessive about protecting himself, and kept a private army of at least a hundred men to guard him.

311

She'd also brought telephoto pictures of the house he'd been building – a tall, pale building with a steeply pointed roof, set into the side of a hill.

'It looks Scandinavian,' I said.

'You're right.' Anna turned the picture round on the table so that it faced her way. 'It was designed by Finnish architects. No expense spared. Marble floors at ground level. Fitness room and sauna lined with birch wood in the basement. Whole building air-conditioned. Bullet-proof windows. It's not confirmed, but we have heard that he's building a nuclear shelter in the grounds by drilling into rock in the side of the mountain and lining the cavity with concrete and steel.'

I came within a micro-second of making some stupid joke about getting a nuclear device for his nuclear shelter, but pulled myself up just in time and said instead, 'The satellite imagery should show that, if the site's still fairly raw.'

When the pictures came over from the States, through the Satcom and our secure computer, they proved brilliantly sharp, and a perfect supplement to the telephoto shots. What the satellite revealed most clearly was the layout of the house and its defences. The building stood on a forested hillside inside a perimeter fence, roughly square, with sides some 400 metres long. The line of the fence showed as a pale gash through the trees, as did the single road running up to the house from a cluster of other buildings on the bottom edge of the compound. The villa was slightly off-centre – closer to the top fence than the bottom – and above it, towards the north-western corner, was a circular helipad. There was also another cleared area, nearer the house, which we assumed was the site of the shelter. A wider shot, of a bigger area, showed the river passing to the south of the site and, away to the right of it, the outskirts of Samashki village.

What caught my eye was an oblong open space in the forest, about two ks to the north-west. From its regular shape, it looked like a man-made field. 'Here!' I said to Sasha. 'This looks ideal as a place to drop into. A good opening in the trees, and far enough from the target.'

'We land there?'

'That's right – and walk in.'

So much was visible on the satellite shots. The telephoto picture showed that the pine-covered hillside was steep, with outcrops of rock among the trees.

When I invited Whinger to make an independent assessment, he came up with the same plan as I had.

'Bugger the fence,' he said. 'They'd have a job to electrify something that long – and where's the power coming from, anyway? It doesn't even look as if it's finished. You could cut throught that, or climb it, no bother. Drop on this football field, or whatever it is, and tab it in. Piece of cake. There may be a patrol on the fence, but I doubt it. The defenders are going to be here, at the bottom, guarding the approach road. There's no other way any vehicle can get near the house.'

'I reckon you're right,' I agreed. 'And when the time comes, the same drill for the QRF: drop on the field, walk in, surround the house and cut it off from its defence force. A couple of guys with gympis and a 66 should be enough to suppress anyone trying to come up the road. Look at these bends in the track – it's quite some climb.'

With the basic plan in place, I was naturally on fire to get going. Whinger and the rest of the lads went off to run the course. Sasha had disappeared to organise our flight, so Anna went with the guys, to interpret, and I was left manning the phones with Terry, the signaller. The sensible thing would have been to get a couple of hours' kip, but although I lay on the bed, my adrenalin was pumping too fast for me to drop off.

At 11.00 a.m. Allway came through from the Embassy, asking if there was anything he could do. I thanked him but said that we were fine, and I gave him an outline of the plan, keeping details of places and timings deliberately vague. When I asked about the international situation, he described it as 'stabilising'.

The next time he called, half an hour later, it was a different story. He said that the Chechens had surfaced, through their representative in London. They claimed they were holding two SAS men hostage, and in return for handing them over, they were demanding not only a ransom of ten million dollars, but also the release of the Mafia players arrested in Britain.

The news made my stomach churn. In making their demand, had the Chechens said anything about Orange? I couldn't ask directly, but had to fence round the subject.

314

'What did they say about releasing our guys? Where's the exchange supposed to take place?'

'We have no information on that.'

'Who did they make the offer to?'

'The FCO.'

'Who's their representative in Britain?'

'He calls himself the Consul.'

My questions brought me no nearer the subject of the bomb. But surely, if the ransom demand had mentioned it, Allway would have told me.

Once again I had to contain my impatience and anxiety.

Around 11.30 I suddenly realised I was starving. I'd been up most of the night and had no breakfast, so I routed out some onions, fried them up, threw in a load of garam masala and turned a tin of beef stew into a power curry. We still had plenty of the rice we'd brought out from UK, so I boiled up some of that, and gave myself a solid meal.

I was in the middle of eating it when Sasha reappeared, all smiles.

'Mmmmmm!' He gave an exaggerated sniff. 'Smells good!'

'Have some.'

'No – you need it. We have long journey to make.'

The Turks had come on side, he said, and we had permission to fly. Better still, he'd fixed an aircraft – a P33, a ten-seat executive jet used by senior military commanders. Take-off would be from the military side of Vnukovo airport at 2.30 Moscow time. We couldn't fly direct, but were to stage through Krasnodar, in the north of the Caucasus, so that the plane could refuel before the final hop of the flight and not have to take on Turkish fuel at the far end.

That meant leaving Balashika at 1.00 – and suddenly time for planning, which had seemed endless, had almost run out.

At 12.30 I put in one last call to Tony, even though I knew it was 4.30 a.m. in the States. He was asleep, but his stand-in, Cyrus, was fully briefed. He confirmed that Orange was stationary on the same site, and that the weather in the region was likely to remain unchanged for the next thirty-six hours.

'You got a big high centred over the west coast of the Caspian, extending all the way to the Black Sea,' he said. 'Predicted wind speeds, three to five knots on 260 degrees. Moon's three-quarter full. Moonrise 1900 local, moonset 0600. Looks like you'll have God's own view of the Caucasus range as you drop in there.'

'Thanks for your help,' I went. 'Tell Tony I'll call him from Kars.'

'OK. And take some warm clothes with you. That place is six thousand feet above sea level.'

FOURTEEN

The P33 was noisy and cramped, with little headroom and hard, uncomfortable seats, but it did the job. There were two regular army officers on board, hitching a lift to Krasnodar, but otherwise Sasha and I had the cabin to ourselves. The seats were arranged in pairs facing each other, and for much of the flight we kept a map of the Grozny area open on our knees, discussing the terrain.

When Sasha started talking about the war he grew animated, cursing the brutality and incompetence of the whole operation. He'd been in charge of one of the Omon special units, and had done what he could to keep his own men under control, but Kulikov, the overall commander of Russian troops in the south, had gone round inciting officers and men to kill every Chechen they could get their hands on.

'Not only Chechen people,' he told me. 'One Omon unit attacked farm. They shoot fifty cows, kill them all. They set fire to cows' food – hay – burn down barns, destroy machines. It was all crazy, mad. What had the cows done to annoy them?'

'Did you get to hate Chechens?' I asked.

'Not hate them. Chechens ordinary people. Not like Afghanis. Afghanis fanaticals. Some Chechens good, some bad.'

As we flew down over the Ukraine there wasn't a great deal to see. The rolling wheatlands had been harvested and most of the stubble had already gone under the plough, so that vast tracts of black earth were showing.

The second leg was a different matter, however. 'We go on the left side,' said Sasha as we re-boarded. 'Then we see mountains.'

As we lifted out of Krasnodar, lying beside a lake in the plain, the pilot climbed slowly on a southerly heading, and soon the Black Sea came in sight, away to our right. Over the coast the plane made a slight left turn and started following the shoreline down, just inland of the water. 'Famous health resorts,' Sasha said, pointing at spots on the map. 'Sochi, Sukhumi, Batumi – many sanatoriums.'

By then the sun was setting over the sea, and on the other side of the aircraft – our left – it threw fantastic light over the forested hills which piled ever higher into the distance until we began to see snow on the peaks.

'Soon we see Elbrus!' called Sasha excitedly. 'Highest mountain in Caucasus. Highest mountain in Europe.'

Screwing round my head to look, I spotted two rounded, snow-covered humps, so high above everything else that they were still catching the last of the sun.

'They're pink!' I exclaimed. 'Like a pair of bloody great tits.'

'Precisely!' Sashsa beamed. 'This is what we would say – *kak dve siski*, like twin tits.' Then he pointed left ahead: 'Grozny over there, behind.' He started in about the war again – how the Russians hadn't been able to make headway against the guerrillas, and had no proper military objectives, so that the soldiers took it out on anyone who got in their way.

He was still talking as the sun's rays at last left Elbrus. The smooth boobs quickly turned a dirty white, stars began to show in the clear sky, and night settled over the Caucasus range.

On our descent into Kars I wondered how the pilots would communicate with the tower. Did someone down there speak Russian, or did both sides talk in English? I never discovered – but we landed safely, to find that the Herc from Cyprus was already in.

Tony's stand-in had been right about the temperature too. As we stepped out of our little aircraft, the cold bit. On that high plateau our breath condensed in the air, and frozen mud crunched under foot. All round the horizon frosty-looking mountains showed faintly in the starlight. Great was my delight when I found mates from the squadron, settling themselves into an empty warehouse with big blower heaters blasting from the corners.

There was no time to socialise or piss about. I said hello to a few of the guys, then quickly sought out the OC of the stand-by squadron, Bill Chandler, who'd got himself an office of sorts in a cabin at one end of the big shed. A scalie had already got his Satcom set up, and Bill was talking to Hereford.

As I approached, he looked up at me, gave a grin and said into the phone, 'Yes. He's here. He's made it.'

When he came off the air, my first question was, 'How do we stand on security inside the squadron? I mean, how many of the lads know about Orange?'

'Nobody yet,' was his answer. 'It's on a need-to-know basis. Obviously the HALO team are going to have to know. It's them and the Chinook crews who'll have to exfil the damn thing. I'm going to tell them at their final briefing. As far as everyone else is concerned, it's purely a hostage rescue mission.'

'That's fine.' I nodded. 'Just remember that Sasha, my Russian partner, doesn't know about Orange either.'

'Christ! This is getting complicated. He's going to find out sooner or later.'

'Not necessarily. If he does, I'll square him. But I'm doing my best to keep him in the dark.'

'That's your problem,' said Bill. 'Meanwhile, can you tell *me* what Orange looks like? You're the only person here who's seen it.'

'Three components,' I told him. 'Two identical black steel cases, roughly three foot by two foot by one. One box about eighteen inches cubed.'

'Weight?'

'The big components eighty kilos each, the small one forty.'

'OK, thanks.' Bill made some notes.

'Tell you what,' I said. 'When Sasha and I go in, if I get eyes on Orange and have to refer to it over the Satcom, I'll call it "three heavy cases". All right?'

'Three heavy cases,' Bill confirmed. 'The latest satellite imagery suggests that they, or it, are in some outlying building to the east of the house.'

'Then that'll be the summerhouse.'

'The summerhouse,' he repeated, scribbling again. 'We're still waiting for confirmation of exfil by Chinook. As soon as we get it we'll pass it through.' Then he said, 'You and your pal had better brief the air crew. The captain wants to be on his way by ten.'

The RAF had set up a temporary base in what was obviously a training wing – a classroom of sorts, with a blackboard, tables and chairs of tubular metal, and garish, incomprehensible Turkish posters round the walls. The only member of the crew I'd met was Alec, the co-pilot, who introduced me to his captain, a solid, fair-haired Scot called Dan. They had maps spread out over two of the tables pushed together, and were using rulers and compasses to mark them up, punching figures into a lap-top.

'OK,' said Dan, inviting me into the discussion. 'There's not much civilian air traffic over this godforsaken area, but there is the occasional night flight coming up over Grozny from Baku, down here on the Caspian. Therefore our aim is to fly a normal civilian track. Your target's Samashki, right?'

'Yeah – we're aiming for an opening in the forest three ks north-west of the village.'

'Roger. The wind's about five ks on two-four-zero, so if we tip you out ten ks west, you should be able to fly yourselves in.'

I nodded. 'That'd be fine.'

'Good. That'll keep us well clear of Grozny. So . . .'
He stood up and stretched before running through a
quick recap. 'We go out on zero-eight-four and hold
that heading till we cross the civilian track from Baku.
Then we turn left on to two-eight-eight and head up
between Grozny and Ordzhonikidze. Our marker
point for the turn is this peak here, Dyltydag. It's over
four thousand metres and fairly isolated, so we should
pick it out all right – but if we can't, the computer will
hack it.'

'What height will we be flying at?'

'Twenty-eight thousand. You'll want plenty of
clothes on.'

I nodded again, wondering at the sight of all those
peaks on the map – a range running for two or three
hundred miles, north-west to south-east, with
numerous 15,000-footers among them . . . We were
going to fly right over the whole lot. All I asked was,
'How long will it take to get there?'

Alec did a few more calculations and came up with,
'One hour five to the turn, then twenty-five minutes to
the DZ overhead. It should be no problem to get you
there. It's not you that's bugging us, though.'

'What is it, then?'

'The exfil. Two Chinooks are on their way from
Cyprus, and we're trying to work out a way of getting
them through this bloody range of mountains. It's a hell
of a proposition, I can tell you. Even if we put extra fuel
forward, right on the border, it's still a fearsome distance

to anyone going in low level.'

'What about coming from the other side?' I suggested.

'From Russia?'

'Yeah. Wouldn't that be a better proposition? The intervening terrain doesn't look nearly so high.'

'We're working on it. But we don't have clearance from the Russians yet – from any direction.'

'Call Anna.'

'Anna?'

'The woman who's been doing our liaison in Moscow. She's shit-hot. She'll fix anything. Colonel Anna Gerasimova, FSB.'

'Sorry, mate – what's that?'

'The Federal Security Bureau, part of the old KGB, hived off.'

I saw the guy giving me an odd look, so I said sharply, 'Write her name down, and the number. She may not be in the barracks now, but she'll be there first thing in the morning. You'll get her on our Satcom link.'

'It's bloody horrible being the passenger,' I warned Sasha, looking down at the tandem rig laid out on the floor, 'because you've got no control.'

'You tell me,' he said cheerfully. 'I do it.'

We'd already had some practices during the morning, back at Balashika, but this was a full-scale dress rehearsal with all our kit on. The two PJIs who were coming with us fitted Sasha into his webbing harness, with hooks at the shoulders and at the waist, linked him to my own harness and pulled him in tight against my front, with both our full bergens strapped to the front of his legs and a single oxygen cylinder on the outside of my left thigh. Trussed together like this, carrying a lot of weight, we found it almost impossible to walk.

'Let's go through the motions again,' I said. 'As the plane approaches the DZ, we move to the edge of the deck. Let's say it's that line on the floor. Go on, then.'

Slowly, awkwardly, moving our legs in unison, we shuffled the short distance to the line.

'OK. Now we're waiting for the two green lights on either side of the opening.' I pointed outwards at head level, right and left. 'When we get them, and a signal from the head loadie, we just lean forward together and topple out. After that, you don't need to do anything except hold the same position. Keep your hands crossed over your chest, like you've got them now. All right?'

Sasha nodded.

'Once we're under canopy, we can take off our masks and let them hang. Then I'll slacken off the straps so that you slide down, about this much.' I held my hands a foot apart. 'That means your feet will be lower than mine, so they'll touch the ground first. Just as we're coming in to land, I'll tell you to start walking. At first you'll be walking in the air, then on the deck. OK?'

He nodded.

Without changing my voice I went on, 'There are two other things you need to know. First, if our chute fails to open, cross your legs and keep them there.'

'And why?'

'So they can unscrew you from the ground.'

He stared at me, and I went on relentlessly, 'The other thing is, keep your right hand up.'

'Why that?'

'So you don't break your watch when you go in.'

At last he smiled and aimed a gentle punch at me. Outwardly he seemed pretty calm, but perhaps not, because he kept sliding off for sessions in the bog.

Meanwhile, I was sorting the kit they'd brought us and repacking it into my bergen. They'd given us plenty of warm clothes, including two free-fall Goretex suits with Thinsulate linings: when zipped together, the jackets and trousers gave us a perfectly windproof outer layer. There were also a couple of sweaters apiece, thermal silk long johns and long-armed vests, and any amount of boil-in-the-bag meals, which we could eat cold if necessary. If all went well, we'd be on the ground for less than thirty-six hours, so I cut down our load as far as I dared, as the combined weight of our essential kit was already formidable.

I had a 203, with eight spare thirty-round mags and two grenades, plus Sig, spare mags, knife, Satcom, GPS, covert radio, kite-sight, binoculars, fireflies, water-bottles, sleeping bag, bivvy bag and cam nets. A lot of the heaviest stuff, like the magazines, went into the pouches on my webbing, but there was still enough to fill a bergen. Sasha had his Gepard and spare mags, plus a pistol and ammunition.

At 9.30 p.m. I went for a final briefing with Bill

Chandler. The met forecasts were unchanged. Orange hadn't moved: the satellite was still getting its signal. 'As far as they can tell, it's not in the main house,' Bill told me. 'If it was inside a big structure, they probably wouldn't hear it. It seems to be about a hundred metres east of the building.'

'OK,' I said. 'As soon as we're on site I'll call you and let you know what we can see.'

After a sandwich and a cup of tea we were ready to go. At the last minute I bumped into Pat, who looked in rollicking form, his bright brown eyes shining, cheeks ruddy, and his teeth flashing white as ever.

'Taking on Chechnya single-handed, are you, Geordie?' he enquired with a big grin on his face.

'Just the two of us. Pat, this is Sasha, a very good colleague from Moscow. Sasha – Pat Newman.'

'Hi, Sasha!' Pat shook hands quickly. 'You want to watch this fellow – he's a dangerous bastard to be with.'

Rising to the banter, Sasha took hold of my webbing and said, 'I keep him tied to me.'

'Quite right! Otherwise he might dump you in it.'

'You look out,' I told Pat. 'The Chechens are pretty handy with their guns. Move a bit faster this time or you'll end up a Figure Eleven again.'

'We'll see!' Pat grinned and gave me a smack on my sore shoulder.

'Eh,' he went, seeing me wince. 'What's the matter?'

'I got nicked there in a bit of a shoot-out.'

'Really! We live in dangerous times. Happy landings, anyway.'

'Same to you, Pat. We'll see you tomorrow.'

As we moved off, Sasha asked, 'What is Figure Eleven?'

'One of the targets we shoot at on the range.' With both hands I drew the silhouette of a man's torso in the air.

For us, down in the back of the Herc, the flight was routine and relatively short. After take-off the pilot climbed hard, under full power, to clear the mountains, and the vibration was enough to loosen your teeth. Then we levelled off, and I went up on the flight deck for a look at the terrain.

Beneath us a sea of snow peaks lay glittering in bright moonlight, with jagged ridges of rock running down from the summits in incredibly complex patterns. I plugged the end of my helmet lead into an intercom socket and said to the pilot, 'Glad we're not going out right here.'

'Aye,' he went. 'You wouldna have much of a chance. Here's our marker summit coming up already. See it?'

Dead on the nose of the aircraft a single snow-clad peak was rising from the horizon, slender and pointed. We seemed to be approaching it at a snail's pace, then all at once loomed closer. While I was staring at it the plane tilted steeply to the left as the auto-pilot made our programmed turn.

Back in the hold, the head loadie signalled us to start getting our tandem rig on, and the two PJIs helped do up the straps, clips and buckles to the correct tension.

So, for the final few minutes, we stood strapped tight together, unable to sit down, barely able to walk. My pulse rate had shot up and my heart was pounding. I'd peed into the Elsan just a few minutes before, but already I had the feeling I wanted to go again. I tried to concentrate on controlling my breathing so that I didn't hyperventilate.

On our own oxygen now, with masks in place, it was impossible to communicate any longer. In spite of the discomfort, there was time – too much time – for my mind to zip back to the fuck-up over France. The big difference now was that Pavarotti, poor bugger, was on the deck, in the hands of the Mafia, and had no chance of flying into me on the way down.

Either side of the tailgate the red warning lights flicked on. The head loadie gave me two fingers. I acknowledged them, and saw him hitch his own harness to a strop hanging from the wall. The tail opened, letting in a blast of searingly cold air. As the ramp settled into its horizontal position the guy motioned us forward, and with another well-anchored loadie steadying us from behind, we waddled to the edge of the abyss, a few inches at each step, stiff-legged as ducks.

One finger from the head loadie. One minute to go. Sixty seconds of sheer terror.

Sasha seemed totally cool, not trembling or shifting about. I could only think, He must have nerves of fucking steel. I found it impossible to think rationally. All I could do was try to keep my breathing rate down and will the seconds to pass faster.

Then suddenly both red lights turned to green.

'Green on!' I yelled. 'GO!'

I gave Sasha a tap on the right arm and as one we leant forward and toppled into a blasting, icy hurricane.

Immediately we were in a face-down attitude, Sasha beneath me. Freezing air ripped past my cheeks, scouring like crystals of ice. Far below and away to our right the snow-peaks shimmered and glinted. I felt the drogue-chute tug at the centre of my back as it deployed behind us, slowing our descent slightly and keeping us stable.

Then, steering with hands and feet, I turned us round until our heads were pointing north. I was still aware of the moonlit snow summits, now out on our left, but there was no time to enjoy the view. Our urgent need was to pinpoint the LZ. It should be showing up as a lighter patch in the black of the forests.

At first I couldn't pick it out and panic threatened. Every second I kept glancing back at the altimeters on my forearms. The hands were unwinding like clocks gone berserk.

At last I got it: a little grey oblong, father to our right than I'd expected, but well within reach. By dropping my right arm and raising my left, I tilted us in that direction. At the change of attitude I found myself dreading the possibility of going into another spin; but Sasha played his role perfectly, remaining passive beneath me, not trying to influence our flight-path, relying on me to steer.

Down, down, down we went. Sixteen thousand, fourteen, twelve . . . The forested hills were gloriously black below us. Far off to our right, beyond the LZ, was a small cluster of lights, which I reckoned was Samashki, too far off for anyone there to spot one little dot falling from the sky. Otherwise the wooded hills were magnificently dark, denoting a total absence of houses. No bright windows, no roads, no moving vehicles.

Ten, eight, six . . .

Our target was growing rapidy into a fair-sized field.

Five . . .

I tugged the release toggle. Away went the drogue with a snap, pulling out the big chute, and with a heavy snatch we were jerked upright, swinging beneath the main canopy. Immediately I unhooked one side of my mask so I could talk again, and released the tension on the harness buckles, so that Sasha sank down until the top of his helmet was level with my chest, giving me a better view of where we were heading.

The pale opening in the forest was well within reach, ahead and slightly to our right. 'See it down there?' I said quietly, pointing.

'Fantastic!' Sasha breathed, on a high. Now I could hear *him* hyperventilating. 'Breelliant!' he went. '*Otlichno!*'

'OK,' I said, 'take it easy, and don't make too much noise.'

I steered for the open patch, glad of the bright moonlight for the view it gave us, but feeling altogether too conspicuous. At least the LZ looked fairly level.

The black trees came up rapidly to meet us. We were over the southern edge of the clearing, sliding towards the centre. As we came in I pulled on both risers, stalling our descent.

'Get ready,' I told Sasha. 'Start walking now.'

Then I flared again: the chute came up and stalled, and a moment later we landed softly on short, frosty grass.

For a few seconds we crouched, motionless, listening. Not a murmur. The breeze carried a thin, clean scent of pines. The opening we'd landed in looked to be about two hundred metres by one hundred, with trees on all sides. Then it was out of the harness, weapons out of their ties and at the ready, and down in a defensive position, facing outwards. Sasha needed no instruction: he moved fast and instinctively.

My hands were lumps of ice. My fingers started to throb and burn as I worked them furiously, open and shut, to get the circulation going while I waited for my GPS to get a fix and confirm we were on the correct location.

As soon as the figures came up, and I saw they were right, we rolled our jumping kit into a bundle, shouldered our bergens and set off towards the edge of the field in search of a place to hide or bury the evidence.

'Big experience for me,' Sasha panted, still breathless with excitement as we hurried forward.

A sudden outburst of noise made me drop flat again. The commotion came from a distance, higher up the mountain to our left: an explosion of high wailing and howling in which several distinct voices rose and fell.

Sasha gave a chuckle. '*Volki*,' he said. 'Wolves. We hear them often during the war. They sing to moon.'

'Jesus!' I gasped. 'They gave me a fright. Do they attack humans?'

Sasha laughed again. 'Never! Wolf very shy animal – keep away.'

The chorus rose and fell for nearly a minute, then stopped as suddenly as it had begun.

By now the moon was on its way down, but still so bright that I hardly needed the kite-sight: the binos did just as good a job. I swept them round, hoping to see some of the ghostly howlers, but they must have been half a mile away.

At the far end of the field, in the direction we wanted to go, there was some object in a corner. The kite-sight revealed it as an old wooden farm wagon, with a primitive hay-rake beside it.

'That thing must have come up a track through the forest to reach where it is,' I whispered. 'Let's take a shufti.'

We moved into the deep shadow at the edge of the trees, then advanced slowly to the corner. There was no fence round the edge of the grass, so I reckoned that herdsmen or boys must look after any animals that came to graze there. As there were wolves about, that made sense.

The wagon had wooden wheels, the back pair twice the size of the front, which were mounted on a swivelling yoke, and it took me straight back thirty years to my boyhood in the north of England.

'Vairy preemitive people, Chechens,' Sasha whispered.

'Yes,' I said, 'but look at this.'

Beyond the cart was a drinking trough for cattle, carved out of a single tree-trunk. I reached down and felt a skim of ice in the bottom. Beside it was a broken-down hand pump for raising water from a well. Staring at it, I reckoned this was a summer pasture, on which some farmer made hay, but that now it had been abandoned for the winter. A moment later I'd found the well cover, made of planks, and lifted it. In went the para bundle, and that was one problem solved.

A rutted track led away through the wood, twisting downhill towards the east. For twenty minutes we followed it, but then the path turned right into the valley, no doubt heading down towards the village, and we had to continue as best we could through the trees, holding our height along the contour.

Our navigation proved spot-on. Seventy minutes out from the LZ, we saw something light-coloured through the screen of tree-trunks ahead, and with the kite-sight made out the perimeter fence of the compound: weld-mesh on steel posts, all glowing coldly in the moonlight.

We came to the edge of the trees and stopped. I whispered to Sasha, 'We'll give it an hour,' and we settled ourselves on the top of a bank which com-manded a close view of the barrier at a point where it turned a corner and ran away down the slope. Lying on

333

our stomachs on a bed of old pine-needles, we looked straight on the fence, which was two metres high and topped by four strands of razor wire on overhang arms canted outwards.

Scanning past it with the kite-sight, I saw that the trees cut down to make way for the barrier hadn't yet been cleared. The trunks had been sawn into lengths, but the tops had simply been dragged out of the way and left in heaps. Perfect, I thought. Ideal for an OP. We can just burrow into one of them and become invisible. No digging or nets needed. We can pick the best spots for observing the villa and checking on patrols.

The more I scanned, the more evidence I saw that the fence was still being worked on. Lengths of metal and odd pieces of wire lay scattered on either side of it, and further up the hill, on the outside, was what looked like a small trailer which I assumed the builders had been using to bring up material. I'd been planning to cut our way through the bottom of the weldmesh, but with this amount of construction still in progress that seemed a dangerous idea. Instead, I decided to take a look at the stretch near the trailer, in the hope that it wasn't yet complete.

For the time being we were out of the wind, in deep shadow, on dry ground, and as comfortable as could be – so I wasn't surprised when Sasha began to snore gently beside me. I turned to look at him, and saw that his head was resting on one arm. Let him sleep, I thought. One pair of eyes is enough here.

Forty minutes later, I gripped him by the arm. He came to silently and was immediately alert. I pointed downhill, along the wire, where I'd seen the glow of a cigarette being drawn on. Then it came again, closer. A patrol was on its way round the perimeter.

I got the kite-sight aligned and saw the smoker immediately: a single man with a weapon slung on his shoulder. At his heel a German Shepherd was ambling, apparently loose.

'Get ready!' I whispered. 'He's got a bloody dog.'

I felt for my knife, down my right leg. I hate guard dogs. You never know whether to shoot them and give away your presence by making a noise, or risk serious injury by trying to get a knife into the bastards.

We lay on the bank like logs. I felt we were going to be all right, because the drift of the wind was from the fence to us, and we hadn't put any scent on the ground by going to the wire itself. Besides, the sentry was an idle sod: he was ambling along, not looking to right and left, but humming to himself between drags. As he passed beneath us, within fifteen feet of our heads, the smell of cheap tobacco smoke filled the air around us. It wasn't surprising that the dog never deviated from its track.

We gave the pair a couple of minutes to get clear, then went for the fence. Close inspection revealed that none of the wire was insulated, and that there was no alarm system that I could see. We moved cautiously uphill towards the trailer, and found it contained drums of more razor wire. Fifty metres beyond it we found what I'd been hoping for: a section of fence not yet fitted with the overhang. In twenty seconds we'd both climbed the weldmesh and gained the cover of the heaped tree-tops.

I reckoned that by the time the sentry came round again – if he made it at all – our scent would have left the frosty surface. With the ground so soundly frozen, our boots hadn't left any traces on the fence itself.

We slipped out from our heap of pine-tops, back into the standing trees, and crept left-handed round the outcrops of rock, following the contour, the hill falling to our right. According to the map, which I'd tried to imprint on my brain from the satellite data, the villa would be below us.

From his station a pace behind me Sasha put a hand on my arm. I stopped to listen. He was pointing down-hill. When I turned my head in that direction I heard what he'd detected: a faint hum, something like an air-conditioning unit. We moved on a few yards, looked over a rocky ridge, and saw the house rising tall from a levelled-out plateau below.

'Hell of a place,' I whispered.

From Anna's photographs I recognised the steep roof and high walls, glowing pale in the moonlight, but the whole place looked more formidable than I'd reckoned. There were three main floors above ground level, a fourth with dormer-windows sticking out of the roof, and some kind of a basement. At the front, on our right, five cars were parked, and on the side facing us a ramp led down to a sunken garage.

'Jesus!' I whispered. 'It's just like the cellar at the Embassy.'

'The Embassy?' I heard Sasha turn his head to look at me.

Suddenly I realised what I was saying. 'You know – in the courtyard . . .' Christ! 'Oh no. Sorry. I was thinking you'd been with us. We stored some kit at the back of the British Embassy in Moscow. There was a garage entrance a bit like this.'

Thank God, he didn't show the least curiosity.

'Beeg house,' was all he said. 'Where are your men?'

He meant that it might be one hell of a job to locate them – and he was right. For the moment I concentrated on the layout of the place.

Akula had good comms, obviously: we could see a couple of dish aerials bolted on to the wall beneath the eaves. There were video cameras mounted on the corners of the building, and what looked like an infra-red device covering the driveway. But half an hour's observation convinced me that there was no patrol immediately round the house: Akula was relying on the fence to keep intruders at a distance.

From where we lay we could see the approach road snaking off down the mountainside to our right, and once I was confident that nobody was moving inside the compound, I decided to recce the track, right down to the barrack huts, or whatever they were, at the bottom entrance.

'Stay here and watch the house,' I whispered. 'I'm going to recce the road. Back in an hour. If there's any development, call me on the radio. If there's a big drama, rendezvous back on the bank outside the wire. OK?'

Sasha nodded, and I slipped away down the slope, keeping off the road but following its line in and out through half a dozen hairpin bends. There'd be no problem about blocking it: in at least three places it came through narrow defiles where the rock had been blasted away; a single vehicle brought to a halt would stop everything coming up. A couple of guys with gympis on the high ground nearby would be able to sort any number of defenders.

At the bottom I came across the guardroom and barrack block that the satellite had seen: low, solid-looking, single-storey structures either side of the weldmesh entrance gates, with several cars and small trucks parked outside. As I watched from above, I saw the guy who'd come past us along the fence return to base, shut his dog into a kennel beside the guardroom and disappear into the building. I checked the time: 4.20. That looked like the end of the night patrol. As I watched, I began to suspect that the reports we'd heard about Akula's private army being a couple of hundred strong must be grossly exaggerated. I reckoned the accommodation below me might house a couple of dozen men at most – so, unless more were billeted some-where off-site, we were up against a pretty small force.

I climbed back a bit, crossed the road and made my way up the eastern side of the compound. There was nothing of interest until, through the trees, I saw the line of a roof above me. This had to be the separate structure identified from satellite imagery, the building in which the trackers reckoned Orange had been housed, maybe a hundred metres east of the villa.

I circled out to the right and came in above it: a rectangular storage shed with no windows and a corrugated roof of what looked like asbestos. I felt my heart speed up. Radio signals would pass straight through that roof. Without any real evidence, I became convinced that the bomb was there. 'The Mafiosi are nervous of the device,' I told myself. 'They don't want it inside the house, so they've put it here.'

Behind the shed was a big heap of what looked like freshly excavated rock. Maybe that was spoil from the nuclear shelter they were digging out of the mountainside. Maybe the shed covered the entrance to the bunker.

To complete my anti-clockwise circuit I had to cross the mountainside above the villa, and it was up there, a couple of hundred feet higher than the house, that I came across the helicopter pad – a circle of concrete in the middle of a shallow natural bowl, from which the trees had been cleared. I could see at once that it was big enough to accommodate a Chinook, but not until I was moving away from the centre did I realise what was positioned on one side. From a distance the object looked like a crumpled garden hut. Creeping up to it, I saw that a tarpaulin was lashed down to rings set in the ground. Close inspection revealed a .50 machine gun, set up on a heavy tripod so it could engage targets in the air as well as on the ground. I felt under the cover and ran a hand down the barrel, thinking that the bastards probably had hand-held SAM systems as well.

Sasha had no action to report, so together we pulled off to a safe distance from the villa and settled in a hollow surrounded by rocks from which I could transmit without fear of anyone hearing.

By now the moon was down, and the night had become much darker. As I assembled the Satcom aerial I said, 'Sasha – I'm working on the plan for tomorrow. I'm going to call for the HALO troop to drop in as soon as it's dark. But during the day I reckon we'll want to watch both the house and another building I've seen on the far side, over there. That means we need to man two separate OPs. You all right on that one?'

'No problem. Many times I do such observation.'

'Good. We'll have radio comms with each other, anyway. Now – let's get this thing working.'

I had the Satcom set up on a flat rock, and now turned it a couple of times until I got a strong satellite signal. Then I draped my sleeping bag over my head to muffle the sound of my voice, and seconds later I was through to the squadron base in Kars.

'Blue,' said a voice I didn't recognise.

'Red here,' I went. 'Can I speak to Bill Chandler?'

'Roger. Wait one.'

I waited, imagining the hangar, guys in sleeping bags around the perimeter, and the squadron CO with his head down in some reasonably secluded corner.

'Geordie?' He sounded lively enough. 'How goes it?'

'Fine. No problems.'

'Where are you?'

'Inside the compound. We've got eyes on the villa. We're maybe a hundred and fifty metres above it.'

'Any sign of our guys?'

'Not yet.'

'Or of the three heavy cases?'

'No, but I think I know where they are.'

'Can you identify the site?'

'Not now.'

'In the summerhouse?'

'Yes. Listen, the drop was spot-on. We've recced as much as we can in the dark. As soon as it's light I'll shoot some footage with the video, get pictures back to you. But basically the plan holds.'

'So . . .' He paused, evidently looking at his notes. 'The same DZ?'

'Yep. It's an ideal place. Looks like a summer pasture. Nobody within miles. I'll get myself up there with a Firefly to guide the lads in.'

'OK, then. We're aiming to drop at 1900 your time. That's half an hour after full dark.'

'Can you make that 1930? I'll need time to get up to the DZ, and I don't want to move in daylight.'

'OK. 1930 it is. That's confirmed.'

'Great. Obviously Pat will want to work out his own plan. But as I see it there are three objectives: first is to cut the road coming up from the barracks at the bottom; second is to secure the summerhouse, third to hit the villa.'

'Roger. How many in the garrison?'

'Very few. Could be twenty. Nothing like the rumours. But they've got a fucking great machine gun set up beside the helipad, and I'm sure there are guys we haven't seen yet inside the house.'

'OK. How's the rest of the garrison deployed?'

'By the time we got here they were all in their pits, bar one.' I told Bill about the sentry patrolling the perimeter, but said we hadn't seen anyone inside the wire.

'Is the helipad big enough for a Chinook to land?'

'Definitely. But we'll have to take out that five-oh first. What's the position on the exfil?'

'I think it's going to be possible from the north. Your Russian friends are playing ball. It looks as though we'll be able to get the choppers up to a place called Nalchik. Then they can hop over the mountain when they're needed, and come back out the same way. They'll be in and out of Chechnya air-space in a few minutes. The only thing is, the met looks a bit dodgy. There's a depression moving up from the south.'

FIFTEEN

It was at 11.30 the next morning that things suddenly started to move. Sasha and I had both made secure OPs, buried under piles of pine boughs about 400 metres apart. Once I'd left him with a good view down to the front of the villa, I moved on round and found a site that commanded not only the summerhouse but also the exit road. There, lulled by an intoxicating smell of fresh resin, I'd crawled into my sleeping bag for warmth, and dozed off for the last hour before dawn.

We'd put our covert radios on listening watch, and agreed that from 0700 we'd come up on the air to compare notes on the hour and half-hour – unless we wanted to alert each other at any other time, in which case we'd give a double jab on the pressel.

At first we hadn't much to report. Sasha told me that a couple more cars drove up to the villa, and one went down. Work started on the fence. I couldn't see the site, but when I heard an old tractor spluttering up and down and men chatting quite close behind me, to my right, I thanked my stars that we hadn't cut the wire.

Once again the weather was fine, but I sensed a change coming. Soon after dawn the sky began to haze over and the air moistened, as if snow was on the way. My priority task was to get video footage of the villa and send it back to Kars, so that the guys would have extra information to back up the satellite imagery and could start working out their assault plan. Now I reckoned I'd better go pretty soon, before the landscape got blotted out.

Breakfast consisted of slimy, cold lasagne which came out of its foil bag tasting of mud, and cold water that tasted of plastic. With that feast down my neck I slipped out of my hide, taking my 203 with spare mags in my pouches, but leaving my bergen, to give myself greater mobility.

The mountainside was so broken by gullies, rocky outcrops and stands of trees that I found it easy to keep in dead ground, hidden from the wire above me on one side, and the villa below on the other. Not that I didn't keep a sharp lookout: before I crossed any open space I scanned repeatedly with my binos in case sentries were posted on vantage points.

I filmed the helipad on my way past, hoping that shots of the .50 mounted on its tripod would give an idea of scale, and came out on a high point above Sasha's LUP. Lying face-down on a rock under some trees, I got good footage of the house, first the front, then the western side with its underground door – making sure I kept each take long enough for members of the QRF to spot detail. I zoomed in for close-up shots of the security cameras and IR devices, then filmed the road going down towards the barracks and the gate. I contemplated going down and taking in the barracks as well, but decided that any extra information I might gain wouldn't be worth the risks involved. My gut feeling told me it was the villa and the summerhouse that we were going to assault. With any luck we wouldn't need to go near the barracks: we'd just block the road to anyone trying to come uphill.

By 9.00 a.m. I was back in my own OP, having filmed the summerhouse as well. My scramble around the mountainside had got me well warmed up and my fingers were nimble when it came to down-loading information from the camera into my lap-top and sending it up via the Satcom to the squadron at Kars.

Within five minutes Bill Chandler came on air to say that the quality of the pictures was excellent. He also confirmed that Orange was still transmitting from the same site, and that we had definite permission to exfil via the Russian Caucasus.

It wasn't until 11.20 that things started to happen. I got a sudden *tsch, tsch* in my earpiece, and there was Sasha, fired up.

'Beeg development!' he went. 'I have seen your men.'

'Our lads?'

'Yes. They came from lower house into upper house.'

'Out of the basement entrance?'

'Yes. Four guards bring them.'

'How did they look?'

'Bad. Zheordie, I am afraid they are smashed up.'

'What did you see?'

'The big man, Pavarotti – his eyes are black. The small one has clothes on his hands.'

'Clothes? Bandages?'

'Bandages. Yes.'

'Where did the guards take them, Sasha?'

'Inside the house. Upstairs.'

'The ground-floor entrance – main door?'

'Yes.'

'OK. Thanks. Keep watching.'

I went straight through to Kars and relayed Sasha's information. Anger ran through me as I lay under my heap of pine branches. My first thought was to take the pressure off our guys by creating a diversion. A 203 grenade into one of the villa's windows would stir things up, all right. Sasha and I could drop quite a few of the home team if they came running out of the house. But a premature attack by just the two of us could well panic the Chechens and make them top their prisoners.

I spoke to Bill again and suggested what I'd been thinking.

'No go, Geordie,' he replied. 'For Christ's sake take it easy. It's great to know the guys are there, but until we've got the bomb secure, the plan must hold. They have to stick it out, and so have you.'

Fuck them all, I thought savagely as I switched off. When it comes to the crunch, all senior ruperts are unfeeling bastards who don't give a stuff about losing guys.

I lay there feeling furious, but not for long.

The next development was almost worse. Shortly before 12.00 I became aware of a drone, faint at first but rapidly growing louder. Chopper, I thought. Then I caught the fluttering beat of a rotor, and a few moments later the thing came swishing and roaring so low overhead that its downdraught made the roof of my OP thrash about, and I had to seize hold of some branches to stop them being blown away.

For perhaps a minute the roar persisted, as the pilot came in to land on the helipad. Then he shut his engine down and the noise fell away to a dying whine.

Sasha was already on the air. 'Zheordie – helicopter in.'

'Yeah. Did you see what sort?'

'Small civilian, passenger aircraft. Three to four persons.'

I knew Sasha couldn't see the pad from where he was, but he would get a look at the incoming party if the people walked the few yards down to the villa.

'They'll probably come down to the house,' I told him. 'Stay on the air and let me know.'

'*Prinyato.*'

A couple of minutes later he said, 'Now they are coming. Three men. I think one is Akula. I recognise . . . Yes, definitely this is Shark.'

'What are they doing?'

'They are coming to the door. Door opens in front. Inside house now. Zheordie?'

'Yes?'

347

'I notice something. When they were five metres distant, door open *avtomaticheskii*. And why? Some persons inside are watching with cameras.'

'That's right. They've got closed–circuit TV. I filmed the cameras.'

My mind was racing. Had the prisoners been taken upstairs for another session of interrogation, this time by Shark himself? Had he brought some ace torturer with him, or maybe a nuclear expert, to find out the truth about the bomb?

I reported the arrival of the chopper to Bill Chandler. 'It could be set to lift our guys out,' I warned him. 'Or the bomb. Is there any way the Yanks can track a helicopter if it takes off from here?'

'I'll ask,' he said. 'I'll pass the message through. You'll tell us if it does move.'

'Of course. What about binning the HALO and bringing the QRF in earlier by chopper?'

'Not a chance.' Bill was adamant. 'We still don't have clearance to fly in Russian airspace. Besides, we need the element of surprise. Our information from Colonel Gerasimova in Moscow is that the defence force is bigger than you think. There's a bigger barracks down the valley with a hundred or more in it. Plus any local guys they can muster.'

'Is that right?'

'Yep. And listen, Geordie, the colonel's done us another favour. She got on to Kelsen, the firm of Finnish architects who built the villa, and faxed us the plans.'

'Oh, great!' I said.

'There's a basement floor,' Bill went on. 'That's got gym, games room, sauna, showers and so on. Then, below that, there's another floor, a kind of sub-basement, marked "Storage". That tallies well with the pictures you sent.'

'*Tochno*,' I went, thinking of Sasha with his eyes on the building and unconsciously slipping into Russian. 'Exactly. That's where they brought our guys out of, that lower door. I reckon that's where they're being kept. When the assault goes in, we're going to need to hit that door first. Wait a minute, though. There must be some internal access from the store area to the upper floor. Isn't anything marked on the plan – a staircase or a lift?'

'There's a lift-shaft, yes.'

'Maybe the lift's knackered. Or maybe it hasn't been installed yet. Plan round taking out that lower door, anyway.'

Shortly before 12.30 Sasha buzzed me up again. Toad and Pavarotti had been taken back underground, looking even worse than before. Pav was walking with a limp, and there was blood showing through the bandages on Toad's hands.

Bastards! I said to myself. Just wait till we get in among them. Bill Chandler had already told me, 'No hostages.' Now, after what Sasha had seen, I was going to feel no compunction about taking out everyone in the villa.

★

The sun never came out that day. The haze of cloud thickened steadily, and early in the afternoon snow began to fall. My problem was exhaustion. I fought it as hard as I could, but I know that I nodded off several times – and when I suddenly came to, just before 3.00 p.m., I couldn't remember where I was. Then, as I moved, snow slid off the flap of my sleeping bag and on to my face. I rolled over on to my front and looked out. Snow was falling hard – a real blizzard, fine flakes slanting in towards me from my right front. The weather was coming from the south-west, from the high mountains.

When I scanned the summerhouse through my binoculars, I saw that a white blanket of snow lay unmarked all round it. Nothing doing there.

I knew that the helicopter hadn't taken off: for one thing, I'd have heard it go; for another, it would never fly in this weather. So Shark must still be in residence. Little did he realise that his time was rapidly running out.

Or was it? A new fear began to needle me. If this weather kept up, with its heavy cloud cover, the HALO jump might have to be postponed. Snow on the ground wouldn't matter – in fact it would make the DZ show up all the better, white in the middle of the black wood – but snow clouds in the air were another matter. I'd better report the conditions to the FMB.

When I tried to go through to Kars, my anxiety rose a notch. No response. I suspected the blizzard was to blame, and that the snow was blocking contact with the satellite. Comms are notoriously fickle. They go up and down, and often there seems no reason. I fiddled with the dish aerial, turning it this way and that, and then moved out of my lair on to a more prominent site. Still no contact. I tried again and again, to no avail.

Lying on my front, I realised how the snow was blotting out every sound. Work on the fence, which had been proceeding intermittently, seemed to have stopped completely, and a heavy silence lay over the compound.

Then I heard a noise of an engine, labouring up the hill from the barrack area. Presently it came into view – a mid-grey, square-bodied truck with big snow tyres, weaving slightly as it slithered over the snow. The driver swung up on to the flat area outside the summerhouse, crunched into reverse and backed to within two or three yards of the doors.

He and another man jumped out, and one of them opened the truck's rear door to release a third. All were wearing dark green overalls and brown fur caps with ear-flaps tied up over the crowns. The driver produced some keys, unlocked the doors of the shed and slid them back. A minute later, out came all three, lugging, between them, one of the components of Orange.

Snow or no snow, there was no chance of me making a mistake – the men were only sixty metres from me, and through the glasses I could see those orange markings perfectly. The sight set my adrenalin racing. Again I had to fight down my instinct to make a direct intervention. A 203 grenade into the front of the van would rearrange Akula's plans pretty swiftly. But, again, that might mean the end for Pav and Toad.

The three men went back in and brought out the second half. I snatched up the Satcom receiver and switched on. Nothing. Again – nothing.

Shit! The bomb was about to disappear, and I couldn't report it.

The men locked the shed, slammed the doors of their truck and climbed aboard. I watched helplessly as the driver started up and drove off downhill, nosing his way carefully through the bends. By now the snow was falling so fast that, even as I watched, the vehicle's tracks were becoming blurred. In a few minutes they'd be obliterated altogether.

In spite of my anxiety, I realised that what had happened carried one small advantage: now, if the HALO drop did come in as planned, Sasha wouldn't see the bomb, and wouldn't know anything about it.

The next hour was one of the most miserable I'd ever known. I spent it shitting bricks that the head-shed might call off the free-fall. They might decide to leave Sasha and me to try and spring the prisoners. I could just hear Bill saying, 'Make your own way out as best you can.' Fucking thanks, I thought. I kept reasoning, No, they can't do that – they'd be four guys down rather than two. But for all my wishful thinking I couldn't be sure.

As the snow kept floating down in a dense pall, I speculated about where the bomb might be heading. Back to Moscow, I felt certain. What if the Chechens used it to threaten the Russian government, just as the Americans had been planning to do? What an irony that would be.

I convinced myself that the blizzard was going to continue all day and all night, and that Akula's men had come up to move the bomb while they still could, before everyone got snowed in.

At last the snowflakes began to thin, and the sky lightened as the storm moved on towards the north-east. I waited till I could see a patch of blue sky among the clouds, then tried the Satcom again.

This time, thank God, the call went straight through.

'Bill,' I exclaimed. 'They've moved the fucker!'

'I know. Where the hell have you been?'

'Nowhere,' I told him. 'The comms went down in a snowstorm.'

'I see. Well, the device has been on the move.'

'I was trying to tell you that. Some guys came and carried off the components in a truck. Bill – how far's Grozny from here?'

'Fifty ks. That's where it's gone. The Yanks have tracked it that far.'

'The damned thing'll be airborne by now,' I said. 'If it's gone off the air again it means it's inside a plane. What do we do?'

'Wait one.'

I held on, hearing nothing but a roar of static. Then Bill came back and said, 'We're going ahead with the drop, weather permitting. We're just waiting for the latest forecast.'

'The sky's clearing here,' I told him. 'It's bloody cold, too.'

'OK, Geordie. I'll come back to you in a minute.'

I waited tensely, longing for the hit to be over and done with. 'Let's just grab our guys,' I said to myself, 'and get out of this arsehole of a place.'

Then Bill came through again. The forecast was good: clear skies behind the storm, and a hard frost. The plan remained on. What was more, they'd decided to advance the drop by half an hour, moving it to the original time of 1900. The two Chinooks were on their way to Nalchik, and would sit there waiting to hop over the mountain as soon as they were summoned.

'We passed all your data to the RAF,' Bill said. 'They've done an appreciation and decided to approach you from the north, down the slope. They don't fancy coming up the valley and over the compound entrance.'

At 5.30 I gave my pressel a double jab and said, 'OK, Sasha. I'm on the move. We're off to the DZ. I'll come round and pick you up. Stay still till I reach you.'

'I wait.'

Stars blazed overhead, and even though the moon hadn't risen yet the night was alarmingly bright, the snow reflecting all the remaining light from the frosty sky. This white blanket was something we hadn't planned for: the patterns on my DPMs were clearly visible, and I could have done with a snow overall.

Moving cautiously, and keeping to bare rock ridges as much as possible so that I didn't leave a continous trail, I worked my way round to the helipad. Sure enough, the chopper was still on the ground – an Alouette, painted some light colour, its rotor blades drooping under a three-inch load of snow. If it remained in position there'd be nowhere for a Chinook to land. No matter – the hostage recovery team could fast-rope down while the aircraft hovered. Then, if we couldn't shift the Alouette, we might have to exfil from the DZ in the forest.

I found Sasha ready to move. Instead of heading out to the left, in the direction of the DZ, we put in a bit of a detour and made our way straight up to the top fence, which was still unfinished. After watching for a couple of minutes we climbed the wire at a point where the wind had blown the snow off a rocky spine, leaving no tracks on the inside. The outside was a different matter. We landed in what turned out to be a gully, filled with snow to a depth of a couple of feet, and we couldn't help churning up the surface as we floundered out of the drift. I snatched up a pine branch and frisked it back and forth behind us, levelling the surface as best I could; but the moonlight was so bright that a trail still showed.

There was no time to mess about. Clear of the fence, we turned left, to the west, through the forest, and again followed the contour. Navigation was simple: I knew that if we held our height, we'd come out on the farm track that led up from the valley to the high hayfield.

Except when we brushed into tree branches, our progress was utterly silent: the dry snow lay like six inches of the softest powder, and our boots made not the slightest sound as they pushed through it.

We reached the track at 6.40 and stopped to listen. Twenty minutes in hand. Suddenly, into the silence, floated a wolf chorus, coming from much farther off than the howling the night before. Turning to look behind me, I saw that the moon had appeared over the eastern horizon, enormous and pale. For maybe a minute the distant, eerie wailing rose and fell. Then it died away.

We moved downhill until we came to the junction and the path that led to the hayfield. It crossed my mind that perhaps, for maximum security, we should continue to push our way through the trees, rather than use the track. But then I thought, To hell with it. There's nobody about. Let's just get there.

By 6.50 we were on the edge of the field, which glowed brilliant white in the moonlight.

'They'll see this, all right, when they jump,' I whispered.

Sasha nodded. I saw him swallow, and sensed that he was just as hepped up as I was.

'I've told them this is the forming-up point, by the old wagon,' I said quietly. 'You stay here, just in case anyone's been following us up. Keep back against that tree-trunk, in the shadow. As soon as I've collected everyone I'll bring them over. OK?'

'*Da, da.*' Sasha nodded vigorously, then said, 'Good luck!'

I punched him on the arm and moved away, skirting the edge of the field to keep in shadow. At 6.55 I stopped to wait, half-way up the long side, and stared to the south-east, way out among those millions of stars. I knew the Herc would be coming on the same path we'd used, flying at 28,000 feet. I also knew that I'd never see it or even hear it. All the same, I couldn't help searching for it in that phenomenal sky. I imagined the tailgate descending, the red warning lights, the guys lined up, three abreast, packed tightly together and laden with all their gear, toddling towards the lip at the back of the cabin floor with good old Pat Newman overseeing.

A minute to go. Maybe the plane was late. No – the SF air crews could hack it to the second. In that case, the Herc must be almost overhead.

I walked out a few metres into the field and stood in the open, feeling very exposed. Twenty seconds to run . . . ten . . . five, four, three, two, one. P Hour.

Now – where were they?

I found I was holding my breath, and had to make a conscious effort to relax. Were the lads on their way? It was almost impossible to believe that twenty bodies were hurtling down towards me at terminal velocity, a thousand feet every five seconds. Twenty-four thousand feet in two minutes. Then the chutes would deploy at 4,000 feet . . .

I counted the seconds, staring upwards, with the Firefly in my right hand. Then at last I heard the magic sound I'd been waiting for: the sudden, rattling, snapping flutter of a chute breaking out. It came from high in front of me, and was quickly followed by another, and another, four, five . . . then several all at once. Holding the Firefly above my head, I punched the rubber button on the base and saw a brilliant flash bounce off the snow.

In the enormous silence of the mountains the thin electronic whine of the unit building up to its next discharge sounded like a jet engine. *Flash* went the light again – and then suddenly in my earpiece there was Pat Newman's voice saying, 'OK, Geordie, I've got you. Close it down. I'm coming in.'

A moment later I saw the angular black shapes of the parachutes gliding across the stars like a formation of giant bats. In the last few seconds I heard the rush of air spilling from the canopies: then suddenly men in pairs were touching down all round me.

Brilliant! I thought – but at that instant, away to my left, a dog began to bark hysterically. The noise was coming from inside the trees, just beyond the old hay cart. I jabbed my pressel switch twice and listened for Sasha to come up on the air.

Nothing.

I jabbed again. The dog was still barking. One of the incoming figures had disengaged from its partner and was coming towards me. I recognised Pat from his rolling walk.

'Get in! Get in!' I hissed. 'That bloody dog.'

Even as I was talking the barking ceased.

The lads didn't need telling. Pat had briefed them already, and in any case their instincts and training made them head straight for the dark edge of the pines,

358

dragging their chutes behind them.

In the shadows, Pat had a quick head count.

'We're OK,' he said. 'We're on. What's the crack?'

'Not sure. See that old wagon on the edge of the field? I left Sasha there. That's our forming-up area. It sounded as though he had a contact. Wait one.'

Two more jabs on the pressel. Still no answer. All round me there was a general scrabbling and scrunching as people rolled up their chutes, and a rattle of working parts as they readied their weapons.

'Whatever's happened, we've got to go that way,' I told Pat.

'OK,' he said quickly. 'Us two'll move up and check it out.'

In the lead, I advanced with my 203 at the ready, every sense on full alert, with Pat ten metres behind me. Our boots, cushioned by the snow, were making no sound, but I knew we'd show up as black silhouettes every time we passed an open area.

At the corner of the field I stopped to scan with the kite-sight. Nothing moved, and I'd just started again when my earpiece hissed twice.

'Sasha?'

'*Da.*'

'Where are you?'

'Same place.'

'What happened?'

'One man came after.'

'Where's he gone?'

'I keell him.'

'What about the dog?'

'I keell dog also.'

'OK. We're closing on you now.'

'*Prinyato.*'

'The guys can come up,' I told Pat. 'There's a cache here for the chutes.'

While the rest of the lads came up I moved on, and was right beside Sasha before I saw him, standing against the trunk of a big pine. The snow on the track beside him was spattered with black-looking stains, which I realised must be blood.

'You OK?'

'Sure.'

'What happened?'

'I am waiting here. The man comes past. I shoot him with knife gun.'

'Where's the body?'

'Here.' Sasha pointed behind him at a dark heap beside the tree.

'And the dog?'

'Same place. Knife also.'

'Was it that German Shepherd that came along the perimeter wire last night?'

'I think.'

I turned to Pat and said, 'No point in trying to hide the bodies. We need to get in and out fast before anyone comes looking. But there's a well here we can dump the chutes in.'

'OK,' said Pat. 'Let's go.'

We bundled the chutes down the old water tank,

threw snow over the cover and hustled on.

I went as fast as I dared, trying to combine speed of advance with maximum alertness. The snow helped by deadening our footsteps, but all the way I was thinking that the surface of the field behind us must look as though a football match had taken place.

We came to the wire at the point where Sasha and I had lain to observe the barrier.

'This is it,' I told Pat. 'Once we're over, we'll be on target in less than a minute.'

'We need to tell base we're on our objective,' he whispered. 'They'll get the Chinooks airborne right away.'

'OK.'

I waited as he quickly set up his Satcom and reported his position.

How long would it have taken for the sentry to make a normal circuit of the fence? How soon would his failure to return be noticed? We had a few minutes yet.

With the set back in Pat's bergen, we went up to climb the wire. Over the fence and hidden in the trees again, we held a quick O-group.

'Now that the device has gone,' Pat began, 'that's knocked out one of our objectives. The summerhouse is no longer relevant. Forget that.

'I've designated three parties. Party A to block the road, Party B to assault the villa, Party C to watch the helipad and prevent any take-off.

'Our objective is to rescue the hostages. But no one else gets out of that building alive. OK?'

He got a few grunts for answer, and went on, 'I've briefed the parties already, Geordie. But for your benefit, Party C consists of two men – these two.' He pointed, but in the dark I couldn't recognise faces. 'Party A, the road, is these three. Two gympis and a sixty-six. That leaves fifteen, counting Sasha. I want to leave two back somewhere to act as sniper-observers. That makes thirteen for the house assault . . .'

Pat had got everything well worked out. I knew he'd laid out plans of the villa, using mine tape, on the floor of the hangar in Kars, and that the team had walked through each phase of the assault. His plan was to keep away from the front of the house altogether, so that we didn't trigger the alarm systems. A basement group would approach from the side and tape a demolition charge to the cellar door. The rear party would do the same to three ground-floor windows at the back.

Split-second timing was essential: the assault had to crack off from both sides simultaneously, and in that first instant one of the snipers would put a 203 grenade through the front door to increase the confusion.

As our ERV, Pat designated the helipad.

We moved out in single file, again at tactical spacing, in an anti-clockwise circle round the target. First stop was the helipad, where we dropped off Party C in good positions among rock bluffs that commanded the pad only thirty metres below them. Next we worked down until we could see the back of the house. Lights were on in most of the windows, but curtains or blinds had been drawn. Some fifty metres above the building we left the main assault group (which included Pat) crouching in the trees.

Round at the side I dropped off the basement group, to wait while I took Party A down to the point I had earmarked on the road. Then I hustled back up, glancing at my watch. The time was just before 8.30.

On the covert radio link I reported to Pat: 'All groups in position.'

'Roger,' he went. 'The assault will go down in figures three minutes. Move on to target at one minute before zero.'

By now the moon was well up, its light filtering through the fir branches. Beside me was Paul Anderson, an EMOE specialist, who was going to blow the door. As we crouched there, waiting, I realised that our breath was steaming in the air. For the past couple of hours I'd been so absorbed that I hadn't noticed the cold.

'Two minutes,' came Pat's voice.

I was hoping to hell the raid would give us some clue about where the bomb had been taken. Maybe we'd find messages, papers, tapes . . .

Suddenly Jim Taylor, leader of Party A, came on the air. 'Stand by,' he said. 'There's a vehicle coming up the road at high revs. What do we do? Hit it?'

'Roger,' Pat answered instantly. 'Take it out. Other groups, close on target *now*!'

We burst out of the trees and ran towards the basement door. In seconds Paul had taped a line of det cord straight down the middle. We stood back, flattening ourselves against the wall.

'Thirty seconds,' came Pat's voice. But before he could carry on the countdown the howl of an electronic alarm broke out from the front of the villa and wound up to a scream. At almost the same instant a brilliant flash split the night, and the thump of a 66 rocket exploding thundered up the mountainside, followed by the rattle of machine guns as Party A engaged the car.

'Go! Go! Go!' Pat screamed.

I turned my head away as Paul closed his clacker.

BOOM!

The door split in half and we pushed through the gap. As I went in I heard more rounds going down in the road-block.

The space inside was full of smoke or dust. Clouds of the stuff caught our torch beams and made it hard to see what there was in the room. Answer – nothing. Bare concrete block walls, bare cement floor, the room empty.

Another door at the back, steel, locked. It took Paul only seconds to make up another charge. Again we stood to one side. *BANG!* In the confined space, the shock buffeted us.

The second door swung open. Dust problems again. But this time through the haze I saw tubular steel storage shelves along one wall. On the floor at the foot of them was a long, dark heap. As my torch beam came on to it, part of the heap moved.

'Pav!' I yelled. 'Keep still! You're OK.'

In a flash I was kneeling in front of him. He and Toad were lying on their sides, head to head, their hands, behind backs, cuffed to the feet of the metal shelving. At first glance I thought Toad was dead – his eyes were shut and his face was white as chalk. When I put a hand on his cheek he felt as cold as a corpse. But at the touch his eyelids flickered.

One of the lads had bolt-cutters in his belt kit. 'Give us a light while I cut these fucking chains!' I shouted. I needn't have yelled, because a torch came on right beside me – but my adrenalin was up and running.

'OK,' Paul said calmly, holding the light.

Leaning over, I saw that Toad's hands were covered with filthy bandages, and that blood had seeped out of them and on to the floor. A couple of crunching snips cut though the chain and released him. Another severed the link between his cuffs. As his hands came free he gave a groan and tried to straighten his arms, but otherwise made no movement.

Pav wasn't in quite such a bad way. He, too, felt cold as death, and his face was a mess, but when I released his hands he brought his arms to the front of his body and curled up like a child.

I hit my pressel switch and called, 'Pat?'

There was a moment's pause. Then, as he answered, his voice was almost drowned by a burst of small-arms fire.

'We've found the hostages,' I went. 'In the basement. We're going to evacuate them into the trees.'

'Roger,' he answered. 'Carry on, and call in the choppers. We're clearing the upper floors.'

'Hypothermia,' Paul was saying. 'Both of them are in a bad way.'

Mentally, I was torn in two. One half of me wanted to stay with my injured mates and see them to safety. The other was burning to get up into the villa in search of Shark and grill him about where he'd sent the bomb.

I glanced round. Apart from me, there were five guys in the group: four to carry each casualty and one to cover them.

'Get them out under the trees to start with,' I said. 'I'm going upstairs. See you in a minute.'

In the far corner of the store-room was a wooden door. A burst from the 203 shot hell out of the lock, and I ran up a bare concrete staircase; knowing that I should wait for back-up but driven on by pure aggression.

Another locked door, another burst.

I erupted into a large and brilliantly lit open area – the recreation floor, with a sauna room, exercise machines and a fair-sized pool, a small swimming pool or a king-size jacuzzi. There was pale wood everywhere, on the floor, the walls and the doors of the sauna and the cubicles. The change in temperature was phenomenal: in one step I'd gone from zero to tropical.

Somebody had been in the pool until a few seconds before. The water was still moving, and a trail of wet footmarks led to one of the cubicles. The door was closed, but beneath it I could see a pair of feet.

Rounds were still going down on the upper floors. Then a heavy explosion crashed off.

'Come out!' I yelled. 'Get out of there!'

I stood off a few feet with my weapon levelled. 'Come out or I shoot.'

The door opened. Out came a man in a white towelling bath robe. From his long, narrow face I knew instantly that this was Akula. His black hair was slicked down with water and his eyes were wide open with fright or surprise. His movements were quite slow and perfectly controlled.

He said something in Russian, or possibly in Chechnyan. I didn't understand it and barked back, 'Speak English, you bastard. I know you can.'

'Who are you?' he demanded.

'Never mind that. I want to know where you've sent the bomb.'

'The bomb? What bomb? I don't understand.'

His right hand was moving up towards a pocket at waist height on the front of his robe.

'Keep still!' I shouted. 'Hands up.'

He raised them reluctantly.

I went forward and jabbed the muzzle of the 203 into his breastbone so hard that he crashed down on his arse.

'Get your hands above your head!' I shouted.

He lay on his back, arms up, while I felt in the pockets of his robe. My fingers closed on a small pistol. I brought it out, glanced briefly at it, and saw that it was covered in gold engraving. I slipped it in my pocket and repeated my question, standing over him with the 203 pointing down at his chest.

'Listen,' I said. 'I know who you are. You are Akula, the Shark. What have you done with the device?'

'I tell you, I have no device.'

'Don't fucking lie to me!' I shouted. 'Or I'll blow your bloody head off.'

That seemed to change his mind. 'You are too late,' he said. 'The device is not here.'

'I know. I'm asking where you've sent it.'

'You are American, yes?' There was a hint of mockery in his voice, of condescension.

'It doesn't matter what I am.'

'Well – you should send message to British Government.'

'Yes?'

'Tell them, release the Chechen men they have arrested.'

'What Chechen men?'

'Twelve persons.'

'What have they done?'

'Nothing. But the police arrested them. Unless they are free, London will be sorry.'

'What are you saying?'

'Only that. London will regret.'

'You mean you've sent the bomb to London?'

I was so hyped up by the thought that Orange was going to be used against us that, without any conscious decision, I fired a burst into the floor beside the Shark's right leg, then another that hit him in the thigh. As the rounds struck, he gave a convulsive jerk, then began to writhe around on his side, blood flowing out fast over the birch floor.

All at once there was a commotion at the far end of the room. A door flew open. As I looked in that direction, Akula tried to take advantage of the diversion and began dragging himself away along the edge of the pool. In a split-second I took in the fact that the newcomer was Sasha, who dashed in with his Gepard levelled. Before I could move or speak he'd opened up with three short bursts. The first missed, but the second caught the Shark full in the flank. As he rocked on his hands and knees, the third raked him again and toppled him sideways into the pool.

Behind me, from the changing cubicle he'd been in, came a sudden noise and movement and the door flew open. Out burst a young blonde woman, stark naked, holding a pistol in her right hand.

Before she could pull the trigger, Sasha cut her down with a burst into her back from point-blank range.

He was on a total high, uncontrollably violent, half mad. He fired two more bursts into the ceiling, splintering the planks, and rushed up to me with a triumphant roar of 'ZHEORDIE! WE KEEL THEM ALL!'

With a couple of bounds he reached the edge of the pool. The man's body was half-floating, face-down in the water, feet on the bottom. Blood had flooded out all round it, staining the water, dark red close in, paler farther out.

'Akula in the water!' Sasha shouted. 'Breelliant! We make him kneel! We make him swim!' Again he let drive a burst into the body, causing it to bob violently up and down.

Men came pounding into the room. Our guys. One, two, three.

'Out!' yelled one of them. 'The place is on fire. Gotta go downwards.'

'Here!' I pointed towards the door.

All five of us flew down the concrete stairs and through the wooden door. The inner store-room was empty. The hostages had gone.

Outside, the impact of frosty air cooled all of us down. I realised I'd been on just as vicious a high as Sasha.

As we drew away from the building and up the hill, we could see flames raging inside the ground-floor windows. Then a great tongue of fire burst out of the roof. Out of breath, I got down on one knee, jabbed my pressel and called, 'Pat?'

'Yes?'

'Geordie here. I'm east of the building. Where are you?'

'Straight above the villa. The Chinooks are coming in.'

'Great. Is there a medic on board?'

'Should be. I asked for one.'

'The hostages are in a bad way.'

'OK. RV on the helipad, soonest.'

'Roger.'

We started through the trees, but we'd only gone a few yards when another explosion burst out above us. I heard later that the guys in Party C saw somebody sneak up into the cockpit of the Alouette, so they put a 66 rocket into its fuel tank.

The fireball lit up the trees all around. By the time

we reached the scene the chopper was blazing from end to end. There was no chance of shifting the wreck quickly.

Over the radio I heard Pat call the Chinook captain and re-direct him to the LZ in the forest.

By now some of our guys had wrapped Pav and Toad in space blankets and sleeping bags and lashed them into nylon stretchers. There followed a desperate struggle, as relays of us carried them along the rough mountainside, bundled them over the wire and lugged them away through the forest.

Towards the end we could hear the Chinooks circling. Then rounds began to go down behind us and bullets came cracking through the trees.

By the time we reached the edge of the field we were sweating like pigs. One man, in the lead, ran out and shone a torch to bring the first Chinook in. At the same moment I heard Pat calling the second to put down an airstrike.

'Into the trees!' he was shouting. 'One hundred metres west of the LZ. One hundred metres and farther.'

The air was full of the heavy, thudding beat of big rotors. Through that came the violent racket of a chain-gun, putting down rounds at an incredible speed, making a noise almost like a chainsaw.

The next thing I knew, one chopper was coming in. The pilot put his nose down right on the torch. A storm of snow was thrashed into the air by the downdraught. We ran through it with our burdens, straight up the lowered ramp. Within seconds everyone was on board and counted, and we were lifting away.

Kneeling between the casualties, I got my back to Toad and shouted, 'Pav. It's me – Geordie.'

When he answered, 'Where've you fucking well been, you old bastard?' I knew he was well switched on.

'Pav,' I said. 'What did they do to Toad?'

'Bolt cutters,' he replied. 'One finger at a time.'

'Ah, Jesus! How many's he lost?'

'Dunno. Four maybe.'

'Bloody hell. Listen, what did he tell them about the device?'

'Nothing.'

'Is that right?'

'Absolutely nothing. Toad was bloody brilliant.'

'So they don't know about Apple?'

'Not a whisper.'

'Thank God for that.'

SIXTEEN

We landed back at Lyneham to find a premier-league flap in progress. The Firm had been shitting themselves so badly that they couldn't wait till we reached Hereford before they started grilling me. Two men had been waiting in the airport arrival hall, and within five minutes of touchdown I was speeding westwards in a chauffeur-driven Rover.

The fact that the British Government was in a panic came as no surprise. When the Chinooks had put us down at Krasnodar in the northern Caucasus, we were amazed to find an RAF Tristar sitting on the airfield, waiting to fly us home. So desperate had the situation become that our normal means of transport, a Herc, had been deemed too slow, and the big jet had been diverted from Cyprus to get us back at twice the speed. The result was one of those disorientating flights which end at practically the same time as they start. We'd taken off at 2200, and three and a quarter hours later we'd landed at 2215 local.

During our brief stopover at Krasnodar I'd spoken to Whinger on the Satcom. Naturally he was frantic to know what had happened, and I brought him up to

373

speed. At his end, he said, the team job was staggering on.

'I was hoping to come straight back and rejoin you,' I told him, 'but I'm off to the UK for a debrief first. Nobody's sure where the Chechens have taken Orange. London looks the most likely. As soon as the dust settles, I'll get my arse back to Balashika as fast as I can.'

'Speak to you soon,' replied Whinger laconically.

Back in England, scene after scene played through my mind as we headed westwards through the night: the chutes of the free-fallers coming in like bats out of the starry sky; the Chechens humping away the components of Orange during the snowstorm; Akula floating face-down in his own pool; the blaze from the villa lighting up the snow on the mountainside with a huge, ruddy glow.

My trouble in the debrief was that I'd already exhausted my small store of information. Talking to the CO in Hereford via Satcom from the Tristar, I'd already given all the details I could, and now, repeating my conversation with Shark for the benefit of the guys from the Firm, I felt as if the record had got stuck in the same groove.

I sat in the back of the car with one man beside me; the other, in the front, kept screwing round to talk. I could only suppose that the driver had full security clearance.

'Go through it again,' said the guy next to me.

'The whole meeting only lasted a couple of minutes,' I said. 'Akula just said, "You'd better send a message to the British Government."'

'And?'

'That if we didn't release the Chechens who'd been arrested, London would be sorry.'

'Was that all?'

'"London will regret." Those were his words exactly.'

'From which you assumed he was sending Orange to London and planning to detonate it there.'

'That's right,' I agreed. 'Couldn't the Yanks track the plane?'

'By the time they knew what was happening it was too late. There were several planes airborne over the Caucasus. Any of them could have been the one they wanted. The most likely candidate was a privately owned Gulfstream that went to Malta, which is one of the Mafia's overseas strongholds. We think the device may have been transferred to another aircraft there.'

'What about at this end?'

'We've got a watch on all major airports. The difficulty is, a small jet could put down in dozens of different places – on a private strip, anywhere.'

'So you think the bomb may be here already?'

'We've got to assume that.'

'And you can't search the whole of London.'

The man next to me made a wry grimace. Once more I thought of the guys in furry caps, carrying the components out through the snow.

'I should have whacked them while I had the chance,' I said.

'What's that?' The man in front twisted himself yet farther round, and I had to explain all over again.

Then I asked, 'But do they know how to detonate the damned thing? *Can* the device be set off without the SCR?'

'Probably, yes. The Americans say it could be, if somebody's had the right training.'

'Bloody hell!'

'Exactly.'

'This Shark – he didn't give any other clue?'

'He never had a chance. He might have, but Sasha rushed in and dropped him.'

I described how the naked woman had come storming out of the changing cubicle, and how Sasha had drilled her through the back. My companions seemed quite unmoved by the saga: their only reaction was that the front-seat guy opened a briefcase and switched on the interior light to show me some mug shots.

'These are what we got off the disk from Moscow,' he told me. 'Allegedly the Chechen Mafia's first eleven.'

'Well,' I said. 'That's Shark, for a start.' The long face, hollow cheeks and heavy eyebrow were unmistakable.

'That *was* Shark,' I corrected. 'You can eliminate him from your inquiries.'

'What about this one?'

He showed me a photo of an even more cadaverous-looking man, but younger. 'That's the brother, Supyan Gaidar. He calls himself Barrakuda. Anna showed me that photo in Balashika.'

'What about this one?'

The third villain bore a strong resemblance to Sasha, but his face was broader and shorter. I shook my head.

'Any of these guys could have been in the villa,' I said. 'If they were, I doubt if they came out alive. The only one I saw was Shark.'

'But this one,' my neighbour persisted. 'You're sure about him?'

'Definitely Barrakuda. He's pretty much like his elder brother.'

'We believe he's in the UK by now,' said the man in front. 'He was last heard of heading for London.'

In camp the atmosphere was no less frenetic. Everybody from the CO down came at me saying, 'Where have they put it? How do we find Barrakuda?' They seemed to think that because I'd been in Moscow, I must be an expert on the Chechen Mafia. They couldn't take in the fact that I knew nothing about the organisation's London dispositions.

Also, people were naturally worried about the safety of our guys still at Balashika, and kept asking questions about the situation there. All I could say was that, if they stayed inside the camp, they'd be OK.

After an hour's further debrief the boss at last realised that I was out on my feet, and told me to get my head down. He saw that there was nothing further we could do until we got some definite leads. So it was that at 0030 British time, 0330 Moscow time, 0430 Grozny time, and the end of the world by my biological clock, I eventually had a hot shower, lay down in my room in the sergeants' mess and passed out.

The next I knew, someone was shaking my shoulder. 'Get up, Geordie,' a voice was saying. 'On your feet. They've seen him.'

'Who?'

'Barrakuda.'

'Ah, Jesus! Where?'

'Central London. A police surveillance team saw him go into one of the flats they've had staked out.'

I blinked and stared at my watch: 6.15. 'What happened?' I croaked.

'He came in a taxi, carrying a small hold-all.'

'OK,' I said. 'I'm with you.'

Tired as I was, I knew I had to go, because I was the only person in England who'd set eyes on Orange.

Half an hour later I was heading back towards the capital, a member of the SP team, kitted out to take part in yet another hit. I knew all the other guys well enough to fit in, and as I'd recently finished commanding an SP team for nine months, we all spoke the same language.

As usual, our orders were unwritten but absolutely clear: our primary task was to recover Orange, but our scarcely less important aim was to silence Barrakuda and anyone found with him. If we got the bomb back and took out the immediate Mafia cell, the whole saga would become deniable. Anything the Chechens might say could be discredited. The operation was to be carried out as quickly as possible.

As our Range Rovers hurtled up the M4 at a steady 100 m.p.h., I noticed that the traffic seemed very light, and realised belatedly that this was Sunday.

In less than two hours we had reached a small warehouse in Notting Hill that had been taken over as a forward mounting base: the wagons drove straight in, out of sight, and the guys tumbled out to get their kit sorted.

By now the Firm had secured plans of the flat that Barrakuda was using. Markham Court was a small redbrick block, dating from the 1930s, in Seymour Place, north of Marble Arch. It belonged to West End Homes, a property company, and in June apartment No. 10 had been taken, fully furnished, on a three-year lease by a firm based in Malta. The area was up-market residential, central and convenient, and in recent years had been heavily infiltrated by Arabs.

The building had only five storeys, and No. 10 was on the top floor. A single lift went up from inside the front door of the building, with a staircase winding round the outside of the shaft. Lift and stairs both gave on to small landings, with two flats on each floor, to right and left. The only other access to each apartment was via a metal fire-escape, which served a back door leading out of the kitchen area.

Only five floors, I thought. The height's no problem. After our sixteen-floor epic in Moscow, this was money for jam in technical terms. The problem was going to be spectators: once explosions started cracking off, people would inevitably assemble to gawp. Still, that was a matter for the police.

The assault was easily planned. There was no need for anything elaborate like an abseil drop off the roof: all we needed was for our Red and Blue teams to arrive at front and back of the building simultaneously and secure the exits. Red would commandeer the lift and at the same time clear the front stairs. Blue would do the same at the back and go up the fire-escape. With the teams co-ordinated by covert radio, we'd blow both doors and storm the flat – the aim being, in the first instance, to overpower the people inside rather than kill anyone and possibly rob ourselves of vital intelligence. Only if we met armed resistance would we use our weapons, and only when the bomb had been found would we get rid of Barrakuda.

On the floor of the warehouse we laid out white mine tape to the exact dimensions of the rooms in the flat, and decided who would clear which. In the building across the street from the target, one startled family had to be evicted from their penthouse so that sniper observers could be installed and listening equipment brought to bear on the windows. Early indications suggested that the flat was occupied by two men.

Meanwhile, a Russian-speaking policeman – a young, dark guy called Michael, who looked more like a student than a police officer – was seconded to Red team, with orders to come up and join us as soon as the flat was secure. Two nuclear technicians from Porton

Down were standing by to neutralise Orange, when or if we found it.

At 10.45 a.m. we were ready to roll. Our CO and ops officer were installed alongside the police in a control room set up in Marylebone police station. I knew that at the last minute, before we went in, the CO would take command of the operation by signing the formal order, but that didn't concern us at the sharp end.

The police team who had Markham Court under surveillance confirmed that nobody had entered or left No. 10 since the arrival of Barrakuda, so we were reasonably confident that we'd find only two men inside.

Red team slipped into the building so easily that we might have been arriving for Sunday morning coffee.

Just as we were debussing a small, heavily veiled Arab woman came out of the block. Funny, I thought, she's just like us, dressed in black from head to foot. She did a big double-take at the sight of us. I thought she was going to dart back inside, but she kept going and walked off along the street.

One of our lads got a foot in the open door, saving us the need to pick or smash the security lock. Then it was three into the lift, two running up the stairs, and the sixth man staying down to guard the entrance.

Outside No 10. I paused till I heard from the commentary in my earpiece that Blue team were in position at the head of the fire-escape. Then I quietly said, 'Placing charge now.' The door had a peep-hole in the centre at head level, but as we'd arrived in total silence the chances that anyone was standing with his eye glued to it seemed exceedingly remote – so I ignored it and went forward to tape the det cord straight down the middle.

With that done, I stood back against the wall, the other guys lined up beyond me.

'Red, all set,' I reported.

'Blue, ready,' came the answer.

'OK then. Stand by . . . stand by . . . GO!'

I closed my clacker. The bang was very sharp and loud in the confines of the little landing, and the front door split in half and caved inwards. I lobbed a stun grenade through the opening, squinted sideways as it cracked off, and burst into the flat.

Two men in shirtsleeves were sitting at a table – or rather, they had been. By the time I entered the room they were half-way to their feet, staggering backwards in shock from the explosions.

'Stand still!' I yelled. 'Hands up!'

I saw immediately that the left-hand man was Barrakuda: a smaller version of Akula, with the same hollow cheeks, but younger, maybe in his late thirties, his features less haggard. He'd been taken completely by surprise. Before he could move two of our guys had him pinioned and cuffed with his hands behind his back. His companion was a big fellow, older and heavier, with stiff brown hair brushed up and back. He, too, was instantly overpowered.

Blue team, bursting through from the kitchen end of

the flat, confirmed that there was nobody else in residence.

A rapid search proved that the device was not on the premises. We looked under beds, in cupboards, behind furniture: there was no recess large enough to conceal cases that size.

From out in the hallway I reported, 'Red leader. Flat secure. No casualties. Device not here. Repeat, device not here. Let's have the interpreter up soonest.'

Now I noticed two small suitcases standing by the wall inside the front door. I picked one up. The weight told me it was full. Back in the living room I saw that our prisoners' jackets were hanging on the backs of the chairs where they'd been sitting. On the table stood an open attaché case made of crocodile skin, which immediately reminded me of the Moscow apartment. This one contained only papers, but among them were two air tickets and two passports with green plastic covers.

The passports were issued by the Republic of Chechnya and made out in Cyrillic script, with Roman equivalents underneath the names. One belonged to Hussein Amadov, the other to Andrei Musayev. The photo showed that Barrakuda was using Musayev as a pseudonym. The Air Malta tickets were made out in the same names. The destination was Valetta, but the flight numbers and dates were so densely printed that I had to stare at them for a few seconds before I could make them out. Then I realised that the tickets were for 21 October – that very day – and that the departure was scheduled for 12.45 p.m. Eh, I said to myself. These guys were about to do a flit.

As I flicked through the documents, Barrakuda watched me without moving, but I could feel controlled hatred emanating from him. I was glad we had him cuffed. I still had my MP5 on its sling over my shoulder, so I moved in on him, jammed the muzzle into the front of his expensive-looking cream shirt and jerked it violently sideways, ripping off two buttons. Sure enough, under the hair on his scrawny chest was the tattoo of a long, slim fish.

'You speak English?'

He said nothing, but lifted both elbows outwards to mean, 'No.'

I gave him a crack on the right ear with the barrel of the weapon, and although the blow rocked his head sideways, he hardly flinched.

I turned to the big man and asked the same.

'A little.'

'Where's the bomb?'

He pretended not to understand. I repeated the question. Again it produced no answer. Then I heard a movement behind me, and there was Mike, the interpreter, in the doorway. Behind him I saw police officers moving in to evacuate the other flats.

'Tell this guy I know who he is.' I pointed at Barrakuda. 'His real name's Gaidar, Supyan Gaidar. Tell him I want to know where they've put the nuclear device.'

As I spoke the names, I saw a flicker of unease run

through the prisoner.

Then Mike started in. His Russian was impressively fluent and fast, but it produced only a negative response.

'He doesn't know what you're talking about.'

'What's he doing here, then?'

This time the man did answer.

'He says he's here on business,' Mike translated. 'It's his first visit to London.'

'OK. Take a look at those papers on the table.'

Mike picked up a couple of sheets and scanned them briefly. 'They're about a shipment of goods from Valetta to Amsterdam.'

'Drugs, I bet.'

A telephone rang, right beside me.

'Pick it up,' I told Mike. 'Answer it in Russian.'

He lifted the receiver and said, '*Da?*' He listened briefly, went, '*Khorosho. Spasibo,*' and put the phone down. Barrakuda was glaring.

'What did they say?' I demanded.

'"Everything's in order. Precisely three hours from now."'

I checked my watch and said, 'Ten twenty-one. That gives us until thirteen twenty-one. Thirteen twenty.'

Immediately the phone rang again.

Again Mike said '*Da?*' and listened, but this time nobody spoke.

'Keep grilling him,' I told Mike. 'Back in a moment.'

I went through the shattered door on to the landing, out of earshot. I knew the telephone line had been tapped that morning so the spooks could trace the calls.

Now that the flat was secure, the SAS ought by rights to hand control over to the police and get out; but I'd had another idea.

I jabbed my pressel and said, 'Red leader. I need to speak to the CO.'

'Here,' said the boss immediately.

I reported the calls and said, 'If they can trace the source, we need to hit it. But I've got another idea.'

'Carry on.'

'The Barrakuda guy's obviously trying to do a flit. He's got his flight out booked for this afternoon. But I'm sure he knows where the bomb is. He knows it's not far away, and that it's set to go off three hours from now. We could try beating hell out of him to get the information, but my hunch is that wouldn't work. On the other hand, if we just keep him on site, he's soon going to start shitting himself.'

'OK. I'll square it with the Director and the Police Commissioner that you remain on target. How many men do you need?'

'Red team will do fine.'

'All right. Blue can pull out, then. The QRF will remain on standby outside.'

'Roger.'

The six guys from Blue team disappeared down the stairs. I put two of our own lads to guard the back door of the flat, two outside the front door, on the landing, leaving myself, Darren Barnes and Mike the interpreter to harass the prisoners.

'Tell him he's not going to Malta,' I said. 'Tell him

he's not going anywhere. He's staying here to enjoy his own little explosion.'

Mike translated. Barrakuda remained impassive but the big guy immediately began to look sick.

'Go through the briefcase,' I told Mike. 'Every bit of paper.' I turned to Darren and said, 'Get a brew on, for fuck's sake. See what you can find in the kitchen.'

He went out and rummaged in cupboards. 'There's tea,' he called, 'but no milk.'

'Black tea, then.'

The big guy started trying to say something to his partner. I waved at him to shut up and asked Mike, 'What was that?'

'Couldn't get it. Must have been Chechen.'

We hustled the two men to opposite ends of the room and sat them on chairs facing away from each other so that they couldn't communicate even with a look.

'Sugar?' shouted Darren from the kitchen.

'Three,' I called. 'Make it four.'

The scene had started to seem surreal. There were these two guys sitting handcuffed, back to back. Outside, London was enjoying a peaceful Sunday. Overhead, the cloud was breaking up, with occasional blue sky showing though. The odd jet went over on its way into Heathrow. Down in the street, cars accelerated as they headed north along Seymour Place.

Somewhere not far off, a nuclear device was ticking its way towards detonation.

I began to feel light-headed, almost as if I was floating.

Darren brought the tea. It was black as pitch and tasted like syrup, but it helped bring me back to reality. I got half the cup down my neck, then noticed some keys on the table beside the briefcase. One of them fitted the suitcase in the hall, but the luggage turned out innocent – spare suit and shirts, pyjamas, shaving kit.

Looking round the living room, I saw that it had old-fashioned mouldings, like fake panelling, on the walls, but that in an attempt to make it look more modern, somebody had put up large, abstract prints of geo-metrical designs, mostly black and white. The furniture was modern too, and expensive, the centrepiece a three-seat sofa covered in white hide.

Time crawled. After what seemed like an hour I found that only eighteen minutes had passed. I'd put my radio on listening watch, to conserve the battery.

Then, at 10.45, I got a double hiss and switched on again.

'Red leader,' I said.

'Your two calls.' It was Joe Darwent, the ops officer. 'The first was from a mobile. Sweeper vans are out, but it was too short for them to get a fix. The second call came from a house in St John's Wood, just north of you. Blue team are on their way there now.'

'Roger. What else is happening?'

'The top brass are meeting in the COBR. The Director's there, with the Home Secretary and a few others.'

'What about the police?'

'They've evacuated your block.'

'Is that all?'

'They're searching suspect houses, but they can't start mass evacuation unless they know where the device is. They might find they were moving people into a danger area.'

'Roger.'

For twenty minutes I sat on the window-sill and let silence go to work. With my covert radio switched on, I heard Blue leader reporting the arrival of his team at the location in Elm Tree Road, behind Lord's cricket ground. Quickly they deployed on both sides of the house and blasted their way in, only to find the place deserted. A search revealed no sign of the bomb.

At 12.10 the big guy began to get restless, shifting his arse around on his chair. At last he said something, which Mike translated. 'He wants to have a shit.'

'He can have a shit if he tells us where the bomb is.' It sounded ridiculous, as though I was bargaining in an attempt to make some child behave well. 'Otherwise he can shit in his pants.'

The man was in obvious physical discomfort, which my answer only increased.

'Tell both of them there's only one way they're getting out of here,' I said to Mike. 'That's by giving us the information we want.'

Mike translated. Suddenly Barrakuda began to talk in Chechen at the top of his voice.

'Shut up!' I shouted – but he carried on regardless, even when I belted him across the side of the head. Soon he was yelling like a madman in a high, hoarse voice. The big guy began to bellow back, and all at once I felt glad, because I saw that stress was getting to the pair of them.

I left them to it, and from out on the landing I called Control. 'They've started arguing like lunatics,' I reported. 'Their nerve's going.'

'It had better break soon,' snapped Joe. 'Things are getting bloody fraught around here.'

'Same here,' I told him.

At 12.25 the big guy shat himself. The smell was repulsive, so I opened a window. Cold air blasted in, but it was better than the stink.

Barrakuda went quiet again. At 12.40, when I stood in front of him, his face looked white as flour, and his eyes seemed to have sunk into his head. After I'd watched him for a few seconds, he said something.

'He wants to make a deal,' Mike interpreted.

'Oh yes?'

'If he gives you the information, will you guarantee him free passage to Malta?'

'Fucking hell! Who does he think he is? Tell him not a chance. Not the remotest bloody chance.'

I waited while the information was conveyed. Then I ostentatiously ripped the lead out of the telephone and said, in a series of short sentences, waiting for Mike to translate each one. 'What's going to happen is this . . . The police have already evacuated the city . . . In ten minutes' time we're getting out too . . . We're not going to wait for the explosion . . . We're going to cuff you to your shitty friend, tie you up and leave you here

. . . Talk now, or it'll be too late.'

That pushed him over the brink. He said something, and I saw Mike's eyes widen.

'What was that?' I snapped.

'He says the bomb is here.'

'Where?'

'In the garage below.'

'Jesus Christ! What garage? These flats don't have garages. We checked that.'

'In the small street behind.'

'What number?'

'Three.'

I hit my pressel. 'Red leader. What street is there immediately behind this block?'

'It's a mews,' said Joe instantly. 'Markham Mews. Why?'

'The bomb's there, in the garage.'

'Say that again.'

'Our prisoner says the bomb's there. In Number Three's garage. I'm coming down.'

I was already in the hall. 'Stay put!' I yelled to the rest of the team.' At the last moment I stuck my head back round the sitting-room door and said, 'Remember, nobody comes in here, and nobody's coming out of here alive.'

I couldn't wait for the lift. I took the stairs four or five at a time, heaving myself round the corners with the hand-rail. By the time I hit the street police sirens were screaming towards the block. A car nearly knocked me down as it swung into the mews. I was aware of a cordon in the distance, with a crowd behind it, and other figures running close to me.

There were the garages, built into little houses opposite the apartment block. One, two, three, numbering from the left. The third had bright blue wooden doors, freshly painted, with a white figure high on the right-hand side. The doors were secured with an old-fashioned hasp and padlock.

'Bolt-cutters!' I shouted. 'For fuck's sake, bolt-cutters!'

There was someone in black beside me, one of the QRF. Bolt-shears appeared in his hands. Two seconds later he had chopped through the soft metal guards around the padlock. I slid the bolt back, padlock and all, and dragged the doors open. The little garage was occupied by a beige-coloured van with the logo WEST END ANTIQUES painted in an elegant rainbow shape across its back doors.

Shit! I thought. Either Barrakuda was lying or he boobed on the number.

The guy from the QRF was more on the ball. He jumped forward, tried the doors, found they were locked, pushed his way between the right-hand side of the van and the brick wall, shone a torch through the driver's window and shouted, 'It's here!'

I was alongside him in an instant. There, in the back of the van, glinted a single, big, black object: Orange, with its two components united. From one corner, wires led to a red box just inside the rear doors.

My breath had gone. I hit my pressel and croaked,

'Red leader, we've found it. In Number Three garage. Locked inside a van.'

'DON'T TOUCH ANYTHING!' snapped a deep voice I didn't know. 'ATO here. We're on our way. Leave everything alone. Get clear of the site.'

We pushed back along the side of the van, trying not to rock it. In the doorway I looked up at the back of Markham Court, convinced that someone must have eyes on the site. More black-clad guys were hovering in the mews, hanging back from the target in uncharacteristic fashion. Their instincts were the same as mine – to go in and smash the timing device immediately. My watch said 1.13: we were within eight minutes of detonation. But they'd heard the ATO tell them to keep their distance, and they were wondering what the hell to do. It wasn't in our nature or training to run away – and in any case, there didn't seem much point. If the thing was about to go off, we'd never get far enough to make any difference.

What we did was to hustle back as far as the main road and tuck ourselves round the front of the apartment block, out of line of sight from the open garage doors. I tried to say something to the QRF guy, but words didn't come, my heart was pumping that fast.

This is fucking ridiculous! I thought. You get round the corner when you're cracking off an ordinary explosion. If *this* thing goes, we'll all be vapour and the building will simply vanish.

There wasn't long to wait or worry. Within seconds a van came screaming down the street. Its tyres squealed as it scorched round the corner into the mews and slid to a halt in front of the garage. Out jumped two men clad in white over-suits from head to toe, like astronauts. Each carried a heavy-looking hold-all full of kit.

'ATO on target,' the deep voice reported. 'Stand by.'

The lock on the van's rear doors held them up for all of five seconds. They flung the doors open and both leant in, on top of the live device, backs to us, reaching forward with their gloved hands. Fifty yards off, in full view, I stood transfixed, holding my breath. If it goes, I kept thinking, will I see the flash in the final split-second of life, or will the shock wave be too fast even for that?

The suspense was excruciating. I felt the whole world must be standing still, that everyone on earth had stopped breathing, like me. Mentally, I took off my hat to the two guys at the back of the van. By God they've got balls, I thought.

Then, after an incredibly short space of time, one of them stood up, turned round and raised both arms in triumph, as if he'd scored a goal. At the same moment I heard the deep voice say, 'Device made safe. Repeat: device made safe.'

I suppose I felt relief. I must have. But I don't remember it now. All I can recall is getting a sudden and intensely vivid mental image of the wretched sister device, Apple, sitting there in its hollowed-out niche beneath the Kremlin wall.

SEVENTEEN

On the plane to Moscow I had the unpleasant feeling that I'd gone back to the beginning and that the whole nightmare was about to start again. Flight number, departure time, type of aircraft, even the cabin crew – all were the same as on our recce trip.

Only I had changed. Instead of looking forward to a new experience and a bit of a lark, I was being driven by a personal compulsion at least as powerful as the jet engines thrusting us through the sky.

The morning papers carried no hint of the previous day's events: the media, thank God, had apparently not had a sniff of the drama in Markham Court and Mews. If they'd picked it up, they'd have had one hell of a story: LIVE NUCLEAR DEVICE DISCOVERED IN STOLEN VAN . . . GUN-BATTLE LEAVES TWO CHECHENS DEAD IN FLAT . . . SAS MAN LOSES FINGERS IN GROZNY TORTURE.

Wretched Toad! Word came up from the Services' hospital in London that surgeons had had to amputate the remains of both little fingers and the third finger on his left hand. When the Shark's men had realised that he was the one with knowledge of the bomb, they'd

395

started in on him with bolt-shears, one joint at a time. But, tough little sod that he was, he'd given nothing away. Pavarotti, who wasn't seriously hurt, confirmed that he'd shown outstanding courage.

According to the headlines, international tension had eased. Even so, there were only about a dozen passengers on the 767. Feeling the need to relax, I got two miniatures of Haig off the drinks trolley, along with a can of soda water, and downed the lot in a few minutes. The Scotch helped to lull my anxiety, and when I stretched out across three seats with a blanket over my head I soon fell asleep, and stayed unconscious for most of the flight.

The arrival hall at Sheremetyevo was as dim and dire as ever, but so few people were coming in that Immigration proved relatively painless. Beyond the Customs, in contrast, the taxi drivers swarmed even more voraciously than usual. Hardened to their methods, I stood still until I spotted a short man waiting at the back of the scrum. He had an open, friendly face, a neatly trimmed red beard, and was wearing a peaked, dark-blue cap. Instead of screaming at me, he was smiling.

I pushed through the mob and said, 'OK. Let's go.'

Outside, the cold bit, and I was surprised to see a dusting of snow on the ground. My guide led the way to a clean-looking grey Zhigudi and held one of the back doors open for me.

'Thanks,' I said. 'But I'll come in front.'

I settled in the passenger seat and asked, 'What's your name?'

'Sergei.'

'You speak English?'

'Some.' He gave a deprecating grin. 'City centre?'

'No. I want to go to Balashika.'

'Balashika!' He sounded amazed.

'Balashika first. Then city centre. Then back to Balashika. How much will all that cost?'

'Dollars?'

I nodded. As he pulled out on to the highway, I could see his mind ticking up figures. 'One hundred fifty.'

'I'll give you two hundred.'

'*Khorosho!*'

He drove fast but well, not taking risks, but watching all the time for openings in the traffic, and taking short-cuts to avoid the blocks at major intersections. When I praised his navigation, he answered in quite fluent English. We chit-chatted about this and that, and when I asked how old he was, he suddenly, with a flourish and a big grin, whipped off his cap to reveal that he was almost completely bald. 'Feefty!' he exclaimed. I refrained from saying that without his hat he bore a strong resemblance to Lenin, but I felt that if I had, he wouldn't have given a damn.

He took the outer ring-road, round the north perimeter of the city. Out in the country there seemed to be more snow, and although the main road was clear, the ground was uniformly white.

As we approached Balashika I felt my anxiety building. I hadn't quite worked out how I was going to handle my re-entry into the camp. The time was 6.30 p.m., and the chances were that the team would be back indoors for the night.

Taxis weren't allowed inside the barracks, so I asked Sergei to wait outside the gate. Luckily the guy on the barrier recognised me, and even greeted me cheekily as *Starik* - Old Man.

I ran up the steps of the barrack block in some trepidation, but again I was in luck. The guys had eaten supper early and gone out again to run a night exercise. Only the two scalies were in residence. I had a word with them, and said I'd be back later. Then it was just a matter of collecting basic essentials from the caving kit: wire ladder, head-torch and bolt cutters, plus a towel, sweater and spare padlocks from my own locker.

In fifteen minutes we were heading back into town, down the all-too-familiar Shosse Entusiastov, past the scene of the fatal ambush. As we went by, I twisted to my left in an attempt to pinpoint the spot. Yes – there was the wooden hut the Mafia had used as a decoy GAI station.

Going against the flow of traffic, we reached the centre of Moscow in thirty-five minutes. Sergei must have been curious about what I was doing, but he had the sense or the good manners not to enquire. I asked him to head for Sofieskaya Quay, and got him to drop me a hundred metres short of the churchyard gateway, at a point where an alleyway ran back between two houses.

'Half an hour, back here,' I said.

'Is good.' He peered at his watch. 'Now seven-thirty. Back eight o'clock?'

'*Tochno*. See you then.'

I was confident he'd return, because so far I'd paid him nothing, and I liked him the more for not having demanded the first instalment of his fee at half-time.

I walked a few steps down the alleyway and waited till I heard the car move off. Then I came back on to the embankment and hurried to the gateway.

Now, early in the evening, lights were on all over the convent building. Scarcely had I entered the yard when two women came walking towards me; but they passed without giving me a look, and a couple of seconds later I was safe in the pitch blackness of the old stable.

The bolt-cutters gave me sickening thoughts of Toad, but they did their work in a trice. I lifted the cover of the shaft, secured the top wires of the caving ladder round the hinges, and threw the rest of it down. Because of the wires, I couldn't close the cover while I was underground, but that was a risk I had to take.

Down in the tunnel the smell was exactly as I remembered it: damp, slime, decay. Of course I was scared – but in my experience the best way to hold fear at bay is to keep moving, so I hurried forward towards the river, anxious to discover if the water level was up or down. It was up. It was within three or four inches of the arched roof. Jesus! I should have brought a mask and dry-suit.

Too late now. At the top of the slope I stripped off my clothes and left them in a heap on top of my shoes.

Then, with the head-lamp back on and the bolt-cutters in my right hand, I waded into the black flood.

The water was cold as ice. I gasped as it reached my crotch, but strode forward hard in an attempt to keep my blood moving. Quickly my whole body became submersed. I made paddling movements with my hands to speed my progress. Soon I was up to my neck, then up to my chin. Down came the roof, down, down. I reached the point at which, with the top of my head touching the bricks, my mouth was under water and my nose just entering it. From now on the only way I could breathe was by tilting my head back and turning my face upwards in the narrow airspace. To do that I had to push the headlamp on to the back of my head so that it didn't foul the roof.

I took a deep breath, ducked under and drove forward, five steps, ten. Desperate for oxygen, I came up in that peculiar attitude, hit the roof with the headlamp, pushed it back, gasped in a breath and inadvertently got half a mouthful of filthy liquid. When I choked explosively, all the grot flew upwards and came back down in my face. The setback left me gasping. For a few seconds I fought panic. Keep still! I told myself. Get yourself together.

With my mouth shut, I took in some air through my nose. Then to my dismay I realised that in going for the headlamp I'd dropped the shears. I felt around with my bare feet. No contact. Had I moved forward a short distance while struggling for air? I shuffled back a few inches and felt around again. Still nothing.

The cold was getting to me. I could feel my legs starting to go numb. If you piss about here any longer, you're going to get cramp and bloody drown yourself, I thought. Leave the damned things. You can manage without them.

I waded on. Then, after one more stop for air, the water level began to drop. My head came clear: once again I could walk and breathe normally.

I came out of the flood shuddering, adjusted the lamp with shaking hands, and ran naked the last few yards to the site. Everything was as we'd left it. Scrabbling with chilled fingers, I dug away some of the spoil under which we'd buried Apple, until I came to the co-ax cables leading down from the SCR. I remembered how carefully Toad had connected them up, tightening nuts with his special spanners. Now I took hold of one in both hands and gave a big wrench. The cable held. I cleared more of it, right down to its junction with the black case, and heaved again, so hard that the whole device shifted, and pieces of spoil tumbled down the front of the heap.

Again I was on the verge of panic. Nothing on earth would persuade me to go back and search for the bolt-cutters again. One last effort: a colossal jerk, and away the cable came, so suddenly that I hurtled back into the far wall of the tunnel, grazing my right shoulder.

I stood shaking, more from fright now than from cold. At least the effort of struggling with the cable had warmed me up.

'Right, you fucker,' I said out loud to the bomb. 'That's you knackered.'

Into the water again. This time the same breathing technique got me through without swallowing any sludge. By sod's law, I expected to tread on the bolt-cutters, now that I no longer needed them, but I missed them again. Back at my clothes, I looked at my watch and found I had ten minutes to make the rendezvous. I towelled off furiously, got dressed, stuffed the sodden towel into my day-sack and hauled myself up the ladder, pausing with my head out the top of the shaft to make sure that everything was clear. Finally I slipped two new padlocks into position, wrapped the old ones in the towel, and crept out of the courtyard into the street.

The wide embankment was clear of cars and pedestrians. I nipped across the road, threw the old locks into the river, and hurried back to the far pavement. I was still walking towards the mouth of the alleyway when Sergei's car came towards me; but by then I was a safe distance from the church.

All the way back to Balashika I was uncomfortably aware that I stank like a sewer rat. But Sergei made no comment, and when I paid him off at the barrack gate I gave him twenty dollars over the odds, so that he went off in high good humour.

My own schedule was tight, but possible. The lads were still out on their night exercise, so there was no need for explanations. My first date with Anna had gone down the tubes; but under our new arrangement she had agreed to pick me up at 8.45, so I just had time for a shower. One hell of a shower it had to be, too. I washed my hair twice to get rid of the smell, and as I scoured myself all over, I felt my spirits lifting.

The worst part of the evening was over. What lay ahead I wasn't sure, but at least there was a promise of some action and excitement.

Comfortable in clean clothes, I again left word with the scalies and headed for the guardroom. I'd asked Anna not to drive in, in case any of the lads saw her and started taking the piss, and I found her sitting outside at the wheel of her little blue Fiat. As I climbed into the passenger seat I got a kiss on the cheek and a waft of heady scent – not the cheap rubbish that the slappers at the hotel had been doused in, but something sophisticated and Western. In the dim light I couldn't see exactly what she was wearing, except that it was a trouser suit. She had a big fur coat thrown back off her shoulders, over the seat.

'Great to see you!' I went. 'Great of you to come. Where are we going?'

'A restaurant called the Taiga.' She turned and gave me a peculiar look, not quite mocking, but definitely amused. 'That's not your kind of tiger, by the way.' She spelled the word out and said, 'It means the forest in Siberia, the wild forest. The restaurant's only a small place. No tourists ever go there. But it has proper Russian food.'

'Sounds good,' I said. 'In fact, it sounds tremendous. I haven't eaten all day.'

'Well,' she said, as she zipped through the gears, 'tell me the story.'

'Sasha must have told you already.'

'He has. But I want to hear your version.'

'You will. But I won't bore you with it yet. Wait till we get there. I need a drink to get me going.'

'All right. It's not far.'

Once again we sped down that damned road, then cut away through the northern edge of the city. I complimented her on the car, on her driving, on her clothes (even though I couldn't see them) – anything to avoid plunging into the saga, because I was afraid that once I'd started, everything would come out.

My mind was whirling as Anna pulled up in a scruffy side-street.

'Here we are,' she announced.

A small, red sign proclaiming TAIGA glowed faintly above a battered wooden door. If you hadn't known what the place was you'd never have given it a second glance. But inside it was like a forest growing in a cave: real tree-trunks, some birch, some pine, divided up little cubicles from each other, and the ceiling was a riot of branches. The air was warm and full of a wonderfully rich, meaty smell.

The waiters were dressed in forest green. From the way one of them sprang forward to take Anna's coat, I saw that she was a star guest. Another man showed us straight to a table in a corner cubicle: he ushered Anna into her chair and held a brief conversation as he poured out two glasses of vodka from a bottle already sitting in an ice-bucket on the table. That was apparently all the ordering she needed to do: no question of menu or wine list.

She raised her glass and said, '*Poyekhali!*'

'What's that?'

'It means "Bottoms up" when you're drinking vodka. It's what Gagarin said when he was about to go into space – "Let's get moving."'

'*Poyekhali*, then.' I clinked my glass on hers, and we both drank. Now I saw that her suit was made of turquoise shot-silk, and that she was wearing a pearl necklace. For the first time since I'd met her, she'd put on visible make-up – not much, but enough to accentuate her good features. She had darkened her eyebrows slightly, which made her eyes look bigger, and a touch of lipstick made her mouth seem more generous. She'd washed her hair, too, and done it so that it stood up in a shiny black curve above her forehead.

'Have some caviar,' she said. 'It's the best thing with vodka.'

She took the lid off a white pot cradled in a bed of ice, revealing a nest of shiny black eggs underneath. At that moment a waiter arrived with a dish of hot toast wrapped in a napkin.

'Please!' she said. 'Dig in. Is that the right expression?'

'Spot on!' I dug deep with a teaspoon, and heaped caviar on to the toast – the best mouthful I'd ever eaten. More vodka, more caviar. She too seemed hungry, eating and drinking level with me. I don't usually pay much attention to food, but the salty fish eggs and ice-cold spirit were such a combination that for a few minutes I really had to concentrate on my taste buds.

'Don't overdo it,' Anna said presently, again with that amused glint in her eyes. 'There are other things coming – Siberian specialities.'

'Why all this Siberia suddenly?'

'That's where I come from.'

'Really!' I looked at her with new interest. 'Tell me.'

She began to talk, quite fast, about how she'd been born in a village called Charysh, three thousand kilo-metres east of Moscow, in the Altai mountains – a primitive community, without electricity in those days, and most of the houses made of wood. Her family had been dirt-poor, but her father was the local school-master, and when Anna had showed intellectual promise at the age of nine, he'd sent her to live with an aunt and uncle in the capital so that she could get a better education.

The waiter brought us hot plates and a bowl from which steam rose in clouds, but Anna was so immersed in her narrative that she didn't immediately notice. Then, breaking out of her reverie, she said, 'Look! *Pilmeni* – dumplings with spiced meat. And this is special cabbage, cooked with walnuts.'

She helped herself and started to eat, but in a vague manner, not focusing on the delicious food. Her mind was out in the mountains and forests, and on she went, talking, talking, as she recalled how the River Charysh froze over in winter, so thick that army trucks could drive across it, and how, when the snow came, it would blanket the land a metre deep for four or five months on end.

Red wine had appeared on the table. I drank some, and kept eating. The little dumplings were irresistible. I lost count of the number I put away as I listened to her stories, fascinated to see a different, softer, more vulnerable person emerging from the tough chrysalis which was all I'd known so far.

Soothing taped music was playing, no more than a gentle background drone. But suddenly, as a new song started, Anna gave a twitch and cried, 'Oh! This one I love.' With a flick of the hand she bade one of the waiters turn up the volume, and the sound swelled into that of a male-voice choir, with a single, clear tenor reaching high above a groundswell of sonorous basses.

To my amazement, I saw her eyes fill with tears. For my benefit she began to translate the story, speaking low and fast as each haunting phrase of the song came to an end. 'A man is running through the taiga . . . He follows the tracks of wild animals . . . A storm is blowing . . . His way is long . . . Hide him in your breast, dark taiga . . . Far away he has left his native land, his mother, his wife and children . . . He will die in a foreign land and be buried there . . . His wife will find someone else . . . But his mother will never find another son.'

By the end, the tears were rolling down her cheeks. I reached over and covered her hand with mine. She looked up, smiled and gave a great shudder. Then she brought out a handkerchief and wiped her eyes.

'I'm sorry. The song is very sad.'

'I could hear that.'

'It reminds me of many things.'

'Anna,' I said instinctively. 'Why have you never married?'

The question seemed to jerk her back to the present. She raised her eyebrows and said, 'Married? I *am* married. My son is ten years old.'

I stared at her in amazement. 'You never told me.'

'Why should I?' She looked amused again. 'That's nothing to do with my professional career.'

'No, but . . . Where is your husband?'

'In Petersburg. He manages a bank there. We drifted apart years back.'

'And your son?'

'Mitya? He's at school here in Moscow. He lives mostly with his aunt, my sister.'

'Where's he tonight?'

'Who?'

'Mitya.'

'With his aunt.'

'And your husband?'

'In the north.'

She was looking at me steadily. 'Geordie,' she said. 'I've sent a message to your people at Balashika to say you'll be there in the morning. You're coming back to my apartment, to spend the night with me.'

'Fantastic!' I took a deep breath. These revelations seemed to be the cue for me to open up. God knows what it was that made me decide to confess. Now that

I'd disconnected Apple, there was no need or logical reason to reveal anything. Yet I knew in my heart that I had to do it. Otherwise, my conscience would never let me rest. It wasn't as if I'd reached this conclusion under the influence of alcohol: all this I'd worked out earlier, when I was stone-cold sober.

'Listen,' I said, looking round our little cubicle. 'I don't suppose the KGB have got this place bugged.'

'Of course not!' She grinned mischievously. 'You're probably the first foreigner that's ever come here. It wouldn't be worth their while.'

'Then I've got something to tell you.'

In the next few minutes I went overboard. I dived in headlong and told her all I knew about Apple and Orange. My mind was moving at incredible speed. I was vaguely aware of waiters removing plates and bringing tea, but I ignored them and rattled on, spilling secrets left and right. Even as I talked, I knew I was betraying my mates, the Regiment, my country, and that I was probably bringing my career in the army to a rapid end. But the accumulation of guilt had become too great to bear, and the act of freeing myself from it brought a feeling of fantastic liberation. I finished on a high, amazed at myself, but exhilarated.

Throughout my performance Anna had watched me as if half-hypnotised. She kept absolutely still, with her eyes fixed on me; yet after a while I realised that she was registering neither surprise nor anger. As before, her predominant expression was one of faint amusement.

When finally I came to a halt, she said, 'You need

some cognac,' and signalled to the waiter, who brought two small glasses and a bottle.

'Armenian brandy,' Anna announced. 'Your famous Prime Minister used to say it was the best.'

'Tony Blair?'

'Don't be ridiculous! Winston Churchill. Cheers!'

We clinked glasses, and I drained mine straight down.

'Aren't you furious with me?' I asked.

'Why should I be?'

'For having double-crossed you all this time.'

'You weren't being very clever about it.'

'You mean you knew what we were doing?'

'Not exactly. But we knew you had some secret agenda.'

'How?'

'Every time you went to the Embassy you were followed.'

'Jesus! But not into the churchyard?'

She shook her head. 'We lost you there.'

'What about that time we went up to the university and we got chased?'

'Those were some of our people.'

'Were they hurt?'

'One was killed.'

'I'm sorry.'

I poured myself some more brandy.

'But when the bomb was lifted – that wasn't you?'

'No – that was the Mafia all right. But Geordie – the Americans will realise that Apple isn't responding to signals. In fact, they must already know something's wrong. What if you get an order tomorrow, telling you to go down and check the device?'

'I'll tell my people at home it's impossible. I'll say the churchyard's been compromised, that the head of the shaft is under guard.'

Her eyes were holding mine.

'Listen,' I said. 'What were you doing that day you came poking your nose into our lap-top?'

She threw back her head and laughed. '*That!* A throwback to my old habits, I suppose: a little private espionage. Of course I was curious to find out more about what you were all doing.'

'But you never got into the program?'

She shook her head.

'What'll you do now?' I asked. 'Now I've told you?'

'Nothing.' This time it was her hand that took hold of mine. 'We'll keep this between us. If you've killed the bomb, that's it. There's no point telling my bosses. They'd only go mad and stir everything up again on the international front. By the way – can I have some more of that?'

She pointed at the bottle. I started and apologised, filling her glass again.

'Besides,' she said, 'it's not as if our own consciences are all that clear.'

I stared at her. 'What the hell do you mean by that?'

'Compact nuclear devices,' she said teasingly. 'CNDs. They are not the exclusive property of the West.'

'You mean . . . you don't mean you've done this to us already?'

'That's rather a crude way of putting it.'

'Are you saying there are CNDs buried under London?'

'Not necessarily *buried*.'

'How many, for God's sake?'

'I'll have to check, but I think the last count was five. I acted as liaison officer on an operation in 1993, when two went in.'

Suddenly I felt punch-drunk – not intoxicated, but rather as though I'd taken too much punishment.

'I don't know what to say,' I began feebly.

'Don't say anything. That's enough talk for tonight.'

THE
WATCHMAN

Elizabeth

(Here's to a dance so many years ago)

ACKNOWLEDGEMENTS

To my agent Barbara Levy, editor Mark Booth, assistant editor Hannah Black and the rest of the team at Century.

He kitenga kanohi,
He hokinga whakaaro.
[To see a face is to stir a memory.]

PROLOGUE

Sunday, 11 February 1996

Northern Ireland

There was a moment when Ray Bledsoe might have escaped with his life. If he had trusted his instincts at that moment – if he had reached for the Walther PPK and emptied the magazine through the side windows of the black taxi as it pulled into the parking bay alongside him – he might just have made it. He'd been an undercover soldier for three and a half years now, quite long enough to know bad trouble when he saw it, and a glance at the skinheads in the taxi had told him that this was the worst trouble of all. As he looked away he could feel their eyes lock on to him in icy, murderous anticipation.

But he had done nothing. The voice that whispered danger was drowned out by the voice screaming Yellow Card. If he opened fire on these men pre-emptively and without delivering the warnings specified on the Yellow Card he could find himself pensionless, dishonourably discharged and on trial for murder. The Rules of Engagement were bollocks, of course, and dangerous bollocks at that, but seventeen years in the Royal Military Police and a couple of well-publicised trials of British servicemen had instilled in Ray Bledsoe a deep-seated anxiety concerning the procedures of contact.

And so he had done nothing. Instead of reducing the taxi's interior to a horror show of shattered glass, jetting blood and brain-sprayed upholstery he had sat tight and reached for the packet of Embassy and the lighter on the passenger seat. Then, lighting up, he had wound down his window an inch or two and allowed the cold February air to draw out the smoke. Played it innocent. You don't gun down carloads of total strangers for no reason, Ray Bledsoe told himself, whatever your instincts. Whatever your misgivings.

But as the sharp air lanced at his face and the Embassy smoke hit his lungs he knew that emptying his Walther into the taxi was exactly what he should have done and that the moment in which he might have acted had passed. He sensed the purposeful exit of bodies from the taxi, saw his side window implode in a terrifying shower of sledgehammered glass, felt a gun barrel jammed cold to his head, smelt vinegared breath and knew himself as good as dead.

'Out, soldier.' The voice low, a Fermanagh accent, smooth as the cocking of a heavy automatic. 'And don't even think about . . .'

Talk, Bledsoe ordered himself, conscious that fear was freezing him, locking down his thought processes. *Blag. Use your bloody gob.* He turned to the glassless window but didn't know what words he used. Might have shouted, might have whispered. Couldn't hear himself.

'I said *out*, yer focker. *Now*!'

The door opening, the honeycombed sheet of safety glass sagging inwards, a blur of shaved heads and

2

tattooed arms, and the gulls screaming and wheeling above them. For all the chance of Bledsoe's reaching the Walther PPK at that moment it might as well have been back in the armoury at Lisburn.

Think. Think SOPs. Think yourself past the fear. Think.

And then, as he indecisively half rose, came the smashing blow to the forehead – a 9mm Browning butt, full magazine – and the blood in his eyes and the cold air and the arms dragging him and what must have been the carpeted floor of the taxi's boot rising to meet his face. He never saw the weapon's second chopping descent.

After an hour he began to come to. He did not immediately understand that he was in a moving car, and did not at once connect the pain at the front and back of his head with a dimly remembered sequence of events involving a PIRA snatch squad. Then he did remember and prayed hard for unconsciousness to return, and when it wouldn't return he lay there for the best part – or the worst part – of another hour. His hands were cuffed, he discovered, and he had been stripped naked. There was a smell of vomit, rubberised carpet and lubricating oil.

Please God, he thought, *don't let them take me over the border and out of the Crown jurisdiction. If they get me past the roadblocks and the border posts I'm a dead man.*

At the time of his kidnap Ray Bledsoe had been preparing to drop off payment for a tout named Proinsas Deavey in a car park. It was a standard dead-letter drop – the routine being that Bledsoe stuffed £200 in used notes in the Embassy packet and dropped it into the left-hand of the two bins by the parking

3

bays, and Deavey swung by a short time later with a soft-drink can to dispose of, surreptitiously pocketed the Embassy packet and made himself scarce. It wasn't an arrangement that either party actively enjoyed, but it had worked well enough up to now.

Deavey was an associate of known Republican players, but a self-destructive mixture of greed and stupidity had put him in the pay of the British security services. Things had started going wrong for Deavey when he set up a small-scale business selling pills and blow in Central Belfast's 'Holy Lands'. Named after its principal arteries – Damascus Street, Jerusalem Street and Canterbury Street – the Holy Lands was the bedsitter enclave serving Queen's University, and students from both sides of the political divide washed their socks, heated their beans and drank their beer there. It was Deavey's bad fortune to have approached a group of ultra-nationalist eighteen-year-olds, who had shopped him the moment he left the bar. Later that evening he had been given a severe beating behind a Falls Road betting office. The punishment squad had identified themselves as members of Direct Action Against Drugs, a known cover organisation for the IRA.

Resentful, half-crippled and robbed of a useful source of income, Deavey had been a comparatively easy touch for the FRU, or Forces Research Unit. The FRU was a small and highly secretive unit set up by the British army for the purpose of cultivating and running touts. It was staffed by soldiers who didn't look like soldiers. Most of them were middle-aged men like Bledsoe – long-serving ex-NCOs with pub bellies, thinning hair and anonymous faces.

Proinsas Deavey was one of half a dozen small-time

4

players that Bledsoe and his colleagues were handling. The former dope dealer had never made contact with any really important players, but the scraps he provided – meeting places, unfaithful husbands, who drank with whom – all assisted in the piecing together of the Intelligence jigsaw. Deavey had sold his Republican soul to Ray Bledsoe in a fish and chip shop outside Carrickfergus for a down payment of £175.

Touts were the bane of the PIRA's existence and their work with touts made FRU members highly desirable to terrorist snatch squads. When it came to his interrogation, Bledsoe knew, the first thing they would demand would be the identity of the touts he was running. The second would be the identity of the special forces personnel he was in contact with – the other FRU members, the Det (or Detachment) soldiers who made up the undercover surveillance teams, the Box (or MI5) teams and, of course, the SAS. Then they would want the radio codes and the rest of the intelligence baggage that he carried in his head.

The PIRA, Bledsoe thought, had almost certainly had him marked down as an FRU member for months. Lifting him now was partly expediency – they badly needed to know the answers he could give them – and partly the desire to raise two fingers to the British government. The larger symbol of that contempt had been the bombing, two days earlier, of South Quay in the Docklands area of London. Like everyone else at the barracks, Bledsoe had seen the pictures on TV, had stared open-mouthed at the devastated City landscape, at shattered office blocks, at streets inches deep in a glittering slush of broken glass. The lorry bomb had killed two people, injured many more and caused millions of pounds' worth of damage. A statement had been issued by the IRA an hour before the explosion revoking the official ceasefire that had lasted for seventeen months and nine days.

It hadn't felt like a ceasefire to Ray Bledsoe. More like business as usual and some of his colleagues said a fucking sight worse. But the bomb signalled a change. The bomb meant that the gloves were off publicly as well as privately. The FRU and the other special forces had been warned to exercise extra caution, to double-check sources, to watch their backs.

But there was only so much, finally, that you could do. Bledsoe's reaction to the warnings had been to request back-up for his drop-off. At his previous meeting with Deavey, Bledsoe had found the tout so jumpy that he had begun to wonder if the little bastard was playing a double game. It wasn't impossible that he'd decided despite everything that he was safer in PIRA's pockets than the army's and had bought his life by promising them an FRU agent on a plate. Or perhaps, even more extremely, Deavey had been PIRA's man all along and had been feeding them false information from the start.

Bledsoe had considered both scenarios highly unlikely – the tout seemed just too solid between the ears to run a sophisticated intelligence scam – but just in case of any funny business he had requested that a second FRU member attend the drop-off in a separate car. Connor Wheen, Bledsoe knew, had parked his Mondeo three hundred yards away near the car park entrance and with any luck he would have witnessed the snatch.

Assuming that he had done so, Wheen would have

put out an alert. Perhaps even now there was an SAS pursuit vehicle a mile behind them, showing no lights.

As he bumped and rolled on the floor of the taxi, however, Bledsoe found it difficult to think coherently. He had never thought of himself as a courageous man. If the car he was in broke through the cordon and escaped over the border there would be . . . what? The interrogation, the stomping kicks to the teeth and balls, the burning cigarettes to the eyeballs and . . . *Stop it*, he ordered himself. *Get a fucking grip. You're a soldier. Act like one. And, more importantly, think like one.*

Think of the details. Think of the SAS team bomb-bursting out of the camp at Lisburn within seconds of the alert, all with kit and weapons packed for action. Think of them hammering out on to the roads in their big Beamers and Quattros.

The ground grew steadily rougher, severely testing the big vehicle's suspension, and Bledsoe prayed for the grinding, rubber-flapping lurch that would signal that the car had punctured itself on an army spike chain. But there was no such lurch and then suddenly there was no movement at all. From far away came the heavy, squealing scrape of a sliding door. The car rumbled forward for a further few seconds and the sliding door rasped once more. A moment's stillness, then the boot sprang open to reveal the hard white glare of strip lights and Bledsoe was hauled, blinking, on to a flattened earth floor. The floor was cold and damp beneath his bare feet, the cuffs cut into his wrists and he could feel his hair stiff with blood. There were voices all around him.

Things took shape before his dark-accustomed eyes. He was in a large, iron-sided rectangular barn,

7

surrounded by expectant-looking men in dark-blue boiler suits. Vapour rose from their mouths, and the excited, contemptuous sound of their voices. In the corner to his left, mockingly normal, stood a John Deere tractor and an ordered pile of plastic fertiliser sacks. At the centre of the wall was a workshop area with pulleys and chains, and at the far end a stud-partitioned office. Ahead of him, parked along the right-hand wall, was an unloaded trailer.

He half-turned, still blinking. The entrance through which the car had come was barred by a pair of tall corrugated-iron doors hung from greased rails, in front of which waited two boiler-suited guards. One was fingering an automatic handgun, the other was pissing a steaming puddle on to the ground. Both were smirking at him with hate-filled, delinquent eyes.

Bledsoe stood there for a moment, swaying. Two thoughts hit him immediately. Where were the Regiment lads going to hit the place from? This was bad, but the other realisation was worse, so much worse that his chest began heaving involuntarily and he thought for a moment that he was going to pass out.

They were going to kill him and probably to blood some of the younger foot soldiers in the process. They were going to make it messy, to see who could do the business without flinching and who couldn't.

The nearest man, a burly red-haired figure, sniggered.

Fuck you, Bledsoe thought, shaking badly now but attempting to rally himself. *PIRA cunt. When the Regiment lads get here – and get here they will, blowing the doors off if they have to – I hope they blow your fucking head from your shoulders.*

8

For a moment things seemed to coalesce in the icy air. Bledsoe was in pain, concussed and very frightened indeed, but he knew what he was going to do. *Breathe*, he told himself. *Clear your head. Ignore the pain. Think.*

And then a dark-blue figure came from one side, slammed a fist into Bledsoe's stomach and brought his knee up hard into the FRU agent's nose, splintering the bone. Blinded by the flash of his breaking nose, gagging for air, Bledsoe went down. *They're going to hit me again*, he thought absently.

He was right. A steel toecap to the balls that froze his mouth into a silent scream followed by a crunching boot to the lower ribs. At least two of the ribs fractured now. His grasp on consciousness wavering, Bledsoe closed his eyes.

Hands took him under the arm, dragged him across to the trailer, slammed him against the iron tailgate and cuffed him to it, arms spread. His legs gave way for a moment and they let him hang there, drooling and half-suffocated, blood pouring down his face from his nose.

Finally he found his feet. Dragged icy farmyard air through his mouth. Opened his eyes a crack. Counted eight of them. Nine – there was one he hadn't seen before, a pale-faced figure with depthless eyes who could have been any age between twenty-five and forty, and unlike the rest was not smiling.

'Name?' The speaker was the one who'd kicked him, a thin, broken-nosed guy.

Bledsoe dragged his head up. Spat blood. Cleared his throat. 'I don't know who the hell you think I am,' he began blearily, 'but . . .'

'I'll tell ye who ye are,' the thin man said. 'Ye're

Sergeant Raymond Bledsoe, formerly of the Royal Military Police, presently seconded to the so-called Forces Research Unit. There's not a deal we don't know about ye, cuntie, ye can thank yer Regimental magazine for that, sae don't go gi'in us any crap.'

Silence. The older man from the car regarded him levelly.

'Ye know what we want,' the older man said, zipping himself into a pair of overalls with fastidious and terrifying care. 'Radio codes, SAS names, tout names – everything. We can start with yer man Deavey if you like, though as ye've probably guessed by now he's not quite the t'ick Paddy you took him for.'

Bledsoe said nothing. Stared up at the strip light, tried to distance himself from the pain of his nose and ribs.

The other man smiled. 'Ye see, unlike yer occupying army, we'll always be here. Deavey had the wit to realise that.'

Bledsoe struggled to keep his expression neutral, not to rise to the bait. Here we go, he thought. As rehearsed. 'I'll talk,' he said. 'But not to you. I'll talk to Adams or McGuinness or any of the executive-level officers of Sinn Fein and I'll give them everything they want to know. Or Padraig Byrne.'

Byrne, ostensibly a Sinn Fein councillor, was known to the security services as the chief of the PIRA's Belfast Brigade. There was purpose and calculation in Bledsoe's insistence on talking face to face with senior players: they were watched round the clock and in the event of a British agent being lifted, as Bledsoe had been lifted, this surveillance would be doubled. His trust in Connor Wheen was Bledsoe's only hope of survival. One or other would come through for him. The alternative was quite literally unthinkable.

'Ye'll talk to Byrne?'

'I will.'

His interrogator looked round the room. Everyone smiled.

'Yer word on that, then, ye'll talk to Byrne?'

Bledsoe hesitated, sensing a trap. Was it really going to be this easy?

The interrogator took a step closer. 'Well?'

He nodded. 'I'll talk to Byrne. No one junior to him.'

The other man nodded and glanced round the assembled faces. The smiles were wider now, displaying contempt, amusement and bad dentistry in equal measure. The man from the car shook his head, pulled a cellophane pouch of Drum tobacco from his trouser pocket and began to roll a cigarette. As he licked the paper the thin, broken-nosed man turned away, took a 9mm Browning automatic from the pocket of his boiler suit, considered it for a moment, then swung the butt back-handed and with full force into Bledsoe's broken ribs.

The pain was indescribable, an explosion of liquid fire in his chest that seemed, once again, to drain the FRU man of all coherent thought. He fell forward, hanging from the tailgate by his cuffed wrists, and for a moment saw himself as the young Provos surrounding him saw him – a pallid, bloody-faced, flabby-arsed forty-fags-a-day chancer, close to his pension and closer to tears. As an agent handler Bledsoe's world had become that of his informers – a world of beer and bar-stools and clapped-out cars. He had fitted in well, but at the cost of his health and fitness. 'There's no disguise like a fat gut!' the instructors had told them at Tregaron, and Bledsoe had laughed along with the others.

Now look at him. Pathetic.

Something still beat in his chest, however, even as he hung there wheezing and gagging. Some ghost of the bloody-minded squaddie he'd once been still hung grimly on. *There'll be a fuck of a bang when the lads blow that door. A fuck of a bang. And the killing spree of all time. None of these Provie cunts would live to . . .*

A hand grabbed Bledsoe's hair and pulled his head level. Through a film of pain he saw a short, square figure walking out of the office area, a figure whose reddened and bony features, slicked-back hair and carefully buttoned Aran cardigan he recognised instantly.

'Would ye be knowing this gentleman?' It was the gun-butt man again.

'Yeah,' said Bledsoe, attempting to sneer. 'Val Doonican.'

That earned him another kick in the balls and this time, as a lurching despair became one with the pain, Bledsoe kept his eyes shut.

The man in the Aran cardigan was Padraig Byrne. No Det unit was about to follow the fucker anywhere. He was already here – wherever here was – and he had probably been here for days. When Bledsoe finally reopened his eyes it was to see Byrne pulling on a boiler suit.

'Pleased to see me, Sergeant Bledsoe? You will be, that I promise.' The voice was light and cultured, and somehow horribly at odds with the raw-boned features. The considered view in Lisburn barracks,

12

Bledsoe remembered, was that Padraig Byrne took it up the arse.

'You see, Sergeant, we've got something for you.'

A book hit the ground with a thump next to the FRU man's feet. *What the fuck?*

'Raymond John Bledsoe,' Byrne continued in his soft wheedling brogue, 'this is your Death!'

There was snigger of sycophantic laughter from the young Provo foot soldiers. Opening his eyes a fraction, Bledsoe saw that the book was a Yellow Pages directory for the Newry and Mourne area. *He hadn't crossed the border, then. There was still hope.*

Please God, he thought, *let Wheen have hooked a follow car on to that taxi. Let there be a Regiment team out there right now, taking out the sentries.*

He hung on desperately to that hope. He suspected that the interrogation was about to start and he didn't know if he had any courage left to bullshit them with. It was going to be very bad – he was certain of that from the number of young guys they'd assembled, and from the hunger and expectancy on their faces.

And then, with a blast of cold air, the sliding doors opened again and a mud-spattered white van drove into the barn, shuddered for a moment in a haze of exhaust and was still. The barn doors were quickly dragged shut, then a terrible high-pitched screaming issued from inside the van. The screaming seemed to go on and on, and ended in a sound that was halfway between a retch and a whimper.

'Do you recognise that voice, Bledsoe?' asked Byrne, continuing his Eamonn Andrews impersonation. 'Yes, all the way from Lisburn barracks, Belfast, it's your old friend . . .'

A second naked and plasticuffed figure was dragged

from the back of the van by two more boiler-suited Provo foot soldiers. He had been severely beaten around the head and upper body, dirt and vomit smeared his chest and legs, and his face was a shapeless blood-smeared mask. In the middle of the room the foot soldiers kicked the new arrival's feet from under him and he fell heavily to the ground.

Byrne looked on, enjoying the moment. 'Good evening,' he addressed the man on the ground. 'And thank you for joining us on this special occasion.'

'Fuck you!' said the fallen man. At least that's what Bledsoe guessed that he was trying to say, but something horrible had happened to his mouth and teeth, and all that came out was a bubbling, gutteral rasp.

Bledsoe stared. Tried to beat back the worst of the fear.

With an immense effort the battered figure squinted around him, found Bledsoe, and winked one blackened and swollen eyelid. As he did so his face took momentary shape and with a sullen jolt of recognition all hope died in Ray Bledsoe.

'That's right,' crowed Byrne exultantly, resuming. 'It's your old mate Connor Wheen!'

I'm dead, Bledsoe thought dully. *We're both dead*.

Byrne watched them, delighted with his coup. A chair was brought from the office and the two men hauled Wheen into it, forcing his cuffed hands behind the backrest.

'I know what you're wondering,' said Byrne to Bledsoe with vast good humour. 'You're wondering if you're still north of the border, so that your SAS pals can drop in on us. Well, you know something . . .' Byrne shook his head at the sheer hilariousness of the situation. '*You're not!*'

14

Bledsoe felt his sanity slipping away. All that remained now was terror, pain and death. His unhinged gaze found the pale-faced man, who stared back at him with ageless, unsmiling intensity. You are in hell, that gaze told him. Welcome.

Byrne turned to the pale-faced man. 'Joseph, as we agreed earlier, I'd like it to be you that does the killing.' His tone was casual, conversational.

'Please,' whispered Bledsoe. 'I'll tell you everything.' His lips were papery and his voice was a submissive monotone. 'You can have the Det list, the SAS list, the tout list, the codes . . .'

Padraig Byrne frowned and looked at him intently for a moment or two as if wrestling with some complex moral or intellectual issue. Then he smiled again and turned back to the pale-faced man he called Joseph.

ONE

Sierra Leone

After an hour's march, Captain Alex Temple held up his hand and the patrol came to a cautious halt. Above them the waning moon was obscured by lurid bruise-coloured rain clouds. In the forest to either side of them insects drilled and screamed. It was fifteen minutes after midnight and all six men were soaked to the skin. They were sweating too, as their dark-accustomed eyes scanned the clearing.

Alex had been right. Above the distant booming of thunder, just audible, was a faint staccato crackle. Gunfire, surely. To his side, all but invisible in the dank shadows, Don Hammond nodded in agreement, showed two fingers – two clicks ahead – and pointed up the trail. *Yes*, thought Alex with fierce joy. *Yes! This is what I joined the Regiment for. This is what I'll do for as long as they'll let me.*

He grinned at the wiry sergeant and glanced round at the four other members of Zulu Three Six patrol as they melted into the dank foliage. Immediately behind him was a sharp-faced trooper named Ricky Sutton, the patrol signaller. At twenty-three, Sutton was the youngest and least experienced member of the team. Covering Sutton's back as he worked was Stan

Clayton, a long-serving and famously mouthy cockney corporal, and on the other side of the clearing, shadowy in the dimness, crouched Lance Wilford and Jimmy 'Dog' Kenilworth, a corporal and a lance-corporal respectively. Like Alex, they were dressed in sodden jungle kit and webbing, and carrying M16 203 rifles and a sheathed *parang*. Beneath the frayed rims of their bush-hats their faces were blackened with cam-stick. All had compasses attached to their wrists and rifles.

At Don Hammond's sign, the patrol members quietly lowered their heavy Bergan rucksacks and began to cache them. Mosquitoes whined around them, settling greedily on their hands and faces. A couple of the men had leeches visible at their necks and wrists, and Alex guessed that they all had at least half a dozen sucking away beneath their wet shirts and combat trousers.

Crouching in the dank foliage, Hammond unfurled the aerial of the sat-com radio, and reported the patrol's position and the direction of the small-arms fire to the SAS base in Freetown. When Hammond had completed the report Alex resumed the lead scout position. Signing for the rest of the patrol to follow, he set off towards the distant gunfire.

This was it, he thought – *this had to be it* – and breathed a silent prayer of thanks to the gods of war. He was thirty-five years old and a commissioned officer, and both facts militated against him. SAS officers, or 'Ruperts' as they were known, were usually directed into planning roles, while the 'chopping' was done by the troopers and NCOs. As a Rupert, Alex was lucky to be here at all. Somehow, against all the odds, it seemed that he had been granted one last adventure.

Zulu Three Six patrol was searching for a missing ITN news crew.

The journalists – reporter Sally Roberts, cameraman Ben Mills and sound recordist Gary Burge – had been missing for more than thirty-six hours now. They had last been seen in the town of Masiaka, thirty-five miles inland from the capital, Freetown. Masiaka was a strategically important staging post, and its mildewed and flyblown bungalows had been much fought over in the dirty war between the Sierra Leone army and the Revolutionary United Front. At present it was in the hands of pro-government forces and so considered more or less safe for Western media teams.

According to the Agence France Presse people who'd been showing them around, Sally Roberts and her team had arrived in Masiaka intending to interview members of a notoriously volatile pro-government militia known as the West Side Boys. The ITN team had hoped to find the militia's commanders at the mildewed and bullet-pocked bungalow that served as their HQ, but on arriving there had discovered that the occupants had decamped eastwards in pursuit of an RUF raiding party.

Undeterred, and against the advice of the other Western press agencies, the ITN team had decided to follow the West Side Boys into the RUF-held badlands and at dawn the next day had set off on the Kissuna Road in a hired car. No one in Masiaka knew what had happened to Roberts, Mills and Burge after that. No one had seen them and no one had heard from them, despite the fact that all three were carrying sat-phones.

From evidence later provided by militia members it seemed that the West Side Boys had followed the raiding party far into RUF territory and that a vicious but inconclusive firefight had taken place near Kissuna, after which the militia had withdrawn back towards Masiaka. During the battle, as usual, most of the combatants had been blind drunk; the RUF on palm wine, the West Side Boys on the plastic bags of raw gin that they habitually carried. A dozen or so fighters, several of them children, had been killed on both sides.

When the ITN team neither returned that night, nor contacted anyone in Masiaka, people began to wonder. At noon the following day, fearing the worst, a BBC news crew filmed an interview with a West Side Boys militia leader called 'Colonel Self-Loading'. Within two hours of the interview, and following a swift triangular exchange of secure calls between Freetown, Whitehall and Hereford, an unedited video copy of the film was running at SAS HQ, Freetown. The HQ was a former security complex on the edge of Lungi airport – a scruffily anonymous cluster of tents, low Nissen-style huts and radio masts. Watching the video clip were Major David Ross, OC of the forty-strong detachment from 'D' Squadron, and Captain Alex Temple of the Regiment's Revolutionary Warfare Wing.

The twenty-minute clip made for grim viewing. Colonel Self-Loading's eyes were red with fatigue, ganja and trail dust but he was certain of his facts: no Western correspondent had spoken to any member of the West Side Boys since their departure from Masiaka two days earlier. And certainly no Western woman.

If the team had been anywhere near the Kissuna battle zone, the colonel told the BBC interviewer, then they had probably been lifted by the RUF. Even now, he said, the woman was probably being asked if she wanted 'long sleeves' or 'short sleeves' – amputation above or below the elbow. Hacking off arms was the RUF's calling-card. Recently, they had extended the practice to genitals. Once mutilated, victims were made to sit in bowls of caustic soda.

'And maybe they eat them, you know.' The young colonel shrugged, reaching under his Tupac Shakur T-shirt to scratch his belly. 'Food is short.'

Colonel Self-Loading was in a position to know about the RUF's dietary habits. A year earlier the West Side Boys had sided with the rebels, sweeping down to occupy Freetown on a manic tide of blood and slaughter, and to the thumping beat of the RUF anthem 'No Living Thing'. The conversion of the West Side Boys to the government's way of seeing things – a conversion which was rewarded by British mercenaries with a thirty-five-ton sanctions-busting consignment of Bulgarian weaponry – was comparatively recent. If Colonel Self-Loading said that the RUF ate human flesh, then they did.

'You see, this is a bad war,' he declared to the camera with all the authority of his nineteen years. 'A very bad war.'

Excusing himself, he explained to the interviewer that he was off to find a 'popsicle' – an iced lolly made of neat gin – and a woman.

'Doesn't look good,' said Alex levelly, when the footage came to a close.

'Nor it does,' said David Ross. 'And I've got a feeling it might be coming our way.'

20

Alex nodded. 'I'll put my lads on standby.'

'Do that,' agreed Ross.

The Revolutionary Warfare Wing, from which Alex's twelve-strong team had been drawn, is the most secretive element of the SAS and the unit's existence has never been officially admitted. Its purpose is the execution of officially deniable tasks and contracts, including the covert training of overseas 'friendlies'. These last have included the Mujahedin of Afghanistan and the Cambodian Khmer Rouge.

On this occasion, rather less controversially, Alex Temple's team were in Freetown as part of a training package for the Sierra Leone army. They found it uninspiring work and between exercises were glad to return to the temporary base they shared with the forty men of 'D' Squadron.

At twenty minutes after 5 p.m. Alex was summoned to the OC's hut for the second time that afternoon. In a few succinct sentences David Ross put him in the picture concerning the kidnap of the ITN team. The squadron would be mounting a search operation that night, Ross informed Alex, and the RWW team would remain on standby at the base to help with the planning of a rescue.

Alex heard Ross out and proposed an alternative plan. The RWW team would mount the search, he suggested, while 'D' Squadron would stand by to effect the rescue.

Ross politely but firmly turned Alex's plan down. The RWW team were separate from his command, their presence in Sierra Leone was being paid for by that country's government and there would be an awkward convergence of responsibilities.

Alex countered that for the purposes of the

operation he would be happy to place himself and his men under the direct command of Ross. If he led the search team 'D' Squadron could be kept intact for the rescue. 'If we find them,' he pleaded with the OC, 'it'll be a "D" Squadron success. If we don't, it'll be an RWW fuck-up.' What Alex didn't need to add was that he had several years' more experience than Ross and was undoubtedly the best man to lead the search.

Ross considered Alex's suggestion. The two men liked and respected each other, and the lean-faced ex-Signals officer was aware that this would probably be Alex's last chance of leading his men into hostile territory. In the end, he gave Alex the nod. Intelligence reports from RUF informers suggested that the hostages had been taken to one of two possible camps. Alex was to divide his men into two six-man patrols and prepare for insertion under cover of darkness.

As he listened to the briefing an hour later and pored over the map table with his men, Alex felt the first fluttering crawl of anticipation. This, he knew from experience, would build to the taut excitement which always preceded action. When the time came, the excitement would give way to an icy, analytical calm. Then, for better or worse, he would do his job.

And on this one, he reckoned, it might well be for worse. Looking at the aerial reconnaissance photographs – at the drab, swampy vastness of the jungle, the tiny gnat-bite settlements and the sullen clay-coloured waterways – it seemed almost unimaginable that they would locate the ITN team. How the hell could they find three people in all of that? And even if one of the patrols did locate the journalists, would they still be alive? Would there be time to scope the place out, accurately assess the enemy's strength and firepower, insert a rescue team and lift the hostages from under the noses of the notably well-armed RUF?

'We have to think positive, gentlemen,' said Ross briskly, as if reading his thoughts. 'The intelligence people have established a link with RUF commanders in the interior. We're assured that if they want to negotiate, the infrastructure exists. Having said that, of course, we can't count on any such thing. We've got to find the hostages and prepare a hard extraction.' He swept his hand over the maps. 'Now, it looks like a huge search area, but the probability is that if our hostages are still in one piece they're being held at one of a pair of jungle camps in the Kissuna sector. These are located as follows' – he overlaid the assembly of aerial photographs with a clear sheet marked up in chinagraph pencil – 'and I've coded them Arsenal and Chelsea. Both, as you can see, are on the Rokel river, and neither is more than ten clicks from our LZ here on the ridge line, which we will call Millwall.'

Carefully, Alex scanned the aerial photgraphs. The camps were just about visible if you knew exactly what you were looking for. They were surrounded by a hell of a lot of jungle, though.

'Search teams will be dropped off at Millwall at 2330 hours tonight,' Ross continued. 'By the time they reach their recce points, judging by past experience, the bulk of the RUF soldiery will be off their heads on dope and palm wine, and security around the camps will be piss-poor. We could approach earlier but the risk of the patrols being discovered would be much greater, with concomitant increase of risk to the hostages.' He steepled his fingers and regarded them levelly. 'As it is you're going to have to go bloody carefully, and remember that just because these buggers are part-time cannibals who like dressing up in weird costumes and chopping toddlers' arms off with machetes, it doesn't mean they aren't at home with sophisticated weaponry. They've got RPGs and all sorts in those camps, thanks to their income from those bloody diamond mines they control, and I don't – repeat *don't* – want to lose any men. You will not, under any circumstances, risk a contact, is that understood?'

Everyone nodded. Alex glanced at the other patrol members. He was the only officer.

'From Millwall,' Ross continued, 'patrols will tab in to their respective targets. Whether or not there's any sign of any hostages, we're going to need full reports concerning numbers, weaponry, fields of fire, disposition of buildings and all the rest of it, OK? By 0230 hours tomorrow, if we haven't located the TV people, I want both patrols back at Millwall for evacuation by Puma. If we have found them I want both patrols to converge on the camp in question and remain eyes-on. Alex, you and one other will then tab back to Millwall and be choppered back to Freetown to brief the Squadron. Any questions so far?'

Along with the others, Alex shook his head.

'The timing of the assault will depend on the intelligence you get back to us and the outcome of any negotiations that take place,' Ross continued. 'It's still perfectly possible that the RUF can be persuaded to return the hostages – Roberts and Co. are an international press team, after all, and the RUF aren't completely indifferent to world opinion.'

Oh no? thought Alex, who had seen the school-age amputees on the streets of Freetown and Masiaka. *You could have fuckin' fooled me.*

24

'Assuming the negotiations fail, the "D" Squadron assault team will go in between twenty-four hours and a week from tonight. Again, any questions?'

And again there were none.

At 11 p.m., the two RWW search patrols boarded a Puma. Showing no lights, fitted with low-noise rotor blades and flown by a pilot in night-vision goggles, the helicopter slipped silently inland, overflew Masiaka and swung eastwards into RUF territory. At 1130, precisely on schedule, the twelve soldiers de-bussed, crouching in the rotor wash as the Puma lifted away from the ridge line and turned back towards Freetown.

Thirty minutes after caching the Bergans the patrol halted for a scheduled comms burst from base. As Ricky Sutton looped a plastic-coated aerial wire over a tree branch, a damp, overbearing heat pressed around them. The sporadic bursts of rifle fire were clearly audible now and over the smell of decomposing vegetation the air carried a faint drift of woodsmoke.

Were the ITN team being held at the camp ahead of them? As always in the presence of danger, Alex felt tautly, intensely alive.

Checking his watch, he joined Don Hammond and Ricky Sutton who were huddled over the 319 patrol radio, waiting for the burst to decrypt. In silence, the three men stared at the miniature green-lit VDU screen.

Black letters leapt into view. Ricky Sutton wiped away the rain.

'HOSTAGES TO BE EXECUTED 14th 1200. INFORM WHEN LOCATED. SEARCH

PATROLS TO SUPPORT D SQN ASSAULT AT 1ST LIGHT. ROSS'

'Fuck me!' breathed Alex, his heart pounding. 'The fourteenth is today. First light's in about four hours. And we haven't even found them yet.'

He'd wanted an adventure.

He'd got one.

TWO

Assault at first light.

That turned everything – *everything* – on its head. The RUF must have issued some impossible ultimatum – the freeing of all prisoners taken by the Sierra Leone army, for example.

The patrol had moved through the remaining jungle as fast as humanly possible. They were very close to the camp now and Alex recognised the random discharges as being those of British-issued SLRs. The sound was a good sign. Unless the RUF were fighting among themselves it meant that they were in party mood, emptying their 7.62 rounds into the river and the surrounding jungle out of a kind of stoned machismo. And perhaps, Alex thought, in anticipation of the killing of the news crew at midday.

'Left a bit,' murmured Don Hammond behind him.

Alex raised a hand in thanks. As lead scout, he was the only member of the team not responsible for navigation – all his concentration went into watching and listening: for the unexplained movement, the shadow that wasn't a shadow, the tiny suck of a boot in clay, the oily straining of a cocking lever.

Listening was becoming harder. In addition to the rifle fire, there was the faint thump and whisper of music. Straining his ears, Alex recognised one of Sierra Leone's big summer tunes – a favourite of the RUF, the SLA and the militias alike – called 'Titti Shaggah'.

Had they posted sentries, he wondered, stilling the five men behind him with a hand gesture. For two minutes the patrol crouched unmoving in the animal track, but there was no sound that shouldn't have been there. They moved on and the ridge line began its gradual descent towards the Rokel river. Step by silent step, Alex negotiated the gradient. The rain was still holding off, but splashing rivulets streaked the treacherous clay incline. They were five hundred yards away from the camp now and through the dense foliage below them Alex could see the yellowish flickering of electric lights. Surely, he thought, they must at least have some bloke on stag.

They had and Alex almost missed him. All he saw, in fact, was the tiny swing of a cigarette coal at the side of the track twenty yards ahead. Stilling the patrol again and deliberately steadying his breathing as the adrenalin flooded his system, Alex moved silently down the skiddy clay, feeling with his feet for the rocks and tree roots that would noiselessly support his weight. *One squelch*, he thought – *one snapped branch or kicked stone – and we're buggered*.

Ten yards now and he could see in the moonlight that the sentry was leaning against the other side of a tree trunk. A tree trunk whose thickness was approximately that of a man's chest. Once again, the arm swung sideways. The hand held a ganja spliff, not a cigarette.

Quietly, Alex drew a short Mauser stabbing knife from his belt webbing. It took him three agonised

28

heart-thudding minutes to cover the last sodden yards of the descent and then finally he was behind the trunk, his nose and eyes full of drifting ganja smoke but his feet secure on the slippery twisting tree roots. Like a striking snake, as his right hand reached across with the knife, Alex's left hand clapped across the sentry's mouth. At the last moment, though, with a desperate outrush of breath, the SAS officer checked his blade. The face beneath his hands was smooth, the neck slender, the struggling body pitifully small. The sentry was a kid – might even have been a girl – couldn't have been more than ten, and almost immediately went limp with terror in his arms. The spliff fell to the ground and went out with a tiny hiss.

Keeping a hand firmly across his captive's mouth, Alex gestured to Don Hammond to join him. The sergeant quickly gagged the child with a sweat rag, tied the slender wrists and ankles with a length of para cord from his belt kit, and concealed the immobilised figure beneath a dense bush in the darkness to one side of the track.

The patrol proceeded warily with the descent. They encountered no more sentries and, as they neared the lights and the music, the ground began to level out until they found themselves close to the edge of the tree line. In front of them a parapet of knotted roots supported a thick tangle of rotting vegetation, beneath which was a drop of about six feet. Beneath this, either drunk or stoned but unquestionably asleep, lay two RUF soldiers. One was wearing a white nylon wedding dress, the other threadbare tracksuit trousers and a combat smock hung with plastic dolls' heads.

Ricky Sutton, keen as ever, drew his commando knife. 'Shall I do 'em?' he mouthed, but Alex shook his head. If the bodies were found the whole camp would go to a state of alert, jeopardising any potential rescue mission. As Ricky sheathed his blade, Alex scanned the area with his binoculars.

Below them, contained within the dark curving sweep of the Rokel river, lay the camp. Roughly oval-shaped, it occupied an area slightly greater than a football pitch. At the nearer, lower end was a large bonfire on to which, at intervals, silhouetted figures heaped wet branches and tree roots, encouraging a thick column of grey-brown smoke. On the higher ground to the east, lit by strings of low-wattage bulbs, two windowless cinder-block huts stood at right angles to the river. Beyond them was a cluster of mud-walled outhouses. On the far side of the river the jungle rose steeply for a hundred metres or so to the ridge line.

Of the hundred and fifty-odd figures visible in the camp, perhaps a score were dancing and drinking around the bonfire, while at least twice that number were milling around the far end, near the huts. The remainder staggered about, singly and in large drunken groups, at the river's edge. Most carried SLR 7.62 rifles, but there were a few AK 47s and RPGs in evidence too. Several of the men appeared to be so attached to their weapons that they were dancing with them.

The sheer numbers of the RUF made any assault of less than company strength hazardous. The cinder-block huts would provide cover for anything up to fifty soldiers each and if the hostages were in this camp they were probably situated close to or inside the huts. Bringing fire to bear on the RUF without injuring them would be difficult. The most positive factor, in

Alex's view, was the topography of the camp. Surrounded as they were on three sides by the vast grey-green bulk of the river, the RUF were like rats in a bag. If all of the SAS firepower was positioned along a single front in the tree line, the bag could be drawn shut. The difficult part was going to be finding, and then extracting, the hostages.

Another plus point was that despite the recent incursion into the Kissuna area by the West Side Boys militia, no serious attempt had been made to implement any form of camp security. The noise, for a start, was considerable. The crack of random discharges tore the air, as did the answering, echoing smack as these impacted in the surrounding jungle. No wonder no one wants to go out on stag, thought Alex, with all this random shooting you'd take your bloody life in your hands. From beneath the sound system, which continued to belt out 'Titti Shaggah' and other local hits, came the steady thump of a generator.

'If I'd known it was a party,' muttered Stan Clayton, 'I'd 'ave worn my dancin' trousers!'

Alex smiled and beckoned the men around him. 'No sign of our people so far,' he whispered, 'but I want to take a closer look. Those huts up the end look promising for a start. Don, I want you to stay here with three of the guys and count heads and weapons. Stan, I want you to come with me. We're going for a swim.'

The cockney grinned, grasping the plan immediately. Quickly the two men stripped off their webbing, leaving their kit in two neat piles. Then, creeping past the unconscious RUF soldiers, they lowered themselves down the tree roots to ground level.

In front of them, bordered by the river, was the camp. To their right were the black-shadowed margins of the jungle. Ahead of them, and falling away behind them into the jungle, was a rough, mud-churned road. Swiftly the two men turned right, paced off twenty yards into the swampy foliage, turned through ninety degrees, took bearings from their wrist compasses and set off through the darkness on a fast-paced eastbound course parallel to the road. Ten minutes later they exited the jungle. The dark sweep of the river was now at their feet and they were well upstream of the camp.

'We'll 'ave to tuck in tight,' murmured Clayton thoughtfully.

Alex nodded. Close up, the Rokel was a vast and terrifying force of nature. The flash floods that accompanied the early days of the rainy season had torn its winter banks away and the normally placid river was now an angry torrent hundreds of yards wide. If Alex and Stan strayed out of the side eddies they could be hurtled miles downstream or drowned outright. Hard in to the bank, however, the risk of detection was much greater. The whole undertaking was very much more dangerous than it had first appeared, but it represented the SAS team's only chance of locating the hostages.

'Let's find ourselves a raft,' whispered Alex.

Soundlessly, they waded into the warm, soupy water, where a regular procession of tree limbs, bushes and other vegetation uprooted by the floods was washing past them in the current. Within a couple of minutes they had secured the perfect vehicle – a twenty-foot branch hung with decomposing foliage.

'Ready?' asked Alex.

'Sure.' Clayton nodded. 'I can always use a few dozen more leeches round my bollocks!'

Carefully they steered the branch a short distance away from the bank and began the smooth, inexorable drift towards the camp. Only their heads showed above water and behind the festoon of rotting weeds they were effectively invisible to the guards on the riverside. Slowly they rounded the bend past the camp's first outposts. It was shallower here and Alex could feel his feet dragging on the river's muddy bed.

Close up, the scene was very much more threatening than at a distance. On the bank, less than ten yards away, a crowd of drunken soldiery staggered around, clutching rifles, machetes and beakers of palm wine. Even over the muddy tang of the river the SAS men could smell the cloying reek of the home-made spirit. From the speakers the RUF anthem 'No Living Thing' punched out, bouncing from the cliffs opposite with a thudding reverberation. Along the shore the glazed-eyed soldiers screamed the choruses.

His face inches from the corporal's, Alex was conscious of Stan Clayton's attempts to still his breathing, to remain absolutely motionless behind the branch. *If they see us*, thought Alex — *if the branch catches on something and swings around — we're dead. They'll hack us to pieces in seconds. Stan's wife will be a widow, his son will be without a dad and it will all be my fault. My fault for turning an important search mission into a juvenile, hairy-arsed, straight-to-video personal fucking adventure.*

The random shooting continued. One man, standing on the bank no more than eight feet from them, casually loosed off a couple of rounds from his SLR as he urinated into the river, and the SAS men flickered an expressionless glance at each other as the

33

7.62 rounds passed inches over their heads and tore into the far bank. A few yards further on a woman with her dress pulled up over her back crouched listlessly in the mud as a bearded soldier drove into her from behind. Around her, a surly and impatient knot of men watched and waited, and masturbated to make themselves hard for when their own turns came.

This hellish scene was repeated at intervals along the bank and more than once Alex caught himself – or so it seemed – staring mesmerised into the eyes of an RUF warrior. His heart appeared to be beating hard enough to disturb the greasy surface of the water. It seemed impossible that he had not been seen.

But the soldiers, it turned out, were less interested in driftwood than in the slopping palm wine buckets from which, at intervals, they refilled their half-gourds and plastic beakers. Those and the half-dozen wretchedly prostrate women on the shore – refugees, Alex guessed, displaced by the fighting.

The current, perceptibly faster now, swept them past the outhouses. The first, Alex guessed from the rhythmic chugging sound, housed the generator. In a second, from which the buckets were being carried, he supposed that they had some kind of distillery. The third, a mud-walled dwelling whose palm-frond roof had collapsed inwards, was anyone's guess, but as they drifted past it the palm wine stink was joined by that of shit.

And then, for no more than five seconds, Alex saw them: three pale-skinned figures, their heads bowed, their hands tied behind them, kneeling in the narrow passage between the two cinder-block huts. They were being guarded by a single uniformed soldier carrying an SLR, smoking a joint and wearing a pink bubble-cut wig.

Alex's eyes widened and he turned to Stan Clayton, saw that the other man had clocked the guard and the captives too. Then they were passing the speakers, and taking the full thumping force and screaming distortion of 'No Living Thing'.

'I think I prefer the Martine McCutcheon version,' murmured Clayton thoughtfully, as an RUF man heaved a wet tree root on to the bonfire and a shower of bright-orange sparks whirled skywards. They were only eight or nine yards from the nearest whooping, rifle-waving soldiers now, but the amplification from the sound system was such that the corporal could probably have yelled at the top of his voice without being heard.

And then, as the firelight dimmed and a column of dense brown smoke replaced the flames, Alex felt the current take sudden hold, swinging the branch and themselves into deeper water. The two men silently struggled to remain concealed and to keep the branch parallel to the shore. They were clearing the camp fast now – the bonfire was already well behind them – but they were moving inexorably towards the Rokel's racing central channel.

'We're going to have to let go,' gasped Alex and heard Clayton's grunt of agreement beside him.

'On three, underwater and kick for the side. One, two . . .'

Alex released the branch, dived, and felt himself lifted by the current and swung with doll-like help-lessness through the dark, churning water. There was a roar at his ears, a sense of vast and indifferent force, then a rock or a boot exploded in a vicious flash of light against the side of his head.

Somehow, even as he briefly lost consciousness, he managed to keep his mouth shut. Hours or maybe seconds later, desperate to breathe, he clawed his way to what he thought was the surface, struck mud and felt himself dragged downwards again by a hand at his collar. For some reason, there seemed to be air at the bottom of the river. He tried to inhale, gagged and found that a mud-tasting hand was clamped over his mouth. Water streamed from his nose. He could breathe again. He opened his eyes.

Clayton's worried grin was inches away. 'You all right, Alex?'

They were in deep, eddying water beneath the bank. The music and din of the camp were still loud, but no longer deafening. Stan Clayton had one elbow under Alex's chin, the other anchored to a solid-looking mangrove root.

'Are you OK?' The whisper more urgent now.

Alex tried to nod and then, retching, vomited foul-tasting water. There was blood in his eyes and his head hurt like hell. Somehow he found a root of his own and passed an unsteady hand over his face. 'Yeah . . . thanks, Stan. Lost it there for a moment. Thanks.'

I was seconds away from drowning there, he told himself. *Seconds away from death.*

'I think we're more or less clear of the camp,' continued Clayton. 'The other blokes can't be far, but I'm a bit worried about them fuckers we 'ad to duck round on our way here. Bride of Frankenstein an' his mate.'

'Let me have a look,' said Alex and with Clayton's help hauled himself up so that his eyes were level with

36

the bank. They were less than twenty yards from where they had descended the tree roots, but of the sleeping RUF soldiers there was no sign. Instead, Don Hammond was leopard-crawling towards him through the shadows, grabbing him under the arms, dragging him by sheer brute force up the slick clay face of the bank.

'I reckoned it was either you guys or a hippo wallowing around out there,' said the sergeant. 'Come on, Stan, grab hold.'

When Clayton was on the bank too the three of them moved back from the river and into cover, and Alex swiftly brought the sergeant up to date concerning the ITN team.

'How did they look?' asked Hammond.

'Alive,' replied Clayton tersely.

'Where are the other guys?' asked Alex.

The sergeant inclined his head towards the bush. 'Just moving the two guards that were here away from the path. We reckoned you'd be coming out about here.'

'Did you kill them?'

'Yeah, course we did.' He looked at Alex doubtfully. 'Are you OK? You look as if you've got some kind of head wound.'

'Took a whack in the river on something. Stan dragged me in by the collar.'

'Well, that'll have saved us all some paperwork. Dead officers we don't need. Are you OK to tab back to Millwall, or do you want me to go?'

'I'm fine to go, Don.'

'You sure? What's eight nines?'

Alex hesitated. The question seemed strangely unanswerable.

'And the motto of the Parachute Regiment?'

Again, Alex was silent. He'd begun his military career with the Paras but couldn't for the life of him . . .

Hammond nodded and glanced at Clayton. 'I'd say you're a bit concussed. I'll tab back to Millwall with Lance and pick up the home-bound chopper. You stay here and set up the assault.'

Alex nodded. The sergeant was right. A single navigation error between here and Millwall – more than an hour's night march through thick jungle – could cost the captives their lives.

'Put it this way, Alex.' Stan Clayton grinned. 'At least if you stay 'ere you're guaranteed to be here for the fireworks. Go back wiv a leakin' 'ead and Ross'll just send some other fucker.'

'OK, guys, OK. I hear you,' said Alex, raising his hands in mock surrender. 'Don, have you managed to draw a map of the camp?'

Hammond nodded, and pulled out a sheet of waterproof paper marked up with outlines and co-ordinates.

'Right,' said Alex. 'The ITN people, when I saw them, were being held in the passage between these two cinder-block buildings here, which you've called Hut One and Hut Two. Was that how you saw it, Stan?'

'Yeah, it was.'

'And from what I could see they looked very tired. Their morale was poor. Each or any of them might be hurt, possibly badly. But I'd say that all three were definitely alive.'

'Guarded?'

'One guy. Pink curly wig.'

Hammond looked at Clayton, who nodded in confirmation.

'Weapons?' asked Hammond, still looking at Clayton.

'My guess would be that there are about a hundred and fifty SLRs in the camp – one for each man. I saw a few AKs and RPGs, too, and there could be anything in those huts.'

'Fields of fire?'

For five minutes Hammond submitted the two men to a detailed debrief. Evidently suspicious of the accuracy of Alex's recall, given the captain's recent knock on the head, he made a point of verifying every fact with Clayton.

With the map filled in with as much detail as Alex and Stan Clayton could provide, Don Hammond radioed Zulu Three Five patrol who were observing the Arsenal camp ten kilometres away and reported that the hostages had been located. The patrol leader, a sergeant named Andy Maddocks, replied that he was pulling out immediately and estimated that he would reach Chelsea in about ninety minutes.

Alex then set off with Zulu Three Six patrol back up the track towards the Bergan cache. En route they checked the captive child-sentry, who was frightened but otherwise unharmed. Before the fighting started, Alex decided, he would release the poor little bugger into the jungle. Would that help him, or even save his life? Quite possibly not, he admitted to himself, but he couldn't play God.

When they reached the clearing where the Bergans were cached, Don Hammond radioed in a sat-com report to David Ross and then kept on going. It was 0145, and he and Lance Wilford had three-quarters of an hour in which to reach the Puma landing zone at Millwall. All things being equal he would be back in Freetown by 0300. The assault – the killing time – would come an hour later at first light when, with a bit of luck, the RUF forces would be sunk in drunken, exhausted sleep.

It wouldn't be a pushover, thought Alex, remembering the red-eyed fury with which the soldiers had roared out the words of 'No Living Thing'. For all their gross indiscipline – for all their raping, mutilating, torture and murder – the RUF were well-armed and they were certainly no cowards. They would fight and they would fight hard. Many of them believed themselves to be impervious to pain, and given the volume of ganja and palm wine they got through of an evening, they were probably right.

What did they intend to do to Sally Roberts and her crew if their demands were not met? Impossible to say, although given the cruelty and contempt with which the soldiers treated the African women at their disposal – gang rape being the least of it – he could hazard a guess at the female reporter's probable fate. The men would most likely be shot and dumped in the river.

But this, mused Alex, glancing at his wristwatch, was not going to happen. Instead, in just under two hours, Sally Roberts, Ben Mills and Gary Burge would be flown out of the camp code-named Chelsea in a Puma helicopter. And with any luck, they would be alive when it happened.

At the bottom of the slope, behind the tree roots, Zulu Three Six patrol sat tight. This time, as well as the sat-com and the 319 patrol radio, they'd brought their individual Motorola UHF sets with them from the Bergan cache. Precisely co-ordinated operations like this one tended to be very comms-heavy. There was a worrying amount of movement near the hostages, Alex noticed, and he found himself straining to watch as the distant figures came and went beneath the strings of yellow light bulbs.

Cool it, he told himself. *For the moment – for just a few hours more until the deadline – the RUF need the news team alive.*

At precisely 0230 Ricky Sutton set up the sat-com to receive Ross's scheduled transmission from Freetown. The incoming message was brief and to the point: Don Hammond and Lance Wilford had been exfiltrated from Millwall and were on their way back to base. Assault time was estimated at 0400.

As the twenty-three-year-old trooper folded away the sat-com aerial, Alex divided his team in half and disposed them in the jungle line in positions commanding broad arcs of fire over the camp. He himself took the western position with Sutton; Stan Clayton and Dog Kenilworth moved to the east.

Attaching the earpieces and throat mikes of their UHF sets, the patrol worked out their individual targets. When the time came, the impression given to the RUF had to be one of devastating force – that they were under sustained attack from all sides. In truth, of course, the rebels would be heavily outgunning the SAS, but they must never be allowed to know this.

The camp's situation, Alex knew, would work against the rescue team. With the looping river at their backs the RUF had nowhere to flee to, and in the event of attack they would have no option but to face the jungle and the opposing fire team and shoot it out.

Desperation would make them very dangerous, there would be a huge volume of fire directed towards the two RWW patrols and once the helicopters were on the ground it was going to be very difficult to return that fire. The hostages and the assault and rescue teams would be right in the thick of it. They'd agreed over the radio that the incoming 'D' Squadron soldiers would wear their bush-hats inside out with the orange band showing and not have any cam-cream on their faces, but it was still going to be very tricky knowing who was who – first light or no first light.

The insects were silent, now, and the temperature finally falling. Around the shallow dugout that was Alex's firing position hovered the scent of the Sierra Leone night – a pungent blend of wet clay, wood-smoke and rotting mangoes. To his left, manning the sat-com and the patrol's 319 set, lay Ricky Sutton.

Alex had agreed with Don Hammond that the patrol would try a second swim past between 2.30 and 3 a.m. to determine whether the hostages had been moved inside for the night. Stan Clayton had volunteered to go again, knowing as he did where the currents were most treacherous, and at 2.45 his narrow form slipped away eastwards, upstream of the camp. As he did so, Dog Kenilworth made his shadowy way to the downstream exit point to drag him up the river's sheer clay bank.

The next fifteen minutes passed slowly for Alex. The RUF posed no great danger to Stan – they were unlikely to be awake, sober and staring into the river at this hour – but Alex had felt the massive and wilful power of the Rokel river at first hand and hoped that the outspoken cockney would play it safe. Eventually, thankfully, the two loomed out of the darkness – Stan

42

officers-to-be with their sports cars and their nightclubs and their weekends in the country. There had been admin classes, report-writing classes and even an etiquette or 'knife and fork' course. Never in his life had Alex felt more like a fish out of water.

The others hadn't all been rich, but plenty of them had been, especially the ones destined for the Brigade of Guards and the other outfits where an expensive social life came with the regimental silver. Alex, whose father ran a small garage and body-repair shop in Clacton-on-Sea, and who had joined the Paras as a private to impress a girlfriend (who had immediately dumped him – thanks, Stella!) found it impossible to imagine what it must be like to have money to spend on Savile Row suits and Curzon Street restaurants and Caribbean sailing holidays at that age.

For Alex, at eighteen, it had been rockfish and chips, Kestrel lager and a brown leather jacket ('sixty-five quid mate, fully lined') from the Pakistani guy who had the stall at the Saturday market. There hadn't been any foreign holidays. 'Why pay to go to the Seychelles,' his father would ask, nodding towards Marine Parade with its icy spray and mournful winter winds, 'when the sea's right here on our bloody doorstep?'

It wasn't meanness, it was just that Ray Temple didn't hold with what he called 'all that pina colada bollocks'. What he did hold with was motor sport and lots of it. Formula One at Brands Hatch, drag races at Santa Pod, stock cars at Belle Vue, bangers at King's Lynn, night races at Snetterton – any occasion involving cigarette advertising, petrol vapour and deafening noise. The Temple family attended pretty much every event in the Castrol motor sport calendar.

And went first class all the way, with enclosure tickets, steak dinners at the motel if it was an overnighter, souvenir T-shirts and the rest.

The old man had been broken-hearted when, inspired by a TV documentary series, Alex had gone for the Parachute Regiment rather than one of the mechanised units. 'Don't be a tosser, son,' Ray Temple had begged him. 'If God had meant us to walk, he wouldn't have created fuel injection.'

But Alex had been adamant and stuck to his guns throughout the tough Para-selection course known as 'P' Company. He wasn't particularly big and he certainly wasn't the archetypal tattooed, scarred-knuckled Tom, but when it came to the specialised skills of the airborne infantryman he was a natural. He was a fast learner, excellent with weapons and always switched on in the field. His superiors marked him down as potential NCO material and posted him to his battalion's Patrol Company.

Unexpectedly, like many a town-raised soldier before him, the young paratrooper developed a passion for the wild, remote terrain in which he and his unit trained. He enjoyed downing pints and trapping WRAC girls with his Patrol Company mates, but found that after only a few days in barracks he missed the freedom and the solitude offered by the mountains and the moors. Shortly after his twenty-third birthday he was made up to lance-corporal, but by then a part of him had begun to wonder if there might be more to army life than the culture of the Aldershot brotherhood, with its relentless cycles of drinking, brawling, mooning, curry-swilling, shag-ging and vomiting.

On impulse, he applied for SAS selection. By then,

perhaps jealous of his promotion, some of his colleagues were beginning to regard him coolly. No one made any specific accusations but the word got around that he was a bit of a loner. There was an unconfirmed rumour that he had turned down the chance to join in a game of 'freckle' – a ritual in which a fresh turd was hammered between two beer mats on a pub table and the least bespattered paratrooper got to buy the next round.

If he had failed SAS selection, Alex would have had a very hard time living it down. But he didn't fail. Along with Don Hammond, then a Royal Fusiliers corporal, and a dozen others of the forty or so who applied, he passed. Badged into the Regiment, he discovered a different sort of soldier – tough, self-sufficient young blokes like himself who knew how to have a good time but didn't need to strike macho attitudes. The best friend he'd made in the Regiment was probably Hammond. As unmarried troopers they'd shared quarters in Hereford, along with a couple of clapped-out cars and – for three ill-tempered months – a Royal Army Dental Corps nurse named 'Floss' Docherty.

When it was announced that Alex was to be commissioned, no one could have been more pleased than Don Hammond. The two had an instinctive sympathy in the field and neither saw any reason why this should be affected by their differing ranks.

And here he was, a dozen years and a dozen dirty wars after signing up, a bloody officer! His father had laid down his plug spanner and laughed fit to piss himself when Alex had told him that he was going to Sandhurst. 'You always were a canny bugger,' he told Alex, shaking his head in disbelief, 'but this beats the bloody bank.' His mother, seeing him in his full-dress uniform for the first time alongside the public-school boys, had wept.

Well, he reflected wryly, flipping up the backsight on his M16 and taking a sip of tepid water from his canteen, he might as well enjoy it while it lasted. The system gave, but the system also took away, and took away faster than shit off a hot chrome shovel. At heart, Alex knew, he was not an Establishment man.

THREE

Shortly after 3.30 there was movement in the camp. A tall soldier carrying some kind of hooked knife was walking amongst the prostrate soldiers, stepping over outflung arms and legs. As he reached the camp perimeter he paused to kick one of the sleeping figures. It was one of the women, Alex saw through his binoculars. With infinite slowness, the woman began to get to her feet, only for the soldier to take her by the hair, wave his bill-hook, and start violently pulling her towards the jungle. Hastily, fearfully, she matched her pace to his. This looks tricky, thought Alex. This looks very tricky indeed. They're making straight for us.

'Coming our way, Alex,' murmured Ricky Sutton beside him.

'Seen,' replied Alex. For the second time that night he drew his Mauser knife. The pair were no more than fifty yards from him now. Whatever you're going to do to her, Alex pleaded silently with the soldier, do it right there. Don't come any closer.

But the man kept on coming. Whatever it was that he intended – the curved knife almost certainly had something to do with it – it was going to make a lot of noise. There were going to be screams. So he was taking the woman into the bush where her evil-spirit howling wouldn't wake the camp up.

Twenty-five yards now, and Alex could hear the woman's terrified keening and the soldier's muttering as he forced her forward. If they tried to evade, to crawl sideways out of their way, the soldier would see them. And if they stayed put . . .

When it came to the moment, instinct took over. Tripping the soldier with his rifle, avoiding the scything blade as both the man and the woman fell, Alex leapt on top of him. For a critical moment the soldier must have thought that a tree root was to blame for the confusion, and that the melee consisted only of himself and the woman, for he made no noise beyond an stifled curse. And then the butt of Alex's M16 met the back of his head with bone-smashing force, and he was still.

Ricky Sutton, meanwhile, had grabbed the woman. Behind his hand she was still keening, the sound a tiny sustained ribbon of anguish. Deliberately, Sutton moved his face into a shaft of moonlight, so that she could see at a glance that despite the black cam-cream he was European, and urgently shushed her. Their eyes met – his taut and pale, hers tear-rimmed and terrified – and she nodded once. She was wearing a thin cotton dress and plastic sandals.

The soldier had to be dealt with and Alex had no choice but to do it in front of the woman. Lifting the unconscious man's head by the hair, he chopped inwards and dragged the blade of the Mauser knife hard through the front of his throat. There was a rushing wet heat from the jugular, a clicking gasp from the severed windpipe, and a brief shivering dance of the legs. Within half a minute exsanguination was complete. The sticky blackness was everywhere.

Sutton, meanwhile, gagged the shocked, unresisting

50

woman with a sweat-rag. Wrists and ankles trussed with paracord, she lay against a shallow incline behind them. Six feet away, the corpse of her late admirer stiffened in the cooling tar of his blood. The SAS officer and the trooper settled back to wait.

At 0350, Alex noticed a tiny shift in the quality of the darkness at the head of the Rokel valley to the east. If he looked a little to one side he could make out a ridge, a tree line, where previously there had been nothing. The minutes passed, the cyclorama paled a further degree, and the misted, dew-charged vastness of the jungle began to reveal itself. There was nothing on earth, thought Alex, to beat the grandeur of the African dawn.

Not even the front at Clacton.

He raised his binoculars. There was the command-post, there were the huts, there were the embers of the bonfire. And there – everywhere – were the sleeping soldiers and their weapons.

Quickly the men re-checked the sightings on their M16 203s. As well as a conventionally calibrated rifle-sights, which they had set to two hundred yards, their weapons had sextant-sights screwed to their carrying handles.

0355, and the pilot of Hotel Alpha, the lead Puma, was now audible on the patrol's UHF sets. His voice was relaxed. 'Coming in on schedule, Zero Three Six. You should see us in three or four minutes. Over.'

'We hear you, Hotel Alpha. Ready when you are. Over.'

Raising his rifle, Alex took up aim on the door of the left-hand of the two barracks-huts. Hut One.

0358. The pilot's voice again. 'Touch-down in

51

two minutes, Zulu Three Six. Repeat, touch-down in two minutes.'

'Everyone ready?' Alex whispered. It was unlikely that anyone had fallen asleep, but it had been known to happen.

They all heard it at the same time. At first it was just a pulse, distant and low. Could have been a heartbeat. And then, with shocking suddenness, the lead Puma was racing towards them over the grey jungle canopy.

A sentry holding a Kalashnikov was the first to stir, and Alex dropped him with a single high-velocity round to the chest.

'*Boyakasha*!' breathed Ricky Sutton to his left and opened up with a long stream of tracer at the guards around the bonfire. The other sentries ran for the cover of the huts, but met a series of lethally aimed bursts from Stan and Dog. As they fell, Alex saw Don Hammond lean coolly out of the side of the helicopter and heard the distinctive *boom boom* of the heavy 5.5″ gun. Chunks of masonry seemed to leap from the walls of Hut One and, as the RUF soldiers poured out like angry ants, Alex snapped off a fast series of shots into the doorway. The area between the huts also held armed men, but these he left alone for fear of hitting the hostages.

Fire was being returned now and with interest. Volleys of 7.62 SLR rounds were snapping through the tree line, shredding the foliage around them and kicking up great gouts of earth. Unperturbed, Stan Clayton and Dog Kenilworth kept up a lethal assault with their M16s. Behind them Andy Maddocks' patrol put down steady fire.

Lowering his rifle so that he was cradling it in his arms, Alex slipped one of the small, egg-like grenades from his bandolier into the launcher tube below the main barrel and swung the weapon towards the eastern-most point of the camp. A glance at the sextant and he fired. The grenade dropped some two hundred and fifty yards away and burst with a fierce crack amongst a group of soldiers who were attempting to bring fire to bear on the helicopter. Returning the rifle to his shoulder, Alex stilled the survivors with a series of single shots.

Working the slide to discharge the used shell-case, he loaded a second grenade into the tube, and aimed it in the direction of the generator-hut. Another miniature schrapnel storm, sending several men running from cover into the open, where Ricky Sutton's unhurried shooting dropped them in fast succession. The camp was in chaos now. The Puma had landed, its rotors still turning, and the 12-man SAS team was pouring out of it, diving for cover and snapping aimed bursts at the RUF rebels who surrounded them.

In response several of the rebels dropped their SLRs and ran. A handful threw themselves on the uncertain mercy of the river. Most, however, making up in aggression and outrage what they lacked in prepared-ness and training, determined to make a fight of it and attempted to fall back on the cover of the two cinder-block barracks huts. Lacking any coherent command-and-control system, however, they found themselves retreating into their own side's defensive arcs of fire. Several of them only managed to make it into cover because their colleagues' long-uncleaned SLRs had jammed.

For a moment, Alex held his fire. As he watched, the incoming SAS team split up. Half raced for the hostages, disappearing behind the huts, half assaulted Hut One. The whoomf of a grenade, a long burst of fire, a staccato flurry of single shots and the building was theirs. A moment later the rescue team reappeared at the sprint, ducking through the rebel fire towards the helicopter. Three of them had limp, half-dressed figures slung over their shoulders. 'Go!' prayed Alex. 'Get them on the chopper and out of here. *Go!*'

The Puma, as if alive to the urgency of the situation, seemed to dance with impatience on her struts as enemy rounds snapped about her. At the controls, Alex could see the helmeted pilot, motionless – a brave man, he thought – and the silhouetted figure of Don Hammond poised at the open door, waiting to haul up the hostages.

The RPG must have been fired somewhere behind the generator. It whooshed a couple of feet over the heads of the rescue team, impacted against the Puma's slanting plexiglas windshield and vapourised the cockpit and the pilot in an orange-white bloom of flame. The blast threw the oncoming rescue team and the hostages to the ground and, as they lay there, the SAS men instinctively covering the journalists with their bodies, a second missile struck the rear of the Puma's cargo compartment. The buckled and burning remains of the helicopter canted sideways and Don Hammond pitched face forwards from the doorway – his clothes, his head and his remaining arm aflame.

Powerless to help from two hundred yards distance, his mind a stunned blank, Alex watched as Hammond tried unsuccessfully to get to his feet. The two members of the rescue team who had not been carrying hostages rose from the ground, raced forward and between them attempted to stifle the flames on the burning sergeant and drag him into cover.

But the RUF were beginning to rally. And while the hostages and the rescuers were covered from fire by the bulk of Hut One, Hammond and the men who had run out to help him were far enough forward to be exposed. Shots snapped around them and Alex heard a lethal-sounding double smack. One of the SAS men staggered and fell. Somehow, supporting his wounded mate with one arm and half-dragging the sergeant's blackened remains with the other, the third man made it to the cover of Hut One, where the hostages were being scrambled through the doorway over the sprawled corpses of dead RUF soldiers.

The SAS team had barely vanished inside the hut when the Puma's fuel tanks went up in a third roaring explosion, and oily black smoke began to twist into the grey dawn sky.

'Zulu Three Six, this is Hotel Bravo, what is the situation?'

It was the pilot of the support Puma.

'Hotel Alpha is down, Hotel Bravo. Repeat, Hotel Alpha is down. Stay back until my signal.'

'Will do, Zulu Three Six.' The pilot's voice was expressionless.

There was a brief hiatus and, forcing himself to postpone all thoughts concerning Don Hammond, Alex undertook a swift assessment.

At least twenty rebels lay out in the open, dead, while a dozen more twitched and gaped and bled amongst them. A further dozen RUF casualties were almost certainly concealed amongst the outbuildings to the east of the camp. Even allowing for a few runners and swimmers that still left a hundred-odd rebels in good combat order.

'Dog,' Alex murmured into his UHF mouthpiece. 'I want you and Stan to cut through the jungle to the point where we got into the river and work your way back towards the camp from the east. We've got to take out that grenade-launcher before the support helicopter arrives.'

'Heard.'

'On our way.'

Still on his UHF set, Alex then called up the assault and rescue team, requested the sergeant in charge and explained that he had sent in two men from the eastern end of the camp to try and force the RUF soldiers to keep their heads down.

'Understood,' came the reply. 'I'll put another four in from this end. If you keep laying down fire from the bush we should be able to keep 'em busy enough to get the chopper in and out.'

A moment later, however, a long volley of 7.62 SLR and Kalashnikov rounds smacked into Alex's position. Heady with the destruction of Puma Alpha, the defending RUF troops had decided to take the battle back to their tormentors in the jungle.

As the firestorm swept their position, spattering himself and Sutton with bark and falling leaf fragments, Alex pressed his face and body into the damp coffee-ground soil. Beside him he heard the unmistakeable whipcrack of physical impact and a shocked gasp.

'Ricky?' he said, fearing the worst.

'I'm hit,' muttered Sutton through clenched teeth, 'in the fuckin' arse.'

Alex's heart sank. How many bloody more, he

thought. If I run into Sally Roberts, the bitch'll wish she'd never been born.

Another volley raked the tree line. Somewhere behind him, the bound woman keened with fear. Reaching for the shell-dressing pack in Sutton's smock pocket and the clasp-knife in his own, Alex cut through the young signaller's blood-sodden DPM trousers, slapped on the dressing, and ordered him to sit tight. To his right Stan and Dog returned fire, pouring a steady stream of armour-piercing rounds on to the RUF positions around Hut Two.

A moment later Alex saw four SAS men slip out of the door of Hut One and disappear around the far side. From the generator area he heard the crack of 203 grenades launched by Dog and Stan and a moment later the familiar stutter of M16s on rapid fire as the assaulters completed the movement. The RUF were now under sustained assault from three directions, trapped in a lethal cage of noise and shrapnel. No RUF man was going to risk standing up for long enough to aim and correctly discharge an RPG in all of that, Alex reckoned. Quickly, he called in the reserve Puma.

The pilot acknowledged the signal and sixty seconds later the big snout-nosed chopper swung in fast and steep, dropping down next to the twisted and still burning wreck of the first. It had hardly touched the ground when the rescue team sprinted out of the barracks-block with the ITN crew over their shoulders. Hurling the journalists through the open doorway like so many sacks of coal and dragging themselves in afterwards, they were away within seconds, dipping and swaying across the grey-green jungle canopy to safety.

On the sat-com, Alex called up Ross. 'Hostages airborne,' he told the CO, 'but we've taken casualties.' Quickly, he brought him up to speed with events.

'Keep me posted,' said Ross tersely, and broke the connection.

Silence now from the RUF – all of their remaining strength pinned down in and around Hut Two. Above them, the sky seemed to be darkening again. Stalemate.

Alex slotted a fresh 30-round magazine into the belly of his weapon. Does the fight have to be to the death, he wondered. The fierce anticipation of the night before was entirely spent. The camp was a butcher's shop now and one or two of the RUF corpses looked horrifyingly young. All that he felt now was revulsion – a desperate longing for the whole thing to be over.

And then Dog Kenilworth's Brummie tones were in his earpiece. 'They're jacking it in. Slinging their rifles out.'

Alex exhaled, permitted himself a moment of relief. 'Any men followed the rifles?'

'No, not so far . . . Yeah, hang on, one's just shouting to Stan now.'

'What's he saying?'

'Dunno. Something meaning "No shooting!", I'd guess. He's coming out.'

'Watch yourselves, OK?'

'Don't worry, Alex.'

One by one the RUF soldiers processed out of Hut Two and the other outbuildings at the eastern end of the camp. From the tree line Alex saw the line of disarmed men, hands raised, shuffling towards the smoking wreck of the first Puma. There, under the watchful eye and trained M16s of the assault team, they waited in disconsolate ranks.

'Andy,' Alex ordered, 'cut across and join Stan and Dog. When it looks as if all the prisoners are under guard, I want the three of you to do a quick house-to-house, check for stay-behinds.'

'Understood,' said Maddocks.

Alex turned back to Ricky Sutton. The trooper was pale and clearly in shock, but managed a wry grin. An SLR round had torn a furrow over the hamstring muscle at the back of his thigh, and despite the two shell-dressings blood was still welling hotly through the gauze.

'Right,' murmured Alex briskly. 'Who had the patrol med-pack?'

'I'm . . . lying on it.'

Carefully, Alex eased the pack from beneath the trooper's chest, found a morphine stick, and angled it into Sutton's thigh. Within seconds, the taut, fearful strain in the young trooper's eyes was replaced with a dreamy vagueness.

Reaching for his UHF set, Alex pressed the transmit button. 'How's it going, lads?' he asked.

'Fine,' came Andy Maddocks' voice. 'No stay-behinds, all badboys disarmed. What shall we do with the weapons? We've got a hundred-odd SLRs, few AKs, RPGs, odds and sods.'

Alex removed a saline drip assembly from the med-pack.

'All weapons, ammo, and comms kit goes into the river.' He thought of the women and children who, raped, traumatised and with one or both arms hacked off by men such as these, were still arriving daily in

59

Freetown. 'And that includes all pangas, machetes, billhooks, whatever. Anything with a blade.'

'Understood.'

Turning to the bound woman, whom he now saw was probably no more than 16 or 17, he fingered the gag from her mouth and tied it round Sutton's thigh to reinforce the shell-dressing. Then finding a vein at the trooper's wrist, he worked in the IV needle. Beside him, crooning distractedly to herself as if to comfort a child, the girl sat blank-eyed.

Within minutes the secured camp had taken on an ordered and familiar aspect, with sentries posted, SAS casualties stretchered and ammunition checks underway. The mood was sombre – even the irrepressible Ricky Sutton lay in morphined silence on his stretcher. Where the bonfire had raged the night before, the captured RUF soldiers sat in subdued lines with their hands plasticuffed behind their backs. Others, moving with dream-like slowness, stacked the bodies of their dead comrades. Beyond them the rain hissed and steamed as it met the smoking shell of the Puma.

On the sat-com, Alex arranged the details of the return to base with David Ross. It would probably be a question of two Chinooks, they decided – one for the SAS team, one to deliver the RUF dead to the government forces HQ. A few yards away, Stan Clayton and Dog Kenilworth manoeuvred Don Hammond into a black body-bag.

FOUR

At breakfast the mood was sombre.

They'd de-bussed at SAS HQ shortly after 6 a.m. and, calling for hot coffee in his hut, Ross had debriefed Alex immediately. Alex's account had been detailed but unemotional and Ross had heard him out in near silence, only occasionally interjecting a brief question. When they were done, an hour or so later, Ross had nodded, his lean features expressionless, and sat for a moment in silence. Alex knew he had liked Don Hammond as much as any of them.

'You did well, Alex. Bloody well. All of you. Another few hours and we would have had three dead UK nationals on our hands, not to mention egg all over our faces. Bearing in mind that we were hitting a hot DZ, it was always going to be a very high-risk operation.'

Alex nodded. At times like these, as both men knew, there was not a great deal to be said. Violent death was the everyday currency of their profession and there was no sense pretending otherwise.

'Just remind me of the daughter's name, Alex.'

'Cathy. I think she was seven last birthday.'

Ross looked tiredly down at his notes. 'Right. Thank you.'

Would I like that job? Alex wondered. *Would I enjoy*

sitting up and watching the clock as my men risked their lives? Would I be able to write the letters of condolence that David Ross always made a point of writing?

The phone at the OC's right hand buzzed. He listened for a moment, then covered the mouthpiece and turned to Alex. 'It's Hugh Gudgeon at Para HQ. The TV people are all in one piece, apparently. They want to thank the leader of the rescue team personally.'

'I haven't got much to say to them, David, to be honest.'

Ross nodded and looked away. 'I'm afraid that won't be possible, Hugh, nor do I want any mention made of the Regiment in connection with this business. Would your chaps very much mind taking the credit? No? Excellent. All right, then. 'Bye.'

Alex had left the CO's hut to shower, shave and clear himself of leeches. This was a rather simpler process than that shown in films like *Bridge Over the River Kwai*. One touch of army-issue insect repellent and the fat, purple-black bloodsuckers fell off. The repellent was useless for anything else – it positively attracted mosquitoes – but it did have this one killer application. Stripping to the skin in the makeshift outside shower area, Alex managed to rid himself of twelve bull-leeches – a personal best.

In the mess tent he joined the rest of the patrol, who had got a head start on the NAAFI baked beans, pale-yolked local eggs and monkey-bananas. And beer, of course. It may only have been seven in the morning, but after a mission it was understood that you popped a few cans.

Alex helped himself to a plate of beans, one of the doughy, locally baked bread rolls and a can of Carling.

The food looked none too appetising in the tent's greenish light, but at that moment Alex could have eaten practically anything. 'Cheers, lads,' he said, thumbing back the tab. 'Here's to a daring rescue!'

'Who was responsible for that, then?' asked Lance Wilford.

'The Paras,' said Alex.

'Ah.' Dog Kenilworth smiled. 'Fine body of men.'

There was silence for a moment.

'Any news on Ricky Sutton?' asked one of the troopers from Zulu Three One patrol, who had been tasked to recce the Arsenal camp.

'Should be OK, is my guess, barring a very sore arse,' said Alex.

'And Steve Dowson?' Dowson was the 'D' Squadron corporal who had been hit while attempting to rescue Hammond.

'Shoulder's a mess but he'll live.'

There were relieved nods, followed by another protracted silence, then Stan Clayton raised a fridge-frosted beer can. 'To Don Hammond,' he said loudly. 'Bloody good soldier, bloody good mate.'

The others raised their own drinks and then everyone started talking at once and the mood lifted. There was no shortage of good Don Hammond stories and it had been one hell of a successful mission.

As Alex drank and listened in silence, the elation of the successful mission faded, to be replaced by the sombre reality of his friend's death. After the third can his mood had not improved and, unwilling to spoil the others' celebrations, he slipped from the mess tent, collaring a bottle of rum as he went.

In his own tent he raised the mosquito net over-hanging his camp bed, sat down and took a deep hit of rum straight from the bottle. He would say goodbye to Don alone and in his own way.

He was about to neck a second swallow when a trooper ducked through the tent flap. 'Sorry, but the Boss wants you.'

Again? thought Alex, pulling himself unsteadily to his feet. *Bollocks*. Glancing regretfully at the rum bottle, he followed the trooper from the tent.

In the hour since their last conversation, David Ross had clearly suffered a change of mood. Irritation now etched the spare features. 'You're going home,' he told Alex abruptly. 'Don't ask me why because I don't know. All I've been told is that you're wanted in London as soon as you can get there.'

Alex stared at him, mystified. What the fuck was going down? Whatever, he'd had enough of this sweaty shithole. 'Can I take a couple of the lads back with me? We can jump a Hercules.'

'No on both counts,' said Ross testily. 'They want you quicker than that. You're being choppered to Banjul and boarded on to a BA civilian flight to Heathrow. For that reason you're taking civilian clothes and cabin luggage only.'

'I didn't bring any . . .' Alex began.

'One of the liaison blokes is picking some stuff up now. Should be back any minute.'

'Is this to do with last night's operation?' Alex ventured.

'Not unless there's some element to the whole thing that I haven't been told about.'

That such a possibility even existed, Alex saw, clearly rankled bitterly with the CO. 'I'll get packing,' he said.

Ross nodded.

Fifteen minutes later, dressed in a flowered bush shirt, over-tight slacks and plastic sandals from Freetown market – all that the liaison guy had been able to rustle up at ten minutes' notice – Alex was watching from the passenger seat of a Lynx helicopter as Kroo Bay and the curving northern sweep of Freetown fell away beneath him. The rain of the early morning had given way to sunshine and now the whole country seemed to be steaming in the heat. Beside him, the khaki T-shirt of the special forces pilot was dark with sweat beneath the arms and where it was in contact with the plastic seat cover.

'Another hot one,' said the pilot laconically over the intercom.

'Looks like it,' Alex replied, settling himself back into his seat. They had the best part of two hours' flying time ahead of them. In twenty minutes they would be in Guinea airspace and in half an hour would be overflying the capital, Conakry. Thereafter they would follow the coastline northwards through Guinea-Bissau and touch down at Banjul at 9.30.

He determined to enjoy the view.

At Banjul he was the last one on to the British Airways flight.

'You must be important,' said the stewardess who met him at the door of the 777. 'They've held this plane for fifteen minutes!' She looked down at his plastic sandals with a lemon-sucking smile. 'Ready to walk the gauntlet?'

His appearance prompted a slow handclap. Around him, the sea of faces was hostile. They had been waiting for him, one angry woman informed him, for over twenty-five minutes. Perhaps next time he travelled he might bring an alarm clock with him?

His seat, needless to say, was right at the back of the aircraft. Toilet class. He was shown there by the lemon-sucking stewardess, and had to endure the eye-rolling and barely disguised impatience of an almost entirely female complement of economy-class passengers.

The stewardess directed him to a seat next to an amply proportioned woman, some fifty years old, who smelt strongly of coconut tanning oil.

She looked him up and down. 'Well,' she murmured purposefully, noting the uncomfortable tightness of his trousers. 'Aren't I the lucky one!'

Alex's spirits sank. How long was this fucking flight? Eight hours? 'Are you all . . . together?' he asked, indicating the other passengers.

'Well, it'd probably be true to say that we're all here for much the same reason,' the woman said with a small smile.

'Which is?'

'To meet Gambian boys, of course. Bit of the old Shirley Valentine.'

'Ah,' said Alex. 'Right.'

'Africans are properly appreciative of the fuller figure, you see. And they know how to woo a girl without ever mentioning DIY or football.'

'Or their jobs?' ventured Alex.

'Or their jobs,' she agreed. 'Quite right. I'm Maureen, by the way.'

'Alex.'

'So what brings you to the Gambia, Alex?'

'Oh, I never talk about my job. Too boring.'

'You came here for . . . *work*?'

Mistake. Serves me right for being a smartarse, he thought. 'I'm in, er, travel,' he explained.

'So you . . . get around a bit?'

'Here and there.' He shrugged.

She nodded. Taxi-ing into the oncoming breeze, the big 777 started its long race to take-off.

'And do you like big girls, Alex?'

Blimey, he thought. Talk about cutting to the chase. 'Did you have a good holiday, Maureen?' he asked her, with what he hoped was professional-sounding interest.

In answer she fished a polaroid photograph from her purse. It showed a young Gambian man, nude except for a pair of sunglasses. He was about seventeen, slender and leaning backwards to counterbalance his evident enthusiasm. The plane hurtled into the air, pressing them back into their seats. 'There's my answer, Alex. Now can I please have yours? Do you like big girls?'

He turned to her, took in the painfully sunburnt flesh, the hennaed hair, the small hopeful eyes. 'Maureen,' he said. 'I do like them. But I've got one waiting for me at home.'

'Hm,' she said, unconvinced.

An hour or so after take-off, breakfast was served. Uncertain of what was waiting for him at Heathrow, Alex ate the lot. With a bit of luck there'd be some lunch, too. Trouble, as every soldier knew, was best faced on a full stomach. And with a well-rested mind. The adrenalin rush that accompanied violent action was invariably followed by exhaustion and Alex slipped gratefully into sleep. One of the few advantages of his present situation – perhaps the only advantage – was that he would be able to see Sophie again and he didn't want to appear completely knackered when he did.

For a long while, scenes from the previous night replayed themselves before his eyes. The smell of rotting mangoes and the river, the clicking of that severed windpipe, tracer scorching across the clearing, the screams of the maimed RUF men, the stillness of the Puma pilot as his aircraft danced beneath him, the Puma enfolded in flame against the sodden grey of the jungle, Don Hammond pitching forward, the smack of SLR rounds impacting into Steve Dowson's shoulder and Ricky Sutton's thigh . . .

The images faded. They were not ready to join the longer-established nightmares in the vault of Alex's memory – it would be weeks and perhaps months before that happened – but they had been faced. He had always tried to make horror his friend.

It showed, Sophie told him, on his face.

FIVE

Sophie Wells was the sister of Jamie Wells, who had
been an officer cadet at Sandhurst with Alex and was
now a Coldstream Guards lieutenant.

Jamie and Alex had met towards the end of the
course. It had been a Friday night and with his ten-
year-old Karman-Ghia out of commission, Alex had
been looking for a lift into London, where he had
arranged to meet a mate for a few beers.

Jamie had not only been driving to London but to
Chelsea, which suited Alex perfectly. Dave
Constantine, the colleague in question, had recently
been posted as Permanent Staff Instructor to 21 SAS
and Alex had arranged to meet him at the bar in the
territorial battalion's King's Road HQ. Jamie,
meanwhile, was going to a party in Cadogan
Mansions, behind Sloane Square.

On their arrival in London Alex stood Jamie a drink
at the bar at the Duke of York's HQ, where Alex was
handed a note. Dave Constantine, he discovered, had
been called away at the last moment to replace one of
the other PSIs on an escape and evasion exercise on
the Brecon Beacons.

Jamie had suggested that the SAS man come with
him to the party, which was being given by his sister.
Alex hadn't been keen; to spend the evening with a

hundred braying Sloanes was very low on his wish-list. 'What does your sister do?' he asked doubtfully.

'You'll have to ask her.' Jamie grinned.

'Right.' Alex smiled grimly. 'I get it. It's a survival exercise. You've had to survive the beatings and the bollockings, so now I've got to survive the Taras and Tamaras.'

Jamie returned his gaze. 'Think of it that way if you like,' he said equably. 'But you might also enjoy yourself.'

'Yeah, right.'

'What have you got to lose?'

Alex conceded defeat.

The party was on the third floor of a nineteenth-century mansion block, and seemed to be taking place on the stairs and in the lift as well. Alex had expected an uncomfortable roomful of red-faced young men in corduroys and tractor-tyre shoes; what he actually encountered was the best part of an acre of dizzyingly beautiful women.

He had also expected to look out of place; in fact, although some of the handful of men present were expensively dressed, most looked as if they had bought their gear off an Isle of Dogs market trader. The look was as fake as their cockney accents and movie-gangster rhyming slang, but Alex reckoned that his cropped military haircut, Essex Stock Cars T-shirt and old Levis would probably pass muster among them.

Alex's first hint of Sophie Wells's existence was when a gold and turquoise whirlwind blew past him trailing scent, silk and male admirers. She came to rest briefly in front of Jamie – for just long enough, in fact, to present her brother with a kiss and an introduction to a dewy-faced teenager in a chiffon micro-skirt –

'she's the new "face" of Prada, so I want you to make absolutely sure she's in bed by 10.30!' – then was suddenly right there in front of him. 'So.' She smiled. 'It's Alex, isn't it? A friend of Jamie's from Sandhurst? How lovely of you to come!'

For a moment Alex gazed at her, taking in the short chestnut crop, the cool grey-green eyes, the Italian silks, the flimsy and very visible lingerie beneath. Where did you begin with a creature like this?

'I'm Sophie,' she continued encouragingly, swiping a couple of glasses of champagne from a passing waiter's tray and handing one to Alex. 'And these dreadful people' – she gestured vaguely around her – 'are my friends. Aren't they ghastly?'

Alex managed a smile. 'You should see mine,' he said. 'Is this party to celebrate anything?'

'My twenty-sixth birthday,' said Sophie. 'My entry into middle age.'

'You look well on it,' said Alex, wishing he could have found something cleverer to say.

'Do I? God, I don't deserve to. You look . . .' She hesitated. 'How old are you?'

'Thirty-four.'

'I was going to say that you look older than this lot' – she waved vaguely at the people around them – 'but you don't. You just look . . . different.'

She held his gaze, Alex noticed, rather than darting her eyes about the room in search of the next flirtation, the next conversational fix. So steady was her regard – so intimate, somehow – that they might have been alone together.

'Well, there probably aren't too many other soldiers here.'

She laughed. 'That's certainly true. But I've met a

few soldiers in my time and they didn't have what you've got – that sort of wary look behind the eyes.' She dropped her voice to an enquiring murmur. 'How did that get there?'

Alex looked away, momentarily uncomfortable, breaking the cocoon that they had briefly spun about themselves. Sophie watched him patiently.

'Jamie wouldn't tell me what you do,' he said eventually. 'I'm supposed to ask you in person.'

She shrugged. 'Oh, I'm a fashion PR. I get column inches in the glossies for designers.'

'I bet some of those designers are grateful for a few inches,' said Alex.

'Alex!' shrieked Sophie in mock outrage. She turned to a man in a canary-yellow biker's outfit and Alex, taking his cue, drifted away. By one of the windows he saw Jamie, glass in hand, talking to the Prada girl. Alex caught his eye and winked, and Jamie flushed a slightly deeper shade of pink than usual. *These are nice enough people*, thought Alex, *but what the fuck am I doing here, precisely?*

He wandered into a large kitchen, fitted out with tiny laser-like spotlights and vast brushed-aluminium units and appliances. The placed looked like a safe depository he'd once guarded. Opening the walk-in fridge, he found himself a cold Mexican beer. The champagne went down the sink.

At one end of the room was a large picture window, looking out over Sloane Street. For several minutes Alex stood there in unmoving silence, watching the northward crawl of red tail-lights towards Knightsbridge. At that moment, it seemed that he was disconnected from everything and everyone that he knew. His SAS career had separated him from his family, promotion had lifted him out of the orbit of his fellow NCOs, and he guessed that both age and background would set him apart from most of his brother officers. He didn't particularly regret any of this except possibly the distance that had grown between himself and his family. This was as much a matter of logistics as anything else: Hereford was a long way away from the Essex coast and London stood between them. He just didn't make it down there often enough.

Nor had he ever been married. He'd had lots of girlfriends over the years but had always held back from proposing to them. There was plenty of time for family life, he'd always reckoned, when he wasn't being yo-yoed around the world by the Regiment. Ireland had discouraged him, too. He'd seen brave soldiers fall apart when their wives and children were threatened. What would it be like, Alex wondered, planning a future with someone? And what sort of person would that someone have to be if they weren't going to end up at each other's throats?

Far below, in Sloane Street, an articulated lorry straddled the traffic where it had jackknifed while attempting to turn into a side street. Long lines of cars had built up on both sides of the road and the faint blare of their protest was audible through the heavy plate glass. Behind him Alex heard the suck of the opening fridge.

'You must be Jamie's friend. Sophie thought you'd done a runner.'

He turned to find a pretty fair-haired girl in jeans and a floaty top jacking open one of the Mexican beers.

'Still here, I'm afraid.' He extended his hand. 'I'm Alex.'

'I'm Stella.' She looked at him appraisingly and grinned. 'She'll be really glad you're still here. She was like *oh no*, he's *gone*, we've completely freaked him out. Not that I'm supposed to tell you that, of course.'

'I can keep a secret,' said Alex.

'Yeah, I'll bet you can,' said Stella, drawing along-side him. 'Interesting view down there?'

They peered down through the summer twilight.

'Fashion's not really one of my special subjects,' Alex told her.

Stella nodded. 'Unlike most *fashionista* babes, there's a lot more to Sophie than her job.'

'I'm sure,' said Alex. 'Are you a PR too?'

'Nah. Sophie does the London PR for my company. I'm a designer.'

Behind them there was a sudden overexcited hubbub. Alex glanced over his shoulder to discover a tall, anxious-looking girl chopping lines of white powder on one of the polished aluminium draining boards. A half-dozen other modelly looking boys and girls crowded impatiently round her. Banknotes were produced and small hoovering sounds ensued. One evenly tanned young man whom Alex vaguely recognised had a violent sneezing fit into a paper kitchen towel. There was nervous laughter from the others, but by the sixth sneeze the blood spatters were clearly visible.

'You don't disapprove?' asked Stella, watching him watching them.

'Me? No.' Alex held up his beer and squinted at the label. 'Personally I'd rather go this way than that way, but . . .' He shrugged.

'Each to his own?'

Alex looked over at the powder-nosed models. 'Or her own.'

The kitchen was filling up. Stella introduced Alex to a film director named Danny Biggs, for whose latest project she was designing costumes.

'What's the picture going to be about?' Alex asked.

'Bunch of geezers turning over a bank,' said Danny. 'Working title "Hair of the Dog".'

'Why do you need a fashion designer to dress bank robbers?' Alex asked him. 'Most villains I've come across are fat, middle-aged white men in dodgy gold jewellery and knocked-off sports gear – the sort of stuff you can pick up in any high street.'

'Well, we 'ave to improve on reality,' explained Danny. 'Dress 'em in ruffled shirts an' Gucci whistles.'

At that moment Jamie appeared with the Prada girl and touched fists with Stella. 'You'd better watch out,' he told her, indicating Alex. 'This man gave us a lecture yesterday on ambushes and surprise attacks. Keep him in view at all times!'

Stella raised an eyebrow. 'I thought you were one of the . . . what do you call them, students? Cadets?'

'I am,' said Alex. 'But I came up through the ranks for ten years first, hence my advanced age. From time to time us old lags get called on to address the Ruperts – that's Jamie and his friends – and pass on a few dirty tricks.'

'Dirty tricks, eh?' mused Stella. 'Sounds interesting.'

As Jamie and the Prada girl exited with their drinks, Sophie reappeared.

Alex's heart thumped in his chest. She was beautiful, he realised, and beautiful in a much more interesting way than the models, with their stick-thin limbs and their dim, drug-dazed faces.

'Hey, girlfriend!' Stella greeted Sophie. 'Look who's still here!'

As Sophie met Alex's eye, the beginnings of a smile touched the corners of her mouth. 'Well! I thought we'd shocked you into flight.'

Alex attempted an answering smile. 'I don't scare quite as easily as you think,' he said.

At the draining board the anxious-looking model was rubbing the last of the cocaine into her gums.

Stella rolled her eyes at the girl. 'Tash, you should cool it with that stuff. I don't want you falling off the catwalk tomorrow.'

'I know, Stell. I've just been like, so busy, yeah? I got this option for the new Virginity campaign and everyone at the agency's like hey, you really gotta do this, they're like *really* big clients and I'm like *whoa*, cool it, yeah? I just want to, like, chill out, y'know?'

'I know,' said Stella gently. She turned to Sophie. 'Dad was asking how you were.'

'Tell him fine,' said Sophie.

'What does your dad do?' Alex asked Stella on impulse.

'He's a musician,' said Stella. 'He used to play bass guitar with a band in the Sixties. And he still does a bit of songwriting.'

Alex nodded. 'My dad's into cars. That's his thing.' He turned to Sophie. 'What about you? How's your old man fill his time?'

'He sells what he calls area-denial systems and the rest of the world calls landmines,' said Sophie. 'Mostly to third-world dictators. That's his thing.'

Alex nodded again. This was clearly sensitive territory. 'And is business, er, good?' he ventured.

'Booming,' said Sophie drily.

They looked at each other for a moment.

'Before you disappear,' said Stella, 'I've just had a thought. Why don't you and this nice young man come to dinner at my place tomorrow night?'

Sophie gazed into Alex's eyes. Her grey–green gaze poured over him like a wave. 'That would be lovely,' she said quietly. 'Are you free?'

'Yes,' said Alex.

'Good.' Sophie kissed him softly but firmly on the mouth. 'See you there.'

Alex watched her go. Stella watched him watch her. 'Smitten, I'd say.' She smiled. 'Definitely smitten.'

'Who?' asked Alex, smiling like an idiot.

'You tell me.' Stella bent and rummaged in her bag. 'Here, I'll give you the address for tomorrow night.' She wrote it on the back of an invitation to a film première. 'Be there,' she told him sternly. 'I'm counting on you, OK?'

'I promise,' said Alex.

Ten minutes later he was walking down Sloane Street with Jamie, who after a promising start had seen the Prada girl stolen away from him by the film director Danny Biggs.

'He told her he grew up hanging around the dog tracks and nicking cars,' protested the disconsolate Jamie. 'The truth is that he went to Eton with me and his father's the Lord-Lieutenant of Shropshire. Bastard.'

'I'm afraid all's fair in love and war, mate,' Alex told him. 'No prizes for second place.'

'I guess not,' Jamie agreed gloomily.

They walked on in silence for a few paces.

'By the way,' said Alex, a little self-consciously, 'it

looks like I'm seeing your sister tomorrow night' – he checked his watch – 'I mean tonight. For, um, dinner.'

'Oh, yeah?' said Jamie, amused at Alex's embarrassment. 'Glad you came, then?'

'I guess I am.'

The next day Alex spent the afternoon at the Duke of York's Headquarters in the King's Road, test-firing revolvers with Dave Constantine. Wondering if he should dress smartly for dinner at Stella's – perhaps even buy some new clothes – he had eventually ditched the idea and stuck to his jeans and a T-shirt.

In the evening he took the tube to Notting Hill Gate and walked northwards up Ladbroke Grove. Stella's flat was on the first floor of a vast white wedding cake of a Victorian house and overlooked a private garden. From a dark staircase he walked into a huge room flooded with pale evening light. Several floor-to-ceiling windows had been opened outwards on to an ironwork balcony, in front of which Stella and a guy with dark hair and a lazy smile were sitting at a table drinking champagne.

'Alex,' said Stella. 'Hey. You made it!'

'I did,' agreed Alex.

Trying to recall the event afterwards, he discovered there were gaps in his memory. He couldn't remember what Stella's boyfriend did – it might have been something to do with the music industry, or possibly with TV, but then again it could have been advertising or PR – and he couldn't remember anything that they ate or drank or talked about at the long table in front of the balcony. For Alex, this was one hell of a lot of information to forget in a short space of time but he didn't really give a damn because everything to do with Sophie – her skin, her hair, her smell, the way she moved – etched itself deeply and permanently into his consciousness.

She amazed him. There were her clothes, for a start – electric blue and, presumably, vastly expensive – which lent her the sheen of an exotic bird. And then there was her slender, delicately rounded body, and the limitless candour of her wave-green eyes. But more than her appearance there was her manner, her almost reckless confidence. Most women Alex had met up to that moment had seemed to watch themselves, to monitor their appearance and the impression that they were making minute by minute. Not Sophie. Sophie didn't seem to give a damn. There was a huge mirror on one wall of the twilit room and though she passed it a score of times Alex never saw her glance into it once. She was just there, beautiful if you chose to think so and if not, well, who cared?

Alex chose to think so. He was entranced and the thing that really got him – the thing that really ducked under his guard – was that she seemed to be as entranced as he was. She just stared at him, quite openly, fascinated.

'What's that smell?' she asked him as soon as she walked into the room. Walking over to Alex she sniffed at him. 'It's on your hands,' she stated. 'A kind of burnt . . .' She pressed his fingers to her nose and then touched her face to his hair. 'But you don't smoke, do you?' she murmured from behind his ear.

'It's gunpowder residue,' said Alex, realising what she was referring to. 'Cordite. You get it from using firearms in an enclosed space.'

'You've been killing people again,' said Stella disapprovingly. 'Honestly, you boys!'

Alex smiled. 'Just trying out some new toys on the range.'

'As one does,' said Stella's boyfriend. 'What sort?'

'Moorsyth .50 super-magnum,' said Alex.

'Ah.' The boyfriend was clearly none the wiser. 'Right.'

'Let's eat,' said Stella.

After dinner they split up. Spooning the sugar crystals from the bottom of her coffee cup, Sophie announced her desire that Alex take her for a walk. It was a warm evening, the streets, the cafés and the pavements were crowded, and it seemed the most natural thing in the world that she should take his arm so as to avoid their becoming separated. At one moment, outside a noisy Portobello Road pub, she stopped in her tracks and turned to face him, placing her hands on his shoulders. When he met her gaze, however, she smiled enigmatically and moved on.

Ten minutes later she suddenly dived into a bar. It was tiny, the walls were yellowed with cigarette smoke and hung with ancient photographs of boxers and footballers. 'Quick!' she told the barman. 'We need some malt whisky. Hurry, it's an emergency.'

'Do you always get what you want?' asked Alex as the waiter placed two tumblers of Laphroaig in front of them.

She frowned. The whisky made its smoky way down their throats. 'I think . . . pretty much always,' she admitted. 'What about you?'

'It's a long time since I've wanted anything as badly as . . .'

She reached for his thigh under the table. 'Do you want me . . . badly?'

'Yes,' said Alex.

Her eyes shone and she compressed her lips with pleasure.

They had finished their drinks and crossed Notting Hill Gate into Kensington Church Street. There, as if at a prearranged signal, both had raised their arms to the same cruising taxi.

In the back, ignoring the seat belts, he put his arm round her shoulders and she kissed his neck before moulding herself warmly against him. Taking his other hand, she placed it on her breast and he felt the nipple harden beneath his probing fingers.

'Mmm!' she murmured.

Laughing, but their movements urgent now, they ran up the stairs to her flat. They had kissed as soon as the door had closed behind them – a long kiss, but one which swiftly proved to be less than either of them wanted or needed.

She led him inside, somehow managing to unbelt him and to remove her blue silk top as she went. An antique velvet-covered sofa offered itself, and by then she was unzipping and stepping out of her skirt. His hand moved to the damp triangle between her legs, hers to the zip of his trousers. He sat back and she lowered herself gratefully on to him, gasping as she felt him thrust hard inside her. Her back arched and her hair fell away from the pale oval of her face. 'I can still smell the gunpowder,' she gasped and drove herself against him, hot and wet, clenching and releasing, rising and falling.

SIX

Sleepily, Alex reached for her. Eyes closed, he allowed his fingers a lazy exploration of her body, felt the desire stir inside him once more.

But Sophie seemed to have changed. Her breasts, for a start, were very much larger and heavier than he remembered, and were now suspended in a loose nylon bra and resting against several warm rolls of flesh. The smell in his nostrils was not that of Guerlain perfume and expensive hairdressing but of sweat, airline cooking and recycled air.

Cautiously he opened an eye. The face that lay inches from his and the breast that he was fondling belonged to his fellow passenger from Banjul, Maureen. And it was Maureen's hand which was firmly cupping his crotch.

'You certainly do like big girls, don't you,' she whispered hungrily. Her fingers tightened round him. 'In fact you're quite a big boy yourself!'

Alex stared at her. The whites of her eyes had a yellowish cast to them, as did her teeth. A centimetre of grey showed at the roots of her hennaed hair. In the opposite aisle, one of the few other male passengers on the flight caught his eye and gave him a leery wink.

'A little bird tells me that you and I are about to join the mile-high club,' she whispered.

Alex struggled upright. 'That little bird is wrong,' he said, searching his memory for the woman's name. 'I'm sorry, I've . . . I've been asleep.'

She looked at him quizzically. 'You seemed so . . .'

'I was dreaming,' he said firmly. 'Of my girlfriend.'

'Ah,' she said, drawing herself upright and pulling an in-flight magazine from the back of the seat in front. 'I see.'

Every detail of her deportment spelt hurt and disappointment – emotions to which Alex guessed she was no stranger. He glanced at his watch: 2.45 p.m. London time. Three bloody hours to go. He felt stale and overtired. Whatever was waiting for him at the other end had to be an improvement on this.

Three men were waiting for him.

They were standing with one of the Customs officers at the EU citizens' immigration desk. One, in a shiny blazer and slacks, looked like a run-to-seed bodybuilder. Salaried muscle, thought Alex. Ex-squaddie, 18K and a clothing allowance. The second, a florid-faced figure in a Barbour coat, had the tired, tolerant gaze of the time-serving civil servant. The third, a younger and more military-looking figure in a Brigade of Guards tie and a velvet-collared coat, Alex vaguely recognised. Box, he thought. MI5.

'Captain Temple,' asked the younger man. 'Could you step this way, sir?'

They hurried him into the Customs offices, down a flight of stone stairs and out into a car park where they convened round a nearly new Ford Mondeo.

'Alex, isn't it?' said the man in the velvet-collared coat. 'Gerald Farmilow. We met at Thames House. I'm Five's liaison officer with the Regiment.'

It came back to him now. He'd been introduced to a bunch of Security Services suits when he'd first taken over the RWW team. This Farmilow character had been one of them.

'I remember, Gerald,' he said. 'I'm sorry – it's been a bit of a long night.'

'Congratulations, by the way,' said Farmilow. 'An excellent result.'

Alex nodded. He felt dry-throated and in need of a shower. And some halfway sensible clothes.

Farmilow glanced at his watch, a wafer-thin sliver of gold and enamel, and nodded towards the red-faced man in the Barbour.

'Alex, George will tell you what this is all about.' He held out his hand. 'I've got to push off back to Millbank.'

A brief handshake and he was gone. Identification effected. Mission completed.

'I'm George Widdowes,' said the man in the Barbour, opening one of the Mondeo's rear doors, 'and this is Tom Ritchie.'

The driver mutely raised his hand.

'I'd also like to add my congratulations to Gerald's,' Widdowes continued. 'I understand you had a major success last night.'

Alex looked at him non-committally and climbed into the car. He wasn't about to discuss Regiment business with these people.

Widdowes nodded approvingly. 'Lips sealed. Quite right. Look, Captain Temple, we've got a good hour's drive ahead of us – we're going out to Goring, in Berkshire – so I'll put you in the picture as we go. Do you smoke?'

Alex shook his head.

The younger man drove, Widdowes sat in the back with Alex. Alex's overnight bag joined a laptop computer that was lying on the front seat. No one spoke until they were crawling along the exit road towards the M4 with the rest of the evening rush-hour traffic, but finally Widdowes half turned in his seat. 'I'm sure I don't need to say this, but it's essential that you don't repeat a word of what I'm about to tell you to anyone. Colleagues, senior officers, other security services people . . .'

Alex didn't bother to reply. Leaning against the back seat of the Mondeo with his eyes half closed, he felt a little of the tension leaving his shoulders.

'Good. Right, then. Had to say that. You know how it is.'

Alex nodded.

'Right . . . Well, here goes. A fortnight ago there was a murder committed in Chertsey, just inside the M25 in Surrey. Know it?'

'Isn't there an MOD arms sales place there?'

'That's right. Which is why the victim – one of our fairly senior people, a man named Barry Fenn – happened to be staying in the area.'

Alex nodded. He was suddenly and acutely aware of his appearance – in his flowered shirt and flip-flops he looked and felt ridiculous. Typical of Box to get you at a disadvantage. 'Go on,' he said levelly.

'You weren't here, obviously, but even if you had been you wouldn't have heard or seen anything about it. We found him, we cleaned him up, we disappeared the body. Officially Barry Fenn died of heart failure in an ambulance en route to St Peter's Hospital, Chertsey. In fact, he was killed in the early hours of the morning in a third-floor bedroom at the White

85

Rose Lodge by a person or persons unknown. The killer – I'm assuming it's one person – disabled the exterior floodlight warning system, scaled the back of the building, climbed in through a window, eliminated our man, returned the way he came and vanished.'

'How did he kill him?' asked Alex.

'Horribly,' said Widdowes, closing his eyes. 'Barry Fenn was a good friend of mine. Had been for twenty years odd.'

Alex waited. Widdowes steepled his fingers again.

'The killer tied his wrists and drove a six-inch nail through the side of his head. When he'd done that he cut his tongue out.'

Alex said nothing. Widdowes' words had fired off a number of warning flares in his mind, but he showed no outward sign of this. The SAS were deeply wary of the other security services, whose human resource management they considered fatally flawed. David Shayler had gone a long way towards making monkeys of Five by publicising their involvement in the Muammar Gaddafi assassination plot and Richard Tomlinson had performed much the same service for Six when he outlined plans to whack Slobodan Milosevic with the help of the RWW. In general it was not a good time to be sharing a sleeping bag with Military Intelligence.

'I'm sorry,' Alex said neutrally. 'I'm sure he was a good man.'

'He was,' said Widdowes.

Alex glanced at his plastic flip-flops and sunburnt toes, and thought of Africa and Don Hammond and the screams of the wounded RUF men. Although the leech marks were still fresh on his arms and legs and groin, the bloody events of the night before already seemed a world away. 'Let's cut to the chase, Widdowes,' he said. 'What do you want from me?'

The MI5 man turned to him. 'We're going to the site of a second murder. Another of our desk officers, a man named Craig Gidley. Exactly the same modus operandi, except that this time the killer gouged his eyes out.'

A moment's silence.

'Go on?' said Alex.

'And we've got reason to think the killer's one of our guys. Or to be precise, one of your guys. An SAS-trained undercover agent.'

Alex stared out of the window. They passed a flooded gravel pit, a coppice, fields.

'We need this man found, Captain Temple, and soon.'

The dead man's house stood a short distance outside the Thames-side town of Goring. A high flint wall surrounded the property; inside, a converted Georgian farmhouse was fronted by a neat lawn, yews and a lime tree. On the gravelled drive in front of the main entrance several cars were drawn up.

Ritchie found a space for the Mondeo, opened Widdowes' door for him and returned to the driver's seat, patting his pockets for cigarettes. Widdowes led Alex round to the back of the house, where two men and two women were sitting at an ironwork garden table. They looked as if they had been there for some time.

Widdowes led Alex round the table, first to the older and obviously senior of the two women, whom he introduced as 'our deputy director', then to the two men, who were respectively a service pathologist and a forensics officer. The final introduction was to an anonymous-looking younger woman whose name was Dawn Harding.

With these formalities complete the pathologist and the forensics man excused themselves and returned to the house. In response to a gesture by the deputy director, Alex and Widdowes took their vacated chairs.

'Thank you for coming at such short notice, Captain Temple,' said the deputy director. She was an austerely handsome woman in her fifties, grey-haired.

Alex nodded cautiously.

'I believe George has brought you up to date with events?'

'In general terms, yes.'

'And with what we want you to do.'

'He's given me a fair idea.'

'And?'

'And my answer to him was the same as my answer is to you: that I'm a soldier, not a policeman. I can track a man through the jungle or over mountains, but not through criminal record databases and security services computer files. You've brought in the wrong person.'

The deputy director looked at her two colleagues and back at Alex. 'You won't need files or records,' she said quietly. 'We know who murdered Fenn and Gidley.'

Alex stared. 'You know who . . .'

'Yes. At least we've got a pretty good idea. And finding him is something we've got well in hand ourselves. What we need from you is more in the nature of disposal. Before we go into that, though, I'd like you to look at the body and see what it suggests to you. George?'

Widdowes stood and led Alex into the house through the back door. Inside, a flag-stoned corridor gave on to an oak-floored front hall, and the hall on to a small, book-lined study. To Alex, as he flip-flopped through, the set-up looked like an expensive one. The furniture was old and dark, and the gilt-framed portraits which hung on the walls looked like originals.

Disposal. Typical Box bullshit. They meant execution.

The owner of the house was lying face down on the study carpet. Although not tall he was a bulky man, and his dinner jacket and trousers looked a size too tight. His hands, blackened and swollen, had been tied behind his back with yellowish cord and it was clear from the severely chafed wrists that he had struggled violently against his bonds. Beneath his face a congealed pool of blood had blackened the worn Persian rug. The coppery smell of the blood hung in the air.

From the doorway Widdowes signalled for Alex to approach the body.

'We've taken the photos and run all the technical stuff. You can move him around if you want.'

There was nothing that Alex wanted to do less, but he put his hands to the body and pushed, and the corpse rolled heavily over on to its back. In this position the full horror of the assault was revealed. The face was an unrecognisable mask of caked blood. Where the eyes had been were now clotted black holes. At the victim's right temple the head of a six-inch flat-head nail showed a couple of millimetres proud of the skin surface. On close inspection the nail head proved to be flecked with rust. For the best part of a minute Alex stared at the body. It seemed to be expected of him.

'OK?' asked Widdowes.

Alex shrugged. 'Just fill me in again on what happened. The Gidleys were having a party, yeah?'

'A dinner party,' said Widdowes. 'A dinner party for four Service colleagues and their partners. They would have arrived at about the same time that you left Freetown to keep your appointment with the RUF.'

'And you weren't there?' asked Alex.

'No,' said Widdowes, a small note of annoyance creeping into his voice. 'I wasn't, as it happens.'

'And the deputy director?'

'The DD was there, yes. In all – including Craig and Letitia Gidley – ten people sat down to eat. By half past midnight the guests had all left, and Craig Gidley locked the front gate and let the dogs out.'

'They were Dobermanns, right? Attack dogs?'

'That's right. They'd been shut up in their kennels while the guests were around. Normally they had the run of the grounds – a couple of acres in all. Better than any alarm, as you can imagine.'

'Not on this occasion,' said Alex soberly.

'Well, no, as it happened. Not on this occasion.' Widdowes rubbed his eyes. It occurred to Alex that the MI5 man had probably had as shitty a day as he had.

'Shortly afterwards Letitia Gidley saw her husband lock the front door. She went up to bed – they had separate bedrooms – and he went into the study announcing that he was going to have a finger of

Scotch and spend half an hour on the computer. That was the last time she saw him alive. She found him here at 9.30 this morning and called the DD.'

'Where's – what's her name – Letitia Gidley now?'

'At a colleague's in London. In a fairly bad way, as you can imagine. Let's go outside.'

Gratefully, Alex followed him into the hall and thence to the porch. The front door was of heavy steel-backed oak. 'This how he got access?' asked Alex.

'Yes. Picked the lock. Very expertly. Come through.'

Widdowes led him the fifty yards or so past the parked cars to the front gate, where he pointed to a telegraph pole.

'See that little box on the line running to the house?'

Alex recognised it at a glance. 'It's a sonic deactivator. Sends a false "secure" signal to the alarm monitoring station.'

'That's right. Have you ever used one?'

Alex chose to ignore the question. 'And it was just the house that was alarmed?'

Widdowes looked at him thoughtfully for a moment before nodding. 'Just the house. These two little charmers kept an eye on the garden.'

He led Alex along the lawn. In the herbaceous border, doubled up among the lupins and delphinia, were the stiffened bodies of two Dobermann pinschers.

Alex whistled appreciatively. 'He's good, this guy. And the wife heard nothing?'

'Nothing.'

Alex nodded. At the front door the two men he had met earlier were loading a body bag into the boot of one of the cars. Ritchie, cigarette in mouth, was giving them a hand.

'How would you have taken out Gidley?' asked Widdowes.

'I'd have done pretty much as this guy did,' Alex answered. 'Wait until everyone's inside and the party's under way, then climb the telegraph pole and disable the alarm. He wouldn't have gone inside the grounds at that stage because of the dogs.'

'How would he have known about the dogs?' asked Widdowes.

'He would have seen them,' said Alex. 'He'd have had this place under surveillance for days, maybe even weeks. He'd have known the dogs' names, when they were fed, everything.'

'So then?'

'Then he would have pulled back from the target and positioned himself somewhere he could count the cars out at the end of the evening. Field, maybe, or a tree. He probably had binoculars. Soon as he was sure the Gidleys were alone, he'd have returned and gone over the wall.'

'What about the dogs?'

'See the way they're lying?' asked Alex, pointing to the twisted bodies. 'I'd put money on his having used poison, meat laced with strychnine. You whistle the dogs over, throw down the meat and then assume a submissive posture face down on the ground. Instead of going straight for your throat the dogs just piss on you. Once they've symbolically dominated you, you see, you're no longer a threat and they can get on with the meat.'

'Big mistake,' murmured Widdowes drily.

'Very big,' agreed Alex. 'They're dead in seconds.

Then our man takes a quick trot to the front door, boosts the lock and . . .' He shrugged. 'That's the how of it, anyway. As regards the why, you tell me.'

'Let's go back to the DD,' said Widdowes.

They returned to the back of the house, where the deputy director was making notes in a small ring-binder. The two men sat down. It was several seconds before she looked up. 'So, Captain Temple, give us your assessment of the perpetrator of this murder.'

Alex hesitated. 'Why me?' he asked her. 'Why pull me out of the Sierra Leone jungle when you could have had Hereford chopper a bloke down this morning? Why waste the best part of a day?'

The deputy director gave the faintest of smiles. 'Because I wanted *you*, Captain Temple, not just some "bloke". I've been led to understand that you're the best.'

Alex looked away. 'Who told you that?' he asked sardonically.

'Commissioned from the ranks at thirty-four after a decade's exemplary service. RWW team leader while still a captain . . . The facts speak for themselves.'

Alex shrugged. He guessed that, one way or another, he'd managed to keep his nose clean over the years. And managed it without brown-nosing the brass, which he privately considered to be his real achievement. 'Let me get this right,' he said. 'You're in the process of trying to locate the man who murdered Fenn and Gidley. Assuming that you do locate him, you want me to move in and eliminate him.'

'That's about the shape and size of it.'

Alex nodded. 'If I'm going to do that, I'm going to need to know everything you've got on him.'

'That's not a problem.'

'And I'm going to need to ask you some pretty sensitive questions.'

'And I'll do my best to answer them, Captain Temple. There'll be no secrets between us. We want this man taken off the streets, and fast. For reasons I'm sure I don't have to go into, I want the whole thing tied up before the police get wind of it. Or, God help us, the press. That means days, Captain Temple. Not weeks. All of this is *urgent*.'

Nodding his assent, Alex looked out across the evening stillness of the garden. Midges whirled in the scented air. Was it his imagination or had she emphasised the word 'captain', as if to suggest that promotion would accompany success. Or that demotion would follow refusal, perhaps . . . Not that he had a hope in hell of getting out of this.

'OK.' He nodded.

The deputy director swept her papers together. 'Good,' she said briskly. 'I'll see you in my office at 9 a.m. tomorrow. By then we'll have photographs and the bulk of the forensic information, and I can give you some of the background to all of this. Meanwhile you'll be liaising with Dawn, who'll take you back to London. Anything you need, just ask her.' With that she got up, briefly extended her hand to Alex – he pressed it, perhaps more gingerly than was strictly polite – and swept into the house.

'I'll wrap up here, Dawn,' said George Widdowes. 'Why don't you and the captain make a move? Unless of course' – he turned to Alex – 'there's anything else you need to see?'

'I don't think so,' said Alex and turned his attention for the first time to the woman who had been sitting in silence at the far end of the table.

SEVEN

Alex's first impression was of toughness: tough grey eyes, tough posture and tough attitude. She had nondescript blonde hair, hadn't bothered with make-up and was wearing a black short-sleeved sweater, black trousers and flat-heeled elastic-sided boots.

The impression didn't last. The clothes, if plain, were clearly expensive and accentuated rather than concealed the smooth curves beneath. If she was wearing no make-up it was because she knew she looked fine without it. And she certainly wasn't tough in the way that the 14th Int women he'd known in Belfast had been tough. Women like Carol Denny or Denise Foley who would match the Regiment guys drink for drink after a good terrorist kill and would have been perfectly happy lying up in a freezing hide with a Heckler and Koch snipers' rifle and doing the job themselves. Denise, he remembered, used to bake a cross-shaped cake every time the Det or the Regiment took a player out.

Nor was Dawn Harding much like the Box girls he'd met over the water. For the most part they had been bright, ordinary-looking types, much more desk-bound and secretarial than their Det colleagues. Most of them, according to Don Hammond – who'd always had a bit of a way with words – were 'gagging for a bit of Regimental pipe'.

But not this one. This one was decidedly unimpressed and it wasn't just because he happened to be dressed like a West African pimp. It was because she wanted to impress on him from the start that there was a distinct difference in status between some johnny-come-lately ex-squaddie and a fast-track MI5 desk officer to be. When she turned to him it was with the polite but very slightly patronising look that all executive-stream Box personnel seemed to acquire sooner or later. 'So,' she said. 'Back to London. Have you got anywhere to stay?'

It was a good question. Since clearing Customs at Heathrow, Alex had not had a moment to himself and he certainly wasn't about to ring Sophie with all these wanky spooks hanging around. He didn't even want to call her from his mobile until he was well clear of them – mobile phones were a pushover in surveillance terms and although it was unlikely that a scanner was being operated from the cars at the front of the house, he didn't want to take the chance.

There was one call he could and would make, though. Tersely excusing himself and deliberately marching a good twenty yards away from Harding, he put a call through to Lieutenant-Colonel Bill Leonard, the CO of 22 SAS. This, Alex knew, was in direct contravention of Widdowes' request, but bollocks to that.

Leonard was still at his desk at the Regimental base at Credenhill, near Hereford. 'Well done last night,' he said quietly. 'Overall, a bloody good show. You're in Berkshire I gather, with friends.'

On insecure lines the Regiment used the minimum of military jargon. There would be no 'sirs' or 'bosses' or departments named.

'That's right. They have some . . . cleaning they want me to do.'

There was a brief silence. Finally Leonard spoke. 'I want you to lend them a hand on this one, Alex. Accepting an upgrade like you did last year means eating a shit sandwich from time to time and this is one of those times.'

'Yeah, but . . .'

'No buts, Alex. This problem of theirs has got to be dealt with and I can't think of a better man than you to do it. I'm sorry, Alex, but that's a must. What I can promise is choice of posting when you're done. You've got my word on that.'

Alex said nothing. By the time he was done, he reflected – if he was ever done – things would have changed. The 'choice' would dissolve, as it always did.

'How's Karen?' he asked. Karen was Don Hammond's widow.

'Bearing up, as is Sue. They've both got people round with them. I'll have someone call you about the funerals.'

Sue, Alex guessed, must have been the wife of the dead Special Forces pilot.

'Help our friends out, Alex. There's no room for manoeuvre on this one.'

The phone went dead.

Dawn Harding drove a two-year-old Honda Accord and drove it with an almost aggressive respect for the speed limit. When she was cut up at traffic lights outside Reading she merely slowed to let the other driver get away, while on the M4, where the pre-vailing speed was around 80, she seemed happy to roll along in the high 60s.

'Saving the engine?' Alex ventured at one point.

'No. Hanging on to a clean licence,' answered Dawn. She gestured towards the traffic pouring past them. 'And I've nothing to prove to a bunch of stressed-out commuters. Where is it you want to go exactly?'

Alex had tried Sophie earlier but got her voice-mail. He got it again now. For a reason that he couldn't quite put his finger on – something to do with wanting to hear her reaction to the news of his return – he didn't want to leave a message. 'Sloane Square,' he answered. 'Anywhere around there.'

'Late-night shopping in the King's Road?' Dawn archly flicked a glance at his shirt.

'No, I've got some friends at the barracks,' said Alex. *And sod you too*, he thought.

'OK. Sloane Square it is. And I'd be grateful if you didn't go chatting to all your Territorial Army mates about this afternoon's events, if that's all right with you.'

He stared at her. 'It's not my habit to "go chatting", as you put it, to my mates or to anyone else. I was a badged SAS soldier before you . . .' He faltered to silence. How old was she? Twenty-five? Twenty-six? '. . . Before you sat your GCSEs,' he finished weakly.

She smiled. 'So, have you ever killed anyone, Captain?'

'I've hurt a few people's feelings!'

Dawn nodded sagely. 'And are you very conscious of your age? Is that a problem for you? After all, most captains must be ten years younger than you. My sort of age, in fact.'

'Listen,' said Alex, 'if you think your superiors' – he

stressed the word – 'have got the wrong man for the job, I'd be very happy to step down. Just stop the car and I'll fuck off.'

'You'll . . . *fuck off*?'

Alex reached over to the back seat for his bag.

'Yes,' he said. 'I'll fuck off.' He looked at her meaningfully. 'There is no aspect of this project that I'm looking forward to, none whatsoever. I've had dealings with Thames House before and regretted it every time. For my money you jokers can dig yourselves out of your own shit.'

'I see. Well, that's certainly telling it like it is. Did it ever occur to you, Captain Temple, that we might all actually be on the same side? Pursuing the same objectives?'

Alex said nothing. At that moment he was at least as angry with himself as he was with her. She'd wound him up and he'd gone off like a fucking clockwork mouse. *You're a dickhead, Temple*, he told himself. *Get a grip.*

She slowed to negotiate the lights at Barons Court. As she pulled on the handbrake, Alex watched the muscles in her forearm tauten. She had long fingers and short, square-cut nails.

'You're saying,' she went on, 'that it's really of no concern to you that some . . . some maniac is torturing and murdering our people?'

'I was only wondering why you couldn't deal with the whole thing in-house.'

'The decision has been made to do otherwise,' said Dawn curtly.

Which pretty much brought the argument to a close. She gave him her mobile and office numbers, and asked him to ring her as soon as he knew where he was staying. Mentally Alex determined not to do this.

'Do you know your way to Thames House?' she asked.

'Millbank, last time I visited.'

'Tomorrow at 9 a.m., then. I'll meet you at the front desk.'

'It's a date.'

Unsurprisingly, she didn't smile. A few minutes later, as she brought the Honda to a halt outside the Duke of York's Headquarters in the King's Road, he nodded his thanks and grabbed his bag.

'Tomorrow,' she repeated, flipping a long brown envelope on to the passenger seat.

Alex hesitated before reaching for it.

'Expenses,' she said. 'According to our records, you don't have a London address. And unless you've left some clothes at Miss Wells's – and my guess is that you're not really the type for that cosy domestic scene – I'd say that you're going to need to add to your wardrobe some time between now and tomorrow. Keep it simple, would be my advice, and dress your age. Harrods is still open for a couple of hours. See you.' She didn't even leave at speed, just drew gently away from the kerb.

He watched after her for a moment, shaking his head with intense dislike. The reference to Sophie had had its intended effect: to let him know that Dawn Harding and her organisation could jerk his chain any bloody time they felt like it. 'Not if I see you first,' he murmured, but knew that his words had no meaning. He and Dawn Harding were locked together for the duration, like it or loathe it. He punched the recall button on his Nokia.

Five minutes later a silver Audi TT convertible pulled to a swerving halt at the kerb. 'Hey, sexy! Looking for business?'

For the first time that day Alex smiled. Sophie was wearing a screamingly loud Italian print shirt and, despite the lateness of the day, sunglasses. The sight of her made his heart dance. 'Jump in,' she ordered.

From that moment, things picked up. Alex explained his clothing predicament, Sophie made a rapid series of phone calls and five minutes later a willowy young man in leather trousers was unlocking a warehouse in Chelsea Harbour. Lights flickered on to reveal at least a dozen rails of men's clothes and several shoulder-high pyramids of shoeboxes. 'Help yourself to anything you want,' the young man told Sophie and Alex. 'I'll find you some bags.'

'What is all this stuff?' Alex asked.

'Mostly bits and pieces from shows and magazine fashion shoots,' Sophie replied. 'A lot of it hasn't even been worn.'

They eventually settled on a selection of items that Alex thought slightly over-fashionable and Sophie disappointedly described as 'somewhere between dreary and invisible'.

'In my world,' Alex explained, 'the grey man is king. How much do we owe this guy?'

'Oh, give him a couple of hundred.'

'Are you sure?'

'Don't worry. It'll get written off as damaged.'

'You lot are worse than army quartermasters.'

Sophie swung the keys of the Audi from a slender forefinger. 'My place?'

In the flat overlooking Sloane Street they heated up a Sainsbury's Prawn Vindaloo, drank Kronenbourg beer from bottles and watched *Goodness Gracious Me*. For Alex, after weeks of rations consumed in exclusively male company, the evening was heaven.

When she saw that he had unwound a few notches, Sophie settled herself against him on the sofa. 'Is it good news that you're back?' she asked him tentatively. 'Does it mean that you've got some time off?'

'Yes and no,' he said. 'I'm here to . . . chase something up.'

'Anything you can tell me about?'

He shook his head. 'I'm sorry.'

'Dangerous?'

He shrugged. 'Doubt it. I've got to find someone, that's all. Brain work, not bullets. So I'm going to be around, yeah, but I'm also going to be coming and going.'

She nodded. 'Is it always going to be like this?' she asked. 'Me asking, you not telling?'

'For as long as I'm in, yes,' he said. 'You mustn't take it personally.'

'I don't take it personally,' she said, with a flash of irritation, quickly suppressed. 'It's just that we've been together for a year now, on and off, and I'd like to feel that I had some . . . access to your life.'

'You have full access to my life,' he told her gently. 'It's just my work that's off limits. And I promise you, you're not missing anything there.'

'But your life *is* your work,' she protested. 'I can see that in your face. All those missions in Northern Ireland and Bosnia, all those dead men . . . I can see them there behind your eyes.'

He shrugged. It was not something he'd ever talked about in much detail. The demons, it was generally accepted, came with the job.

'I want all of you, Alex. Not just the burnt-out remains.'

He frowned at his Kronenbourg bottle. At the edge of his vision an RUF soldier crouched in blood-sodden shock, his lower jaw shot away. Behind him staggered the blackened figure of Don Hammond. There was a full company of such men quartered in Alex's head now.

Blinking them away, locking on to Sophie's grey-green eyes, he smiled. 'I'm all here. And I'm all yours.'

EIGHT

Alex presented himself at the front desk of Thames House at a couple of minutes to nine. Dawn Harding was waiting for him there, briefcase in hand, and signed him in. 'We're wearing Italian today, are we?' she said, noting his Gucci loafers and running an appraising glance up and down his grey Cerrutti suit. 'I thought you Hereford boys were more comfortable in Mr Byrite.'

'I know the importance you civil service types attach to appearances,' Alex said equably, fixing his visitor's badge to his lapel. 'You wouldn't want me to let the side down, now would you?'

He followed her into the lift, where she pressed the button for the fourth floor. 'And you found somewhere to stay all right?'

'I managed to get my head down.'

'I'm sure you did.' She stared without expression at the brushed-aluminium wall of the lift. As previously, she was dressed entirely in black and wearing no make-up, perfume or jewellery. Her only accessories were the briefcase – large, black and plain – and a military issue pilot's chronograph watch. This spareness did not, however, disguise her femininity. In some curious way, Alex mused, allowing his gaze to linger around the nape of her neck, it highlighted it. Or at least it made you wonder.

The lift shuddered to a halt. 'A word of advice,' she said flatly, checking her watch as she marched out into a grey-carpeted corridor flanked by offices. 'The correct form of address for the deputy director is ma'am.'

Alex smiled. 'So who are you, then? Matron?'

She gave him a withering glance. 'Dawn will be just fine.'

The deputy director's office was at the far end of the corridor. Dawn left Alex in an ante-room containing a leather-covered sofa and a portrait of Feliks Dzerzhinsky, founder of the KGB, and disappeared through an unmarked door.

She reappeared five minutes later. Alex was still standing – the leather sofa was so slippery he could hardly sit on it – and she led him into an office which would have been sunlit had not the blinds been partially lowered. This, Alex guessed, was to prevent glare rendering the computer monitors illegible. There were three of these on a broad, purpose-built desk, along with a telefax console and a tray piled high with what looked like newspaper cuttings. Maps, books and a large flat-screen monitor covered most of the walls, but a painted portrait of Florence Nightingale and a signed photograph of Peter Mandelson romping with a dog went some way towards softening the room's essentially utilitarian lines. At the near end half a dozen leather-and-steel chairs surrounded a low table bearing a tray with a steaming cafetière and four civil service-issue cups and saucers.

Behind the desk, silhouetted against the half-closed blinds, sat the deputy director and once again Alex was struck by her handsome, clear-cut features and elegant appearance. Today she was wearing a charcoal suit, which perfectly complemented her shrewd blue eyes and the expensively coiffed gunmetal of her hair.

To one side of her, both hands thrust deep into the pockets of a suit which had probably once fitted him better, stood George Widdowes. To Alex, the studied informality of the posture looked like an attempt to play down his subordinate status.

The deputy director rounded the desk and held out her hand. 'Since we're to be working together, Captain Temple,' she told him with a practised smile, 'I think we should at least know each other's real names. I'm Angela Fenwick, and my full title is Deputy Director of Operations. Dawn Harding and George Widdowes you know. Welcome to Thames House.'

As they arranged themselves in chairs around the table, Angela Fenwick leant forward and pressed down the plunger of the cafetiere.

'Boom!' whispered George Widdowes. No one smiled.

Angela Fenwick turned to Alex. 'I'd like you to know that nothing that is said in this office is recorded, unless you ask for it to be, and nothing you say here is in any way on the record. Basically, you can express yourself freely and I hope you will. The corollary is that you are not to make any mention of what I am about to tell you to anyone, in or outside this agency – and that includes your Regimental colleagues, past and present – without my express say-so. Do you have any problem with that?'

'No, I don't think so.'

'Good. Coffee, everybody? George, will you be mother?'

When Widdowes was done, Angela Fenwick leant back in her chair, cup in hand, and turned to Alex. 'Craig Gidley's murder,' she said. 'Did that remind you of anything?'

Alex glanced at the others. They were looking at him expectantly.

'You can speak openly in front of George and Dawn.'

Alex nodded. 'PIRA,' he said. 'Belfast Brigade took out those two FRU guys by hammering nails into their heads. Early 1996, it must have been, just after the Canary Wharf bomb. Left the bodies at a road junction outside Dungannon.'

'That's right,' Fenwick agreed. 'Can you remember where you were at the time?'

Alex considered. 'In February 1996 I was in Bosnia,' he said. 'I was part of the snatch team that grabbed Maksim Zukic and two of his colonels for the War Crimes Tribunal at The Hague. But we heard about the Canary Wharf bomb pretty much as it happened, and later about the FRU guys too.'

'Ray Bledsoe,' added Widdowes. 'And Connor Wheen.'

'Yeah, that's it. Bledsoe and Wheen. We didn't see that much of the FRU when we were on tours in the province, but I probably met both of them at various times.'

Angela Fenwick frowned. 'Am I right in thinking that you were number two on the sniper team when Neil Slater shot the Delaney boy at Forkhill?'

'Yes, that was a year later.'

'The information about the weapons cache at the Delaney farm came from a tout originally cultivated by Ray Bledsoe.'

'Is that so?' said Alex. 'We tend not be told stuff like that.'

'Why didn't you tell me last night that you thought there was a PIRA connection to the murders?' asked Dawn Harding accusingly.

'You didn't ask me,' Alex answered mildly. 'But I was pretty certain of it as soon as Mr Widdowes here mentioned six-inch nails.'

Angela Fenwick nodded. 'I just wanted to establish that you knew about the Bledsoe and Wheen incident. And you're right, the roots of this thing do indeed lie in Northern Ireland. But they go back a little further than 1996. Back to Remembrance Day in 1987, in fact.'

'Enniskillen,' said Alex grimly.

'Precisely. Enniskillen. On the eighth of November in 1987 a bomb was detonated near the war memorial in that town, killing eleven people and injuring sixty-three. A truly horrendous day's work by the volunteers.'

Alex nodded. Widdowes and Dawn, sidelined, were staring patiently into space.

'The day after the explosion there was a crisis meeting attended by six people. Two of those – the former director and deputy director of this service – are now retired. Of the remainder one was myself, one was George, and the others were Craig Gidley and Barry Fenn. I was thirty-nine, a little younger than the others, and I had just been put in charge of the Northern Ireland desk.

'The purpose of the meeting was to discuss something that we were acutely aware of already: our desperate need to place a British agent inside the IRA executive. As you'll probably be aware, we had a pretty extensive intelligence programme running in the province at the time. We had informers, we had 14th Intelligence Company people, and we had touts. What we didn't have, however, was anyone close to the decision-making process. We didn't have anyone sufficiently senior to tip us off if another Enniskillen was in the wind and there couldn't be – there absolutely couldn't be – another Enniskillen.

'So basically we had two choices. To turn a senior player or to insert our own sleeper and wait for him to work his way up. The former was obviously the preferable choice in terms of time but in the long run it would have been much less reliable, as we could never be sure that we weren't being fed dis-information. We tried it, nevertheless. Got some of the FRU people to approach individual players that 14th Int had targeted and make substantial cash offers for basically harmless information. The hope was that we could hook them through sheer greed and then squeeze them once they were incriminated. Standard entrapment routine.

'But as we half expected, none of them went for it. Even if they had any ideological doubts – and in the wake of the slaughter at Enniskillen one or two of the players certainly did have ideological doubts – they knew only too well what happened to touts. Apart from anything else, they knew they'd never be able to spend any money we gave them. So they told our people where to get off and in a couple of cases published their descriptions in the Republican newspaper *An Phoblacht*. Which, as you can imagine, made us look pretty damn stupid.

'So the decision was made to put in a sleeper. Not someone who, if he was lucky, might be allowed to hang around the fringes of the organisation and report back snippets of bar talk. Not a glorified tout, in other words, but a long-term mole who would rise through the ranks. Someone who had the credentials to rise to the top of this highly sophisticated terrorist organisation, but also the courage, the commitment and the sheer mental strength to remain our man throughout. We would need someone exceptional, and identifying him would be a major project in itself.

'Operation Watchword, classified top secret, was planned and run by the four of us – myself, George, Gidley and Fenn. It had a dedicated budget and a dedicated office, and no one else in the Service was given access of any kind. It was to be divided into three stages: selection, insertion and activation. Our man, once we found him, would be known as Watchman.

'Selection began in October 1987. The first thing we did was to make a computer search through MOD records. We were looking for unmarried Northern Irish-born Catholics aged twenty-eight or less and ideally those who had been the single children of parents who were now both dead. We looked at all the armed services. From the list that we got, including those with living parents and siblings, we eliminated all the officers, all those above the rank of corporal or its equivalent and all those with poor service records – for drinking, fighting, indiscipline and so on.

'We were left with a list of about twenty men, spread across the various services, and at that point we borrowed a warrant officer named Denzil Connolly from the RWW.'

Alex nodded. He had never met Connolly but

knew of him by reputation. A right hard bastard by all accounts.

'Connolly dropped in on the various commanding officers and adjutants. He didn't enquire directly about the individuals we were interested in, merely asked if he could make a brief presentation and put up a notice calling for volunteers for Special Duties, which pretty much everyone knew meant intelligence work in Northern Ireland. Afterwards, over a cup of tea or a beer, he'd ask the adjutant if there was anyone he thought might be suitable. Self-sufficiency, technical ability and a cool methodical temperament were what was needed. If the target name failed to crop up he'd bring out a list that included the man in question. He had been given a dozen possibles, he'd say. Could the CO grade them from A to D in terms of the qualities he'd mentioned?

'By Christmas we had the numbers down to ten, all of whom answered the selection criteria and had either been directly recommended or assessed as As or Bs. The ten were then sent to Tregaron to join the current selection cadre for 14th Intelligence, bumping the course numbers for the year up to about seventy. You probably know more about the 14th Int course than I do, Captain Temple, but I believe it's fairly demanding.'

'It's a tough course,' said Alex. 'I think it prepares people pretty well for what they're going to encounter as undercover operators.'

Angela Fenwick nodded. 'Well, of the ten we sent on the course, four were among those returned to their units as unsuitable by the staff instructors at the end of the first fortnight. The other six were pulled out of Tregaron by us at the same time, although they assumed that what followed was part of the normal selection course. They were housed in separate locations in the area where our Service's psychiatric people interviewed them over several days to assess their suitability.'

'Why not let them just go through the normal 14th Int selection course?' asked Alex.

'Because there was a big difference in what we wanted out of them. Working undercover is lonely and solitary work but ultimately you're still part of a team. You're still a soldier on a tour of duty, and there are plenty of times in an undercover soldier's life when he can let his guard down, put aside his cover, socialise with his colleagues and be himself. The man we were looking for, on the other hand, would have no such opportunity. Once inserted he would probably never speak to another soldier again. He'd be giving up everything and everyone he'd ever known. We needed to know that he was capable of that.'

'And there were other factors,' added George Widdowes. 'We didn't want our man known as one of those who successfully completed the course. As part of his cover story he needed to have failed. And to have failed early enough for it to be believable that he couldn't remember much about the other sixty-odd blokes on the course. We didn't want our operation to compromise the security of the ones who passed.'

Alex nodded. 'Yes, I see what you mean.'

'The other thing at that stage was that we had to separate our six men from each other in case they figured out what they had in common and put two and two together. It wasn't a huge risk, but even at that stage we had to be one hundred per cent security conscious.'

'Right.'

'We interviewed the six,' continued Angela Fenwick, 'and, as George explained, they assumed the process was part of the normal 14th Int selection. Four of them we were happy with, the other two we sent back to Tregaron. The four we liked the look of were bussed one at a time to different points in an MOD training area in the North-West Highlands near Cape Wrath, given rudimentary survival and communications kit, and ordered to dig in. It was January by then and conditions were atrocious, with blizzards and deep snow.

'Over the next three weeks, although they were never more than a few kilometres from each other, none of the four men saw each other or another human being. They were given their instructions by radio or through message drops and ordered to carry out an endless series of near impossible tasks – marching all night to food drops where there turned out not to be any food, processing unmanageable amounts of data, repairing unmendable equipment, that sort of thing – and made to do it all on next to no sleep and in the worst possible physical conditions. The idea, obviously, was to test their mental endurance, and although the four never saw them they were in fact being monitored throughout by a three-man team from the SAS training wing at Hereford.

'At the end of the three weeks they were each put through an escape and evasion exercise. This culminated in their being captured, given a beating and driven to a camp near Altnaharra where they were subjected to forty-eight hours of hard tactical questioning by a team from the Joint Services Interrogation Wing.

'After this the four were assessed by the instructors. One was in a very bad way by then and clearly unsuitable – I think he ended up having a nervous breakdown and leaving the army. Two were reckoned to be tough enough but essentially more suited to teamwork than a solo placement and were taken back to Tregaron to continue the 14th Intelligence course. The fourth one – the one they recommended – was a Royal Engineers corporal named Joseph Meehan.

'We had been hoping that Meehan would be the one they went for. He was young, only twenty-three at the time of the Watchman selection programme, and very much a loner. So much so, in fact, that his CO had been worried about his long-term suitability for regimental life. At the same time he was highly intelligent, highly motivated, and had an exceptional talent for electronics and demolitions. As it happened, he was also on the waiting list for SAS selection.

'For our purposes he seemed to be perfect. We needed someone young – it was going to take years rather than months to get him to a position of authority within the IRA. And of course we needed a loner. As far as we were concerned he had everything.

'Anyway, Meehan it was. From Altnaharra he was helicoptered down to London and installed in one of our safe houses in Stockwell. At the point at which George and I first met him, in February 1988, he still thought he was on the 14th Int course. He thought everyone did a month's solitary in Scotland. Even said he'd enjoyed it.

'We told him the truth. Explained exactly what we wanted of him. Said that if he took the job his soldiering days were effectively over. That he'd never be able to see his army mates again. He told us what he'd told the psych team a month earlier, that he hated the IRA with every bone in his body and would do or say whatever was necessary to destroy them.

'Knowing Joe Meehan's life story as we did, we were inclined to believe him. He was the only son of a Londonderry electrician who, when the boy was twelve, attracted the attention of the local IRA for accepting a contract to rewire a local army barracks. Meehan senior was kneecapped, his business was burnt out and he was chased from the province, eventually resettling in Dorset. Joseph went with him, left school at sixteen, and apprenticed himself to his father, but by then the old man was in a pretty bad way. He was crippled, drinking heavily and going downhill fast. He died two years later.'

'Was there a mother?' Alex asked.

'The mother stayed behind in Londonderry,' said Widdowes. 'Disassociated herself from the father completely after the kneecapping. Asked Joseph to stay behind when the father left and when he wouldn't she shrugged and walked away. Ended up remarrying a PIRA enforcer who ran a Bogside poolhall.'

'Nice,' said Alex.

'Very nice,' agreed Widdowes. 'And that was the point when Joseph joined the British army. One way or another he was determined to avenge his father's treatment. His hatred of the IRA was absolutely pathological – he described them to our people as vermin who should be eliminated without a moment's thought.' Widdowes blinked and rubbed his eyes. 'And from our point of view this was good. Hatred is one of the great sustaining forces and

115

Meehan's hatred, we hoped, would keep him going through the years ahead. When we told him the nitty-gritty of what we wanted, he didn't hesitate. Yes, he said. He'd do it. We had our Watchman.'

NINE

'Training Joseph Meehan took six months,' said Angela Fenwick, staring out over the grey-brown expanse of the Thames. 'We would have liked to have given him more time, but we didn't have more time, so we packed everything into those six months. He lived in a series of safe houses, always alone, and the instructors came to him. Without exception these were the top people in their respective fields and permanently attached to Special Forces or Military Intelligence institutions on the mainland. For obvious security reasons no serving personnel were let anywhere near him. To start with we put him in one of the accommodation bunkers at Tregaron. Isolation conditions, of course, and we bugged the room and tapped the phone.'

Alex knew Tregaron well. Two hundred acres of windswept Welsh valley, rusted gun emplacements and dilapidated bunkers, all of it behind razor wire. He'd blown up a few old cars there as part of his demolitions training. Bloody miserable place to stay on your own, especially in winter. 'Who did you put in charge of him?' asked Alex.

'An RWW warrant officer, who provided us with progress reports and so on. We started off by getting a couple of the Hereford Training Wing NCOs to put him through their unarmed combat course, and sharpen up his advanced weapons and driving skills. Apparently he managed to bring the unarmed combat instructor to his knees by the end of the third session.'

'Impressive,' confirmed Alex. 'I wouldn't fancy trying to deck one of those guys.'

Fenwick nodded. 'At the same time we had an instructor from Tregaron taking him through his surveillance and anti-surveillance drills, and generally familiarising him with intelligence procedures – drop-offs, dead-letter boxes and so on. After this we brought in a rapid succession of people to teach him individual skills like covert photography, lock-picking, bugging and counter-bugging, demolition and so forth. You probably know most of the specialists in question?'

'Stew for locks?' asked Alex. 'Bob the Bomber for dems?'

'Well, it's not exactly how they were introduced to me,' said Angela Fenwick with a smile. 'But I think we're probably talking about the same people. We had a couple of our own Service people bring him up to speed on computers, too. The technology was obviously less advanced than it is now but it was clear even then that the intelligence war was going to be fought every bit as keenly in cyberspace as on the ground.

'Meehan learnt very fast indeed, especially the technical stuff. According to his service record he'd always been a natural with electronics and the SAS demolitions people described him as the best pupil they'd ever had. The usual routine was that he'd do the physical stuff in the mornings and the classroom stuff in the afternoon. The Tregaron people updated him on the geography of the province and told him the locations of all the drinking houses, social clubs, players' homes, safe houses et cetera, to the point where he could almost have got work as a minicab driver, and at least once a day they ran him through different aspects of his cover story. Like all the best cover stories, this had the advantage of being ninety-five per cent true. Only nine months of it would have to be fictionalised. Nine months and a lifetime's beliefs.'

Alex was impressed by Fenwick's grasp of the salient details of the operation. She certainly seemed more on top of things than most of the MI5 agents he'd met in the field. He was also beginning to feel the beginnings of sympathy for Meehan. *If the ex-Royal Engineer was twenty-three in 1987*, thought Alex, *he's just a year older than me. We were probably learning much the same things at much the same time. The difference being that I was learning them in company with a bunch of mates and going out on the town on Friday nights and he was stuck in an isolated bunker in Tregaron with a tapped phone. Poor bastard.*

'Anyway,' continued Fenwick, 'the instructors hammered away at him pretty much full-time, seven days a week. We had a couple of the JSIW people come down and take him through his story until he was practically reciting it in his sleep. And, of course, we played the usual mind games, getting him to memorise complex documents, waking him up in the middle of the night to check minute aspects of his cover, that sort of thing. Every room in the house was plastered with pictures of IRA players, so even in his time off he was taking in information.'

She paused. To either side of her George

Widdowes and Dawn Harding sat in trance-like silence.

'After three months we moved him down to Stockwell for a couple of days so that the Watchman team could spend some time with him and from there it was on to Croydon for a couple of months of advanced fieldcraft training with our service instructors. By that stage we were very much concentrating on demilitarising him, on knocking the professional soldier out of him. For that reason his time at Croydon was deliberately made as unstructured as possible. We fed him junk food, beer and roll-ups, slowed his metabolism down, sent him on the sort of exercise that involves spending the day in a pub. There's a test we set field agents that involves selecting a total stranger in a public place – pub, launderette, that sort of place – and seeing what information you can extract. There was a checklist we had – name, address, phone number, car registration number, job description, place of birth, spouse's maiden name, credit card number . . . It's not an easy skill but Meehan got to be very good at it indeed – and he always made the other people think that they were the ones doing the questioning. All in all, he was a natural. A fantastic find.' She coughed and patted her throat. 'Sorry, as you can see I'm not used to doing so much talking.'

Standing, she walked to a small table beside her desk and poured herself a glass of Evian water. George Widdowes half rose, as if about to pat her on the back, but caught Dawn Harding's eye and sat down again. The room, Alex noticed, was becoming uncomfortably stuffy.

'After Croydon,' Widdowes said, 'we put our man

through his first real test. We sent him back to the Royal Engineers two weeks before the 14th Int selection course was completed – the course, that is, that we'd pulled him out of several months earlier – and told him to get himself kicked out of the regiment. Left it up to him how he managed it.

'What he did was to go around telling everyone he'd been kicked off the 14th Int course because he was Catholic and Irish-born. He made it look as if this had really dented him – he started drinking a lot, picking fights, getting his name on charge sheets and so on. He'd already visibly put on weight and was a long way from being the lean, mean fighting machine the Engineers had originally sent up to Tregaron. There was an insubordination charge, a complaint of insulting behaviour by one of the civilian catering staff and some incident with a pub bouncer in Chatham – all slippery-slope stuff. The end came when one of the warrant officers discovered some detonator cord in his locker in the course of a room search. He claimed that it was a mistake, that he'd signed it out for instruction purposes and forgotten to sign it back in again, but the CO wasn't having it and Meehan was out on his arse.'

Alex whistled quietly and Widdowes shrugged. 'It was the only way. The whole thing had to be believable – we couldn't risk asking the CO to fake up a dishonourable discharge. Enough people were in the know already.

'Immediately after his discharge Meehan moved back to London and got a bed in a working men's hostel in Kilburn. Within a couple of weeks he'd picked up work with an emergency plumbing and electrical repair outfit run by a local tough called Tony Riordan. He stuck with Riordan long enough to figure out all the scams and fiddles, and generally acclimatise himself in the role of jobbing electrician, and in the evenings, like any other twenty-three-year-old, he'd hit the bars. As we hoped would happen before too long in that area, he ran into a few exiles from Belfast and Derry, and picked their brains about job prospects over there. Wasn't a political guy, he said, just had family over there and wanted a change.

'He ended up being given a few names. Nobody who'd seen the quality of his work thought twice about recommending him. And finally, over the water he went.

'The first thing he did over there was to visit his relatives. There was his mother, of course, still living over the pool hall in Bogside, and there were the usual uncles and aunts and cousins scattered around the place. He looked them all up, said his hellos, paid his respects. He didn't advertise the fact that he'd been in the army, but he didn't try to hide it either. Just told anyone who asked that he'd got fed up and left.

'He saw his mother for the first time in more than ten years, but made no secret of how he felt about her walking out on the family. The boyfriend, by now a pissed old fart approaching sixty – bit like me – tried on a bit of Republican stuff, told him there were people he should meet and so on, but Meehan wasn't buying. Didn't want to know, he said. Wasn't interested.

'By the autumn he was living in Belfast. A cousin who was a chartered surveyor – highly respectable guy, married, kids, house in Dunmurry – offered to take Meehan in until he'd found his feet. Meehan stayed there for eight weeks or so, sorted himself out a job with the service department of a store in the city centre, a sort of Tandy-type place called Ed's Electronics, and moved into a rented place a few streets away from his cousin. He also started seeing a girl, a hairdresser called Tina Milazzo. She was a careful choice – Catholic, clearly, but not part of any obvious player set-up. Her family were immigrants and her parents ran a café in the Andersonstown Road. The Milazzo family were known to us because of Tina's brother Vince, who fancied himself as a hotshot driver and all-round dangerous dude, and liked to hang out where the players hung out. He would never have been allowed within a mile of any real action because he was a loudmouth, but he was tolerated.

'After that, it was basically a question of waiting. We sent Barry Fenn out as his agent handler and Barry used that waiting period to run through the various communications procedures – something we always try to do if we can, because it reassures the agent in the field that the systems work. So we were pretty well informed about the assimilation process.'

'Did Fenn handle anyone else?' Alex asked.

'No. He was Meehan's dedicated handler. We didn't tell Meehan that, though.'

'Why not?'

'Well, I suppose because we didn't want to worry him by suggesting that PIRA might have sussed out the others. They hadn't, of course, but we didn't want him concerning himself for one moment with those kinds of issues. Anyway, once Meehan was in place we told him that henceforth the drops and meets would be initiated by him rather than by us, and that we'd be pulling Barry back – or 'Geoff' as Meehan knew him – until he reported that a definite approach had been made. We knew this was likely to be months rather than weeks, because we'd agreed from the start that Meehan would adopt a strictly "not-interested" posture vis-à-vis any Republican stuff.'

'Wasn't there a danger that PIRA would take him at his word and leave him alone?'

'I think we pretty much made him irresistible. As well as working at the shop he let it be known that outside work hours he was happy to do repairs at home. Transmitter-receivers and computers that no one else could fix, that sort of thing. The more complex the problem, the better he liked it. It was only going to be a matter of time before the word got around that one of the guys at Ed's was a circuitry wizard and a few quiet checks started to be made. And of course we also had Vince Milazzo shooting his mouth off about his sister's new bloke who'd been in the army but had got pissed off and walked out.'

'And they bit?'

'Eventually they bit. To our relief, as you can imagine. It had been more than eighteen months since Enniskillen by then, and in that eighteen months we'd had eight soldiers killed in Ballygawley, six at Lisburn and two in the Buncrana Road. More than thirty-five men had been seriously injured and that's just the army statistics. I can't honestly remember how many civilians and UDR members had been murdered in the period, but the pressure on this Service to get a man in place was unbelievable.

'The way it happened was that one evening in June 1989 a couple of fellows were waiting for Meehan when he finished work. Suggested he came for a quiet drink and drove him to MacNamara's, which is very much a volunteer hang-out. Asked him if he took on private work. He said he did, but nothing political,

124

which they seemed to accept. One of them then took him out to the car park and showed him an army Clansman radio. Asked if he could fix it.

'Well, obviously he could have fixed it in his sleep, but he refused, said he wasn't touching it. When they asked him why, he told them that he recognised the radio as army issue and wanted no involvement with that sort of business. Then he thanked them politely for the drink and walked off. They didn't try to stop him.

'But of course they were back a few days later, and this time it was six of them and they didn't take him to a bar, but to the first floor of a house in the Ballymurphy area. They'd done some checking, they told him, and they had some questions that needed answering. They were still polite, but it was clear that if the answers weren't good enough he was in serious trouble.

'It was the moment he'd rehearsed a thousand times. Sure, he'd been in the British army, he told them, and he'd never tried to hide the fact. His family knew it, his girlfriend knew it and his employer knew it. He also told them what had happened to his father and how he had been chased from the country a decade earlier. With his father dead, he explained, he no longer had any family on the mainland, so he'd come home. All he wanted now, to be honest, was to carry on with the work he was doing, bank a decent salary and be left alone to get on with his life.

'They heard him out. As a Royal Engineer, they said, he must have been involved in demolitions.

'Sure, he told them, and for the first time allowed a note of bitterness to creep in. He'd been a qualified demolitions instructor and at one time had considered a career in the quarrying industry after leaving the army. With his dishonourable discharge, however, all that had gone up in smoke.

'Tell us about the discharge, they said, so he did. He'd been stitched up, he explained, and all for a couple of lengths of det cord. All the instructors kept bits and pieces in their lockers – signing the stuff in and out every day took bloody hours. It wasn't as if it had been drugs or live ammunition, they'd just had it in for him for being a Mick. But then that was the Brit Establishment for you – heads they win, tails you lose. But what the fuck, he still had the skills. No one could take the skills away.

'They listened and then drove him back to his flat. Nothing much was said, but this time when they handed him the Clansman he took it. They gave him a number to ring when it was ready.

'After this encounter, which he described to Barry in detail from a public phone near his home, the communications from Meehan via Barry Fenn almost dried up. It became clear to him that he was being watched almost full-time. He was certainly being tested; a few days after mending and returning the Clansman a woman called round at his flat at seven in the morning with an Amstrad computer in a plastic bag. It had crashed, she told him, and she needed a data-recovery expert.

'He unpicked the mess, downloaded the data and discovered that it contained details of the security system of one of the city-centre banks. It was obviously a set-up: if the security was beefed up in any way they'd know he was a player for the other side. So we did nothing about it at all – didn't even bother to tell the bank. And of course there was no raid.

126

'A couple of weeks later the first two men turned up at his flat on a Saturday morning. As far as we can work out he was taken on some kind of tour of the city. Various introductions were made and the day ended at a drinking club.

'Over the next few months a gradual process of indoctrination took place. The people that he met were low-level players for the most part, and I guess they flattered Meehan and showed him a pretty good time. A charm offensive, if you can imagine that. Our instructions to him, relayed via Barry, were to allow himself to be drawn out. We wanted him to give the impression of "coming to life", both socially and politically.

'Tina Milazzo certainly helped with this. Sources on the ground told us that she gave the impression of enjoying the nightlife and the conspiratorial atmosphere, and the company of the other girlfriends. She probably sensed that the other men were respectful of Joe, that they had plans for him and that this reflected well on her. Whatever, she fitted in. She helped the thing along.

'Over the months that followed we heard almost nothing from Meehan. We wanted him to dig in, to live and breathe Republicanism, and we told him that he should only contact Barry if he had anything really vital to report.

'Nothing vital came up. The killings of soldiers and others continued, but we considered it highly unlikely that Meehan was anywhere near the inner circles where such things were discussed and planned. It would be years, probably, before that would be the case. But he was on his way. Shortly before Christmas 1989 a seventeen-year-old named Derek Maughan was picked up by a team of volunteers after stealing a car and joyriding around the outskirts of the city. It was not the first time this had happened, it was decided to make an example of him, and he was driven out to waste ground and a nine-mil round was put through his kneecap. From the front, as he was just a lad, rather than from the back. Now as it happened, one of the volunteers on the snatch team was touting for the FRU and within a couple of days of the shooting we had the names of all those involved.

'The driver was one Joe Meehan. That year this agency was able to give the Cabinet Office a very special Christmas present. The assurance that a sleeper was in place in the Belfast Brigade. That, finally, MI5 had a man in the IRA.'

TEN

There was a lengthy pause. Dawn Harding, as if to make a tacit point about self-control, sat motionless and without expression. George Widdowes stretched in his chair and recrossed his legs. Rising and marching briskly to her desk, Angela Fenwick lifted the telephone and ordered sandwiches for four. From a desk drawer she took a clear plastic folder. Inside was a sheaf of photographs, which she handed to Alex.

He examined them one by one. There was an early Meehan family shot taken in a kitchen: the father standing in his shirtsleeves, the blowsy bottle-blonde mother smoking by the stove and the pinched, worried-looking boy – even then the image of his dad – crouched over his homework. In the school photo, scrubbed and hairbrushed, young Joseph didn't look much happier, but he appeared to have cheered up a bit for the holiday snap in which, aged about eleven, he and his mother were sitting at a folding table by a river with a caravan in the background. Another shot, possibly taken on the same holiday, showed the boy triumphantly holding up a small trout. Almost a smile on his face.

And then there was Meehan aged about fifteen taking part in a cross-country race. The seriousness and the pinched look were back by then, and had been joined by something else – a tenaciousness, a hard intentness of purpose. The same expression was waiting behind the level gaze as the sixteen-year-old apprentice stood with his visibly frail father in front of their van ('Lawrence Meehan, Electrical and General Repairs').

And finally as a squaddie. A formal sit-down shot of the battalion in shirtsleeve order. Meehan in civvies posing with two fellow privates in front of an armoured personnel carrier. Meehan in issue overalls doing something complicated at a workbench with a soldering iron. Meehan and a couple of mates brewing up on exercise beneath a rockface.

And that was it. A life in ten photographs. Not conventionally handsome, but intelligent-looking. Not naturally one of the lads, but the sort you could rely on to stand his round. Not a natural tough guy, perhaps, but a fast learner. And without question a bad enemy. A real implacability behind the pale, narrow features and the rain-grey eyes.

'So this is him,' said Alex eventually and, catching Dawn Harding's scornful expression, immediately regretted the statement's pointlessness.

'This is him,' said Angela Fenwick. 'The Watchman. Our PIRA mole.'

'I'm assuming the story you're telling me has an unhappy ending,' said Alex.

'I want you to know everything,' said Fenwick. 'I want you to know exactly what sort of man we're dealing with. I want you to know everything we know.'

Alex nodded. He was busting for a piss. He said so and Dawn Harding stood up. En route, she officiously hurried him past several open office doors. *For fuck's sake*, he thought.

130

'Aren't you coming in?' he asked her when they reached a sign marked Male Staff WC. 'Just in case I catch sight of something I shouldn't.'

'There won't be much to catch sight of,' she said.

When they got back to the deputy director's office the sandwiches had arrived. In Alex's place two files had been placed on top of the Meehan photographs. They contained ten-by-eight-inch colour photographs taken at the scenes of the murders of Barry Fenn and Craig Gidley, and the respective pathologists' reports.

'None of these to leave the building, please,' said Fenwick. 'Dawn will show you a room where you can go through them when we've finished.'

Opposite Alex, Widdowes was galloping through his sandwiches as if fearful that they were going to be taken away from him.

Alex picked up one of his own, and was about to bite into it when a thought struck him. He froze and Dawn Harding raised an eyebrow. 'I've just realised something,' he said. 'Yesterday morning I left an RUF sentry who can't have been more than eleven tied to a tree. I meant to let him go when we pulled out.'

'Sounds to me he's pretty lucky to be alive at all,' said Angela Fenwick.

'I doubt he *is* still alive,' said Alex. 'The survivors of the raid will be looking for scapegoats.'

'Can't make an omelette without breaking eggs,' said Widdowes through a yellow-toothed mouthful of bacon, lettuce and tomato. 'Africa's a bloody basket case, anyway. It's not what the rest of the world does to them, it's what they do to themselves. God, the stories you hear.'

'Sally Roberts is apparently telling anyone who'll listen that she was carried to safety in the strong arms of the SAS,' said Fenwick.

'We told her we were Paras,' said Alex. 'Where did she get the SAS stuff from?'

'She told the *Telegraph*'s stringer that none of the men who rescued her had shaved or washed for several days and that they wouldn't talk to her in the helicopter. The Paras always chatted her up.'

The ghost of a smile touched Alex's face but he said nothing.

'Right,' said Widdowes, placing his sandwich plate on the carpet and wiping his mouth with a spotted handkerchief. 'Shall I take over?'

Fenwick nodded and glanced quickly at Dawn. Alex sensed a current of empathy between the two women from which George Widdowes was excluded.

To begin with, Widdowes explained, things had looked good. From Meehan's occasional brief reports to Barry, and from information provided by touts and informers, it was clear that he was serving out some kind of initiation period. He was regularly called out for driving jobs, moving other volunteers from area to area, and transporting punishment squads and their victims to locations where beatings and kneecappings were administered. The IRA liked its volunteers to have a clear understanding that severe penalties were handed out to those who disobeyed them.

Meehan was also used as a 'dicker', standing on street corners looking out for manifestations of security forces personnel. Only the more experienced dickers, Alex knew, were used for 'live' operations. If a hit was planned on a border post a series of walk-pasts would be organised in the course of which the dickers would look out for any of the tell-tale signs – additional sentries, increased patrols and defences – that the operation was known about. A tout might have talked, anything might have happened, but the net result of a security lapse would invariably be the same: an SAS killing team waiting in ambush and a series of funerals attended by Gerry Adams and Martin McGuinness. The job of the dickers was a vital one to the PIRA and many operations were cancelled or postponed because of a dicker's instinct, honed to a sensitive edge on a thousand street corners, that 'something wasn't quite right'.

The first indication that Joe Meehan was moving up the terrorist ladder came in August 1990 when he reported to his handler that he'd been asked to act as a dicker on a bank robbery in the Cliftonville Road. The Northern Ireland desk made no move to inform the local security forces and the robbery went ahead. A female teller suffered a badly broken nose when she was punched in the face after attempting to press a panic button and a little over £8500 in cash was taken.

After the bank job, things went very quiet. In a twenty-second call on a public phone the following morning Meehan informed Barry that he was now being watched round the clock, although he had given his fellow volunteers no sign that he was aware of this. As far as the serious players were concerned, he said, he was still very much on probation. A lot of the volunteers couldn't quite get their heads round the idea of trusting an ex-soldier.

Somebody must have trusted him, however, for he finally got his turn. A three-man team was assembled to recover a weapon from a cache in a churchyard near Castleblayney and Meehan was one of them. Again, he was able to inform Barry of the upcoming operation and again MI5 allowed it to take place unhindered. In the normal course of events the weapon would have been dug up by an SAS team, bugged for tracing purposes and rendered harmless – 'jarked' in special forces parlance, then reburied and left for recovery by the IRA.

On this occasion, however, it was decided that the risk that PIRA might discover the jarking and suspect a security leak was too great. No suspicion, however slight, must taint the Watchman. Whatever the cost, the weapon had to remain intact.

And the cost was very nearly fatal. Within two days a Royal Welch Fusiliers patrol had come under fire in Andersonstown and their lieutenant had had the stock of his SA 80 rifle shattered by a high-velocity round. The patrol returned fire but the trigger man escaped across the rooftops. The weapon, later identified from the spent rounds as a US Army-issue M16, was never found. MI5's silence ensured that no watch was placed on the cache for the weapon's return.

'We were playing a very dangerous game,' Widdowes admitted. 'But if the slightest suspicion had attached to Watchman, even long after the event, then we would have lost him. That M16 was our entry ticket, if you like. It's probably still out there somewhere.'

From his knowledgeable tone Alex surmised that Widdowes had spent some time on the ground in the province. 'What would you have said if that lieutenant had been killed?' Alex asked.

'I would have said the same thing that I said about

the piccaninny in Sierra Leone two minutes ago: that you can't make an omelette without breaking eggs. We had to get a man into PIRA. He had to be above suspicion. At some stage we were probably going to have to weather a loss.' Widdowes delivered himself of an uneasy smile. 'I can see that you disapprove, Captain Temple.'

'No,' said Alex. 'It's just the way you put it.'

'We're in the same business, Captain Temple, and fighting the same enemy by all means at our disposal. The language is neither here nor there.'

Alex nodded. He thought of Sierra Leone, of a Puma helicopter swinging low over the jungle canopy beneath a bruise-dark sky. How would Don Hammond's relatives be weathering their loss, he wondered.

'Moving on,' said Widdowes firmly. 'The recovery of the M16 marked the end of Meehan's probationary status. He was in. One of the boys. And slowly, surely, the intelligence followed, increasing in quality as he rose through the ranks. For a couple of years between 1993 and 1995 we had really useful stuff coming in. A little of it we were able to act on; most of it we weren't – not without compromising him – but it was all grade A information.'

'The Cabinet Office was happy?' asked Alex drily.

'The Cabinet Office was very happy,' said Widdowes. 'And so were we. He gave us the location of a training camp in County Clare in the Republic, for example, and we were able to establish a covert OP in order to identify everyone who came and went. He gave us details of a PIRA safe house in Kentish Town in London, and we successfully installed a watcher team next door to monitor all arrivals and communications. Both of those represented major intelligence breakthroughs. And he gave us other things: names, vehicle registration numbers, surveillance targets, touts who had been set up to disinform FRU agents . . . It was a rich seam and while it lasted we mined it.'

'While it lasted?' asked Alex.

'Sadly, yes. For about two years Watchman gave us 24-carat weapons grade intelligence. And then, over the months that followed we began to notice a decline. At first it was barely noticeable. The information kept coming in – initially via Barry and later via a secure e-mail line to this office – and it all continued to look good. Names, possible assassination targets, projected dates for mainland campaigns – it was all there. But it had become subtly generalised. There was a lot of stuff about "policy". It had stopped being the sort of information it was possible to act on.

'Eventually there came a point where Angela, Craig Gidley and myself sat down and went through the message files, did some hard talking and came to the regretful conclusion that, for want of a better expression, we were having our pissers pulled. The general consensus at first was that Meehan had lost his nerve. On the rare occasions where he provided raw intelligence it came in too late for us to do anything about it. For example, there was an RUC officer who died because we only heard about the plan to murder him forty minutes before it took place. We put an emergency call out to his CO but the guy was in his car, driving home, and one of Billy McMahon's boys shot him outside an off-licence. You probably remember the incident.'

Alex nodded. The RUC man had been named

Storey and it had been his habit of stopping off for a packet of Benson and Hedges every evening that had sealed his fate.

'The intelligence was either too late or it was second-source,' continued Widdowes, 'by which I mean that it was information that we were going to get from someone else anyway – touts or whoever. It looked OK on paper, but on the ground it was never quite good enough and we were forced to admit that we'd probably lost him. He'd gone native, lost his bottle – whatever.'

'Couldn't you pull him out?' asked Alex.

'We tried to but he went silent on us. Wouldn't respond to any request for contact. In late 1995, when it became clear that he'd moved out of his flat, sold his car and gone to ground, we started to close things down. We pulled Barry Fenn out for a start, in case he was compromised, and didn't replace him.'

'You turned Meehan loose, effectively?'

'We left the e-mail link open. He could have contacted us any time. But he didn't. By mid-1996 we were sure that he had turned – that he was now one hundred per cent PIRA's man. There were two bombs, one in a Loyalist pub in the Shankill Road, one in a supermarket in Ballysillan, and the word coming in from the FRU's touts was that they'd been set by Joe Meehan. A total of seven dead. Lives might or might not have been saved in the Watchman's early days but now they were most definitely being lost. And the joke of it in the bars in Ballymurphy and on the Falls Road – the real hilarious fall-down-laughing joke of it – was that we'd trained him. That the PIRA's top electronics and explosives man was British army-trained.' He shook his head. 'What happened in

February 1996 to the FRU people, Bledsoe and Wheen, you know. They were killed on the orders of Padraig Byrne – that was pretty much common knowledge. What you won't have heard is that the man who actually whacked those nails through their heads was – to our certain knowledge – Joseph Meehan.'

Alex winced. 'You had proof of that?'

'Everyone knew. Apparently there were at least a dozen people there when it happened. Word is they were blooding all the young guys.'

'And Meehan was completely beyond your reach by this time?'

'Yes, completely beyond our reach. There was only one thing we could do and we did it. We fed him into the jaws of PIRA's paranoia. We sent a story to the *Sunday Times* purporting to have been written by a former undercover soldier from 14th Intelligence's Belfast Detachment. In the article, among a lot of other stuff, the supposed soldier mentioned that for several years MI5 had been running a senior IRA mole and went on to describe three or four intelligence breakthroughs that the mole had made possible. The stories were true and in each case the information in question was known to Meehan.

'We then immediately went through the motions of attempting to place an injunction on the *Sunday Times*, but at the same time made sure that the attempt wasn't successful. A few days later we dropped the word in the Falls that Joe Meehan was playing both sides and one of his mainland bank statements arrived at the Sinn Fein office. We pay our people pretty decently and the best part of three and a half K was going into his account every month.

'After that we never heard another word – either from him or about him. He just vanished. We had a tout chat to Tina Milazzo but she hadn't seen him for months. Not since he "got weird", as she put it. Our assumption until a couple of weeks ago was that he'd been executed some time in the spring of 1996. Interrogated, probably, and then shot.'

'Until Barry Fenn's murder,' said Alex quietly.

'Exactly. At which point we realised that he was alive.'

'You were – are – certain that it's Meehan, then?'

'It has to be him,' said Widdowes. 'He knew Fenn and Gidley, he used a hammer and nail, he used entry and exit methods that only a man with highly specialised training would use.'

'So what exactly do you want me to do?' asked Alex, although he was already certain of the answer.

Widdowes looked at Angela Fenwick and after a brief pause it was Fenwick who spoke. 'There were four of us on the Watchman team,' she said tautly. 'And Fenn and Gidley are already dead.'

Alex nodded. Despite her professional control he could hear the fear in her voice.

'Basically,' she said, 'we need you to kill Joseph Meehan before he kills us.'

ELEVEN

'So give me one good reason why you can't take the whole thing to the police, let them catch the guy and have him stand trial for murder,' said Alex.

He and Dawn were sitting in the cafeteria at Thames House. Beyond the armour-plated ground-floor window, the river moved brownly and sluggishly seawards. At the end of the counter steam rose from the electric urns as the staff prepared for the four o'clock tea rush. Like everywhere else in the building, the room was stiflingly overheated.

'Too many people would be compromised,' answered Dawn, in the tones of one dealing with a child. 'Surely you can see that?'

'I can see that your Service would come out of the whole thing looking bad, yes. The press would crucify them.'

'And your Service too,' said Dawn patiently. 'We made the Watchman a spy, but your lot made him a killer and it's the killer we're after now. We're in this together, like it or not. If my people go down, your people go down too.'

'It'll come out sooner or later. These things always do.'

'Not necessarily. No one's seen or heard of this man Meehan for years. We find him, you chop him –

finito, end of story. He's certainly not going to be missed.'

'You think you'll find him?' asked Alex quietly.

The grey eyes hardened a fraction. 'Don't you think we will?'

'If he doesn't want you to find him, he'll go to ground somewhere.'

She raised an ironic eyebrow. 'Somewhere that only you Special Forces boys can follow, right?'

Alex shrugged. 'I might be able to help you with the way that he thinks. Give you an idea of the sort of place he'd look for.'

She sighed. 'Look, we have the Service's best psych team dealing with the way that this man thinks and our best investigators looking for him. Any suggestions would, I'm sure, be very helpful, but we do, in fact, have the matter well in hand. What we'd really like you to do is wait and, when the moment comes, move in and eliminate him.'

'Is that really all you think we're good for?'

'On this occasion, I'm afraid that it's all we need you to do.'

They sat in uncomfortable silence. Outside on the river, a succession of interlinked barges moved upstream against the current. She had no real idea, thought Alex, what she was asking him to do. What it was like to look another human being in the eye and then kill him. How, in those moments, a few seconds could stretch into infinity.

It's all we need you to do.

A belated flicker of concern crossed her face. She frowned. She seemed to be aware of the direction his thoughts were taking. 'It's not up to me,' she said. 'I'm just here as a go-between.'

He nodded. It was as close to an apology as he was ever likely to get. 'So when did you join the Service?' he asked.

'Six years ago.' She forced a smile. 'I answered the same advert as David Shayler, as it happens.'

'What did it say? "Spies wanted"?'

'It said: "Godot Isn't Coming".'

'Who the hell's Godot?'

'A character in a Samuel Beckett play called *Waiting for Godot*. The other characters wait for him.'

'And he doesn't come?'

'No.'

'Sounds unmissable. So you knew this was an MI5 advert?'

'No. But I knew it had been placed by an organisation with a bit of . . . sophistication to it.'

'Right,' said Alex. 'Because of this Godot stuff.'

'Exactly.'

'We watch a fair amount of Samuel Beckett's stuff up in Hereford. Are you glad you answered that advert?'

'Yes.'

'And are you free this afternoon?'

She looked at him suspiciously. 'No. Why?'

'When I've looked through the photographs and the pathology reports, I'd like to go back to Gidley's place. There are a couple of things I need to check.'

'I thought we'd established that you were leaving that side of things to us.'

'Dawn, I need to see what Meehan's exact movements were the night before last. If I'm going up against him, I have to know how he operates.'

'I very much doubt there'll be anything to see.'

'That depends on what you're looking for. Trust

me, I'm not going to be wasting your time.'

She regarded him expressionlessly for a moment and nodded. 'OK, then, but like I said, I'm tied up this afternoon. It'll have to be tomorrow morning.'

'I guess that'll have to do. Tell me something off the top of your head.'

'What?'

'Why is Joseph Meehan murdering the MI5 officers who ran him?'

'I heard you ask Angela Fenwick the same question. She said she didn't know.'

'I heard her say it. But what do you think?'

'I think he went native, like George said.' She shrugged. 'Why do any terrorists do what they do? It's an armed struggle. We're the enemy.'

'But why choose such an extreme method of killing people? And why take out Fenn and Gidley who, let's face it, were pretty much at the fag-end of their careers?'

'He killed the people he knew. To Meehan, Fenn and Gidley represented the heart of the British Establishment. As do George Widdowes and Angela Fenwick, presumably.'

Alex shook his head. 'I don't think he killed them for symbolic reasons. As Brit oppressors or whatever. I think he killed them for a specific reason.'

She narrowed her eyes. 'What makes you think that you can see inside this man's head?'

Alex shrugged. 'We're both soldiers. Soldiers are methodical. They believe in cause and effect. What's the point of carrying out an elaborate, ritualistic murder that no one will ever know about? That you know will be immediately covered up?'

'Perhaps he's mad.'

'Do you know something?' said Alex. 'For a moment there we were almost having a conversation.'

Dawn held his gaze for a moment, then reached to the floor for her briefcase. When she straightened she was her usual brisk, businesslike self. 'As well as the photographs and reports on Fenn and Gidley I've got some keys for you. They're for a top-floor flat in St George's Square in Pimlico. You can stay there if you need to or' – she hesitated for a fraction of a second – 'you can make your own arrangements.'

'Thank you,' said Alex neutrally.

Barry Fenn, he saw, had been a weaselly, narrow-shouldered man. From the photographs, in which he was wearing bloodstained pyjamas and was sprawled half in and half out of bed, it was clear that he had been woken from sleep. According to the pathologist's report he had struggled briefly and ineffectually before being struck on the back of the head with some sort of cosh. The six-inch nail had been hammered into his temple while he was semi-conscious and his tongue, it appeared, had been hacked out as some sort of afterthought. Livid and hideous, it had been placed in the unused glass ashtray beside the bed alongside a book of matches. There was less blood than there might have been.

Looking at the photographs, Alex realised that his earlier identification with Meehan had been dangerous and stupid. Beyond their training and a similarity in age, he had nothing whatever in common with this maniac. Dawn was right: the man was a psychopathic murderer and had to be stopped.

The pathologist's report on Craig Gidley indicated that, like Barry Fenn's tongue, the victim's eyes had been cut out after the fatal hammerblow had driven the nail through his temple. To Alex this confirmed that the mutilations were there for a purpose other than to cause suffering. As a message, perhaps?

But a message for whom? For MI5 as a whole? For George Widdowes or Angela Fenwick in particular? Whatever the message, it was clear that either Widdowes or Fenwick was next on the Watchman's list.

Would he get them? Alex wondered dispassionately. Would he catch them and kill them? Forewarned and with all the protective resources of MI5 at their disposal, they would be much harder targets than Fenn and Gidley had been.

But then the Watchman was clever. He had been taught by the best – in many cases the same people who had taught Alex – and he had clearly forgotten none of it. The combination of professionalism, sadism and sheer insanity he embodied was terrifying.

What did he want? What was the man trying to achieve?

Alex stared at the photographs of Meehan as if his gaze could somehow penetrate their surface and unlock the man portrayed in them. But the more he shuffled them around, the less they seemed to reveal. Just those pale, skinned-whippet features and that watchful, guarded gaze.

He looked tough. Not in the sense of being intimidating, but in the sense of being a hard man to break. He'd duck and he'd dive but one way and another he'd keep on going. There were a thousand looking like him on the streets of Belfast – dingy, forgettable figures hunched into donkey jackets. Alex could see why he'd been such a perfect undercover man.

Would MI5 find him? Meehan would have to make a serious mistake first and there was nothing to indicate that that was going to happen. Mad he might be, but careless he clearly wasn't.

Alex turned to the large map of Britain on the wall. Where would Meehan be hiding out? No, turn the question round. Where would he – Alex – be hiding out if he were Meehan? In a city, among the crowds? No, he'd be in danger if he revisited his old London stamping grounds. He couldn't risk going anywhere there was an Irish community. The arm of the IRA, like its memory, was long.

Meehan would know that MI5 would leave no stone unturned in their search and that unless he had built up a completely watertight new identity they would find him. He'd have to have a new passport, driving licence, social security number – everything. Just checking in and out of bed-and-breakfast houses was not going to be enough. He'd have a base somewhere. Somewhere he could hide.

Somewhere he could plan the next killing.

Alex arrived back at Sophie's flat shortly before seven, having arranged to meet Dawn Harding at nine the next morning. She'd pick him up, she told him, where she had dropped him off the night before – outside the Duke of York's Headquarters in the King's Road.

He found Sophie changing. 'We're going out,' she told him, swinging round so that he could zip up the fastening of her cocktail dress. 'One of my clients – Corday – is launching a new fragrance range and I've helped organise a little party for them. The perfume's called "Guillotine" and all the women have to wear a red velvet ribbon round their necks as if they've been beheaded.'

'Do you mind if I give it a miss?' Alex asked wearily, loosening his tie. 'I'm not really in the mood.'

'Oh, don't be boring, darling! I'm sure you've had a horrible day doing whatever secret things you've been doing but so have I. It's been impossibly grim at the PR coalface. Come and drink some champagne at Corday's expense, and then . . .'

'And then?'

'And then you can take charge of the evening. How's that?'

Alex agreed. If Five were going to leave him twiddling his thumbs while they pursued their investigation, then he might as well enjoy himself. And he wanted to please Sophie who, after all, was putting him up. He didn't even have to drive the next morning – Dawn would be doing that, presumably at her usual infuriating crawl. So he might as well chill out. 'So where are we going?'

She raised her chin to tie her red velvet ribbon. 'Hoxton Square.'

'Where's that?'

'Alex, sweetie, which planet have you been living on for the last few years? Hoxton is only the most desirable *quartier* in London. You can barely throw a stone without braining some famous artist, model or designer. It's celebrity city!'

'Right, well, just introduce me as a friend of your brother's. Say I work in security or something.'

She frowned and pouted into the mirror, checking her make-up. 'Security's a bit dingy-sounding, darling. Can we manage something a bit more upscale? Something dot.com, perhaps?'

'OK. I'll have a think.' He rubbed his eyes. Various subconscious worries were still nagging at him. 'I realised something dreadful today, that I'd left a rebel sentry – a boy, can't have been much more than ten – tied to a tree in the middle of the Sierra Leone jungle a couple of days ago.'

Sophie wriggled her toes experimentally in her raw-silk shoes. 'I know. It's awful how forgetful one gets. Do you want to ring someone about it?'

Alex stared at her disbelievingly. 'He's probably dead by now, or at the very least missing an arm.'

'Shall we go?'

As they swerved through the traffic in the silver Audi TT, with Sophie impatiently cutting up every vehicle that had the temerity to draw alongside her, Alex tried to improve his mood. Things could be worse, he told himself. He was being paid to waste time in London – an opportunity that most soldiers would give their eye-teeth for – and he was sleeping with a rich, beautiful and highly sexed girl who gave every sign of thinking he was the cat's pyjamas. He was on his way to a party to drink champagne with said highly sexed girl, and in two or three hours they would tumble into bed and tear each other to pieces.

So what was pissing him off, exactly? Was it that he seemed to be spending his life being shuffled about by women? Alex had nothing against working with women but right now his life seemed to be run by them. In the past whenever girlfriends had started making noises about permanence and commitment, Alex had started making noises about the incompatibility of soldiering and married life. And he had meant it. He had seen his colleagues go down like ninepins, their tiny independence skewered by the demands of ratty, frustrated wives. The wives hadn't started ratty and frustrated, but they soon got that way when they discovered that the system could only accommodate them and the kids as sideline players. As Stan Clayton had once explained to him: getting the trouble-and-strife up the duff before an overseas posting was like spitting in your beer before you went for a piss!

Seeing the results – vengeful, careworn wives, fragged-out blokes worrying about money and their families' security from dawn till dusk – Alex had sworn to have nothing to do with any of it. As far as he was concerned the deal was that you promised nothing that you weren't prepared to give, had a good time for as long as it lasted and got out before things turned nasty. He had a sort of honour system, which went something along the lines that if a woman made it plain from the start that she wanted marriage and kids then you didn't waste her time. Otherwise, you went for it.

Something told him, though, that with Sophie it was going to be different. For a start he was not in control of things. He didn't automatically call the shots, as he'd always done before. She moved easily and fluently through a world in which, if he was honest, he felt insecure. And while she respected his skills and knew that there was another, darker world in which he moved with ease and fluency, she never allowed herself to be overimpressed by him.

Ultimately, he wasn't sure of her. This made things exciting, but it also made things . . . difficult.

As they swerved round a traffic island in the TT, tyres screaming, Alex told himself that he ought to take a train up to Hereford and pick up his car. Behind the wheel of the Karman-Ghia he could at least pretend that he was in control of his life. For the time being, though . . .

What the hell?

TWELVE

When they reached Hoxton Square Sophie ignored the double yellow lines and parked right outside the venue. This was a former electricity showroom turned gallery, and paparazzi were already drawn up at either side of the entrance. As Alex and Sophie hurried in there was a brief burst of flash – presumably in case they were celebrities whom no one yet recognised.

The party was on the first floor and the place was already crowded. On the far side of the room Alex caught sight of Stella laughing with a group of models. The sound system was playing Juliette Greco, two women in tricolore hats were spraying perfume at anyone not fast enough to get out of their way, and the sharp smell of 'Guillotine' cut the air.

'Come and meet Charlotte,' said Sophie, taking Alex's hand and sidling purposefully towards a slight, dark-haired woman who seemed to be dressed in 1970s wallpaper. 'She's the oldest of the Corday sisters. You've heard of the Corday fashion house, haven't you?'

'Why don't I go and find us a drink?' Alex suggested, disengaging his hand.

Within moments he had been swallowed up by the crowd. Around him brief snatches of conversation and shrieks of laughter rose like waves above the music and were inaudible again. A gravel-voiced broadcaster whom he vaguely recognised but had never met threw her arms round his neck, kissed him on the mouth and asked how the new restaurant was going. He told her that it was still serving human flesh and moved on, leaving her open-mouthed.

People pushed past, flickered a glance at him in passing to establish for certain that he was not someone that they needed to know and vanished. Alex wanted to speak to none of them – he simply couldn't summon up the interest. Over the months that he'd been seeing Sophie he'd attended quite a few of these occasions and he'd come to the conclusion that London society was peopled almost entirely by fuckwits. From the outside it looked glamorous, all late-night restaurants and beautiful girls and champagne, but in truth, he had discovered, it was very, very dull. For every genuine achiever there were a hundred style journalists, fashion parasites and cokehead aristocrats desperately jockeying for recognition. None of them seemed to have any awareness of a world beyond their own tiny circuit, and listening to the endless loop tape of their conversation about clothes, accessories, drugs and parties bored him out of his mind.

There were exceptions. He liked Stella and of course he liked Sophie – more than liked her, in fact.

But why was it, he wondered, that the whole scene that she was involved with made him feel so dead inside? And – equally importantly – why was it that situations involving real death made him feel so acutely alive? How was he supposed to square those facts with the idea of – one day, at least – settling down?

'Bloody Mary?'

Alex looked down to see a tiny, large-busted girl in

a tricolore cap, holding a tray. She giggled. 'Or Bloody Marie-Antoinette, I suppose I should say.'

Alex took one of the glasses and drank. It was almost fifty per cent pure vodka and fiery with tabasco. 'Bloody strong, whichever.'

She laughed. 'I know. I thought I'd loosen this lot up a bit. Come the revolution, they'll all be for the chop.'

'They certainly need culling,' said Alex morosely, taking a deep hit of his drink. It occurred to him a few seconds later that he was feeling rather over-sorry for himself. These people weren't so bad. He threw back the remains of the drink, helped himself to another and took a deep swig. He began to feel very much more cheerful. Get a life, Temple, he told himself. Have some fun for a change!

'Shall I just stay here?' she asked. 'Let you help yourself?'

He smiled. Small girl plus big tits equals hard-on. 'You could do worse,' he said. 'Are you one of the caterers?'

'Sort of. Part-time. I'm actually trying to get into the fashion business.'

'You should speak to Sophie Wells. She's over by the entrance, or was when I last saw her.'

'She's a right snotty cunt,' said the girl, as Alex took a third glass. 'D'you know her?'

'Mm. A bit.'

'Which bit?'

'Go on.' He smiled. 'Piss off before we're all in trouble!'

'Hey, Alex from Clacton!'

'Stella! How's it going?'

She gave him an uneven grin. 'All right, apart from the smell of this perfume. It's like fish guts at low tide.'

153

'I guess the original guillotine wasn't too fresh,' said Alex.

'What have you been up to?' she asked. 'I haven't seen you for a bit.'

'I've been in Africa,' said Alex.

'Yeah? How was that?'

He shrugged. 'Tell me something, Stella.'

'OK.'

'If you wanted to hide – if you absolutely had to hide, life or death – where would you go?'

'I'd go where I always go,' she said, as if the question were the most normal one in the world. 'The past.'

He stared at her. Heard someone calling her name.

She smiled and the crowd drew her away. 'Believe me,' she said, fluttering her fingers. 'There's nowhere like it.'

He found Sophie again and was just about to hand her her drink when something irregular registered at the edge of his vision.

At the entrance, by the glass doors, two tall heavy-set figures were forcing their way past the security guards. The guards were doing their best, but they were no match for the red-faced, guffawing new-comers. One of them, a beef-fed, tiny-eyed giant of at least six foot two inches in height, was wearing a rugby shirt while the other, city-suited, was only a shade shorter. The crowd backed away from them uneasily.

'Shit!' said Sophie quietly at Alex's side. 'Gatecrashers.'

She stepped with confidence into the path of the two men. 'Look, guys . . .' she began. 'This is a private . . .'

'Charlie,' roared the taller man, throwing a massive arm round Sophie's shoulders. 'Take a look at what I've . . .'

But the other was forcibly slapping a passing guest on the back. '*You, sir!*' he brayed. 'Are you – by any chance – an *arse-bandido*?'

Both gatecrashers had public-school accents, Alex noted. Everything about them spelt money and arrogance. Well, they were about to get what was coming to them.

'So, my darlin'.' The bigger of the two reached drunkenly for Sophie. 'You were saying . . .'

A split second before his hand reached Sophie's chest, a fist crunched into his nose. The blow carried with it every ounce of resentment that Alex had ever felt towards the privileged classes.

'*Alex!*' he heard Sophie scream. '*No!*'

The man turned to Alex, amazed. Blood poured from his flattened nose as if from a tap and streamed down the front of his rugby shirt. The other man stood there, swaying. There was a moment of absolute silence, then the bleeding man drew back a fist the size of a bowling ball.

Alex swerved, felt the wind of the blow pass his cheek and, half turning, seized the oncoming arm by the wrist. Forcing his shoulder into his attacker's armpit, and using the Hooray's own weight and momentum, he threw him hard on to his back. The giant frame seemed to pinwheel in the air for a moment and then crashed down over a crate of champagne bottles.

'*Alex!*' screamed Sophie again.

He sensed rather than saw the second man's rush. Grabbing a Bollinger bottle by the neck he turned and swung it with all his strength. The bottle smashed against the man's skull with a crunching, gassy sigh and in a white explosion of foam. With spectacular effect his head turned blood-red, his eyes rolled upwards and he crashed to the floor. Screams joined the spatter of broken glass and the groans of the first attacker who was writhing beneath one of the caterers' trestle tables.

The pushing started, then, and the panic. A drinks table went over, then another, and within seconds the floor was covered in spilled champagne, canapes and broken glass. Someone activated the fire alarm. Hanging over everything was the acrid stench of 'Guillotine'.

'*Alex*!' Sophie screamed for a third time, waving her fists at him. 'What do you think you're doing?' Around them, people were jostling for the exit.

'What do you mean?' asked Alex, dropping the smashed bottleneck. 'Did you really want those pissed-up yobs grabbing at you?'

'They were two boys who'd had too much to drink, that's all. It's *you* who's ruined the party!' She stared despairingly at the departing guests and then down at the fallen men. 'Could someone please ring an ambulance?' she pleaded.

'*Boys*?' asked Alex, amazed. 'Look at the fucking size of them. I can't believe you're siding with them.' He turned to her thoughtfully and smiled. 'But then I suppose they're your type, aren't they?'

'Don't be so *stupid*. You *totally* overreacted and you know it. You could have . . .' She shook her head, incoherent with anger. Beside her, one of the caterers was dialling 999.

'Killed them?' Alex regarded the fallen and bloodied figures dispassionately. The first man, still

156

groaning, appeared to have badly injured his back and the second was unmoving and bleeding copiously from the head. 'No such luck, I'm afraid. I'd say your perfume got its publicity, though.' He sniffed the air. 'Stella was right, it is a bit fishy.'

She rounded on him, eyes blazing. 'And what the hell would you know, you . . . you *psychopathic hooligan?*'

Alex began to laugh. He couldn't help himself. 'I'm sorry!' he managed eventually. 'Really, Sophie, I'm sorry.'

Drawing back her hand she slapped him as hard as she could across the face and marched furiously off.

Alex caught up with her. 'Please,' he said. 'I'm sorry, Sophie. Really I am. I wasn't laughing at you. It's just the whole thing.'

She shrugged him off. Her voice was shaking with anger. 'The *whole thing*, as you call it, has turned to shit. I open up my life to you, introduce you to my friends, and you just . . . just crap all over them. You can make your own fucking way home and you needn't bother to call me again. Find someone else's life to smash up.'

At this moment, as they stood there facing each other, speechless, the little waitress with the big bust appeared at the foot of the stairs. 'So, is this a good moment to talk about work?' she asked Sophie brightly.

Sophie glanced at her uncomprehendingly. 'No,' she said quietly. 'It isn't.'

The waitress shrugged. 'Told you she was a cunt!'

Alex watched Sophie slam the door of the silver Audi. When the snarl of her exhaust had died away he reached into his suit pocket. The safe-house key was still there.

THIRTEEN

The first hour of the drive up to Goring in Dawn Harding's Honda was conducted in near silence. Alex had a mild hangover and was feeling a bit guilty about the way the previous evening had turned out. He shouldn't have laughed, he told himself.

The trouble was, the row had exposed all the differences that existed between them. He couldn't be bothered with most of her friends, when all was said and done, and he couldn't be bothered to obey the rules that people obeyed in her world. She considered him an unreconstructed macho dinosaur, and in return he found her spoilt, shallow and over-privileged. They brought out the worst in each other.

And yet they wanted each other. Often.

The night in the Pimlico flat had been a cheerless one. A 1970s Bulgarian defector might have felt at home in the place, with its stained orange carpet and fusty, boarding-house smell, but Alex could have done with something a little less Cold War.

He should get some flowers, he told himself, present himself at Sophie's front door that evening with an apologetic face and a big bunch of roses. Would roses do the trick? They were supposed to, but then in Sophie's picky and obsessive circle roses might be considered naff.

'Do you like roses?' he asked Dawn.

She looked at him suspiciously. 'Why?'

'If someone gave you roses, what would you think?'

'A man, you mean?' she asked.

'For the sake of argument, yes.'

'I'd think either he was trying to get something from me, or he was apologising.'

'Right.'

'If they were really special, though . . . I mean if they weren't just those boring, limp, half-frozen things you buy at the tube station in a twist of cellophane but properly scented old English roses grown in a garden, well, I might at least listen to what he had to say.' She glanced at him shrewdly from the driving seat. 'In trouble, are we?'

'No. Just wondering.'

'Ah. Wondering. Well, my experience is that most girls do, in fact, quite like to be given roses.' She narrowed her eyes at the road ahead. 'Even the posh ones like your Sophie.'

He nodded. He guessed he was going to have to say goodbye to any kind of private life for as long as he was working with Box.

'Can I ask what you're actually doing to locate this Watchman character?' he asked.

Her expression remained unaltered but her eyes froze over. 'Put it this way,' she said. 'We've got pictures, we've got DNA, we've got dabs, we've got handwriting, and we've got vocal and facial recognition systems in place. I think you can say that we're adequately covered.'

'And Widdowes? What are you doing to protect him?'

'George Widdowes is an experienced intelligence officer.'

'So were Fenn and Gidley. Didn't help them much when laughing boy showed up, though, did it?'

'Forewarned is forearmed.'

Alex shook his head despairingly and rubbed his eyes. 'You don't get it, do you?' he said quietly. 'Meehan will kill him. He's programmed to do it and he will do it.'

She was silent for a minute or two.

'OK,' she said. 'I'll tell you. We're setting up a lookalike at his house. A Special Branch guy. We've got the place ringed with police marksmen. George himself has been pulled out of circulation.'

'You think that'll work?'

'Look, I admit we were a little bit slow off the blocks with Gidley, but we're very much on-message now.'

'On-message,' said Alex. 'Right.'

'This Watchman,' Dawn went on patiently. 'He's one man, he's on his own, he's got no support system to speak of. It's not constructive to be too afraid of him.'

'He's a murderer,' said Alex. 'He's Regiment-trained. And he's spent several years in the field with the most sophisticated terror organisation in the world.'

'You sound as if you admire them.'

'Professionally speaking I do admire them. If I'd been born a working-class Catholic over the water I'd probably be a volunteer myself and most Regiment blokes will tell you the same thing. It doesn't mean you aren't prepared to do your job and waste as many of the fuckers as you can, but ultimately when you put a bullet through one of those boys and you look into his dying eyes you can see yourself as you might have been, and that's the truth.'

From the long habit of counter-surveillance, Alex glanced up at the rear-view mirror. The small movement and the dizzying motion of the reflected cars reminded him how much vodka was still in his bloodstream and he pressed the button to lower the passenger window. Fresh air rushed in. The sun had not yet burnt off the dew in the fields. 'The PIRA are good,' he continued, 'and the thing they're better than anyone else at is security. They won't hesitate to cancel a hundred-man operation if one dicker's instinct tells him or her there's something not quite right – that one too many cars has passed or that a man's coat's hanging wrong or there are no birds in a hedge where there should be birds. Our man Meehan will have absorbed all that. He'll wait as long as it takes. That's why I respect him. And that's why you people should respect him too.'

'Respect him, yes,' Dawn agreed, her eyes fixed on the road ahead. 'Fear him, no.'

'Given a choice between fear and arrogance,' said Alex mildly, 'I'll take fear every time. Nothing gets you killed faster than arrogance.'

'We'll see, shall we?'

'I'm afraid we will, yes.'

They settled into a sour, antagonistic silence.

When they got to Goring, Alex asked Dawn to park several hundred yards from the house. 'I want to approach the place as the Watchman would have done,' he explained. 'See it as he would have seen it the first time he came down here.'

'No one noticed any strangers in the village,' said Dawn. 'We've asked a few questions about that.'

'He wouldn't have been noticeable,' Alex told her. 'My guess is that he would have come on foot first time round, probably in hiking gear and on a wet Saturday. Or by bicycle, perhaps. Anorak hoods, clear glasses, cycle helmets – they're all good disguises. Those just-passing-through, rambler-type people are invisible in a semi-touristy place like this. You see them at the side of the road eating a sandwich and swigging a soft drink, but you don't really see them. You couldn't describe them two minutes later.'

She nodded. They continued in silence along the roadside.

Dawn frowned. 'But what would he . . .'

'Shush a minute,' said Alex, cutting her off. The Gidleys' house was just coming into view and he wanted to see it – had to see it – through the Watchman's eyes. At his side, as he marshalled all his senses and instincts to this end, he was vaguely aware of Dawn bristling with irritation.

Women, he thought.

Meehan would want an OP – a place he could observe from without being seen. Somewhere away from the road and out of range of the dogs, but close enough to check out the arrangements. He'd have planned for at least a week's surveillance. He wouldn't have compromised with just a day or two. He would have gone up with food and water and a bag to crap into, and noted everything. Where would he have watched from? A building? Were there any other buildings in sight? No. No farm sheds, garages, outhouses, nothing. Their absence would have been one of the factors that attracted Gidley to the house in the first place. So was there anywhere at ground level he could lie up? Didn't look like it, because wherever he lay the wall surrounding the property would block his vision. He wouldn't be able to get enough height on the place. The contours were against him.

Man-made OPs? There were telegraph poles running along the road and connecting to the property, and it was theoretically possible that he'd nicked a BT van and overalls to fit the deactivator. But he wouldn't have been able to stay up there for long enough to establish anything worthwhile – within moments of his appearing the Box security people would have been on to BT to check him out.

Trees, then. Alex had reckoned from the start that Meehan had gone for a tree, but he'd wanted formally to eliminate all other possibilities. There were a horse chestnut and a sycamore overhanging the road on either side of the Gidleys' perimeter wall, but he dismissed these. Tempting, but just too close to the house and the orbit of the dogs. Besides, in consideration of the security hazard they posed, all the trees near the property wall had had their lower limbs sawed off. Climbing them would have necessitated scaling equipment and any climber would have had to take the risk of being seen either from the house or the road.

On the opposite side of the road was a field of young corn bisected by a public footpath. Mature trees stood at the side of this path at irregular intervals. Alex scanned them from the road. The ideal observation point was a large beech, from whose boughs a clear hundred-and-fifty-yard sight line on the house and grounds was available. Without a word, with Dawn sighing behind, he marched down the road,

163

swung his leg over the stile into the field and moved at pace towards the tree. His head was clear now, his brain singing with the pleasure of the pursuit. 'I'll have you, you bastard!' he murmured to himself. 'I'll fucking have you!'

They arrived at the foot of the beech and Alex climbed expectantly over the elephantine grey roots. Meehan, he was sure, would have climbed the trunk on the far side from the road, using ropes and scaling equipment. Carefully, he examined the trunk. Nothing. No sign, no scar. *Shit*! It *had* to be this tree. But the trunk showed no sign at all, not a single scratch, scar or abrasion that might have been made in the last month. After searching the fine-grained silvery surface for more than twenty minutes he was forced to concede that if Meehan had used this tree he had not climbed it by the trunk. Nor were there any branches hanging anywhere near the ground.

Dawn remained expressionless, but Alex could tell that his frustration gave her quiet satisfaction. Finally, and meaningfully, she glanced at her watch.

'Come on,' he said, marching her further up the path.

The next tree that might have afforded a view over Gidley's property was a horse chestnut. Its large leaves and candle-like white blooms made it a lot harder to see out of but at the same time, Alex noted, a lot harder to see into.

Maybe, he thought. Maybe. Warily, he circled the trunk. Like the beech, it was fine-skinned and any scratch would have shown. But once again, there was nothing.

'Is it possible,' asked Dawn demurely, 'that you might just be barking up the wrong . . .'

'No!' he snapped. 'It bloody isn't. He was here somewhere.'

'You're sure?'

'I'm sure. Now please . . .' Desperately, he scanned the tree's spreading skirts and his eyes narrowed. There was one place, just one, about ten feet from the ground. 'Come with me,' he ordered her. 'Step where I step.'

Followed by Dawn, he moved into the shadowed, dew-sodden grass. When he was below the lowest point of the bough he motioned her to be still and crouched down. Half closing his eyes, he felt carefully around the wet ground as if he were blind. It took five minutes, but eventually he found what he was looking for: a plug of pressed soil the size and shape of a cigarette packet. 'Got you,' he breathed.

'What is it?' asked Dawn.

In answer he felt quickly around and eased another plug from the ground a foot away. 'He had a ladder,' said Alex. 'He didn't want to go up the trunk using a scaling kit and leave marks, so he used a ladder and a rope and went up here. Then afterwards' – Alex held up the soil – 'he filled in the places where the feet of the ladder went. It hasn't rained since then, so . . .'

'Why go to that trouble?' asked Dawn. 'Since we know it's him and he knows that we know.'

'He's a perfectionist,' said Alex. 'It's about doing it right, whatever the circumstances. About leaving no trace.'

'A sort of Samurai code?' mused Dawn.

'That sort of thing,' Alex agreed. 'What I think he did here was to get a decorator's ladder – one of those aluminium self-supporting jobs – tie one end of the rope to it, throw the other over the branch, pull the branch down and tie off the rope. Then he grabbed the branch and up he went.'

'Dragging the ladder up behind him on the rope. Neat. Too bad we haven't got a rope or a ladder.'

'We've got me,' said Alex. 'And we've got you.'

'Oh, no!' said Dawn firmly. 'No *fucking* way!'

'Way, baby!' said Alex with a grim smile. 'Shoes off.'

'Tree-climbing's not part of my job, *baby*!'

'And saving your colleagues' life? Is that part of your job? Personally I couldn't give a monkey's, but . . .'

'Why can't you go up alone?'

'I could, but it would mean my standing on your shoulders and I'm not sure you could manage that.'

'Try me.'

'I'd love to.'

'You know what I mean.'

They tried it. She genuflected; he took her hands and stepped on to her shoulders with his bare feet.

'Do you have any idea how much I paid for this sweater?' she breathed, trembling with strain.

'Take it off,' said Alex cheerfully. 'I won't be shocked.'

'Fuck you!'

She couldn't straighten up. She tried – gave it her best shot – but in the end she simply couldn't.

'Why don't we try it the other way round?' he suggested reasonably.

'Why don't we just get a ladder from the house?'

'If this doesn't work we will, OK?'

Sullenly she took off her shoes, placed them together on the wet grass as if on a wardrobe shelf, took his hands, stepped on to his shoulders.

'And . . . up.' He straightened. 'Take your hands

away from mine when you're ready. Grab the branch. Good, now pull yourself up. Try and get your leg over.'

'I thought that was your speciality,' she gasped. Then she looked down at him nervously. 'What now?'

'Move as close to the end of the branch as possible, so that it's weighed down.'

She did so. He took off his shirt and threw it up to her, ordered her to tie it round the branch, which she did. 'And now these. Tie the legs together so that they make another link of the chain.' He threw her his trousers. She tied them to the shirt. He was now naked except for his boxer shorts. 'How silly do I look?' he asked.

'From up here? Very.'

'You sure the knots are sound?'

'I've done some sailing. Trust me, they're sound.'

He hauled himself up as if using a rope ladder, unknotted his shirt and trousers – part of the haul he had bought with Sophie – and quickly re-dressed. 'OK, do you want to stay here? Or climb with me.'

She hesitated. He could see a small muscle working in her jaw. 'I'll come up,' she said eventually.

'Right. You know what we're looking for. Anything, basically.'

'You really think we're going to learn anything?'

'I think we have to look.'

They climbed for ten minutes, the ground fell slowly away beneath them and the dark-green leaves enveloped them. As they moved upwards they found tiny but unmistakable signs that someone else had recently done the same thing and by dint of hard searching were able to follow a trail of lichen blurs, pressure marks and trodden fungi.

'Look up,' said Alex at intervals, which Dawn correctly interpreted as 'Don't look down'.

Finally, breathless, she turned to him. 'I can't get up there.' 'There' was the broad junction of several branches with the trunk some thirty feet from the ground.

'He managed it,' said Alex.

'Well, I can't,' she breathed. 'It's just too long a reach.'

'I'll get you up there,' Alex said.

'Must you?'

'Yeah. I'm pretty sure that's where he watched from. I'm going to lift you and sit you there, OK?'

'OK,' she said uncertainly.

He braced himself opposite her, placed his hands on her waist and looked into a pair of grey eyes from which she was struggling to keep all signs of fear. Beneath his grip, however, he could feel a faint involuntary trembling. When he lifted her she almost made it – she was absurdly light, somehow, for someone so bad-tempered – but the fine black wool of her sweater gave a poor grip and she slipped down again between his hands. The sweater, meanwhile, slipped up.

'I'm sorry,' he said sincerely, staring at the neatly voluptuous contours of her scarlet satin bra. 'I didn't mean that to happen.'

She wrenched down her sweater. *Blimey*, he told himself. *Who'd have thought that beneath that stroppy exterior* . . . 'Try again?' he suggested.

Now sheer anger got her up there. Once settled, she stared out over the fields.

He clambered up behind her and saw what she saw. The trunk and the adjoining branches formed a solid enclosure within which, without too much discomfort, it would have been possible to remain for hours. Before them the alignment of the heavy, densely leaved chestnut branches afforded a perfect long-distance view of the Gidleys' property. Only the area directly behind the house was invisible.

'He was here,' said Alex. 'He was here for days. Look, you can see the worn place in this fork where he wedged his foot. And here, this shined place where he sat. This was where he planned Gidley's murder.'

'If I weren't so utterly terrified of heights,' said Dawn quietly, looking around her, 'I'd say it was rather beautiful up here.'

Alex stared at her. 'You're really afraid of heights? Phobic?'

She returned his stare openly and frankly. 'Like I said, terrified. This is the highest I've ever been off the ground outside a house. Skyscrapers make me feel faint. I couldn't even go up the Eiffel Tower.'

'So why didn't you tell me?'

She looked him in the eye. 'You didn't exactly make it very easy, did you?'

He was silent for a moment. 'I guess not. I'm sorry. You're a trooper, Dawn Harding, and I'm a bastard.'

She nodded thoughtfully. 'Yes, I'd pretty much go along with that. I might add the words "patronising" and "sexist" while I was about it.'

'Fair enough.'

'And request that if we're going to continue working together you don't take out your frustrations on me every time you get an order you don't like, or your Sloaney girlfriend gives you a hard time, or you don't get laid, or whatever.'

'OK.'

169

'And most importantly that you get me to the ground in one piece.'

'I promise.'

Together, as best they could, they searched the branches around them for anything that Meehan might have left. In the end it was Dawn who found it: an inch-long stub of pencil slipped into a knot hole near their feet. Working it out with his pocket knife, Alex managed to slip the pencil into his shirt pocket without directly touching it.

'Forensics'll be interested to see that,' said Dawn. 'Do you think there's anything else?'

They searched every inch, but found nothing else. Ten minutes later they were back on the first branch, ten feet above the ground.

'Ever done a parachute course?' Alex asked her.

She shook her head.

'OK, I'll jump and then catch you.'

He hit the ground, rolled and stood himself up. Soon, she was hanging from the branch with her bare feet on his shoulders. One after the other, he took her hands. She wobbled.

'OK,' he said. 'Now put my hands under your arms.'

'No funny business?'

'As if!'

Gently, he lowered her down the front of his body. When their faces were level and her mouth inches from his, he stopped. He looked into her eyes. Was there the ghost of a smile there?

They had lunch in a nearby pub. Ploughman's lunches, with in his case a beer and in hers mineral water. A sharp morning had turned into a warm day and they sat outside at a bench.

'You did something today you wouldn't have thought yourself capable of,' Alex began.

'Oh, spare us the squaddie pep talk, please. I went up that tree this morning because . . .'

'Because the thought of being bested by a yob of a soldier was something you couldn't face. Worse even than your fear of heights, right?'

She shrugged and smiled. 'Perhaps. I never said you were a yob, though.'

'No?'

'No. Though you certainly are one. And proud of it – after all, it's a solid-gold chick puller, isn't it, being in the Regiment?'

'Didn't you get laid last night either?'

'As a matter of fact I did,' said Dawn mildly.

There was a heartbeat's silence.

'So, who's the lucky guy?' Alex asked, rather more sharply than he intended.

In answer Dawn just laughed and shook her head. 'That pencil was a good find,' she said, cutting a pickled onion in half. 'Forensics can get stuck in. There should be dabs.'

'There won't be,' said Alex. 'He meant us to find it. It's a message.'

'How d'you know that? How d'you know he didn't make a mistake? Just leave it there?'

'He wouldn't do that. He doesn't make mistakes.'

'That's just your ego talking. You're Regiment-trained, he's Regiment-trained. In your mind you can't make a mistake, therefore he can't make a mistake.'

'All that I'm saying is that trained guys like him don't make mistakes concerning operational procedure. You arrive at an OP with a pencil, you leave with a pencil, end of story.'

'OK. So what, in your opinion, is the message?'

'I think it's part and parcel with the nails. Some kind of reference to the undercover days. That knot hole was rather like a dead-letter drop, didn't you think? Perhaps returning the pencil is his way of saying that things have gone beyond words. That the only possible medium of communication left is murder.'

She stared at him.

'My guess is that he's way ahead of us,' said Alex. 'My guess is that he knew you'd bring in someone like me and so he put that pencil where only someone like me would find it.'

'I found it,' said Dawn.

'You know what I mean. It's a message for me. As if to say hello, brother. I was wondering when you'd be along.'

'You think he wants to be caught?' asked Dawn.

'I don't know about that – but I know he means to do a fair bit more killing first.'

Dawn frowned. 'I'm not supposed to tell you this, but there's something that probably wasn't in those reports you were given. They analysed the nails that were used to kill Fenn and Gidley, and found something very strange indeed.'

Alex looked at her.

'They were well over fifty years old. Nails haven't been made by that process or of that particular alloy since before the Second World War.'

'The pencil,' said Alex. Using a paper napkin he removed it from his shirt pocket. It was of dull, plain wood, and bore no marking of any kind.

They peered at it. 'I'll bet you anything you like it turns out to be the same age,' said Dawn.

'Any idea what that's all about?'

'Search me.' Dawn half smiled. 'Except that you've already done that once today, haven't you?'

'Not as thoroughly as I'd have liked,' said Alex. 'I'm sure there are a few more surprises in store.'

'More than you'll ever know,' said Dawn.

FOURTEEN

That afternoon Alex took a train to Hereford, picked up his car from the garage where it had been repaired, collected some clothes from his flat and drove out to the SAS base at Credenhill. There he went straight to see Lieutenant-Colonel Bill Leonard, the CO. Leonard was expecting him, and the Adjutant showed Alex straight through to the spare, utilitarian office with the steel furniture and the black-and-white photos on the wall.

'So how's it going with the Box investigation?' asked Leonard, pushing away the laptop computer at which he had been tentatively poking. The CO was a short, broad-shouldered Yorkshireman with untidy brown hair, an enquiring blue gaze and fists the size of frozen chickens. A few years back he had played rugby for the army and many of his former opponents still bore the scars to remember him by. Bill Leonard was a far cry, Alex had always considered, from the public-schooled Ruperts who had preceded him. This was one of the reasons why Alex had decided to approach him and to disregard the order from Angela Fenwick not to discuss the Watchman case with his SAS colleagues.

'They're not letting me anywhere near it,' said Alex. 'My job is basically to wait on the sidelines until they find the guy, and then go in and waste him.'

'Are they going to find him?'

'Doubt it. He may be nuts but he's still a lot faster on his feet than they are. They've set up some lookalike in the home of the guy they suspect is next in line, but he'll suss it a mile off.'

Leonard nodded. 'I've seen his file. He looks pretty switched on. Or he certainly was then. You think he'll whack this next bloke?'

'I reckon I can probably cut down the odds of that happening if they'll let me. But you know what they're like.'

'I know exactly what they're like. What *are* you doing?'

'Well, I'm doing what I'm told, which basically means fuck all. The trouble is, I suspect this guy's expecting someone like me to come after him.'

'He'd be a fool if he didn't expect that,' said Leonard, studying his massive fingers. 'You think he'll have a go at you?'

'If I get in his way, yes.'

'You want to draw a Sig or something from the armoury?'

'It might be sensible. What I'd really like to do is speak to anyone who trained him. Are any of those blokes still contactable?'

Leonard frowned. 'It was a fair old time ago, but you could give Frank Wisbeach a ring. His name's in the file as one of the Watchman instructors.'

'Do you know where I could find him?'

'He was driving a minicab in town the last I heard of him, poor old sod. Clarion cabs, I think they're called.'

'It might help to have a word,' said Alex. 'Anything

that gives me an angle on Meehan and on the way his mind might be working.'

'If you do get an inside track, there could be a lot we can learn. About agent stress, breaking points and so on. We need a lot more information on that sort of thing.'

'Well, if I find myself face to face to him, I'll ask him what exactly turned him into a serial killer,' said Alex.

'How many people do you have to take out before they classify you as a serial killer?' Leonard wondered aloud.

Alex shrugged. 'Four, I read. Up to that point you're just a killer. After four you're serial.'

Leonard smiled wolfishly. 'Like us, you mean?'

It was an hour before Frank Wisbeach returned Alex's call and when he did he was apologetic, explaining that he had been on an airport job. He was free that evening after 7.30, he told Alex, and they arranged to meet for a drink at a small pub on the outskirts of the city.

Driving back into town, Alex wondered what he should do about Sophie. For starters give her a call, he thought, and dialled her home number on his mobile. It rang unchecked; she hadn't put the answering machine on. He tried her mobile number but got the message service.

He didn't want to leave a message, he wanted to speak to her directly. Something about the morning's encounter with Dawn Harding had made him want very much to sort things out with her.

Later, he told himself. Later.

The Black Dog was not a pub that many Regiment members went to and this was why Alex had chosen it.

It was a dim, dingy sort of place with an over-loud jukebox and the sour smell of spilt lager and cheese-and-onion crisps. Frank Wisbeach arrived shortly before eight and Alex was a little shocked by the sight of the gaunt figure in the cheap windcheater who had been his first Close Quarter Battle instructor.

'How are you, son?' asked Wisbeach, transferring a crumpled inch of roll-up to his left hand for the duration of their handshake. 'I heard they made you an officer.'

'They did,' said Alex. 'I'll be shuffling paper for the next few years.'

'Don't knock it, son – think of the pension. You're knackered before your time in this game. If it's not your knees it's your back. All those bloody Bergan runs.'

Wisbeach certainly looked knackered, Alex reflected as he bought the first round. It was the old story – that of the regimental hard-man who couldn't quite hack it without the army's visible and invisible support systems. Frank Wisbeach had left the SAS at the end of the 1980s after a distinguished career as an NCO which had taken in Oman, the Falklands War and several tours of Northern Ireland, and signed up with a private security company with training contracts in the Middle East. Alex was uncertain of the details, but the word was that a big client had then defaulted on months of back pay and expenses, bankrupting the company and several of its employees.

A series of bodyguarding jobs followed, but by then Wisbeach had been too old a dog to learn the ways of spoilt pop stars and bored Arab wives. A short fuse, an unwillingness to suffer fools gladly and a taste for the drink had ensured a swift professional decline, and by the mid-1990s he was living in a caravan and manning the doors in a provincial nightclub.

'So what brought you back to Hereford?' Alex asked, placing the other man's pint of bitter in front of him. 'I heard you were down in Luton.'

'Marriage, mate. Marriage brought me back. I came up for a reunion with a few of the lads from the Regimental Association and somewhere along the line – I can't quite remember the details but a pub lock-in was certainly involved – I found myself proposing to Della. Arse on her like a four-tonner but a nice smile and a half-share in a hairdressing business on Fortescue Road. Frank, my lad, I thought, it's time you settled down. Ever drink so much you pissed yourself?'

'No, I don't think so.'

'I was doing that most nights. And shitting myself too at weekends. There comes a point you review your options.'

Alex nodded sympathetically.

'So I married Della – fuck knows what she sees in me, but there you go – and picked up a bit of cabbing to help with the bills. Best thing I ever did. You ever been married?'

Alex shook his head.

'Take my advice, son, save it. Let the army look after you for as long as it wants to and then find a woman with a comfy pair of tits on her and a bit of money of her own, and hang your fucking boots up.'

'Sounds good,' said Alex.

'It is good, mate,' said Wisbeach, one-handedly rolling himself another cigarette. 'It is good.'

The deftness of the gesture reminded Alex of the skilful combat instructor that the older man had once been. 'You taught me a lot, Frank.'

Wisbeach shrugged and put a match to his roll-up. 'You were a good soldier, son. Saw that straight away.'

'That's not what you said at the time!'

'Well, you've got to dish out the old bollocks, haven't you. That's what you're there for on Training Wing.'

Alex smiled. 'I guess. Do you remember a guy called Joe Meehan?'

Sparks of wariness appeared in the other man's eyes. He seemed to sink into his cigarette smoke. 'It's a long time since I heard that name mentioned. A very long time.'

'You trained him, didn't you?'

'Who wants to know?'

'Bill Leonard suggested I speak to you.'

Wisbeach nodded slowly. 'Did he indeed. What's the whisper on the lad you mentioned, then?'

Alex wondered how much to confide. Sober, Wisbeach retained the Special Forces' soldier's habit of discretion. He hadn't even admitted to knowing Meehan. But pissed-up . . . 'The whisper is that he went over the water and they turned him.'

Wisbeach looked Alex in the eye and Alex saw from the slow freeze of his expression that the former NCO had guessed what he had been ordered to do. Knew that he was looking for Meehan in order to kill him.

For several moments neither man spoke. Above their heads, a pseudo-Victorian fan paddled stale cigarette smoke around the ceiling. On the jukebox, All Saints sang in mournful harmony.

'I'm sorry for the both of you,' Wisbeach said eventually, regarding his nicotined fingers with a kind of depthless exhaustion. 'There's no fucking end to it all, is there?'

179

'No,' Alex agreed. 'There isn't.'

'How will you . . .'

'I don't know,' Alex said. 'I just have to locate him.'

Wisbeach seemed to come to a decision. 'Joe Meehan was very good,' he said briskly. 'Technically you couldn't touch him. He was one of those people weapons always worked for. I was the same, so I knew it when I saw it. Mentally, too, he was very tough. Not in a laugh-it-off sort of way like most Regiment blokes – more like one of those Palestinian or Tamil Tiger suicide bombers. He was a true believer, if you know what I mean.'

'Was that a strength or a weakness?'

'Well, you wouldn't have wanted to go out on the piss with him, put it like that. He was a total loner and dead serious all the time. But then we weren't training stand-up comedians, we were training secret agents and assassins. In fact, I felt sorry for the poor bastard.'

'Why?'

'Because guys like that always destroy themselves in the end. They just bash on and on, never giving up, until there's nothing left of them.' He stared at the huddle of customers near the window and took a deep swallow of his beer. 'I'm told they're burying young Hammond in the morning.'

'That's right,' Alex confirmed.

Wisbeach shook his head. 'Africa, eh. What a fucking dump of a place to cop it. Get you another?'

'Yeah. Same again please.'

Wisbeach made his way to the bar. As he returned with the two full glasses three teenagers wearing earrings and flashy sports gear pushed roughly past him, spilling both drinks. None bothered to look round or to apologise.

'Excuse me, lads,' said Wisbeach mildly, turning to them. 'Bit of an accident. Do you mind filling up these glasses?'

The three looked round, incredulous and sniggering. 'Fuck off, Grandpa,' said the heaviest, whose doughy features were topped by a greasy centre parting.

Bloody hell, thought Alex. Here we go. 'Forget it, Frank,' he called out across the room.

But the ex-NCO was not of a mind to forget it, and placed the spilt drinks carefully on the bar. 'Come on, lads,' he said, the ghost of a smile touching his features. 'Don't let's spoil the evening with bad manners.'

At waist level, where the barman couldn't have seen it even if he'd been looking, there was the flash of a blade.

'You heard me,' said greasy-head. 'Now *fuck off*!'

Wisbeach frowned, as if disappointed. Then a heavy-knuckled hand shot out, grabbed the knife-wielder's neck and squeezed hard. There was a moment's absolute stillness. The Baha Boys boomed on the jukebox.

Wisbeach's knuckles tightened. The knife dropped to the floor and its owner's mouth snapped convulsively open, issuing a spray of half-chewed potato crisps and phlegm on to Wisbeach's sleeve.

The ex-NCO grinned. 'Good here, isn't it?' he said to the other two louts. His tone was conversational. For the first time that evening, thought Alex, the old bugger looked genuinely cheerful.

As anoxia kicked in, greasy-head's eyes crossed, the shiny nylon of his Adidas track pants darkened with urine and he sank half-conscious to his knees. When Wisbeach finally released him he lay retching and sobbing on the floor beneath the bar. If the barman had noticed anything, he showed no sign of having done so.

'Two pints please, lads,' Wisbeach said quietly, addressing the two survivors of the incident. 'You can bring them over to our table.'

Stunned by the sight of their leader's humiliation, they nodded their agreement.

'Better?' Alex smiled when they had taken delivery of their drinks.

'Much,' said Wisbeach. He leaned forward. 'Listen, son, don't go around saying you got this from me, but if you really want to know about Joe Meehan, the person to talk to is Denzil Connolly. Denzil was on one of those Khmer Rouge RWW training packages with me – a really shit-hot instructor – and he was in charge of Meehan at Tregaron before they dropped him over the water or whatever the hell they did with the poor sod. The two of them spent two or three months living in each others' pockets. So if anyone knew him . . .'

'Any idea where I'll find Connolly?'

'Sorry, mate. Not a clue.'

Alex nodded and the two men drank their beers in silence.

'Want another?' asked Alex eventually.

'I won't, thanks,' Wisbeach replied. 'I've got a couple more hours' driving.' He stood up, gaunt and tall, and extended a hand to Alex. 'Fuck of a business, son.'

'Yours or mine?'

The ex-NCO smiled. 'Watch yourself, OK?'

FIFTEEN

Five minutes later Alex was walking towards Hereford city centre. The encounter had depressed him, Don Hammond's funeral was tomorrow and he felt like cheering himself up.

As he left the outskirts of the city the streets got busier. There was a slight drizzle but this hadn't deterred the good-time crowd and noisy groups were swinging from bar to bar along the shining pavements, anxious to pour their salaries down their throats as rapidly and with as much shouting and laughter as possible. As the noise and the Friday night smell of beer and cheap perfume swallowed him up, Alex felt his spirits lift. A fat blonde girl winked at him and her friends giggled and screeched – he recognised them as part of the troopy-groupie crowd that often hung out at The Inkerman in the hope of being 'trapped' by young SAS troopers.

'Yo, Alex!' It was Andy Maddocks from 'D' Squadron and Lance Wilford of the RWW, dressed to kill in their civvy going-out clothes.

'Hey!' said Alex, moving out of the way of the lurching crowd on the pavement. 'What are you flash buggers doing back here?'

'Big turnaround after the hostage-rescue,' said Andy Maddocks. 'They're sending another squadron out next week.'

'And the RWW team?'

Lance Wilford shrugged. 'You disappeared, Don's dead, Ricky Sutton's having his arse mended in hospital . . . I guess they felt they ought to send in a new lot. Give the SL government their money's worth.'

Alex nodded. 'They pulled me out for a liaison job,' he told the other two men in answer to their unspoken question. 'I'm up here for Don's funeral tomorrow.'

The others nodded soberly and then, brightening, Maddocks turned to Alex. 'Why not join us for a few bevvies? And possibly a chat about the weather with a trio of nymphomaniac nurses, preferably still in their uniforms?'

'And suspender-belts,' added Lance wistfully.

'Sounds good to me,' said Alex.

A few minutes later they were crammed into a smoky corner table with pints in front of them. Andy, unwilling to waste time, was craning his head from side to side, looking for spare women.

'I thought you were married, Andy,' murmured Alex.

'Separated. Wendy binned me when the squadron got back from Kosovo.'

'Any particular reason?'

'Mental cruelty's what she told the lawyer. Which I suppose is as good a way as any of saying that she was shagging a footballer.'

'A footballer? You're kidding?'

'No, she and some friend of hers who goes out with one of the reserves took to going to all the United home games. With predictable fucking consequences.'

'Manchester United?' asked Lance.

'No, you womble, Hereford United.'

Lance reflected. 'I was going to say, if it'd been a Man U player it'd almost've been worth it. I'd let Ryan Giggs shag my wife.'

'You haven't got a wife. Giggsy wouldn't want to shag any woman that'd marry you. What'd he want to bother with some slag from . . .'

'Are you calling my future wife a slag?'

'Well, she is, isn't she? Be honest.'

They all laughed, Lance loudest of all.

This is good, thought Alex. This is real.

'So, do you reckon you'll be getting any Hereford United tickets?' Lance asked, after a short drinking break.

He ducked just in time to avoid Andy's fist.

'Where did the mental cruelty come in?' asked Alex.

'Told Wendy I didn't want kids,' said Andy. 'Couldn't bear the thought of having a son or a daughter who lost its dad. It's one thing being killed, it's another lying there knowing you're going to break your child's heart.'

'So why d'you marry her in the first place?'

'Price she put on her virtue. No white dress, no snakey-snakey.'

Alex nodded. 'Where did you go on your honeymoon?'

'Belfast,' said Andy. 'With the rest of the squadron . . . Lance, mate, I think we're in business. Go and ask those three to come over. Her in the blue top and the two with her.'

'Why me? You go!'

'You're a fucking corporal, now get your arse over there.'

Alex would have said it was impossible to get anyone else round the table but somehow the three managed to jam themselves in. One of them, a cheerful, round-faced girl with what Frank Wisbeach would without question have called 'comfy tits', was practically sitting on his knee.

'Whassat?' she asked, squirming uncomfortably.

'My mobile,' said Alex apologetically. 'What's your name?'

'Gail,' said the girl, snapping her lighter beneath a king-size Pall Mall. She smelt of make-up and Pernod and synthetic perfume and her hair – inches from his face – was a curtain of wheatish blonde, as flat as if it had been ironed. Next to him, Andy Maddocks was very seriously informing the girl in the blue top that the three of them were gay.

'Bollocks!' said the girl in the blue top. 'We know what you are. We sussed you ten minutes ago from the tans.'

'And the muscles,' said Gail, reaching across the table to tweak Lance's tattooed bicep.

'And the crap haircuts,' volunteered the third girl to shrieks from the other two. 'We're not fucking stupid.'

'It was worth a try,' said Andy. 'I was going to suggest you try and convert us to heterosexuality.'

'And just how would we do that?' asked the girl in the blue top.

'Well . . .' began Andy.

For an hour the six of them sat, drank and laughed. Alex could feel himself getting drunker and drunker but the fact didn't worry him in the least. He had never been a regular pub-goer but right now he was having the best time that he could remember. This was the reality, this smoky bar corner and the press of the crowd and the laughter of his mates and the weight of Gail's thigh against his and the tableful of empty glasses. If he was going to take his officer status seriously, he supposed glumly, he was going to have to wind this sort of activity down.

So how should he play it? Up or out? Stay with the army in the knowledge that the best was behind him or bale out and take his chances in civvy street? The latter sounded more tempting but what would his life actually consist of, given that soldiering was the only trade he knew? Babysitting overpaid celebrities who – at best – would treat him as a paid accessory? Waiting in the rain outside the fashionable restaurants where Sophie and her friends went? He couldn't see himself taking that route. He didn't want to end up like Frank Wisbeach, taking his frustrations out on delinquent teenagers.

Contract soldiering, perhaps. Working for the highest bidder. Fucking up the lives of third-world citizens on behalf of multinationals like Shell or Monsanto?

All in all, he thought, he'd rather go back to Clacton and take the garage off his dad's hands. But then he couldn't quite see Sophie hunched up against the sea wind eating haddock and chips from the bag, or chucking a rubber bone for the dog, or watching *EastEnders*.

Sophie. He should give her a bell.

'You're a quiet one, aren't you,' said Gail. 'You haven't said a word in ten minutes.'

'Sorry,' he said. 'I was thinking.'

'What about?'

'The future, I suppose.'

'Well, we could start off with another drink.' She glanced at her two friends, who were subtly but definitely paired off with Andy and Lance.

'Same again?' he asked her. 'Pernod and black?'

'Yeah. I'll come with you.'

On their unsteady way to the bar, he found his arm encircling her waist and her body moving into alignment with his. He felt her hip-joint articulating beneath his hand, the soft weight of her breast against his side.

'You're an officer, your mate said.'

'Er, yeah.'

'You don't sound like an officer.'

He grinned. 'What do I sound like?'

She frowned and pouted up her lips. 'Oh . . . I don't know. Like the others, I s'pose.'

'Well, that's what I am like.'

'You're not, though. They're, like, dead laddish and up for a laugh, and you're not like that at all. You just pretend to be.' She narrowed her eyes, leant against him and lowered her voice. 'I bet you're a right hard bastard. Have you got a girlfriend? Don't answer that – of course you have. Just don't tell me about her.'

'As long as you don't tell me about your boyfriend.'

'I haven't got a boyfriend.' The crowd propelled them forward against the bar. 'I've got a bloody husband, worse luck.'

Alex turned to stare at her but at that moment the barman materialised in front of them, eyebrow raised. Alex ordered himself a sixth pint and a Jameson's whiskey chaser, and Gail her fifth Pernod and black-currant. 'Married?' he asked flatly.

'He's away. With someone else.' She glanced up at him. 'Don't ask, just be nice to me.'

She was pretty, he thought. Pretty eyes. And a mouth and body to chase the ghosts away. He slipped his hand under the bottom of her sweater, felt the taut waistband of her jeans and the warm flesh above.

The drinks arrived and they backed away from the bar.

'Where d'you live?' he asked her.

'I don't want to go there,' she said. She touched his cheek with the back of her fingers. 'What about you?'

'Walking distance.'

In the flat he bolted the door and closed the curtains as she walked slowly around, touching things.

'There's dust everywhere.' She smiled.

'I've been away. Coffee? And I've got some Bushmills somewhere?'

'Sounds good.'

In the kitchen area the strip light was on the flicker. Alex was kissing her against the wall and she was running her hands up his back when the kettle boiled.

In the bedroom there was a jumble of mostly green kit against the wall – waterproofs, thermals, medical packs, a water purifier, sleeping bags and stuff sacks – into which, earlier that day, Alex had tossed the shoulder-holstered Glock pistol and accessories he'd signed out of the armoury at Credenhill.

If Gail noticed this, she made no comment, just lowered her drink and kicked off her shoes. 'Music?'

In answer Alex directed her to the miniature sound system and pile of CDs that sat, as dusty as everything else, on a shelf.

'This is the strangest collection I've ever seen,' she said wonderingly. 'Miles Davis, Britney Spears,

Johann Sebastian Bach, the Teletubbies, *Bridget Jones's Diary . . .*'

'It belonged to a guy who got killed last year,' said Alex. 'I think there were some Christmas presents for his family among it.'

She shook her head. 'The lives you people lead.' She switched the system on and selected the Britney Spears CD.

On the bed, or rather on the double mattress that served Alex as a bed, they undressed each other. She was wearing a tight lilac sweater which she pulled away from her face as he took it off so as not to smear her make-up. Beneath it, she amply filled a black lace bra. Smiling, she allowed him to search behind her back for a moment before pointing to the rosebud clasp at the front. He undid it and lowered his head. Her fingers knotted in his hair.

Finally they were both naked. She was pale-skinned and soft as ice cream, and there was a dreamy-eyed passivity about her which he found a vast relief after Sophie. She was his – all of her, unconditionally and for as long as he wanted.

Breathing in her muskily synthetic aura – part pub, part Boots perfume counter – he ran his hands over the impossible softness of her breasts. When he reached the inside of her thighs she gasped and drew her knees apart.

She tasted, in some curious way, of Alex's memories of his childhood, of sweat and closeness and sea spray, of the time before he had killed anyone. She moved like the sea too – slowly and from somewhere deep within herself. After a time he moved back up her body, manoeuvred himself inside her and forgot about Sophie altogether.

SIXTEEN

She left early, while he pretended to be asleep. He woke for a second time to find a note on the pillow and a daytime telephone number – a work number, he guessed.

Why had she left? Not wanting to spoil things with the awkwardness of a morning after? He smiled – in many ways theirs had been the perfect relationship.

He shook his head and immediately wished he hadn't. It felt as if there was a cannon ball rolling around in it. The inside of his mouth was parched and sour, his stomach felt uneasy and he had a morbid thirst. Not for the first time he reflected that it wasn't the drinks that made you pissed that fucked you up, it was the completely unnecessary ones that you drank when you were already pissed. It was those Scotches that you ended up with just because it felt right, somehow, to wind the evening up with a glass of spirits in your hand.

The thought of whisky made his gorge rise, and he staggered to the bathroom and the cold tap. On the way he trod heavily on his old Casio Neptune watch – it had survived worse – and arrived at the sink just in time to throw up. Don Hammond, an enthusiastic drinker who had always tried to persuade Alex to put in more pub hours, would have been proud of him.

It wasn't until he had showered and dressed that he remembered the Glock. It was still there, thank God, as were all the heavy little boxes of 9mm ammunition. What would have happened if any of it had left the flat in the pocket of a girl he'd picked up in a pub, he shuddered to think. He'd always been the first to take the piss out of those Box clowns who had their laptops nicked from their cars.

The Glock that he had chosen was the model 34. In the past he'd used the 17, the most popular 9mm Glock model. It held up to nineteen rounds, hardly ever jammed and in general was a dream to use. The 34, developed for competition use, was basically the same gun but with the accuracy advantage of another inch of barrel. It wasn't the easiest weapon to conceal, but it still weighed in at just under two pounds fully loaded and if it came to aimed shots, Alex had decided, that extra inch between the sights might just make all the difference. He had fired off a few magazines on the range and had been stunned by the weapon's performance, given that the general rule for automatics was that at a range of more than twenty yards you were lucky if you could hit anything smaller than a front door.

From the armoury he'd also drawn a silencer and a laser dot-marker sight, which he reckoned ought to cover most eventualities.

And a knife. A standard-issue Government Recon commando knife with a 6.25-inch blade. The instinct that Alex had about Meehan was that he wasn't a firearms man. Firearms were crude, noisy and remote – he would regard it a failure to have to resort to them. Meehan, Alex was sure from his modus operandi so far, was a close-up man. A blade man.

Retrieving his watch, he saw that it was almost 9.30 and rang Dawn. She was no party girl. She would be up and about.

Her mobile rang twice and then she answered it.

'Up and about, Miss Harding?' he asked her. 'Bright-eyed and bushy-tailed?'

'Is that Captain Temple?' she enquired in a brisk, businesslike way that told Alex immediately that she was not alone.

'Yes. It is. Can I talk, or are you . . .'

'No, I'm not. What do you want?'

'I just wanted to make sure you were enjoying this' – he peered through the curtains – 'rather damp morning. And not fooling around in bed. Did you tell me what his name was, by the way?'

'Look, Captain Temple, if you've got something to say . . .'

'I thought I'd let you know where I was. In case you were missing me.'

'In your dreams. Where are you?'

'Hereford. I'm chasing up one of our man's ex-teachers.'

'You think that'll be useful?'

'I think it's all we've got, for the moment. I'll keep you abreast.'

'You do that. Oh, and, um, the object we found. It was the age we thought it might be. And bearing the right prints. Congratulations, Captain.'

The phone went dead. Why did he have this irresistible desire to wind Dawn Harding up? Alex wondered. Because she was such a straight arrow? Such a company girl? And whom had she been sleeping with, anyway? Some keen young computer buff from Thames House, no doubt. Some pillar of the

Orienteering or Mountain Biking Club. Alex could just see him, weedy and pale, leaning back against the pillows, having a moody post-shag Dunhill. Except that he wouldn't smoke. He'd probably be a vegetarian. A vegan. Drink ground-up acorns instead of coffee.

By ten, having gulped down a half-pint glass of lager from the store in the fridge (an old morning-after trick of Don Hammond's) Alex was feeling a little better. Ready, in fact, to undertake part two of the standard hangover cure – a full English fried breakfast.

More cheerful now, and gratified that the finger-prints on the pencil stub had conclusively linked Meehan with the killings, Alex made his way to a café. The downside to the discovery was his certainty that the find had been intended by Meehan. It had almost been a greeting to his pursuer.

For all his instincts concerning the Watchman, Alex mused, he really had no idea where the man might be holing up. One possibility was that he was moving around the fringes of one of the larger cities with transients and unaccountables – squatting, perhaps, or moving between cheap hostels and bed-and-breakfast houses, or hanging out with travellers. If in trouble, the rule went, seek out those who also have some-thing to hide. The Watchman, however, also had to avoid the Irish Catholic communities among whom visiting PIRA players moved, so perhaps he was avoiding the cities.

A second possibility was that he had constructed himself a completely false identity – driving licence, bank accounts, credit cards and the rest of it – and was living in a rented flat and passing himself off as a salesman or some other itinerant professional in a small provincial town.

But something told Alex that this was not the man's style. Frank Wisbeach's words reinforced the idea of Meehan as the victim of some grandiose delusion. A man of unwavering seriousness, the old NCO had said. No detectible sense of humour. A 'true believer'. Alex had met 'true believers' before. The phrase was used to describe soldiers who believed that the purity of their calling somehow singled them out from the rest of humanity. They tended to subscribe to ideas of 'the warrior's path' and 'the mediocrity of civilian life'. 'Green-eyed boys' they'd called them in the Paras. This didn't stop them being good soldiers – quite the opposite in many cases – but it did mean that their behaviour could get a bit weird if unchecked. The Watchman's murder project definitely had the 'true believer' edge to it and it was for this reason that Alex didn't quite believe that the man was pretending to be Mister Average and driving a Ford Escort. It didn't go with the apocalyptic nature of his actions. If he saw himself as some mystical bringer of vengeance (as so many of these nutters seemed to) then he would ensure that his surroundings were appropriately Gothic and elemental. A forest, perhaps. Something like that.

Did he own a vehicle? Probably, but Alex guessed he would use it only sparingly. Vehicles showed up on CCTV, people noticed and remembered them and they were powerful transmitters of forensic evidence. Stolen cars were especially bad news if you wanted to keep your head down.

Alex addressed his breakfast – black pudding, bubble and squeak, eggs, beans, mushrooms, two fried slices and a mug of tea. The business.

He was just supposed to do the chopping, he

reminded himself. Fine, except that the only time Five were likely to get anywhere near Meehan was when the former MI5 agent had finished his killing spree and was ready to give himself up. Killing Meehan at that point would be little more than a gesture.

Right now Meehan would be watching Widdowes, just as he had watched Fenn and Gidley. He'd be lying up nearby, entirely aware of the lookalike and the rest of their strategies, waiting for the moment when they stopped fully believing that the attack would come. The moment when they persuaded themselves they had won. And then, with blinding and brutal speed, he would strike.

Alex had to persuade the Box team to let him take over – or at least participate in – the guarding of George Widdowes. He'd have to get the MI5 officer back into his house so that, like a tiger to a tethered goat, Meehan would be drawn to his prey. The idea was a good one. It could work. He'd have to talk to Dawn about it. They would have yet another row. He discovered he was rather looking forward to it.

Don Hammond's funeral was the usual sombre affair. There was an obvious police presence, some blocking off the traffic, with many of the officers carrying side arms.

Less obvious was the standby squadron, who were waiting in Range Rovers at several of the surrounding crossroads, armed with MP5 Heckler and Koch sub-machine guns.

Alex arrived in the dark Principles suit that he used for Regimental funerals and metropolitan area sur-veillance, and was nodded through by the adjutant, also suited. In the church there were somewhere between a hundred and fifty and two hundred people. There were several rows of soldiers from the Credenhill base, all looking uncharacteristically smart in their Number Two uniforms, and in front of them a tight group of friends, relations and other uniformed soldiers surrounded Karen Hammond, Don's widow, and Cathy, his daughter.

Moving hesitantly forward, Alex met Karen's eye. She smiled and beckoned him, and a place was made for him in the row behind her. Silently she reached out her hand and equally silently Alex took it. She's as brave as Don was, he thought, turning to the coffin which stood, flag-draped, in the aisle. On it lay his friend's medals, his blue stable belt and his sand-coloured SAS beret.

Who dares wins.

Not every time, thought Alex, catching sight of eight-year-old Cathy Hammond's grief-whitened face. Not every time.

In the churchyard Alex allowed his attention to wander as the chaplain spoke the now familiar words of the funeral service. His eyes travelled over the bare heads and the bemedalled uniforms, and the relatives' dark coats and suits. Karen and Cathy were both weeping now, and Karen's family pressed protectively around them. The eyes of the other soldiers, for the most part, were downturned. Alex himself felt empty. Tears were not what he owed Don Hammond.

And then, as the three shots were fired over the open grave, Alex's wandering gaze met a pair of eyes that were not downturned – that were levelled with deathly directness at his own. The man, who was wearing a nondescript suit and tie, and had a curiously ageless appearance, was standing on the other side of the grave behind Karen's family, and Alex realised with stunned disbelief that he knew this narrow face and pale unblinking stare, that he had seen photographs of this man in Thames House, that he was standing just three yards away from Joseph Meehan, the Watchman.

As their eyes locked, Alex felt his scalp crawl and his heart slam in his chest. *No, it was impossible.*

Impossible but true. It was Meehan and he had come to scope out his pursuer. In the icy flame of his regard was a challenge, a statement of ruthlessness and contempt. I can come and go as I please, it said – even here, even now, in the secret heart of your world – and there is nothing that you can do to prevent me.

And Meehan was right. At that moment there was nothing in the world that Alex could do. Sympathy for Karen Hammond and the dignity of the occasion paralysed him. He couldn't speak, let alone jump over the open grave and grab the man by the throat.

There was a loud clatter overhead as three Chinook helicopters flew past in formation. Alex held Meehan's pale gaze, but the ranks of mourners shifted as they looked upwards, and when they re-formed, moments later, the cold-eyed face had vanished.

Alex peered desperately over the open grave as the churning helicopter blades faded away, but the fly-past had marked the end of the service. As the Hammond family and their friends moved away from the graveside, the regimental personnel held back, Alex among them. Short of elbowing his way through the uniformed men he was trapped.

Finally, the crowd began to disperse. Moving as fast and as forcefully as he was able, given the circumstances, Alex made his way to the churchyard exit.

There was no sign of anyone resembling Meehan either inside or outside. Running to the head of the road he challenged the two uniformed troopers on duty there. Had a man in his mid-thirties just passed them – fair-skinned, dark-haired, five ten, grey suit . . . tough-looking . . .

The words spilt out but the troopers shook their heads. No one like that. No one on his own.

Ignoring the curious stares of the exiting mourners, Alex ran on ahead of the roadblock to the nearest Range Rover and repeated the questions.

Same answer. No one answering that description.

Shit. *Shit*. Had he imagined seeing Meehan? Had the image of the man been preying on his mind to the point where he was beginning to hallucinate? Was Meehan now stalking *him*?

Tucking himself into the roadside, Alex called Dawn on his mobile and – in guarded terms, given that he was using an open line – reported the incident.

'How sure are you that it was him?' Dawn asked.

'Not a hundred per cent. And if it was he could be anywhere by now.'

'Why would he want to show himself like that?'

'Check me out, perhaps. Let me know he can come and go as he pleases.'

Dawn was silent. Alex could tell that she was unconvinced that the man had been Meehan.

'Look,' he went on, 'I've got a possible regimental lead. It's not much but it's a possibility. Someone who knew our man. Someone he might have talked to.'

'Do you need my people's help?'

'No. Leave it to me.'

'OK, then. Keep me informed.'

She broke the connection and Alex looked around.

Several people were staring at him and he self-consciously brushed down his suit. He had meant what he said to Dawn. Meehan could be anywhere by now. There was no chance of catching him without involving the entire Hereford and Worcester police forces and probably not even then. And, if he was honest with himself, he *hadn't* been a hundred per cent sure it was Meehan.

Much more constructive to work out where his base was. There had to be some secret location he returned to between the killings. An inner-city flat? A hostel or bed and breakfast? A caravan park? The only person who might possibly have a clue as to the whereabouts of that location – and it was still a hell of a long shot – was Denzil Connolly. Of those who trained Meehan, according to Frank Wisbeach, Connolly was the only man who really got to know him. If he could find Connolly, Alex reflected, he was in with a chance of finding Meehan. He might, at the very least, learn something about the man he was pursuing.

'Looking for a lift back to camp?'

It was the driver of one of the Range Rovers and Alex accepted gratefully. At the Credenhill base he made his way to the sergeants mess, where he was formally invited in – as an officer, he no longer had the automatic right of entry.

After an SAS funeral there was always a big piss-up. Alex had been to more of these than he cared to remember and if there were ever times that the Regiment genuinely resembled the family it claimed itself to be these were they.

The mess was a large room dominated by a bar and furnished with oxblood Chesterfield furniture. The floor was carpeted in regimental blue and the walls were hung with paintings of former SAS soldiers, captured flags and weapons, and the plaques of foreign units. An impressive collection of silverware was also on display.

Men poured in in groups, animated now and relieved that the austerity and the tears of the funeral were behind them. A sheepishly grinning Ricky Sutton arrived on crutches, newly released from hospital, and was greeted with a ragged cheer. Most of the men headed straight for the bar, and by the time the Hammond contingent and the other wives and relatives were ushered in there were the makings of a fine party.

Alex, still shaken by the incident at the funeral, did not immediately move to join his friends. Seeing Bill Leonard, he cornered him and asked him if he had any idea of Denzil Connolly's whereabouts.

The burly lieutenant-colonel did not look best pleased to be questioned on this subject. Curtly he assured Alex that the Regiment had no contact information of any kind on Denzil Connolly. Then, excusing himself, he moved away.

The Hammond family came in, and Alex was among the group who moved to greet them.

'Don really loved looking for trouble with you fellers,' said Karen, teary-eyed and shaky but somehow still smiling. 'I'd never have tried to take him away from all that.'

'He was the best,' said Alex gently. 'Best soldier. Best mate.'

She wept against his shoulder for a few moments, then wiped her eyes and put on a brave grin. 'Where's that posh girl of yours, then? Don told me she was a smasher!'

'She couldn't come,' said Alex. 'She got stuck in London. Work.'

Karen smiled. 'Well, don't leave it too long. You'll need a nice smart wife when they make you a general.'

'Yeah, well, it hasn't quite got to that yet.'

'Don't leave it too long, Alex. Promise me.'

He smiled. 'I won't, Karen. I promise.'

For now, though, there was something he had to follow up and he made his way to a knot of old lags who were clustering around the RSM at the bar.

'Afternoon, Alex, you warry old bugger. I mean sir,' said the RSM, addressing his beer glass. 'Word is you enjoyed yourself last night!'

The others smirked.

'I may have taken a drink,' admitted Alex. 'Or two.'

'In mixed company?'

'That's not impossible either.'

The RSM nodded. 'Well, you look like shite today. Serves you right. Poor old Don, eh.'

'Poor old Don,' Alex echoed. 'He had a very bad last minute and I hope Karen never hears the details of that. But you should have seen him hanging out of that chopper with the SLR and Kalashnikov rounds screaming around him, blazing away with the old five point five. Talk about Death from Above.'

The RSM nodded approvingly. 'I hear you didn't do so badly yourself?'

Alex shrugged. 'We were lucky. We could easily have lost a lot more guys. Next time they should just let the hostages get eaten or chopped to pieces or whatever.'

'You said it,' said the RSM, wordlessly handing his

glass back for refilling. He glanced at Alex's suit. 'Heard you'd been pulled out of Freetown ahead of time. Spooky business, I heard.'

'That sort of thing. I'm trying to get hold of someone you may be in touch with. Denzil Connolly.'

The NCOs looked at each other.

'Long time since I heard that name,' said a sniper team leader named Stevo. His tone was careful.

Alex said nothing. There was no communications web more intricate, secretive and subtle than that which existed between British army sergeants. He had been part of it once, but it was closed to him now. He could only file his request and wait.

'There was some strange stuff with Den Connolly,' said the RSM, glancing at Alex. 'And that looks like an empty glass in your hand. I thought you officers were supposed to set an example.'

For the time being, Alex knew, that was as far as things would go. An overfull pint glass was handed splashily over. Someone spoke through a microphone over the laughter and hubbub. There was going to be an auction of Don Hammond's kit, with the proceeds going to Karen and Cathy.

Two hours later Alex's head was singing with Stella Artois and the shock of seeing Meehan at the funeral had receded. Stepping out into the sudden silence of the evening drizzle, he made his way across the tarmac to the guardhouse. After the original Sterling Lines barracks in Hereford, the Credenhill camp seemed a vast high-tech sprawl – more like a software park or an airport than anything else. Sticking his head into the guardhouse, he asked if someone could ring for a minicab to take him back into Hereford. As it turned out, one of the duty policemen was going that way and offered him a ride.

Denzil Connolly. The name bounced back and forth in Alex's mind. In case anyone just happened to remember anything, he'd left his mobile number with Stevo and the RSM.

There were two ways to catch a predator like Meehan. One was to peg out a bait and lure him into the open, the other was to find his lair and stake it out.

If necessary, Alex intended to try both.

Back at the flat, he rang Sophie. Her home number was engaged, her mobile switched off. Depressed by the afternoon's events, fuzzy-headed with alcohol, he considered giving Gail a ring. For a long and tempting moment he felt her body against him, soft and unresisting.

At the last minute he decided otherwise. Changing into a sweat top and shorts, he made his way outside to the pavement and began jogging towards the outskirts of the city. It was raining harder now, the light was beginning to go and most of the shops were closed. The pavements were all but deserted, but once again Alex was visited by the unpleasant suspicion that he was being watched.

Get a grip, he told himself. *Paranoia isn't going to help*.

Soon he was on an empty road leading southwards. The rain, cold and clean, lashed his face and hands, his breathing steadied and found its rhythm, and his mind began to clear. He had to watch his step, he told himself, or at least be a bit more discreet. Last night he would probably get away with on the grounds that his best friend had just been killed and everyone was entitled to go crazy from time to time, but if he made a habit of it people were going to start thinking he was losing his grip. And when that occurred, well, you only had to look at Frank Wisbeach to see what happened when a good soldier started to unravel.

Fired with a new resolve, he pushed himself hard on the five miles or so back to Hereford. The rain continued, it was lancing down now as the light faded, and he could feel the beginnings of a new blister on one heel.

Back in the flat he showered and tried Sophie again. Same result: home engaged, mobile switched off. Quickly he dressed, packed a suitcase, locked up the flat and climbed into the pearl-white Karman-Ghia. Pointing the bonnet towards the Ledbury Road, he set out for London. He was glad to have the car back and to feel the cheerful growl of the 1835cc engine as the rain lashed the windscreen in front of him. Ray Temple had accepted the thirty-year-old shell in lieu of a debt two years earlier and rebuilt the car from the wheels up, selling it to his son for the altogether bargain price of £5000.

The car could really move, but on this occasion Alex made sure to keep well within the speed limit. Whatever the alcohol limit was these days, he was uneasily certain that he was in excess of it. He'd only had a couple of pints at the funeral – well, perhaps it had been three – but there had probably been a fair bit left over from the night before. Having said that, he'd run the best part of ten miles before starting to drive, which would have burnt off a few units, surely?

Best to take no chances, to take a leaf out of the Dawn Harding school of motoring. While waiting at traffic lights outside Cirencester he dialled her number. 'So what are you up to?' he asked her.

'What business is that of yours?'

'What's his name, Harding?'

'Grow up, Temple.'

'Can we make a date for tomorrow morning?'

'Any particular reason?'

'Nothing I can talk about on an open line. How about breakfast?'

'OK. Eight o'clock outside my office building.'

The phone went dead.

In Western Avenue, as he entered London, he spotted a rose seller standing in a lay-by. He was unlikely to find any florists open, Alex thought, so he bought twelve quid's worth – the rest of the man's stock. Mindful of Dawn's words, he took off the cellophane wrappers and bunched the blooms all together. The roses were pretty knackered-looking and certainly had no scent to speak of – they still looked as if they'd been bought in a lay-by, in other words – but they were better than nothing.

Half an hour later he was parking the Karman-Ghia in Pavilion Road, off Sloane Street. The rain had stopped and the pavements and the roads shone silver beneath the street lights. Tucking the roses under one arm and tidying his hair with the fingers of the other hand, he made his way towards the building containing Sophie's flat.

Glancing up at her window he saw her, wearing the white towelling bathrobe that she'd stolen from the Crillon Hotel in Paris. She was in her bedroom, staring out eastwards over the city. And then a second dressing-gowned figure appeared beside her, placed an arm round her shoulder.

Who the fuck was that, Alex asked himself, his heart plummeting. Stella, perhaps? But he already knew it wasn't Stella. Running back to the car he rummaged inside his travel bag, pulled out a pair of image-stabilised Zeiss binoculars and focused on the two figures.

It was a bloke. Some fashionably stubbled fucker. And very much at home, thank you very much, with his arm round Sophie, who looked like the cat who'd had the cream. Well, she certainly hadn't wasted any bloody time, had she?

Stupid bastard, he thought, hurling the roses up the middle of Pavilion Road.

Stupid bastard!

SEVENTEEN

'So,' said Dawn, stirring the cup of brick-red tea that the café owner had just placed in front of her. 'Is this going to be a long argument or a short one?'

'I've paid for a long one,' said Alex.

She regarded him bleakly. His call to her after the funeral, Alex realised, had counted as a mark against him. She thought that he was getting flaky, that he had started seeing things.

'Look, I've got a hell of a lot to get on with. What is it you want?'

'I want to talk to you about George Widdowes. I don't think your lookalike idea is going to work. I think the only way we're going to stop Meehan is by setting a trap. By putting the real man back into the house as bait.'

'No way. We're on top of the Widdowes business. The man we've got looks very like George indeed. He's wearing George's clothes, driving George's car into London every day . . .'

'Meehan will have guessed that you'd try that,' said Alex impatiently. 'He'll have checked him out.'

'Only from a distance, going by our find at the Gidleys'. That tree must have been a hundred and fifty yards from the house. He'll never know the difference from that sort of range.'

'The tree was a general OP for watching security procedures and checking out the dogs. He'll have had a closer look than that at Craig Gidley before killing him, believe me. Probably set himself up at the side of the road earlier in the day and checked him in through the gates. He knew Gidley, just like he knows Widdowes. A glance would have been enough. And a glance has probably been enough to tell him that you're using a lookalike right now. That's why nothing's happened. That and the fact that the area is almost certainly swarming with Box employees with sniper's rifles. You have to remember that our man's served in Belfast and South Armagh. He's got a nose for that sort of thing.'

Her silence told him that he was right about the concealed marksmen.

She placed her teaspoon carefully in her saucer and frowned. 'Look, at least as things stand we're keeping George Widdowes alive.'

'Sooner or later Meehan's going to discover where you're keeping him,' said Alex. 'He'll follow him back from work. There are only so many exits from Thames House and yes, I know about the underground car parks and the tunnel and the rest of it and so, sooner or later, will he. Meehan will stake them all out, one by one. It may take a month, it may take him a year, but sooner or later he'll do it. He'll catch Widdowes leaving the building and follow him back to wherever it is you've put him. Where is it that Widdowes lives, officially?'

'Hampshire,' said Dawn.

'All these guys tied up in Hampshire while Widdowes goes off his head in some crummy safe house in Docklands or Alperton or Gants Hill, waiting for a bullet between the eyes? At the moment Meehan's calling all the shots – we've got to stop retreating and take control of this thing.'

Dawn pursed her lips thoughtfully.

'At least put the idea to Fenwick,' Alex continued. 'And if she agrees in principle, then let's go down to Widdowes' place and check out the possibility of setting up an ambush.'

'I can't promise anything,' she said eventually. 'But tell me what you want to do and I'll put it to the deputy director.'

'Can you please slow down,' said Dawn, 'we're not going for the land speed world record.'

They were heading up the M3 to Hampshire, this time in the Karman-Ghia. Alex had told her that he didn't think he could take another journey with her at the wheel and she had retorted that she was perfectly happy to be driven – it would make a change, in fact.

To Alex's surprise – and to Dawn's irritation, he suspected – Angela Fenwick had agreed to his request to recce Widdowes' house with a view to returning the agent there and luring Meehan into a trap.

George Widdowes lived a short distance outside the village of Bishopstoke in the Itchen valley. Longwater Lodge, where he lived alone, had once been attached to the much larger Longwater House, now a management college. Surrounded by trees and shrubberies, and set back some fifty metres from the road, the lodge was bordered at its far end by a carrier stream of the River Itchen, which flowed through the grounds of the main house.

Alex and Dawn had parked a quarter of a mile away outside the Pied Bull pub in the village's main street and had ambled out towards Longwater Lodge as if they were a young couple who, on impulse perhaps, had taken the day off. After the rain of the previous day the fields had a summery freshness and the steady hum of bees rose above the grumble of the distant main road.

The Lodge looked empty. The curtains were drawn, no cars stood outside it and a brand-new For Sale sign stood at its gate. The sign had been Dawn's idea and she had somehow ensured that it was up within the hour. Any enquiries to the London estate agent whose name it bore would have been met by the explanation that while the owner of the property wished to announce his intention to sell in the near future, the agency had not yet received full instructions.

Alex had been surprised by the speed with which the idea had been implemented and that Winchester estate agents were quite so receptive to sweet-talk from the security services. 'Oh, we've got friends everywhere,' Dawn had glibly informed him. 'We're quite big players in the property market.'

The purpose of the sign had been to enable her and Alex to reconnoitre the property. If we want to have a good look, she had told him, then we might as well do it the easy way and walk straight up the drive. Anybody watching will simply assume that we're a couple who are interested in buying.

Turning his back on Longwater Lodge, Alex scanned the surrounding countryside. Still green cornfields bordered by hedgerows and oak trees on the higher ground; water-meadows in the valley, with willows and poplars shading the river. Hundreds of acres visible and a thousand places where an experienced man might be lying up. The Watchman was out there somewhere, keeping the house under observation, but you could send in a battalion of paratroopers with dogs and helicopters and still not find him. With the first indications of a search he would simply fade away.

Alex stared over the road into the sunlit green valley. He knew he would never be offered an obvious give-away like the flash of a binocular lens, but for an optimistic moment or two he stared anyway.

From the humpback bridge crossing the river, the two of them examined the Lodge and its surroundings. The property comprised about an acre and a half in total. The road on which they stood swept right-handed round the front of the garden, and was separated from it by a wall of about five feet in height and a neatly clipped yew hedge.

'That's where our people go in at night,' Dawn told him. 'They climb over the wall once it's dark and keep the place under surveillance through night-vision goggles.'

'How do they get here?'

'By Land Rover. Park up a hundred yards away round the corner.'

'He'll have sussed them out on night one,' said Alex. 'You can count on that.'

Dawn shrugged. 'You may be right.'

'I am right,' said Alex. 'He's almost certainly watching us right now. Give us a kiss!'

'In your dreams.'

'I mean it. That's what normal couples do when they're looking at houses. They hold hands. They kiss each other. It means they . . .'

'I know perfectly well what it means.' Turning, she kissed him glancingly on the left cheek.

He frowned. 'Oh, come on, Bunnykins, you can do better than that. Think how happy we could be here. Think of little Bethany and Jordan and Kylie running into the house with bunches of flowers and bouncing on our bed on Saturday mornings. Think of the songs you'll sing as you bake the bread and scrub the floor. Think of the jam you'll make.'

'You're sick, Temple.'

'I'm not sick, Bunnykins, I just want a proper kiss. I'm not necessarily talking tongues at this stage, but I do think it should be convincing.'

'Don't be disgusting. And stop calling me Bunnykins.'

'I will if you kiss me right now, mouth to mouth, for a minimum of five seconds. If not, I'm afraid you go on being Bunnykins.'

With a long-suffering sigh she turned to him and placed her arms round his neck. Her mouth was very soft. She even closed her eyes.

'There,' he said finally. 'That wasn't so bad, was it?'

She was silent for a moment. 'I've had worse,' she said.

He placed his arm round her waist, sensed her body stiffen, then felt an answering arm creep unwillingly round his waist.

'How many marksmen?' he asked.

'Most nights two, I think. One somewhere in the front here, one round the back of the house. I doubt anyone could get past them to the house without being seen.'

'I'm not so sure,' said Alex. 'Let's walk around the garden. Lots of pointing to the ground, please. Lots of saying that's where we'll have the sweet peas and let's put some crocus bulbs in here and oh dear, we'll never get camellias to grow in this chalky soil.'

'You're really determined to make me look and feel absolutely as stupid as possible, aren't you,' she murmured.

'No, I'm not. I'm just trying to stop you looking like an MI5 desk officer – someone Meehan would suss at a glance. Like I said, he's probably watching us right now. If I were him, I'd be. Let's look round the back.'

'What are you hoping to find, exactly?'

'He'll have scouted the place, looking for a way in at night. Somewhere he can get into the property without being bumped by the security people. I'm searching for that way in.'

'Do you know how you'd do it?'

'I'm pretty sure I do but I'd just like to walk around for a bit. What about you? How would you get in?'

'Shoot the guards, perhaps? Silenced rifle with night sights?'

'That'd certainly do it,' said Alex, pointing at the house as if discussing a loft conversion, 'but he hasn't killed anyone except his targets so far.'

'He killed Gidley's dogs.'

'Dogs are just security products. Everyone kills dogs. But my take on Meehan is that he doesn't want to leave a trail of supplementary human corpses. Pride in his work would prevent that.'

'Is this you identifying with him again? Is this the way you see killing? As work to take a pride in?'

He laughed. 'You're the one who's hiring the hit man. You tell me. And follow this path round, please. I want to have a quick look at the river bank.'

'You think he'll come by river?'

214

'That's the way I'd do it. Quick cuddle here, I think, under the weeping willow.'

'Must we?'

'I'm afraid so. It's just too romantic a spot to miss.'

'Oh, yeah? And just what constitutes a romantic spot, in your view?'

'I think anywhere can be, if you're with someone you really, really . . .'

She folded her arms. 'Go on.'

'Kiss me, Harding!'

Her eyes were as flat as a snake's. Slowly, she placed her arms round his neck and her lips against his. Through his shirt and hers he felt the small pressure of her breasts. Then she stepped back.

'That didn't register very high on the Richter scale,' he protested.

'We're supposed to be married,' she said, turning to look at the house. 'Not in love.'

They continued along the bank. The river was slow and deep, its shining surface almost viscous-looking in the sunlight, the bank-side foliage perfectly reflected. Six feet below, emerald weeds wavered and trailed over polished gravel and chalk.

He's watching us, thought Alex with absolute certainty. And he's saying to himself: are these two the nice young couple that they seem to be, or have they come to hunt me down and kill me? 'Here,' he said. 'This is where he'll come. Don't stop. Keep walking. He'll approach silently from a couple of hundred yards upstream – no one will see him in a black wetsuit once the light's gone – and he'll climb out between these two banks of bullrushes.'

'Are you sure of that?'

'I'm positive. It's exactly where I'd do it. You're

covered by the bushes on the bank and the rushes in the water, you're the minimum distance from the house – you definitely don't want to have acres of lawn to cross – plus there's a sort of underwater chalk bar like a step you can use to climb out. He's already tried it. When we walk back past you'll see a boot scrape in the algae on the chalk bar and a couple of reed clumps that look as if they've been twisted by someone pulling himself out. He's rehearsed it.'

Dawn crouched to examine a clump of yellow flag iris. 'How do you know it was him?'

'Well, who else is going to have been climbing in and out of the river in George Widdowes' garden? He'd probably have been wearing a weight belt to counteract the buoyancy effect of the wetsuit and keep himself low in the water on his approach. There was a snapped root where he might've tried hanging the belt in the dark. He wouldn't want to leave the water wearing it.'

'You spotted all that in the time it took us to walk past that bit of bank?'

'I knew what I was looking for. What I expected to see.' He thought of Sierra Leone and the frothing brown torrent of the Rokel. 'I've made the odd river approach myself. Bit rougher than this, but the principle's the same.'

'So what are you suggesting? That we have one of the marksmen up a tree, waiting for Meehan to climb out. Sort of a hippo shoot?'

'While your shooters are here he won't come,' said Alex. 'It's as simple as that. Plus he already knows about the lookalike. Probably knows his name, address and home phone number by now.'

'So what are you saying?'

216

'Get rid of the shooters, the lookalike, everything. Pull them all out and move George Widdowes back in. I'll move back in too, along with a back-up guy, and we'll set up an ambush of our own – a proper killing team. Sooner or later Meehan will have to come and then we'll waste the bastard.'

'What back-up guy?'

Alex's immediate thought was of Stan Clayton. 'Someone from Hereford. One of my people.'

'There's no question of any other non-Five people being involved, I'm afraid. This is a top-secret operation, not a get-together of your barrack-mates.'

'Listen,' he said quietly. 'They aren't just my barrack mates, they're the people with the best training and experience of this kind of close-up surveillance in the world. Guys who've spent days at a time lying up in the undergrowth next to IRA arms caches, or waiting for Bosnian war criminals. With all due respect to your guys, I've seen them in action and they stick out like the bollocks on a dog. One other guy from my RWW team, that's all I'm asking.'

'I can pass on the request, but I can tell you right now what the answer's going to be.'

Alex shook his head. 'You still don't get it, do you?'

'I get it only too well. You want to turn this into a Regiment operation. Well, I'm afraid it's all a damn sight too sensitive for that.'

'What you mean is that you don't trust anyone else to keep his mouth shut about what is basically one of the most disastrous fuck-ups in your service's history. You're afraid that if word gets out that one of your agents not only turned into one of PIRA's top nutting boys but crowned his brilliant career by torturing and killing a choice selection of your desk officers, that people just might start asking questions about your service's competence to handle intelligence affairs in the province. They might decide the Treasury got better value for its money from some other agency. The Firm, for example.'

At the mention of MI6, Thames House's hated rival, Dawn Harding all but bared her teeth. 'You are out of your depth by some distance, Captain Temple. You have been placed under the authority of my service and you will kindly respect that authority.'

'Even when its orders are illegal?'

Dawn's expression tightened. 'Let's behave like grown-ups, shall we? We both know what has to be done, we both know why. Like I said, I will pass on your request but I can tell you now what the response will be: if you need back-up, MI5 will provide it. Assuming, that is, that they go along with your plan at all.'

Alex nodded expressionlessly. 'Let's go and check out the house.'

She nodded and followed him towards the Lodge.

'After all,' he added drily, 'we have to make sure there's going to be room for the children's play area.'

Half an hour later the two prospective buyers of Longwater Lodge were sitting in a quiet corner of the Pied Bull. On the walls framed photographs of local cricket teams were displayed, along with horse brasses, winnowing fans, malt shovels, scythe handles and other redundant rural artefacts. A truce had been agreed between them.

'It strikes me,' said Alex, when their sandwiches and drinks had been served to them, 'that your deputy director is probably in the clear. That there's a good chance she's not one the Watchman's targets.'

Dawn narrowed her eyes. 'What makes you say that?'

'Fenn had his tongue cut out, OK?'

'OK.'

'And Gidley had his eyes cut out?'

'Yup.'

'Widdowes, if he gets him, will have his ears cut off.'

'What makes you say that?'

'Well, I figured it might be that three wise monkeys thing. See no evil, speak no evil, hear no evil.'

She nodded. 'I thought of that as soon as I saw what he'd done to Craig Gidley. The suggestion being that when they were alive they saw, spoke and heard evil, and only now that they're dead . . .'

Alex nodded. He had thought it was a pretty brilliant deduction on his part and was rather disappointed that she had reached the same conclusion, and reached it first.

'The thing I was going to say,' he pressed on, 'is that there are only three wise monkeys. So assuming your man Widdowes is supposed to be the third, that puts Fenwick in the clear.'

'Two points,' she said. 'One, we're dealing with a psychopathic murderer here. Assigning logic or structure to his actions and assuming that he will abide by this logic and structure is asking for trouble. He will do what he will do, period. Two, look at this. I did an Internet search for the expression "wise monkeys".

From her jacket pocket she took a folded piece of paper. It was a printout, Alex saw, a printout of a London auction house web page.

Lot 42 – 'Four Wise Monkeys'. Netsuke, Thirteenth Century

This is a highly rare and important piece, in that it shows four wise monkeys, rather than the more coventional three. The monkeys were introduced into Japan from China in the eighth century AD by a Buddhist monk of the Tendai sect, and are believed to have been associated with the blue-faced god Vajra. Originally there were four monkeys, namely Mizaru (see no evil), Mazaru (speak no evil), Mikazaru (hear no evil) and Iwazaru (know no evil). As in this piece, Iwazaru was always represented with his hands placed over his heart. By the fourteenth century, however, the fourth monkey was absent from most representations, as he is from the best-known example, the seventeenth-century carving over the doorway of the Sacred Stable in Nikko, Japan. The presence in this early piece of the fourth monkey emphasises the essentially ambiguous nature of the traditional instruction. For while at one level the refusal to see, hear and speak evil will afford spiritual protection, at another level it lays the postulant open to charges of moral disengagement – of a closing of the heart.

Alex read the sheet and handed it back to Dawn. 'Four monkeys, then,' he muttered. 'Do we reckon that our Watchman knows about the fourth?'

'It took me less than a minute to find this on the web.'

'I guess you're right,' said Alex.

'And there's another thing,' Dawn went on. 'Do you remember the pictures of Meehan you saw in Thames House?'

Alex nodded.

'Do you remember the one in the kitchen of their house in Derry? The one with both his parents in it? Well, if you enlarge it you can see that there are some brass ornaments on the shelf. There's a bell shaped like a Dutch girl, and a miniature camel, and a little square thing that I'd bet a month's salary is a statuette of the wise monkeys.'

Alex nodded. 'Well, that does seem to wrap it up,' he said. 'And to put your Miss Fenwick squarely in the frame as the fourth monkey.'

'That's rather what we feared.'

'You might have mentioned it,' said Alex. 'Like I said before, anything that helps me to know him better will help me to deal with him.'

'We were rather hoping you might deal with him before the projected number of his victims became . . . an issue.'

That evening he was changing into a tracksuit in the Pimlico safe house, preparing to go for a run, when his mobile rang. It was Dawn, although she didn't announce her name. 'You've got what you wanted,' she said peremptorily. 'Our friend returns to his house in Hampshire the day after tomorrow.'

'Do I get any of my people?' asked Alex.

'No. You either use ours or you go without.'

'Understood.' He frowned. 'Look, you don't fancy a drink or something, do you?'

'Didn't the roses work, then? I forgot to ask.' Her tone was amused.

He paused. Took a deep breath. 'Do you fancy a drink or not?'

But the phone had already gone dead.

EIGHTEEN

'So,' said George Widdowes. 'You're really sure about this? You're sure that you'll be able to tackle Meehan when he comes?'

'Yes,' said Alex. 'I am. So far he's had everything his own way. He's been able to pick the time and the place. Now we're going to force his hand.'

The MI5 desk officer and the SAS captain were sitting in the ante-room to Angela Fenwick's office in Thames House.

'Tell me,' said Widdowes.

'Basically,' explained Alex, 'we bait a trap. As you know, there's a For Sale sign outside your house. What's going to happen is that you're going to move back there for a few days and in three days' time you're going to supervise the loading of all your stuff into a removals van. Is the place very full?'

Widdowes shook his head tiredly. 'Not very. This is strictly necessary, is it, all this house-moving routine?'

'We've got to do it properly. And it'll make sense to Meehan. You're afraid and you feel isolated out there by yourself, so you're moving back to London. Maybe you've even been ordered to move back to London. Whichever, you're going to miss the place and, given that there are a couple of armed policemen patrolling the property, you decide it'll be safe to stay there for the last few nights.'

'You reckon that'll bounce him into having a go?'

Alex nodded. 'I reckon it will. And if he doesn't come in the next forty-eight hours he certainly will after he sees the furniture van being filled. He'll know that this is his last chance – that if he doesn't take you now all his surveillance has gone to waste and he'll have to start from scratch again.'

'You think we can set the whole thing up without spooking him?'

'Well, that's the question. Anything smells funny and he won't come – he's PIRA-trained, after all. If you just moved back into the place without any security, for example, he'd be very suspicious indeed and let the whole thing go. My guess, though, is that when he sees those armed cops he'll think that you reckon you're safe.'

'The armed police won't put him off?'

Alex smiled and shook his head.

'So why won't he just wait until that evening and follow the furniture van? Follow it to my supposed new house or flat?'

'Because it won't be going anywhere. The loading'll finish about six, and then the van will be driven a couple of hundred yards down the road and parked up in a lay-by to wait for the next morning. Local removal firms often do that so that they don't have to pay their crews overtime.'

'Why not wait until the next day and then follow the van?'

'Because it might go anywhere – a storage facility, for example – and then he'll have to start searching for your new place from scratch. Besides, he'll know that wherever you go will be ultra secure in comparison with your present place. He'll know that the Hampshire house offers by far the best chance he's likely to get.'

'And you'll be waiting for him?' said Widdowes doubtfully.

'Basically, yes. I'll hide up by the river and when he comes I'll shoot him at short range with a silenced weapon.'

'How will you make sure he doesn't know you're there waiting for him?'

'He won't know,' said Alex quietly. 'Count on that. I've set up ambushes before.'

In the car park beneath Thames House, a little over twenty-four hours later, Alex squeezed into the boot of the car that was to masquerade as Widdowes'. The BMW saloon had been customised with a boot-fitted surveillance lens and bullet-proof windows.

'Are you going to be all right in there?' Widdowes asked.

'Yeah, I'll be OK. Hand us in my kit, could you, and put your own stuff on the back seat.'

The drive took an hour and a half in total and by the end of it Alex was feeling light-headed and nauseated from the exhaust fumes. When Widdowes finally sprang the boot open, it was in the near darkness of the garage at Longwater Lodge. Illuminating his watch, Alex saw that it was a few minutes before 5 p.m. 'Right,' he said, when he had stretched his legs for a moment or two. 'This door leads directly into the house?'

'Yes.'

'And is there a room without any windows?'

'There's a cellar, yes.'

'Perfect. I'll set up my stuff down there. Can you get me there without leading me past too many windows?'

Widdowes nodded and opened the door to the house. Alex, feeling slightly ridiculous, followed the tall Barbour-coated figure on his hands and knees. They reached a door, which Widdowes opened. Alex swung himself on to a descending staircase and took his bag from the older man, who then flicked a light switch and followed him down into the cellar.

It was a decent-sized place, and not too damp. In front of him was a large Potterton boiler, switched off. Against the other walls stood a wine-rack, a carpentry workbench, several bundles of magazines bound with baler twine, a case of Eley shotgun cartridges and a battered travelling trunk.

'I've got a camp bed,' said Widdowes. 'I'll bring it down for you.'

While he was upstairs, Alex unpacked his case. He left the clothes inside, and arranged the weaponry and kit on the carpentry workbench. There was the Glock 34, its silencer, the laser dot-marker sight on its factory-fitted slide, a spare lithium battery for the laser sight, two boxes of twenty-five hollow-point 9mm rounds and the Recon knife. There were also a sleeping bag and a tin of black waterproof cam-cream from a survival shop in Euston, a pair of fisherman's felt-soled boots from Farlow's of Pall Mall, and an all-black Rip Curl wetsuit, weight belt and jet fins from a diving equipment store in Fulham. For Alex, not usually an enthusiastic shopper, the knowledge that he'd been spending MI5's money had made for a pleasant morning.

When he reappeared with the camp bed Widdowes appeared disconcerted by this array. In fact, he looked badly scared. His features were flushed and his eyes flickered uneasily about him. Hardly surprising, thought Alex. It couldn't be anything but terrifying to know that you were next on the list of a proven psycho like Meehan.

'Are you OK?' Alex asked.

Widdowes nodded. 'Yes, I'm OK.' He laughed nervously. 'You've certainly brought the full armoury with you.'

'I'm not taking any chances with this bastard,' said Alex. 'He's going straight in the fucking ground. Have you got your own weapon?'

Widdowes reached inside his jacket, withdrew a Colt .38 revolver, spun the chamber and returned it to the shoulder holster.

Alex nodded. Privately he thought that if it ever came to a one-on-one between Widdowes and Meehan the MI5 man was as good as dead, but he guessed that the heft and weight of the Colt were a good confidence booster. He turned to Widdowes. 'Look, I know you're an experienced field agent and I don't want to get your back up, but a handful of rules for the duration, yeah?'

Widdowes nodded.

'Avoid windows. I doubt he'd try and shoot you but better to be safe than sorry, so if you must go past a window keep moving. Whether inside or outside the house, don't ever present a static target and don't whatever you do speak or shout out to me – don't worry about warnings, if he comes anywhere near here I'll see him before you do. I'll have him covered. Behave at all times as if you were alone in the house.

Have you met up with the two police guys?'

'Yes. They're MI5 people, in fact, in police uniforms.'

'That's fine. Basically what we need them to do is mooch around the front of the house. Just wander about between there and the road, and stick their necks into the back garden every so often. They should stay together most of the time, smoke the odd fag, that sort of thing. They've got to look like lazy and incompetent jobsworths: out to grass and no threat to anyone. Can you make sure they understand that?'

Widdowes nodded again.

'Otherwise, just observe your usual routine. It might help if you put an empty bottle or two out each night – give the impression you're hitting the old vino. That'll encourage him to think . . .'

'Yeah, I know what you're saying. Nerves shot, soft target . . .'

Alex looked at Widdowes. His darting glances, uneven colour and paper-dry lips confirmed that he was very frightened indeed. He put a hand on the older man's shoulder. 'George, mate, we're in this together and I'm fully aware that your part is the harder one. Honestly. If you can think of a better way of nailing this fucker I'm on for it, believe me.'

Widdowes pursed his lips and nodded.

'I'm also sorry to put you through a non-existent house move, but again . . .'

'That's OK,' said Widdowes, forcing an unconvincing smile. 'I've been meaning to sort through all this junk. Get my life into some sort of order. What do you want to do about eating?'

'Well, it gets dark at about eight o'clock and I want

227

to get into position about then. So if we have a feed at seven-ish?'

'I'll knock something up. You're going to wait for him in the river, aren't you?'

'That's the idea.'

'Have you considered how you're going to get into position without him seeing you? I mean, we have to assume he's watching the area around the house. Quite possibly from close up.'

'You're going to have to drive me downstream to somewhere I can get into the river and work my way back here. Somewhere he won't see me get out of the car.'

'That's no problem. I can take you up to the next road bridge and you can get back through the grounds of Longwater House. There's no one there at the moment, the place is closed up.' Widdowes frowned. 'But how do you know Meehan won't be down there? How do you know you won't run into him?'

'Because he won't want to go in blind. He'll come from the direction he can watch the house and the guards from, which is upstream. You can't see anything at all from where I'm going, except trees.'

Widdowes slowly nodded. 'Right. Got you.'

'Is there a pub in the downstream direction? Some reason you might be going that way?'

'There's an off-licence in Martyr Worthy. If I come back ten minutes later with a Thresher's bag . . .'

'Good enough. Now I'd suggest you get upstairs. Maybe take a cup of tea to the two cops – give you an excuse to brief them about looking useless.'

'What will you do?'

'I'll be OK, don't worry. See you at seven.'

Widdowes nodded and smiled wryly. 'I'll tell you

one thing,' he said. 'If this guy Meehan succeeds in taking me out there are going to be some long faces at Thames House.'

Alex looked at him.

'Angela Fenwick, for a start,' continued Widdowes. 'She's in line for the directorship, that's why the deaths of Fenn and Gidley have pissed her off so royally. If she loses any more of her desk officers it's going to start looking very much like carelessness. Her star and that of her familiar could well start to decline.'

'Her familiar?' asked Alex, surprised by the bitterness and vehemence of his tone.

'Dawn Bloody Harding. Zulu Dawn. Dawn of the Living Dead. From the moment she joined the service she hitched her wagon to Angela's – that's why her progress has been so meteoric. For as long as Angela's riding high, Dawn's up there with her. But if Angela falls, then Dawn goes down too. Don't overlook the political side of all this, chum. You've been brought in to safeguard the upward mobility of a political cabal.'

'I'm here to safeguard you, George. The rest doesn't interest me.'

Widdowes nodded philosophically and shrugged. 'I'm sorry. You're right – it's not your worry. Getting cynical in my old age, that's all.'

When he had gone Alex unrolled his sleeping bag on the camp bed, lay down and stared at the cellar's plasterboard ceiling. Eventually he closed his eyes. It was going to be a long night and he would do well to get some rest. In his pocket, his mobile throbbed.

'Yeah?'

'It's Dawn Harding.'

'Zulu Dawn!'

There was a silence. 'Where did you get that name?' she asked accusingly. 'Have you been . . .'

'It's one of my favourite films,' said Alex breezily. 'How are you?'

'Fine,' she said curtly. 'Is everything OK down there?'

'So far, yes.'

'How's George holding up?'

'He's under a bit of stress but he's keeping it all together.'

'You think Meehan will come tonight?'

'Might. Bird in the hand and so on.'

There was a pause.

'Are you . . . OK?' she enquired.

'Do I detect a note of concern?' asked Alex, unable to keep the smile from his voice.

'No, you don't!' she snapped. 'I simply need to know you're in good shape. I don't want any more corpses on the pathologist's slab.'

'Don't worry,' said Alex, the vision of Dawn suspended high above the ground in her scarlet underwear flashing past his eyes. 'I'll keep myself in good shape for you.'

She disconnected. Alex returned his gaze to the ceiling and his smile faded. He had ninety minutes in which to rest up. He closed his eyes.

Shortly after seven Widdowes woke him. The MI5 officer was carrying a plateful of cheese and ham sandwiches, a Granny Smith apple, a Mars bar and a two-litre bottle of still mineral water. 'Sorry,' he said. 'It's not quite up to Gordon Ramsay standard. I assumed you'd want mustard on the ham?'

'Yeah. Great.'

'I meant to ask. What do you want to do about washing?'

'I don't,' said Alex. 'You can smell toothpaste and soap on the air. I won't be using either until Meehan's dead. And hopefully I won't be needing a crap till then, either. As far as pissing's concerned, well, from time to time you'll find this Evian bottle on the stairs.'

'Got you,' said Widdowes without enthusiasm.

Alex ate and drank for five minutes in silence, then loaded the Glock's magazine with nineteen rounds and slapped it into the butt. Pointing the handgun at the wall, he pressed the button activating the laser sight. A small red dot appeared on the wall, scribbling fine lines of light as Alex moved the weapon. Satisfied, he thumbed the system off again. Then he stripped, pulled on the wetsuit and buckled the sheathed Recon knife round his calf. The Glock went into a plastic thigh holster on a lanyard. Blackening his face and hands with the cam-cream, he pulled up the neoprene hood of the wetsuit. The clothes that he had just been wearing went into the waterproof stuff sack that had previously held the wetsuit. The boots and fins went into a carrier bag. 'OK,' said Alex. 'Let's do it. What's the light like outside?'

'Going fast,' said Widdowes.

They made their way back to the garage, Alex climbed into the boot and Widdowes drove off, stopping briefly to converse with the uniformed men at the gate. The ensuing drive took no more than three minutes, but took them well out of the sight of anyone who had been observing the house. Quickly, watching out for other cars, Widdowes let Alex out of the boot, handed him the stuff sack and drove on. The whole operation had taken no more than ten seconds.

Crouching in the cow-parsley on the river bank, Alex peered around him in the fading evening light. Above him was the road, which was narrow and unlikely to see too much traffic between now and tomorrow morning. To his left was the road bridge. He could just make out a narrow walkway beneath this, but access to it was largely obscured by nettles, elder and other roadside vegetation. Sliding down the bank, Alex pushed through undergrowth into the darkness beneath the bridge and cached the stuff sack of clothing there. Attaching the weight belt round his waist, he undid the Farlow's boots and tied them to the belt by the laces, then pulled on the jet fins and lowered himself into the water.

The carrier stream was about six feet deep at the edge and deeper, he guessed, in the middle. Despite its smooth surface, the current was considerable. Cautiously, he began to move forward. The boots at his waist dragged a little, but this was more than compensated for by the powerful jet fins, just as the buoyancy of the wetsuit was compensated for by the weight belt. With it he was able to move silently with only his head above the surface, without it he would have been wallowing about on the surface, leaving a wake like a speedboat.

Tucking in to the side of the river, trailing his arms at his side, he concentrated on moving with absolute silence and the minimum of water disturbance. After fifty yards he passed a high fence, which he guessed was the boundary of the Longwater estate. A few hundred yards, Widdowes had said. He swam silently on. At one point the river shallowed, running over a broken bottom no more than a couple of feet deep and Alex was forced to leopard-crawl six inches at a time against the weight of the tumbling water. With relief, however, he soon felt the river bed falling away beneath him.

After a hundred yards, he grabbed on to an over-hanging root, swung himself into the bank and took stock. Soon he would be coming into the area that he had to assume was under night sight surveillance. Meehan might be several hundred yards away, scoping out the property from a concealed hide, or he might be much closer. He could be lying up in the river as little as fifty yards upstream. From now on Alex would have to move with extreme caution.

A couple of yards ahead there was a faint splash. A small sound, but enough to set Alex's heart racing. Something had been thrown or dropped into the water. Was Meehan waiting on the bank above him? Had he seen him? Shrinking into the knotted roots beneath the river's mud and chalk banks, Alex froze, his heart pounding. Slowly, an inch at a time, he reached for the knife, withdrew the razor-sharp blade from the scabbard, held it inches beneath the surface. And then, against a faint patch of light, he saw the questing head of the otter, cutting an arrowhead wake through the water. Going hunting, he guessed with dizzying relief.

When he had caught his breath he moved on, keeping hard in to the bank, driving against the current with the fins. Through the trees to his left he could see the vast dim bulk of Longwater House, now, and ahead of him the lights of the Lodge. What was Widdowes up to? he wondered. In the short time they had spent together he had developed a sympathy for the man. Not much in Widdowes' manner suggested it now, but he'd probably been a competent enough operative in his time. Box's Belfast agent handlers were not fools, for the most part (although one or two of them were and Michael Bettany had been a traitor too, jailed for spying for the Soviets), nor were they cowards. No one who had seen what had happened to Fenn and Gidley, though, would be anything but afraid.

Alex was suddenly filled with a loathing of Meehan. They all moved in a dirty world, that much was accepted, but to do what he had done, well, that was something else. Chopping bits of people's faces off, hammering nails into them . . . What the last hours of those two poor bastards from the FRU must have been like was beyond imagining.

Alex moved silently upriver in the deep black shadows beneath the bank. He was invisible now, a creature of the night. He came to a halt beneath the slender curving trunk of a willow, a place he had noted when he visited the house with Dawn. Above him was the yellowish haze of the lights from the Lodge, five to six yards ahead of him was the silhouette of the reed-bed and the bushes through which he had calculated that Meehan would make his exit.

Feeling beneath the water, Alex found a sturdy root and, quickly exchanging his fins for the Farlow's boots, attached the fins to the root by their straps so that they hung in the current a foot beneath the surface. Could he find them again? Yes, they were just below this willow root. Should he take the weight belt off? He tried it, felt himself rising in the water and hastily reattached it. Where to go? Inching forward, his feet found a shelf that would take his weight. Gratefully he sensed the thick felt soles of the fishing boots grip the slippery chalk. If he'd settled for commando-soled boots, as he'd originally considered, he would have had a hard night ahead of him. His right arm found a corresponding elbow of willow root to hook through. He was now facing the current and the direction that Meehan would come. Between him and Meehan's projected exit point was a clump of sedge and the outer skirt of the willow's foliage. As long as he kept still, he would be invisible, even if Meehan was using night sights.

For his part, Alex had decided against night sights. Partly because of their unwieldiness in the water, partly because the intensified green images would compromise his night vision. He knew what he was looking for and he knew where to look. Even when the lights went off in the house there would be a close to full moon. And it would be when the lights went off that Meehan would come.

For an hour Alex remained there, unmoving, his eyes scanning the river ahead of him. In low light conditions, he knew, you saw better with your peripheral than your direct vision. Very slowly, a limb at a time, he kept himself moving underwater, gently contracting and relaxing his muscles. Partly to stave off cold and avoid cramping, which despite the wetsuit was a very real threat, and partly in order to remain alert.

Of all the ambushes that Alex had ever set up, this was by far the least satisfactory, in that he was operating alone and without back-up. He would go for a heart shot as Meehan pulled himself out of the water, he decided, when both his hands were occupied. The silenced double tap would punch the life out of the former agent before his brain had had a chance to take in what was happening. He'd be dead before his knees bent and the Watchman's rule of terror would be over.

The first man Alex had killed had been during the Gulf War in 1991.

He had been part of a four-man Sabre team tasked to knock out a Scud missile dump at al-Anbar, west of Baghdad. Under the command of an NCO named Neil Slater they'd been choppered in by night and left to forage for cover. The cold had been extreme – they'd been sent in wearing little more than light-weight 'chocolate chip' battledress and shirts – and there had been no cover of any kind. Within the hour they were frozen to the bone. The four of them – Alex, Neil Slater, Don Hammond and Andreas van Rijn – had made a quick recce and Slater had made the decision to lie up for the rest of the night in a disused berm a couple of hundred yards from the dump. None of them had slept; instead they had huddled together against the cold and the wind-borne snow that whipped mercilessly about them.

The next morning, half-frozen, they had seen a convoy of Iraqi T-55 tanks rumbling towards them – the most terrifying sight Alex or indeed any of them had ever witnessed. Desperate, they had buried themselves in the detritus at the bottom of the berm – Iraqi ration tins, ammunition boxes, rubble, old tyres, discarded cam-netting and the decaying corpse of a goat – and prayed. The Iraqi tank crews, anxious to relieve themselves after several hours in their T-55s, had surrounded the berm. The Sabre team were pissed on, they were shat on and Alex's thigh was agonisingly burnt by a discarded cigarette end, but they were not discovered. And eventually, after four ghastly hours, the tanks had rumbled away into the desert.

As soon as the SAS team had judged it safe to move Slater had radioed in the tanks' position and direction of travel, and called in the air strike on al-Anbar. Its purpose was twofold: to destroy the missiles grouped there for transportation to mobile missile launchers and to kill a man known as Marwan.

'Marwan', to the Allied intelligence forces based in Saudi Arabia, had for several weeks been little more than an occasionally occurring code name in the welter of enemy radio traffic. It was thought from the contexts in which he was mentioned that he might be a senior technician of some sort. Then an intercepted transmission between the al-Anbar base and Baghdad command had suggested that 'Marwan' might be a man known to the Allies as 'Guppy' – an Iranian scientist who had changed sides during the Iran-Iraq war and now ran the missile research plant at Sa'd 16, in north Iraq. It was the Sa'd 16 team who had developed the al-Husayn – the long-range version of the Russian Scud that could be fitted with chemical and biological warheads. According to the transmission, 'Marwan' was due at the al-Anbar base that evening, suggesting that the missiles might be about to be checked over and dispersed.

If 'Marwan' was indeed 'Guppy', then it was essential that he be killed, just as it was essential that the missiles should be destroyed while they were all in one place. Neil Slater's instructions were to call in the air strike, assess the subsequent damage and ensure that there were no Iraqi survivors.

The air strike was at the same time the most dramatic and the most appalling event Alex had ever witnessed. The Tornados had screamed in, their missiles drawing a deceptively faint diagonal trail, and the Scud jet-propellant had gone up in an eyeball-searing roar of light and heat, hurling vehicles, machinery, weapons and human body parts in all directions. The explosions had been followed by a terrible screaming and by the sight of disjointed figures writhing on the charred ground. And by the smell, the meaty stench of burning human flesh.

'Go!' Neil Slater had screamed. 'Go, go, go!'

And they had gone. Above them the sky was black with smoke, as if a solar eclipse were taking place. Initially Alex had thought that they would encounter little or no resistance, that the entire Iraqi strength had been killed or maimed in the air strike. But this was not the case, as rapidly became clear. As the team advanced, moving in skirmish order across the twilit noon landscape, they came under sustained fire from a slit trench. A group of Iraqis must have been lying up in a bunker and escaped the firestorm unleashed by the Tornados.

The four SAS men hurled themselves into cover behind a Panhard Landcruiser which had been blown on to its side by the blast. From directly in front of them the Iraqi fire team immediately brought a withering hail of 7.62 rounds to bear on the vehicle from their Kalashnikovs. Between the two sides lay the charred, twisted and smoking bodies of the missile support crew, the lingering screams of those who had not yet died cutting through the stinking air. Thirty yards in front of them was an anti-aircraft gun emplacement, surrounded by the bodies of the men who had manned it. To twenty-six-year-old Corporal Alex Temple, who had never been on a full-scale battlefield before, it was a scene straight from hell.

'What range do you reckon?' Neil Slater asked him calmly, as Kalashnikov rounds screamed and ricocheted against the Landcruiser's blackened and twisted flank.

'I'd say fifty metres,' said Alex, struggling to keep his voice steady.

Slater nodded and removed a grenade from his bandolier. The grenade's gold top told Alex that it was the high-explosive type, rather than anti-personnel or white phosphorus.

From the other side of the Landcruiser came the whoomfing crack of a Russian grenade. Hand-thrown, guessed Alex, but not quite far enough.

Calmly Slater checked the sextant sight on his weapon's carrying handle and slid the HE grenade into the 203 launcher tube beneath the barrel of his M16. 'Fifty metres it is,' he said. 'Cover please, lads. Time for a delivery of Gold Top.'

'Pasteurise the fuckers,' whispered Andreas van Rijn, Slater's second-in-command.

As the three of them poured aimed shots from their M16s at the Iraqi position, Slater leaned coolly from cover, glanced down once at the sextant sight and fired.

The egg-shaped grenade hit the ground a few feet beyond the trench, bounced once and exploded noisily but harmlessly on the desert floor, shredding a thorn bush.

Quickly, Slater reloaded. This time the grenade fell short, but close enough to blow a half-hundredweight of sand and scrub into the trench.

The fire from the Iraqi trench intensified, and it was at that moment that the SAS team guessed they were facing elite troops and 'Marwan' was in the enemy trench. This was the only possible explanation for the Iraqi team's failure to surrender, given that they faced almost certain obliteration: they had been ordered to defend the missile scientist with their lives.

A second Russian pineapple grenade bumped laboriously towards the Landcruiser, exploding deafeningly up against it. A spatter of Kalashnikov fire followed.

'Our turn, I think,' said Slater grimly, shaking his head against the blast. This time the gold-top 203 grenade fell straight into the enemy trench and Alex watched as a shattered assault rifle flew into the air alongside the severed arm that, until a moment earlier, had held it.

'Full fat!' murmured Andreas van Rijn appreciatively. 'Full fucking fat!'

The firing did not cease. At least three Iraqi soldiers were still capable of manning a weapon and were bravely continuing to do so, forcing the SAS team to remain flattened behind the wrecked vehicle. At intervals Alex and the others were able to squeeze off a few rounds, but not to great effect. In small-arms terms it was a stalemate. But the SAS had their 203 grenade launchers.

Inexorably Slater reloaded. He had the range now, and dropped a fourth HE grenade into the Iraqi trench. This time the explosion was followed by silence and then a low groaning sound.

With his hand, Slater ordered absolute stillness. The SAS team froze. Nothing, just that long-drawn-out groaning. All of them were uncomfortably aware that sooner or later more Iraqi troops would converge on the place. Probably sooner. The destruction of al-

Anbar would certainly not have passed unnoticed.

Quickly, Alex switched magazines and as he did so his eye caught a blurred movement behind the anti-aircraft emplacement to their left. A fraction of a second later a tall khaki figure was sprinting towards the Landcruiser, holding a Kalashnikov and – Alex noted in something like slow motion – a pale-green Russian cylinder grenade.

From a kneeling position Alex pulled the heavy M16 203 to his shoulder. The moment seemed to go on and on. He saw the courage and the blazing intention in the Iraqi's eyes, heard his sawing breath and the desperate driving of his feet, dropped his foresight to the oncoming man's chest, saw his upper body half turn to accommodate the grenade throw – only twenty-five yards to go now – aimed, smoothly exhaled and punched six high-velocity 5.56mm rounds through his sternum.

For a moment, as a little over a pound of bone, muscle and lung tissue leapt from the Iraqi soldier's back, his eyes met Alex's. There was surprise there and perhaps a measure of disappointment, but not much more.

Is that all, Alex asked himself wonderingly? Is that all it is to kill a man?

The volley pitched the Iraqi backwards on to his own grenade, from which he had withdrawn the pin before starting his run. Untypically of the item in question and of exported Russian grenades in general, it worked perfectly, shredding the soldier's heart through his ribs after a delay of exactly four seconds.

A frisson passed through Alex as he clenched and unclenched his toes in the Farlow's boots. He had been in the river outside Widdowes' house for nearly three hours now, his dark-accustomed eyes endlessly quartering and scanning the space ahead of him, his senses pricked for any noise or smell that was in any way foreign to the place. He was cold, but not critically so – a layer of body-temperature water lay between his skin and the wetsuit's neoprene lining. The stiller he kept, in fact, the warmer he was.

The MI5 men had played their parts perfectly, pacing loudly around the grounds with cigarettes and torches, announcing their flat-footed presence to any who might be observing. You certainly wouldn't need night sights to know that the Thompson Twins were in town.

But of the Watchman there had been no sign. A heron, broad-winged and graceful, had lowered itself from the sky a little after nine o'clock and taken up residence among the reeds close to where Alex expected the Watchman to exit the river. The perfect early warning system, thought Alex. Not even Joseph Meehan could shimmy past a heron without disturbing it.

He'd felt nothing at the Iraqi's death. And nothing afterwards, when they'd killed all of those still alive. In most cases the double taps that they had delivered had represented a merciful release from the terrible burns caused by the Tornado's incendiary missiles and the exploding Scud propellant.

They'd found a man who might or might not have been 'Marwan' in the trench, dead from shrapnel wounds to the head and blast injuries. He'd been unarmed and wearing khaki overalls of a different design from the others. In his pockets they had found a Tandy calculator, an ID card and a wallet containing pictures of his family. All these, along with a half-melted Toshiba laptop computer found near the anti-aircraft emplacement, had been bagged and returned to base. The operation had been judged a one hundred per cent success.

Alex had felt nothing and thought he'd got away unscathed.

NINETEEN

The Watchman did not come and with first light Alex swam silently downstream to the bridge, exited the water and re-dressed himself in the clothes that he had left hidden there. The cold of the river and the length and intensity of his eight-hour vigil had left him desperately tired, and for a long time he could not stop himself shaking. He couldn't even bring himself to think about further nights spent the same way.

In truth, it had always been unlikely that the Watchman would come on the first night of Widdowes' return. He would want to watch and wait, to weigh up the chances of the whole thing being a set-up. In Meehan's position Alex wouldn't have come on that first night.

But now, hopefully, Meehan would have had a chance to see that the arrangement was exactly what it seemed to be: a nervous public servant guarded by a pair of competent if rather dilatory policemen. Widdowes was getting the sort of protection that an important criminal witness might get, or the senior officer of a regiment that had served in Northern Ireland.

Alex sat beneath the bridge for a further couple of hours. Slowly the darkness became wet grey dawn, and at 6 a.m. he heard a car come to a halt above him and a voice quietly call his name. Hurrying out with his kit, he dived into the boot of the customised BMW and lay there while Widdowes went through the motions of going for an early-morning drive.

Back in the garage the MI5 man looked at him with concern. 'You look completely knackered,' he said. 'Are you OK?'

'I'll live,' replied Alex. 'How are you?'

'I did what you said: cooked myself supper, watched *Newsnight*, and hit the sack. Even managed to sleep.' Widdowes hesitated. 'I'm grateful for this, Alex,' he said quietly. 'Man to man and forgetting all the inter-service bullshit, I'm really grateful. You're putting yourself on the line and that means a lot. Is there anything I can do in return?'

'Yes,' said Alex wearily. 'Stay alive. And sort us out some breakfast.'

'Any preferences?'

'Everything,' said Alex. 'The full bollocks.'

'My pleasure. Would you like a bath?'

'When Meehan's dead,' said Alex.

Widdowes nodded. From the drive came the sound of a car on gravel and voices. The MI5 'policemen' were handing over to a new pair.

In the cellar, meeting his exhaustion head-on, Alex pushed himself through a hard exercise routine followed by a series of stretches. The wetsuit, the boots and the rest of the kit were laid out to dry – a pointless exercise, really, but one which imposed a level of formality and routine on the situation.

When the breakfast came, preceded by the smell of fresh coffee, Alex ate fast and in silence.

'You're sure you want to stay here while I go to work?' Widdowes asked eventually.

'He won't try to kill you in the car,' said Alex with certainty. 'And I doubt he'll even bother to follow you. He knows where you're going, he'll know from the cops on the gate that you're coming back here. Just keep the windows up, the door locked and head straight for Thames House. You'll be fine – the guy has to sleep some time.'

Widdowes nodded. 'I'd better make a move. Sure you'll be OK?'

'I'll be fine.'

The two men shook hands and Widdowes departed. Placing the Glock 34 on the ground beside the camp bed, Alex climbed into his sleeping bag, closed his eyes and slept.

For the next two nights the Watchman did not come. Each evening Alex lowered himself into the river by the bridge, swam upstream and began his long vigil. He went to exactly the same position each time, hooked his arm round the underwater root, lodged his feet on the chalk shelf and waited.

Time passed with unreal slowness. As his eyes searched the gloom ahead for any sign of movement, his mind seemed to separate itself from his body, to undertake journeys of its own. Sometimes it seemed as if he were not in the river at all, but flying, or sleeping, or driving. He was visited by the familiar ranks of ghosts – the Iraqis with their charred faces and smoking chest cavities, the bullet-shattered IRA volunteers, the blood-slicked Colombians and RUF men, the frost-stiffened Serbs. All of them milled about him in an ever-changing tableau, gravely displaying their wounds, endlessly reprising the instant of their deaths. To kill a man, Alex had long understood, was to fix a moment in time, to have that moment with you for ever.

And now, with considerable formality, he was planning another death. A death that, in his mind's eye, he had seen many times. The Watchman, carried downstream by the current, would surface in the moonlit water three or four metres away and begin his silent ascent of the bank. With his right hand Alex would thumb on the infra-red sight, move the red dot to the centre of his target's chest, fire and keep firing. The coughs of the silenced Glock would be all but inaudible. The body would fall back into the water, swing towards him on the warm stream. That was how it would be.

But the Watchman didn't come. Alex waited, primed to kill, but the river remained just a river, a place of gnats and weed and flag iris. And with each grey morning he doubted his sanity more, wondered whether despite all his experience he had miscalculated. Would the BMW come and collect him once more? Or had his instincts finally deceived him? Was Widdowes even now lying mutilated and dead on the floor of Longwater Lodge?

Each morning, however, the car did come and the routine was the same. Breakfast, coffee and then sleep. A heatwave struck, and the windowless cellar became stifling and airless during the hours of daylight.

Daylight that Alex never saw. He woke each afternoon at around three, exercised, cleaned the Glock and prepared himself – all without leaving the cellar. Dawn Harding usually rang at about five thirty, shortly after she had seen Widdowes leave Thames House. Their conversations were brief – beyond discussing the ups and downs of Widdowes' state of mind there was little to say.

When Widdowes returned he would cook supper for the pair of them, take Alex's food down to the cellar as if the SAS officer were a medieval prisoner and then – at Alex's insistence – eat his own in front of the TV upstairs, as he had always done.

On the fourth day the furniture van arrived and the loading-up began. Alex managed to sleep through most of the bumping and swearing that was taking place on the floors above, but was still awake by 2 p.m.

Tonight, he thought, squinting through the 5.32-inch barrel of the Glock at the smooth curl of its rifling. Tonight the bastard has to come.

And if he doesn't?

If he doesn't then I bow out. Apologise. Kiss Dawn's stillettos. Submit to whatever grim routine she and her department choose to inflict on me.

It was a full moon that night as Alex waited for his prey and the sky was cloudless. Even after midnight a little of the heat of the day seemed to hang about the river and above Alex's head a cloud of insects danced on the warm air. In front of his hooded, blackened and immobile face water-boatmen made tiny dashes over the surface film.

The lights had been switched off in the house for more than two hours when he saw the faintest of dark shapes drifting downstream towards him. It was about thirty yards away and a foot or two out from the bank. An otter? he wondered. No, too large and immobile. Too dead. A log, then? Maybe. Or maybe just a large clump of weed. River keepers had been cutting the weed on the fisheries upstream and great rafts of it had been drifting downstream earlier that night.

But weed was usually lower in the water than this.

Quickly, Alex scanned the area to either side of it, allowing his peripheral vision to play on the shape. Nearer now, he saw that it was a large branch, splayed and leaved. But a branch which was holding hard to the bank and moving steadily towards him.

Behind his cage of roots and reeds, Alex narrowed his eyes. Was the branch going to barrel into him? Why was there a branch in the river at all in the middle of this breezeless night? Adrenalin began to trickle into his system. He pressed the Farlow's boots hard into the chalk and stealthily withdrew his arm from the grip of the underwater root. His hand held the Glock now and the safety catch was depressed for action.

Opposite the reeds, several yards upstream, the branch seemed to catch and halt. Alex's heart slammed against his ribs and his left hand joined his right on the butt of the Glock. Inch by inch he raised the weapon.

Nothing.

No movement of any kind.

Certainly no sign of anything human making for the bank.

Perhaps the branch was just a branch. Perhaps it had just happened to snag itself at the exact spot that he had been watching. Perhaps . . .

Alex blinked. Before his dark-accustomed eyes the moonlit ripples jazzed and swung.

And then – with blinding, heart-stopping force – a shining black figure exploded out of the water just inches from Alex's face. Its teeth were bared in sub-human fury, a blade was whistling downwards in its fist.

Instinct wrenched Alex from the knife's path, but a moment later a rock-like fist slammed into the side of his jaw, white light burst before his eyes and he tasted blood. Alex went down, dropping the Glock, but somehow managed to draw the commando knife from its sheath on his calf. Twisting as his attacker's blade sliced through the water, desperate to regain the initiative, he hurled himself straight at the other man's throat.

The other's reaction was identical: defence by attack. The two met in a ferocious dogfight of stabbing and flailing limbs and Alex felt an icy sharpness rip down his thigh. He was losing this fight, a part of him realised dispassionately, and it was a novel experience. His opponent was at least his equal in speed, determination and sheer savagery.

If not his superior. Alex struggled to get his knife arm out of the water and into his opponent's face but the other seized his wrist and forced it down with vicious and almost inhuman strength. A knife flash in the moonlight, a desperate swerve and the neoprene hood was flapping loose at the side of Alex's head and his cheek was hot with blood. The two men's legs locked taut – stalemate – and then in the moment before they bore each other underwater Alex drew back his head and slammed it into his opponent's nose, felt the smashing crunch of breaking bone.

Desperately swinging at the broken nose with the heel of his free hand, Alex attempted to drive the shattered bone chips backwards into his opponent's brain, but managed only a glancing blow. For a fraction of a second the eyes of the two men met and they were each other's mirror image: hooded, bloodied and snarling like wolves.

Underwater now, throwing his whole weight into the attempt, Alex wrenched desperately at his own knife arm, but the other's grip on his wrist was as inexorable as a steel vice. Baring his teeth, Alex bit into the fist that enclosed him until he felt his teeth meet through the gristle, but still the grip did not weaken. Instead, the blade flashed past his face again and although he wrenched his head away he felt the icy burn of its passage through his cheek. He should shout for the MI5 men, he realised numbly, but then there was a second explosion of light as his opponent's knife hilt hammered into the base of his skull, his face was forced underwater and there was no longer any breath to shout with.

Soon his lungs were screaming and his legs flailing beneath him, kicking at the Glock as it swung on its lanyard. He grabbed for the other's knife hand, couldn't reach it, punched at where he thought the smashed nose ought to be and clawed blindly for the eyes. But the grip on his head was as immovable as that on his knife arm, he'd had no chance to grab any air and finally his mouth gagged open to admit a choking inrush of water. Anoxia came fast and he felt his hands sleepily release their grip on the commando knife.

And then, in some dim, drowning corner of his consciousness, Alex sensed that he was being dragged upwards. Retching, he vomited up the best part of a litre of river water and as he struggled for air he was aware of a hooded face poised above him.

'So,' said the face quietly. 'You're the one.' There was a hint of a Belfast accent.

Alex said nothing. His chest was agony and points of light danced in front of his eyes 'Do it,' he rasped contemptuously. 'Kill me and be on your way.'

'I'll not kill you,' the Watchman murmured,

251

reversing his knife in his hand. 'That'd be too much like killing myself.'

The Watchman's arm became a blur, a third blinding whipcrack of pain bloomed behind Alex's eyes and this time he lost consciousness altogether.

TWENTY

Dawn Harding arrived at 5 a.m. with a Service doctor and the same forensic pathology team that had attended to the body of Craig Gidley. Above him, Alex heard them take the stairs up to George Widdowes' bedroom at a run, heard the abrupt halt of their footsteps as they discovered the horrendous carnage there.

Alex himself was lying naked on the camp bed wrapped in a single blood-sodden sheet. The MI5 security duo who had found him unconscious on the bank had removed his wetsuit and dressed his wounds as best they could from their first-aid kits, but in the end he'd told them to leave it for the doctor. His left cheek had a deep transverse gash along the line of the bone and his right ear had been almost cut in half – two hours after the event blood was still welling down both sides of his face. With the left arm he'd been exceptionally lucky – the cut was deep but the knife had missed the subcutaneous muscles and his hand function seemed unimpaired. The wound to the left thigh was over a foot long and had bled copiously but again no important muscle function seemed impaired. Alex guessed that the tough double-layer neoprene of the wetsuit had gone a long way towards preventing more serious damage.

He supposed that he ought to be a bit more worried about his skull. He'd always been a thick-headed bugger – his dad and several of his instructors had told him that – but he had received two very violent blows indeed and the pain when he tried to move his head was excruciating: of a different order even from his gashed face.

But the pain at the back of his head shrank into insignificance when he considered the scale of his failure to protect the life of George Widdowes, who now lay upstairs in a three-foot-diameter pool of clotting blood with a gag in his mouth, a six-inch nail through his right temple and his severed ears on his pillow.

As soon as he could move Alex had insisted that the security men help him up there and the huge blood loss had told him immediately that Meehan had cut Widdowes' ears off before ending his victim's life with the hammer and the six-inch nail.

What can those last moments have been like? Alex wondered speechlessly. What had been the order of the fear that Widdowes had felt when faced with Meehan and his knife? And the pain as the ears were sawn through? What had that been like, coupled with the knowledge of the obscene killing that was to follow?

Impossible to imagine. And whatever the nature of these experiences, it had been he – Alex Temple – who had gifted them to George Widdowes.

Arrogance had overruled caution. He had placed himself in the front line without back-up and by doing so put another man's life at risk. In part, he realised with appalling clarity, his actions had been driven by sheer competitiveness, by the simple urge to prove Dawn and her organisation wrong.

He had dared and George Widdowes had lost.

His failure, personal and professional, was absolute.

He had never felt such despondency. Never felt such icily unquenchable rage.

Dawn made her way downstairs with the doctor, a T-shirted man in his forties with a faint South African accent whom she introduced as Max. Both looked stunned by the slaughter upstairs.

Without hesitation the doctor stripped the sheet from Alex and scanned his body.

Dawn glanced down at his bloodied nakedness and then turned to the wall. '*Shit!*' she murmured. 'What a *fucking* mess. I see he almost took your ear off too?'

'Didn't mean to,' said Alex blankly. 'Just slashed at me, going for my eyes. I asked your colleagues to stick the bulldog clip on to hold the whole thing together.'

'Probably saved the ear,' said Max. 'I assume this was all done with a knife?'

'Yeah. Commando type.'

'Had any tetanus shots recently?'

'Three months ago.'

'AIDS test?'

Alex closed his eyes. 'He was trying to kill me, not fuck me.'

'Get one done. Any other injuries?'

'Couple of good bashes to the base of the skull. Probably with the steel hilt of the knife.'

Max felt gingerly beneath Alex's head. 'Does that hurt?'

'Doesn't feel great.'

'Could be fractured. I'll book you an X-ray. Meanwhile, I'd better get you stitched up. You'll probably find that it hurts less and the time goes quicker if you talk.'

Alex raised an eyebrow at Dawn.

Max caught the look. 'Yeah, you can talk in front of me. I've certified three murdered desk officers as having died of natural causes in the last month, I think I'm suitably compromised.'

Dawn took a deep breath and, as Max selected a suturing needle from a case, moved back a pace or two. 'What happened?' she asked, looking coldly down at Alex.

'He got the jump on me. Basically, I was wrong to have continued with the set-up here after you refused me a back-up man.'

Dawn caught Max's eye and with a flick of her head indicated that he wait upstairs. Pulling his needle through, the doctor left it hanging.

'So George Widdowes' death was my fault, was it?' Dawn demanded as soon the door had closed above them.

'No,' replied Alex levelly, 'it was my fault. It was an error of judgement on my part. I'm not ducking responsibility for that.'

'So you had a Glock and he wasn't carrying a fire-arm of any kind?' asked Dawn.

'That's correct,' Alex confirmed. 'Or if he was carrying a firearm he dropped it pretty early on in the game. So we both pulled knives.'

'Go on,' said Dawn.

'I broke his nose, bit his left knuckle pretty deeply and stabbed him a couple of times in the upper body. It obviously wasn't enough to put him down or stop him doing what he wanted to do, but I hurt him, I think. He won't be feeling good right now, and his face and hand will be visibly damaged.'

'How long did this fight go on for?'

'Oh, three or four minutes probably.'

'And how would you rate him, professionally speaking?' she asked.

Alex shrugged and immediately wished that he hadn't. 'Better than me, obviously,' he answered wretchedly. 'It was weird, though. He was totally aggressive, but . . .'

'But?'

'But when the point came he chose not to kill me.'

'Why, do you think?'

'Well, he said something just before he hit me on the head and knocked me out. Something along the lines of . . . oh, killing me would be like killing himself or something. Some psycho bullshit.'

'You saw him clearly?'

'No. For a start he was covered with black cam-cream, for seconds he was wearing a wetsuit with a hood.'

Dawn remained expressionless. 'Can you remember anything at all about him?'

Alex looked away. Once again, he saw the icily staring figure at Don Hammond's funeral. Had he simply constructed that image in his mind from the MI5 photographs?

'He's about my size and build. And right-handed. And he hasn't got a beard or moustache. That's all I'm certain of.'

'That doesn't exactly narrow it down a great deal.'

'I know,' said Alex. 'And I'm sorry. I'm sorry about the whole thing.'

Dawn looked at him, shook her head and punched out a number on her mobile. At the pick-up she

257

relayed Alex's description and the nature of the Watchman's injuries. Afterwards she walked round the cellar, examined the gashed wetsuit and the small pile of Alex's belongings.

'We've got people covering the ground for a ten-mile radius,' she told him. 'Helicopters, tracker dogs, everything. Country-wide the police'll be looking for a man in his mid-thirties, around five foot eleven and strongly built, with a broken nose and injured hand. We've put it around that he's a paranoid schizophrenic, armed, who's escaped from the high-security wing of Garton Hill. Do not approach, et cetera.'

Alex was silent. There was nothing useful left to say.

Five minutes later Max whip-finished the sutures on his cheek. 'Right,' he said. 'Let's get on with that ear. Tell them upstairs I'll be at least another forty minutes.' He turned back to Alex with a rueful smile. 'Think sweet thoughts, my friend. This is going to hurt.'

That afternoon Alex was driven in a private ambulance to the Fairlie Clinic in Upper Norwood, London. In theory this facility is available to the paying public; in practice it is reserved for the use of the security services. Several supergrasses, Alex had heard, had received reconstructive facial surgery behind its unremarkable doors.

There, he was walked to a windowless private room and his clothes were placed in a locker. A male nurse brought him a cup of tea, a painkilling dose of Volterol and Coproxamol, and the use of a radio tuned to Classic FM. The rest of the day passed slowly.

258

Shortly before midnight Alex awoke to hear his mobile phone juddering in his locker. It was still switched to vibrate, he realised. He was lying in total darkness against cotton pillows, the painkillers had worn off and his stitches were burning.

'Alex,' came the voice, quiet but insistent. 'It's Stevo, man.'

'Stevo?' he asked blankly, then remembered talking to the sniper team leader at Don Hammond's post-funeral piss-up. 'Stevo, yeah, tell me! How are you?'

'Fine, man – listen, I don't know what you want Den Connolly for but I can tell you we've had all manner of lairy buggers asking after him recently.'

Box people, thought Alex. Might have guessed it.

'Basically the lads have kept schtumm,' Stevo continued. 'But I'll tell you what I know.'

'Go on.'

'He left after the Gulf and hooked up with some outfit doing marine security in the Mediterranean. Don't know the details, but apparently he started hitting the Scotch or the job went arse-up or whatever and the next thing anyone heard was he was into armed robbery.'

'Yeah?'

'Word is, he was the trigger man on that job off the North Circular.'

'Park Royal?' murmured Alex. 'A security van? Something to do with cashpoints?'

'Yeah. Basically three of them did the Bank of Scotland for a million and a half. Not a massive take, but good enough for Den and he fucked off to Spain.'

'D'you know where?'

'A village outside Marbella called El Angel. One of the lads went down there last summer. Apparently

Den got some Spanish front guy to buy a bar for him and hangs out there.'

'What's the bar called?'

'Pablito's. Nice little place, apparently. Den's in a bit of a downward spiral, though.'

'And officially no one knows about this place?'

'Bill Leonard certainly doesn't, because he called us in a week ago and asked if anyone had any ideas where to find him. Then there were a couple of obvious Boxheads in Saxty's asking after him. We all assumed it was something to do with the Park Royal job.'

'How do you know it isn't?'

'I don't know. I reckon you'd tell us the form if it was anything like that.'

'I promise you, I'm not going to grass him up.'

There was a brief silence. 'The RSM was wondering: is it anything to do with a certain former student?'

Alex smiled and, as so often before, marvelled at the subtlety and accuracy of the Regiment's NCO grapevine. 'Speak no evil, hear no evil, see no evil,' he said eventually.

'Like that, is it? Wise monkeys?'

'Something like that. Thanks, Stevo.'

TWENTY-ONE

He offered Dawn his resignation the next day.

'You can't just . . . *walk out*!' she protested. 'You're the only one to have seen Meehan face to face.'

'He's the one who's seen me, not the other way round, and I don't look exactly anonymous with these stitches all over me. I won't be able to get within miles of him.'

'And Angela Fenwick? What's going to happen when he comes after her?'

'Your people are going to have to stop him,' said Alex. 'It's as simple as that.'

She stared at him. 'Alex.' She hesitated over the use of his name. 'Please. Don't make me beg you to finish the job.'

'It's more likely to be Meehan who's finishing the job,' said Alex wryly, touching his bandaged face.

'Alex.' she lowered her voice. 'You can catch him and you can kill him. You're the best. That's why we came to you.'

He glanced over at her. Today she was dressed completely in steely grey – the grey of her eyes. 'What would it take,' she murmured, 'to keep you on the case? In charge of the case, calling the shots?'

Would you credit it, he thought. *She's actually schmoozing me*. He closed his eyes. He'd never yet walked away from a challenge.

261

'You could have whatever . . .'

'Spain,' he interrupted her flatly.

She stared at him.

'We have to fly to Spain. There's someone we need to see.'

He gave her a censored version of the facts. She listened in silence.

'I don't see why you can't simply tell me who this man is, so that I can send someone over to talk to him.'

'He won't talk to you or to anyone you send,' said Alex firmly. 'It's got to be me. Once I've talked to this guy I'll hand the information over to you and you can do what you want with it. You brought me in for my specialised knowledge – you might as well get your money's worth.'

She looked at him uncertainly and he shrugged. If he could help MI5 nail Meehan it might make up in some small way for his negligence towards George Widdowes. It was all that he had left to offer.

'If anyone knew Meehan,' Alex continued, 'it was this guy. Day after day, week after week, down at that bunker in Tregaron . . . You get to know someone pretty damn well under those circumstances. You talk to each other because there's nothing else to do. Blokes I've trained – I know things about them their wives certainly don't.'

She nodded, took her mobile from her bag and left the room. By the time she returned he had finished the coffee. Her eyes travelled over the ugly, black-scabbed stitches that cut across his face.

'Angela's flying to Washington this morning for two days and I think we can assume she'll be safe from Meehan during that time. But it means we have to get to Spain pretty much immediately and be back within forty-eight hours. Do you think you can travel in that state?'

They went first-class that afternoon. At the Fairlie Clinic they knew all about short recovery times, and the male nurse who had attended Alex the day before gave Dawn a swift tutorial on the care of knife wounds and packed a kit containing all the bandages, dressings and painkillers that she would need.

At Heathrow, at Alex's insistence, they had bought a beach bag and swimming kit. In Alex's case this had meant a pair of blue shorts, in Dawn's a red bikini that Alex had exchanged for the severe one-piece she herself had chosen.

'We've got to fit in,' he told her as the plane circled Malaga airport. 'The more official we look the less he'll tell us. If we look like a couple of civil servants on expenses I can guarantee that he won't even speak to us. And we both know you look good in red!'

She'd ignored the last comment and reluctantly agreed, as she had agreed that no official mention would be made of their contact's name or location, and that whatever she learnt from the visit no criminal prosecution would be set in motion.

'The other thing you have to remember,' Alex had told her, 'is that the world our man occupies is not run by *Guardian* readers but by hard-core criminals. The deal with girlfriends is that they wear a lot of lipstick, they're treated like princesses and when it's time to talk business they make themselves scarce. So when I feel that point's coming I'll expect you to do just that, OK?'

'I don't know why you need me along at all,' she complained.

'To make the whole thing kosher. Our guy's sure

to have some sort of woman in tow and a single male visitor unbalances the household. He constitutes a threat, a sexual challenge, a physical invasion – all sorts of negative things. A man with a girlfriend, however, is quite another matter. You and his *chica* can push off and talk about blonde highlights or vibrators or whatever and leave the men to put the world to rights over a bottle of ten-year-old malt.'

'I can't wait.'

'Look, we want a result, we've got to press the right buttons.'

She narrowed her eyes. 'And all that male-heroic, bimbo-girlie stuff is a million miles from your own enlightened, neo-feminist views, right?'

'Absolutely,' said Alex. 'I'm the original new man, me.'

The seat belt sign came on and a broad swathe of brilliant Mediterranean blue appeared beneath them. It was 4.15 local time.

The drive from Malaga airport took the best part of forty minutes in their hired Mercedes. It was a beautifully clear day, the air was warm and the pace of the traffic on the coast highway leisurely. From Malaga to Marbella seemed to be one long strip of holiday, golfing and marina developments. Some of these were completed, some were still at the bricks-and-mortar stage and all offered extravagantly generous terms to potential buyers.

'We should put a deposit down on a condo.' Alex yawned contentedly as they bypassed Marbella. 'We can retire here and play golf when we finally hang up our shoulder holsters.'

'Endless boozing with retired villains,' said Dawn acidly. 'I think not.'

'Oh, get a life, girl! The sun's shining. We're on the Costa del Sol. Let's at least try to enjoy ourselves.'

'There's something very creepy about this place. Where are all the young people, for a start?'

'Having sexy siestas would be my guess. That or lying on the beach.'

'Hm. Planning the next Brinks–Mat robbery more likely.'

'Look,' said Alex, 'there's the sign for El Angel.'

They drove past the turning and on to Puerto Banus, where they had booked accommodation for two nights. The Hotel del Puerto, they discovered, was a class act. A fountain surrounded by dwarf palms played in the reception area and their luxurious balconied room overlooked the port.

The room was a double. Alex had no reason to suspect that Connolly would check their accommodation, but he knew two singles would definitely spook him in the unlikely event that he did bother. Dawn had not been enthusiastic about a shared bed and Alex had drily promised to sleep on the floor.

And here they were. Beneath them sparkling white yachts rocked gently at anchor, and on the quayside expensively dressed holidaymakers sauntered past the bars and shops. Even Dawn brightened at the prospect before them and when Alex suggested they went down for a snack she readily agreed.

He unzipped his bag on the double bed, stripped uncomfortably to his boxer shorts – the wound in his thigh was particularly painful after the journey – and replaced his jeans and T-shirt with lightweight chinos and a Hawaiian shirt printed with dragons. The stitches he covered up with Elastoplast. 'How do I look?' he asked Dawn.

'Like a beaten-up pimp,' said Dawn. 'If you'll excuse me, I'll change in the bathroom.'

She re-entered in a short cocktail frock in her signature dove-grey and the faintest suggestion of scent. Her hair and her eyes shone. Alex stared at her.

'You look . . .'

'Yes, Captain Temple?'

'. . . as if you're on holiday.'

'Good,' she said. 'Let's go.'

They chose a bar more or less at random. It was a little past five in the evening, and the glare had lifted from the sea and the gin palaces in front of them. The tables near them held middle-aged men in yachting gear and much younger women with implausibly huge breasts.

Their food arrived, plus a couple of Cokes. Alex had warned Dawn that some fairly serious drinking lay ahead. From his pocket he took a small plastic container holding a dozen ephedrine tablets. These, drawn from the Fairlie Clinic, had the dual effect of sharpening the senses and keeping drunkenness at bay. 'Bottoms up!' He grinned, downing two of them and handing the container to Dawn.

'Cheers!' rejoined Dawn rather more soberly. She took two and placed the container in her bag for safe keeping.

'Glad to see you're taking deodorant,' observed Alex, peering down into the bag. 'Things could get a bit sweaty.'

'Funny guy,' said Dawn. 'It's actually a can of Mace. Anyone tries any monkey business – including you – they go down.'

'Riot girl, huh?'

'You bet.'

The drive took fifteen minutes.

El Angel was a very different proposition from Puerto Banus. Not so much a village as an arbitrary strip of land between the highway and the sea, it comprised a clutch of new and not-so-new hacienda-style developments. The largest of these – a bowling and fast-food centre – was windowless and uncompleted, and from the weathered appearence of its plasterwork had clearly been so for some time. A large painted sign showed the development as its architects had envisaged it – bustling, youthful and cosmopolitan – but in truth it looked merely forlorn.

Parking the Mercedes on the highway, Alex and Dawn followed the track towards the sea. This passed through low scrub and between areas which had clearly once been intended to be gardens. Now, however, they only contained builders' rubble, rusting angle iron and other construction detritus. The evening breeze carried a strong smell of dogshit.

Dawn winced as thistles tore at her ankles. 'Perhaps I'm not so ideally dressed after all,' she remarked, glancing down at her strappy sandals.

'You look fine,' said Alex.

The path led on to a custom-built road flanked by white-rendered houses. Some of these were occupied and had cars on their drives and defiant little gardens of bougainvillea and hibiscus in front of them, but most stood empty.

Alex was struck by the desolation of the place. These deserted villas were, in a very real sense, the end of the road. You would come here and slowly forget everything.

Dawn must have been feeling the same, because to his amazement she slipped her arm through his. 'In every dream home a heartache,' she murmured.

'Yeah. I'm beginning to feel seriously in need of a drink.'

'This bar *is* actually on the sea, is it?'

'That was the impression I got,' said Alex. 'Shall we ring one of these bells and ask?'

They looked at each other, laughed nervously, then Dawn strode over to the nearest house. The sign read 'Tangmere'.

The door was opened by an elderly man in a cravat and an RAF blazer. A vague housecoated figure, presumably his wife, peered nervously behind him.

'We're looking for Pablito's,' began Alex, shielding his stitched-up ear with his hand.

'Over the road, face the sea, track at eleven o'clock between Sea Pines and Casa Linda. ETA three minutes. Calling on young Denzil?'

'Yes.'

'First-rate chap. Darkish horse, of course, but then that's the rule rather than the exception out here. Tempt you inside for a minute or two? Raise a lotion to the setting sun?'

'Perhaps some other time,' said Alex guiltily, seeing the poorly concealed desperation in the other man's eyes.

'Very good. Dunbar's the name. Usually here.'

Alex and Dawn set off down the track and saw the bar almost immediately. It was a blockhouse of a place, finished in a rough brownish render which matched the stony seashore. A neon design, not yet illuminated, showed palm trees and a sunset. Around the building stood half a dozen wooden benches and plastic-topped tables. A rusting motorcycle leaned tipsily against one wall.

'I am *definitely* overdressed,' said Dawn, picking her way awkwardly over the shingle.

'Whereas my pimp's outfit is spot on.' Alex grinned.

As they approached Pablito's they saw that they had taken a very indirect back route and that, in fact, a narrow road led straight to the front entrance. The swing doors in front of the building were half open. Inside, the place looked more spacious than its exterior suggested. A bar ran the length of one wall and on one of its stools a fat, heavily tanned man in a sarong, perhaps forty-five, was watching football on a wall-mounted television. Behind the bar a twenty-something woman with bleached blonde hair polished lager glasses. A cigarette smoked in an ashtray at her elbow.

As Dawn and Alex peered over the swing doors, the woman assumed a practised smile. 'Come on in, loves. We're still in injury time, as you can see, but make yourselves at home. What can I do you for?'

Alex turned to Dawn. From the corner of his eye he could see the blonde woman staring at the dressings on his face. 'What's it going to be, pet?'

Dawn smiled sweetly at him. 'Ooh, I think a Bacardi Breezer might just get me going!'

'One BB coming up. And for you, my love?'

'Pint would be nice.'

The man on the stool scratched his stomach and looked up. 'Tell you, that Patrick Viera's a bloody liability. Someone's going to put his lights out one of these days. Staying locally, are you?'

'Puerto Banus,' said Alex.

'Very nice. Come over on the 1615?'

Alex nodded, helped Dawn on to a bar stool and

with due consideration for his lacerated thigh, sat down himself.

'Exploring the area, then?'

The features were puffy with alcohol, but the eyes were shrewd. And beneath the gross brick-red body, Alex saw, were the remains of a disciplined physique. On the broad forearms were the marks of tattooes removed by laser.

'We wanted to get away from things for a few days.' Alex winked at Dawn and allowed his hand to stray to the dressing on his cheek. 'And as you can see, I've had a bit of a bang-up in the motor. We reckoned we were due some quality time.'

'Well, you've come to the right place for that.' The fat man's eyes flickered over the knife wounds. 'What game you in, then?'

'Den, love, leave the poor man alone,' said the woman, clattering over to the optics in her high-heeled mules. 'He hasn't set foot in here more'n two minutes and already you're . . .'

'No, it's OK,' said Alex. 'I'm a physical training instructor. And Dawn, well, Dawn's one of my best customers, aren't you, pet.'

She giggled. 'I hope so.'

This was the explanation that they had agreed on. If pressed, the suggestion was to be that Dawn was married to someone else.

The fat man nodded and returned to the football, shaking his head at intervals to mark his disapproval of Arsenal's failure to wrest control of the game from Sturm Graz. As the final whistle blew he swung round on his bar stool and extended a large hand to Alex. 'I'm Den. Big Den, Dirty Den, Fat Bastard, what-ever.' He moved behind the bar and slapped the woman's tight, white-denimed rump. 'And this is Marie. Pull us a bevvy, love.'

'Leave off! And for Gawd's sakes put on a bleedin' shirt.' The woman reached for a lager glass and winked at Dawn. 'He wouldn't stand for it if I went about with my chest hanging out – I don't see why I should when he does!'

'When you've got a body like mine,' said Den, 'you should share it with the world.'

He emptied a half-glass of Special Brew in a single swallow, slapped his vast belly, reached for his cigarettes and leant confidentially towards Dawn. 'You know, I'm known locally as something of a fitness guru,' he murmured.

Dawn giggled again. 'Well, I approve of your gym,' she said, looking around her at the football pennants and the signed *EastEnders* posters.

Other customers began to arrive. Alex and Dawn nursed their drinks at the bar and listened to the amiable banter around them. Everyone else, it was clear, was a regular. Equally clear was that this unremarkable beach bar was a meeting place for expatriate criminal aristocracy. For the most part they were expensively if a little garishly dressed. The women looked a lot more like Marie than Dawn, favouring bleached-blonde feather cuts and uncompromising displays of orange cleavage. The men went for Ross Kemp buzzcuts, pastel leisurewear and extensive facial scarring.

Den acted as host, drinking steadily and determinedly himself and ensuring that others' glasses were full. To Alex there seemed to be no clear line between paid-for and complimentary drinks. No money was demanded of him and he assumed that he and Dawn were running up a tab.

At nine o'clock on the dot the Dunbars appeared, nodded courteously to Dawn and Alex, shook hands all round, drank a whisky and soda and a gin and tonic respectively, and left.

'The old boy flew Spitfires over the Western Desert,' Den told Alex afterwards. 'Ten confirmed kills. Now he's living on twenty-five quid a week. I let him run up a tab and then cancel it when Remembrance Sunday comes round. Least I can do.'

Alex nodded.

'I get him talking sometimes,' Den continued, lighting a cigarette. 'Dogfight techniques. Aerial combat. And I tell you, get him on to all that stuff and you see the old hunter-killer light come back into those eyes. Know what I mean?'

Alex nodded again. He could feel the ephedrine now, racing through his system. Beside him Den ashed his cigarette and took a deep draught of Special Brew. The big man was sweating. Behind them the wives shrieked, Dawn among them.

Alex excused himself. He needed a piss.

Edging through the crowd he made his way outside into the neon twilight and peered around. By the palm trees would do. Behind him he heard feet crunching on the shingle – some other bloke on the same errand, he guessed.

Then something determined in the tread – some grim regularity – told him that it wasn't. As he half turned, glimpsing a heavy-set silhouette topped with the shine of a shaven head, a massive forearm locked chokingly round his throat.

'Forget the fitness bollocks, chum, who the fuck are you and what the fuck do you want?'

The voice was low – almost a whisper. Alex

272

struggled desperately to break free and lashed back with heels and elbows. The blows landed on flesh and bone but without result. The arm at Alex's throat was as solid as teak and tightening. Pinpoints of light appeared before his eyes and there was a rushing at his ears. His attacker clearly didn't expect an immediate answer.

It was probably the ephedrine that gave Alex the extra couple of seconds of consciousness in which his scrabbling fingers found the other man's crotch. Grabbing a sweaty handful of trouser, he clamped his left fist tight over the other man's scrotum and squeezed with all the force he could muster.

A high-pitched gasp of pain sounded in his ear and the arm at his throat loosened a fraction. Enough for Alex to whirl around, still clutching and twisting the other man's groin in his left hand, and hammer two rock-hard punches into his lower ribs with his right.

Evading a furious, windmilling series of counter-punches Alex staggered back, gagging for breath. He could see the man clearly now, a muscle-bound enforcer with a spider's-web tattoo inked across his thick neck. Alex had vaguely registered him in the bar earlier. The tattoos were certainly prison work.

His face distorted with pain, the gorilla advanced on Alex, who backed away fast. This wasn't about interrogation any more, it was about revenge. At that moment a slender figure rose from the shadows beside the entrance and a jet of spray cut the air.

The enforcer roared with the unaccustomed shock, pain and anger. His hands clamped themselves to his eyes, and Alex took advantage of the moment to kick him as hard as he could in the balls. With an agonised sigh, the man crumpled to the shingle.

'Can't leave you alone for a moment, can I,' said Dawn, stepping into the light from the neon sign and returning the Mace to her bag with a self-satisfied smile.

'I guess not,' said Alex, his heart pounding with adrenalin. He looked down at the groaning figure at his feet. 'Did you follow me out?'

'Put it like this – I thought all that traditional East End hospitality was a bit too good to last.'

'Well . . . Thank you!'

'What the bloody 'ell's goin' on 'ere, then?'

Framed in the bar's entrance was Connolly, drink in one hand, cigarette in the other. From the surprised look on his face the scenario was not at all the one he expected. I was supposed to be the one on the ground, thought Alex. Begging for mercy and admitting to being a police officer, presumably.

Connolly's look of surprise was quickly suppressed and he gave the fallen man a brisk kick in the guts. 'Get up, yer big fuckin' nelly!'

The enforcer writhed and Connolly turned concernedly to Alex. 'Sorry, chum, was Kev here being impertinent?'

'He asked me a question and then tried to strangle me before I had a chance to answer.'

Connolly shook his head, marched into the bar and returned with a jug of water, which he emptied over Kev's head. 'You just can't get decent help for love nor money these days . . .'

Slowly and unsteadily Kev dragged himself to his feet, clutching his groin. His T-shirt was sodden and a dark orange stain covered the left side of his face, where the Mace pepper spray had struck him. He managed a rueful grin, his eyes still streaming, and extended a shaky hand to Alex. 'Sorry, mate, over-reacted a bit there!'

'No problem,' said Alex, amazed that the man was able to stand at all. Now that the adrenalin from the fight was ebbing away the stitches on his own face were beginning to throb.

'All friends again?' asked Connolly with a dazzling smile. 'Marvellous. Kev, take the lady inside, open a bottle of champagne – the Moët, not that dago muck – and make her comfortable. And wipe yer boat race while you're about it!'

The gorilla nodded meekly and signed that Dawn precede him through the swing doors.

'I'm sorry about that, mate,' said Connolly, turning back to Alex. 'But you'll understand I've got to keep an eye on the security side of things.'

Alex nodded.

'You're not Old Bill, I know that much. But you're something. That's no sunlamp tan on your hands and neck, any more than those are car crash injuries on your face and arm. And I didn't see the rumble just then, but . . .'

'Stevo sent me,' said Alex quietly. 'I didn't want to alarm Marie.'

Connolly emptied his glass. 'Stevo? I don't know any Stevo.'

'Jim Stephenson from "B" Squadron in Hereford. That Stevo. I'm Regiment, Den.'

'Go on.'

'I'm in "D" Squadron. Seconded to RWW, like you were.'

'So when did you join?'

For five minutes Connolly subjected him to a series of questions about Regiment personalities, extracting details that only an insider would have known. He slipped in a trick question, asking if that idle short-arse Tosh McClaren was still around and Alex confirmed that yes, Tosh McClaren was still around, and he was still 6 foot 2 tall. After a time, Connolly appeared satisfied that Alex was who he said he was.

Sensing this, Alex looked him in the eye. 'Listen, Den, I'm not trouble, OK? I just want to talk.'

Connolly stared at him in silence. He looked tired, puffy-faced and a little sad. And strangely vulnerable, thought Alex, for a man who had once been known as the SAS's toughest NCO.

'You're not a talker, son, you're a shooter. It's written all over your face.'

'I'm looking for someone, Den, that's all. Help me and you can rest easy about the Park Royal job. No more cover stories, no more looking over your shoulder for the cops.'

'What the fuck's the Park Royal job?'

'Den, I'm family. Trust me.'

'Oh, yeah? So who's the girl? Well handy with the Mace, it looked like.'

'She's just a girl. Nothing to do with anything.'

Den stared at his empty glass in silence, flipped his cigarette into the gathering darkness and nodded. For a moment, behind the flushed features, Alex saw the taut wariness of the Special Forces soldier. Then the dazzling smile returned and a large hand was placed on Alex's shoulder. 'Come on, son, we're wasting good drinking time. Tonight's on the house, yeah?'

He steered Alex back inside and moments later Marie was sliding Alex a glass of champagne and a shot-glass of Irish whiskey. Someone, to applause and laughter, began to sing 'My Yiddisher Momma'.

Some time later Dawn reappeared beside him. Her cheeks were flushed and she seemed to be genuinely enjoying herself. Under the circumstances it seemed natural for Alex to slip his arm round her waist, and for her in response to incline herself against him. For a moment he felt the soft pressure of her breast against his side.

'Thank you,' he said again. 'That could have turned nasty, one way or another. How are you getting on with the gangster wives?'

She placed her champagne thoughtfully on the bar. 'They're good fun. I like them. Any progress?'

'I've dropped a name or two. Told him who I really am. Not who you are, though. Far as he's concerned, you're just my girl.'

'Mm. Lucky me.'

'The main problem is that he thinks I'm some sort of hit man. Possibly even come over here to whack him. He's very jumpy. I think the best thing I can do is to tell him the real reason I'm here and hope that calms things down.'

'I agree. And this is looking like a rather serious conversation if I'm supposed to be some no-brain blonde bimbo.' She pouted. 'Which I clearly am!'

He ran a finger down her cheek. 'It's just that you play the part so well.'

'Now why am I suspicious of a compliment like that, I wonder?' she asked.

There was another burst of singing from the floor of the room. Someone had sat themselves at a piano and was banging out old Cockney songs.

'Are we within earshot of Bow Bells here, do you think?' mused Dawn, throwing back the remains of her drink.

'Basildon, maybe,' said Alex. 'Not that I've got any quarrel with that, as an Essex man myself.'

Den Connolly suddenly appeared beside them, sweating and massive. 'Before I'm too pissed to understand a word you're saying,' he asked Alex, 'who exactly was it you was after?'

Alex dismissed Dawn with a nod of his head and a pat on her dove-grey behind. 'Joseph Meehan. Code-named Watchman. You finished him for Box.'

Connolly nodded. 'I ain't officially here,' he said eventually, his words slurring. 'I ain't officially anywhere. But you know that.'

Alex nodded. 'I know the score from Stevo. No one hears your name. Ever. And if you can give me what I need you can rest easy about that other business.'

'You gimme your word on that?' Connolly glanced meaningfully down at the assembled company. 'My friends'd be very pissed off if . . . They're my family now, y'understand – forget fuckin' Hereford, RWW, all that old bollocks.'

Alex looked him in the eye. 'I give you my word.'

Connolly pursed his lips and nodded slowly and vaguely to himself. 'Tomorrow. Lunchtime. Bring your . . .' He gestured vaguely towards Dawn, who was whispering confidences to Marie. 'Meanwhiles, order anything you want. Open bar, like I said.'

They left around 2 a.m. Not because Alex thought that Connolly might relent and talk to him that night, but because he felt that he needed to prove his credentials to the ex-NCO. He had to show proper respect. Leaving early would have been regarded as very graceless. So he had stuck around, downing drink after drink, and looking suitably impressed by the tales

278

of blags, slags, grass-ups, fit-ups, bent coppers, unnumbered shooters and all the rest of the hard-man mythology. Dawn meanwhile rested wide-eyed at his side, with her arm draped lightly round his waist. They looked, in short, like any impressionable young couple who happened to have stumbled into a bar full of criminals.

When the last goodbyes had been said and they'd finally reached the car, Dawn blinked hard several times and reached in her bag for the key.

'You OK to drive?' asked Alex blearily.

'I've actually drunk comparatively little,' said Dawn. 'I always get rum and a Coke in that situation – that way you can just keep your glass filled with Coke and no-one's the wiser.'

'Well, ephedrine or no, I'm well and truly bladdered, I'm afraid,' Alex slurred. 'But mission accomplished, sort of.'

'Get in,' said Dawn.

At the hotel they stood together for a moment in front of the open window. The port and the yachts were lit up now, and the sea was an inky black below them. A tide of drunken benevolence washed over Alex. 'You were great,' he said feelingly, placing a hand on her warm shoulder. 'Especially Maceing that bonehead of Connolly's.'

She smiled and inclined her cheek to his hand. 'You've already thanked me for that. I enjoyed myself. What d'you think tomorrow holds?'

'Dunno. All that lunch invitation stuff was just to buy himself time. The more of his hospitality he can persuade us to soak up, the less bad he's going to feel about us leaving empty-handed. At the moment he accepts that I'm kosher and you're just the sweet thing

I happen to be travelling with, but he's worried about who comes after me. Where it's all going to end.'

'What's he got to hide, Alex?' she asked gently.

'Enough.'

'So what promises did you make him?'

Careful, Alex told himself woozily. She doesn't know about the Park Royal job. 'Oh, I strung him along . . .'

'You think he'll talk to you tomorrow?' Dawn asked sharply. 'Because tomorrow's all we've got. In thirty hours Angela gets back from Washington and any time after that . . .'

Alex nodded. She didn't need to spell out the danger that Meehan posed. Privately, he was far from convinced that Connolly would talk to him, but he couldn't see how else the situation could have been handled. The alcohol was pounding at his temples now and the knife cuts were beginning to pulse in unison.

'Why don't I get those dressings off?' she asked him. 'Let a bit of fresh air at your poor face. Lie down on the bed?'

He could quite easily have removed the dressings himself, but lay there breathing in her jasmine scent and her smoky hair, and the faint smell of rum on her breath. She was OK, was Dawn, he decided. A bit of a bitch at times and the most irritating bloody driver he'd ever met, but what the hell? She had a tough job. He could live with her downsides.

And she really was quite seriously pretty with those cool grey eyes and that soft, secretive mouth. Without especially meaning to, and with a vague stab at discretion, he glanced down the grey linen front of her dress as she inched the dressing from his cheek.

She didn't seem to be wearing any sort of bra and he recalled with a rush of pleasure the feel of her breasts against him in the bar.

'That's not fair,' she said reproachfully.

'What's not fair?'

'Here I am, doing my big Florence Nightingale number and all you can do is stare down my front, panting like a dog. You're supposed to be an officer and a gentleman.'

'No one ever said anything about being a gentleman,' said Alex. 'And I'm not panting, I'm breathing.'

'Well, stop it. And shut your eyes, or I'll rip your ear in half again and you wouldn't like that, now would you?'

Alex smiled, and tried not to think about George Widdowes' ears lying grey and bloodstained against the pillow. The same thought evidently occurred to Dawn, for her movements abruptly hardened and became businesslike.

When she had finished she stepped out on to the balcony with her mobile phone. 'Can you give me a moment?' she asked, punching out a number. 'Personal call.'

He took himself into the bathroom. The boyfriend, he thought, and felt a sudden urge to hit Dawn's unknown lover very hard in the face. Several times, preferably.

He glanced in the mirror, at the angry black stitch-tracks across his face. *You look like shite, Temple*, he told himself. *You'd be lucky to trap some swamp donkey from Saxty's looking like that, let alone this foxy little spook. Get real.*

By the time she returned he was down to his boxer shorts and looking for the Nurofen.

'Turn round,' she said. 'Let me look at that thigh.'

Alex obeyed. Five minutes later she folded her arms. 'OK,' she began. 'This is the deal. You get the bed and the blankets from the cupboard, I get the quilt on the floor.'

'I'll go on the floor. You take the bed.'

'Normally I'd accept like a shot, but given the extent of your injuries I've decided to be generous. No arguments, Temple, OK?'

Alex inclined his head and climbed into the bed. Dawn went into the bathroom. When she returned to the quilt on the floor she paused for a moment in front of the window, a slight and entirely feminine figure in her white T-shirt and knickers.

Alex groaned. For the first time that day he found himself in severe physical pain.

TWENTY-TWO

'You're not going to throw up again, are you?' Dawn enquired.

'I don't think so,' whispered Alex. 'But you couldn't just ask that waiter for a half of lager, could you?'

'Are you insane?'

'No, I know it sounds bad but it works. And since it seems to be impossible to get a decent fried breakfast in this hotel . . .'

'This is Spain, Alex, not the Mile End Road. Why don't you just lie back and get some sun, and stop being so scratchy?'

It was 10.30 and they were on adjoining sunloungers by the hotel pool. Dawn was wearing the red bikini they had bought at Heathrow, but not even this could raise Alex's spirits. A bad hangover had coincided with an acute bout of guilt and depression concerning George Widdowes.

The day before had been enjoyable and there had been an air of promise about things – a sense that the mistakes of the past might somehow be redeemed by a little energetic detective work. Now, everything seemed curiously pointless. If he weighed up his career and balanced the harm he had done and the deaths he'd caused against the long-term good, he was unable to state – as he'd once been able to – that on balance the good came out on top. It didn't. The bad came out on top.

Den Connolly had clearly felt that moving from unattributable operations for the RWW to boosting security vans on the North Circular Road was little more than a side shuffle. It wasn't a question of going into crime – you were already there. You had already spent so much of your career so far outside the normal boundaries of behaviour that almost anything seemed logical and reasonable.

The trouble with crime, though, was criminals. They were stupid, for the most part, and greedy. And boastful, judging by last night, and sentimental, and seriously lacking in taste. No, he decided, you'd have to put your own outfit together. A few good, reliable blokes. Apply military standards of security, planning and execution.

And then what, assuming you did the bank and made your wad?

Buy a bar and a big telly, and listen to war stories and get fat?

Dawn raised her head from the sunlounger and peered at him irritably. Her face was shining with sunscreen. 'What was it you said yesterday? Cheer up? Get a life? The sun's shining?'

Alex turned to face her and felt the day's first pale flicker of lust. The red lycra strap of the bikini top hung undone on either side of her and a single pearl of sweat lay in the small of her back. For a moment he stared at it, wondering how her skin would taste, then a waiter with a tray approached.

'*Una cerveza para el Señor, por favor,*' murmured Dawn. '*Y un naranja fresca para mi, gracias.*'

'*Si, Señora.*' The waiter nodded and disappeared.

'That sounded very fluent,' said Alex.

'Yes, I told him you needed an enema for your bad mood.'

'What I need is not to have drunk so bloody much last night.'

'I expect you've done worse in the service of your country.'

He grunted. The knife wounds were beginning to heal, and in consequence to itch like crazy. 'I forgot to ask – did you manage to rescue my weapon from the river?'

'The Glock? Yes. Plus your knife and a silenced Sig Sauer that Meehan must have been carrying. And while you were out for the count, by the way, we managed to get tissue scrapings and a couple of hairs from under your fingernails.'

'Well, I certainly held on tight. But surely you don't need any proof of who you're dealing with?'

'Every confirmation helps. But our main hope is that we might be able to learn something about his whereabouts. The Forensic Science Service can tell you a hell of a lot from a hair.'

Alex looked at her doubtfully. 'Good luck with that. The hair may well turn out to be more helpful than laughing boy down the road.'

'If he's not going to tell us anything, why ask us to come back?'

'He'll probably produce something just to swing the immunity deal I promised him. The question is whether we'll be able to rely on what he produces.'

Dawn frowned at him. 'Look, about this immunity deal . . .?'

'Dawn, the chances are that if you've got nothing

on him now then nothing's going to come up in the future. And you can swing it, can't you, if he leads us to the Watchman?'

'It's a hell of a big "if".'

The drinks arrived. Alex drank down his beer in three long swallows, thought it probable for several minutes that he was going to vomit, then suddenly felt better.

Dressed, they strolled through the port, where Dawn bought herself a scoop-neck top and a pair of skin-tight white jeans, and high-heeled mules. To look the part, she explained. Basic tradecraft.

Back at the hotel she changed into it all, adding a Wonderbra.

'Blimey!' said Alex, impressed. 'All you need now is a forty-a-day Rothman's habit and a boyfriend on *Crimestoppers*!'

'If we hang around at Pablito's long enough I'll probably end up with both.'

Alex raised an eyebrow. 'I thought you were already taken. Mr Lucky-boy in London.'

Dawn rolled her eyes and swung her bag over her shoulder. 'Let's go.'

Pablito's appeared deserted. The swing doors were locked, the tables untenanted and wasps swung threateningly around an overflowing litter bin.

Checking his watch, Alex knocked at the entrance.

The door was opened by Marie, who was wearing a pink velour tracksuit. 'Come in. 'Fraid Den's still sleeping it off. You look a treat, my love. Cup of Nes?'

'Lovely,' said Dawn.

When the coffee was ready they carried it upstairs. Above the bar was a small landing giving on to a bedroom and bathroom, and a sun-baked roof terrace. On a large rectangle of plastic matting at one end of this, naked but for a faded pair of Union Jack underpants, lay Denzil Connolly, snoring. An ashtray had overturned at his side and a nine-tenths-empty bottle of Bell's whisky lay just beyond the reach of his outstretched arm.

'He likes to sleep under the stars,' said Marie. 'I had to put down the matting 'cause the bottles kept smashing and then he'd roll on the pieces in the night. He's a big feller, as you can see.' She folded her arms in a long-suffering gesture. '*Den, love, we've got company.*'

The sleeping figure stirred and the eyes half opened in puffy suspicion. 'Wha' the fuck you . . .' Seeing Alex and Dawn, he closed his eyes again, groaned and writhed like a hippopotamus. 'Wha's fuckin' time?'

'Twelve. And Alex and Dawn are here.'

'Who? Oh, yeah, right. Give us a hand up.'

He struggled to his feet and Marie led him inside. There were unpleasant noises from the bathroom.

By the time they sat down to lunch on the terrace half an hour later, however, Connolly appeared fully recovered. Bullish, even, in his vast shorts and polo shirt. They ate fish and oven chips with vinegar and mushy peas cooked by Marie and drank ice-cold Spanish beer.

'You two should get a place over here,' Connolly said expansively. He winked at Dawn. 'Can you cook, love?'

'You betcha.'

'Well, then. Sorted.'

'It would be nice, wouldn't it, Alex?' said Dawn.

'I'm afraid I'm not quite in the early-retirement

league,' said Alex. 'Maybe I could set up a little security outfit, though. Country clubs, golf clubs . . .'

'Protection?' asked Marie brightly.

'Well, I wouldn't put it exactly like that . . .'

The meal, and later the afternoon and early evening, wore on pleasantly enough. Alex had taken a couple more ephedrine tablets at the hotel and so was happy to maintain a steady intake of cold beer. Connolly drank Scotch from the start, occasionally topping up his drink with a splash of mineral water, and by mid-afternoon Alex estimated that the big man had sunk a good third of a bottle. This, he knew, was when you got the best of a heavy drinker: in the five- or six-hour window following recovery. The whisky seemed to have little effect on Connolly other than to cheer him up and he proved a vastly entertaining host, telling story after story about the criminal fraternity who were the bar's main – if not only – clientele. No mention was made of his own exploits, however, nor of his military past.

At four o'clock Marie drove them to San Pedro, where Connolly was a member of a country club. In practice this simply meant a change of bar and Alex tried to moderate his alcoholic intake. Dawn did her rum-and-Coke trick, always managing to have a full glass at her side, but for Alex it was harder. Connolly, he sensed, needed to know that he was in the presence of a kindred spirit. He needed company on the long alcoholic journey that would end in oblivion in the early hours of the morning. He needed to see Alex keep pace with him. This was the price for the information that he had to offer.

At six they returned to El Angel, where Maria prepared the bar for the night's trade and microwaved a frozen chicken-and-pineapple pizza to keep them all going. Despite having drunk more than two-thirds of a bottle of Scotch, Connolly appeared solid as a rock and capable of continuing for ever. Alex, by contrast and despite the ephedrine, was beginning to feel decidedly light-headed. It was a very hot day and he had downed a good dozen beers in half as many hours. Surreptitiously palming a glass and a salt cellar from one of the tables he disappeared into the Gents. There he poured a good teaspoonful of salt into the glass, added water and waited while it dissolved. Gritting his teeth, he took a hefty swig. As soon as the salt hit the back of his throat he retched convulsively, bringing up the last few drinks in a warm gush. Twice more, he forced himself to repeat the exercise. By the end of it he was white-faced and nauseated, but reckoned he had probably bought himself another couple of hours of drinking time.

Soon, the first customers started to arrive and the routine of the night began to repeat itself. Connolly appeared to be in expansive form again, greeting every new arrival with huge enthusiasm, roaring with laughter at their jokes and dispensing drinks liberally.

Alex began to despair of ever getting him alone. Had the big man, he fell to wondering, remembered a single detail of their conversation the night before? Or had he and Dawn simply been two vaguely recognised faces who, for reasons unknown, had turned up to keep him company?

The evening passed in a beery, pissed-up blur. He had drunk himself sober, Alex found, and with every minute that passed his irritation grew. He should have known better than to force through this trip on the word of a known head case like Stevo. All that he had done was compound his failure to protect Widdowes by promising information that, when push came to shove, he couldn't deliver. 'I'm not confident about all of this,' he confided to Dawn at about 11 p.m. 'Last night I was convinced he had something to tell us but now I think he's just stringing me along. That is, if he remembers what I said to him last night, which I'm seriously beginning to doubt.'

'I think you're wrong,' said Dawn. 'I think he's trying to come to a decision. I think we're in the best place we could be right now.'

Alex stared at her, amazed. Her tone was both complicit and intimate. Her usual operational scratchiness was nowhere to be found.

'Trust me, Alex,' she added, turning her back to the bar and placing a proprietorial hand on his shoulder. 'I've seen this sort of thing from informants before. It's a sort of dance they do, like cats walking round and round a place before they sit down.'

'I'm glad you think so,' said Alex, pleasantly conscious of the small pressure of her hand. 'I was going to say that I thought we'd blown several grand of your agency's budget on a wild-goose chase. That you might have some serious explaining to go through when you get back to Thames House. Swanky hotels and bikinis and all the rest of it.'

'Oh, the bikini won't be wasted,' said Dawn airily. 'But take my advice. Let Connolly come to you. He knows why you're here, all right.' She winked. 'Trust me!'

'I do trust you.'

'Well, I'm not sure if I should trust you with all these Costa Crime *femmes fatales*. I've seen a couple of real vampires eyeing you up.'

'Well, then your observational skills are better than mine, girl, because I haven't clocked them.'

She tapped the mobile phone in her jeans-jacket pocket. 'Would it surprise you that there was a call made to the hotel this morning asking to be put through first to your room and then to mine?'

'And?'

'And the caller discovered what he wanted to know, which is that we had the same room number. That I'm really your girlfriend, not some scalp hunter from Box or Special Branch.'

Alex smiled. 'Well, I'm glad we've got that straight.'

She gave him a long, cool glance. 'Will you do something for me?'

'What?' he asked, inhaling the smoky jasmine of her scent.

'If we get anything from Connolly will you go all the way for me?'

He narrowed his eyes. 'What exactly do you . . .'

She leant towards him, took his bottom lip between her teeth and bit him. Not hard, but not softly either. 'Stay on the case. You and me together. As equals. No more bullshit, no more fighting. After all,' she murmured, 'we are supposed to be sleeping together.'

He stared into her level grey eyes, dazed by her closeness.

'So, lovebirds, whassup?'

It was Connolly, swaying in front of them.

And Marie. 'Dawn, love,' she said, 'I've come to borrow you. You know the words to "Stand by Your Man", don't you? We need more chorus members.'

'Ooh, lovely,' trilled Dawn.

Connolly waited until the women had gone, then nodded towards the stairs.

On the roof terrace they drew up chairs. A bottle of Paddy's whiskey, two glasses and Connolly's cigarettes were arranged on a low table. The fat man poured the drinks. 'Joe Meehan, then,' he said, raising his glass. 'What's the story, morning glory?'

'How much do you know about what you were finishing him for?' asked Alex, sipping the whiskey, feeling the dark burn of its descent.

'Officially, nothing. Except that it was clear he was going over the water. And going in very deep, given the attention he was given. And I also knew that he was very good. Almost certainly the best man I ever trained.'

'No one told you anything?'

'No, we were left to draw our own conclusions. I'll tell you something, though. They made a big thing about the secrecy of the operation. It was an RTUable offence even to mention it.'

'Well, notes are being compared now.'

Connolly waited, his glass steady in his hand, immobile.

Alex leant forward. 'You were right about Ireland, obviously. He went in deep, joined the Provies, worked his way up.'

'Brave lad.'

'He was,' agreed Alex. 'Until the whole thing went arse-up. They turned him, Den.'

'Not possible,' said Connolly flatly. 'They never turned that lad, I'd bet the bar on it. He was the best I ever saw. The most committed. He'd never have fallen for all that tinpot Armed Struggle bollocks.'

'They turned him, Den,' Alex repeated. 'He joined Belfast Brigade's Nutting Squad. Made bombs for them. Personally tortured and murdered those FRU blokes – Bledsoe and Wheen.'

'Not possible, mate,' said Connolly again matter-of-factly, tapping the filter of a cigarette on the table and lighting it. 'I just don't believe you.'

'It's true and it's verified. The province's worst nightmare, and the Regiment and Box put him there.'

Connolly shook his head in disbelief. Closed his eyes, briefly. 'So now you're after him, yeah?'

'Look, I don't know what happened over the water, Den, but the man's certainly killing people now. Three in the last couple of months.'

'And so you've been pulled in to kill him.' Connolly took a drag of his cigarette, sipped reflectively at his whiskey and stared out over the sea.

'I need to find him. Put any spin on that you like.'

Connolly shook his head. 'You can fuckin' whistle, chum.'

'Den, mate, you've got a nice set-up here, and you've been good to me and Dawn. But do you really want to spend the rest of your life looking over your shoulder, worrying that someone's going to grass you up? Worrying that every new customer might have an extradition order and a warrant in his pocket? Armed robbery, Den. Think about it. It pulls down a heavy score.'

From the other man's expression Alex could see that he had thought about it, often. 'Are you threatening me?'

'No. What I'm saying is that I can make that worry disappear. For ever. But I'm going to have to have something very solid to offer in return. If you've nothing to give me I'll disappear, and everything will carry on as it was before.' He emptied his glass and poured himself another. 'I'm not threatening you, Den, I'm just making you an offer. Take it or leave it.'

293

For several minutes they both stared out at the sea. From below them, in the bar, came the muted sound of singing and laughter.

'There was a thing Joe told me once, about his childhood,' Connolly began abruptly. 'He spent his teens, it must have been, with his dad in the West Country – Dorchester, was it, somewhere like that – and every summer they'd go caravanning. Lake District, New Forest, Norfolk Broads, all over. Just the two of them. Now on one of those trips, he told me – can't remember which – his dad parked up the caravan and they set off for a hike across country.

'Usual enough story – they went a bit too far, weren't quite sure of their bearings, weather turned nasty on them, so rather than footslog it back they decided to try and find a bed and breakfast. No B&B for miles, as it turned out, but what they did find was the entrance to a big old house. Deserted, with boarded-up windows and that kind of thing. The place had obviously been secured at some point, but the padlocks and the notices on the gate had been vandalised and it was pouring with rain and in they went. It was getting dark by then, and the plan was to shelter for the night and make tracks back to the caravan park in the morning.

'So anyway they got inside, found a dry corner and got their heads down. The old man's a bit worried by this point, being a law-abiding sort of bloke, but the boy's in heaven: he and his dad are having the adventure of a lifetime! Morning comes and they find that there's not just the house – there's a ruined church and a river and some falling-down cottages and a couple of shops – a whole village. All completely deserted. Obviously been locked away for years.'

'Like Imber, on Salisbury Plain? Or what's that Royal Armoured Corps place in Dorset – Tyneham?'

'Exactly. Just like that. So they have a bit of an explore. The dad's still a bit jumpy but as I say, the boy's having the time of his life. He climbs into the church through a window, jimmies a door open and finds his way down to the crypt. Now I can't remember the exact details but somewhere down there, locked away in boxes or cupboards or something, is all this antique gear.'

'Gear?'

'Covert resistance stuff. Transceivers, morse sets, one-time pads, time-pencil detonators – that sort of thing, all packed away in greaseproof paper. So he takes some bits and pieces up to his dad, who can't believe his eyes, because although the gear's all World War Two vintage it's still in mint condition.'

'A cache in case of enemy invasion,' suggested Alex.

'That's what they eventually figure. And they find other stuff, too, hidden away beneath the other houses. Electrical bits and pieces, radio components, ironmongery, what have you. A real Aladdin's cave for a young lad.'

'So how come no one had found this stuff before them?'

'I dunno. I'm guessing that it was because the only other people who'd been near the place for decades had been dossers and tramps. A few bikers, perhaps, and maybe the local satanist coven but . . .'

Alex nodded. 'Go on.'

'Well, the boy's all for helping himself to the gear but the old man puts his foot down. They haven't committed any offence yet, he says – it's not

trespassing to walk through an open gate, after all –
and he doesn't object to their having a look at all this
stuff, but they're not taking it away. So they poke
around, Dad explains how it all works, and then they
pack it away again, reseal the boxes and off they go,
make their way back to wherever they left the
caravan.

'Anyway, to cut a long story short, Joe persuades
the old boy to shift the caravan to a farm a couple of
miles away and they go up to the old house every day
– creeping around like a couple of commandos, Joe
said, and having a good old sticky beak at all this secret
resistance gear. Happiest time he ever knew, Joe says.
Best days ever. And when it's time to go home, he
tells me, he does a funny thing. He goes and buys his
own padlock and chain, and locks the place up
properly. Puts up all the old notices again – MOD
Property, Strictly no Entrance to the Public and so
on.'

'Why does he do that?'

'Not sure. My guess is that it was something to do
with deep-freezing the experience. Sealing it away.
And also to do with the fact that his dad could have
made a lot of money out of flogging the gear without
anyone being any the wiser but chose not to out of
principle. There were a few of the old Mark III
transceivers down there, apparently – the SOE
suitcase jobs. They'd have to be worth a few grand
apiece now. I suppose Joe didn't want anyone else
having them away.'

'You know what I'm going to ask you next, don't
you?' said Alex.

'Yeah and I'm afraid I honestly don't know the
answer. I really don't. All I can remember is that the

place was on the edge of one of the national parks – Peak District, Snowdonia, Dartmoor . . . You must've trained people yourself – you know how you listen to what they say and you don't quite listen, and sometimes you deliberately forget.'

Alex nodded. He knew what the other man meant. Part of you kept friendship at arm's length when you were sending a man into a situation of acute danger. 'So why was he telling you all this?'

'It was a place we went in Wales – an MOD property in Eppynt Forest we were using for an escape and evasion exercise. There was a line of clapped-out cottages there and he said it reminded him of this place he'd once discovered with his dad, and told me the story.' Connolly frowned and blinked, and downed his whiskey. 'There was one other thing. The last time I saw him before the Box people came to take him away, we were up at the camp at Tregaron. We shook hands and I wished him luck, and he smiled and held up a key. At the time I had no idea what he was on about, but . . .'

'You think it was the key to that property?'

Connolly shrugged. 'Who knows?'

'And you can't think of any detail that might point to where this place was?'

'Alex, it was a dozen years ago. Anything was possible in those days and everyone you met had a weird story to tell. These things wash over you.'

'Happiest time he ever knew?' mused Alex.

'Best days ever,' confirmed Connolly and flicked his cigarette butt over the low parapet on to the beach.

'Leaving out Scotland for the moment,' said Alex,

thoughtfully kicking off his deck shoes, 'you've got the Lake District, the Peak District, the Cheviots . . .'

They had been back from Pablito's for less than ten minutes. Marie had called them a taxi and they'd left the hire-car at El Angel.

'. . . the North York Moors, the Dales, Kielder . . .'

'Alex,' said Dawn quietly, turning to the open hotel window and the twinkling lights of the port, 'could you please shut the fuck up and kiss me?'

Alex blinked. A warm tide of ephedrine-tempered alcohol raced through his bloodstream but for some imponderable reason his mind was clear. He stared at her. The Dawn Harding that stood before him now was no relation whatever of the vengeful bitch that he had been so unwillingly paired with in London. This Dawn Harding's face was flushed, her eyes were bright, her posture was challenging and expectant. A warm breeze touched her hair. With great care – this was definitely no time to fall flat on his face – he crossed the room towards her. His hands found the small of her back. Her eyes closed at his touch, her lips parted and she pressed against him, breathing hard. Wanting all of her at once – mouth, eyes, neck, breasts – he practically lifted her off her feet.

'Quick,' she murmured, her fingers in his hair. 'Get me out of these clothes.'

Alex kissed her again until she was gasping and her fingers had left his hair and were scrabbling at the buttons on his shirt.

She tore the last two, but by then he had pulled the tight white top over her head and unsnapped the fierce little Wonderbra. Her breasts were pale, their upper curves touched by a slight pinkness from the morning's sun and very faintly damp. She tasted of sweat and smoke.

Falling to his knees, he forced himself to slow down, explored her stomach with his mouth, ran the tip of his tongue down the line of tiny translucent hairs that descended towards the gilt stud of her jeans. Popping the stud, he eased down the zipper and began to pull down the jeans.

They stuck. He pulled again and she staggered, giggled drunkenly, and fell on to the bed with her legs in the air and the white Versace jeans around her knees. Taking one of the leg-ends, he tried to pull it over her feet. 'They're too bloody tight,' he breathed, swaying.

'Come on, Captain,' she said, looking up at him archly. 'If you can take down a Scud launch site behind enemy lines, surely you can manage my jeans in a hotel bedroom!'

Bracing his foot against the edge of the bed, Alex gave an extra-hard tug. They jeans came off in a rush and he fell heavily backwards on to his stitched thigh. The pain was intense and for a moment he lay there on the floor in his own half-undone trousers, swearing and laughing.

After a moment Dawn peered over the edge of the bed and saw the blood rapidly beading through the cotton. Lowering herself to Alex's side, she eased the trousers off and then hurried to the bathroom for cotton wool and surgical spirit. 'That's rather blown the romantic mood, hasn't it?' she murmured, pressing a swab to the wound. 'Still, while I'm down here I might as well have a look at the rest of the damage.'

As she poured and dabbed, Alex said nothing. The

surgical spirit was cold against his skin. The sway of her small, neat breasts over his body proved a very effective anaesthetic.

He lay there as she eased off the dressings on his face and arm. He had been right in his early guess that a sensuous body lay beneath all that formal puritan grey. Her palely curvaceous form was overlaid with the faint musculature of one who exercised when there was nothing better to do with her time, but not otherwise. Her stomach was flat but soft, tapering towards the dark-blonde scribble of her pubic hair.

To tend to his arm she hunkered down over his hand. As bees to honey – as she must have known they would – his fingers moved upwards to meet her. She closed her eyes, pressed herself briefly and slickly against his palm, then continued in a businesslike way with her ministrations. 'Wait,' she told him a moment later. 'I'm concentrating.'

'So am I!'

'Let me get these bandages off – I'm not into sex with Egyptian mummies.'

To remove the dressings from his face, she sat astride him so that Alex could feel the damp heat of her crotch against his chest. But her expression was serious, and when he reached for her breasts she frowned absently and slapped his hands back down to his chest. 'I hope you don't behave like this with all those army nurses.'

'We don't get nurses in the SAS,' breathed Alex. 'We get some sweaty corporal called Dave or Ginge.'

'I told you to leave them alone. I'm going to have to be very rough with you if you don't.'

'I've been roughed up by experts.' Alex grinned. 'I can take it.'

A moment later she straddled him and lowered herself on to him. For a moment she was still, then he felt a series of hot, updrawing waves. Nothing mattered except the absolute intensity of the feeling that – for all their antagonism – he knew they shared at that moment. And then, with a desperate dying cry which might have come from either or both of them, it was over and Dawn gently subsided on top of him. She seemed very young – almost childlike with her scrubbed face and sleepy eyes. 'That was fun,' she murmured. 'Wasn't it?'

'It beats arguing.'

She settled herself against his shoulder. 'Please, will you be nice to me from now on?' she asked. 'I mean really, really nice?'

'I promise,' murmured Alex.

'And will you kill for me?'

He looked at her.

She wrinkled her nose at him and grinned. 'Well?' she asked. 'Will you?'

He smiled. 'OK.'

TWENTY-THREE

'OK,' said Angela Fenwick. 'The position is this . . .'

It was 10.30 a.m., and Alex and Dawn were seated with the deputy director in her office. Florence Nightingale looked benignly down from the walls; the cafetiere steamed on the table between them.

Despite her overnight flight from Washington Fenwick looked fresh, groomed and alert. Alex and Dawn, by contrast, who had taken an 8 a.m. flight from Malaga, were looking rather less impressive. Alex, in particular, had a raging thirst and a cracking headache that reminded him of its presence with every step that he took. The knife cuts, well on the mend now, were itching crazily.

Dawn, for her part, was paler and quieter than usual. They had not discussed the events of the night before – their departure from the hotel to the airport had been a hurried one – nor had her behaviour towards him changed greatly. But there had been little things. In the queue for Customs she had turned to him and pressed her face into his shoulder. In the taxi from Heathrow she had settled herself, catlike, beneath his arm. There was a complicity between them.

And for all that he was feeling lousy, the time spent with Dawn – and the few hours spent in bed with her

– had reshaped things in Alex's mind. He didn't want to back out now, he wanted to go all the way, whatever the cost. He wanted to see the Watchman dead at his feet.

And it was possible – more than possible. Meehan had seemed uncatchable but he wasn't uncatchable. He was a man and men sooner or later made mistakes.

Confiding his childhood memories to Denzil Connolly had been Meehan's first mistake and sparing Alex's life had been his second.

'We got the analysis of those Meehan tissue samples back yesterday evening from the Forensic Science Service labs,' Fenwick continued. 'And they told us something rather interesting.'

She opened her briefcase and removed a paper. 'The hair that Captain Temple extracted for us has been confirmed as Meehan's against DNA samples from the other crime scenes, and it showed abnormally high medium-term traces of a substance known as perchloroethylene. Known as PCE, perchloroethylene is a solvent used in the tanning process. Due to its high toxicity – I won't bother you with the details – PCE is on the European Community's black list of chemicals whose use is strictly controlled. In this country, however – never a front-runner in environmental terms – these controls are regularly ignored by industry and run-off from tanneries into rivers is often accompanied by excess PCE levels.

'Now we've been on to the various ministries overnight, and we've talked to the National Rivers Authority and all the water companies this morning, and between them they've provided us with a list of nine tanneries from which high levels of PCE run-off have been . . .'

There was a knock at the door, and a hurried entrance by a young man holding a folded document and a book. 'Excuse me, ma'am,' he said, handing the articles to her. 'These have just been couriered over from Room 1129 at the MOD.'

'Excellent,' said the deputy director. 'Thank you.' She glanced at the document – a map, as it turned out. 'Dawn, would you be so good?'

Taking the map, Dawn rose from her seat and pinned it out on the display board opposite them. It was a map of England and Wales, flecked with larger and smaller areas of red.

'Following your call early this morning about the possibility of our man holing up at an old MOD property,' said Fenwick, 'I spoke to a couple of people in Whitehall. This map apparently shows everything, large and small, that they own. Quite a portfolio, isn't it? Billions of pounds' worth of land.'

Alex stared at the map, daunted by the sheer scale and number of the holdings. There had to be several hundred of them.

'If we could add the tanneries, please, Dawn,' said Fenwick, handing the younger woman a printed list.

Dawn stared at it, and reached for the first black mapping pin. 'Hurley, Staffordshire,' she read out. 'On the River Blithe.'

And the second: 'Mynydd, Powys, on the Afon Honddu.'

And the third: 'Beeston, Lancs on the River Douglas.'

She continued to the end of the list.

She stood back and the three of them stared at the map. The pins were spread erratically over the country, with a slight cluster detectable between

Birmingham, Coventry and Northampton.

'From what the FSS people say,' Fenwick went on, glancing down at the report, 'PCEs in this sort of concentration would only to be encountered within a few miles of source. So in the case of somewhere like Hurley, for example, we don't have to follow the river system seventy miles across country to the coast. We can just draw a circle of a few miles' diameter around the plant. The FSS figure was three miles, so let's say six to be on the safe side. Any of these locations strike anyone as the sort of area you might take your son on a caravanning holiday?'

'The mid-Wales one looks good,' said Alex. 'So does the north Yorkshire and the Dartmoor. Any of those three, definitely.'

Fenwick nodded. 'Dawn, take all the data down to the computer people. We need Ordnance Survey printouts of the tannery areas, with all suitable MOD properties highlighted. It's almost certainly safe to eliminate airfields, working bases et cetera – the details of the various properties seem to be listed in this book they sent over.'

Dawn nodded briskly and gathered up the materials.

When she had gone Fenwick turned enquiringly to Alex. 'Everything healing satisfactorily? I understand you put up quite a fight in poor George's defence.'

'The Watchman did what he came to do,' said Alex shortly.

Fenwick pursed her lips and looped an errant gunmetal tress behind one ear. She was a handsome woman, Alex thought, if a bit on the cold side. Those blue eyes could freeze you to the bone in seconds. 'It doesn't take a Nobel prize winner to work out that the next in line for Mr Meehan's attentions is myself,' she said with a slight smile.

'I'm afraid it looks that way,' Alex agreed. 'What precautions are you taking?'

'As few as possible, I'm afraid. I have to continue doing my job and I have to continue to be seen to do it.'

'Have you moved house? Varied your routine at all?'

'There's no point, I'm afraid. I live as if expecting an assassin as it is and I have done ever since I inherited the Northern Ireland desk. I know you have your doubts about some of our people, Captain Temple, but I assure you the arrangements in place are good. Apart from anything else I have to receive ministers and diplomatic visitors and, well, all sorts of people. I can't just up sticks and move to some suburban safe house.'

'Bet you wish you could at times,' said Alex. The image flashed into his mind of Fenwick lying in a pool of blood with a nail through her head. She was certainly keeping up appearances, he thought. Perhaps she's worried that if she looks rattled or fails to show up for work she could lose out on the directorship.

'Perhaps I do, Captain Temple.' Fenwick folded her hands in her lap for a moment, then one of the phones on her desk started flashing, and she marched over and picked it up.

'I'll wait outside,' said Alex and left the office.

A minute later Dawn reappeared in the ante-room. In a couple of sentences Alex told her of his concerns for her boss's safety.

'She lives in a private block in a gated estate in Chelsea,' said Dawn. 'It's one of the most secure addresses in London. There's CCTV everywhere, a security guard on the entrance, passes to get in and out, everything. No one – no window cleaner, no visitor, no one – gets within fifty yards of the building without security clearance. The whole place is fully modified for at-risk personnel – one-way windows, departure from an underground car park, the police a couple of minutes away in Lucan Place . . .'

'He'll be checking the place out,' said Alex. 'Probably even as we speak.'

'I know,' said Dawn. 'And that's why we're checking out anyone who goes near it and pulling in anyone who can't be personally vouched for by a resident or security staff member. Believe me, the job is being done and done properly.'

'Does she live alone?'

'Drop it, Alex, please,' Dawn said sharply. 'Our job now is to find the wasp's nest – the place he always returns to – and kill him there.'

He nodded. 'OK. Just wanted to . . .'

'I know. Let's go back in.'

For a couple of minutes Dawn's fingers raced over one of the keyboards on Angela Fenwick's desk and the large flat-screen display on the wall opposite them flickered into life.

First, an enlarged area of Ordnance Survey map came up, with the village of Hurley, Staffordshire at its centre.

'No National Park or particular tourist area nearby,' said Dawn. 'There's Blithfield Reservoir, but I don't think Meehan Senior would have driven a caravan halfway across the country to see that. Otherwise, the area on the screen is at the central point of a square formed by Stoke, Derby, Wolverhampton and

Telford. Not high on the list of tourist must-sees, I'd say.' She struck the keyboard and two small areas of red appeared on the screen. 'Vis-à-vis suitably sized MOD properties in the area, we've got an RAF storage facility here near Yoxall and an old TA depot outside Colton but neither of them is less than a couple of miles from the River Blithe.' She looked up at Alex. 'I'm assuming that the conclusion we're drawing is that he is staying beside the river and using it for drinking water, rather than gathering water from the river and drinking it somewhere else.'

Alex nodded. 'He's probably got some sort of filtration system, but obviously nothing too sophisticated. Could well be using standard issue Puritabs. In the UK you tend to allow for water-borne bacteria and pesticides but not for heavy-duty chemical toxins like these PCEs or whatever they're called. And yeah, he'll definitely be holed up somewhere with its own water source rather than transporting a heavy canteen several miles across country. He'll be on the river itself – we know he likes them.'

Angela Fenwick nodded grimly. 'Next possibility?'

Another section of map flashed up.

'Mynydd, Powys. Much more deserted, obviously. Area of outstanding natural beauty and definite tourist area in the summer months. Good for fishing, too, and we know Meehan and son enjoyed that. But no MOD properties nearby. The army and marines pass through the place pretty regularly on exercise but we don't actually own anything in the catchment area at all. Not so much as a Nissen hut on the Afon Honddhu.'

'Go on,' said Angela Fenwick.

'Beeston, Lancashire, on the Douglas, halfway

between Wigan and Southport. No MOD facility on or near the river. Nothing touristy about the area, particularly.'

'Go on.'

They went through all nine of them. For Alex's money there was one definite front runner – a small tanning plant on a stream named the Hamble, which ran off Black Down on the western boundary of Dartmoor. This was the one he would have chosen – this or the Mynydd one in Wales. Both were remote but served with metalled roads; both were close to popular tourist destinations; both offered vast areas of wild country in which, if need be, an experienced soldier could survive for weeks. 'It'll be one of the two, I'm sure of it,' he said.

'We've got nothing registered to the MOD on either river,' said Dawn doubtfully.

'Suppose the MOD has recently sold the property,' suggested Alex. 'For the last hour we've been looking for MOD properties and for a small village with a church, because we know that Meehan specifically mentioned the existence of a church. But if the property was classified secret, at some point, and so not marked on any map, and was recently sold . . .'

Fenwick nodded. 'Yes, that's true. There's no reason to suppose that it's marked on current maps – I can't believe the MOD bothers to inform Ordnance Survey whenever it sells and declassifies property. And of course it wouldn't be included in the MOD's current portfolio either.'

'From Meehan's story,' said Dawn, 'doesn't it sound as if this place, or at least its original purpose, has been forgotten? That nobody really knows why it was classified in the first place? It can't have been set up much later than 1940 and there's been a lot of inter-departmental paper shuffling since then.'

Fenwick reached for a phone, pressed the scramble button and dialled a number. 'Is that 1129? Jonathan? Angela Fenwick here . . . Yes, bless you for that, Jonathan. Look, I want you to do something further for me. Go back five years and check for top-security-rated but untenanted MOD properties abutting the following rivers and within five miles downstream of the following grid references. Got a pencil?' As Dawn scrolled back through the maps, Fenwick read out the tannery locations. 'And if five years doesn't throw anything up,' she continued calmly, 'then try ten and then fifteen . . . Yes, soonest, please. Ring me back the moment you find anything.'

Replacing the phone, she turned to the others. 'With a bit of luck he won't be too long,' she said. 'Shall we call up for some more coffee and some sandwiches?'

In the event, they finished the sandwiches before the call from Room 1129 came in. As she listened, Fenwick took notes. 'And that's the only one?' she concluded. 'Right. I'm grateful. Thank you.' She turned to Dawn. 'Can you get the Hamble map back up?'

Alex felt a sharp prickle of excitement.

From her chair, Fenwick aimed a red laser pointer at the screen display. 'Right,' she said. 'A recent source of perchloroethylene pollution is this building here – a small tanning plant presently engaged in litigation with the National Rivers Authority. One and a half miles downstream of the plant is Black Down House and its outbuildings, including the shell of a church, standing on some forty acres of land.

Evacuated in August 1940 by order of the War Office for reasons pertaining to national security and later classified as a secret location under the Act in relation to Operation Gladio. For the last eighteen months, following sale by auction, Black Down House and its outbuildings have been the property of Liskeard Holdings, an Exeter-based property development company. Their present condition is unknown.'

The three of them looked at each other.

'What was Operation Gladio?' asked Alex.

'An anti-communist stay-behind network set up immediately after the war by SOE and MI6, and funded by the CIA. To be activated in the event of a Soviet invasion. The idea was that agents should be put in place and materials hidden at secret locations so that any Western European country that was rolled over would be in a position to resist, communicate with the outside world et cetera.'

'And Black Down House was one of those locations?'

'So it seems,' said Fenwick.

'So all that kit Meehan found as a kid has sat there for fifty years, waiting for an invasion that never came?'

'Longer, probably. Britain established a stay-behind force as early as 1940 in case of German invasion. After the war a lot of the facilities were simply reassigned. Everything to do with Gladio and the stay-behind units has been classified top secret ever since, although bits and pieces have come out, particularly in Italy. Returning to the present day, however, it looks as if we might have found our man's base. Congratulations, captain.'

'How do you want to handle it?' asked Dawn.

'I think I should just get down there as soon as possible,' said Alex. 'Stake the place out, try and identify him, and, uh, kill him, basically.'

'Killing him would be best,' confirmed Angela Fenwick.

TWENTY-FOUR

Dawn drove. They were carrying too much unusual baggage, she insisted, for them to risk being picked up for speeding. And Alex, sooner or later, would nudge the car up to 80 or 90 mph. It was in his nature.

Alex shrugged and sat back, and with the Range Rover tucked well into the slow lane, they made their steady way westwards. Their purpose, Alex had reluctantly agreed with Angela Fenwick, was to recce the area and determine their next step. There were to be no cowboy heroics or one-man initiatives as there had been at Longwater Lodge. If further manpower was needed then MI5 would provide it. And with this Alex had had to content himself. On his right he could see Stonehenge, like an assembly of frozen NAAFI chips.

'I'm beginning to enjoy our little trips away together,' said Dawn.

Alex squeezed her thigh. 'This might not be quite the honeymoon that Spain was,' he warned her. 'Worst-case scenario we could run into a contact. Have you had any time on the range recently?'

'Just the odd twenty-five rounds at lunchtime,' she answered. 'And then mostly for fun. I did my time on a watcher team, though, and I can't imagine surveillance has changed much since then.'

'So what weapon did you draw this morning?'

'A Walther PPK. Call me old-fashioned but . . .'

Alex was surprised. The PPK was a highly service-able weapon but famously unforgiving in the hands of a beginner. As a straight blow-back pistol it had a very stiff recoil spring and a pretty snappy perceived recoil as well. 'You don't have any trouble racking the slide?' he asked her. 'Or working the double action trigger?'

'I've got nice strong fingers,' she replied, flexing them on the steering wheel. She glanced at him side-ways and he smiled.

Turning, he cast an eye over the rear of the vehicle. He had tried to think of everything and if in doubt he had overspecified. There were sleeping bags, a stuff sack of spare clothing, dry boots, maps, compasses, binoculars and a jumble of other articles that a couple on a hiking holiday might carry with them. Mounted on a steel frame on the back of the Range Rover was a trail bike. It hadn't occurred to Alex to drive a motorcycle down to Dartmoor, but the moment he saw it in the MI5 vehicle pool he realised just how useful it might prove in that terrain. For that reason two sets of motocross goggles and helmets lay among the hiking gear.

There were also a handful of rather less common items: two pairs of night-vision goggles for a start, and a box each of 9mm and .38 hollow-point rounds. Had the car been stopped and searched by the police there would certainly have been a raised eyebrow or two.

'When we get there,' said Alex, 'I want you to promise to do what I say. If I say pull back to the vehicle, for example, I want you to do just that, OK? No arguments, no bullshit.'

'Fine by me. Just run through the schedule.'

'We'll do a single pass past the place, see what we can see. Then push on for a couple of miles and park up – I've chosen somewhere on the 1:15,000 map – a car park by a transport café. Then we'll cut back across country – there's a streamside path that should take us to the boundary of the estate – work our way round, and see what there is to be seen.'

'You think we'll find him?'

'Who knows what we'll find. Or how long we'll have to wait.'

'This is just a recce, right? You're cool with that?'

'Just a recce,' Alex confirmed.

'On the other hand, if you get him bang to rights . . .'

'You don't get men like Meehan "bang to rights",' said Alex flatly.

'Negative thought leads to negative action,' said Dawn.

'Spare me the fucking zen, Harding.' He intertwined and cracked his knuckles. The slow drip of adrenalin into his system had begun. 'Don't worry, you'll get a corpse, one way or another.'

Two and a half hours later they were driving north from Tavistock across the western plain of Dartmoor Forest. The roads were narrower now, and Dawn edged the Range Rover carefully between high banks edged with fern, hawthorn and bracken as a solitary kestrel pinwheeled above them. At intervals, as the banks fell away, a vast and baleful reach of heather revealed itself.

'Follow the sign for North Brent Tor,' said Alex, 'and then for either Chilford or Hamble.'

To their left a series of rocky outcrops stood like iron teeth against the sky. This was the Watchman's terrain, Alex was sure of it.

'We should pass Black Down House on our right any minute now,' said Alex. 'Take it as slowly as you can without looking suspicious.'

They drove for ten minutes down a side lane which was little more than a farm track. Not many people came down here, Alex reflected, noting the lane's poorly maintained surface and overgrown verges.

And there the house finally was, set well back from the road, its windows boarded and its decades-old paintwork weather-streaked and flaking. Beyond it the ground fell away sharply towards the river. There was no sign of any other buildings. Nor, apart from a temporary steel barrier which had been erected in front of the former gateway, was there any indication that the property had been developed in any way since its sale. No structural supports had been erected, and the overgrown trees and bushes surrounding the building had clearly been untouched for years. The air of neglect surrounding the place was palpable.

'Not the most inviting place in the world,' said Dawn as the property slid from view.

'I think that's rather the point,' Alex observed. 'Like the fact that you can't see much of it from the road. There's a church and several outbuildings down there somewhere, plus twenty-odd acres of woodland.'

'No vehicle anywhere near it.'

'No. Which makes me think he might not be around. After all, he'd have no particular reason to to hide it.'

'But it does beg the question as to where the hell he is,' said Dawn worriedly.

'First things first,' said Alex. 'If we're going to recce the place I'd much rather he wasn't around. As long as your boss goes straight from Thames House to the Chelsea flat she should be safe enough – assuming the security's everything you say it is.'

Five minutes later they parked the Range Rover on the cinder forecourt of the Cabin Café. For appearance's sake they went in for a cup of tea and a slice of sponge cake. There were several other people in there, the majority of them wearing brightly coloured anoraks and carrying map cases.

Alex's and Dawn's appearance, by contrast, was decidedly sombre. Alex was wearing grey wind-proof trousers and an old combat smock; Dawn had on black jeans and a lightweight forest-green jacket, and her hair was concealed beneath an army surplus jungle hat. Both were wearing nondescript hiking boots.

When they had paid, Alex and Dawn began to walk back up the road in the direction from which they had come. Both were carrying rucksacks and Alex now had a pair of high-powered binoculars round his neck. Once out of sight of the café, the pair cut left-handed into a field and descended the few hundred brambled yards to the river.

Or to the stream, for the Hamble was hardly a river. Not at this time of year, anyway. Such water as it contained tumbled quietly from pool to shallow pool, brimmed darkly for a moment and hurried on. A sheep path ran above it, disappearing at intervals but soon reprising its dry erratic track. Hanks of wool hung from a barbed-wire fence.

They slid down the nettled bank to the water and for twenty minutes Alex set a fast pace up the stream bed. The day was a warm one, despite the fact that afternoon was swiftly becoming evening, and soon they were both sweating. Alex's thigh swiftly began to throb where the stitches pulled at the wound, but he consigned the discomfort to a distant part of his mind.

They covered the ground fast. The banks of the stream were eight or nine feet high and the foliage had clearly not been cut back for years, allowing them to stay well-concealed from any watching eyes. Despite the absence of any vehicle, Alex was not convinced that the Black Down estate was unoccupied and a careful study of a large-scale map had convinced him that this was the safest approach. Meehan could not watch the entire half-mile perimeter, he could only patrol it, and Alex suspected that he slept through the day.

The estate, they soon discovered, was surrounded by a chain-link fence topped with razor wire. This was not new – long streaks of rust discoloured the galvanised metal – but at ten feet high it was still effective enough. The banks flattened at the point the stream met the perimeter, so that the lowest chain-linked strands went to within inches of the stream bed. The fence continued in both directions and there was every reason to suppose that it surrounded the estate entirely. It was clearly not proof against determined assault, but it would undoubtedly have deterred the curious over the years.

Alex and Dawn crouched in the shadows beneath the bank.

'What d'you reckon?' asked Dawn.

'I reckon I'm going to have to go in underneath it,' Alex answered.

Removing his rucksack, he took out a lightweight folding shovel and began digging in the stream. After ten hard minutes, and having hauled out several large rocks by hand, he had cleared a twelve-inch space beneath the lowest strands of the fence and the stream bed.

'OK, all clear?'

They looked around them and Alex quickly undressed. Naked, he burrowed up the stream bed and under the fence. The water was surprisingly cold. When he was through Dawn wrapped his clothes in a bin liner and threw them to him over the fence. The other kit followed. 'Remind me to take those stitches out,' she hissed as Alex re-dressed.

Quickly, they ran through their contingency plans. She would wait where she was and call him on his mobile if there was anything to report, and he would attempt a search of the Black Down estate. Switching his mobile to vibrate, he melted into the woods. His progress was slow. He moved in total silence, continuously scanning the ground in front of him for trip wires and booby traps, and the landscape as a whole for any sign of surveillance.

Soon he was at the edge of the woods and from a well-concealed position among a patch of overgrown thorn bushes was able to rake the area with his binoculars. There was no sign of life and as far as he could see the area of tall grass, nettles and cow-parsley in front of him was untrodden.

Slowly, and with infinite care, he moved from the cover of the woods into the shadowed stream-bed. The water was deeper here and he was soon soaked to the waist. It wasn't the approach route he would have chosen, given a choice, but unlike the nettle-choked field, the exposed rocks would leave no trace of his passing. The day was still warm. The sugar in the tea that he had drunk had made him thirsty and with a flash of irritation Alex realised that he had not filled his canteen. Drinking the stream water, as they had discovered from the forensic samples, was probably inadvisable.

Rounding a corner he saw the church. It had a square tower and a blankly ruined look. Where there had once been windows there were now gaps around which, at some long-ago point, mortar had been roughly trowelled. At one time a road had led past the main house and down alongside the river. The church and its small graveyard lay at the end of this road, or what remained of it. Trees and bushes had forced their way through the dried-out surface and long-unchecked vegetation pressed from both sides. Beyond the church was a line of dilapidated single-storey dwellings.

Having noted the layout of the place, Alex drew himself back into invisibility beneath an overhanging alder bush. With his binoculars he used the slowly failing light to scour the area around the church and then rang Dawn. 'I'm in position,' he murmured. 'Since I've got no idea where our man sleeps or even if he's here, I'm just going to hang back and sit tight. How are you?'

'OK. Nothing to report here.'

Where would Meehan stay, Alex wondered. In the house? In the church? In the crypt, underground? Did the house have cellars? Wherever it was, it would be somewhere where he would have plenty of warning of any arrivals.

By the property's new owners, for example. Angela Fenwick had discovered that Liskeard Holdings were having trouble securing planning permission for the hotel and conference complex that they hoped to build on the site, and that was why the property remained in its ruined state. But presumably there had been a fair amount of coming and going by architects and others.

Alex reasoned that Meehan probably slept and concealed himself somewhere beneath the church. The chances were that if the house had a cellar it would be damp and uncomfortable, and subject to occasional visits – the church was much older and much more securely built. Church crypts were stone-walled. They were usually dry.

At 8 p.m. Dawn rang. 'Still waiting for Godot?' she asked.

'Yup, you?'

'The light's almost gone, as you can see. I was thinking I should get back to the Range Rover. Twitchers don't twitch in the dark.'

'OK. Be in touch.'

Two hours later his thigh was itching unbearably and his back aching from immobility. How many hours have I spent lying up like this, he wondered. A hundred? More? And how many times has the whole thing ended in failure, in merely getting up and going back to base?

He was going to have to make a decision, sooner or later, about whether to risk taking a closer look at things. Was Meehan due back tonight? Was he already there? Was he, at this minute, watching Alex – the hunted turned hunter?

Alex shuddered, both at the thought of being scoped out by Meehan and at the memory of the former agent's terrifying strength.

No, he thought. *I'll go in now.*

Slowly he eased himself from cover and continued the silent passage upstream that he had started hours earlier. In his pocket, fully loaded, was the Glock.

Soon, the house was in view above him. The ruins of a flight of steps led down from the road fronting the house to the stream at the bottom of the slope. If he started to climb, he would greatly increase the chance of being spotted if Meehan was in residence. If he stayed where he was, however, he would never learn anything.

A step at a time, he moved up the slope. With the passage of years and neglect, the brickwork steps had cracked and he could feel their uneasy shift beneath his feet. Finally he reached the top and the front door. Was it locked? No, the lock had been kicked in and the flaking door swung open easily. Glock in one hand, Maglite torch in the other, Alex went in. He was in a front hall, a place of rotting floorboards, fallen masonry and the smell of dead animals. Fag ends and empty bottles greyed with plaster dust lay about and there was an old coat in the fireplace. Anything of any conceivable value had been stripped away – there was nothing there except walls and floor.

Taking a pair of thick socks from his rucksack, Alex pulled them over his boots. They would muffle the crunching sound of his movements and help conceal the tracks of his Danner boots on the floor. Quickly he moved from room to room on the ground floor, but found nothing. A few empty tins and a gutted mattress lay around, but there was no sign that the place had been occupied by anyone other than tramps and vagrants – and that a long time ago. There was no cellar.

Upstairs the story was the same: gutted rooms,

fallen plasterwork and the darkness of the boarded-over windows. At some point a pigeon had trapped itself in there and its half-feathered skeleton lay on a bedroom mantelpiece.

Where had Meehan and his father slept that night all those years ago? Wherever it was, there was no sign that he had bothered with the place since.

Outside, it was now quite dark. Pulling on his night-vision goggles so that the scene leapt into eerie green daylight, Alex descended the slope again. At his ear was the tiny mosquito whine of the goggles' battery-powered electronics.

Carefully he made his way towards the dilapidated cottages. As with the church, a rough attempt had been made to make these safe by slapping mortar around the gaps where there had once been windows. One of them – the only one with an intact roof – seemed to have been designated a store of some kind, and its back room proved to be packed with ancient cardboard boxes containing electrical and woodworking items. Raising the goggles and flicking a pen torch beam on these, Alex identified dark-brown bakelite transformers and junction boxes, rows of dusty radio valves, plaited electrical flex, fibrous early Rawlplugs and other items whose use he could only guess at.

And nails, of course. From half-inch to six-inch. Alex pocketed a couple for the forensics team, flicked off the pen torch, lowered the goggles and went outside again.

The mobile throbbed against his thigh.

'You OK?' asked Dawn.

'Looking around,' murmured Alex. 'No sign of him yet. This is definitely the place, though – I've found a stack of those old nails. You OK?'

'Fine. Take care.'

'Sure.'

He slipped the phone back into his pocket and moved towards the pale bulk of the church. This time the door was locked. Alex considered climbing in through a window, dismissed the idea as too likely to attract attention and reached into one of the chest pockets of his smock.

It was a couple of years since he'd done the lock-picking refresher course at Tregaron and the goggles didn't help, but Alex's movements were reasonably confident as he inserted a pick into the church door. The lock was a standard pin-tumbler type and it was no more than a few minutes before the door swung inwards.

Pocketing the pick and the torque wrench in favour of the Glock, Alex scanned the place. As in the house, anything of any value as architectural salvage had been removed and above him only a few roof beams remained. Broken tiles and mounds of pigeon shit littered the stone floor.

The door was to one side, low and arched. Again, it was locked, and this lock was no high street Yale. It took Alex almost half an hour of delicate work with the spring-steel pick to solve all the pins and bring them to the shear line, and he breathed a heartfelt sigh of relief when he felt the plug's smooth rotation beneath his torque wrench.

Beyond the door was a descending spiral staircase. The stone treads felt worn beneath Alex's soles as he crept downwards, peering before him through the goggles. There was very little ambient light for them to magnify and he seemed to be descending into a dim green haze.

The crypt appeared to be empty but for a wooden bier of the type once used in funerals. Lifting the goggles, Alex risked a quick sweep with the Maglite torch, only to have his initial observation confirmed. There was nothing else – no chests, no cupboards, no sign of habitation – merely walls and floors carved with memorial inscriptions and a cool stone emptiness. Nor were there any doors to further chambers.

Think, Alex told himself. *Go back to basics.* Meehan told Connolly that the equipment he found was in the church. The Operation Gladio hiding place had to be proof against sophisticated enemy search teams and a locked door would have constituted no protection whatever against a determined GRU or Spetznaz outfit.

Once again, he searched the place with his torch, running its beam over the walls and floors, and the inset stone tablets with their florid carvings.

He almost missed it, and he would never have found it had he not known that it had to be there somewhere. A memorial brass inlaid into the floor in one corner of the room. Worn, as if by the passage of many feet, and inscribed 'To the memory of Samuel Calvert, born 1758, laid to rest 1825. My sword, I shall give to him that shall succeed me in my pilgrimage.'

Gladio, thought Alex. The word means a sword, doesn't it?

The brass lifted with a knife tip. Beneath, supporting it, was a heavy iron grille. And beneath the grille were steps.

TWENTY-FIVE

Alarm screamed in Alex's mind. He was getting himself deeper and deeper into a situation from which retreat was impossible.

His plan, to which Angela Fenwick had agreed, had been that he should make an initial sortie into the property to search for evidence of Meehan's presence and then pull back, so that an MI5 team could replace him. If Alex encountered Meehan while undertaking his recce, however, he was to kill him on sight. From Fenwick's point of view, Alex knew, this would be the ideal outcome. No more Watchman, no more complex and expensive deployment of Service personnel, no more threat to herself or to her ambitions.

And to be honest, thought Alex, it would suit him too. It would balance the books for George Widdowes' death. There was also the undeniable truth that a happy Angela Fenwick meant a happy Bill Leonard, and a happy Bill Leonard could mean promotion.

Plus, of course, the world would be rid of a psychopathic murderer. If Meehan were waiting in the darkness at the bottom of those steps, or if he were to return to the church right now, Alex would be trapped. Better by far to pull back, to get Fenwick to send reinforcements.

Pulling out his mobile he tried punching in Dawn's number. The sudden beep indicating that there was no signal strength made him jump and his heart race, and he realised just how on edge he was.

Meehan could come back at any moment.

Pulling the grille and the brass plate back into place from below – the gaps in the grille had deliberately been made wide enough to allow this – Alex began to descend the steps. The room at the bottom, he saw with a quick, relieved sweep of the goggles, had no human occupant. It was a burial chamber and the rectangular stone slab at its centre had probably once supported a tomb.

But not now. Now the walls were piled deep and high with green-sprayed steel cases whose contents, according to the white stencilled legends on their sides, included time pencils and other varieties of detonator, delay fuses, carborundum grease, pocket incendiaries, Eureka beacons, S-Phones, Mk III Transceivers, Welrod pistols and an assortment of grenades and mines. It was a far more comprehensive list than Connolly had described, thought Alex, staring for a wondering moment at the scores of cases. Overcome by curiosity, he prised open the lid of a case marked 'Grenades – Gammon type'.

Inside, neatly packed, were a dozen bizarre-looking appliances, each consisting of a bakelite fuse housing and a cotton bag. The idea, Alex assumed, was that you filled the bag with plastic explosive – maybe chucking in a handful of nuts and bolts for good measure – and lobbed the whole thing into the middle of an enemy patrol. Very nasty indeed.

The transceivers packed into their little leather suitcases, by contrast, were objects of great fascination, with their miniaturised sockets and grilles and dials. If I get through this in one piece, thought Alex, I'm coming back for a few of these, and perhaps a couple of the Welrods too. Take them up to Sotheby's or Christie's . . .

This sub-crypt, it was clear, was where Meehan lived. At one end of the room were cardboard boxes containing new own-brand supermarket tins – soups, beans, spaghetti, peas – chocolate bars, and packet foods. A packing case held fresh oranges, potatoes and green vegetables. No onions, probably because of the strong smell they gave off while cooking. Among the food was a small plastic rubbish bag containing crushed tins, sweet papers, withered orange peel and a brown apple core. The last two looked less than forty-eight hours old.

There was also a plastic water-purification system, a tiny MSR stove and fuel bottles, a pair of mess tins, plastic cutlery, a comprehensive medical kit – the suture-set recently used, Alex noted – and a washbag. In the corner of the room above this area a fresh-air duct led upwards into the darkness, presumably voiding behind some decorative element on the tower.

At the other end of the chamber, folded neatly on the floor, were Meehan's clothes – nondescript camping-store items for the most part, and a pair of worn cordura hiking boots. From one of these an inexpensive Suunto compass trailed a para-cord lanyard.

On the slab, weighed down at each corner, was a good-quality photocopy of an architectural blueprint. The building in question was entitled Powys Court (Block 2), Oakley Street, London SW3. A roll of similar blueprints lay to one side and a flash of the Maglite served to confirm that all related to the same building.

What was it that Dawn had said about Angela Fenwick's flat? A private block? In a gated estate? One of the most secure addresses in London?

Heart pounding, Alex scanned the place, felt through the modest pile of clothing. There was no sign of any weaponry – Meehan had it all with him. He tried thumbing Dawn's number on his mobile but couldn't get a signal.

Shit!

Racing up the steps, he hurriedly replaced the grille and the brass plate. Moments later, pulling the crypt door shut behind him, he was running from the church towards the main gate. Meehan was about to move on Angela Fenwick – he was sure of it.

He was over the gate in less than a minute and, having got well clear of the premises dialled Dawn again. This time he got a tone and she picked up immediately. 'Powys Court mean anything to you?'

'Yes, it's Angela's place. Why?'

'Meehan's got the architectural blueprint. He's probably there right now.'

'Where are you?'

'Couple of hundred yards beyond the entrance to the house there's a lay-by and a sign saying Chilford.'

'OK. Two minutes.'

Packing the night-vision goggles into the rucksack, he waited impatiently for the headlights of the Range Rover.

She was closer to five minutes. 'I've rung Angela,' she told him. 'Told her to get out.'

'And go where?'

'Safe house. She's agreed to stay there for the next twenty-four hours and surround the place with Special Branch people.'

'Can she get there without being followed?'

'She was on her way home from Downing Street. The driver will throw in every move in the book, make sure they're not followed.'

Alex looked dubious.

'Don't worry,' said Dawn. 'He's very good and very experienced. Ex-army, as it happens.'

'Go on.'

'She wants me up there soonest. I have to help her run things from the safe house.'

Alex nodded. 'And I'll stay down here. Sooner or later this is where he's going to come back to and when he does I'll be ready.'

'I'd have liked to stay with you.'

'I could certainly have used an extra pair of eyes and ears,' said Alex, unloading the gear from the back of the Range Rover.

'Is that all I am to you?' she asked with a half-smile. 'A handful of body parts?'

'You know what I mean.'

'Have you got everything you need?'

Alex patted his smock pockets and checked the rucksack. 'Torches, lock-picks, Glock, ammo, night sights, knife, scoff, first aid, spare clothing, water-proofs, cam-netting . . . Looks OK. To be on the safe side I might take the bike and some petrol. Don't like being without a vehicle. Oh, and some drinking water – I'm not poisoning myself with that shite from the stream.'

He opened the back doors and collected a couple of bottles of water and the helmet, goggles and ten-litre

330

fuel can that went with the motorcycle.

'Sure you'll be OK?' Dawn asked as he lifted the bike from the transportation frame on the back of the Range Rover and rolled it towards the pile of supplies.

'Yeah. He's not getting the drop on me twice, don't worry.'

'Professional pride.' She smiled. 'Honour of the Regiment!'

'Something like that.'

She nodded. 'OK, then. Take care. And remind me about those stitches.'

'They can wait.'

She kissed him on his good cheek. 'So can I. Be careful, Captain Temple.'

'On your way, Harding,' he said, touching his hand to her hair.

He hid the bike in the woods opposite the entrance to Black Down and covered it with bracken and pine branches. The machine was an Austrian KTM 520cc EXC, and had been sprayed a matt khaki. The green plastic fuel can was full, and attachable to the rear of the seat by means of a rucksack and bungee cord. He left a helmet and pair of goggles attached to the handlebars. Then, shinning backwards and forwards over the steel barrier, he moved the rest of the kit into the grounds of Black Down House.

No cars passed. There had been traffic on the road earlier in the evening but now it seemed to have dried up. Crouching by one of the gate piers, he checked his watch. It was twenty minutes before midnight.

Quickly Alex considered his position. His target could arrive at any time, and the sooner he got himself out of sight and into position the better. But into which position – Meehan was far too security-conscious simply to climb over the barrier each time he wanted to get into the property and might approach the church from any point along the half-mile or so of boundary fence.

But whichever direction the man was coming from, Alex knew it was to the church that Meehan would go.

He settled himself to wait. He had chosen a position in daylight – in the long grass midway between the woods and the church. The Watchman would return tonight, he was sure.

This was the end game.

TWENTY-SIX

As the night progressed the temperature fell. Dampness enclosed the Black Down estate, the waning moon clouded over and shortly after midnight the first drops fell. Within the hour the grass was bowed and the stream hissing with rain.

Alex tried to ignore the increasing cold and the sodden weight of his clothing. He was lying on uneven ground behind a fallen and rotting tree with the rucksack cached at his side. His face was blackened with cam-cream, long grass surrounded him and cam-netting covered his body. Rain streamed down the grip of the Glock 34. The rain would conceal him, but it would also conceal Meehan. 'Come on, you bastard,' he murmured. 'Come on.'

He prayed that Meehan would return. Surely the man didn't have a place in London. London was a very tightly regulated city, it was next to impossible to sleep rough without some helpful cop or social worker directing you to the nearest shelter. And asking for your name. And having a bloody good look at you.

Nor would he be able to return to his Kilburn haunts. Irish London was far too dangerous a place for him to approach since MI5 had spread the word that he'd been touting for them. Every Provo sympathiser would know his face, unless he'd had it altered beyond all recognition – and that was a damn sight harder to do than was popularly supposed.

No, he'd come back down here, lie low for a bit, catch his breath. He'd been successful so far by dint of extreme caution, he wouldn't want to blow it now with only Fenwick left to kill.

And something told Alex that the tide had turned. Something about the sight of those supplies – the tinned supermarket food, that austere little pile of kit – told Alex that the Watchman was nearing the end of his watch. And when that happened he – Alex Temple – would be ready. He welcomed the hardness of the earth beneath him and the cold sting of the rain. It kept him on edge.

Shortly after 4.10 – he had just checked his watch – there was the low sound of a vehicle passing by on the road and the brief flicker of headlights. The sound was swallowed by the falling rain, the lights faded to nothingness.

Ten minutes passed. Alex hunkered down beneath the cam-netting, his body taut with anticipation, his eyes narrowed against the rain which streamed from his forehead. In front of him the foresight and backsight of the Glock were aligned on wet darkness.

'Come on,' he mouthed, adrenalin jolting through him as he thumbed down the safety catch. '*Come on.*'

Nothing.

It had just been a passing car.

The sick ebb of anticipation.

Or had it been Meehan? Had he parked up nearby and made his way back over the fence? Alex scanned the darkness in front of him through narrowed, night-accustomed eyes, methodically quartering the jigsaw of interleaving grey shapes. From the subtle difference in tones, he identified the faint outline of grasses, ground foliage and tree branches, and noted their sodden, rhythmic response to the driving rain. All was movement, but movement of an inanimate regularity.

And then a blur of grey within many blurs of grey, Alex's peripheral vision caught a movement that was irregular, hesitant, pulse-driven. He looked directly at it, lost it, looked away and had it again. The shape was frozen now, as if scenting the breeze.

And now moving again. Could it be a fox? A badger?

Not that shape. That animal was human.

Adrenalin kicking in.

Heart-rate increasing.

Thumb to safety catch. The Glock streaming rain. Range what? Perhaps thirty-five yards?

Come on, you bastard. Come on . . .

Thirty, perhaps, but the rain dramatically reduced visibility. *Shit!* As the foresight and backsight wavered into grey alignment so the target seemed to disappear.

Come closer.

Should he charge him. Just race over there and try and drop him as he ran?

No. His target had the advantage. Knew every inch of this . . .

The figure crouching now, half standing.

Alex hugged the sodden ground. *Come on*, he prayed. *Come this way*.

But the figure seemed to be in no hurry. Infinitely cautious, it moved against the monotone backdrop of the woods, seemed to dissolve, reappeared further away. Alex could hear movements now, footfalls through the undergrowth.

He decided to follow.

Leopard-crawling through the wet grass, he made his way slowly to the edge of the woods. The figure was standing beneath a tree now, scanning his surroundings.

Five more yards, thought Alex, and I'll be close enough for a shot. There was a broad beech trunk in front of him and Alex used its cover to stand up. In front of him the figure had moved away again.

Silently, Alex followed. They seemed to be on some sort of grass path; their progress was soundless.

Grandmother's footsteps.

He had him now. The figure – it had to be Meehan – was standing motionless against some dark evergreen bush. Three more silent paces and the kill was a certainty. Alex raised the Glock in front of him, straightening his arms, minimising the distance.

First pace. Fast. *Step it out.*

Second pace. *Keep going.*

A split second before the trip flare exploded, Alex felt the wire just below his knee, ligament-taut, and then the world around him exploded into blue-white light.

Out of sheer instinct he hurled himself sideways to the ground. Blinded, and with his hard-won night vision destroyed, he could see nothing outside the area lit by the phosphorous glare. All beyond it was black.

Shit!

The flare smoking and crackling. The sound of running feet and Alex stumbling blindly after them, Glock in hand, face whipped by branches.

Meehan was making not for the church, but the house. Fifty yards behind him now, Alex tried to blink away the searing blast of light imprinted on his retinas.

But it stayed there, dancing in front of his vision so that he could barely see as he ran.

He slipped in the mud, went down hard and, picking himself up, ran straight into a tree stump and fell again, setting the knife wounds screaming in protest. A hundred yards ahead of him he saw the other man race into the house. Meehan's night vision was unimpaired – he had deliberately kept his back to the trip flare.

Somehow Alex reached the front door. Behind him, in the wood, the flare was no more than a popping smoulder on its steel picket. His night vision was shot and he was following a presumably armed man into a lightless house.

Shit, just when the Maglite could have helped him, he'd left it outside in the rucksack. On the other hand the torch would betray his own position . . . Crouching motionless just inside the front door in the musty darkness, Alex listened intently.

The crunching of feet on fallen plaster, then silence except for the rain on the roof tiles. Meehan was above him.

How did the layout of the house go . . . *Think*.

Twenty stairs up, that much he remembered. The top corridor T-branching to left and right – Meehan was in the left wing, his location confirmed by a dull thump. *What did he have up there?*

Do or die, thought Alex. Let's go and see.

As silently as possible he crept up the stairs. The photo imprint of the flare was still in front of his eyes, but the beginnings of night vision were returning to him. He could see the top of the stairs now and the corridor. To the left were three doors, one of them opened.

He had left them all closed, he remembered.

Bracing himself, readying the Glock, he burst into the room. It was empty, but the boards previously covering the window opening had been booted outwards and rain was spattering the floor. Alex raced over towards the opening, guessing that Meehan had had some sort of rope or other escape route readied there. The thump must have been Meehan hitting the roof of the porch below.

An instant before Alex reached the window, however, the floorboards collapsed beneath his feet with a desiccated sigh. There was a burst of dust and crumbling lath and plaster, and then there was no support at all and Alex felt himself pitched downwards through the choking darkness. He hit the hall floor below hard and unevenly, smashing on to one elbow and the back of his skull.

Son of a bitch – Meehan had booby-trapped the floor with rotten boards and cut out the beams. Painfully, Alex got to his feet. His parachute training had ensured that he had automatically rolled with the fall and saved himself a broken limb but he was badly shaken.

Had Meehan made a break for his vehicle, or was he waiting outside with his weapon cocked, ready to blow his pursuer away?

A distant scream of tyres on the wet road gave Alex his answer. Still dazed, he shook his head, dislodging a gritty cloud of dry plaster. Time to go, he whispered mechanically to himself. Time to go. Meehan already had a clear two minutes' start.

The rucksack. Run. Find it.

He slipped on the wet ground again, wrenching the stitches, but was beyond pain now. Safety-locking and

338

holstering the Glock, pulling the rucksack of kit to his shoulders – both sets of actions seemed to take for ever – he forced himself in the direction of the main gate. The fall through the floor seemed to have affected his balance and he had to concentrate hard in order to place one foot in front of the other. Keep going, he repeated to himself, desperately attempting to order his thoughts. Not dead yet. Not dead till you're dead. *Keep going.*

It took him a clear minute to climb the gate and he managed to gash his thumb badly on the barbed wire while doing so. When he finally made it to the top, he sucked the blood from his shaking hand and looked blearily around him. To his left, perhaps a mile away, a tiny thread of light showed for a moment. The Watchman had gone east.

Keep going.

Even pushing the bike was difficult to begin with, but eventually he got it to the road, hauled off the night-vision goggles and pulled on the motorcycle goggles and helmet. With the aid of the pen torch – his hands were still shaking badly – he checked the tank. It was full and probably held nine or ten litres of unleaded petrol. The jerrycan in the cotton rucksack bungee-corded to the rear of the seat held approximately the same again.

The KTM had an electric start and burbled immediately into life. Cautiously, Alex let out the hydraulic clutch and moved forward. The power was there, smooth and immediate, but the knobbly moto-cross tyres gave him the sensation that he was riding on marbles. The seat was hard, narrow and unyielding. This was not a machine that lent itself willingly to roadriding.

Go, he ordered himself. *No lights*. The roads were empty and Meehan had to be allowed to think that he had got away. Alex had no night vision, though. He had been wearing the image-intensifying goggles for too long.

Too bad. Drive. And fast.

No lights.

At speed, it was like riding a road drill. The KTM could do 80 mph on tarmac but it wasn't what it had been designed for, and the knobbly tyres shook Alex to the bone, blurred his vision, made the teeth dance in his mouth. And with no lights . . .

Faster. Risk everything.

Rain lashed his face, the white lines on the road were barely visible and when the front wheel touched them the whole machine seemed to twitch and skate.

Accelerate into the bends. Find speed.

The main road. North to Okehampton, south to Tavistock.

Roulette: 50–50; red or black.

South. His fists tight on the domino grips, his body ice-cold in the sodden clothing, the black sutures biting into the knife-cuts.

Ignore the pain.

He saw nothing for two miles and then, far ahead of him, a tiny worm of light travelling not south, but east. If it was Meehan, he had turned off the main road at right angles. He was heading for the centre of Dartmoor and taking the narrow road at well over 70.

Shit. Bastard still had at least four miles on him. Once he made it to a road with a bit of traffic on it he'd just vanish.

Taking a deep breath, Alex swung the KTM left-handed off the road and into the wild darkness of the open moor. His only chance of staying with Meehan was to cut across country. As the crow flew Meehan was only a couple of miles away, but by road he was more than twice that.

Alex accelerated aggressively, felt the near sublime sensation as the tyres bit hard into the rough moorland. Doing the job it was designed for, the bike seemed to gather Alex up, to bind him furiously to itself. The supercross suspension had been set at a very harsh level with a minimum of compression and rebound, but Alex was soon glad of this when the front wheels hit a rock. For a moment man and machine were flying through the darkness, then the wheels came down with a testicle-crunching double smash that would have consigned a non-performance bike to the scrap heap and a less blindly determined driver to an Intensive Care ward.

But with body and brain screaming vengeance, Alex didn't give a fuck. The pain and fatigue were distant things now – all that mattered was that he dominate this leaping, howling beast of a motorcycle. He could see nothing. He was aware of a track of sorts beneath him and the glow-worm thread of the vehicle ahead and to his right, and that was all. The rest – the whipping cold, the shotgun volleys of rain and mud, the desperate grip of his hands and heels – barely registered.

In a rational state of mind he would never have been able to do it. In the event, instinct grabbed the controls from fear and good judgement. Instinct looked ahead, instinct held its line, instinct squared the front wheel into the rain-slicked rocks and hummocks, and as the four-stroke engine screamed beneath him Alex knew a crazy, weightless release.

What the fuck, he thought. *If I smash myself to pieces, then so be it.*

Gradually, he closed the gap between them. Did the Watchman have a plan, he wondered, or was he just distancing himself from Black Down with all speed.

Almost there. Almost within safe range of him. The road across the moor was about twenty miles long, and Alex needed to be well locked on to Meehan before they encountered any more traffic. As things stood he didn't even know what sort of vehicle the other man was driving.

But he could at least see his lights now, all the time. Assuming that it was the man he was after. If it wasn't, well, that was the end of it.

Shit. Another vehicle had joined the car that he hoped was Meehan's. Swinging hard right-handed, Alex made for the road. Within the minute the front wheel of the KTM had dived into a cut and Alex found himself flying over the handlebars to land in an awkward heap in the marshy heather. He was not badly hurt, but his confidence in his bike-handling abilities took a dent. And by the time he had got himself up and righted, and restarted the KTM, neither car was in sight. More carefully now, Alex steered the bike to the road.

After the thrill of flying over moorland, it was back to the murderous vibration of the road. Speed helped a little, but only a little. Throttling back, Alex pushed the KTM up to 85 mph, and after five minutes, to his vast relief, tail-lights appeared in front of him.

The rear of the two cars was a newish red Toyota driven, as far as Alex could see through the rainswept rear window, by a man in a hat. A Countryside

Alliance sticker showed in the back window.

Swinging outside the Toyota, Alex peered through the rear window of the front car, a battered-looking dark-blue BMW. This driver seemed to be bareheaded. The car was much muddier than the Toyota.

It could be either of them. Alex stayed hard on the tail of the rear car, his eyes locked to the driver. The hat looked like a tweed one, the sort habitually worn by Inspector Frost on TV.

Both cars slowed down and Alex fell back fifty yards. They were approaching a village – a sign read Two Bridges. The Toyota driver seemed to be waving his right hand about inside the car – what the fuck was he up to?

And then something about the patterns he was inscribing suddenly made sense to Alex. *He was conducting!* He was listening to a classical music station and conducting it with his finger.

Nothing anyone had said about Meehan had suggested that he was a music fan. Nor was it credible that, at a moment potentially fraught with danger, he would be allowing his concentration to be dispersed in this way. Joseph Meehan was, as Frank Wisbeach had said, a 'true believer'. He had just survived an expert assassination attempt. Under the circumstances he was hardly going to be singing along to Classic FM.

Meehan had to be the guy in the BMW.

Alex was glad he had reached a decision because the two cars separated on the eastern side of the village. The Toyota swung right towards Ashburton, the BMW forked left to Moretonhampstead.

The first fingers of light were now visible at the horizon, and Alex braked and waited at the roadside as the BMW pulled away from the village. He had no intention of being spotted in Meehan's rear-view mirror. As long as he kept his lights off, he told himself . . .

As soon as the BMW was out of sight Alex restarted, gritting his teeth against the pulverising vibrations and dropping back the moment the red tail-lights came into view again. The signpost indicated that it was ten miles to Moretonhampstead and he very much doubted that Meehan was going to turn off the main road.

More worrying was the petrol issue. Meehan, it was logical to suppose, had just returned from London when he appeared at Black Down House. He must have had some nearby place to park the car. Would he have a full tank of petrol? Was he carrying any with him?

The KTM's tank probably held about nine litres. Four-stroke engine, thirty miles to the gallon . . . say a hundred miles, max, before he needed to fill up again. If Meehan needed a refill before then, fine. Alex could ride in and shoot him with the silenced Glock at the petrol station. Ride away before anyone realised what had happened.

If Meehan didn't need petrol before Alex did, then Alex was in trouble. Meehan would simply outrun him.

He came to a decision. He would follow Meehan until his own petrol gage indicated half-full. Then he would call Dawn Harding on his mobile, give her Meehan's position and let her Service's people take over. This was their speciality, after all.

The arrangement was professionally responsible, but also gave him a reasonable chance of sorting the whole thing out himself, which he very much wanted to do. He needed closure, as – he suspected – did Meehan. Their destinies had intertwined. One of them had to kill the other.

TWENTY-SEVEN

From Moretonhampstead the dark-blue BMW took the Exeter road and then turned sharply northwards up the valley of the river Exe towards Tiverton. Hanging well back in the half-dark, Alex was still fairly certain that he had not been seen.

At Tiverton the BMW turned eastwards again. He was making for Taunton, but it seemed that caution was leading him to avoid motorways in favour of much smaller roads. From Taunton, Alex guessed, he would work his way across country to Salisbury.

At first it appeared that Alex was right. Meehan drove through Taunton and continued eastwards on minor roads for twenty-five minutes. And then, a mile or two short of the village of Castle Cary, Alex rounded a corner to see the BMW at a lay-by three hundred yards ahead of him. Meehan must be taking a piss, he thought, braking sharply.

Shit! The fact that he had stopped on seeing Meehan's car rather than driving straight past would unquestionably have set alarm bells ringing.

As nonchalantly as he could, he wrenched open the cotton bag, pulled out the jerrycan and filled the KTM's half-empty petrol tank. Then he slipped the jerrycan back in the bag, bungee-corded it to the back of the seat and stretched as if he'd only woken up ten minutes earlier. With luck, Meehan would mistake him for a local. The muddy trail bike was hardly the most likely pursuit vehicle.

A palely anonymous figure – a figure that Alex had last seen lit by a trip flare – exited the roadside hedge. Unhurriedly, Alex swung his leg over the KTM and pressed the start button, intending to pull level with the car and shoot Meehan where he stood.

When he was still forty yards away, however, he saw Meehan turn towards him, handgun at full stretch. A series of rounds whipped past Alex's head, and as he desperately braked and ducked he saw Meehan leap into his vehicle and accelerate at high speed down the road.

Pulling out the Glock, Alex fired half a dozen rounds after him, but without visible effect. Right, he thought. Gloves off. Let's cock, lock and rock.

There was no hanging back now. As Meehan took the BMW screaming through the village at close to 80 mph, Alex followed close behind. For the first time in his life he prayed for a police vehicle. A whooping siren and a set of flashing blue lights and his problems would be over.

But of course there was no police vehicle to be seen. Instead, Meehan hurled himself northwards, pulling every trick out of the evasive driving hand-book that he could remember. But Alex had done the same course with the same instructors and was driving the more manoeuvrable – if also by far the more dangerous – vehicle. He quite simply locked on and stayed there, dropping back and outwards a few yards every time the road straightened in case Meehan slammed on the brakes at high speed – generally considered the most effective countermeasure against a following motorcycle.

In this fashion – Meehan racing ahead, Alex hanging grimly on to his tail – they screamed up through Radstock and Weston to the M4. Still no police and precious little traffic. It was Saturday, Alex realised belatedly. And it couldn't be more than six thirty. Seven at the latest.

At junction 18 of the M4 Meehan pulled hard over on to the motorway and joined the slow-lane traffic at 70 mph. Flattening himself to the KTM's narrow seat, eyes streaming behind his goggles, Alex followed as the BMW swung across to the fast lane: 90 mph, 95. The vibrations from the KTM's tyres were turning his muscles to Plasticene. His body ached, he had a cracking migraine and was having difficulty focusing his eyes.

Touching 100 mph now.

Just hang on. One of us, sooner or later, is going to run out of petrol.

There was nothing, now, beyond staying with Meehan. It was all he had to do. Just stay on.

The Severn Road Bridge. At breakneck speed, Meehan crashed the barrier and Alex followed. He had a momentary impression of a man in a fluorescent yellow rain jacket peering from a cabin, then the tableau was far behind them and they were swerving through the buffeting winds and rain of the westbound motorway towards Newport.

A screaming turn north next, up the Usk valley. Alex was all machine now and all pain. There was no thought beyond pursuit. At times it seemed as if he and the Watchman were one, controlled by the same hand, racing to a final rendezvous that they both craved.

Which of them would last longer? They roared through Usk, Abergavenny, Tredegar and Cefn Coed. And still the unearthly emptiness and the sense of driving the dawn before them. They were in the Black Mountain country now, among hills known by name to every SAS member, past and present. There was Cefn Crew, rearing blackly over the reservoir, there was the foreshortened bulk of Fan Fawr, there was the jagged ridge line of Craig Fan-ddu. These were the rocks that they had trained over, month after month, sweating and freezing and cursing as they dragged their aching bodies and their rock-filled Bergans over the windy granite peaks.

And then, as the dark blue BMW hurled up the thread-like Cwm Taf valley ahead of them, Alex suddenly knew where the story was going to end. For there, towering over them all, was the pitiless mother of all the Black Mountains – Pen-y-Fan. Every SAS selection cadre knew Pen-y-Fan – they were harassed up and down its grey, shale-strewn sides until they hated every unyielding inch of it. One of the final elements of selection into the Regiment was named 'the Fan Dance', as it started and finished with an ascent of the mountain.

The track briefly straightened. On the wet, pot-holed surface the trail-bike was coming into its own and the gap between the two vehicles was narrowing. Slamming to an angled halt, pulling out the Glock and wrenching the goggles from his eyes, Alex released a fast volley of shots at the disappearing BMW. The first few missed, ricocheting from the roadside shale, but then as Meehan threw the car into the approaching bend his rear driver's-side tyre was suddenly shredded rubber.

The BMW's overturning was both appalling and beautiful. The right-hand side of the car seemed to tuck into the shale-strewn verge for a moment and then the black guts of the machine were suddenly skywards, the roll completing itself with a shuddering crash back on to four wheels.

The vehicle came to a smoking rest beside the road, its windows glassless, then Alex saw the wiry figure of Meehan drag himself painfully out. The former agent was obviously injured, perhaps seriously, but he began climbing immediately, scrambling desperately over the rocks and fallen slates up the western face of the mountain. Slowly, warily, Alex rode the KTM towards the abandoned car. Reloading the Glock and unscrewing the silencer — silencers tended significantly to reduce muzzle velocity — he set off after the fleeing figure.

The two men climbed for several minutes, Alex remaining a steady fifty metres behind Meehan, until the vehicles were toy-like on the road below. As they climbed so the wind's roar grew, dragging at them, deafening them, and punching at their clothes. Meehan, despite his injury — he seemed to be dragging a leg — was setting a ferocious pace and Alex felt the sweat streaming down his back as he followed.

At a thousand feet a shadowy rain squall crossed the face of the mountain. Meehan turned, his face pale and contorted with pain, and sent several rounds spattering about his pursuer.

Granite chips flicked lethally about Alex's face and then a rogue shot, deflected by a rock, punched through the cordura rucksack on his back. Ricocheting from the Maglite torch, the 9mm round tore downwards and outwards through the flesh of the SAS officer's back.

Shit. *Shit!*

It felt as if someone had laid a block of ice across him. There was no pain, although he knew that the pain would come. He could feel the blood coursing down his back.

Ignore it. Eyes on the target.

Flattening himself against the rock face, Alex saw Meehan's progress was becoming erratic. He was flailing around – the shock and the injury sustained in the BMW shunt were taking their toll.

Finally, in a shower of flaky shale, he fell, rolling limply down the hillside to a grassy outcrop a little above Alex's position. His automatic – dropped – spun past Alex on to the rocks below.

Warily, Alex approached Meehan, who lay face down on the springy turf. Correct procedure would have been a double tap to the back of the skull, but he felt he owed this man more than a dog's death.

He turned the fallen man over. The thin, pale features were instantly recognisable and twisted themselves into a wry smile. Blood oozed from a cut in his head.

'Lucky shot, boyo, blowing that tyre.'

The accent took Alex straight back to Belfast. 'I've no doubt of it,' he said and quickly began to search the fallen man. There was a sheathed Mauser knife and several spare magazines, and a pocketful of loose 9mm rounds, but no other firearm.

Meehan pursed his lips. 'Did I hit you back there?'

Alex felt around his back. The hand came back bloody. 'Yeah. Another lucky shot, I'd say.'

Meehan looked away. 'So are you going to waste me or what?'

Alex didn't answer. Reaching for his mobile he dialled Dawn's number.

She answered on the first ring. 'Alex. Thank God. Where are you?'

He told her.

'And Meehan?'

Something made Alex hesitate. He looked down at Meehan. 'Dealt with.'

A faint smile touched the former agent's lips.

'Stay there,' Dawn ordered. 'Don't move. I'll pick up a flight to Brecon – be with you in an hour.'

'We're not going anywhere,' said Alex wearily, and rang off.

'So,' Meehan repeated, almost bored. 'You goin' to follow orders, soldier, and waste me?'

'You didn't waste me when you had the chance. Why?'

'Wasn't part of the plan.'

'Can we talk about that plan?'

Meehan was silent for a moment, then the corner of his mouth twitched. 'Good place for us to meet, don't you think?'

Alex smiled and nodded.

Curiosity touched the pale features. 'How did you find out about Black Down?'

'A conversation you had,' said Alex.

'Connolly?'

'Yup.'

Meehan nodded. 'I never told Den Connolly where the house was. Something stopped me, even then.'

Briefly, Alex explained how forensic analysis had discovered the solvent in his system.

'Poisoned, was I?' said Meehan thoughtfully, looking across the valley towards Fan Fawr. 'I hadn't allowed for that, I'll admit.'

'Connolly said you never turned tout.'

'Nor I did. Not ever.'

Alex stared at him. 'So what . . .'

Meehan looked wearily away. 'Just do your job, man, and give us the double tap. Get the fuck on with it.'

'I want to know.'

'Just do it.'

'None of it makes sense. Don't you at least want it to make sense?'

'You wouldn't believe me.'

'I might.'

The two men stared at each other. Around them the wind scoured the rocks and flattened the grass. The place was theirs alone.

'How much do you know?' asked Meehan eventually.

'I know about Watchman. I know what you were sent over the water to do. I know that the whole thing went bad, agents were killed, all hell broke loose.'

Meehan nodded. 'Whatever you've been told by Five, who I'm assuming you're working for right now, remember that it had a single purpose: to persuade you to kill me. Would it be fair to say that?'

'I guess so,' said Alex.

'Right. Well, remember that. And remember too that I'm a dead man. I've no need to lie.'

'I'll remember,' said Alex and moved down the slope to collect Meehan's weapon.

TWENTY-EIGHT

'The first thing you have to understand,' said Joseph Meehan, 'is just how much I've always hated the IRA. My father was a good man, religious and patriotic, and they crippled him, humiliated him and expelled him from the country he loved. Drove him to an early grave. And there have been thousands like him – innocent people whose lives have been destroyed by those maniac bastards. Whatever else I tell you I want you to remember that one fact. I hate the IRA, I always have hated them and I will take that hatred to my grave.'

He paused and the lids narrowed over the pale, fathomless eyes. 'I'm assuming that Fenwick and the rest of them told you the background stuff – the Watchman selection process and the rest of it?'

Alex nodded.

There was a curious blankness to Meehan's words. They were passionate, but delivered without expression. 'When I got over there I started off living in a flat in Dunmurry and working at Ed's – they tell you about that?'

'The electronic goods place?'

'That's right. Ed's. Ed's Electronics. And I was dating this girl called Tina. Nice girl. Grandparents came over from Italy after the war. Had a loudmouth brother called Vince who worked in a garage and fancied himself as God's gift to the Republican movement. Tried the bullshit on me a couple of times but I told him to fuck off – said I didn't want to know.

'That pissed him off, and he made sure that the local volunteers found out that I'd served with the Crown forces – thought they might give me a good kicking or something. Course they did no such thing, they're not that stupid, but a couple of them started watching me and asking the odd question, and they soon found out I knew my way around an electronic circuit.'

Meehan touched his head and regarded his bloody fingertips.

'I'll spare you the details but there was the usual eyeing-up process and I started to hang out with these half-dozen fellers who thought of themselves as an ASU. They weren't, of course – they were just a bunch of saloon bar Republicans. I did a couple of under-the-counter jobs for them – radio repairs – and then a much heavier bunch showed up. Older guys. Heard I was interested in joining the movement. I'd said no such thing, but I said yeah, I was sympathetic – more sympathetic than I'd been in the past, anyway.'

'And?' asked Alex.

'And they didn't fuck around. Asked straight out if I wanted in. So I said yeah, OK.'

'Must have been satisfying after all that time.'

'Yes and no. These guys were pretty hard-core. I knew there'd be no going back.'

'So what happened next?'

'There was a whole initiation process. I was driven to a darkened room in north Belfast and interviewed by three men I never saw. What was my military history with the Crown forces, what courses had I done and where had I been posted? Was I known as a Republican sympathiser and had I ever attended a Republican march? Had I ever been arrested? Where in Belfast did I drink . . . Hours of it. And why the fuck did I want to join the IRA?

'I told them I was fed up of living as a second-class citizen simply because I was a Catholic. I told them that I'd been in the Brit army and felt the rough edge of discrimination over there. Said since my return to Belfast I'd come to feel that the IRA spoke the only language the Crown understood. Parroted all the stuff I'd learnt from the Five instructors, basically.'

'And they bought it?'

'They heard me out and it must have gone down OK, because I was told that from that moment on I was to make no public or private statement of my Republican sympathies, not to associate with known Republicans, had to avoid Republican bars et cetera. I was put forward for what's called the Green Book lectures – a two-month course of indoctrination which took place every Thursday evening in a flat in Twinbrook. History of the movement, rules of engagement, counter-surveillance, anti-interrogation techniques . . .'

'The old spot on the wall trick?'

'All that bollocks, yeah. And at the end of it I was sworn in.'

'How did that feel?'

'Well, there was no going back, that was for certain sure. But I was finally earning the wages I was being paid.'

'Go on.'

'I started off as a dicker. I was told to hang on to my

job so my volunteer activities were all in the evenings and at weekends. And this started to cause problems with Tina. She was a sympathiser, but not to the point where she was prepared to give her life over. She wanted to do what other girls did – go out in the evening, go round the shops on a Saturday . . . Anyway, I arranged a meet with Geoff, my agent handler – you would have known him as Barry Fenn – and he just said do whatever the fuck makes the bloody girl happy. Buy her a ring, get her up the duff, whatever. He felt it was vital for what he called "my integration into the community" that I stuck with her.

'So we got engaged, which was fine by me. And almost immediately afterwards I'm told I'm spending my two weeks' summer holiday in a training camp in County Clare in the Republic. So Tina hits the fucking roof. Me or the movement – choose. So of course I chose as I had to and she walked, and that was the end of it.'

'Was that . . . difficult?'

'I saw it as a sacrifice. A sacrifice for the greater good, which was nailing those PIRA bastards.' He paused for a moment, then the toneless voice continued: 'At that time I thought that all the evil was coming from the one direction.'

Alex watched him thoughtfully. Squaddies, by and large, did not express themselves in such abstract terms. Even the average regimental padre tended to steer clear of words like 'good' and 'evil' and 'sacrifice'. For the first time since they had found themselves face to face, Alex wondered about the other man's sanity.

'How was the camp?'

'Pretty basic. Weapons drills, surveillance,

interrogation scenarios. I had to wind down my skills to volunteer level, which is a fuck's sight harder than it sounds.'

'I can imagine. Were you upset at the break-up with Tina?'

Meehan looked away. 'There was something I only found out later. She was pregnant at the time. She had the child – a boy – but never let me see him . . .'

Alex nodded, letting Meehan take his time.

'After I came back from Clare I was either working at Ed's or on call for the movement. I did a year or so's dicking and then I was seconded as a driver to one of the auxiliary cells, which is what they call their punishment squads.'

Alex grimaced. 'Shit!'

'Yeah – *shit!* – exactly. In theory we were supposed to be keeping the streets safe for Catholics to go about their business, in practice we were kneecapping teenage shoplifters. It was fucking evil – especially since I'd seen the same thing done to my dad. But that was the point. To make it as horrible as possible. To see if I had what it took. A bit of interest was being paid to me by then.'

Alex raised his eyebrows.

'A man called Byrne. Padraig Byrne. CO of Belfast Brigade at that time and later on the Army Council.'

'Ah.'

'Yeah. He'd been told I'd been a Royal Engineer and had bits and pieces sent to me for repair. Computers, mostly. There was one job where some information had to be recovered and it turned out to be details of a bank security system.'

'Fenwick told me about that.'

'Yeah, well, it wasn't too difficult to figure that one

out as a plant – if the security was beefed up, they'd know that I was passing the information on.'

'But you did pass it on.'

'I passed everything on. But London's policy was not to move on anything that might compromise my cover. Which at that stage I was bloody grateful for, because my impression was that the Provos still didn't a hundred per cent trust me. Especially Byrne. It was like . . . have you ever done any fishing?'

Alex shook his head.

'It was like when you've got a fat old carp nosing at your bait. He wants it, he's desperate to believe that it's safe, but his instinct tells him no. And that's how Byrne was. I could tell that he wanted to believe in me, but . . .' Meehan shrugged. 'I'd been doing a lot of driving. Scouting jobs mostly, with me in the lead car keeping an eye out for trouble and the players or weapons or whatever in a second vehicle following behind. Important, I guess, but still auxiliary stuff. I was never allowed anywhere near any operational planning.

'And then in late 1990 early 1991 things moved on. I was contacted by Padraig Byrne at Ed's and told that I was part of a weapon-recovery team. We were to dig up an Armalite from a churchyard in Castleblayney and deliver it to a stiffer back in Belfast – some ex-US marine sniper, I think it was. I reported all this to Fenn via a dead-letter drop and he told me to go ahead and not to worry, they'd jark the weapon and follow it in.

'Well, they followed it in all right, but they didn't jark it and the stiffer used it against a patrol in Andytown a couple of days later. Luckily – for all that he was supposed to be a real deadeye – he missed, but that was more to do with the patrol spotting him than there being anything wrong with the rifle. We returned it to the cache the next day, it was never jarked and as far as I know it's still in circulation . . .'

For a moment Alex saw an expression of murderous bitterness flash through Meehan's eyes, then the blankness was back.

'Whatever – I must have passed some sort of test in Byrne's eyes, because immediately afterwards I was sent to join a bomb-making cell who were working out of a basement on the Finaghy Road. The cell had a problem. What they were trying to do was to get bombs into police or army bases, which could then be detonated remotely and the problem was that the Crown forces maintained a twenty-four-hour radio-wave shield around every vehicle, building or installation that could possibly be of interest. They needed someone to work out a signal that could penetrate the shield.

'Well, I found one. I found a frequency they hadn't thought of, and as soon as I had, and it had been tested by a feller we had working as a cleaner in one of the police stations, I passed it back to Fenn and told him to factor it into the installation defences. The next thing I knew I was being congratulated by Padraig fucking Byrne. They'd had a success down in Armagh, detonating a remote-controlled bomb inside a base there. Bessbrook. Three soldiers had been seriously injured and a cleaner – a Catholic woman, as it happened – had been killed. And serve the bitch right, according to Byrne, for taking Crown money.

'I rang Fenn that night from one of the public phones at Musgrave Park Hospital and asked him what the fuck was going down. He told me they'd had to let the bomb go by. There had been several failed detonations in the previous few months and there was suspicion at the top levels of the organisation that a British agent was defusing them. I told him it was more likely that the button men were so fucking solid they couldn't do the job properly and that was why the bombs hadn't been going off, but he just changed the subject. I was to carry on as usual. The O'Riordan woman – the cleaner – was an unavoidable loss. The soldiers would be well cared for. Finish.

'I realised that part of what Fenn said was true. There was no question mark in Byrne's mind now – I was well and truly in. That's how it seemed at the time, anyway. Looking back, I can see that I was so preoccupied with the O'Riordan woman's death that I missed the single vital fact I'd been . . .' Meehan doubled up and bared his teeth. For several long moments he was silent, neither breathing nor moving. Finally he seemed to relax and slowly straightened.

'Are you OK?' asked Alex, aware of the question's ludicrous inadequacy.

Meehan managed a smile. There was now a dark, wet stain on his shirt-front. 'Never better!' he gasped. 'Top o' the world!'

Alex waited while Meehan drew breath.

'I worked with the cell for about eighteen months. There were five of us. A QM, an intelligence officer, two general operators – one of whom was a woman – and myself. We were a bomber cell, which is why we had Bronagh with us. It was reckoned that a woman was better for planting devices in public places.'

'And all the time you were reporting to back to your London handler?'

'I was.'

'What sort of stuff?'

'Names and addresses of volunteers, registration numbers of cars, possible assassination targets, anything.'

'By dead-letter drop? By phone?'

'By e-mail mostly, from about 1991 onwards, using machines that had been brought into the shop. I'd bash away in my back room and no one took a blind bit of difference: I was just the anoraky bloke that fixed the computers. Dead-letter drops and meets are all very well, but if you're discovered you're dead. This was perfect: I'd transmit the information then delete all traces of the operation. And I was usually able to make sure that the owners of the machines I used got a cash deal, so there was no record of their having passed through the shop.'

'Sounds as if you were earning your Box salary.'

'Fucking right I was.'

'Fenwick said you lost your nerve.'

Meehan closed his eyes for a moment. The accusation didn't merit a reply.

'Our cell was involved in shooting an RUC officer at the off-licence in Stewartstown Road. I scouted in the stiffers and drove them away from the scene. London knew the hit was going to happen because I'd told them a couple of days earlier what the score was – in fact, I e-mailed them a detailed warning – but the hit went ahead.'

'I heard you gave less than an hour's warning.'

'Bollocks. They had forty-eight. And an hour would have been enough anyway. No – they let it happen and that was when I understood that something strange – no, let me rephrase that, something fucking *evil* – was going down. That the reason I thought I was there – to get intelligence out to where it could save lives and do some good – wasn't the reason at all.'

'So what was the reason?'

'I'm getting there. Does the name Proinsas Deavey mean anything to you?'

'No.'

'Proinsas Deavey was a low-level volunteer who occasionally did some dicking and errand-running. A nobody, basically. I saw him about the Falls from time to time and the word was that he was involved in low-level drug-dealing. Anyway, apparently he tried flogging the stuff to the wrong people and he was picked up by the auxiliaries, who gave him a good kicking. Bad idea, because by that stage Proinsas has a habit himself. He's desperate for money. So when he gets a call from the FRU he's a pushover.'

Alex nodded.

'Now I don't know about any of this until I get a call at work from Padraig Byrne. Some time around Christmas 1995, it must have been. Padraig was what they call a Red Light by then, meaning he was known to the Crown forces as a player, so he had to keep a very low profile. I was told to go round to his place after closing time, making sure I wasn't followed.

'When I got there he told me that Proinsas had got drunk, turned himself over to one of the nutting squads and confessed he was touting for the FRU. In theory PIRA's always run an amnesty system for touts – spill your guts and you're off the hook – but in practice it's more likely to be a debriefing followed by two to the head. In this case, untypically, the nutting squad was bright enough to consult Byrne and he told them to hang on to Deavey – he'd debrief the man himself. Which he did and then set up Proinsas to feed disinformation back to the FRU.

'Now at this stage you have to remember what's going on politically. The Crown forces don't know it yet, but the ceasefire is at an end. Southern Command's England Wing is about to detonate the Canary Wharf bomb and Padraig Byrne – a very ambitious man, remember, keen to move from the Army Council to the Executive – sees a chance for a spectacular of his own. He's going to take out a pair of FRU agents.

'He tells me this. He tells me something else. I'm a junior member of PIRA GHQ staff by then – a sort of assistant to the Quartermaster General. There's been a major technical updating and I've had to play a big part in that – training operators and so on.

'Byrne wants me to kill the FRU guys. In person, in public, in front of a big volunteer crowd. The ultimate commitment, the ultimate statement of loyalty. Do that, he says, and you're on the Army Council, guaranteed. You can forget all that paperchasing at GHQ – you'll have proved yourself heart and soul. So of course I say yes – what the fuck else can I say – and ask for details. And he fills me in. Tells me exactly what's going to happen.

'So the next day I work late at Ed's. File an encrypted report to London on a client's machine, wipe the hard disk – people are wising up to the insecurity of e-mail by then – and hope to God that the FRU people are pulled out in time. I ask to be pulled out too: the finger's going to be pointed straight at me if these guys are miraculously whipped off the streets just days before they're due to be whacked. Byrne, like I said, is a very sharp, very switched-on operator.

'The next day I got a call from the rep of a company called Intex, saying they'd ceased production of the software I'd enquired about. Intex was Five, of course, and the call meant that my message had been received and I was to sit tight.'

Alex stared at him. 'Let me get this right. Are you saying that Five knew that Ray Bledsoe and Connor Wheen were due to be picked up, tortured and murdered, *and did nothing*?'

'Yes. That's exactly what I'm saying. A bunch of us were driven down to a farmhouse on the border that the nutting squad often used for interrogations and executions – a horrible bloody place, stinking of death. The boyos, needless to say, were pissing themselves with excitement at the chance of seeing a pair of Brit agents chopped at close range. The hours passed and I tell you I have never prayed like I prayed then: that London would pull those boys out in time.

'They didn't, of course, and Bledsoe and Wheen were brought down to the border that evening. I had drawn a Browning and a couple of clips from the QM, so that I could at least make it fast, but in the event I wasn't even able to do that.'

Meehan fell silent. His eyes were as cold and blank as pack ice.

'They had a generator there and one of those heavy-duty compressed-air staple guns . . . Do you have any idea what happens when you fire one of those things into someone's eye?'

Alex opened his mouth to speak, but found that he could say nothing.

'As the eye explodes – and it goes fuckin' *everywhere* – the staple blasts its way out through the roof of the mouth. The guy's kicking, meanwhile, and pissing himself, and generally going berserk, but the thing he can't do is make any sound, because his blood and his sinuses are pouring out of his nose and mouth. The pain has to be beyond anything you can imagine . . .'

'You did that?' whispered Alex disbelievingly.

'No, thank God, some other volunteer did it – to Wheen. But the point is not who did it, the point is that Five, knowing what Byrne and his nutting squads do, *allowed it to happen*. They had the information and they deliberately failed to act on it.'

'So what happened next?'

'Byrne figured that Wheen was the tough guy and Bledsoe – if he scared him enough – was going to do the talking. Well, he scared him all right. The guy was out of his head with sheer terror. But just to make sure, Byrne had the volunteer do Wheen's other eye. And then – just to make the point that it was Bledsoe who was going to do the talking – he cut Wheen's tongue out. Have you ever heard a man trying to scream when his tongue's been cut out?'

Alex shook his head.

'It sounds like percolating coffee. Anyway, I stood there, my brain fuckin' turning itself inside out at this sight – terror, horror, disbelief, whatever the fuck – and telling myself one thing: *smile, or go the same way yourself*. And everyone else was smiling, but I tell you they were all pretty quiet at that point.'

Alex nodded.

'So then Byrne told me to do Wheen once and for all so I pulled out the Browning ready to give him one. And Byrne says no. Hands me, of all things, a fuckin' lump-hammer and a six-inch nail . . .'

'And you did him with that?'

'It made this kind of . . . plinking sound,' said

Meehan reflectively. 'The guy died immediately.'

'And Bledsoe?'

'Bledsoe coughed. Told them everything. Every last thing he knew. It took hours – almost light by the time he was finished.'

'And?'

Meehan nodded expressionlessly. 'Yeah, I did him too. Same way. And as I did so I promised myself that the people responsible would know the pain and the terror that these brave men had known. Whatever it took – *whatever* it fucking took – I would make them understand.'

'Surely the people responsible were Padraig Byrne and his Provos,' suggested Alex quietly.

'Those people were evil,' said Meehan, 'but they knew they were evil. They looked evil in the eye, they embraced evil and they knew themselves for what they were. Fenwick and her people, though, were evil at a distance. They never saw the floor of that PIRA abattoir running with blood and shit, never had to look at brave men like Wheen and Bledsoe dying in indescribable terror and agony and tell themselves: yeah, I did that . . .'

'Wise monkeys,' murmured Alex.

'For every action, there's a reaction,' said Meehan. 'My father taught me that. The universe demands balance. For as long as the lives that I had taken were unavenged, there would be no balance.'

Alex stared at Meehan. Was this insanity? he wondered. Or was it logic? Or both?

'Within the week I had been promoted to the IRA's Army Council and Padraig Byrne to the Executive. I continued to file reports to London, but I no longer had the slightest confidence they would be acted upon. I warned them of two bombs: one in a Shankhill pub, one in a Ballysillan supermarket. Both were made by men I had trained, both were set by Bronagh Quinn. Five dead, in total, and over twenty injured. Women and children mostly, in the supermarket. One little girl was blinded when the lenses of her glasses were blown backwards into her eyes.

'There are seven people on the Provisional IRA's Army Council. At the first meeting I attended I looked round the other six faces and I realised that I had done at least as much for the movement as any of them. I had dicked, trailed, scouted, bugged, planned, organised, designed, strategised and taught. I had brought the movement's bomb-making skills into line with the best in the world. And finally, with my bare hands, I had killed. By ignoring every warning I ever sent, Fenwick and her people had made me part of the thing I had dedicated my life to destroying. Can you imagine – *can you imagine* – what that feels like?'

Alex said nothing. Didn't move. Carried on the buffeting wind – distant at first and then louder – was the pulse of an approaching helicopter. If Meehan heard it he ignored it.

'At that first meeting a former OC of the Armagh and Fermanagh Brigade got up. Nasty bastard, name of Halloran.'

'Dermot Halloran,' said Alex.

'The same,' confirmed Meehan. 'And he didn't fuck about. He told us, "Boys . . . We have a problem. We have a mole." There had been indications for some time, he said, that information concerning upcoming operations was reaching the Crown. Top-level information, not foot-soldier stuff. In recent days, he said, these suspicions had become cast-iron.

MI5 had an agent in place – an agent whose minimum possible level of seniority was membership of the GHQ staff. That put every man in the room squarely in the frame. The Executive had men on the case, he went on. It was a process of elimination, and until that process had run its course it had been decided that all operations and meetings should be suspended.'

The rhythmic beat of the helicopter's engine and the slash of its rotors was very close now, filling their ears. The sound seemed to hold its volume for a moment, then died away. Again, Meehan showed no sign of having heard it.

'Presumably,' said Alex, 'they wanted to see who cut and ran.'

'That was my calculation. If they'd been sure they were going to identify the mole they would have just let the wheels turn. Said nothing.'

'So what did you do?'

'I drove back to the city and went home. There was a nutting squad waiting for me and I knew then that Five had sold me out. Well, I'll spare you the details but there was a fuck of a battle. I dropped a couple of them, dived through a window and drove like fuck for Aldersgrove.'

'The airport?'

'Yeah. I was on a flight to the mainland within the hour. From that point I was totally on my own. The next morning I cleared the account MI5 had been paying money into all those years and set about establishing a new identity.'

'Did you contact MI5?'

'Are you joking . . . If I'd contacted them they'd have dropped my co-ordinates to PIRA. Within the week of my leaving Belfast every Provy stiffer in the

369

Command was on my tail as it was. No, Five didn't want me alive and compromised – my story would bury them.'

'But why do you think they ignored all those warnings and let Wheen and Bledsoe and the rest of them die?'

'I thought for a long time that they simply couldn't risk me. That if they'd started acting on my warnings they'd have had to pull me out, whereas as things stood I was their man inside the IRA, the justification for their budget, their meal ticket from the Treasury. That was what I thought at first.'

'Go on.'

'And then – finally – I figured it out. There had to be another British mole. An agent who had been in place not for years but for decades. A man I'd been set up to take the fall for.'

He fell silent for a moment.

'It was something Barry Fenn had said years earlier about there being suspicion in the senior ranks of PIRA that a British agent was defusing the bombs the organisation was making. At the time, all that I heard were the words that applied to me – i.e. "suspicion", "PIRA" and "British agent". I didn't stop to ask myself the vital question: *how the fuck did Barry Fenn know what the senior ranks of PIRA were thinking? I didn't know, so how did he?*

'They had someone all along. One of the very top men, is my guess. And in case such a man ever came under the faintest suspicion of providing information to the Crown forces, it would be necessary to have a decoy set up. Another agent who could be exposed, proved to be the real source and fed to the wolves.'

Alex shook his head and sank back against the

granite. 'Enter the Watchman,' he murmured.

'Congratulations!' said Dawn Harding. 'I do believe you've got there at last.'

She was standing above and to one side of them, and her Walther PPK was levelled straight between Alex's eyes.

TWENTY-NINE

She had brought back-up with her, a blank-faced man in a flying jacket carrying an MP5 Heckler and Koch sub-machine gun.

Had the two of them found Meehan dead, Alex knew, there would have been no problem. Anything that Meehan might have told Alex would have been cancelled out by the fact that Alex had killed him – the SAS officer could hardly broadcast a story that culminated with a murder committed by himself.

But with Meehan alive and Alex in possession of the facts about Watchmen – even just the basic facts – the position was hopeless. A glance at Dawn and the icy flatness of those sea-grey eyes told him that she was prepared to watch him die rather than risk him telling the story. Their one-night stand, and that is all it had been, after all, counted for nothing – less than nothing.

You stupid . . .

She and her back-up man would kill the pair of them, and place their disposal in the hands of a cleaner team. One thing was certain: neither body would ever be found.

Having said that, he was still holding the Glock. Still had Meehan's Browning in his pocket.

'Why isn't this animal dead?' Dawn asked, glancing scornfully at Meehan.

'I wouldn't worry yourself,' said Alex coldly. 'I don't think he's going to grow much older.'

She shook her head sorrowfully. 'You *idiot*,' she spat. 'You arrogant fucking *idiot*, Alex! Why didn't you do as you were asked? Can't you see what you're forcing me to . . .'

She continued, but Alex was no longer listening. He was holding his Glock in his right hand; with his left, which was concealed beneath his smock, he was trying to inch Meehan's Browning from his waistband. His only chance of escaping what would effectively be an execution was to trust Meehan. The man was two parts insane to one part brilliant soldier, that much was obvious, but . . . The Browning was clear of the waistband, now, and heavy in his hand. With infinite slowness he lowered it to the ground beneath his smock.

'And this man,' Alex asked Dawn, indicating the expressionless figure of Meehan. 'Can you begin to imagine what your people have forced him to do? To torture and kill British agents? To stand back and watch as bombs that he has designed cut women and children to pieces?'

Alex's question was designed to allow him to turn to the former agent. Catching the other man's eyes, he glanced downwards once, saw from the swift flicker of response that Meehan had understood him, felt the first unmistakable rush of adrenalin.

Prepare. Breathe. Only the target exists. Hear nothing, feel nothing, see nothing. Only the target.

Without warning, Alex propelled himself forward. He rolled once, his wounded back smashing with agonising force into the granite rock face, then the air screamed and ruptured as rounds from the MP5 impacted around him. The back-up man's first shots had been fired from the hip and as Alex tightened on the trigger of the Glock – *foresight, backsight, focus, exhale* – he saw the familiar movement as the weapon was pulled to the shoulder.

The back-up man had just closed his left eye in preparation for the aimed killing shot when both the Glock's 9mm rounds punched through his chin and thence his cerebellum, spraying the rocks behind him with red and ending his life in less than a third of a second.

Dawn's Walther was swinging towards Alex and the back-up man was still falling to the blood-shined granite when Meehan fired. The single round took Dawn in the centre of the chest, dropping her to her knees as if praying. As her Walther fell from her fingers, Meehan instinctively lowered the Browning for the double tap to the head.

Alex signalled for him to hold his fire and scrambled back up the hillside towards her.

'Dawn?' he said quietly, making safe and pocketing the Walther. 'Can you hear me?'

But Dawn Harding was very close to death. Meehan's shot had taken her through the sternum, and oxygenated lung blood was frothing at her mouth.

'Dawn?' he repeated, feeling beneath her T-shirt for the sucking chest wound and sealing it with his thumb. '*Dawn!*'

She raised her head and managed a painful smile, showing reddened teeth. 'Tell Angela . . .' she began. 'Tell her I . . .'

She fell silent, and tears ran down her cheeks. Then the blood came with a rush, pouring from her mouth on to her chest, and her head sank down and she died.

Switching off all feeling, Alex wiped his Glock on his shirt and placed it between Dawn's unresisting fingers. Taking the Browning from Meehan, who handed it over without hesitation, he cleaned it and placed it in the dead back-up man's right hand. The scenario wouldn't hold up for very long, but any investigation would lead the police straight back to MI5, at which point the case would disappear from the register anyway.

He turned to Meehan. 'Thank you,' he said.

'She was going to kill you,' said Meehan quietly. 'Don't go through the rest of your life wondering.'

'I won't,' promised Alex.

The ghost of a smile touched Meehan's pale features. 'We'd have made a good team, you and I,' he said.

Alex looked at the man who had shot Dawn Harding. 'We probably would,' he said emptily. 'How badly are you hurt?'

'Does that make any difference to anything?'

Alex didn't reply. Staring over the valley he watched as sunlight and shadow raced each other across the flank of Fan Fawr. Then, taking the MP5 from where it had fallen beside the dead MI5 agent, he searched the corpse for spare magazines.

Finally he turned back to Meehan. 'Do you think you could ride a motorcycle?' he asked.

THIRTY

The members' writing rooms at the Carlton Club are reached by means of a corridor leading off the Small Library, and overlook St James's Street. There are four of them, and each contains a desk surmounted by a blotter and a sheaf of the club's writing paper. The walls are lined with books, and in reading room number four the majority of these are blue-bound records of the club's minutes and proceedings from the Second World War to the present day.

It was now a fortnight since the events on the western slope of Pen-y-Fan. Walking a half-mile up the road from the wrecked BMW, Alex had stolen a battered Fiesta from outside a hillwalkers' hostel, driven to north London – an area with which he had no connection – booked into a bed-and-breakfast hotel in Tottenham under a false name, and spent the days that followed allowing his wounds to heal and planning his next move. His single trip into Central London had been an underground journey to Oxford Circus to withdraw cash from a dispensing machine and he had been back in Tottenham within the hour. On the tube he had read the *Daily Telegraph*'s elaborate account of the 'Civil Servant love tryst' that had 'ended in tragedy' in the shadow of the Black Mountains.

The shot that had creased Alex's back had been acutely painful for several days and would certainly leave a spectacular scar, but had not required any medical attention that he himself had been unable to administer with the help of Dettol and bandages. The knife cuts, with their stitches finally removed, were now no more than pale and occasionally uncomfortable reminders of the fight outside George Widdowes' house. On his thirteenth day at the bed and breakfast he had rung the offices of MI5.

As Alex entered number four reading room at the Carlton Club, he heard the clock in the library strike 11 a.m. Angela Fenwick rose from the desk facing the window, turned and extended her hand to him. 'Captain Temple,' she said, nodding dismissal to the elderly club servant hovering at the door. 'Right on time.'

Alex inclined his head, shook her hand in silence and seated himself in the proffered armchair, a tautly upholstered object of oak and azure leather. Fenwick herself resumed her place at the desk, angling her chair towards Alex. She looked older, thought Alex. Sharp lines had been incised at the corners of her mouth and her skin had a dry, desiccated quality that had not been apparent at their last meeting.

She steepled her fingers, a gesture that Alex remembered from his first briefing with her. 'Given that you have just killed two well-liked members of my Service, Captain Temple, I thought it advisable that we meet on neutral territory rather than at Thames House. I thought it might be more . . . comfortable for you.'

Neutral territory, thought Alex, glancing around him. Like fuck. 'I have no regrets whatsoever about killing Dawn Harding and that other amateur trigger man of yours,' he said coldly, 'given that they were trying bloody hard to kill me. Presumably on your direct orders. And you might as well know right now . . .'

'Captain Temple . . .'

'. . . that I will do the same to any . . .'

'*Captain Temple*! I have not come here to argue with you. I fully accept that circumstances led you to defend yourself. Reciprocally, I would ask you to accept that agents Harding and Muir acted as they did towards yourself in the belief that it was in the best interests of national security.'

'Trying to murder a serving SAS officer?'

'Put it how you like.' Fenwick's gaze was ice and her voice was steel. 'The point is that these events have happened and you and I must now discuss . . . modalities.'

'Does that mean that you want to hammer out some kind of deal?'

'That's exactly what it means, Captain Temple, so let's get right on with it. Be assured that I am enjoying this meeting no more than you are. Firstly, do you wish to continue with your army career?'

Alex shrugged. 'I want to be in the position to choose to, if that's what you mean.'

'Very well. I give you my word that you will be left alone. No complaint will be made about your conduct. All that I require is that you never speak of the events surrounding Meehan and the Watchman operation. Not to your colleagues, not to Bill Leonard, not to anyone.'

'And meanwhile you work out how to get rid of me,' said Alex with an ironic smile. 'What's it going to be, an accident on the firing range? A climbing fall? Some mystery virus?'

'Captain Temple, I . . .'

'Because let me tell you, if anything happens to me – anything fatal, that is – a package will be delivered to the offices of a certain national newspaper. That package will contain an MP5 machine-gun together with various expended cartridge cases – all bearing fingerprints, an affidavit sworn before a solicitor by me and a recording of a conversation I had with Dawn Harding on the drive down to Black Down House, in which she discusses in some detail the trapping and killing of Joseph Meehan. It's not watertight, but it's enough to sink you.'

Fenwick pursed her lips but otherwise remained expressionless.

'I've got a copy of the tape here,' continued Alex, taking a Sony Walkman cassette player from his pocket. He pressed the play button.

'*Negative thought leads to negative action . . .*' came Dawn's distinctive voice. '*Just promise me that if there's any chance of taking Meehan out . . .*'

To Alex's amazement he saw Fenwick's eyes sharpen with tears. She turned away from him instantly and pretended to examine her notes. When she looked up again, steely as ever, it was as if the moment had never been. 'Very well, captain. I take your point and I acknowledge that you have the wherewithal to do us serious damage. Let me respond by saying that if you ever discuss or disclose details of this matter pre-emptively – without provocation from my Service – then we will move to defend ourselves in the most . . . vigorous way. Certain accusations will surface – deeply damaging accusations, both of a criminal and sexual nature. You will lose your pension, your credit rating and your reputation. Serious doubts will be cast upon your state of mind. We will do, in short, whatever is necessary to discredit and ultimately ruin you.'

Alex nodded. He believed her. 'Mutually assured destruction,' he murmured.

'Quite so, Captain Temple. A highly effective deterrent in my experience. Do we have a deal?'

Alex met her unwavering gaze, saw in it an iron determination the equal of his own. 'We have a deal.'

They shook hands and there was a long silence. Fenwick stared down at the traffic.

'Are you in contact with Meehan?' she asked eventually.

Alex shook his head. 'No.'

'Rest assured we will pursue him.'

'I'm sure.'

'And we will find him.'

The ghost of a smile touched Alex's features. 'If you say so.'

Fenwick hesitated. 'Captain, would you like to know the real purpose of the Watchman operation?'

'Meehan worked that one out. He was a fall guy – there to take the drop for some longer-established mole. If the shit ever hit the fan and your senior man was threatened, there had to be someone else who could be revealed as a British agent. Meehan was that man.'

Fenwick nodded. 'That's correct. And the longer he stayed in place, the more believable it would be that he was the only mole if he had to be exposed.'

Alex stood up, closed his eyes in frustrated disbelief and shook his head. 'But you sent . . . how many is it now, must be at least a dozen soldiers and civilians to their deaths? To terrible deaths, mostly. And all for the sake of a single intelligence source? Do you honestly think that's a price worth paying?'

'Look, captain, given what we know about each other I think I can trust you with this. The point is that the man the Watchman was dummying for was not just *a* mole, he was *the* mole. The ultimate intelligence source. Have you heard of an agent code-named Steak Knife?'

Alex's eyes widened. 'I've heard about Steak Knife and read about him in the papers – all that stuff about Brian Nelson and the FRU handing over PIRA players' addresses to the UVF – but I didn't know that he actually existed. I assumed that was all black propaganda.'

'Well, of course it is, in part,' said Fenwick with a pale smile. 'But Steak Knife exists all right. And when the history of espionage finally comes to be written, our running of him as an agent will be seen as the greatest coup of them all. He's the very top man, Temple – an international household name – and he's working for British Intelligence.'

'You mean . . .' Into Alex's mind swam the now statesmanlike image of the figure he'd seen a thousand times on magazine covers and on television.

'I do mean,' said Fenwick. 'I'm not prepared to sit here and actually name him to you, but yes. He's ours.'

She looked over at Alex who, still standing, was staring bleakly out of the window over St James's.

'Do you begin to understand the scale of the field of battle now, Temple? Forget the casualties – you always get those. At the end of the day, as you well know, there's always the equivalent of the boy left tied to the tree in the Sierra Leone bush. You have to see the big picture.'

Alex closed his eyes. Felt his fingernails cutting into the flesh of his palms.

'The point to grasp,' continued Fenwick, 'is that having a direct handle on IRA policy has saved hundreds, perhaps thousands . . .'

'I can't,' said Alex flatly.

'Can't what?'

'I can't forget the casualties. I can't forget the Wheens and the Bledsoes, and the women and kids blown to smithereens in the supermarkets. I can't forget the boy tied to the tree. The human level – the level on which that stuff happens – is the only real level as far as I'm concerned. The rest is bollocks.'

'Well, that's hardly a very adult attitude. Your Service career's unlikely to prosper if that's how you think.'

'I'm sure you're right,' said Alex. He pulled a book from the bookcase at random, opened it, stared sightlessly at the page for a moment and returned it. 'You were lovers, weren't you? You and Dawn?'

Fenwick said nothing.

'I always used to tease her. Who's the lucky bloke you wake up next to, I used to say, missing the obvious by a mile.'

Fenwick sat unmoving, as if carved from stone.

'And now she's dead,' Alex continued. 'I watched her drown in her own blood on the side of Pen-y-Fan, and the last thing that she said before she died was your name. And you still – *you still* – think that this whole thing was worth it . . .'

He moved towards the door, glanced back at the

motionless figure. 'Have a good life, Fenwick. I'd tell you to go to hell, but I reckon that you're probably already there.'

Marching through the dining room and down the main staircase with an alacrity rarely seen in that august institution, Alex departed the Carlton Club. It was midday and after an unpromising start the sun was making a go of it.

Pausing for a moment at the club portals, Alex took out his phone and scrolled through the numbers stored in its memory. After a moment's hesitation he selected one.

'Yep?'

'It's Alex.'

There was a long silence. In the background he could hear the sound of female voices, shrieks, laughter. In the foreground, her breathing.

'Sophie?'

'Yes,' she said quietly. 'I'm still here.'

POSTSCRIPT

London

By 4 p.m. it was already dark and the rain-slicked pavements of Mayfair gleamed beneath the street-lights. As the driver nosed the big Jaguar into the electric glare of Piccadilly, Angela Fenwick turned to the HarperCollins publicity girl for a final confirmation that she was looking presentable, that everything was in place. Swivelling her head so that both sides of her face could be assessed, she received the publicity girl's smiling confirmation. Presentation, Angela knew, was everything at these affairs. Photographers would do anything to catch celebrities off guard – even a new-born celebrity like herself, who had only emerged blinking into the flashlight of public regard a week earlier.

The launch at the club last night had gone wonderfully well, she mused, but then it wasn't every day that a senior member of MI5 went public with her memoirs. Everyone had come: Tony and Cherie – Cherie looking *lovely*, as usual – Gordon and Sarah of course, Patrick Mayhew, Mo Mowlam looking like something out of the *Arabian Nights*, Salman Rushdie (and boy, did that man owe her a favour), Tony Parsons . . . And Peter of course – *dear* Peter – with head held high since his vindication in the Hinduja passport business. The evening had been a triumph, with the only sour note struck by a scuffle between the security people and a rather tiresome group of civil rights demonstrators. In a way even that little embarrassment had worked in their favour. A paparazzo had been at hand to photograph the incident and the picture had made the cover of the *Evening Standard*.

The publishers had been marvellous, all in all, pulling out all the stops, footing the not inconsiderable bill without a murmur. 'We can only sell your memoirs once, Angela,' they'd told her. 'So let's go for broke!'

And they had. Naturally she hadn't put in any of the really top-secret stuff; that went completely against the grain. But there had been plenty of colour, plenty of telling detail and plenty of human touches. She'd even managed to include a couple of David Trimble's famous 'knock, knock' jokes, a good Martin McGuinness fishing story and the account of how, on April Fool's day 2000, Jack Straw had officially requested that she tap Ali G's phone.

On a more serious note she'd well and truly stuck it to those bastards over at Vauxhall Cross. That had been the real pleasure – kicking MI6 in the teeth. Without ever saying so directly, she'd managed to paint a picture of smug, pin-striped, public-school, all-male arrogance – an arrogance that spilt over with wearying regularity into reckless freebooting on the international stage. Bosnia, Russia, Serbia, Iraq . . . What the sacked MI6 whistle-blower Richard Tomlinson had started with his exposé of Britain's overseas Intelligence Service, Angela Fenwick had finished.

The career-ending deal had been presented to her shortly after Downing Street had been presented with the facts concerning the violent deaths of four Service employees. Her failure to protect her people, she had been told, indicated a dangerously cavalier attitude. Resign, she had been told. Go now, honourably and with a full pension. Jump before you're pushed.

It wasn't just the murders, she'd guessed. The Home Office had wanted one of their own sort at the helm at Thames House – it was as simple as that. A white, heterosexual, privately educated male. Someone who spoke their language. Someone they could do business with. Someone who'd behave in a civilised manner concerning Security Services budget deals rather than fighting tooth and nail for every penny. It wasn't to do with the Watchman murders, ultimately. The murders were just an excuse.

So she'd jumped. They'd won. And she had started collecting up all the notes she'd made over the years. And *A Career Less Ordinary* had been born.

Annabel, the HarperCollins publicity girl, had been particularly sweet and in the run-up to publication the two of them had become quite close. Not quite close enough to fill the aching void left by Dawn, of course – eighteen months after Dawn's death Angela still thought of her protégée every day – but close enough for Angela to look forward to the upcoming publicity tour, and the nights *à deux* in the big provincial hotels.

The tour itself would start tomorrow; today was the big London signing. They'd decided to do just the one, at Waterstones in Piccadilly. The event had been well advertised and according to Annabel, who'd phoned ahead to the shop, there was a good crowd building.

The driver swung the Jaguar across the traffic in a swashbuckling U-turn, pulled up outside Waterstones, and hurried round to open the passenger door.

Dismounting, Angela noticed a tramp in a grease-shined windcheater lounging by the bookshop's main entrance. As she passed him the stubbled, wild-eyed figure raised a can of Special Brew to her in ironic celebration. To add insult to injury he was sitting immediately beneath a poster of herself and her book. The former civil servant averted her gaze in displeasure. The PM *hated* the sight of derelicts in upscale shopping areas – he'd told her so himself – and yet one still saw sights like this. Weren't Waterstones responsible for their own stretch of pavement? she wondered irritably. She'd get Annabel to have a word with the manager.

Inside the shop Angela was shown to a staffroom, where she left her coat, shook hands with the Waterstones floor manager, declined a cup of coffee and greeted Dave Holland, the ex-RMP officer responsible for her personal security.

'Your fans look docile enough,' said Holland, who had just returned from a recce of the shop floor. 'I'm happy if you are.'

'OK, David, let's do it,' said Angela, briefly unsnapping her handbag to check that she had a pen. She had – an old MI5-issue Pentel.

The signing desk had been arranged at the centre of the shop floor, facing the Jermyn Street exit. It was flanked on one side by dump bins of *A Career Less Ordinary* and on the other by an array of photo floodlights. Behind a rope barrier a dozen photographers waited with Nikons primed. The big photo opportunity involved a handshake with Judi Dench, who played 'M' in the James Bond films. There was a new picture upcoming, and even though 'M' was actually supposed to be the director of the hated Six, Angela was forced to admit to herself that the showbiz association was a flattering one. There was Judi now, approaching from the opposite side of the shop. They'd met once before, at a small dinner at the Ivy.

As the actress approached the desk, and John Barry's *Goldfinger* theme played over the shop's PA system, Angela's heart quickened. This was *fun*!

The two women greeted each other and sustained a long handshake for the cameras. Angela ritually presented the actress with a signed copy of *A Career Less Ordinary* and told her – truthfully, as it happened – that she'd always been a big James Bond fan.

At the photographers' request there were more posed shots. Then Judi Dench took her leave of the event with an actressy twinkle and a flutter of her fingers, Angela sat down and the signing session began.

Soon she was into the routine of it. *Smile, ask the name, sign, hand the book over. Smile, ask the name, sign, hand the book over. Smile . . .*

Angela was enjoying herself, enjoying the attention and the curiosity of the public. There were old-school types in Royal Artillery ties, purple-haired goths, spook-watching journalists, hygiene-deficient conspiracy theorists, radical feminist academics and a host of other London types. One by one, beneath the watchful gaze of Dave Holland, who stood to one side of the desk, they moved forward with their copies of the book.

At the author's side Annabel beamed proprietorially, keeping an eye on the *Daily Telegraph* profilist who was due to interview Angela after the signing. With the exception of a single freelancer the photographers had departed.

Smile, ask the name, sign, hand the book over. Smile, ask the name . . . A pair of Waterstones assistants kept the pyramids of books around the desk stocked from packing cases.

'Geoffrey!' Angela murmured to a particularly well-connected political commentator. 'How sweet of you. How are Sally and the children?'

The writer replied courteously and moved away. His place was taken by a horsy woman in a Puffa jacket.

'What name?' Angela asked mechanically. In the queue behind the horsy woman she caught sight of the stubbled face of the tramp she had seen outside the shop. To her surprise, despite his wild appearence, he was carrying a copy of the book. The horsy woman's lips moved soundlessly.

'I'm sorry?' said Angela, 'I didn't quite . . .'

The woman repeated a name – her husband's, she explained – and Angela signed and then abruptly stopped. Where the hell did she know that face from? The features were wind-roughened and the clothes dirty but there had been a time, she was sure, when this man had been somebody.

But then so many people had been somebody once.

The horsy woman retired and the man handed Angela his copy of *A Career Less Ordinary*. He was smiling, he smelt of beer and the streets, and there was something both intimate and expectant in his smile.

Am I meant to know him?

'What name?' she ventured.

'You don't remember?' he said quietly. 'Angela, I'm disappointed! It's Joe, Joe Meehan.'

Beyond thought, but not yet connected to terror, she started to take the book, to open it to the title-page. And then, gasping, she saw its starched covers close over her hand. She had lost control of her fingers. It was as if they were frost-bitten. Her whole body was frozen.

It had been she – Angela – who had ordered Dawn to take a foot-soldier and eliminate Temple when he had called in to say that he had captured Meehan on Pen-y-Fan. The chances that the former agent had told the SAS officer the truth about Operation Watchman were just too great.

And then, just hours later, Dawn and her back-up man had been found dead. Of Temple and Meehan there had been no sign. Well, she'd found out Temple's whereabouts soon enough but Meehan . . .

Joseph Meehan was dead and buried.

He had to be.

She'd believed it and not believed it. When she left the Service she'd been stripped of the close protection team that had surrounded her for so many years. And, now – here was the irony – there was no one she could go to and say: this man may be alive. And if he is alive he will try and kill me . . .

The weeks had become months and the months had become a year, and still there had been no sign of Meehan, and finally she had begun to relax. Her official security had been stepped down to just one officer and she had begun to tell herself that the Watchman was indeed dead . . .

Dave Holland, recognising at some unconscious level that things were wrong, that the moment was horribly out of joint, stared at the desk. His eyes narrowed as the bearded man held his principal's gaze. What the fuck was going down?

Angela Fenwick, he belatedly realised, was terrified. Paralysed with terror, like a bird faced by a cobra. She couldn't even move.

At Holland's side the photographer had realised something was up too. The big F3 Nikon was already moving up towards his face. Beside the desk the *Daily Telegraph* writer stared in puzzlement at the motionless tableau. Then Meehan pulled out a Browning automatic and jammed the point of the barrel beneath Angela Fenwick's chin.

Mayhem. Dave Holland was aware of a distorted screaming, of panicked bodies falling in slow motion to the floor, of the languid *chakka-chakka-chakka* of the Nikon's motor-drive.

He dived for the gun, but impeded by the press of bodies around him fell disastrously short. A shot, meanwhile, rang out simultaneously with the Nikon's final exposure. This image, which British newspaper picture desks would suppress but which would be syndicated worldwide, showed Meehan in profile. He looked almost courteous. Angela Fenwick's expression, by contrast, was one of uncomprehending terror as a spectral tiara of skull fragments and other matter leapt from her head.

The moment after the shot rang out – although no one would remember this afterwards – Joseph Meehan turned to a man in a battered leather jacket who was standing at the back of the crowd. A long look passed between the two men, a look identical to that which had once passed between them in St Martin's churchyard, Hereford. Then Meehan placed the barrel of the Browning automatic into his mouth, pulled the trigger for a second time and blew his brains into the fiction shelves.

No one noticed the man in the battered leather jacket slip out through the heavy glass exit doors into Jermyn Street. In his hand was the edition of the *Evening Standard* in which the signing session had been detailed. Climbing into the passenger seat of a silver Audi TT convertible which was idling at the kerb, he reached out and, after a moment's hesitation, touched the chestnut-brown hair of the girl behind the wheel. She, in her turn, fractionally inclined her head towards him. A close observer might have detected a certain wariness between the two of them.

But there was no observer. The car pulled quietly away and by the time the first police sirens were audible, the couple had vanished.

LAND OF FIRE

Exclusive! Read the first two chapters of the new Chris Ryan book, soon to be published by Century.

CHAPTER ONE

"Air raid warning red!"

Autumn in the South Atlantic. 3.32 pm on 25th of May on a bright, cold afternoon in the narrow inlet of San Carlos Water, East Falkland. The alarm call sent a shiver through the British fleet and my war turned bloody.

This was Argentina's National Day. In enemy sorties before lunch missiles from HMS Coventry had shot down two A4 Skyhawk bombers over the sound with a third destroyed by small arms fire. But an hour later the bombers had returned to exact revenge, damaging Broadsword and hitting Coventry with three bombs, capsizing her and killing nineteen men.

Now the bombers were back again.

The tannoy message meant that the long range radar of a ship on the forward picket line had detected hostile aircraft in descent towards the island on a strike mission profile.

Minutes earlier a Sea King helicopter from HMS Invincible had set me down on the main deck of the SS Northland, a 15,000 ton roll-on roll-off container ship. There were four of us from D Squadron SAS under the orders of my brother, Troop Sergeant Andy Black. The other two were Tom, one of my great mates, a huge and unflappable Fijian corporal, and Doug Easton, the troop troublemaker, who had just made selection. Doug was a bullet-headed tearaway from East London, violently aggressive and forever forcing his opinions on people. He and I had never hit it off.

The Squadron was scheduled to undertake a major operation in the next couple of days and we were hunting for a missing container of stores. Some clerk in Portsmouth had screwed up on the cargo manifest and our vital laser target designators had ended up on the wrong ship. I was twenty years old and the operation would be my first time under fire.

A stench of diesel and avgas. The cavernous main hold was jammed with giant helicopters and massive crates with spare engines for Harrier jump jets. Teams of RAF technicians, crabs in our language, were labouring to bolt the rotors into place on a twin-engine Chinook. Andy sent Tom and Doug forward and took me aft with him to check the lower vehicle deck. He wanted to keep me apart from Tom on account of how when the order to leave for the Falklands came through, Tom and I had been out drinking. We were shitters in some stinker's house and missed the flight out to Ascension Island with the rest of the Squadron and had to catch a later plane. Andy hadn't forgiven me yet. A veteran of the Oman campaign, he sported the droopy tash and long hair of a seasoned SAS and took no nonsense from anyone, officer or ranker.

As we searched for a stairwell we met a couple of airmen coming forward. "How do we get down from here?" Andy asked. One of the men jerked a thumb over his shoulder and hurried on without stopping.

"Fucking crab," Andy grunted. "Shitting himself in case the Argy planes come back."

You couldn't exactly blame him though. It was bad enough being on a troop ship, but with holds full of fuel and ammunition these guys were sitting on a bomb, literally. The war was becoming very real. I had seen enemy aircraft blown out of the sky over the anchorage and ships burning from missile hits.

We clattered down into the bowels of the ship. The lower deck was shadowy, crammed with long lines of all-terrain vehicles, Land Rovers and 8-ton medium trucks packed to the roof with stores and chained to the deck by their axels.

"Take fucking hours to search this lot," Andy said. "We'll need more light. Hang on here, Mark, while I go back for a couple of torches. And keep your eyes open for anything worth nicking — if the crabs haven't got there first that is."

Hampered by my bulky life vest, I squeezed past a rank of bucket loaders belonging to the Royal Engineers and a grim contingent of battlefield ambulances. From up above came the sounds of a tannoy blaring. Probably another aircraft warning. The Argies were throwing their full weight against the landings.

Andy returned with torches and we set to work. As we moved along the lines I was quizzing him about the up-coming mission. Rumour had it the squadron was to be sent into the Argentine mainland. If true, it would be a major escalation of the war. I knew Andy was bothered by it because he had set me down for the reserve squad, which meant I was unlikely to be picked and it was pissing me off not a little.

Among a fleet of BV lightweight tracked vehicles, the kind that can go across the ice cap if you need to,

I made out four of the squadron's trucks. The first contained bivvy bags and groundsheets as listed. I counted the bundles as best I could in the semi dark. The canvas flap at the back of the next truck was partly unsecured and I squirmed underneath to take a dekko inside. Jesus, I thought disgustedly as I played the torch around. The neat packs of arctic clothing and spare sleeping bags had been hollowed out in the middle to make a hiding place. Some pisser was kipping down in here. I pulled the canvas back for a better look. A man. And whoever it was had dug out a sleeping bag and there was a torch ready to hand, an army issue water bottle and the remains of a meal from a ration pack. Fucking crabs, I thought, they get better fed than we do and still they nick our grub.

Feeling around among the bundles, I turned up a camera and a miniature tape recorder, quality looking items both. Along with them was a piece of electronic kit I didn't recognise, a flat grey plastic box around six inches long by two and a half wide with an extendable aerial like a transistor radio but no tuning dial, only a tiny red button which glowed to show it was switched on.

I was about to go back and show Andy what I'd found when there was a rustling noise from the front of the truck. A rat after the remains of the food? But then it seemed too much noise for a rat. A man. And who-ever had been living here was still around by the sound of it. Right, I'll have you, I thought and launched my-self across the piled stores. There was a frantic scuffling as a body tried to get away. I got a hand around a limb in the darkness, arm or leg I couldn't tell. "Come on, get the fuck out of there," I said, heaving.

A foot came out of the blackness and connected

with my face with a force that rocked my head back against the steel frame of the roof. The torch went flying and the crack I had taken felt as if it had broken my jaw. My head was singing and I could taste blood in my mouth. I was angry now. Okay, I said to myself, if that's how you want to play it, fine. I let fly a punch with all my twelve stone behind it. My fist connected with something solid. There was a gasp and a whimper and the struggles ceased. This was better. Locating a foot, I dragged my opponent out into the half-light near the truck tail to take a look at him.

The guy was wearing combat fatigues, which meant he was army. I'd been expecting a crab or a sailor. Maybe he had nicked the gear too? He was so slight he looked more like a boy than a man. "Who the fuck are you?" I demanded. The little bastard struggled violently and tried to knee me in the groin. I raised a fist. "Leave it out." He went limp again. I lowered the fist. "Now then, what's all this?" I figured he had to be some kind of cabin boy or whatever from the crew, probably scared to death by the bombing and hiding down here when he should be topsides.

In answer he twisted like a snake, diving under my arm to reach the roof flap. I was ready for him though. Flinging myself after, I dragged him back, rolling him over and pinning him down. He fought and squirmed, scratching and biting furiously. It was a while since I'd fought with a kid his size and it didn't feel right somehow. I was worrying I'd break a bone or something. Eventually though I got him pinned down by sheer weight. I straddled him between my knees and laced his hands across his chest so he couldn't move, though he continued to snarl and wriggle like a wildcat.

"What's your name then, arsehole?"

His response was to spit in my face. I cuffed him a couple of times across the mouth to teach him manners and he shut up. His wrists were so thin I could hold them both together one-handed while I searched his tunic for ID. It was while I was patting him down that I realised something was wrong – and not in the way I had been thinking. He was a skinny little devil, all bones and muscle and padded out in odd places. In addition to a combat jacket several sizes too large, he had on a roll-neck sweater with a T-shirt underneath. Ignoring his squirmings, I pulled these up, revealing a narrow ribcage and a flesh coloured sports bra hiding a pair of adolescent tits.

My cabin boy was a girl.

I let go her hands and sat up.

The torch was lying nearby. I snapped it on. Definitely a girl. The dark hair was ragged and plastered to her grimy face. She was unkempt and pale but the dishevelled appearance and dirt could not disguise the fineness of the features or burning intensity of the eyes. Younger than me; seventeen or eighteen at a guess. There was a reddening mark on one cheek where I had hit her. I reached down to touch the place.

Her eyes flashed hatred. A hand swept out of the gloom, fingers curled like talons to rake my face.

I knocked the blow aside.

"I didn't mean to hit you!" Well, I hadn't. I'd thought she was a bloke. "What are you doing down here anyway?"

"*Bastardo!*"

A girl, I was thinking. How she had got here I couldn't imagine, unless maybe she was some crab's bit of fluff smuggled aboard at Portsmouth. I hadn't seen a girl in six weeks. There were rumoured to be a few serving on the Canberra but we had never got near enough to find out. Or she could be a journalist stowed away on board to get a scoop on the campaign . . ?

Then it dawned on me that she'd just spoken in Spanish. I ran my gaze around the nest in which she had been lying up, taking in the items I'd found, the camera, the tape recorder, the radio-type device.

And it hit me. Jesus, I thought, the bitch is a spy. She's down here vectoring the bombers in on us.

That moment she flew at me again.

I called Andy over. Even against the two of us she continued to put up a fight. She could kick and punch like a bantam weight. My teeth were still aching and Andy took a poke in the eye that left him gasping. Eventually we got her tied down with some straps off a vehicle and Andy told me to watch her while he went off to find an officer.

After that everything started to go rat shit. The ship's captain and the ops officer took one look at the girl, still spitting and snarling, and the kit she had with her and told Andy and me on no account talk to anyone. I described the scene in the back of the truck, how I'd guessed she had a homing device, which was what it seemed the thing was. There were long faces as the officers tried to figure out how an enemy agent had managed to breach their so-called impenetrable security cordon. No one knew how she had got on or whether it was at Portsmouth or Ascension Island where the ship had stopped en route. Small wonder we had been taking such loses to air attack.

By this time they had brought a couple of seamen down and told them to get the kit off her. They set to work grinning. The bitch fought and kicked but it didn't do her any good. In a trice she was spread-eagled against a bulkhead and every shred of clothing, ripped away. Legs spread, arms outstretched, she was backed up against the wall and her wrists lashed to steel shackles. It was freezing cold down below decks but in the overhead light her olive skin was beaded with sweat.

Front on, she looked pathetically young and emaciated. The half grown tits shrunken with cold, the dark bush oversized between the skinny thighs. I felt no anger now, only pity and disgust. I wondered what they were going to do with her. This was war and in war spies were shot.

I knew the procedure. I'd been through it myself on the escape and evasion exercise during the SAS initiation test in the Brecon Beacons before the war. Next she'd have the full treatment; the body cavity searches, the physical and verbal abuse, the threats, the hooding and banging on the walls and door to induce disorientation. I could have told them they were wasting their time; that she was never going to talk, but it wouldn't have done any good. The two seamen stayed in attendance to see she didn't kill herself. Though God knows how she was going to manage that the way they had her trussed up.

I felt sick as we climbed back topside, the captain explaining that we weren't to talk about this, not to anyone. It was all top secret. In other words a cover-up was in force. We were to forget the girl, forget the homing device; none of it had ever happened. But I couldn't get the image of her spread-eagled against

402

that bulkhead out of my mind.

Tom and Doug were waiting on deck. An officer told us to get our kit together and a helicopter would fly us back to rejoin the unit.

That was when all hell broke loose.

CHAPTER TWO

The attacking aircraft were A4 Skyhawks of the Argentine Navy based at Rio Grande on Tierra del Fuego. Equipped with a pair of 500-lb free-fall iron bombs each, the planes' targets were the closely packed transport vessels moored in the narrow inlet of San Carlos Water off the beachhead.

It was a dangerous mission. Our ships were protected by radar controlled anti-aircraft guns and state-of-the-art missiles, including the deadly Sea Dart carried aboard the Type-42 destroyers positioned at the mouth of the inlet. Sea Dart was a fifteen-foot long missile weighing half a ton. On firing, its rocket booster accelerated it up to twice the speed of sound within three seconds and it could pluck an aircraft out of the sky at forty miles range. Already today Sea Darts had claimed three attacking jets and the pilots were under no illusions as to the risks they faced.

Sea Dart had one weakness. It was primarily designed to fight the Russian Navy in an open sea war. Against a low level target, operating against a background of clutter from the land, it was less effective. And this afternoon the Argentines had exploited that weakness to deadly effect. Screaming off the land at near wave height, aircraft had hit the destroyer HMS Coventry capsizing her with a loss of nineteen men.

The catastrophe left a yawning gap in the air defences of the San Carlos beachhead. The only guard vessel now left was the smaller frigate HMS Broadsword, herself damaged in an earlier attack. Her Sea Wolf missiles were of an advanced type designed to counter sea-skimming missiles fired by submarines, so new they were still under test. They were highly accurate but their range was just two and a half miles. No time for a second shot.

As the low hills and fractured coastline of the islands loomed ahead, the lead aircraft dropped to three hundred feet and commenced its run up the coast. The pilot twisted and turned, weaving among the valleys. His instruments would be able to detect the pulse of enemy radar beams feeling for him, striving to pick his plane out from the jumble of returning echoes bouncing off the hillsides. Travelling at 500 knots the four aircraft split into two sections for the final attack to divide the gunners' attention.

The lead aircraft appeared to be headed directly for the centre of a massed group of store ships.

An urgent warning pealed from the tannoys: "Air Raid Warning Red!" There was a panicky rush for the upper decks by some of the civilian seamen. They had seen Coventry turn into a fireball and go down and they didn't want to be caught below when it happened to their ship. From previous drills I knew we had about a minute and a half from the warning before the bombs started to fall. I looked towards the south west and saw a dark shape loose itself from the land and come streaking down the sound. The next instant the twin 20 mm WW2 vintage Oerlikons opened up, bam,

bam, bam, bam. From all around guns on ships and land were firing and the air was full of smoke bursts, but the planes flew on unscathed. I saw a rocket plume flash up from one of the hills. Someone having a go with a Blowpipe, but Blowpipe didn't engage crossing targets well and this one ran wild onto a hillside.

Four and a half miles out and the lead planes were so low the wash from their jet engines was striking spray from the surface of the inlet. The firing became a crescendo. The racket was unbelievable; the deep boom of 4.5 calibre main guns of the warships joined by the hammer of cannon fire and the shrill stammer of GPMGs. All the gunfire seemed to be falling short, bursting in front of the planes and making the water dance. To me, watching from the deck of the Northland, it seemed incredible that planes could fly through flak that thick and survive.

Ships that had way on them were manoeuvring frantically to get clear. Northland, though, had no steam up. She was a sitting duck. Four hundred yards short, the pilot of the lead Skyhawk released his bombs. I saw them fall clear, dropping towards us as the jet screamed away overhead, two black dots growing larger by the second and I thought, fuck, they were coming right at us. *We* were the target. Doug had thrown himself flat on the deck; he hated air attacks and didn't like ships much better. I was thinking this is where we all die, but I couldn't tear my gaze away.

The first bomb hit the water twenty yards from the port quarter with a mountainous splash. "Missed, you bastard!" I shouted aloud. Bombs had a delay function, an impeller in the tail that had to spin a set number of turns after dropping to release the firing pin so that it could move forward on impact and trigger the detonator. Flying so low meant they had to be released at exactly the right moment or the sods wouldn't go off.

It was my last coherent thought before the world burst in around me.

In fact the first bomb bounced so fast I didn't have time to see it off the surface like a skimmed stone and struck the ship's side, piercing it and passing upwards through the engine room, killing three men and emerging again through the deck without exploding. I don't recall anything of the impact because a fraction of a second later the second bomb struck us amidships and this time the impellor had done its stuff. The firing pin released and the bomb exploded in the main hold with a force that burst open the deck where I was standing and threw everyone nearby off their feet.

I remember a bright flash and then I must have been knocked unconscious for a few seconds. When I came to I was lying on my front. My clothes were blackened and I was surrounded by smoking wreckage. The decking was all ripped and a roaring jet of flame licked upwards. Ammunition was popping off down in the holds, punctuated by the heavier whoomp of petrol tanks going up.

I stood up and realised that the ship had taken on a list. It was like walking uphill. A hand grabbed me. It was Andy. His hair was all singed and I remember wondering if mine was the same. He was shouting at me but I couldn't make out what because of the noise and because the explosion had left me temporarily deafened. He thrust a survival suit into my hands and pointed to the side. Time to abandon ship. A survival suit was a once-only garment you pulled on over your outer clothes before jumping into the water. Its seals were supposed to keep you dry and alive long enough to be rescued, provided help came pretty quick. Without a suit the average person had a fifty-fifty chance of swimming fifty yards in these waters before hypothermia got him.

I was about to put it on when I saw the two seamen who had been guarding the girl come tumbling up a companionway from below. There was no sign of the girl with them. The bomb must have shattered the lower deck level and those guys had legged it. They weren't about to risk their lives for the sake of a spy.

I didn't know why I should either, unless it was maybe because I was the one who had found her and started it all? I looked around for Andy but he had disappeared. Presumably he figured I could look after myself. The ship didn't seem to be about to go down this second and the fire hadn't reached the forepart yet. I decided I had a good chance to reach her and fetch her out.

In a way it was easier than I had thought. I nipped down the ladder onto the cargo deck level. There was a lot of smoke eddying around but no actual flames yet. One guy passed me carrying a kit bag; he must have been back to his cabin. I went down two more ladders. The emergency lights were on but there was less smoke. All the alarm bells were ringing. The noise of firing was muffled but I could hear big thuds of mortar bombs or gas tanks going up which kept me moving forwards and down. The tilt on the deck didn't seem to be getting any steeper so I figured I wasn't about to drown yet.

When I reached the stern, there she was where they had left her still lashed up to the ringbolts. I untied her wrists and she sagged against me like she was all in. Her clothes were in a heap on the deck. I started pulling them over her arms and legs. There didn't seem much point in rescuing her if she was going to die of cold the second I dropped her in the water. She got the message and inside a couple of minutes I had her more or less dressed. I gave her the survival suit, it made one less thing to carry, and hustled her back to the ladders.

There seemed to be a lot more smoke and heat around now. Also the angle of the deck was suddenly worse. I pushed the girl ahead of me up the ladder. She had recovered some of her strength or else she was scared because she went up like a squirrel. I guess after six weeks aboard she knew her way about.

Half way up the next ladder conditions were vile. Flames were spreading into the stairwell. The ladder had broken free from several of its supports and swayed ominously as we went higher. I was having to climb one handed, using the other to push the girl on. She was slowing now, because of the flames. Another explosion shook the hold. More ammunition going up. Bits of debris were raining down from overhead and the bulkhead next to the hold was smoking or steaming, I couldn't tell which. I concentrated on trying to breath in shallow gasps to keep the smoke out of my lungs. The ladder seemed endless and the handrail was hot to touch.

We reached the landing at the top somehow only to find the door leading out on deck wouldn't open. The watertight latches were closed fast. Some bugger had sealed us in to die. The girl was going limp again through the effects of smoke. I propped her up against the wall and took a hold of the top latch. It didn't budge. Heat or the ship's list must have wrenched the frame out of true. I looked around but the passage behind was filling with flames. There was no other way out. I heaved on the latch again and was rewarded with a slight movement. A series of violent tugs at last worked it free. Now for the bottom latch. This was worse. It was so tightly jammed, nothing I did would make it move. Inky smoke was belching up the stairwell making it impossible to breath. In desperation I pounded on the steel door with my fist. "Let us out, you fuckers!" I might as well have been pissing into the wind for all the chance there was of being heard.

I grabbed the handle of the top latch again with both hands, swung myself out over the stairwell and crashed both legs together against the jammed hatch. The impact jarred my spine but I thought I felt the latch move. I pushed off again with my feet, praying I wouldn't somehow fall off and drop twenty feet in to the burning hold, and gave a second mighty kick and this time the handle snapped free with a clank.

Out on deck things weren't a whole lot better, except that it was possible to breathe more freely. The ship was burning furiously amidships and listing heavily. Secondary explosions were shaking the hull as fuel tanks continued to detonate below decks. It was obviously only a matter of minutes before she went down. A few disciplined types were trying to run hoses into the flames but most of the crew were launching life rafts and jumping overboard in their haste to get off the ship in case she blew. Many of the floats were overcrowded and men were being washed into the sea. A frigate nearby had boats in the water picking up survivors and helicopters were swooping down to pluck people off the deck.

I pushed the girl ahead of me along the deck. Now

I could hear men screaming down in the hold. She stood, swaying with exhaustion, surveying the scene of devastation. In her eyes was a glow of triumph. Something inside me snapped. They could be my mates down there. I seized her by the scruff and forced her to the edge of the shattered deck looking down into the inferno. "Now it's your turn!" I screamed at her.

A hand caught my shoulder. It was Andy again, his face blackened by smoke and flames. "What the fuck are you doing, Mark?" he yelled. "Come on, we've got a boat waiting."

The adrenalin rush had left me light headed and I'd been on the brink of committing murder. If she was a spy then the girl was more valuable alive. I was turning back from the fire when the ship gave a sudden lurch that sent us all sprawling. A burst of flaming smoke spewed out from the burning hole amidships. I felt my hair crackle. Andy pulled me to my feet and dragged me back out of harm's way.

Gasping, I looked around. "Where's the girl?"

But she was gone.

The One That Got Away

Chris Ryan

New edition of the number one bestseller to coincide with the 10th Anniversary of the Gulf War

The new edition of this breathtaking story of extraordinary courage includes a new 5,000 word account of the aftermath, the way the former members of the patrol have fallen out and documentary evidence that settles once and for all what really happened on that fateful mission, and a new section of so far unpublished photographs.

The SAS mission conducted behind Iraqi lines is one of the most famous stories of courage and survival in modern warfare. Of the eight members of the SAS Regiment who set off, only one escaped capture. This is his story.

Late on the evening of 24 January 1991 the patrol was compromised deep behind enemy lines in Iraq. A fierce fire-fight left the eight men miraculously unscathed, but they were forced to run for their lives. Their aim was to reach the Syrian border, 120 kilometres to the north-west, but during the first night the patrol accidentally broke into two groups, five and three.

Chris Ryan found himself left with two companions. Nothing had prepared them for the vicious cold of the desert winter, and they began to suffer from hypothermia. During the night one of the men was to disappear in a blinding blizzard. The next day a goatherd came across the two survivors. Chris's remaining partner went with him in search of food and was never to return. Left on his own, Chris Ryan beat off an Iraqi attack and set out alone. His greatest adventure was only just beginning.

This is the story of courage under fire, of hairbreadth escapes, of the best trained soldiers in the world fighting against adverse conditions, and of one man's courageous refusal to lie down and die.

arrow books

Stand By, Stand By

Chris Ryan

A man at war with the enemy and his own demons

The second number one bestseller from the author of *The One That Got Away*

Never has there been a more graphic account of the SAS in action, never a thriller so authentically grounded in the twists and turns of undercover warfare.

Geordie Sharp, a sergeant in the SAS, is struggling to pick up the threads of his army career. Wounded in the Gulf War, he returns to Hereford to find his home life in tatters. As he trains with Northern Ireland Troop, a murder in his family fires him with personal hatred of the IRA. Posted to Belfast, he discovers that his adversary is Declan Farrell, a leading player in the Provisional IRA. Sharp sets out to stalk and kill his man.

arrow books

The Hit List

Chris Ryan

When a tycoon apparently falls from his yacht and drowns, the two secret service operatives who have in fact murdered him are also killed. The top secret governmental organisation that had employed them needs to find new recruits. Peter Slater, a former SAS soldier, is working as a games master in a public school. When he foils an attempt by terrorists to kidnap an Arab boy, the boy is hurt and Slater is sacked. Down on his luck he is framed for the murder of his girlfriend, and blackmailed into working for MI7. The missions he is asked to undertake on behalf of the British Government become so evil that he finds himself preferring to die rather than complete these missions successfully.

'Heart-in-mouth action'
Mirror

'A covert-double-crossing-twist-in-the-tale plot ... intelligent and entertaining'
Maxim

'A helter-skelter adrenaline rush ... a gripping read'
Irish Independent

arrow books

Zero Option

Chris Ryan

The sequel to the bestselling *Stand By, Stand By*

SAS Sergeant Geordie Sharp, locked in a desperate private battle
with the IRA, is required to undertake two top-secret missions, in
full knowledge that, if they go wrong, the authorities will deny all
involvement.

In the first operation he serves as commander of a hit team on a
Black or 100 per cent non-attributable task assigned to the SAW,
the Regiment's ultra-secret Subversive Action Wing. The target is
an Iraqi who defected to Libya after the Gulf War. The aim is to kill
him and leave no clue as to the identity or origin of the assassins.
The hit team will have to be absolutely clean and if anyone is
killed, the body will have to be recovered or vapourised with
explosives ...

Returning to base, Sharp finds he must also carry out a high-level
political assassination in mainland Britain. If he fails, his four year
old son will die at the hands of the IRA. Trapped between
opposing forces in a fight to the death, he twists and turns
through a nightmare maze, desperately seeking some way of
averting tragedy. Who will be hit hardest – Geordie Sharp or the
British government?

arrow books

Land of Fire

Chris Ryan

1982. The Falklands War. Young SAS trooper, Mark Black, risks his life to capture an Argentine girl spy. To knock out enemy bombers a daring mission is planned against a fortified airbase on Tierra del Fuego. Black and his fellow SAS are sent ahead to reconnoitre. Detected by the enemy, they must fight their way out ...

Twenty years on, now a senior NCO, Black is back in the South Atlantic, haunted by memories he thought he has buried. Once again Argentine forces are being secretly readied for an assault on the islands. A team from the crack SAS Mountain Troop is inserted by submarine. But has the mission been compromised from the start? When fate throws Black back together with the girl from his past, he is faced with a conflict of loyalties. Can he trust her now? And can they escape in time to destroy the enemy bombers and prevent all-out war?

'A rampaging boombuster'
Mirror

'Tough, high-testosterone stuff, gripping'
Herald

'Takes your breath away'
Northern Echo

arrow books

Greed

Chris Ryan

Greed is an explosive story of what happens when terrorism, money, love and jealousy combust.

Five men. One Robbery. A deadly game of greed, revenge, and betrayal is about to begin.

Fresh out of the SAS, Matt Browning is down on his luck. He owes £500,000. If he doesn't get the money soon, he dies. From nowhere, he is offered a lifeline. A hit on al-Qaeda, sanctioned and helped by MI5. Matt gathers a small team of former SAS men to steal $10 million in gold and diamonds from the world's most deadly terrorist organisation. MI5 will give them all the equipment and information they need. No charges will ever be pressed.

Matt thinks it's the perfect crime. Safe, quick , and patriotic. But after the money is stolen, the killing starts.

Someone is taking down the members of the team one by one. A silent, expert assassin is stalking them, gruesomely murdering both them and their families. And Matt knows he's next.

'lean prose delivers all the action with the usual trenchant force... The plot moves like the proverbial express train'
The Good Books Guide

'Hard as nails'
Mirror

arrow books

Tenth Man Down

Chris Ryan

When an SAS team is sent to train government troops in Kamanga, a poverty-stricken and war-torn republic in the dark heart of southern Africa, Geordie Sharp is caught up in the most dangerous and difficult assignment of his military career. At the outset of the mission a juju, or witch doctor, predicts that ten whites are going to die, and as the prediction starts to come true one by one down they go.

In the south of Kamanga rebel forces have seized the diamond mines which produce the bulk of the country's wealth. The aim of the crack government unit is to recover these lucrative assets, with Geordie Sharp and his squad providing much needed back-up.

When the SAS men see that the rebels are boosted by ex-US Navy SEALs mercenaries, they begin to sense a hidden agenda. Before they can discover what it is, Sharp and two others fall into rebel hands. His comrade Whinger dies a hideous death, but Sharp manages to escape.

At last Sharp stumbles onto the secret which is drawing such strong international interest – only to realise that he himself may have been exposed to a lethal dose of radiation in the process.

Is he the tenth and last of the juju's victims?

'Hard as nails'
Mirror

arrow books